THE COMPLETE

COMPENDIUM OF THE HEART

By RJ Hunter

COMPENDIUM OF THE HEART

COMPENDIUM OF THE SOUL

COMPENDIUM OF PASSION

Follow RJ Hunter on Twitter: @RJHunter3000
Like Compendium Of The Heart Trilogy on Facebook:
www.facebook.com/COTH.Trilogy

ISBN: 1507680902

ACKNOWLEDGEMENTS

This book is dedicated to the memory of my mother, Gabriel Rose Culley, my father, Albert Charles McKinlay Hunter, my sister, Janet Carol Miller, and my brother, Geoffrey James Hunter who were all tragically taken before their time.
I would like to thank Julia, for her expertise on nursing, and for her research, especially in books two and three. Thanks to Alex for his technical knowledge, to Matt for his artistry, to Ben for his advice on the usage of the English language, to Ollie for being quiet.
And lastly, thanks to you, the reader for taking the time out of your lives to read my book. I hope you enjoy it, as much as I enjoyed writing it.

CONTENTS

COMPENDIUM OF THE HEART
An epic love story

PROLOGUE

Please excuse this unusual approach, and allow me to introduce myself. My name is Lizzie Marchmont, and I'm one of the characters in this book. In fact, I would go further than that and say, I'm one of the main characters, but some would say differently.

Can I ask you a few of questions? Do you think you could ever venture off the straight and narrow, and live on the wild side? Do you think you are so steady and predictable, that nothing you do will ever shock, or go against the grain? Could you get married, and live contentedly, knowing you were still in love with somebody else? Let me try another one, do you think you could re-kindle a relationship with a person, who you grew to fear and detest, over twenty years earlier? Odd questions, don't you think, and questions that I've pondered over for many years now. But maybe, we'll have some answers by the end of this book.

The story, incidentally, is in three parts and starts in the early 1960s. It then goes through to bring us up to the 80s. I think it'll be one of the most powerful and disturbing, love stories you'll ever read, and certainly one you wont forget.

I've heard it said that some people can change quite dramatically from bad to good and vice versa, if they have a mind to. Personally, I say once bad, always bad. But then, I'm not Sally Peddlescoombe.

During the next few pages you'll meet me, and get to like me, I hope. I can be shocking at times and rather outspoken - that's why I'm talking to you now. Basically, I'm a good person. Yes, I'm a true blue conservative and a staunch capitalist, and I like my drink. But who doesn't enjoy a good tipple if they work hard and deserve it? I do get ratty and I do like to get my own way - but for someone who runs their own business, I see this more as an asset rather than a fault. I also have a heart of gold, and I'm rather a good person to have around when the going gets tough. Sally would tell you, after all, it's her who this story is really about, Sally is my best friend. I met her many years ago at university, and I love her like she was my own sister. We all have one really good friend, someone who we'd willingly lay down our lives for. Well, it's like that with Sally and myself.

You are about to read her story, but it isn't all hearts and flowers. Life has a habit of throwing up the unexpected, and kicking us in the teeth when we are down. But it's how you react that marks you out as a person. Do you just lie there and take it, without so much as a whimper, or do you pick yourself up, rise to the challenge, and stare defiantly into the face of adversity?

Well, Sally did just that, and it almost cost her, not only her sanity, but everything she had ever cherished, and cared about, including her life. I know, because I was there with her, through most of it.

Lizzie Marchmont

1. THE POOL

SPRING, 1983

As Sally stared down, her breath came in rapid gasps. She felt her heart pumping wildly and struggled to keep her balance. It was all the shouting and screaming that had distracted her and made her nearly fall before she was ready.

Closing her eyes she tried to block out the noise and concentrate on what she was about to do. She inched forward slowly, until she could grasp the edge with her toes. Fear and excitement confused her mind as she hesitated, for what seemed like an eternity. No, she couldn't back out, not now. She opened her eyes and inhaled sharply, as finally she let go and launched herself out into the void that accepted her so unconditionally. It all felt strangely surreal, and for a few moments she could no longer hear the noise from below, only the sound of the wind rushing past her ears, as her lithe body cut through the air like a knife.

The water was a lot colder than she had anticipated, but it had been worth it. A wonderful sense of achievement came over her as she rose to the surface and saw several onlookers gazing with admiration.

It had been a beautiful dive, and one that she used to perform like it was second nature during her schooldays. Now, it seemed as if diving from such a height had proved something, like it were some kind of yardstick measuring just how far she had come these last couple of years.

With slow, graceful movements, Sally glided effortlessly through the water. She reached the end of the pool, turned, and with a powerful thrust of her long legs, catapulted herself off the side to complete her quota of lengths. She had always been a proficient swimmer, and was glad she had finally got back into the habit of keeping herself in trim, especially after such a long lay-off.

It was a mild day and the pool was unusually busy, probably due to the welcome appearance of the long-awaited spring sunshine. There was a young mother with two small and very noisy children, a boy having a swimming lesson, an extremely hirsute man practising his front crawl, and a group of teenagers, preening, posing and doing dive bombs into the water, much to the annoyance of the lifeguards. However, Sally had decided to make the most of it. She preferred the breaststroke to the crawl, thinking it better for toning her bust and shoulders. Besides, by cheating and keeping her head above the surface, she could avoid swallowing vile gulps of chlorinated water, and also prevent the unsightly red eye syndrome that could draw so many distasteful assumptions.

Sally Peddlescoombe had been a member of the Powertone Health and Fitness Club since it had first opened, and had been one of its most regular members. In the early days she would work out on the multi-gym three times a week, and practice aerobics along with her swimming routine. Life for Sally seemed so full and enjoyable, with everything happening at such a fast pace. She had all she could possibly need and never doubted for a moment that it could ever change.

By gradually building up her fitness regime, Sally was now starting to reap its benefits, what with her revitalised energy, a few pounds of weight gained and the welcome return of her confidence, she was now feeling good again. It was time to pick up the threads of her life once more, and look positively towards a brand new future.

Glancing up at the clock, as she finished another length, Sally realised the time - she was due to meet Lizzie at one.

She swam towards the shallow end and climbed out of the pool with athletic ease and made her way to the changing rooms. There were other women there, whom Sally had seen on numerous occasions. She would smile and greet them but never went further than the usual pleasantries. Removing her one-piece swimming costume, and stepping into the hot shower, she glanced at some of the other women's bodies and couldn't help comparing them to her own. Although she had no reason to be ashamed of her figure, Sally was very conscious of her appearance.

Throughout her thirty nine years, she had denied herself luxuries few women could resist in order to maintain the size ten she had kept since her teenage years. In fact, Sally's age often came as a surprise to many. Despite being the mother of two daughters and a son, she was always being mistaken for someone much younger.

Now however, this might not be the case. The loss of her husband, William - killed in a car accident at the age of forty one, two years earlier, had taken a heavy toll on Sally. There had been times when the grief all became too much for her, and she had felt like simply ending it all. But something deep down within her soul would always rise up and push her forward into another day. Sally's grief would often just lie dormant, waiting for an opportunity. Then a trigger, perhaps something completely innocent and mundane - like receiving junk mail addressed to William, or coming across an item that had been locked away, such as the tie-pin he had worn to graduation. All this would block out any rational thought, and reduce her to a sobbing wreck of despair.

At first, Sally had worried how the children; twenty-year old Jonathan, Laura, 19, and fifteen year-old Penny would ever get over it. But in reality, it had hit their mother much harder.

Sally had met William while they were at university. She immediately fell for his often-silly sense of humour and warm charm that always seemed so natural. He had a certain spontaneity about him, which excited her, as she would never quite know what he was going to do next. She knew William would do well, just by listening to his words. Words that would hold her in a trance-like state, especially when he told her of his ambitious plans for their future.

In the years before his death, William had strived unselfishly to provide the best for his beloved family. The Peddlescoombes lived in a beautiful, five-bedroom, detached house near to the Thames at Twickenham, in Middlesex. The house was mock Tudor and was set back in a quiet, leafy cul-de-sac. The children had loved the vast, secluded garden, where they used to play hide and seek in their own little private forest, or climb the many trees bordering the perimeter. It was a haven for them, where there was always something exciting to do. William had even built a tree house, made from planks of brightly-painted wood. It was very sturdy and had its own little front door, windows and a sloping roof. The children would pull up the ladder when they were safe inside and pretend to hide from wild animals, or be castaways on a desert island. Once, Jonathan was showing off and fell to the ground, breaking his arm. Laura and Penny laughed believing he was being silly as usual. But they cried for hours thinking how beastly they had been when it was discovered that poor Jonathan really had hurt himself, and his mother had to take him to hospital.

The children and their friends would have their own sports day, with sack races and slow bicycle-riding competitions on the lawn. Sally would busy herself providing rounds of sandwiches and orange squash in plastic beakers for the thirsty participants. During the autumn they would collect conkers together and have epic battles in the conservatory. Usually this would end in tears, with one of them having to retire early due to bruised knuckles.

"You must try to win and not give up so easily," William would tell his children when they grew frustrated or got hurt and didn't want to play again.

Lizzie had already taken control of the café at the Powertone, and was sat, calmly waiting in typical Lizzie style. She was surrounded by expensive-looking carrier bags from her earlier shopping trip, and was defiantly smoking a foreign cigarette to the disgust of the tracksuit-clad staff. Like William, Sally had also known Lizzie from her student days back in the sixties. It was Lizzie whom Sally had turned to immediately after William's death. Lizzie helped pick up the remnants of her broken friend, and like someone who was repairing a much-loved fragile vase, she had slowly helped Sally try to fit the pieces of her shattered life back together again. At times Lizzie had felt utterly drained, as she had suddenly become the supporting pillar to not only her best friend, but the rest of the family too. Sally would put on a brave front for the children and help them through a grief they didn't understand. But who was left for Sally and her fierce pride that prevented her from even thinking of asking for help. Lizzie just automatically took the role upon herself, and carried on because she loved both Sally and William with all of her heart, and had shed many a tear herself.

To Lizzie, the Peddlescoombe's represented all that was good and right about life. Deep down she knew, that had the tragedy happened to her, she would have acted exactly the same, because that was the way they had both been brought up.

"Sally, Sally, over here!"

Sally smiled as she heard the familiar, confident voice, and walked over to join her friend.

"You look absolutely divine darling as always," beamed Lizzie, summoning a waitress. Sally wasn't sure if Lizzie was being her usual catty self, since she had only just daubed on her make-up in the changing rooms, and was dressed simply in jeans and T-shirt.

"Thank-you Lizzie, sorry I'm late," replied Sally as she gave her friend a hug and a peck on the cheek.

"I'll have another glass of dry white wine, and make sure its cold this time!" Said Lizzie brusquely to the unsmiling waitress. "They don't even have Chablis in here!" She continued, glaring at the surroundings critically.

Sally ignored Lizzie's remarks and ordered a coffee. An alcoholic drink was the last thing she felt like after her long swim.

"Sally, I'm not being sarcastic but you really do look wonderful. I'm glad you've reverted back to your natural blonde look, it so suits your lovely blue eyes. Perhaps, I should take up this keep-fit nonsense myself," said Lizzie, lighting up another cigarette. "I'm glad to see you're finally putting some weight back on as well, although, I don't think either of us need worry about our hips in here!"

"Lizzie, you're starting to sound like an old hag!" Replied Sally jokingly. "But thanks for the compliment, I've put on almost a stone since the last time I saw you." Sally looked serious and reached out for Lizzie's hand. "I know you're worried about me, but really, I'm fine now. I've reached the end of a long, dark tunnel. I can't spend the rest of my life moping around feeling sorry for myself. Its taken a long time, but I think I'm over the worst now. I'm getting fit again, and I've also gone absolutely mad and treated myself to a new summer wardrobe - the girls will be so jealous!"

"Sally, you know me, I can't help worrying about you," replied Lizzie, squeezing her friend's hand. "I'm sorry, I know I can be such a nag at times, but, I've noticed a real difference in you. The sparkle has returned to your eyes, and yes, you're certainly starting to look like the Sally of old. I'm so glad, but I knew you would get through it, given time."

There followed a brief moment of silence as the aroma of aftershave lotion wafted across the table. Its sickly, sweetish smell permeated the air all around them, and they both instinctively clutched their noses like mischievous schoolgirls. However, they couldn't resist peering around at the other customers to see who had the nerve to wear such an effrontery to the senses. Hearing a chair scrape the ground, they looked over to see a large, shaven-headed man wearing sunglasses, and dressed immaculately in a navy double-breasted suit. He had a jagged scar running down the left side of his face, and sat down at a nearby table, ordering a cold beer.

Both women grinned and sipped their drinks. However, the silence remained, and Lizzie got the impression that her friend had something on her mind.

Sally asked for a glass of water as she sat back and thought about what she was going to say. Lizzie, meanwhile studied the lunch menu with a look of utter disdain on her face, before turning to the waitress, "Chicken salad, no onions! What are you having Sally?"

Usually, swimming would make Sally ravenous but today for some reason, she seemed to have lost her appetite.

"I'll just have soup of the day please." As soon as the waitress had taken the order, Sally sat forward in her chair. "I'm going to sell the house, Lizzie. I've been thinking about it for some time, and I've finally come to a decision. Living there is a constant reminder of William. He's gone, and the only way I'm ever going to let go of him is by moving away. I can't live in a shrine, which is what I'm doing now. Can you understand that?"

"Of course I can darling," replied Lizzie looking anxious. "Whatever you decide to do, I'll help you all I can, you know that. But what about Jonathan and the girls, and where will you go, has it really come to this, Sally?"

"It's only Penny who I'm concerned about. Laura is in London doing her nurse training and Jonathan, well - I hardly ever see him, and anyway, I think he's going to move into a flat with some of his friends from university. Lizzie, they only come home when they're broke or to get some washing done. It's ridiculous having such a large house with only Penny and myself to live in it. Don't you think so?"

Lizzie sighed and finished her wine.

"You still haven't said where you're going, somewhere near I hope. There's a lovely house for sale on the green, it would just suit you - its got a..."

Sally quickly interrupted before Lizzie got too carried away with her house on the green.

"I'm going back to university, to Falcondale, as a mature student. By going back to where it all began is the only way I'll ever get over what has happened. It'll do me good to get the old brain working again, but I'll have to find a buyer first and that could take an eternity."

Lizzie was completely taken aback by what Sally had just said.

"I'm sorry, but I don't quite understand your reasoning, Sally. How can you possibly escape the past, only to plunge straight back into it again. Do you really think it's wise to go back there, after all these years?"

"I know it must sound absolutely crazy to you Lizzie, but it's something I just have to do. Anyway, I'm only going back to study, at the ripe old age of thirty nine - I'm not going to another planet." Replied Sally, slightly irritated.

"Have you told the children yet?" Asked Lizzie, still shocked by the news.

"Yes, I have, and it turned into the most awful row. We've never argued like that before. Jonathan got very angry and said I had no right to sell their home, then he just stormed off and I haven't heard from him since."

"Please don't do anything drastic. Just promise me, you'll take a step back and give yourself plenty of time to think."

"Thank-you, Lizzie. You don't have to worry, I am a grown woman!"

The café began to fill up with a wide assortment of fitness enthusiasts of all shapes and sizes. Some of whom were attired in quite bizarre, figure-hugging outfits, which Lizzie thought totally inappropriate for an establishment meant for eating. She cringed as loud pop music suddenly blared out over the sound system, making conversation quite an effort. They asked for the bill, but as Lizzie was gathering together her collection of carrier bags, she beckoned Sally closer.

"Our highly-scented friend in the sharp suit appears to have taken quite a fancy to you. He's done nothing but stare since he arrived."

"That's absurd!" Smirked Sally, "It's you he's probably interested in, after all you're much more sophisticated than I am!"

"I hardly think so darling, for a start, I look like the back end of a bus! I've got wrinkles, and let's not forget about the haemorrhoids either. I don't think a dashing hunk like that would go for an old maid with piles, do you?"

"You've left out the varicose veins Lizzie, come on now - let's not be modest!" Giggled Sally.

Several diners glanced around to see two glamorous, mature women leave the café holding on to each other in fits of laughter.

Outside, they hugged each other fondly, before making their way to the car park. It made Lizzie feel good to hear Sally laugh again, even if it was at her own expense. She stopped and turned to her friend, "Please don't think I'm speaking out of turn, but perhaps it is time you met someone else. It's wrong for a woman like you to be alone. I think you should get out more and don't keep punishing yourself like this. William's death wasn't your fault."

"You're right Lizzie, but only if the right person comes along. I'm in no hurry - its just taken longer than I thought to move on."

Lizzie eyed her suspiciously, and knew there was more to this.

"I think you're holding out on me, Sally. There's something else isn't there?"

Sally looked down at the ground, as she thought about what to say.

"Do you remember years ago, I told you I had a crush on William's brother, David?"

"Yes, now you come to mention it, I do. How funny, but I don't think William would have been very happy though?"

"No, of course he wouldn't," replied Sally, hesitating. "But there was more to it than that, Lizzie."

"What do you mean?"

"I fell in love with David, and I actually loved him more than William. I feel so awful, Lizzie."

"Oh my god, and you still went ahead and married William?"

"Yes, I did - it was so wrong of me. But I couldn't destroy William by telling him, I'd chosen the wrong brother."

"Sally, you should have told me. So this has been causing you even more pain, the guilt of loving, David?"

Sally nodded, "Is it possible to be in love with two men at the same time - two brothers?"

"That's a new one on me. Did poor William ever suspect you loved, David?"

"No, I don't think so, but please don't put it like that, it sounds like I had an affair with David."

"I'm sorry Sally, but in the circumstances, I can't blame you for wanting to go back to Falcondale. Did anything ever happen between you and David back then?"

Sally felt awkward. "No of course not."

"Nonsense, try pulling the other leg, it's got bells on!"

"Lizzie, I just don't know what to do for the best."

"Is David still there?"

"I don't know," blushed Sally.

"You're a bad liar, Mrs. Peddlescoombe! It's blindingly obvious to me, what you should do - go back to Falcondale!"

Sally stood impassively, as Lizzie casually flung the carrier bags into the boot of her BMW. She then blew her friend a kiss, and arranged to phone her the next day. Sally walked over to where her own car was parked, thinking about what Lizzie had suggested about meeting someone else. It certainly hadn't been something high on her priority list, and as for David, she didn't know if she could or really wanted to go through all the emotional turmoil of getting involved with him.

She sat inside the car and started the engine, and as she did so, the radio came

on. She gasped, as she recognised the song, and leaned forward to switch the .
off. But something caused her to hesitate, and she slowly sat back in her seat. A.
first it was just a slight watering of her deep blue eyes. Then a steady trickle soon
turned into a flow that began to stream down her cheeks. It gained momentum
until she gave in to the huge, heaving sobs of anguish that still tore at her soul. The
anguish that had been part of her life for so long.

The song ended and the DJ's chirpy banter rudely interrupted her moment of
sorrow.

"Hey folks, that was way back to 1962, with Bryan Hyland's *'Sealed With A
Kiss.'* Does anyone out there remember what they were doing then. It was the year
Marilyn Monroe died. Give me a call, the phone-lines are open!"

Sally switched off the radio, and feeling angry with herself, searched in her bag
for a tissue. She never thought of herself as a weak person, so why did she react
like this? She thought things were improving, which they were, but now this again.
As she was trying to regain her composure, she heard heavy footsteps and glanced
into her rear view mirror. It was the flashy aftershave man from the café walking
towards his car. It was the same man who, unbeknown to Sally been stalking her
these past few months. She couldn't quite see his face because of the sunglasses,
but something about him disturbed her. She couldn't help but notice the huge,
gleaming white limousine he was driving.

 Frank stared in at her, but she quickly looked away, not wanting anyone to see her
in such a state.

2. FALCONDALE

For many, those first few weeks at university were quite a traumatic time, and for Sally Carlington it was no different. She had arrived as a slim, shy, eighteen-year from Middlesex. It had been the first time she had really been away by herself, apart from a school trip to France the year earlier. But this was all so different, now she was alone in Falcondale, deep in rural Wales, and not knowing a soul. Her parents had driven her, along with all the paraphernalia that freshers were inclined to bring with them at the start of a new term.

It was early Saturday afternoon, on the 29th September, 1962. After a very brief look around the campus, her parents had left her. They had a bridge game that evening and wanted to get straight back. The fifty pounds Sally's father gave her as he kissed her on the cheek could do nothing to alleviate the teenager's fears of impending loneliness.

"Don't forget to phone will you, darling - we love you, work hard now," and that was it, they had gone. Sally was an only child, and although she seemed to have everything she could want, her upbringing wasn't what you would call, happy. Her father, a civil engineer and her office manager mother, weren't bad parents in any particular way, they were just cold and distant, as if they didn't really want children. Sally was never taken out on trips, and rarely given dolls or toys to play with. Her parents could certainly afford them, but they just didn't bother, and Sally was generally left to her own devices. Christmas time and birthdays were usually depressing, non events, and as Sally got older, she began to dread them. It meant sitting at the same table as her parents, trying to make conversation, and feeling the tense, awkward atmosphere. So, in many ways, coming to Falcondale was a blessing, but only if she could settle in, and get used to the vastly different way of life.

She plonked herself down on the sturdy iron-framed bed and looked around at the small squalid room despondently. In one corner stood a grubby, cracked enamel sink with a college towel hanging from the rusting iron rail below it. Just above the sink, was a worn-out mirror, which had obviously fallen down several times judging by the numerous filled-in holes dotted around the edges. To the side of this was a threadbare, but somewhat homely-looking wing-back armchair. Next, stood a huge, dark, towering wardrobe which gave Sally the spooks. Then, there was her desk. This was a vast monstrosity of a thing, proudly bearing the graffiti and initials of long-departed students, carved into its heavily waxed surface. She stood up and went over to sit at the desk. Running her fingers over the dark wood, she imagined herself being there, toiling away all alone, during the coming winter months.

Finding the room quite stuffy, Sally went to open the small sash-cord window. It was stuck and took all of her strength to wrench it free. It was worth the effort though, as the cool breeze felt refreshing on her face. She pulled back the garish, yellow-flowered curtains as far back as they would go, then, poking her head out of the window, she noticed the view wasn't nearly as bad as she had expected. The courtyard below was very pleasing to the eye, with the circular flower bed still a beautiful mass of colour, as it overflowed with a multitude of dahlias and begonias.

She sat back on the bed once more and opened the thick, brown envelope bearing her name. It had been given to her on arrival by a thin, bureaucratic-looking woman, who sat behind a desk, looking most important. Inside were numerous typed sheets giving details and background information about the proud learning institution she had enrolled in. One sheet told her which degree courses were available and how she could combine three different subjects during her first year. Sally quite liked this scheme as it would give her the opportunity to study a totally unrelated topic. She could then drop the subject at a later date if she found it wasn't to her liking. Sally had already elected to study English as her core subject, but now History and Classics began to intrigue her as well.

Flicking through more pages, she came across a map of the town and surrounding areas. This was accompanied by a list of interesting places to visit, things to do, and suggested walks around the hills and countryside. Another sheet mentioned the fact that the following Tuesday was Matriculation Day, with a welcome speech to be made by the college president, in the assembly hall. Sally sighed, Tuesday was an eternity away. The problem was today, and how on earth was she going to get through it. She tried to think rationally, and came to the conclusion that most of the other new students probably felt the same - lonely and depressed at being stuck in such a remote and strange place.

She heard some activity outside and returning to the window, saw other newcomers arriving and heading into the entrance of the building. Like her, most had been brought in by their parents and looked somewhat bewildered. Her heart went out to them as she noticed the long, sad faces as they struggled with their various cases and bags. Sally wondered if her face looked like that too.

Putting the papers aside, she decided to take the initiative and venture down to the recreation lounge on the ground floor. Perhaps she could meet some of the others and make some new friends.

Several of the various societies had set up trestle tables in the enormous lounge and were eagerly touting for new members to join them in their seemingly exciting pursuits. Sally immediately joined the Hill Walking Club, but was in two minds about committing herself to the Shakespeare Society. She had loved the Bard's works while at grammar school and would welcome the chance to act out Romeo and Juliet in full costume. As she deliberated and let her imagination flow, a tall, broad-shouldered man of about forty five approached her.

"Good afternoon, Miss, my name is John Meredith, I'm the Dean of Students," he said with a distinct air of authority. "I am here purely for your welfare, and if you ever want to talk to me about anything, no matter what - my door is always open."

Sally introduced herself and thanked the Dean. She immediately liked him and felt re-assured by his calm manner and regard for her well-being. A kindly woman from the Falcondale Christian Society then came forward and offered Sally a cup of strong-looking tea and a rather tempting cream cake to accompany it. Sally graciously declined the offer, but accepted a glass of home-made lemonade instead. Taking her drink, she decided to step outside for a breath of fresh air, after literally being overwhelmed by goodwill.

Wooden bench seats were neatly arranged around the perimeter of the courtyard, and Sally sat herself down on the nearest one she could find. She needed a few moments just to sit and gather her thoughts. The university had done much to welcome the new students and make them feel relaxed, and she now began to realise, that given time, she probably would get to enjoy her time there. Looking up at the mass of over-looking windows, Sally tried to locate which room was hers, but they all looked the same. She then smiled and felt a sense of relief to see that everyone else appeared to be blessed with the same vile curtains as her! She finished her lemonade and decided to go back in and join the Shakespeare Society after all.

As she was about to stand, the sound of pop music began to blare from an open window. Sally looked up again and tried to locate the source of the music, thinking who on earth could be so down right rude and ignorant.

"Do you like Billy Fury?" Inquired the male voice.

She turned to see a tall, fair-haired young man sit down on the bench beside her.

"I really don't know. All I can hear at the moment is just a loud din!"

The well-dressed young man laughed and offered her a cigarette, which she declined. "So you're a fresher are you? You'll have to get used to noise like that at university - it gets worse!"

"Are you a student here?" Asked Sally.

"I sure am. I don't believe I've had the pleasure, my name's Frank," he replied, looking deeply into the pretty blonde's, blue eyes."

She told him her name but the double entendre was lost on Sally.

"Today's my first day - what's it like here?"

"It can be quite a shock to the system, especially if you're from a big city. But, we have ways of making our own fun here at Falcondale," he smirked. "What's your major?"

"English, but I may try Classics and History." She replied, feeling herself going red for no particular reason. He laughed and sat back, as she watched him take a long drag from his cigarette.

"I'm glad you said no, I like that in a woman, it shows spirit. Besides, it's not ladylike for a pretty little thing like you to smoke."

Sally didn't quite know how to take that, and felt even more embarrassed. However, she did enjoy a few more minutes of seemingly polite conversation with the stranger. He went on to tell her things about some of the lecturers which made her laugh. Although she now felt quite relaxed in his company, she had no real experience of talking to men, especially those like, Frank Gant.

She glanced at her watch and made some excuse about having to go back inside. Sally then thanked the young man for taking the time to speak to her and stood up to leave. He walked the few yards to the entrance with her, before gallantly opening the door with an extravagant theatrical flourish.

"Are you one of the society representatives?" She asked, thinking he may be a Shakespearean.

"No, not exactly, but I am a representative of sorts. I stand for the 'Fun Society' and you'll find us practising what we preach at the Black Lion tonight. Why not come along, you'll enjoy it."

Sally smiled and went back inside feeling in much better spirits. A few of the others had decided to brave the recreation lounge and were chatting with the various university officials. However, instead of remaining, Sally decided to go back upstairs, unpack and see about getting her room into some sort of habitable condition.

As she climbed the stairs she could again hear the music from earlier. It seemed to get louder with each step she took, until finally, as she walked along the corridor, her worst fears were confirmed - the racket was coming from the room immediately next to hers!

The University of Falcondale was situated in mid-west Wales, just on the outskirts of the market town bearing the same name. The town was tiny, not really much more than a village. It was surrounded by lush green hills, which were inhabited by a large population of sheep. Often the sheep would wander down to the campus, where they could be found grazing in the grounds or on the sports fields without a care in the world. The town's main shopping area and focal point was the High Street. Here, the dozen or so shops only stocked what was completely necessary, and would all meticulously close dead on one o'clock for lunch, and for the whole afternoon on Wednesdays. A few enterprising individuals in the past had opened shops exclusively with the student in mind. These, like the Beatnik Shop had unfortunately not taken into account that the vast majority of students were broke after the first couple of weeks of term, and were not even there during the summer months. At the beginning of the High Street was a memorial to those lost in the two world wars, and in the centre of town stood a very proud-looking clock tower, which was joined to the town hall and public library. Then, as the street veered to the right, one could see the impressive steeple of St. Mark's church in the background. Although the town was certainly no shopper's paradise, it was home to an excellent fish and chip shop, Pedro's Bistro, several bohemian coffee bars and quite a selection of pubs, much to the delight of the university's rugby fraternity.

After the initial shock of small-town living had set in, many students became very attached to this idyllic little community where town and gown co-existed in relative harmony.

Sally was housed in Lloyd-Evans Hall, which was the oldest of the three main living quarters. It was a large, archaic building, comprising of four main residential blocks in a square formation, with the courtyard in the centre. On each corner stood eerie-looking towers, which to many of the students, resembled Dracula's castle. Sally's room was situated in the inner sanctum overlooking the entrance block and the huge, gothic, ivy-covered archway, that led into the courtyard.

The university, during the early sixties still maintained a strict policy of segregation regarding male and female students in the halls of residence. The students were also obliged to follow a code of conduct, especially when out and about in town, where they were seen as representatives of an old and established learning institution.

Sally had just about finished hanging up her clothes when she was disturbed by a loud knock at the door. She couldn't think who it might be, and even thought for a moment that her parents had come back to take her home.

"Hello! I'm Lizzie Marchmont - your new neighbour. I thought I'd come and introduce myself. The music's not too loud is it?" Then, before Sally had a chance to reply, the girl had half entered her room and was having a good look around. "Oh, what a super room - much nicer than mine!"

Sally stared in disbelief at the vision in front of her. This odd Lizzie character had jet black hair, piled high into an enormous beehive, that almost reached the top of the door frame. She wore a knee-length fake, leopard skin coat, which was open at the front to reveal tight black slacks and an equally tight black sweater. Although Lizzie's make-up was immaculately applied, Sally had never seen pink lipstick and black eyeliner put on so thickly. It looked a bit ghoulish, and Sally immediately thought this weird apparition blended in very well with the gothic surroundings.

"I'm very pleased to meet you, Lizzie," Sally responded, offering her hand somewhat warily. "No, the music's just fine. Billy Fury's one of my favourites!"

Lizzie was noticeably flattered and beamed, "There's a few of us going into town tonight - do you fancy coming along? Don't worry, none of us know each other - we're all new. Anyway, it's better than what the Christian Society has arranged for us, unless of course you like tea and biscuits on a Saturday night!"

The two girls laughed, and Sally said she would love to go along with them. Although she did wonder whether they would all be dressed so outrageously. After Lizzie had gone back to her room, Sally looked through her sparse wardrobe, thinking perhaps she should have brought more clothes with her. Finally, she settled on a modest check skirt and V-neck purple sweater. But what about the college scarf, should she wear that too?

She needn't have been concerned, as only Lizzie was dressed to shock. The other six girls were all wearing pretty much the same as Sally. They had met downstairs in the lobby area, and although there were many new students milling around, most of them preferred to play safe and stay within the confines of the university. Here, they could attend organised functions rather than venture out into unknown territory so soon after arriving.

"What are you drinking Sally?" Called out Lizzie, as the group of girls trooped into the Crown, their first port of call.

Sally didn't quite know what to say. She had never been in a pub before, and had only ever drank the occasional glass of wine or sherry at home. However, she didn't think sherry sounded very sophisticated, so she asked for a Martini, since that's what her parents would often drink in the evenings. As she heard no sarcastic or derogatory remarks from Lizzie, Sally assumed her choice was acceptable. Some of the other girls seemed to be in the same predicament, and one poor soul, a plump girl called Pauline looked scared out of her wits and had to endure the boos and hisses of the whole group after asking for a glass of Tizer.

Inside the pub, the wallpaper and ceiling were tinged a dark nicotine yellow, and the air was thick with pipe and cigarette smoke. The atmosphere was anything but congenial, with the few mainly elderly regulars sitting around tables coughing, playing dominoes and having the occasional snort of snuff. They either totally ignored the group of young women or stared at them in grim silence. Lizzie downed her drink in one, and turned to Sally, "I don't think we'll be hanging around in here too long - see anyone you fancy!"

"What about the Black Lion?" Laughed Sally, knocking back her Martini. "I met a bloke this afternoon called, Frank. He said he would be in there!"

"Ok, it's the Black Lion, if we can find it," called out Lizzie, as she led the girls back outside.

The party didn't have to look very far as the pub in question was situated in the centre of the street, and was the most popular in town. It was well accustomed to being taken over by vast swarms of inexperienced students. Once inside, the younger clientele watched in amusement as the girls tried a variety of cocktails, screamed with laughter and played endless records on the jukebox. The noise could be heard all along the street, as the whole pub became infected with the party atmosphere.

Sally, with her slender figure soon found she had a natural talent for the 'Twist', and quickly began to attract admiring glances. Other students began to arrive and tables and chairs were pushed aside to make room for the dancing.

"Do you know what?" Slurred Lizzie, putting her arm around Sally's shoulder. "I think you and I are going to be good friends. Come on, let's go over to the jukebox. Do you like Helen Shapiro? I'm going to get my hair done like hers on Monday!"

"I'm sure it'll look fantastic!" Replied Sally, a little bewildered. She was on her fifth Martini now and was glad she had Lizzie to keep her upright.

"Why don't you get your hair done too Sally, we could go together!"

Sally stared at this odd girl in disbelief, not knowing if she was just immature or plain silly. But she had grown to like Lizzie as the evening had progressed, and now, also felt they would indeed become great friends.

They pushed their way through the crowd towards the jukebox, but had to wait their turn, as two men were already putting some records on. One was very tall with neat, blonde hair and dressed in a blue sports jacket and grey flannels. The other looked like an Elvis Presley clone, with thick black hair immaculately slicked back. He wore blue jeans and a white T-shirt with the sleeves rolled over.

"Hey, put Chubby Checker on - I feel like twisting again!" Shouted Lizzie to the two men. They both turned, and stared, amazed at the sight facing them.

"I will if you dance with me!" Yelled back the one in the T-shirt, as he simultaneously combed his hair with one hand and flattened down the sides with the other.

"It's a deal!" Screeched Lizzie, as she teasingly began to dance alone while her new partner hurriedly selected the record.

Sally couldn't help catching the gaze of the other young man. It was the same one who had spoken to her earlier in the afternoon. He looked longingly at her, letting his eyes greedily survey her figure from top to bottom.

"Hello, it's Sally isn't it? I'm so glad you decided to come after all. The dancing can wait, let's go and sit in the corner, and you can tell me all about yourself."

Sally was quite over-powered by the strong smell of aftershave lotion, and felt distinctly uncomfortable under Frank's gaze. She wasn't sure about him, but he was certainly very handsome, as Lizzie had so indiscreetly pointed out earlier during a lull in the music.

On the way back to Lloyd-Evans Hall the girls were still singing and laughing noisily. A couple of the more inebriated ones decided to follow Lizzie's example and remove their high-heeled shoes, finding them quite a hindrance after an evening's merrymaking. The night had turned out to be wonderful with everyone, except Pauline, having had the time of their lives. In fact Sally and probably a fair few of the other girls had never known anything quite like it. The evening had been the perfect tonic to allay the fears most of the students had been harbouring since arriving at Falcondale.

Walking a few paces ahead, Sally noticed Lizzie and Ken staggering along giggling together as if it were the most natural thing in the world. She watched intently as she saw her friend push Ken playfully, then link her arm through his. Sally found Lizzie's lack of inhibition quite refreshing and it prompted her to do the same with Frank. Although thrilled at Sally's impulsiveness, Frank then decided to take matters a stage further, and in one swift action, put his arm around Sally's waist and pulled her towards him.

She felt secure being held by him, and for a moment, as they neared the gates, she wondered if she should invite him back to her room. The mere thought of this seemed to arouse her deeply, but she wasn't sure whether this was due to Frank's sheer animal magnetism or simply the idea of blatantly breaking one of the university's most strictest and fervently-enforced rules. There were certainly no shortage of notices pinned up around the campus reminding everyone that no male students were permitted in female halls of residence after 9pm. The university authorities, realising the vulnerability of some of the freshers even went so far as to post night watchmen in some of the halls as a precaution.

Pauline was certainly well aware of this particular rule, and noticing the ever increasing band of male students following the group, took it upon herself to remind the others of the consequences should they choose to transgress.

Frank and Ken were also knowledgeable of this rule and had, through experience found a number of alternative ways of gaining access to most of the buildings. They probably would have succeeded on this occasion had it not been for Pauline purposely alerting the night watchman of their approach.

"Shit! It's bloody old Stan, we'll never get in there tonight," muttered Ken as the bright beam of a powerful torch lit up his face.

"Bloody fat bitch, why couldn't she keep her mouth shut," replied Frank, loud enough for Pauline to hear.

"You'll have to say your goodbyes here folks - rules are rules, as you two young gentleman know full well." Said the watchman, as he began ushering the girls inside.

Sally turned to Lizzie but saw she was otherwise engaged, giving Ken a passionate goodbye kiss.

"Do I get one as well?" Asked Frank, pulling Sally towards him. There was no time to protest, even if she had wanted to, for Frank's mouth quickly engulfed hers and for the first time in her eighteen years, Sally was to experience the intimacy of a full French kiss.

"Disgusting," said Stan as he turned from the two entwined couples and went back into the building.

Sally's first real kiss however, was to be a bit of a disaster. After a few moments of keeping her eyes tightly closed, her head began to spin erratically, and she thought she was about to pass out. She pushed herself away from Frank, and gasping for air, staggered back and stumbled straight into a dustbin. She only just about managed to stop herself falling over completely, but could do nothing to prevent the lid clattering noisily to the ground, shattering the still of the night.

Like a shot, Stan was back outside. He sent the two lads packing and angrily scolded Sally and Lizzie like two naughty children, before bringing them both inside and bolting the doors.

The following morning, Sally was to experience yet another of life's rich experiences - a hangover! "I'm never going to drink again Lizzie. I feel just awful, and my head is pounding."

"That's what they all say," moaned Lizzie, her hair a tangled mass, with last night's make-up smeared across her face.

"No, it's true, I made such a fool of myself. I've never danced like that before, and certainly not with a man!"

"Come on Sally, don't go all prudish on me. You enjoyed yourself just as much as I did."

"Well, yes I suppose I did." Sally then recalled something else, " But Lizzie - I kissed that Frank bloke! Oh my god!"

"Yes you did, and you fell back into that smelly dustbin!"

"Whatever must he think of me?"

"I think he liked you. But you have to admit - it was funny!"

"For you it might have been, as for me, I wont be able to face anyone again, and as for Frank, I doubt he'll want to see me anymore."

During the afternoon, Sally had at last begun to feel like her normal self. Apart from popping out to the shops, before they closed, she hadn't ventured out of her room at all. The communal telephone had been very active as usual and she knew that Lizzie had received a call. Before long, Lizzie was tapping at her door.

"You'll never guess who that was?" She said, in a highly excited state.

"I've no idea," replied Sally, not really interested.

"It was Ken, you know - from last night!"

"Really! What did he want?"

"What do you think, silly, he wants me to go out with him, tonight!"

"That's wonderful, Lizzie - he's very nice," continued Sally, not wanting to sound too despondent.

"Did I detect a hint of jealousy in your voice just then?"

"No, of course not, I'm just very happy for you that's all." Answered Sally a little defensively, before adding. "Well yes, I was a tiny bit jealous, since I seem to have blown my chances."

"So why don't you come along with us, it would be great fun."

"Have you never heard of 'two's company, three's a crowd'?"

Oh well, I'll just have to have both men for myself!"

"What do you mean Lizzie, you're joking with me aren't you - is Frank going too?"

"Yes, silly Sally, of course Frank's going," laughed Lizzie. "In fact, it was his idea that we all go out for a drive in the country."

The four students were to spend several evenings together during the course of the next few weeks. Lizzie seemed perfectly suited to Ken, he was just as outgoing as her, not only in personality, but in dress sense too. They both thrived in each other's company, and at times seemed in competition to see who could shock the most. Frank and Ken were both senior English students and knew all the places to take the girls for a good time.

Sally however, hadn't really had a proper boyfriend before, or at least one where she wasn't chaperoned and continually watched by her mother. She had gone out with Tim, the neighbour's son for a year, and had even let him kiss her on the lips, but their relationship seemed to drift more into one of friendship, rather than intimacy. Now she felt quite overawed by it all really and a little nervous. She had wondered at times why her mother had never explained to her about boys. One minute she was being treated like a child, then she was suddenly whisked off and dumped at university as if she had grown into a woman overnight.

Now, Sally felt she was being misunderstood. She loved to enjoy herself like the other students, but she also wanted more, something deeper, something more spiritual. She wanted to learn and meet other people, not just the rebellious and hedonistic party crowd, but people with different interests, people who were going places, who could uplift her. Frank was certainly fun, but he seemed to be taking her in the opposite direction.

It wasn't long before Sally discovered Frank to be incredibly conceited, manipulative, and he had a vain streak that even outshone Lizzie's! He was also only interested in seeing her when it suited him, and they always had to go to places where he wanted to go. This was usually well away from the other students, and it was always Sally who seemed to pay for everything, while Frank would drink heavily and try to kiss and grope her in the back of his Ford Consul. When she protested he would get angry and call her frigid and old-fashioned. Once, he made her get out of the car and walk back to campus in the dark, because her money had all been exhausted. Sally was now in a position where she had to keep asking her parents for cash, which she hated, but she continued to allow herself to be used in this manner.

Frank would often ignore her, especially in front of other female students and openly criticize her for staying in her room to study. Then, he would just change completely and say nice things and take her out dancing, or to places she hadn't been before, all paid for by Sally of course. At times she felt frightened of Frank, he seemed to have a psychological hold over her which she couldn't explain. Sometimes, she would find this fear quite stimulating, or if she could admit it, even exciting. He had a certain power about him that others picked up on. Often the other students would treat her differently, like she was some sort of gangster's moll. She felt owned by him, and in some ways, even safe, like he would look out for her and protect her, despite the regular bad treatment she received from him.

Frank was very reticent about his background, and would get very defensive if Sally asked him questions. She knew he came from Bristol, had a father who was something big in medicine, and there was an older brother. But that was about all the information she could glean, and she only got those snippets after a night's drinking had loosened Frank's tongue. He certainly would never have told her his brother, Giles had done everything right since the day he was born. Giles excelled at school, at sports, and had left Oxford with his master's degree, ready to enter the heady world of stock-broking. At home, the talk was always of Giles, and how great he was and what his latest achievements were. An example had now been set that the younger Frank, or Francis as he was known at home, would find impossible to match, and how he resented it.

Frank did try, especially during his early years, before his anger had taken root. He too showed a remarkable aptitude for sports, namely rugby and gymnastics. But the problems really began after he was expelled from an expensive public school. Frank had racially abused the son of a wealthy foreign tycoon. Then, after a teacher had rebuked him and accused Frank of being a red-necked philistine, he retaliated by swearing at her, and splitting the woman's lip with a violent punch to the face.

"What's a philistine, father?" Asked the young Frank, as his father read the expulsion letter.

"It's something you should damn well know - have you never opened a bible lad?" Roared Hugh Gant, as he sent Frank sprawling with a blow from the back of his hand. "Why on earth can't you be like Giles and make me proud. You're a bloody disgrace to the family, now get out of my sight."

That's how Frank's relationship with his father remained right through his teenage years, he was constantly trying to live up to an ideal that he wasn't cut out for. While all the time Giles reaped the rewards of being his father's favourite son.

One day, Frank really thought he could win over his father's affections. He had gained a place at university, and eagerly pointed out Falcondale on the map, as his father sat at the breakfast table.

"Do you seriously believe that I can tell my friends at the golf club that my youngest son is at Falcondale?" Remarked the older man angrily.

"But father, it's university - you always said I had to get into university. It's what you always wanted for me."

"You might as well say you're studying in the outer reaches of bloody Siberia for all the good it'll do you. When I said university, I meant Oxford or Cambridge - nothing less. Falcondale takes the chaff from the wheat, the rejects, the bloody imbeciles that nobody wants."

"No, it's not true, Falcondale is a good university, one of the best." But Frank's words were to fall on deaf ears.

It was sometime later, when Frank was drinking with Ken in one of the pubs in town that he decided to let his friend in on his plan. Frank was sick of being broke and having to use and con women to get money. He felt, that coming from a wealthy family he should automatically have what he needed. But of course, his father kept a tight hold of the finances where Frank was concerned. He beckoned Ken over to one of the tables near the window, and told him to look across the street.

"There's nothing there, Frank - just an old lady coming out of the post office with a shopping trolley."

"Yes, I can see that, you moron, you have to see the bigger picture."

"Okay, an old lady with a shopping trolley locking the post office door!"

"Precisely!" Exclaimed Frank, taking a gulp from his beer. "Now look and learn. The old lady runs the post office alone, and every week she locks up for lunch and goes off to do her shopping. It's always the same routine, and she's gone for half an hour. There's several thousand pounds of cash, just waiting for us to claim."

"Steal, you mean?" Replied, Ken, quite shocked at what he was hearing. "It's a post office, Frank, stealing from the crown. If we get caught we'll go down for years."

"Whatever! It's tiny - it's only a bloody sub-post office, it's not the bank of England. Now, listen, I've been going in to buy stamps and watching what happens. She never locks the safe, its too much for her to keep opening it again. Besides, she's been doing the same thing for years and nothing has ever gone missing."

"But we can't break through a locked door, people would see us?"

"She has a little dog, and she always leaves the back door open in case it needs to go out. All we have to do is get into the back yard, get the money, and we can be gone before she even gets to the first shop!"

"Amazing, Frank. You've got it all figured out. When do we do it?"

"I'll let you know. It'll be easy, no fuss, no witnesses, just lots and lots of cash!"

In her moments of doubt, Sally would often think how well she and Lizzie had done by getting boyfriends so quickly, literally on their first day at campus, that must surely be a record. The fact that she was going out with probably, the most handsome, and lusted-over man at college had certainly put Sally on the social map. But, it was left to Lizzie to put things into perspective.

"We've got to hang on to what we've got. We're stuck out in the middle of nowhere, and there's not exactly a surplus of desirable men available is there?"

Lizzie was right, the thought of not having a boyfriend and being alone was something Sally couldn't bear to think of. In the meantime, she decided to let things go on as they were with Frank, and see what develops.

However, one evening in December, Sally had some work to do for a forthcoming seminar, and walked the short distance to the university library. She pushed open the heavy swing doors and went over to the desk, returned some books and made her way to the Classics section. It wasn't too busy at the time, which pleased Sally. She had grown rather attached to the library and felt very relaxed and at peace there. She took her time and gazed up at the thousands of books lining the high shelves. It was so deathly quiet, she could even hear her own footsteps on the carpeted floor. Not finding what she was looking for, she then wandered into the inner recesses, and walked past a section full of musty-smelling old tomes that looked like they would fall to pieces if anyone touched them. She walked around the hall again, but still couldn't find what she wanted.

Sally had been to the Classics section several times before, but that was when she was studying Greek tragedy, and had to find works on Sophocles and Euripides, but now she was swatting up on Greek warfare and was a little lost. She began to feel self-conscious, as some of the students sitting huddled over desks, had noticed her predicament. Sally decided to take the initiative and ask one of them, but as she was about to walk over, she became aware of someone standing next to her.

"Hello, you seem a bit lost - what are you trying to find?"

Sally turned and gazed up into the hazel eyes of a dark-haired student, probably a few years older then herself. His eyes, although intense, seemed to be warm and smiling at her. For a few moments there was a silence, until it dawned on both of them that they were staring straight at each other.

Sally's mind went blank, and she felt herself starting to blush.

"Oh, I'm, I'm, looking for something about ancient Greece - it's for a seminar."

"Ok, but can you be a bit more specific. This section is all ancient Greece. Perhaps I can help - I did Classics in my first year," whispered the student politely.

Sally's composure returned, "It's about the causes of the 'Polynesian war'," she whispered back.

The student couldn't help smiling, "I don't think so. Please trust me on this one - is it the Peloponnesian war?"

"Oh yes, that's it, silly me - I was just having a blonde moment!" Replied Sally, almost dying of shame.

The student went to a shelf and selected several heavy files.

"Here, these will help you." He then beckoned her to sit at his table. "I did exactly the same seminar as you, it's very easy. Within these hallowed compendiums are essays written by past students on pretty much every subject. Nothing you're doing is new, it's all been done before."

"How amazing, I would never have known, and I was about to do it the hard way. So every single subject is covered, you say?" Gasped Sally, highly impressed.

"Well, not exactly every subject!" He replied, giving her a mischievous grin, "But certainly everything you need to know."

He then began picking out various excerpts and told Sally to make a note of them.

As he was busy flicking through the pages, Sally took the opportunity to get a good look at him. She noticed how well-shaped his large hands were. Then, as she allowed her eyes to slowly inch their way up his strong arms, she saw that he had quite an athletic physique. She imagined him to be some sort of sportsman, a rower perhaps. He was wearing a tatty old fisherman's jumper, which seemed to suit his craggy, slightly weather-beaten face. With his unruly mop of hair, he reminded her a little, of Paul, from the up-and-coming band, the Beatles. She then watched fascinated as the different shades of light enhanced the bold outlines of William's features. He seemed so happy and content in what he was doing. He then suddenly closed the book and turned to face her. She felt embarrassed that he'd caught her staring at him. She thanked him quickly and got up to leave, but he reached out and took her arm.

"I'll be here for a while on Friday afternoon. I can bring some of my old notes for you."

"Thank-you," she smiled. There was a brief pause and Sally found herself agreeing to meet him again in the library.

"But I don't even know your name?" He asked, as they walked to the exit.

"It's Sally, Sally Carlington!" She whispered back like a naughty child, "See you on Friday."

Back in her room Sally found it impossible to concentrate on her work. Her mind kept wandering back to the young student she had met so briefly that evening. She smiled as she recalled him with his pile of compendiums, as he called them. She felt excited, and tried to remember the low tone of his voice, the slight but definite accent, the wide smile and his sparkling eyes. He seemed so knowledgeable, but not in a pompous or big-headed way, like Frank would have been. He just seemed so genuine and charming.

Again, Sally tried to concentrate, but her mind was too distracted. She thought about going next door and telling Lizzie - she would be so amazed.

But wait, what's happening, thought Sally? He's only going to lend me some notes. That's nothing to get all excited about. Anyway, she's seeing Frank, and they're going out on Thursday - it's her birthday. Sally suddenly felt a pang of guilt, and went to lay on her bed. But again her thoughts returned to the library. Eventually her eyes began to get heavy, and she drifted off to sleep, just wondering what his name could be?

3. THE SOCIAL CLUB

William, like Sally was awake early the following morning. He quickly showered, dressed and drank a cup of coffee, before pulling on his old threadbare duffle coat, and set off for a walk. Although the really cold weather was still to come, the mornings were beginning to turn quite chilly. Usually, William would get up at around eight, and then it would take him until at least mid-morning to wake up properly. Going for a walk this early was certainly something new to him, but he just felt the urge to get out and breathe the chilly dawn air. He stepped out into a fine drizzle, which was cool and refreshing to his face, and headed off to wander around the town's deserted streets. Perhaps he would have gone back to fetch his umbrella in normal circumstances, but today didn't really seem normal.

William had a lightness of spirit about him, as if he didn't have a care in the world. But then, he didn't really have any proper worries, not like some. He was anxious about his finals coming up next year, and he had been deeply shocked by the death of his screen idol, Marilyn Monroe earlier in August. At the time he thought he'd never get over losing her. Then there was the concern over the recent Cuban missile crisis. William had been certain that a nuclear war between America and the Soviet Union was imminent, and everyone was going to die. However, he had learnt recently, and with great relief that Khrushchev had agreed to dismantle the bases and take the missiles back to Russia. But that was William, he would often present an unconcerned face to the world, and sometimes pretend not to really care, but in reality he was extremely compassionate, and cared very strongly about many issues affecting society.

William was twenty two years old, and had grown to love Wales with a passion. His mother was a local teacher who had met his father, a Canadian serviceman, while he was stationed in Britain during the war. They subsequently married, had two sons and lived on the outskirts of town, before later moving to Niagara-on-the-Lake, in Ontario. William's mother however, had always insisted that her sons go to university back in her home town, and be a part of the principality she loved so dearly.

William and his younger brother, David had spent many a happy day hiking around Snowdonia with their father, or playing in the sea at Aberystwyth while visiting from Canada. However, William's favourite place was the nearby lake. Falcondale Lake was set among lush, rolling green hills, in an area renowned for its outstanding natural beauty. With water lilies growing in abundance, and bordered by tall, sweeping bulrushes, the lake was popular not only with anglers, but hikers and artists alike. Although fishing was William's real passion, he did enjoy the tranquillity the lake exuded, and would often sit on the bank, reading, or simply be lost in his own trail of thoughts. During the warmer weather he would take his rowing boat, along with his fishing tackle and a packed lunch, out onto the calm water, and spend a whole day there. Once he caught a 25lb carp, but no-one believed him. He wished he'd kept the fish as proof, rather than return it back into the water, as he always did.

But now, William was hooked, hopelessly and deeply. He couldn't stop repeating Sally's name over and over in his mind. He had seen her several times around campus, but even though the university at Falcondale was one of the smallest in the country, it could still be difficult to meet people outside one's own circle of friends.

He couldn't quite believe his luck when he saw her in the library, looking so lost and in such need of help. Had Marilyn come back to him after all? At one point he had even got up from his work to go to her aid, but hesitated when it looked as if she had found what she was looking for. He had then sat down again, his mouth dry and heart beating excitedly. Then, she was in his vision once more, still searching for her books. He had another chance - taking a deep breath he walked straight towards her.

As he got closer, he noticed she was slighter in build than he had first thought, and her hair, under the bright lighting was a glorious shade of strawberry blonde. It was longer than the current style and she wore it pinned up high at the back.

William's eyes had caught hers as he first spoke, and he was immediately captivated by them, so clear and such a very deep blue. Although he was trying to whisper, he felt his words had come out awkwardly. She must have taken him for a complete idiot he thought, as he remembered taking in her fine features, the high cheekbones, the delicate outline of her full lips. He broke into a smile as he recalled her mistakenly saying, 'Polynesian war' instead of 'Peloponnesian.' He remembered her beautiful smile, her perfect white teeth and how he wanted to take her in his arms and kiss her there, and then.

He had returned to his table, and noticed she had left her black and amber university scarf on the chair. He called her back in a hushed whisper, but she couldn't hear him. He thought about running after her, but once he had picked the scarf up, he just wanted to hold it close to him, the same scarf that had caressed her beautiful neck. He had to touch it, to inhale her delicate, feminine fragrance. He would keep it for her until they met again. Before putting the garment safely into his coat pocket, he held the scarf to his lips and kissed it, as he whispered her name.

William knew Sally was seeing Frank, and the very thought of it revolted him. It was common knowledge among the second and third years that Frank Gant was a parasite. He and his sidekick, Ken would actively seek out new female students, especially pretty ones like Sally. Then, with a gutless cunning they would seduce their victims, who were mostly lonely and very vulnerable, and take from them every penny they could. This would usually only last a couple of weeks, before they moved on to someone else. Frank took a perverse delight in what he did, and would openly brag about his many conquests, and who the next poor soul would be.

Ken put the bottle of pale ale to his mouth and deftly levered off the cap using his teeth. He then threw the object across Frank's room towards an overflowing bin. It missed and rolled a short distance, before having its path blocked by a pile of muddy rugby kit and stinking socks. Frank had a room on the second floor of the Old Building, which was used to house the third-year students. It was believed that the more quiet and genteel atmosphere would be conducive to those studying for forthcoming finals. However, in Frank's case, it was just another privilege to be abused.

"It's about time you got this dump cleaned up isn't it, how can we bring girls back here? You're such a slob, Frank!"

"Crap! The room needs a bit of character. Anyway, the girls love it like this, it brings out their animal passions!" Cursed Frank between belches, finishing the remaining dregs of his beer.

He then walked over to the bin and tried unsuccessfully to crush the rubbish down with his winkle-picker clad foot. Then, getting annoyed, he opened the door, belched again loudly in the direction of a group of chattering cleaners and dumped it on the corridor floor with a menacing crash. The women looked icily at Frank as he went back inside, slamming his door shut.

It all went quiet back out in the corridor, except for the steady drone of a distant vacuum cleaner. Then, the loud chattering voices began to start up again, always in their native Welsh, and often interspersed with bursts of raucous laughter, much to Frank's displeasure.

From last term, the cleaners had refused to enter Frank's room. It certainly wasn't because they were squeamish about the mess in any way. In fact, many of the women had spent most, if not all of their working lives at the university and very little could shock them. It was an incident concerning a sixteen-year girl, called Carol, that had been the cause of the women's outrage.

Carol's mother, also a cleaner had got her daughter the part-time job the previous summer. Like many her age, Carol had left school early and without any qualifications. She already had another part-time job, as a waitress in one of the coffee bars, which was often used by the students.

As a late developer, Carol was now beginning to like her figure. After going through a pre-pubescent stage where she could only have described herself as skinny, she had at last, grown out of her child-like shape. To Carol's delight, she was now able to experiment with many of the new clothes coming into fashion. She had long slender legs, a narrow waist and her small breasts were showing distinct signs of enlargement, much to her relief. Although no beauty, Carol certainly wasn't unattractive and could boast of several admirers in town. She had a very pale complexion, shapely lips, and what could be described as a homely sort of face. Her hair was a mousy brown and usually tied back in a ponytail.

She was enjoying her job at the university, it could be hard work, but Carol got on well with the other women, and the atmosphere was always light-hearted and jovial. She knew a few of the students from her coffee bar job, but this was only to say hello to. It was very rare that townsfolk and students socialised together. Carol, probably would have known of Frank. Most of the locals did, and there were a few who would like to see him get his just rewards.

It had been a warm day in June, and Carol had been given a section of six rooms to clean. Because of the heat, Carol, just wore her underwear beneath the pink overall, which was the standard uniform. On this day however, Carol wasn't wearing a bra. She thought nothing of it, after all, it was hot and she rarely saw students in the halls of residence during the day.

She had cleaned Frank's room for the past two days and detested it. Not knowing it was his room, she had wondered what sort of creature could live in such a manner. Then, on the third afternoon, he came back while she was inside.

He reeked of alcohol and looked quite the worse for wear. He leered at her before making a remark, which she couldn't really understand. With that, she would have left the room, but he insisted she stay and finish her work.

Mrs. Selwyn, the supervisor had already told her to just empty the bin, then vacuum the floor and not to spend too much time in there. However, Carol had noticed a large red wine stain on the carpet, and not wanting anyone to accuse her of shirking, she had got down on her hands and knees and was scrubbing hard.

After a short while she became aware of someone else in the room. She glanced up and saw Frank standing in the doorway. He was staring straight down the front of her overall.

"Scrub harder!" He grinned, "That's what I like to see, come on harder!"

Carol gasped and looked down, and to her horror, realised he could see everything, right down to her knickers. Frank made no attempt to divert his eyes, and just carried on staring. As she straightened up and tried to regain her composure, he came down heavily beside her, and before she realised what was happening, he had slipped his hand inside her overall and was feeling her breast.

"What are you doing?" She screamed at him, but still his large hand remained firmly in place. Carol tried to get to her feet, but ended up falling backwards, with Frank coming down on top of her. She felt the buttons on her overall being ripped off, as he pawed at her greedily.

"Come on you little hussy, it's what you want isn't it? I've seen you in that coffee bar, you're desperate for it."

Carol tried with all her strength to push him off, but Frank was too strong. He pulled the top of her overall completely apart and leered at her body, before biting hard on her exposed nipple. Then, reaching down, he ran his hand along her thigh, and up, towards her knickers. Carol screamed even louder and Frank froze.

In a flash, Mrs. Selwyn was standing over them.

"Get off of her, you swine!" With that, she began slapping and kicking at Frank, who just rolled off the teenager, and lay on the floor laughing hysterically.

"The Dean's going to hear about this, you'll see - you animal!" Shouted Mrs. Selwyn angrily, as she helped the distraught Carol to her feet. The other cleaners rushed to the room to see what the commotion was. Then, as Mrs. Selwyn led the sobbing girl out into the corridor, Frank stood up.

"It'll be that little whore's word against mine. She's the one who started it."

"No, he's lying Mrs. Selwyn, I was just cleaning the room, honestly," uttered the shocked Carol.

" Who do you think they'll believe?" Cursed Frank, as he approached the women menacingly. "My family's wealth is totally beyond your comprehension. Now fuck off!"

Frank won. He knew he would, and Carol lost her job. A few of the women who Frank had used his charm on, even believed his side of the story, and felt that Carol had led him on, and she was the one to blame. However, that was before Mr. Meredith, the new Dean of Students had taken up his post.

Ken reclined in the armchair in Frank's room and put his feet up on the desk. "You've been seeing that Sally for over two months, and you still haven't mounted her. You're definitely losing your touch, Frank! How about letting me have a try?"

Frank was busy getting ready, but stopped what he was doing to go over and put his face up close to Ken's.

"You can hardly talk, you bloody peasant. You've let that Lizzie walk all over you. I've heard the way you grovel to her, like a snivelling toad!" He then opened the wardrobe to select a shirt, before adding in a mocking tone, "You don't have to worry about attending to Sally's needs. I've got a special birthday treat planned for that little filly."

They both laughed as Frank buttoned down the collar of his freshly-laundered Ben Sherman, before pulling on a round-neck sweater. He was a meticulously fussy dresser, and thought the combination of him looking smart, against the more rebellious outfits that Ken wore, was one of the main reasons for their many successes with women. It also meant they could approach girls who dressed in vastly differing styles. Sally and Lizzie were prime examples of this.

Now Frank's patience was wearing thin. He wanted a positive outcome with Sally as soon as possible, which would finally conclude matters. Another priority had arisen, and he wanted to start work on his new victim immediately. With a final glance in the mirror, he practiced his smile, picked up his sports jacket and headed off with Ken, to the social club.

Frank knew Pauline would be there, he had seen her on certain nights serving drinks and clearing tables. He remembered her from the night he first danced with Sally, but he hadn't been too impressed then, as she had been a bit too chubby for his tastes. Now however, Frank was amazed at the transformation coming over Pauline. She hadn't quite got the look perfect yet, but she was rapidly losing the pounds and replacing them with sexy, feminine curves - in all the right places. He knew he would have to get in first, before she really got noticed.

Frank undressed her with his eyes, envisaging what she would be like without her spectacles, and with her long, dark hair all tousled and hanging down, or better still, spread out over a pillow.

However, Pauline was very shy and needed her confidence boosted, and at first seemed rather embarrassed when Frank initially spoke to her. He had deliberately made a mess of his table, and spilt a drink in the knowledge that it would take her a couple of visits to put things back in order. She had blushed when he first made contact, and asked her name. But, Frank had been very pleased with the response, and after that early exchange, he started to seek out Pauline to serve his drinks. She soon noticed this, and began to return his glances and smiles.

Pauline Chater was in the second week of her part-time job at the social club. Her parents were anything but wealthy, and had scrimped and saved to get her to university. Now, and like many of her fellow first-years, she had found it difficult to manage her money, and most of it had been frittered away. Pauline, however, certainly wasn't a party animal, and she had initially spent her money wisely on books, pens and even a typewriter, so that her essays would always look immaculate when she handed them in. But lately Pauline had been spending money on make-up and more up-to-date clothes, and she was feeling the pinch.

She had been on a constant diet ever since that night when she'd been out with Sally and Lizzie to the Black Lion. She had embarrassed herself by ordering Tizer, and had then sat away from the others, stuffing in crisps with Jenny, who was also a bit of a misfit. It had upset Pauline to see how well Sally and Lizzie had danced, and how slim and attractive they both looked. She hated how popular the two girls were with the opposite sex, and vowed later that night, before she had cried herself to sleep, to do something about it.

Now, Pauline, with her new figure and new look was just like them, and she wanted to show herself off. She too, wanted to be the centre of attraction, to be treated like a woman, and be lusted over by men, instead of being an object of ridicule.

Pauline had despised herself for being fat and being so out of control. She had attended several schools when she was younger, but had left each one following long periods of truancy. She had then refused point blank to return to the last one, after the bullying and insults got too much to bear. She could easily remember all the names she had been called, names that had cut into her like knives, and had slowly undermined every ounce of confidence she possessed.

Pauline could remember vividly the time her mother, in desperation, began taking her to see a child psychiatrist, but Pauline would clam up and refuse to speak a word. She would sit on her chair staring vacantly down at her feet, or just gaze out of the window, lost in her own tormented world. Even after several visits, Pauline never spoke to the psychiatrist, nor even looked at her.

It was eventually decided by the school board to put Pauline into a special school. One which picked up the pupils from home each day by bus, and then returned them later in the afternoon.

On her first day, she was brought into the school by her mother, who had been told by the headmaster to tell Pauline, that it was simply a visit, and she could go home after. In his office, Mr. Napier told Pauline all about the school, and why, in view of her truancy it had become necessary for her to attend it. He asked her why she was so unhappy, and getting no response, he reached over and took her hand telling her she would be safe at the school and no-one would bully her again. Pauline's mother pleaded with her to at least give it a try, but Pauline couldn't believe either of them, and once again she looked away and refused to speak.

Mr. Napier began to lose patience. He then invited Pauline to see the classrooms, and as she stood up, he took her arm tightly, so that she couldn't get away and pulled her out into the corridor. He told Pauline's mother to leave, and the distraught woman put her hands to her face and wept helplessly as she watched her daughter being dragged away screaming to meet her new classmates.

"This is Pauline, and today is her first day, so be nice to her and remember how scared you all felt on your first day. Now, come on Pauline, please open your eyes, no-one is going to hurt you."

Mrs. Hurst, Pauline's new teacher was very experienced with damaged and vulnerable youngsters, and Pauline found it easy to open her eyes to the gentle tone of the teacher's voice, as she allowed herself to be led to her new desk. The class was quite small, with fifteen other boys and girls, all of Pauline's age. It was certainly different to what she had been used to before. Mrs. Hurst indicated towards the blackboard, and Pauline listened as the rest of the class read out aloud;

"Today, we welcome Pauline to Class Three. We hope that she will be happy here, and will stay with us for a long time to come."

The pupils then took it in turns to stand up and tell Pauline their names. Some of them were physically disabled, while others appeared tiny, frail and weak. A few had conditions like, asthma and eczema, while two were considerably overweight, even more so than Pauline.

The children weren't expecting their new classmate to cry, and they had to wait patiently, while Mrs. Hurst attended to her out in the cloakroom. When Pauline was eventually able to return, she felt that perhaps, she could be happy there. All the children had suffered in their own personal way, and now they were here together, united as one big family, just like brothers and sisters. Pauline, at last felt she belonged.

It had been a long time since she had smiled, but as Pauline settled in and got to know her new friends, she learnt how to laugh again. She also found that she had an aptitude for learning, and soon became one of the brightest pupils at the school. There was even a party given for her when she won her place at university, the first pupil ever to achieve this. She was congratulated by all the teachers, and was thrilled when Mr. Napier had said how proud he was of her achievements and what a great day it was for the school. Mrs. Hurst told her what an excellent role model she had been to the other children. Even Pauline's weight had dropped significantly, once she had become more actively involved in school events. Pauline had at last found her missing childhood.

The Social Club, according to Pauline, seemed the ideal place to put herself in the shop window. She probably wasn't the type to do bar work, but jobs around the area were hard to come by, and would usually be offered to someone living locally first. She had little experience of life on a social scale and certainly wouldn't have had knowledge of the leers, gestures and lewd remarks she would be confronted with when going about her new duties. It was this naivety that may have held her in good stead. For Pauline was, in most situations, totally oblivious to the frequent scenes of drunkenness going on around her, especially after rugby matches. She was seemingly unaffected by most of the remarks she was subjected to. She just concentrated on what she had to do, and appeared to do it well, even if it wasn't part of her personality to flirt, indulge in small talk or appreciate crude jokes.

Pauline had two good friends at university, Jenny and Maureen, both were very similar to her in some respects. All three were, what could be described as, bookish, hardworking, and very straight-laced. Their essays were always in on time, and they never missed a single lecture. The three of them were quite plain in their looks, dress and manner of thinking, with perhaps, Pauline now having a distinct advantage over the other two regarding looks. Now though, since Pauline had started her job, her dress sense had become much more in vogue with what many of the other girls at that time were wearing. This had caused both Jenny and Maureen to make a few innocent remarks, possibly tinged with a hint of jealousy, and perhaps a little fear.

They were certainly fascinated by Pauline's metamorphosis, and began venturing into the club purely to observe her. Just being in that environment made them feel naughty and rebellious. They never drank, but just chatted and looked around, hoping that someone special might just walk into their lives.

Jenny and Maureen certainly noticed the attention Pauline was getting from Frank, and they were almost as excited as Pauline herself.

"I thought he was seeing that pretty, blonde girl, you know, what's her name?" Said Jenny, looking rather puzzled.

"You mean, Sally," replied Pauline sternly. "No, not anymore. He told me it's all over between them. It's me he's interested in now. He said he knows someone big at Shepperton Studios who could get me into films!" The two girls then craned their necks to stare at Frank, while Pauline rushed off back behind the bar, still not believing the university heart-throb could possibly be interested in her.

It was Thursday, 13th of December, and Sally's nineteenth birthday. Lizzie had given her a set of beautiful, silk lingerie, presented in a magnificent box, complete with ribbons and a lovely big, purple bow. She had also promised to lend her a very expensive Yves St. Laurent dress for the evening, even though it was probably a little short for Sally's liking. They had both been to the hairdresser's during the morning, where Sally had decided to ere on the side of caution, and just have a few inches taken off, rather than copy Lizzie's new look - peroxide blonde!

On their return they checked for mail, and Sally had been delighted to find her pigeon hole in the post room was crammed full of envelopes. She was pleased she had made so many friends since her arrival, and now felt far happier than she had been recently. For once she felt free of her parents rules and regulations, and enjoyed being in charge of her own destiny.

Back up in her room, Sally soon found places for her cards, but she saved Frank's until last. It certainly wasn't anything particularly exciting - it just contained the usual clichés and some hand-written text telling her to be ready for seven o'clock that evening - for what was going to be, the best day of her life. However, knowing Frank, it was bound to hit Sally hard financially, and that thought alone caused her to worry. Intrigued, she put Frank's card up on the mantelpiece, behind the clock she had brought from home.

In the time she had been there, Sally had transformed, what was once a cold, depressing, prison cell into something decidedly more habitable. Now, her room reflected her own tastes and style, with various pictures and posters of pop stars adorning the walls. She had even brought some brightly-coloured scatter cushions from town, which added the perfect finishing touch. She could now look upon her room as her own little home-from-home.

As it was her birthday, Sally decided to play some music on the new record player her parents had sent her. There were also a few bottles of Babycham in the back of the wardrobe, she opened two, then went and sat cross-legged on the floor, and began to go through her record collection. Lizzie had just popped back to her room to get the dreaded dress, but seemed to have been gone for ages. However, just as Sally got up to tap on Lizzie's wall, her friend returned.

"What kept you? I was about to call Whitehall 1212!" Exclaimed Sally, offering Lizzie one of the Babychams.

"I'm sorry, I was just reading one of the letters I got earlier, and didn't realise the time." She replied, laying the dress out neatly on Sally's bed. Lizzie, then tried to hide her face. But it was obvious she was tearful. Concerned, Sally put her drink down and asked what was wrong.

"Sally, I don't know what to do, I got this letter from my sister, it's just so awful, and on your birthday too." Lizzie then began to sob, as she passed the envelope to her friend. Sally quickly turned off the music and read the contents;

Dear Lizzie,
I'm sorry this letter is so short and to the point. I do hope things are going well with you at university, way out there in deepest Wales. It's very difficult to contact you by phone - it's either engaged, or you're out! Please try to keep in touch, we must all try to stick together, especially now. You can't just run away from things, Lizzie. I had to give up a lot for Mum, and now she needs us all.

I wish there was some other way of telling you this, but Dad has decided to have Mum committed. He feels that it's all getting too much, trying to keep her at home. Mrs. Gardener does all she can, but she's getting too old, and anyway, Mum's condition has deteriorated since you last saw her. There is more, but it's something I can't put in a letter. Please phone as soon you can, as there's much I need to tell you.
With love,
Janice
P.S. Bobby and Sandy are staying with us for the time being.

Sally glanced at Lizzie, not quite sure what to say. It was unnerving seeing her best friend like this. She was always so strong and confident, and didn't seem to get upset by anything. Sally handed back the letter, and sat down next to Lizzie, putting an arm around her shoulder.

"Dad can't do that, have Mum committed, not without saying anything. It can't be true. I don't know what Janice means." Cried Lizzie, as she clutched the letter tightly, and began rocking to and fro. She then glanced at the door and suddenly leapt up, and ran from Sally's room. "I've got to phone her, I can't bear it."

However, there was only one telephone on that floor, and already a queue had formed waiting to use it. "Lizzie, please come back - you need to think this out first!" Called out Sally, to deaf ears.

"Why can't they put in another damned phone - they know how busy this one gets! It's like living in the dark ages!" Shouted Lizzie, out of pure frustration. The other girls in the queue, some standing and yawning in dressing gowns, just stared at her in silence, as if she had gone mad. She heard one of them mutter something about it being the time of the month, then she heard giggling, before storming back along the corridor.

Sally was waiting in the doorway looking worried.

"Please Lizzie, stop. I can't bear to see you like this, let me help you." She said, beckoning Lizzie to sit on the edge of the bed. "You know, sometimes it's best to confront your problems, before they really get out of hand." She then passed her friend a tissue, before taking one herself.

"I'm so sorry Sally, I feel so awful about ruining your birthday. I've even got you crying now. I'm just a silly cow. Look, please try the dress on and we can see how it looks."

Lizzie, then scooped up the expensive garment and held it up for Sally to see.

"No, Lizzie, I can't try it on, it wouldn't seem right."

"Thanks, Sally, for all you've done." Replied Lizzie, tossing the dress aside. "You're a great friend, and I think what you said was right. I've got to go home, I must. I'll leave a note for Ken downstairs, and perhaps, if you see him, you could explain what's happened."

"Look Lizzie, I'm coming with you. I can't let you go like this - you need support. Don't worry about my birthday, it's nothing compared to your problems. You're more important - I'm coming, and that's final!"

It came as a surprise even to Lizzie, that she could actually pack a hold-all, and an overnight case, then get changed, and be ready to leave, all in less than thirty minutes.

Sally struggled to lift the heavy case into the tiny boot of Lizzie's, Austin 35. When she eventually succeeded, she placed her own small bag onto the rear seat, then stepped back in amazement to look at the odd-looking little vehicle.

"What on earth is this thing? It looks like a cocktail onion on wheels!"

"Meet, Isaac, the best car in the world!" Exclaimed Lizzie proudly. "Isn't it just wonderful, and so unpretentious. Come on let's go. Have you left the note for Frank and Ken?"

"That'll be £3'6d thank you, Mrs Davies."

"Bless you, Mr. Morgan. Now I wont have to go out again for a few days," she replied gracefully, tying the strings of the plastic rain hood under her chin.

"How's business at the post office these days?" Asked the shopkeeper, as he loaded the bread and dog food into the old woman's shopping trolley.

"It's very quiet at the moment, but it'll pick up once the students get their grants topped up again."

"Don't talk to me about students. Bloody noisy bunch there are!"

"It frightens me, Mr. Morgan, these youngsters of today - they have no respect for their elders. Not like in my day. Just to think, my Thomas lost his life in the war fighting for the likes of these people. It's all wrong you know, and the police - they do nothing about it, especially that Constable Price, and you should see the mess on the streets of a Sunday morning. It's getting worse, you mark my words."

"I know, Mrs. Davies, you're right." Replied Morgan, having had the same conversation with the postmistress now for as many years as he could remember.

"Just think, the university will be breaking up soon, and we can all enjoy a bit of peace and quiet. Look, it's raining again, you'd better hurry and get indoors." He helped her down the step, and breathed a sigh of relief, once she was out of the shop. He was hungry and wanted to close for lunch. Morgan shut the door and reached up towards the bolt. It was then that he heard the music. It was definitely music, he thought, possibly that rock 'n' roll that was all the rage. It was still some way off, but was getting louder by the second. Mrs. Davies must have heard it too, for she stopped and was looking around to see where it was coming from. In fact, the whole of the high street seemed to come to a halt.

The sound of Del Shannon's *'Runaway'* playing at full blast on the car's radio drowned out the purr of the E-type Jaguar's powerful engine as it sped dangerously along the street. People crossing the road, quickly leapt out of its path and back onto the pavement for safety. They stared in awe as the sleek, shiny sports car filled the narrow road, causing other vehicles to give way to the majestic beast.

Although the rain was starting to come down quite hard now, the two male occupants preferred to keep the convertible roof down, and the music turned up full.

Frank felt like he and the car were one, and he marvelled at how they both complimented each other so perfectly. It was if they had both been created solely with each other in mind, and no matter what the consequences were going to be, it felt right that he should be driving it. He was high on adrenalin and greedily thrived on the attention that he and the car were creating.

Frank slammed his foot on the brake and brought the machine to a screeching halt, to allow a young mother to wheel her pram over a zebra crossing. Ken then stood up from the front passenger seat and yelled sexual innuendo at the woman, who, feeling threatened quickened her pace to escape the unwanted attention. Frank then howled with laughter as he hit the accelerator hard and felt the car surge forward, knocking Ken backwards into the plush, leather seat.

Substituting his own car for his father's Jaguar wouldn't have called for any major feat of ingenuity on Frank's part. His father was away on a convention, and it was perfectly normal for Frank to go back to Bristol on a regular basis, especially if he wanted something. But now, Frank had the cash to buy his own Jaguar. The robbery at the post office had gone like clockwork, just like he said it would. It literally took just a few minutes. Even when they had to break the back gate down, no-one seemed to have heard them.

Frank had then taken it upon himself to book a suite for the night, and a table for two at one of the most prestigious hotels in Wales, the Falconbury, which is about five miles from the university. Frank felt smug, and couldn't wait to get his plan into action. Sally would surely be ecstatic at this chivalrous and romantic gesture, and when he produced his secret weapon - a necklace, 'borrowed' from his mother, bedding Sally would be a mere foregone conclusion.

Laughing, they sped off again, towards the main gates of the university. Frank had to swerve sharply, to avoid hitting an oncoming truck, and then - like a fairground roller-coaster, the car plunged through a large puddle, sending up a wave of filthy, brown water from its thick tyres. This drenched an elderly woman, struggling with a shopping trolley. The sudden shock of the cold water, and the close proximity of the car knocked her off balance, and she fell heavily to the ground. The vehicle disappeared into the distance, and a well-dressed man and the young woman with the pram came rushing to Mrs. Davies' aid. She was still conscious, but very pale, and struggling for breath. They made the old lady as comfortable as possible and stayed with her until the ambulance arrived. Mr. Meredith told her, he would take the groceries back to Morgan, who could look after them for her.

The jaguar skidded to a halt on the gravel drive outside Lloyd-Evans Hall of Residence. Frank switched off the engine and got out of the car. He strode purposely towards the building, before noticing an envelope bearing his name was attached to the door.

It only took a few seconds for his confident, well practised grin to turn into an ugly grimace. Frank screwed up the note tightly in his fist, and hurled it to the ground in a fury. He screamed out a torrent of abuse, and faces that had been peering out of windows, quickly disappeared back inside. Frank then leapt back into the car, and they sped off as quickly as they had arrived.

Tonight was meant to be Frank's special night. He had planned it all, everything was ready. He had gone to a great deal of trouble for Sally, and he expected his just rewards.

There was another envelope waiting for Frank. It had been in the post room for several days now. It was from John Meredith, the Dean of Students, requesting Frank's attendance at his office to answer several serious complaints the university had received regarding his behaviour. However, Frank never found any real reason to venture anywhere near the post room, and wouldn't have known the meeting was set for the following morning.

It had been Ken, who had thought of the obvious solution to Frank's current predicament, when he began to tire of his friend's irritating bad mood.

"Look Frank, Lizzie's gone too, I'm in the same boat. At least you can get that Pauline as a replacement for Sally."

A hint of a smile came over Frank's face, as he realised, the evening might turn out to his advantage after all.

4. GLOUCESTER

Lizzie flicked the indicator switch in the centre of the dashboard over to point right. The noisy intermittent flash was more like the wink from some hideous-looking beady eye, as it momentarily illuminated the interior of the tiny car. Both women were tired and hungry when they finally reached Gloucester. It had taken a good deal longer than Lizzie had expected, as the journey had been hampered by a constant, oppressive drizzle.

Sally was now having very grave doubts about whether this was a good idea. After all, Lizzie's family affairs were really nothing to do with her, and they may take offence at a stranger arriving on their doorstep uninvited at such an awful time. However, she decided not to share her misgivings with her friend, as it would only add to her problems.

Lizzie had tried to explain the situation during the journey, but at times she literally had to shout, in order to be heard over the drone of the car's engine. Lizzie, told of how, several years earlier, her mother, Margaret Marchmont had been knocked unconscious in a sailing accident while on holiday in the Mediterranean. She had to be resuscitated, but not before her heart had stopped for sufficient time to cause irreparable brain damage.

Sally had sat in silence throughout much of the drive, and listened intently as her friend recalled how the family chose to look after their mother themselves. She was totally incapable of doing anything for herself, but at home she could at least be surrounded by people she loved. Most of the responsibility of tending to Margaret had fallen on Janice, the eldest daughter. It was Janice who sacrificed a promising career at Cambridge to nurse her mother. Although, the family were well off, they rarely called in outsiders to help cater for the needs of a once-proud and dignified woman. Only the long-serving housekeeper, Mrs. Gardener was permitted to assist where necessary.

The situation only changed when one day, Janice decided to get married. The constant physical and emotional strain of caring for such a demanding patient had begun to tell on her. No-one seemed to know how long her mother's suffering would last, and it had been generally assumed that Lizzie would automatically take over the responsibility. Robert, her little brother was too young, and anyway, he was destined to follow in his father's footsteps and become a lawyer. However, it certainly came as a shock to the family, when they discovered Lizzie had ideas of her own. Understandably, much resentment came from Janice, who had since tried to make Lizzie feel guilty at every given opportunity.

Lizzie's father, Edward - not an easy man to get along with, was actually quite impressed with his youngest daughter's streak of ambitious determination. It wasn't that Lizzie didn't love her mother any less, it was because she had seen Janice losing her best years, and becoming resentful and worn out in the process. Janice's marriage to Graham was seen by some as a farce, but who could really blame her after she had given so much.

As for Lizzie, she had an insatiable zest for life, and was naturally far more out-going than her often-gloomy sibling. For Lizzie, the thought of spending her youth, and allowing her spirit to die in such a lonely and depressing manner was simply unthinkable.

Now, to learn from Janice, that her mother may be committed to an asylum, had been more than enough to evoke feelings of guilt. It was this guilt, that Lizzie had always refused to accept, but now it was flooding her conscience.

As they neared her home, Lizzie began to feel very aware of the way she was dressed, and how her hair looked. She grimaced, while picturing her sister glaring at her disapprovingly, uttering ruthless and callous remarks. Even within the dark exterior of the car, she noticed the glare from the pink, glossy varnish, so lovingly applied to her long, manicured nails.

When they finally reached Lizzie's home, something made her park the car a short distance away, even though it was still raining quite hard. She began to feel distinctly uncomfortable, and noticed that most of the lights were on, which in itself was very odd, considering her father's frugal nature.

Perhaps, she should have tried a few more times to get through on the telephone, or maybe just driven straight to Janice's house, which was quite nearby. But she was here now, and there was no backing out.

Tentatively, Lizzie made her way up to the front door, while reaching into her handbag for the house keys. She then heard a dog bark from inside, but it was a pathetic little yap, and certainly not the sound, Sandy, the family's golden retriever would have made. Sally immediately sensed Lizzie's apprehension and remained a few paces behind.

Lizzie slowly pushed open the heavy oak front door and took a step inside. She was then confronted by a tiny, snarling Yorkshire Terrier, resplendent in a bright yellow ribbon, tied tightly to the top of its head. It bared its sharp, little fangs and barked ferociously, before beating a hasty retreat, as the gaudily-dressed, peroxide blonde advanced upon its territory. Lizzie, totally oblivious to the creature's efforts to instil terror into her, suddenly felt her mouth water as she caught the subtle, and delicious aroma of something exotic coming from the kitchen. Her finely tuned nostrils also detected something else - perfume. She wondered who might be visiting at this hour. Her sick mother obviously wouldn't be wearing expensive scent like that, and it was hard to imagine Janice in anything more than lavender water.

Lizzie, didn't have to wait long to meet the wearer. From the direction of the dining room, she heard the sound of dainty, feminine footsteps heading towards her.

"Poppy! Poppy! You stop that awful racket now. Do you hear me, you naughty little dog?"

A tall, slim, and very elegant-looking woman, aged about forty appeared, then stopped dead in her tracks at the sight of Lizzie, standing open-mouthed in the hallway. It was hard to make out who was the most puzzled.

"Hello, Pamela, I've come to see my father, is he here?" Asked Lizzie, now back to her usual, confident self.

The woman bent down and scooped up Poppy, before replying in an assured voice, "Oh, hello, Lizzie. What a surprise! Yes, he's here, please come through to the lounge, we've just finished dinner."

Unlike, Janice, Lizzie had always liked Pamela. She had been her father's secretary for more years than she could remember, and always took the time to seek Lizzie out and chat to her. However, although it was not unusual to see Pamela at the house, it did seem odd for her to be there during the evening, and having dinner with her father. Lizzie cast a bewildered look back to Sally, and the two women followed Pamela into the lounge.

"Who is it darling, what was all that damned commotion - not bloody carol singers again?"

Lizzie immediately recognised her father's loud, and often-gruff voice. He coughed, and almost choked on his cognac, as he saw his daughter unexpectedly enter the room behind Pamela.

Edward Marchmont, successful lawyer and freemason looked as if he'd just seen a ghost. He brought the large brandy glass down noisily to the table, wiped his mouth with a napkin, then rose to his feet.

"Lizzie, for god's sake, why didn't you say you were coming? Good heavens, it's lovely to see you girl, but what a surprise! My word, come over here - let's get a good look at you."

"Dad, don't make such a fuss, I'm not a film star - well not yet, anyway!" Smirked Lizzie, obviously pleased to see her father.

Edward gave out a hearty laugh.

"Let's get you a drink. Are you hungry?" Then, noticing Sally, he seemed even more surprised. "Why, you've got someone with you - who's this beautiful creature? Welcome young lady, don't be bashful, what's your name?"

Edward seemed to be going a bit over the top, and Lizzie knew he was uncomfortable. She kissed him on the cheek, removed her coat, and gazed around the large, oak-beamed room. It seemed to look so different to when she was last there over two months ago. It didn't even smell like the home she knew, the whole atmosphere of the house had changed. She noticed that many of the ornaments and little curios that her mother had collected over the years were missing. None of the items were valuable in monetary terms, but they did give the old place its charm and character. Even the Christmas tree, although lit up, and looking rather spectacular wasn't the same as when the girls used to decorate it.

Lizzie turned to her father and decided to get to the point.

"I had a letter from Janice - it was about Mum. Is she upstairs? Janice said you were going to put her into some awful place. I want to see her." There was emotion in Lizzie's voice. She again looked about her, "Where's Bobby and Sandy?"

Edward gave Pamela a sidelong glance, then picked up his drink and walked over to the fireplace. He was a tall, thickset man of forty eight, an ex-army colonel, with short, black thinning hair, flecked with grey. The immaculately trimmed moustache made him even more distinguished looking. He cut an imposing figure, shoulders well back, and still wearing his charcoal-grey business suit. The flickers from the fire reflected in his blue, piercing eyes, and the warm glow gave his face a puce, dangerous look, as if an uncontrollable rage was brewing just below the surface.

"Don't worry about Bobby, he's staying at Janice's. The dog's there too. We thought it best. So what else did your sister have to say in this enlightening missive. Did she mention Pamela at all?" He asked, swirling the cognac around in his glass.

"Janice mentioned that Bobby was staying with her, but she said there was something else. That's all I know." Replied Lizzie, averting her eyes from her father's gaze.

"I see. It looks like I'll have to clarify things for you," he continued in a condescending manner, as if he was about to explain some legal complexity to an imbecile.

Lizzie was in fact, Edward's favourite daughter. He loved her sense of adventure and volatile temper, that was so similar to his own. He had wanted to explain things to Lizzie in his own way, to at least allow her to get through her first term at university unhindered by emotional distractions.

"Perhaps, your friend would be good enough to wait in the library, Elizabeth, while we have this little chat."

"No!" Replied Lizzie defiantly, expecting the worst whenever she was called by her name in full. "Sally has been a good friend to me, and I want her here!"

Edward, Pamela and Lizzie all then stared over at Sally, who suddenly felt positively embarrassed and now wished she hadn't come at all.

There was a long, silent pause, until Edward finally asked Sally to be seated, before beckoning his daughter over to him. Sally watched intently from the corner of the room, as Lizzie reluctantly sat herself down in a large, leather armchair opposite her father.

Although Sally could only make out the odd word, it was obvious that Lizzie was getting very upset. After a few moments she saw Lizzie's face redden, and she stood up sharply and glared down at her father.

"I don't want to hear anymore of it!" She shrieked, unable to believe what her father had just told her. "How can you do this to Mum, it's totally disgusting."

Lizzie cast her eyes at Pamela, who was still clutching Poppy, and was now looking very distressed herself. Lizzie's mind was in turmoil - she wanted to challenge and banish this impostor from her home, and vent her anger on Edward, the father she had once loved and respected. How could he be carrying out this unspeakable act in her very home, and with Margaret upstairs.

Pamela quickly moved aside when she saw the young woman moving menacingly towards her, but to her relief, Lizzie just brushed past her and hurried upstairs to find her mother.

Lizzie was mortified to learn that Pamela, apart from having an adulterous relationship with Edward, had now moved into the family home, and was occupying the same bed that Lizzie's parents once shared together.

Sally's discomfort continued. She glanced around the room looking for something to fix her eyes on, while all the time, trying to remain inconspicuous. She was praying Lizzie wouldn't be too long seeing her mother. The atmosphere was unbearably tense, and Sally felt it would be totally inappropriate to pass the time indulging Lizzie's father in small talk. However, she couldn't help noticing Edward go to Pamela and put his arm protectively around her shoulder. Edward kissed Pamela lightly, but affectionately on the lips and forehead. He had temporarily forgotten about Sally sitting quietly over in the shadows. He glanced across, and for a second their eyes locked. Edward felt angry in the knowledge that a complete stranger had not only witnessed such an undignified family argument, but had now seen him in a moment of intimacy with his mistress.

Sally was equally embarrassed and was more than relieved to hear Lizzie calling her from upstairs. She followed her friend's voice into a bedroom, just off the landing. It was extremely warm inside and smelt like a mixture of excrement and paraffin. The latter smell was emanating from a Sankey Senator heater, which was turned on full, and backed up against the fireplace. The room was quite dim, lit only by the artificial glow from the heater, and a bedside lamp. Sally looked around and noticed a commode next to the bed and a wicker wheelchair parked next to a large antique, mahogany dressing table.

"I want you to meet her. This is Margaret Marchmont, my mother."

Sally, her eyes adjusting to the dimness, looked down at a once-beautiful, but now wasted woman in her mid-forties. She was lying peacefully on a single bed in what was, one of the spare rooms. She noticed Margaret's clear, sparkling brown eyes as they stared out at nothing but emptiness.

"Hello, Mrs. Marchmont, it's a pleasure to meet you," said Sally awkwardly, as if she were speaking to a child. But there wasn't even a flicker of acknowledgment from those brown eyes, they just carried on staring blankly.

"Can your mother hear me, Lizzie?"

"I honestly don't know. Apparently, there's nothing wrong with her hearing," replied Lizzie, gently stroking the side of her mother's face. "Mum, can you hear me? It's Lizzie. I've come all the way from Wales, to see you. I'm at university now. This is my friend, Sally."

Lizzie reached down and took Margaret's hand.

"Look, Sally, that's answered your question, she can hear us - she's squeezing my hand."

As the two girls made Margaret more comfortable, Sally saw a completely different aspect to Lizzie's personality - a benevolent, caring side that she had never seen before.

"If only you could have met her before the accident - you would have loved her. She was so refined, so reserved - a real lady, and she could be very witty too. My mother was the most wonderful person. Sometimes, I wish I was more like her."

"You are, Lizzie, believe me." Replied Sally, her voice quaking with emotion.

"But I couldn't look after her, not like Janice - do you despise me for choosing university?"

"Lizzie, I can tell how much you love your mother, just by seeing you with her. I don't think badly of you for what you did. It took a great deal of strength and courage for Janice to look after her all that time. Equally it took courage for you to choose not to succeed her. Personally speaking, I think your mother needs proper medical care. Perhaps, you and Janice could find an alternative solution to the mental hospital."

Lizzie looked at her friend thoughtfully, "Sally, I can't even think straight at the moment - look at my hands, I'm shaking like a leaf. I'm so angry with him. I've never faced up to my father like that before, but I'm correct, aren't I? He can't have that Pamela living here - it's not right."

Sally nodded her head in agreement, and followed Lizzie back downstairs. A nagging feeling was warning her not to say anymore in case she may regret it. But still, she felt totally helpless as she allowed herself to be sucked into a domestic crisis that really, she wanted nothing to do with.

"So where are we going now?" She asked, as Lizzie began to put her coat on.

"I'm certainly not going to stay here!" Was the short reply. "We'll go over to Janice's and stay there for the night - she wont mind."

Once the two girls had left, Edward went up to check on his wife. He turned the heater off, and sat on the edge of the bed, studying her face.

"It must have been nice to see Lizzie again, Margaret. She's doing so well at university, I'm very proud of her." As Edward kissed his wife, and put the light out, he didn't notice the large tears welling up in her eyes. He said goodnight, closed the bedroom door, and made his way back down to Pamela.

Thursday evening turned out to be quite eventful for Pauline as well. Although, she wasn't due to work in the club that particular night, she had arranged to go there with Jenny and Maureen a little later on. The student's Sports and Social Club was really nothing more than an old war-time Nissan hut, with various bits added over the years. Now it was the hub of university life and for many, the place to meet friends and perhaps, make new ones. Pauline had spent the afternoon at a history lecture, then had gone straight over to the library with her two friends to write her notes up and complete an essay. Although, the work wasn't due in until early the following week, it was her last essay before Christmas, and Pauline wanted to make sure she was ahead of everything. Jenny and Maureen left early to go to the refectory for supper, but Pauline, still sticking religiously to her diet, had stopped going there some time ago. Besides, being seen eating in 'refec' didn't quite fit in with Pauline's new image nowadays.

At about 6.30pm, she packed up her books and headed back to Thomas House, her hall of residence. She would have preferred to stay longer in the library and finally finish her work, but she didn't want to be one of the last one's there. Most of the other students were winding down and getting ready to go home for the holidays.

Once back in her room, Pauline fell asleep on her bed for what seemed like hours, but it was in fact only about twenty minutes. It was the loud knocking at the door, and hearing her name being called that had roused her from her sleep.

At first, she had briefly dreamt that she had been back at school. Here, the pupils were allowed to sleep on camp beds in the gymnasium for half an hour after lunch if they wanted. Often, and to Pauline's delight, the duty teacher would be Mr. Bridges, a New Zealander, who worked part-time and taught Geography. To her, he was the most handsome man she had ever seen, obviously apart from, Paul Newman, or the singer, Adam Faith, perhaps. His soft, deep voice would sound so gentle and comforting to wake up to. Pauline, of course never hinted to anyone that she had a crush on Mr. Bridges, that remained her secret.

The remnants of Pauline's brief dream were finally dispelled when she opened the door, to find the impatient caller was none other than, Ken - armed with a dozen red roses. She eyed the look-a-like renegade from West Side Story suspiciously, as he stood in the chilly corridor dressed in white T-shirt and blue jeans. He smiled not an unpleasant smile, with a cigarette dangling loosely from the corner of his mouth. He then hastily pushed the flowers into Pauline's arms before anyone came along and saw him. She gasped with surprise, no-one had ever given her flowers before. There was a card attached to the roses, which she eagerly tried to read without her glasses. Ken, meanwhile leant back against the wall and calmly smoked his cigarette. He let his eyes wander up and down Pauline's body, while she flicked back her tousled hair and tried to make sense of the spidery writing.

Within moments, her face lit up, and she had to re-read the card to make sure she wasn't imagining things.

"Yes, yes, I can go, but half an hour's very short notice!" She exclaimed excitedly.

"That's typical Frank, he doesn't like to be predictable!" Replied Ken, now realising Pauline's potential himself.

"Where's he going to take me?" She asked, now wide awake and eyes sparkling.

"It's a surprise, so make sure you wear something nice, Pauline!"

Once Ken had gone, Pauline hurried downstairs to Jenny's room.

"Jenny! Jenny! Quick, open the door, I've got some great news!" Jenny appeared at the door, with Maureen directly behind her, "Pauline, what's happened?"

"It's Frank, I'm going on a date with him - tonight!"

Sally was amazed at the very obvious differences between Lizzie and her older sister. Janice, although still only twenty five, displayed the beginnings of premature ageing. Crow's feet were appearing around her eyes, and grey hairs were clearly visible in her mousy bob. But it wasn't only this, Janice had a pale, worn-out look about her that betrayed her years. She was painfully thin, and to some, her face could be described as gaunt. When she spoke, her tone was monotonous, and her use of language was plain. It was as if every word she spoke caused her intense suffering.

Janice had just been putting the empty milk bottles out when she saw the visitors walking up the path towards her. At first, she didn't quite recognise Lizzie in the darkness and drizzle. Even when Lizzie called out to her, she remained indifferent and showed not a hint of pleasure at seeing her sister after so long.

Janice was wearing a grubby, white dressing gown, made out of towelling material. She shivered and pulled it closer together as a gust of wind whistled around her ankles. She hastily closed the front door and led the girls inside.

Sally drew in a deep breath and wondered how this latest reunion would work out, as the sisters reluctantly swapped pleasantries. At least Janice wasn't quite so cold towards Sally, and even gave her a hint of a forced smile.

Janice lived in a three-bedroom, 1930s, semi-detached house, just on the edge of Gloucester. The house was a direct reflection on her often-morose character, and contained just the bare minimum for moderate human comfort. In the front room, Lizzie and Janice sat themselves on a grey, fabric settee, with black plastic armrests. This, formed part of a three-piece suite, and like its two fellow armchairs, was pushed back against the wall. The room looked as if it had been set up for a party, but no-one had arrived.

On one side of the room, stood a bulky black and white television set, which was blaring away to itself. The incessant arguing of the two politicians was irritating, but Janice made no attempt to turn it off. A wooden radiogram took pride of place along the opposite wall, and upon this, stood a tiny, imitation Christmas tree, with large gold baubles and strands of silver tinsel draped across its branches. In one corner, stood a standard lamp, with a yellowing shade depicting canal scenes from Venice. Several pictures were dotted around the walls, again featuring Venetian gondolas. These were apparently a gift set given to Janice and Graham for their engagement. The wallpaper was a light tan colour, patterned with gold and russet falling autumn leaves. Small clusters of balloons were hanging from the ceiling and lengths of paper streamers stretched from each corner of the room, to gather and meet in the centre.

The most striking feature however, was the brand-new, pink pile carpet. This was Janice's pride and joy, and when Lizzie proceeded to light a cigarette, her horrified sister scuttled out of the room, only to return immediately, clutching an ashtray.

Janice glared at Lizzie, "Why on earth didn't you phone first? Graham and Bobby have already gone to bed, and I was about to follow. I take it you received my letter then?"

"Yes, I got it," quipped Lizzie, as she stroked the excited Sandy. "We've just come from Dad's. I saw Mum, and she looked so pathetic just laying there, almost angelic. It's just so sad. I also saw Pamela. Why didn't you tell me Dad has a thing going with her? It was such a shock."

"I was going to tell you," snapped Janice. "That's why I said in the letter to contact me. You never listen - you always have to do things your way!"

Lizzie breathed in sharply, "I just can't believe you allowed this to go on right under your nose. You should have stopped it, Janice!"

Even Sally was shocked at this outburst, and looked across at Janice, for her response - which was immediate.

"How can I stop Dad, you silly mare. I see you haven't changed for the better during your absence. You're still a rude, spoilt, insensitive parasite!"

Lizzie was visibly stunned by the ferocity of Janice's remarks.

"Parasite? So, that's it, we're back to the university issue again," stormed Lizzie. "Well, Janice, I'm sick and tired of your petty jealousy. You could have done the same as me. But no, you enjoy playing the martyr too much. Because it gives you the excuse not to try anything, and that's why you hate yourself so much, and live like this. No, Janice, you're the parasite. You feed on my guilt and try to drag me down to your level - but I'll never stoop that low!"

"What do you mean, live like this?"

"Well, look at this house for a start, and all these vile decorations," Remarked

Lizzie, now with the bit between her teeth. "You've done nothing to it, apart from put this awful carpet in."

"We're quite happy with the way it is," replied Janice haughtily. "Besides, Graham is a very spiritual man, and doesn't believe in having too many material possessions. We have what we need and no more."

"Come on Janice, you only married him because looking after Mum was getting too much for you. I can't blame you for that, but why Graham? He's a bloody bore, and he's an extremely seedy character!" Lizzie then looked around the room, critically, "Is this really what you want out of life?"

"I want you to leave, that's what I want!" Janice was seething and pointing towards the door. "Where were you when Mum needed your help? When she had to be got up, washed, dressed, fed and then cleaned up after she'd soiled herself? You were out with your bearded, beatnik friends, sitting around in coffee bars, talking a lot of rubbish!"

"It was philosophy actually!" Sneered, Lizzie, ignoring the order to leave.

"Well, I loved my mother, and was proud to look after her!" Replied Janice.

Lizzie turned her back on Janice and paced the room, hastily lighting another cigarette. Her hands were shaking and her make-up, usually so immaculate, was in in dire need of a quick renovation.

Sally was also shaking, she couldn't believe two sisters could attack each other in such a manner. The silence in the room was now intense, apart from the steady tick of a sun-shaped wall clock, mounted above the fireplace. Sally glanced at the time, and realised her birthday was finally over. She felt exhausted and longed for a hot bath, and a nice comfortable bed.

Lizzie, ready for another onslaught rounded on her sister, but Sally was up, and now stood between them like a boxing referee. But, before she could say a single word to pacify the two combatants, an ear-piercing shout did the job for her. The three women all looked to the small figure standing in the doorway.

"Please stop shouting - you're scaring me. I don't like it." Uttered the little boy, still clutching his now-cold, hot water bottle.

"Bobby! Bobby! I'm sorry, we didn't mean to frighten you," called out Lizzie, as she went over to hug her little brother.

The boy was shivering in his pyjamas, but soon broke into a smile when he saw his sister. He had much of his father's proud features, and dark curly hair, but more prominent were the big, brown doe-like eyes, he shared with his mother.

Sally was greatly relieved and thankful that this horrid, bitter argument had been laid to rest, at least for the moment anyway. She looked at Janice's stern face, and saw so much sadness, that she had to reach out in a re-assuring manner, and gently touch Janice's arm.

Janice looked blankly at Sally, and pulled her arm away.

"I'm so sorry, whatever must you think of us? We don't always fight like this - its just been a difficult time you see." Forcing a smile, she then politely added, "You can both stay here tonight, I'm sure you must be very tired. I'll go and make us all some tea and sandwiches."

Graham was a tall, thin, anaemic-looking man, with receding red hair, and a pale complexion. He was aged about thirty, but could have passed for someone many years older. He stared grim-faced at Lizzie as she continued to cuddle and make a fuss over Bobby. If first impressions were anything to go by, then Sally immediately understood why her friend had been so hateful to him earlier. Janice, it would appear, had found the perfect partner. Sally however, was also very aware that Graham had a certain presence about him, despite his feeble physical appearance.

He beckoned the two sisters into the living room, leaving Sally to entertain young Bobby, who was immediately smitten with his pretty new friend.

"You are going about things the wrong way," said Graham, in a low but authoritative tone. "You must not waste anymore energy fighting yourselves, especially under my roof. A great wrong has been committed. Not only has your father's adulterous actions effectively ended his marriage to your mother, but it has split his family, and is now causing grave concern to his children." Graham's voice seemed to get louder and more powerful as he spoke. "Your father is committing a serious, moral crime, and both of you must protect your mother from its consequences. You must also save your brother. He should be at his own home, not living here, having his life and schooling disrupted. When you have shown your father the error of his ways, he will come to thank you one day, for not only saving his family and all it stands for, but for saving his mortal soul. Janice and Lizzie, you must stand together as one and forget your differences. Remember, you are on the side of good and what is right."

Even Graham was surprised by the outcome as he continued with his stirring call to action. He expected complete loyalty from Janice, but never expected to bring Lizzie to a near-frenzy, and have her baying for both Edward and Pamela's blood.

Graham was a chiropodist, and had met Janice while attending to her mother's feet on home visits. In order to see Janice more frequently, he had taken it upon himself to visit the house on a weekly basis, and read scriptures and psalms to Margaret. This was in his other role - of lay preacher.

Now, having married the eldest daughter of a wealthy man, there was no way Graham was going to allow the likes of Pamela Cartwright to come into the equation and complicate matters concerning Edward's will, by becoming the next Mrs. Marchmont.

Sally was glad to finally get to bed in the room she was sharing with Lizzie, but on this occasion she was rather relieved, as she found Graham more than a little spooky. The room, like the rest of the house was characterless, chilly and bare, and Sally even found herself missing her old lumpy mattress back at university. She yawned and felt her teeth chatter as she folded the cold nylon sheet over the eiderdown, and slid down, deep into the bed to get warm.

While she waited for Lizzie to return from the bathroom, Sally stared up at the ceiling and began to think about where Frank may have taken her. She did feel awful about letting him down, but Lizzie had to come first on this occasion. Perhaps, there was some way she could make it up to him. As she allowed her mind to wander, she again thought back to the student she had met in the library.

She knew it would be impossible to get back to Wales in time to see him, and wondered if there was any way of contacting him. Perhaps, she could telephone the library and explain the situation to the librarian, perhaps it would be the same person who was on duty the evening they had met? Or maybe, Lizzie could drop her off at the station in the morning, and she could make her own way back to Falcondale. But no, that was ridiculous, the more Sally thought about these options, the more she realised she was clutching at straws and not thinking rationally. She was tired and needed to sleep, but as she closed her eyes, she then began to think about the Christmas Dance the following evening. They had both been so looking forward to it - would they still be able to go? Obviously, it was an inappropriate time to ask Lizzie, so she tried to dismiss it from her mind. Anyway, Lizzie may still need her support when she and Janice go over to confront their father in the morning, and demand he send Pamela packing.

It had been decided that Sally would wait for Lizzie at Janice's house, and then the two girls would return to Wales in the afternoon. This was very much to Sally's relief, as she certainly didn't want to be in the firing line when the two sisters took on the might of their father, on his home territory.

5. THE DINNER DATE

Set in nearly five hundred acres of rugged Welsh landscape, the family-owned, Falconbury Hotel was in fact, a huge, converted country house, complete with additional annexes, function rooms and its own golf course.

The hotel was enormously popular with hill-walkers, pony-trekkers and just about anyone seeking the chance to escape the rat-race for a while. The interior of the main house was distinctly Edwardian, and one could easily conjure up images of Miss Marple or Poirot strutting their stuff among the potted plants and ornate railings.

Pauline picked up her glass and sucked the remaining dregs of her cocktail through the two straws. She made a slurping sound, as if she were just finishing a delicious, frothy milkshake, and looked around anxiously to see if anyone had heard her indiscretion. She glanced towards Frank, who was still busy at the bar ordering more drinks, before delving into her bag for her compact.

Despite Pauline's part-time job at the social club, she still wasn't what could be classified as a drinker. She was certainly aware of cocktails, and had seen people drinking them in those old Hollywood movies, but as yet, she hadn't been called upon in her line of duty to ever provide one.

Frank however, was very knowledgeable when it came to not only cocktails, but seemingly every known drink to man. It was he, who suggested she try a Pina Colada, and to Pauline, it was delicious - even better than a snowball, her other favourite.

She lifted up the tiny mirror, and checked her face. It had all been such a rush, and the last thing she wanted was to be a disappointment to Frank. She knew her cheeks and ears would be red - that always happened, even if she just had a sip of anything remotely alcoholic. Dabbing on more powder, she brought the mirror closer to her face to ensure her eye make-up was perfect. Maureen and Jenny had done it for her, by copying a page from a fashion magazine. Pauline was still very much a novice at such things, anyway - it would have taken her far too long, and she didn't want to be late on her first ever date.

At least her hands had finally stopped shaking, perhaps it was the effects of the drink. Putting back the compact in her bag, she heard Frank laughing with the barman, maybe they knew each other. She watched him as he turned and began to walk back to their table, holding a tray of fresh drinks. Pauline couldn't help smiling at him, after all, he looked so handsome and dashing in his dark blue suit, and sleek, back-combed hair.

Somewhere in one of the function rooms, she could hear a private Christmas party taking place. Every so often the laughter would intensify when one of the white-shirted waiters threw open the double doors, to push in another trolley laden with further supplies of beer and wine.

Pauline and Frank were seated in a vast bar area that was often used to hold meetings or lavish wedding parties. Tonight however, the early entertainment was in the form of a solo pianist, who was currently going through his extensive repertoire of Christmas carols. These were combined with requests from the dozen or so other customers in the bar. The pianist was situated on a raised wooden platform, which was also home to the largest, and most beautiful Christmas tree Pauline had ever seen. It stretched right up to the high ceiling, and was dripping with masses of colourful decorations of every kind. Pauline had never felt so grand and sat back in the sumptuous, armchair and wished the evening would go on for ever.

The conversation had at first been quite strained and awkward. Pauline's social skills when concerning members of the opposite sex was still very limited. She attempted to try and keep the topic confined to general campus talk and revision technique. Frank however, who believed he had few difficulties communicating with women, soon became bored with this, and turned the subject towards cars, in particular E-type Jaguars.

"A new one can set you back well over two grand. But if you have the right contacts you can usually get a good deal. There's not much that can beat it at 150mph!" He had been intrigued to know how impressed she had been, when he had arrived to pick her up. But in reality, Pauline had been oblivious to the car. She had only been interested in Frank, and to her, the Jaguar was just another facet of him to be admired.

She soon discovered that, apart from cars, he loved to talk about himself, and how wealthy his family were. But when asked a direct question about them, he went on the defensive.

Pauline however, was to regret mentioning that she had recognised Frank in some of the framed pictures back at the club. They were all connected with rugby matches, and she had to endure Frank telling her endless stories of the many dangerous tackles he and his friend, Ken had made, and the match-saving tries he had scored, snatching victory from the jaws of defeat.

Frank made two further visits back to the bar, and Pauline was more than relieved when the waiter came over to tell them that their table in the restaurant was ready. Frank rose to his feet a little unsteadily and motioned for Pauline to link his arm. She felt her spine tingle at this first physical interaction between them. Holding on to him tightly, she inhaled the strong aroma of his sweet-smelling aftershave as he pulled out a chair for her at the table.

From Pauline's awkward manner and the way she studied the menu with a pained look on her face, it became apparent to Frank that his companion was quite new to dining out. He summoned over the waiter, and after deciding upon which champagne he wanted, proceeded to order dinner for both of them.

Looking around the impressive dining room, with its magnificent, crystal chandelier, Pauline felt far too excited to eat, and just took a couple of mouthfuls of the rack of Welsh lamb, Frank had ordered. Besides, as a result of her rigid dieting, she now seldom felt hungry and was in total control of her eating habits.

The waiter replenished her glass with more champagne, and Pauline let out a little squeal of delight, which made Frank laugh. He then began doing impersonations of some of the lecturers at the university, which in turn made Pauline giggle uncontrollably, and down even more champagne. She accidentally knocked one glass over and blushed, as the restaurant suddenly went quiet and the other diners stared over at her disapprovingly.

"Frank, I've never been drunk before - isn't it weird? I don't think I can stand up. It's so funny - there's two of you, which one is real?"

A couple sitting at the next table had stopped eating completely, and were staring in disbelief at Pauline, as she fought a losing battle trying to get her dessert from the plate, up to her mouth. Eventually, she gave up after the spoon totally missed its target and fell to the floor with a loud clatter.

The couple quickly looked away, as Frank turned to face them aggressively. He then stood up, and moved menacingly towards their table. As he was almost upon them, he abruptly changed direction to the couple's relief, and bent down to retrieve Pauline's spoon. Wiping the utensil on a serviette, and passing it to her, he placed his hands on her shoulders, and decided to take things a stage further.

"Do you like dancing, Pauline? There's a band playing here later tonight."

"I can't dance to save my life," she replied, her speech now quite slurred. "Would you teach me, Frank?"

"It would be a pleasure, a nice slow one, I think." He smiled at her and went to re-fill her glass, but she placed her hand over the top.

"No, Frank, please. If I have anymore you'll have to carry me home."

After the pianist's final rendition of *'White Christmas'*, he left the stage to muted applause, and was replaced by The Blue Jets, who wasted no time belting out, Johnny Tillotson's, *'Poetry in Motion'*.

Pauline was still very giggly, but after a few dances under Frank's guidance, she seemed to get the hang of it it quite well. Although, she had never done the Jive, or the Twist in public, she had often seen others dance in the students club and had secretly practised in her room with Jenny and Maureen. Now, it just took Frank to add the final touches.

Frank liked the way Pauline moved. She certainly wasn't as lithe and as athletic as Sally when she danced. But now, having had a few drinks, Pauline had completely lost her earlier shyness, and was allowing her own distinctive sexuality to emerge, a sexuality that Frank was determined to exploit later that night.

However, to Frank's frustration, Pauline actually began to sober up after a while, and despite his insistence, she still refused to drink anymore. But, perhaps, her hesitancy to drink might not necessarily be a problem after all, he re-assured himself. She hadn't objected to him getting close to her during some of the dances, and she didn't exactly push him away when he put his arm around her on returning to their table.

At the interval, Frank went to the bar and brought Pauline a Tizer, and himself, a large whiskey. Then he went over to the lead singer of the group and spoke a few words to him. The singer looked at his watch and nodded, then Frank brought him and the rest of the band a round of drinks.

Pauline took Frank's hand and led him back out onto the dance floor as soon as the band struck up again. She reminded him about his earlier promise to teach her the Tango, but now it was getting late and Frank had other plans for Pauline.

"Okay folks, this one's just for you lovers out there, and in particular for Pauline and Frank. Yes, that's right, Pauline, this is for you!" The singer then waved over at her and began to sing, *'Moon River'*.

Pauline was in raptures, "This is from, *'Breakfast At Tiffany's'*," she beamed excitedly, "Have you seen it, Frank? It's wonderful, I think Audrey Hepburn is simply fantastic, don't you?"

Frank wanted to tell her to shut up, but instead, he led her out onto the centre of the dance floor. He pulled her close to him, so she couldn't see the bored expression on his face, and she responded by reaching up to place her arms around his neck. How marvellous, she thought - to be here with him, the two of them dancing like this. How would she ever explain it to Jenny and Maureen, they would never believe that Frank was such a romantic. She knew all those awful things she'd heard about him, couldn't have been true. They were just a pack of lies, spread by girls who were simply jealous. She pressed her head against his chest and felt as if she were floating on the clouds.

Frank let his hands wander up the side of Pauline's waist, and as they reached higher, he felt the outline of her bra, and discovered exactly where it was fastened and by how many hooks. He felt her bosom nuzzling gently against his ribs, as they slowly moved around the now, half-empty dance floor. He noticed how wisps of her raven hair had worked themselves free, and were now partly obscuring her eyes, and dangling loosely around her pale neck. She gazed up at him, her face slightly flushed in contrast, and smiling warmly.

He saw that her top button had come undone, and let his eyes hungrily explore her ample cleavage, so beautifully encased in a delicate, white lace bra. Pauline sighed with pure contentment, and held him tighter.

Frank continued with his mission, and let his hands slowly work their way back downwards. Her blouse was made of silk, and he could feel the smoothness of her skin through the soft material. He reached her hips, and let his eyes close, as he searched for the tell-tale signs of a suspender belt. Feeling himself beginning to grow, he shifted position so that Pauline would feel the hardness of his erection pressing against her.

The song ended and Pauline felt as if she were about to faint. Her skirt was very tight, and she had never been in such close proximity with a man before. She wished she hadn't drank so much and made a fool of herself. She wanted to go home, and was just about to ask him to drive her back, when he grabbed her hand.

"Come on, let's go out and get some air," and before she knew what was happening, he was pulling her out into the cold garden. No sooner had they got out, when Frank spun her around and began to kiss her passionately.

At first she responded, and allowed his tongue to delve inside her mouth. Then, his hands were all over her again, like during the dance, only this time, worse. He was breathing heavily and stank strongly of stale drink and cigarettes. Pauline felt the wind being knocked out of her, as he pushed her back against a stack of folding chairs. His hands were on her breasts, and squeezing hard. It hurt her, and she reached up and tried to pull them off, only to discover they were now burrowing their way up her skirt. Again, she removed his hands, and told him to stop, but he simply lunged at her breasts again. There was a sudden clatter as Pauline's glasses fell to the ground. While she was off guard, Frank managed to get most of the buttons undone on her blouse, and began licking and biting her neck and shoulders as he crouched over her.

"Frank, please stop it, you're hurting me." Begged Pauline.

Frank did stop, but it wasn't because of Pauline - it was because of the other couple who had been in the restaurant. They had also come out into the garden, but after recognising Frank, they quickly went back inside.

Frank picked up Pauline's broken glasses, "Look, I'm sorry, I'll buy you a new pair. Are you alright? I was only messing around - you see the effect you have on me!" He then laughed and reached into his inside pocket to take out a joint. "Here, do you want some of this?"

Pauline was cold and trying to button her blouse, "No, I don't smoke. I want to go home now."

"Come on, everyone smokes weed these days, Pauline."

"Please Frank, can we go back inside?"

He sat on a low brick wall and lit the joint. After taking two long pulls, he offered it again to Pauline. She took the joint, and tried to scrutinise it without her glasses, before passing it back to him.

"Well, you're a real square Pauline, I thought you would be more fun than this?"

She began to sob, and Frank took his jacket off, and hurled it across to her.

"Here, put this on"

"I'm sorry, I've been a disappointment to you," she whimpered, reaching out to catch the jacket. Frank ignored her, but as she turned the jacket around to put it over her shoulders, something fell out of the pocket. Pauline looked down at the gold necklace, laying next to the empty box. She picked it up and saw that a heavy pearl was attached to the chain. It was gripped in an elaborately-decorated eagle's claw.

She looked excitedly to Frank.

"It's beautiful - is it for me?" Then, getting no answer, she realised she was being far too presumptuous, and went to hand it back to him.

Frank was seething. He had planned to give his mother's 18ct gold necklace to Sally over dinner. He would then seduce her, start a row, ask for the necklace back - then return it as good as new. It was as simple as that. But now he was beginning to realise, he could do the same to Pauline.

"I was going to give it to you after the last dance, but now's a good a time as any. Here, let me put it on for you." He squirmed at what he'd just said, but he wanted her desperately, and was prepared to go to any lengths to bed her that night.

"Frank, I don't know what to say. No-one has ever given me anything like this before!"

"You're worth it, Pauline. Listen, I'm sorry for all that business about the joint. It's just no fun being stoned by myself. You could always eat a little piece?"

There was a brief, uncertain pause. "I'll do it for you Frank, but only this once."

They returned to the dance, and Frank got more drinks, spiking Pauline's in the process.

The Blue Jets finished another song and Frank practically had to carry her back to the table.

"I can walk you know, I'm not a baby," slurred Pauline, as she slumped down heavily on the chair. She looked at him with glazed eyes and head swaying from side-to-side, "When is that dope stuff going to work? I swallowed it ages ago."

"You wont know until it hits you," he replied, himself now slurring. He then reached across to pick up his drink, only to spill it into her lap. Pauline let out a gasp of surprise, then began to giggle hysterically. "Oh look, Frank, I've wet myself on our first date!"

"I think it's starting to work!" Laughed Frank.

Pauline could hardly stand now, and Frank was thankful the band was playing a slow number as he hauled her across the dance floor, towards the elevator.

"Frank, I don't feel well, I need to lie down," she muttered incoherently, but he either couldn't hear her above the music, or didn't want to. She clung to him tightly, not daring to trust her legs, in case they buckled beneath her. The whole of the bar seemed like one big blur, and Pauline had to keep opening and closing her eyes in an effort to control the spinning.

The singer spoke into the microphone, as he watched Frank and Pauline's progress with amusement. "Thank-you all for being such a great audience. We hope you've enjoyed the evening - now it's time for our last song, and we go back to that wonderful Drifters hit, 'Save The Last Dance For Me'. Goodnight folks!"

Pauline was carried over Frank's shoulder for the last part of the journey. She could vaguely recall him slapping her hard across the bottom, as he staggered from the elevator towards the suite. She thought she was falling into a deep, dark void and struggled to remain conscious. She had no idea where they were, but knew Frank was there, with her, to keep her safe.

Pauline bounced several times as she hit the bed. It was soft, and the eiderdown felt refreshingly cool. Thinking she was at home, and in her own bed, she started to let the powerful urge to sleep have its way. It was then, that she felt her clothes being roughly yanked off. First, her shoes, then she was rocked side-to-side, and felt her damp, tight skirt being tugged down past her hips.

"Jenny! Jenny!" She called out in her confused state of mind, wrongly thinking her friend was helping her. She felt the strong hands again, those same hands she had fought off before, grabbing and clawing at her.

"Please don't hurt me," she pleaded, her voice weak and muffled. She was pushed, face-down onto the bed, and her blouse and bra were torn off. Feeling cold, she tried to cover herself with the eiderdown, but Frank's hands were on her again - now working their way down her body, rolling and pulling. She reached down and desperately tried to hold on to the elastic top of her knickers, but she couldn't resist him, he had too much strength.

Pauline could smell the same breath again, close to her face. She thought she could make out Frank's features in the dim light, before he buried his tongue into her mouth. She struggled for breath, and forced her head away from him.

She tried to will her mind to work, to think clearly, so she could awake from this horrific nightmare. She gasped as a razor-sharp pain shot through her breast, and felt his teeth gnawing at her nipples. Again, she pushed him away, only to feel the stubble on his chin, as it scraped down across her stomach.

She then felt his burrowing tongue licking around the insides of her thighs, like some rabid animal trying to devour her. She heard him moan as his tongue found its way inside her. In other circumstances she may have enjoyed this new sensation, but Frank was far too rough, and she begged him to stop.

She brought her arms up to the top half of her body, in an attempt to hide her nakedness. Her skin was sore and sticky from Frank's saliva, and she tried to crawl up the bed, away from his intrusive invasion of her privacy. She was viciously grabbed and pulled back down, before feeling the whole of Frank's weight, as he clumsily lowered himself down on top of her. She felt his manhood, large and erect trying to find its way between her legs. She wriggled and tried to get out from beneath him, but now he was pushing hard, in a piston-like, rhythmic motion. Unable to move, Pauline gasped, and let out a short scream as he finally entered her. The pain was excruciating, and she remembered shouting, "No! No!" As she cried, and dug her finger nails into his flesh.

She didn't know how long it took, as she kept drifting in and out of consciousness, but she knew it was finally over, when his body seemed to go into spasm, and he let out a long moan of pleasure, before spurting his seed inside her.

Pauline knew she was going to be sick, but even if she could get away from Frank - there was no way she could manage the few feet to the bathroom.

Frank rolled off, and began fumbling for his cigarettes. He noticed Pauline clumsily trying to get off the bed.

"Look at the state of you, Pauline - you look like a trollop!" He smirked.

"I feel so ill - I think I'm going to be sick," she gasped weakly.

Frank tried to move out of the way, but he wasn't quick enough. He leapt off the bed and looked down angrily at his soiled shirt.

"You disgusting bitch - see what you've done!"

Not being able to help herself, Pauline managed to flop her head over the side of the bed, and without realising, vomited over Frank's jacket, which was lying on the floor.

"Cost me forty guineas, that fucking suit, now look at it! Bloody ruined - you fat slut!" He clenched his fist and moved to strike her, but when he saw the state of her face, he stopped himself just in time, not wanting to get his knuckles dirtied.

Frank hopped around the hotel room in a drunken rage, trying to pull his trousers on. He staggered, and fell against a low table, sending bottles and glasses crashing to the floor. Then, as he was about to leave, he paused in the doorway, and looked down at Pauline, her head dangling limply over the side of the bed. He walked across to her and calmly unfastened the necklace, and put it back in his pocket.

"Frank! Frank! Are you there? Please help me, I think I need a doctor." She whimpered, heaving once more. But Frank never heard her, for he had already gone.

Edward turned the page of his newspaper. He had been glaring at it for the last fifteen minutes as he sat at the breakfast table - but his mind had been elsewhere. He poked his head around the large pages and forced a brief smile at Pamela, who remained silent. She knew after all these years as his secretary, how much Edward enjoyed his moments of peace and quiet. He looked at Pamela again and watched as she went about her usual breakfast routine. She always had a generous helping of prunes, followed by orange juice, a soft boiled egg, with a slice of toast, and finally, tea. However, today Pamela seemed content to just sip her orange juice. She became aware of him staring, and became embarrassed, as if she were a child again.

"What's the matter, dear? You haven't touched your egg, and Mrs. Gardener always does them exactly how you like them."

Pamela sighed, and put her napkin down.

"It's all that bad feeling last night. I wish I could have done something to help."

"I know dear, damned unpleasant business all around. I was a total ass last night, and I know it. I handled the situation with Lizzie absurdly. God knows, I've turned her completely against me now."

He left the table and went out through the French windows into the garden. Edward had taken quite a bit of time off recently, to attend to matters with Margaret. Now he missed his work sorely and felt utterly frustrated. There had been a sharp frost that morning, and the well-manicured lawn bore a crisp, white carpet of ice. He stepped onto the patio, reached into the pocket of his tweed sports jacket, and produced his pipe. After he'd filled it with tobacco, he lit the pipe and began to think about some of his up-coming legal cases, and decided it might be prudent to shut himself away in his study for a while.

He could clearly hear Mrs. Gardener's voice coming from one of the upstairs windows, as she got Margaret up, and ready for another abysmal day of emptiness. Edward hadn't seen his wife that morning. Normally, during a working week, he would call in and see her, before heading off to the office. Although, she would be in bed, she was always awake and always staring blankly. It made him wonder if anything was going through her once, brilliant mind. At weekends, he would wait until Mrs. Gardener had got Margaret dressed and presentable, before going in. It was nice to see her in one of her better dresses and wearing a little make-up, as if for a moment, things were back to normal.

His mind turned to last night once more, and he realised that he should have spoken to Lizzie just as he had always done, which was more like a friend than a daughter. They had always been able to take each other into their confidence, it was a special bond that existed between them. But last night, he had spoken to her like she were a stranger, and had failed in every way to get his true feelings across.

He had wanted to tell her how much he loved his family, and how difficult it was for him to accept that he had lost his wife forever, and all that remained of her was a seemingly empty shell. Edward kept his grief to himself, but he wasn't the type of man who could live a full life without having his physical needs met by a woman whom he could love, and love like he had once loved Margaret. He had mistakenly assumed his children would just automatically accept Pamela, especially since they seemed to like her, and she was practically a part of the family already. He knew Lizzie would have understood his feelings. She would have respected his honesty and candidness, and would have hugged him, knowing that whatever he decided, would be the right thing for all of them.

Why on earth didn't he drive to Wales and speak to Lizzie himself? Yes, that's what he should have done - tell her the truth. Now he was guilty of acting in a most despicable manner by allowing her to learn the details from Janice, who was not averse to over-exaggeration.

He put his hand up to his brow and walked out onto the lawn, the frosty grass crunched beneath the thick, leather soles of his brogues, as he wearily searched his mind for an adequate solution.

Some sort of commotion then rudely shook him out of his soul-searching. Edward heard shouting, which appeared to come from back inside the house.

Lizzie and Janice had let themselves in through the front door. Ignoring Poppy's protestations, they ventured towards the living room. They heard the sound of someone humming, and presumed it was Mrs. Gardener doing some light cleaning. They certainly didn't expect to find Pamela, wearing rubber gloves and packing family photographs into a carrier bag. One photograph was of Edward and Margaret's wedding day, the rest were mainly of the children at various stages of their childhood. A cardboard box had been placed on the table, and this contained many of Margaret's personal items. One set of shelves had been completely cleared, only to be replaced by Pamela's collection of various bits and pieces. In fact, downstairs, there was very little evidence to suggest Margaret still even lived at the house.

"Oh stop yapping, Poppy. It's probably just the dustmen!" Called out Pamela, as she petted the tiny dog, before dropping a photograph of Margaret, waterskiing in 1946, into the bag. "If you don't behave yourself, we wont be able to live here. Now stop your barking this instance!" Pamela then heard something behind her, and turned to see Lizzie and Janice staring coldly at her from the doorway.

Janice charged straight at Pamela, violently knocking the smaller woman to the floor. She snatched the carrier bag and screamed at Pamela; "Look, you witch - this is our lives you're stuffing into this bag. Don't you realise that you're destroying our family? I hate you! Get out!"

Pamela looked absolutely terrified and brought her hands up to protect herself as Janice began kicking out at her wildly. Poppy ran bravely to Pamela's defence and snapped at Janice's heels as the onslaught continued.

Mrs. Gardener came rushing into the room and pushed the assailant away. "Janice! Janice! Stop! You'll kill her. Please! Your mother's in a dreadful state upstairs."

"I wont stop until this bitch is out of our home!" Roared Janice, her eyes almost red with anger.

Lizzie, feeling that she too ought to be making her presence felt, went and stood loyally beside her sister. She looked down at Pamela, and was about to say her piece, when she saw blood was oozing from Pamela's lip, and she seemed to be having some sort of a shaking fit. Lizzie put her hands to her face in shame, and sank to her knees next to the stricken Pamela. Now, for some unexplained reason, she wanted to hold Pamela, to help her, to protect her, but Poppy growled viciously at Lizzie, and kept her at bay.

Edward sat on the floor holding Pamela tightly in his arms, gently stroking her hair. Any sudden movement would make her cry out with pain and cling to him for dear life. Poppy sat next to them, and every so often would jump onto Edward's lap to lick his face.

"Will she be alright?" Asked Lizzie, breaking the awful silence, "Perhaps we should call an ambulance?"

There was no response from Edward, he didn't even look up at her. Lizzie was about to ask again, but thought better of it, and went into the lounge where Janice was anxiously pacing.

"I think you really hurt Pamela, kicking her like that."

"I didn't mean to. I just saw her with the photo and saw red," replied Janice, guiltily.

They waited an hour before Edward finally came out of the living room with Pamela. She was deathly pale and still obviously very shaken up. He called Mrs. Gardener to him and whispered some instructions before dismissing her. Edward remained quite calm and collected, in fact even solemn as he cleared his throat and stood in the centre of the room, supporting his unsteady mistress. He motioned for both Lizzie and Janice to sit down, and the two sisters went over to the settee, looking at each other, not sure what to expect.

"In a few moments I'll be driving Pamela home." Said Edward, in a soft and slightly quaking voice. "Mrs. Gardener is upstairs, packing some of her things. The rest, I shall remove later."

He looked directly at Janice, then Lizzie, and was still unsure whether he should tell them what was really on his mind. He felt Pamela gently squeeze his hand, and drew encouragement from her touch. The two girls were stunned and unnerved by this strange, emotive side their father was displaying, and they noticed immediately, the incredible bond between him and Pamela. It was something that disturbed them, and they were incapable of realising the true depth and meaning of a relationship which they could find so appalling.

Lizzie and Janice, despite their victory were more than pleased to leave their father's house. However, in their hurry, they failed to hear the sobbing coming from Margaret's room. The sobbing that grew louder and louder, until it became unbearable and tore at the very centre of Edward's troubled heart.

Mrs. gardener sat the woman, who had been her employer and friend for more years than she chose to remember in her wheelchair. Margaret would then sit by the window, so she could gaze out onto the lawn and admire the rose bushes when they were in bloom. It was a beautiful garden and one that she enjoyed tending herself, not so very long ago.

Mrs. Gardener however, may or may not have known about Edward's secret - that Pamela was Lizzie's natural mother. Certainly, if she did know, it was something she would never speak of, and rather than betray her employer's trust, she would sooner take the secret to her grave.

Mrs. Gardener would always find the time to speak to Margaret, and she would always address her as Mrs. Marchmont. She would never know if Margaret could hear or interpret the information, but it was something she felt was important. She would talk of the small, but necessary things in life, things that she found interesting herself, local news, like who had got married recently, the cost of living, and the ills of society. That was always a popular topic of Mrs. Gardener, and one which she felt she could never quite understand. On that particular morning, before the rumpus, she had been telling Margaret, as she brushed her hair, about the birth of her new grandson, Charles - named after the young Prince. She spoke of all the presents and knitted clothes the baby had received, and how he looked so much like her own son.

Following the awful scene downstairs, it was now taking a great deal of effort for Mrs. Gardener to try and calm Margaret. She had never seen her cry like this before, despite some pretty awful rows between Mr. and Mrs. Marchmont, in the early days, but this was something different.

"The shouting's all over now, there's nothing to worry about. I even heard Mr. Marchmont say he was going to get proper, trained nurses to come in and look after you. I'll still be coming in as well, but more for the housework and for little Bobby of course. It'll be lovely to have him home again, especially for Christmas, along with Lizzie. My word, how that girl's grown! She's turned into a proper, young lady now, and at university too." However, as Mrs. Gardener continued, she became aware of Margaret reaching out for her. She took the woman's hand, but noticed she was trying desperately to say something. Moving her head closer, Mrs. Gardener listened intently, as Margaret struggled to get her words out.

"I can't hear you, Mrs. Marchmont, try to speak just a little louder."

Then, in no more than a faint whisper, Margaret managed to speak, just one word.

But, despite further prompts from Mrs. Gardener, Margaret wouldn't say anymore. The housekeeper then ran downstairs and called Edward.

"Are you sure she spoke, I'm not entirely convinced," asked Edward, looking down at his wife.

"Your wife said, 'Pamela', it was as clear as day. I would stake my life on it, Mr. Marchmont."

Edward sat down next to Margaret, and placed his arm around her shoulders.

"Darling, you are going to stay here with me, like you always have. We will never be apart. I've told Pamela to leave, and she won't come back here again. I've been a fool. I had no idea, I'm so, so, sorry, I hurt you, my dearest." Edward thought he saw a hint of a smile on Margaret's face, but he dismissed it, and got up to go back downstairs.

6. THE CHRISTMAS DANCE

It was midday, and a bleary-eyed Frank stood at the bar in the social club. He downed his pint, ordered another, then lit up his first cigarette of the day. He inhaled deeply, only to break into a frenzied coughing fit, before continuing with his version of the previous night's events.

"I could have killed her. She totally ruined the suit I brought for graduation. Crazy bitch couldn't hold her drink and puked up everywhere."

Ken listened intently, but couldn't help laughing at his friend's misfortune.

"You should make Pauline pay for it. Where is she anyway, her two stupid mates were asking for her earlier?"

"Damned if I know, I expect the inconsiderate little trollop is still pebble-dashing that hotel room." Sneered Frank, leaning slovenly against the bar. "I just stormed out in the end, it must have been about three in the morning - she was lousy in bed anyway."

Ken laughed, "What about the bill, how much did it cost you?"

"No idea," replied Frank, smugly, "That's her problem. Anyway, it wont come to anything like the cost of my bloody suit. Come on, lets go for a spin in the jag, I've got to get it back tomorrow."

They left the club and walked through the campus towards the administration building, as Ken wanted to see if he could get some tickets. It was a cold, frosty Friday, and the day of the university's Christmas Dance.

"I'm telling you Frank, the only place you'll get tickets now is at the Dean's office. Just think, you'll be able to see Meredith's secretary, the one you fancy - what's her name, Mrs. Parker, isn't it?"

"It's Jane actually," drawled Frank, "I'm on first name terms with her," he added dryly, taking out a metal comb from his pocket, and pulling it through his hair.

They decided to check the post room first to see if any tickets might just be laying around, waiting for people to collect. Ken flicked through a pile of mail and assorted messages, but apart from what looked to be Christmas cards there was no sign of any tickets. However, he did notice an official-looking envelope addressed to Frank.

"It's probably just the usual crap, asking for my accommodation fees. They'll be lucky!" Cursed Frank bitterly, as he tore the letter open.

"Shit!"

"What is it, Frank?"

"It's from that bastard, Meredith. Says I'm to attend his office regarding complaints about my behaviour."

"When is it?"

"Today, ten o'clock."

"But that was three hours ago!" Exclaimed Ken, as he took the letter from Frank. "Look at the date, its been here for ages. Don't you ever check for mail?"

"Fuck him. If that boring swine wants to see me, he can come looking."

"Maybe you should go and see your friend, Jane. She might be able to get you out of this mess. Besides, it'll give you a chance to chat her up and get us a couple of tickets for tonight."

Frank grinned and swaggered along the corridor, towards the Dean of Student's office. He passed grand-looking paintings of long-departed dons and group photographs of previous graduation days, which he paid no attention to. As he neared Mrs. Parker's office, he noticed a cabinet full of sporting trophies. He gazed through the glass at the cup he once held aloft, after he'd captained the rugby team's memorable, victory over their nearest rivals two years ago. Those days were long gone now, as Frank's hedonistic lifestyle had reduced him to being a mere substitute, if he was fortunate enough to get picked.

While he waited by her empty desk, Frank noticed that a pile of tickets for the Christmas Dance had been left out. He winked at Ken, and took the opportunity, to slip a few of them into his inside pocket. A couple of minutes had passed and there was still no sign of Jane. He then sat on her desk and browsed through some papers he saw in the out box. Most were petty warning letters to students, regarding things like, noise and drinking. Reading a letter, which was addressed to one of the rugby team, he howled with laughter and had to read it again. No, he thought, this can't be serious - excessive breaking of wind in the halls of residence during the small hours!

He was disturbed by the sound of the adjoining door being opened, and looked across to see, Mr. Meredith standing in front of him.

"What on earth do you think you're doing?" Barked the Dean.

Frank stood up, and glared at him, angered by the Dean's tone of voice. "I'm waiting for Jane, what do think I'm bloody well doing?"

"Mrs. Parker is at lunch. How dare you come into her office and go through confidential papers." Scowled Meredith, returning Frank's glare.

The younger man, unnerved by the Dean's confidence and assertive manner, sighed as if he were bored, then put the papers back down on the secretary's desk.

"You're Frank Gant aren't you?" Demanded the Dean, moving closer, so that his face was just inches from Frank's.

Frank took a step back, then hurriedly produced the letter from his pocket.

"That's right, I've come about this. You see, Mr. Meredith - I got a bit held up." Smirked Frank, noticing the Dean's short, military-style haircut, and the hard stare from his cynical eyes. Meredith had served with Montgomery's Desert Rats, during the war, and was still very much indoctrinated with the army way of life.

"Don't try and get smart with me, Gant." Snarled Meredith, "You should have been in my office at ten o'clock this morning. Where were you?"

Frank looked down to avoid his tormentors gaze, and tried to get his drink and drug fazed mind to co-operate.

"I'm sorry, Mr. Meredith. I've been studying hard lately, and I woke up with such a severe headache, I had to take some aspirin and go back to bed."

The Dean smelt the alcohol on Frank's breath, and recalled a complaint about him splashing the old lady in town yesterday. Mrs. Davies had subsequently died of heart failure in hospital, and the post office was closed until further notice, due to a police investigation taking place. He looked at Frank with total disgust, and tried desperately to contain his anger.

"Now, let's get this straight, Gant. I've received some very serious and disturbing complaints about you, and these matters need to be resolved. I have the authority to send you down, and withhold your degree. That is of course, if you have the ability to pass your finals. There'll be another letter in the post forthwith. Now get out of my sight."

It was well past midday by the time the young chambermaid reached the Falcon Suite. The hotel was three quarters full, with many guests enjoying the hospitality of a cheap night's board with the Christmas dinner and dance stopover offer. The hotel would rather let rooms at a discount, or as part of a special package, than let them stand empty. They would never lose out, since most of the guests were there for a good time and wouldn't notice the subtle price increases on most of the drinks.

Carol had been lucky to get the job at the hotel so soon after the awful incident with Frank back at the university. She loved her new position and was motivated by the fact that the hotel promoted from within. Many of the staff in senior positions had started out on the bottom rung of the ladder, just like Carol, and now at last, she had the opportunity to shine, and show what she was capable of.

Today, Mrs. Crayford, the Head Housekeeper had entrusted Carol with the Falcon Suite, one of the most luxurious and expensive rooms in the hotel.

Carol had been delighted to take on this new responsibility, and went about her work with a lightness of spirit. However, as she let herself into the suite with her master key, the smell of vomit was overpowering. Being dark inside, she went straight over to pull back the curtains and open a window. It was then that she heard a groan come from the bed. Carol was quite startled, as she didn't expect anyone to still be in the room during the afternoon. Checkout was at ten thirty, and she had knocked first before entering, as was customary.

She quickly checked her list to make sure it wasn't her mistake, then swallowed hard as she took in the state of the suite. There were several cigarette burns on the carpet, a champagne bottle lay on its side, accompanied by two glasses, one of which was shattered into dozens of tiny pieces. A torn, expensive-looking, silk blouse was draped over a coffee table, with its ivory buttons ripped off. A pair of knickers were dangling from a bedside lamp, stockings and a suspender belt were strewn across the bed, and a lace-trimmed bra, was lying next to a man's crumpled jacket, both covered in vomit.

Slowly, Carol went over to Pauline, being careful not to tread in anything she might regret. As she got closer, she picked up a pair of broken spectacles, which she placed on the bedside table.

"Are you awake Miss, can you hear me?" There was no response, apart from another groan. Carol was just about to try and rouse her again, when Pauline suddenly sat bolt upright and grabbed the startled girl by the hand.

"Who are you? Where am I?" Cried out Pauline, staring wide-eyed and looking frightened and confused, before collapsing back onto the bed.

Carol ran from the room to alert the housekeeper.

"It's awful, Mrs. Crayford, she looks like she's dying!" Blurted out Carol. "She hasn't got a stitch of clothing on, and there's all these bite marks on her - like she's been attacked by an animal!"

"Take control of yourself, Carol dear, now lets go together and see this poor lass."

"I would have helped her, but she's been sick everywhere. What shall we do?"

The housekeeper remained calm and reached down to a huge bunch of keys hanging from a chain attached to her waistband.

"Hush Carol, wait out here for me." With that, Mrs. Crayford unlocked the door and walked into the suite. She was inside for about two minutes, before she appeared back at the door and called Carol inside.

"The poor child's got a hangover. She's never drank before. We'll need a taxi to get her back to the university. She'll have a sore head for a while, and it'll damn well get worse when she gets the cleaning bill for this room. I've never seen anything like it - the suite will be out of use for days."

Mrs. Crayford then led Carol back inside, "Now my dear, I want you to help this girl clean herself up, then we'll have to get her out. I know her name, and I'm going down to speak to the duty manager, to see how we'll handle this. You've a lot to learn about the hotel business."

Pauline was now sitting on the edge of the bed, holding her head in her hands. She looked up slowly, as Carol approached.

"Oh my god, what has happened to me?"

"The housekeeper said you had too much to drink," replied Carol, trying to be helpful.

"Where's Frank? There was a man, where is he, did you see him?"

Carol felt a shiver run down her spine at the mention of Frank's name. "No, Miss. You were alone. I can call down to reception and ask them?"

"No, please don't. Can you help me, where's my glasses? I'm not sure if I can stand."

Carol reached across for Pauline's glasses. One lens was gone completely and other was shattered, as was the frame.

"I can get some sticky tape and see if I can repair them."

Pauline nodded, and tried to get up.

Carol had already fetched a robe from the bathroom, to cover the student's modesty, but as she stood, Carol couldn't help but gasp, when she saw the blood on the sheets.

Pauline glanced around and realised her nightmare had in fact, been for real. Her first instinct would have been to break down in despair and cry for something she had cherished so dearly, but had now been so cruelly taken away. However, that would have been the Pauline of old. For this Pauline, the crying days were over.

Before she was free to leave the hotel, Pauline had to suffer the indignity of being driven back to town by the manager, in order for her to withdraw practically every penny she had in her savings account. This was to pay for the cost of cleaning and repairing the hotel suite. As she handed over the money, Pauline reached up to her neck. She had remembered the beautiful necklace Frank had given her last night. She felt her heart sink to find it was gone. She pleaded with the manager to let her go back up and look for it, but he wouldn't listen, and ordered her off the premises. She did though, manage to retrieve Frank's jacket, before it would have been thrown away. Carol had kindly cleaned it up for her, and had then placed it in a bag. Pauline felt a certain affinity with the jacket, they were both Frank's property.

Pauline breathed in the fresh air and gazed out of the open taxi window, as she finally returned to the campus. Watching the green hills go steadily past, she tried to piece together the events of last night. There was so much she couldn't remember. One thing however remained crystal clear in her mind, despite the thumping headache. It was Frank who had pursued her, who had asked her out, who had wined and dined her. It was Frank who had taught her how to dance, and it was Frank who had planted his seed inside her. Now, as far as Pauline was concerned, she was his woman, his property. But more importantly, he was her man.

Sally hated the silence and longed for something to say that might cheer Lizzie up. Her friend had said very little about what had happened when she and Janice had confronted Edward.
"Yes, it went really well. Pamela has gone, Mum is going to stay at home, with nurses coming in to look after her, and Bobby is going back home as well."

Sally tried to get more details, but to no avail. It seemed to her that Lizzie was still harbouring issues or she was totally ashamed of how things had panned out. She decided not to question her friend anymore, and would just wait until Lizzie felt ready to talk again.

They passed through a small village, and Sally noticed the time displayed on the clock-tower. He would be there now, she thought, as Lizzie had to brake sharply for a red light, causing her to curse. Sally suddenly felt her heart begin to race, for some reason, she felt that the young student at the library, could still be there, waiting for her.

"Lizzie, when we get back, I just want to pop into the library for a few minutes. How much further have we to go?"

Lizzie looked sidelong at Sally with a puzzled look on her face.

"We should be back in about forty five minutes, but why on earth do you want to go to the library on a Friday afternoon? Everyone else will be getting ready to go the dance or will be going home for Christmas. You do surprise me sometimes, Sally!"

"I wont be long. You can go back to Lloyd-Evans, I'll see you there. It's just that I've got a seminar early next week, it's the last one, I'm pleased to say." Replied Sally, trying her hardest to sound convincing.

"I'm glad I never took Classics, that's all I can say!" Said Lizzie, dryly. "Well, I suppose I can have a bath, while you're there. You wont be long will you? I'm sorry to be such a bore, but I feel so low at the moment, what with all that stuff at home, and now all this driving."

"Lizzie, I think you've stood up to it remarkably well. I certainly could never challenge my father like that."

"Thanks Sally, I really appreciate that. Perhaps we could cook something nice in the kitchen, get a bottle of wine, and just stay in my room tonight?"

Sally smiled at her friend, it was so unlike Lizzie to be this low. "What about Ken, don't you want to see him later?"

"Sod Ken!"

"Oh Lizzie!"

"I really can't be bothered. Besides, he'll want to go to the dance, and I don't feel up to it tonight."

They finally reached the campus, and Lizzie pulled up outside the library. As Sally got out of the car, her friend called her back.

"About this morning, Janice and I were right weren't we? It's just that I haven't been able to stop thinking about it. I feel so awful about Pamela, she's really quite a nice person."

"I think you should wait a day or so, then phone your father. I don't think everything is all quite over yet."

Sally waved Lizzie off, and walked the few yards towards the library. She would never describe herself as a nervous sort of person, but now she felt a strong, tingling sensation in the pit of her stomach. She climbed the few steps, then realised she hadn't even looked in a mirror since early that morning. She seemed to be alone, so she opened her bag, and did a quick touch-up job on her make-up. Feeling more confident, she pushed the heavy, swing door, but it appeared to be locked, how odd, she thought? Glancing down at her watch, she noticed it was four in the afternoon, the library doesn't usually close so early, not even on a Friday.

"Been shut since twelve young lady," called out the campus postman, as he walked past. "Often shuts early this time of year, if no-one's using it."

Sally thanked him and turned to go, but the postman called after her, "Is your name Sally, by any chance?"

"Yes, it is, but why?"

"There was another student here earlier, a lad called, William, he told me he was meant to meet someone inside. Closed, I said, the poor boy looked quite upset. Anyway, he mentioned your name, and I said I'd look out for you in passing, and see you got the message he left for you on the board outside."

Sally drew in a sudden deep breath, she had not thought to look there. Excitedly, she thanked the postman again, and knew that everything was not lost after all. She hurried back into the porch, and glanced at the notice-board expectantly. She saw a large poster confirming what the postman had said about the library's closure, then, just a little below it, among the notes and leaflets telling of forthcoming church services, was a piece of folded paper with her name written on it. She removed the drawing pin, but her fingers were cold, and she fumbled a little, as she tried to open it out.

Dear Sally,
I brought your seminar notes. Sorry about the library being closed - I didn't know!
I've left them in the post room for you. Perhaps, you might be at the Christmas
Dance tonight. I do hope so, I'd love it if you saved me a dance! If not, then I'll

wish you a happy Xmas, and will look out for you next term.

William Peddlescoombe.

P.S. I have your scarf!

Sally re-read the note, and whispered to herself, so that's his name, William, William Peddlescoombe. After picking up the notes from the post room, she walked briskly back to her room, desperately thinking of a way to persuade Lizzie to come to the dance that night. They both had tickets, and it would be such a pity to waste them. Putting herself in Lizzie's position, she wondered what her friend would do. It didn't take much working out, in fact, it was obvious - Lizzie would be totally straight and honest with her.

"Sally, I just can't believe it! I can't leave you alone for five minutes! When did you meet this William, with the funny-sounding surname?" Inquired Lizzie eagerly, "My word, you're a fast mover, and I thought I knew you!"

"It was only very recently," replied Sally, blushing. "Anyway, it may come to nothing, oh, Lizzie, I wish you could see him!" Sally got visibly more excited as she described her encounter with William, and it was infectious, Lizzie was soon out of the doldrums, and now, persuading her to come to the dance would be that much easier.

"Look, Sally - I'll be just fine here, honestly. I want you to go. I've already ruined your birthday, and I certainly don't want to spoil your chances with this bloke in the fisherman's sweater!" Said Lizzie sitting at the dressing table and proceeding to apply her false eye lashes. "I can be so selfish, and miserable at times. I'm very lucky to have you as a friend."

"Yes, I know!" Joked Sally, "But why can't you come to the dance and be miserable there? And why are you putting on your eye lashes, if you're not coming?"

Lizzie started laughing, "Ok, I'll come for one drink, and one dance, maybe!"

"Fantastic! Shall I go to my room and get the Babychams?"

"Yes, please do, but aren't you forgetting something Sally - what about Frank?"

"Sod Frank!"

"Oh, Sally!"

"Frank's not going to the dance. He said he doesn't want to toady up to all those lecturers, and listen to a lot of boring speeches. So, while the cats away..."

Frank and Ken had been the first to arrive at the assembly hall, where the university's annual Christmas Dance was due to take place. They knew this particular venue very well, for it was here that most of the examinations were usually held. However, for Frank, the hall filled him with dread - it just reminded him of those annoying re-sits he was always having to take, and all the valuable drinking time that had been wasted because of them.

A temporary bar had been set up at one end of the hall, while at the other, stood the stage, where so many degrees had been proudly handed out over the years. Situated in the centre, and around the edges, were several large trestle tables. These were covered with white, linen tablecloths, and several volunteers were busy helping to set the places. In the past, each faculty would have their own separate tables, but this year, the students would be able to sit where they wanted. The eating arrangements for lecturers and university officials would remain the same. Tables would be made available for them up on the stage, where they would be less susceptible to the ritual barrage of bread rolls being thrown straight after the president's speech.

Following a rousing rendition of the university song, it was customary for lecturers to go amongst the students and help serve the main course. The eating of Christmas dinner in the evening had now been a tradition at Falcondale for well over a hundred years. Once the feasting was over, all able-bodied men, and women, were required to assist in moving tables and chairs to create a space for the dancing. Faculty and officials however, were only expected to remain for the first dance. Very few though, adhered to this unwritten rule, or were brave enough to stay longer, for fear of being made a laughing stock by students already high on Christmas cheer.

As the guests arrived, they were given a glass of extremely mild, mulled wine, which often had the habit of getting much stronger as the evening progressed. The guests would then mingle around the foyer looking for friends, or to see who was going to sit where. The atmosphere was always congenial, and for many students and staff, this annual event was probably the most enjoyable on the social calendar.

As the hall began to fill up, a low chanting could be heard in the distance. The chanting grew louder by the second, and for those of a nervous disposition, or for first-year students, who had never heard it before - it could be quite a scary and awesome experience.

Soon, the deafening cry of Die! Die! Die! totally made any conversation in the hall quite impossible. Guests either quickly made their way to the tables, or just stood dumbfounded, and watched as the main doors suddenly burst open.

The noise was coming from the university rugby team, and its army of followers. It was an episode that occurred every Saturday of term, but on a much smaller scale. The team, whether in victory or defeat would tour the town's pubs, before eventually making their way back to the social club, or in this case - the assembly hall. They would sing or shout as loudly as they could and hold aloft the player who had scored the most tries. Although deemed an honour, this was quite a dangerous practice, as invariably the supporting crowd were very inebriated and would often stumble, letting the said scorer crash heavily to the ground. The chant of 'Die', was in fact 'Dai'. This was the name of a legendary player, 'Dai The Dragon', who had scored the winning try in the final of the Welsh College's Shield, despite having the end of his nose bitten off. He later refused to take part in any celebrations until the players of both teams searched the pitch for his missing body part. The nose now takes pride of place, sitting in a bottle of alcohol behind the bar at the social club. Tradition has it, that the next scorer of a winning try in the final of the WCS will have to drink the contents of the bottle as a mark of respect.

Needless to say, the university has never won the shield since.

Usually, Frank and Ken would have been up near the front of the procession, but tonight, Frank preferred to remain at the bar. He wanted to get his priorities right and be in a prime position to act accordingly at the merest hint of a desirable female, without having a vast herd of drunks swarming around him.

It certainly suited Frank, not having Sally there, judging by some of the gorgeously turned out beauties on display. He downed his pint and cheered excitedly as the beer-sodden crowd surged in. Then, together with Ken, they started to bang their empty glasses on the bar, in tune with the deafening rhythm.

Those in the immediate vicinity quickly divided like an ugly parody of the parting of the Red Sea, to allow the new arrivals access to more alcohol. Once everyone had been served, some sense of order began to return to the event, and the students were asked to take their seats. It took several minutes for over a thousand people to finally settle. Frank and Ken scanned each table with a trained eye, and it was then, that Frank noticed, Pauline. She was sitting up at the far end, near the stage. He was rather surprised that she had been able to attend something like a dinner and dance, bearing in mind the condition she had been in, when he had left her earlier that morning. He wasn't quite sure if she had seen him yet, but he noticed she was with her two friends, Jenny and Maureen. They probably had an evening of toadying up to the faculty planned, he thought, as he gazed further along to where Meredith was sitting. Frank's mouth drawled as he saw the Dean was busily chatting away to his beautiful secretary, Jane. She looked more stunning than ever, even at a hundred feet away. She was dressed in a striking, dark green ball gown, that highlighted her green eyes perfectly. She wore her auburn hair shoulder-length, and had her make-up immaculately applied. Jane was probably one of the most attractive women at the event, and Frank wondered where their respective partners could be. He grinned as he finished yet another pint, and imagined himself seducing a married woman right under the Dean's nose. There's just something about an older, attractive, and unobtainable woman. Forbidden fruit perhaps.

"Frank, stop leering at that bloody Jane will you, and look at this!"

Frank turned and followed Ken's gaze, over towards the main doors.

"Holy shit! Blonde bombshells or what! I never thought Sally could look like that!"

In fact, several others took notice and watched in total admiration as Sally and Lizzie made their entrance. Sally was dressed in a figure-hugging, black taffeta dress, that accentuated her shapely figure beautifully. With her blonde hair slightly cascading, and her blue eyes sparkling, she looked simply dazzling. Even the gorgeous Jane looked over in awe, and had to concede she had come second best that night. Lizzie also looked stunning, but in her own rebellious way. She, in direct contrast, looked just like Cinderella, dressed in striking blue and yellow velvet, that produced a startling combination of colour, as it complimented her latest Monroe-like hair do.

Ken couldn't contain himself any longer, and stood up to summon the two stunning students over to the table. He and Lizzie were delighted to see each other, which pleased Sally, as she could see straight away, that her friend was getting back to her usual self.

"Ken - you look so handsome in a suit. You should wear one more often!" Remarked Lizzie in a teasing manner. But Ken couldn't find an answer straight away, he just glared at her amazed. "Is that really you, Lizzie?"

"Of course it is, you fool! Have I been away that long?"

Sally wasn't quite so enthusiastic to see Frank, she had been rather hoping it would be somebody else. However, she had to admit, he did look rather fetching in his black dinner suit and bow tie.

"Hello, Frank. What a lovely surprise to see you here. I didn't think you wanted to come?"

"What the hell do you think you're playing at?" He growled, with a crazed look in his bloodshot eyes, before grabbing her arm and leading her to the bar. Sally, realising he was drunk prepared herself for public humiliation. Frank ordered himself a large whiskey, then, becoming aware that he was making a spectacle of himself, toned down his act a little. He then smiled at Sally and lifted her arm in a sweeping motion, so that he could run his eyes admiringly up and down her expensive dress.

"What's the matter, Frank. Didn't you want to see me?"

Frank moved in closer towards her, "Look, I'm sorry, that was stupid of me. You look incredible, Sally, absolutely gorgeous. It's just that I had last night all planned out for you. It was meant to be the evening of your life. So what was so important that you had to stand me up?"

Before she could answer, he pulled her violently towards him, knocking over several glasses on the counter in the process. He then kissed her passionately in full view of the other guests. Frank's anger at Sally and his earlier plans for Jane soon melted away, as he felt the familiar stirring down below.

Sally, feeling distressed, quickly managed to disentangle herself from Frank's grasp, and began to explain about Lizzie's problems at home. She hoped it would be enough to placate him and keep his simmering rage under some sort of control.

"I'm so sorry, Frank. I had no idea. I didn't know it meant so much to you. Surely, yourself and Ken managed to occupy yourselves while we were gone?"

Frank paused for a moment before answering, "No, in fact I had rather a boring night. I had a few drinks at the club, then went to bed. I wanted to get up early, so to speak." The irony however, was lost on Sally. He took a step back, wanting to continue his visual inspection. Then, after telling her to do a turn, he pulled her towards him once more.

"Listen Sally, there's a wonderful hotel not far from here, how about I take you there for a nightcap?"

"You look as if you've had enough nightcaps already. Let's stay here for a while, the dancing will start soon."

Frank was now determined to get his way.

"It's a fantastic place, you'll absolutely love it," he continued, putting his arm around her.

To Sally's relief, Frank didn't get the chance to push the hotel idea any further. The moment was interrupted as Ken appeared excitedly, "Come on you two, the soup's getting cold. They'll be plenty of time for all that afterwards!"

They walked the few yards to the table, with Sally linking Frank's arm. He gallantly pulled out a chair for her, as he grinned, thinking about when he should try the necklace trick. He decided to bide his time a little, and wait for an opportunity to crumble some cannabis resin into her Christmas dinner. That would loosen Sally up a little he smirked to himself.

The atmosphere in the assembly hall was very jovial, and even the rugby crowd were acting with remarkable restraint. As usual, the lecturers serving the students were coming in for their customary round of jovial abuse and harassment. Even before dessert was over, some of the teaching staff, eager to get the first dance over with, were busy pushing tables and chairs aside. The free wine, included with the meal soon ran out, and once more, the bar area began to get crowded. Frank and Ken were involved in a drunken discussion with two other students sharing the table about which was the hardier sport, soccer or rugby. The conversation was getting quite ugly, so Sally and Lizzie took the opportunity to join the lengthy queue outside the ladies powder room.

7. THE STORM

For a moment she was sure she could hear ringing. Ignoring it, the girl carried on lathering her hair. Lloyd-Evans Hall was practically deserted that night, with many of the residents either having gone home, or attending the dance. The second-year student leant over the sink and began rinsing off the shampoo, then, as her ears became unblocked, she heard it again - it was definitely the telephone ringing. She was in no particular hurry as someone else would probably answer it eventually. The girl gathered up her wash things and headed back to her room. She was returning home for Christmas early the following morning and wanted to get as much packed tonight as possible.

The thought that she might be the only one left on her floor frightened her as she neared the ringing telephone. Usually, there was always some sign of life in the building - laughing, shouting or the beat of music playing somewhere.

"Hello, Lloyd-Evans Hall." She said, listening intently for a few seconds, but there was no answer. "Hello, is anyone there. Can you hear me?" She knew there was someone on the other end, as she could hear a faint breathing sound and what seemed like someone trying to speak. The girl immediately assumed it was another of the crank calls they would sometimes get, and replaced the receiver, before hurrying back to her room and locking the door.

Edward put down the telephone, poured himself another large brandy and paced up and down his study. Even though there was a good fire burning, the room felt cold, and Edward himself, felt colder still. A bitter sense of loss had taken grip of him, and it had increased its frozen, black hold, until it seemed like it was squeezing the very life out of his sad heart.

He heard the heavy footsteps coming down the stairs, and walked out into the hallway to meet the doctor.

Doctor Weller, a portly man in his mid-fifties, who always sported a colourful bow tie placed his hand on Edwards shoulder.

"Margaret wouldn't have felt a thing old boy. Brain haemorrhage, I'd say. In fact, I'm damn well certain of it. You knew it was on the cards, Edward."

"Thank-you Cecil. Do you think it was because of the arguments with Lizzie and Janice?"

"Yes, it's very possible, but we'll never know for sure. Look, Edward, I need to write out a death certificate for Margaret."

"Yes, of course, please come into the study. It all sounds so formal, and so final."

The doctor noticed Edward was close to breaking point.

"I think I'd better write you up for something, just to take the edge off things."

Edward shook his head, and began to pour them both a brandy.

"It's like she was just waiting, waiting to see Lizzie again, to know Bobby was coming home and the dog and..."

"And what?" Asked the doctor, taking a seat at Edward's desk.

"I think she had to know that I wasn't about to put her into a hospital."

"You've done your best old chap. It's all so very tragic. Listen, I don't think you should be here on your own tonight. Have you contacted anyone? What about the girls, or Mrs. Gardener?"

"I've just tried to ring Lizzie in Wales. The poor girl must have just got back. I couldn't speak to whoever it was who answered the phone. Cecil, what's happening to me for Christ's sake?"

The doctor stood and went over to Edward, "It's understandable man. Your wife has just died and you're in shock. I'll try Mrs. Gardener in a moment. Then, when she gets here we can call Janice. I think someone will need to be with you when the undertakers come."

"Yes, you're right, Cecil. I hadn't even thought of that" Edward sat and buried his head in his hands. He was fortunate to be able to release his pent up emotions in front of a man he'd known as a friend since the war. He sat quietly, as Dr. Weller filled out Margaret's certificate, before ringing Mrs. Gardener to ask her to come over.

"Do you remember France, Edward, and the heavy fighting near Caen, all those years ago?"

Edward looked up, his face racked with pain.

"It's something I'll never forget. It was June '44. We didn't finally capture it until July. But why do you ask?"

"You mentioned Lizzie, and I was reminded of that young soldier."

Edward swallowed hard and took a gulp of his brandy.

"Lieutenant Thomas Cartwright was his name. The poor chap had the most terrible wounds. But I couldn't just leave him there to die, Cecil, not like that."

"No Edward, you managed to get Thomas to me, then you stayed by his side and preyed for him as his life slowly ebbed away."

"He asked me to reach into his pocket. There was a letter addressed to his wife, along with a blood-stained photograph of her with their baby. We both knew he would never see them again, but what could we do?"

"There was nothing I could do Edward. But you did something. You didn't want him to die all alone in a foreign country."

Edward began to sob.

"Thomas told me the name of his wife - It was Pamela, and the baby was called, Elizabeth. He couldn't wait to get back home to see them. I remember thinking of Margaret and Janice at the time, and how awful it would be, never to see them again." Edward had to stop in order to regain his composure before continuing, "He told me how he loved to keep reading Pamela's long letters. She would give him news of little Lizzie's progress, and tell him how much she loved him. Listen to me, Cecil - see what a sentimental fool I've become."

Cecil patted his old friend on the shoulder, and felt a pang of emotion himself.

"But, you helped him Edward. You took a letter from that dying, young soldier under your command, and delivered it safely to his wife. You then told her how much he loved them."

"His death was my fault, I had to tell her that too. I was in command, and I led him and others like him to their deaths. It was all so unnecessary. It was me who killed him!" Cried out Edward, feeling the torment deep down in his soul.

"No!" Shouted Cecil. "The war killed him, not you. You were just doing your job, obeying orders. You gave life, by taking in Pamela, and bringing up her baby as if she were your own. You gave Lizzie a wonderful life, a life with purpose and with opportunity. You helped Pamela through an ordeal that nearly destroyed her. There was no-one else she could have turned to. Others would have given up by then, but you gave Pamela work as your personal secretary. You gave her a job where she could always see Lizzie and watch her grow up into a magnificent young woman. Edward - it wasn't a crime to fall in love with Pamela."

Edward took in a deep breath and stood up. He took out his handkerchief and wiped his eyes.

"Thank-you. I'm fortunate to have a friend like you. That all happened a long, long time ago. Perhaps, it's best just to try and forget. But what you did tonight worked. By making me talk about those events released so much of the pain that has been dragging me down."

"Look, old chap, you must be strong. You're a good man Edward, and now your family need you. Pick up the phone and tell them the truth."

"I've told Pamela it's over, Cecil. She's gone."

"I certainly didn't approve of Pamela moving in here, and I think you should have kept things quiet. But what's done is done. You love Pamela, and she loves you. I would give it a bit of time, then get her back, Edward. The girls will soon come around, and Lizzie, especially needs to know the truth. She thinks you and Margaret are her parents, now she'll lose who she thought was her mother, only to find she's just gained another one - her real mother."

"Yes I see what you mean. But I will always be her father, no matter what."

"You will indeed, Edward, and what a great father you are."

Edward then paused thoughtfully for a while.

"Should I do it, Cecil? Should I really get Pamela back?"

"Yes, Edward, it's meant to be," replied the doctor, opening the door to Mrs. Gardener.

Edward, meanwhile emptied his glass, cleared his throat and lifted up the telephone once more. Again, he heard the continual ringing tone as his call went unanswered. Mrs. Gardener stepped into the study looking pale and anxious.

"I'll go up and attend to Mrs. Marchmont, before they come and take her." She said sadly.

"Thank-you, I would be so grateful." Replied Edward, as he heard a female voice on the end of the line. He immediately recognised it as the girl who had answered earlier.

"Lloyd-Evans Hall, hello."

"Hello, I'd like to speak to my daughter, Lizzie Marchmont." Said Edward, "Please, it's very urgent."

After a short while, the girl returned, "I'm sorry, she's not in her room. She may be over at the dance. Can I take a message?"

A great cheer went up, as finally the president finished his long-winded speech, one that had been continually interrupted by the sound of musicians warming up behind him. Despite the speech not really being much different to last year's, nobody seemed to mind, and the president smiled proudly upon receiving such a noisy ovation.

Jenny and Maureen clapped enthusiastically, but their attention had been distracted by the irrational behaviour of their friend, Pauline. They stared at each other looking somewhat bewildered, before turning their attention to Pauline once more. The two girls had been extremely worried about her after she hadn't returned following her date with Frank. When she did finally get back, she looked ghastly, and Jenny and Maureen had put her straight to bed with a couple of aspirin. They both stayed close after she had fallen asleep and whispered re-assurances, as terrifying dreams made Pauline's body writhe in torment.

"Look at those marks on her!" Gasped Maureen, "Perhaps she was attacked by someone - maybe it was him, that Frank bloke? Look at her clothes, that lovely blouse - they're totally ruined."

"No human could do that," replied Jenny. "I think she was attacked by some sort of animal, a wolf, perhaps - maybe there's wolves in Falcondale?"

They were more than relieved when Pauline finally woke after a few hours. However, she was reluctant to speak of how the date went, and then worked herself into a frenzy ranting on about an expensive necklace she had lost, and how Frank would be so angry. The girls wanted to call the campus nurse over, as they were so concerned. But eventually, they managed to calm Pauline, and persuade her to take a bath.

The girls however, were to be even more confused when their friend returned from the bathroom, looking and feeling much more refreshed, only to declare she was going to the dinner and dance that evening. Jenny and Maureen then had to search frantically through their limited wardrobes to find something suitable for Pauline to wear.

The applause stopped, but Pauline carried on clapping, as if she were in some sort of trance.

"Pauline! Pauline! Are you alright, can you hear me?" Called out Jenny anxiously, "Perhaps, we should take her back, Maureen. I don't think she should have come tonight in the first place."

Pauline, then stared at Jenny, before forcing an unconvincing smile.

"I'm ok, honestly - it's just so hot in here. Let's go and get another drink."

"You've had enough already, Pauline. Come on, we'll take you outside for a while."

"There's nothing wrong with me, Jenny. Stop treating me like a child!" Exclaimed Pauline indignantly. "I'm going up to the bar."

Jenny decided it wasn't worth pursuing the matter any further and sat back down to finish her lemonade.

Sally waited patiently in the powder room, while Lizzie seemed content to spend the rest of the night touching up her bright red lipstick.

"Sally, this dress makes me look absolutely enormous! Why on earth didn't you say something? I look like a total dog!"

"Just get a move on, Marchmont!" Replied Sally, giggling, while her friend continued to vainly survey herself in the unflattering mirror. "Lizzie, you look just fine. Do you realise we've been away for twenty minutes. Frank and Ken will be legless by now."

Lizzie snapped her bag shut and followed Sally back out into the hall.

"Have you seen this William chap yet? It could be a bit awkward with Frank here too."

"There's really nothing in it!" Replied Sally, going on the defensive. "Anyway, I expect he knows I'm seeing Frank. I think the whole of Falcondale does."

Lizzie stopped and turned to Sally, sensing something wasn't quite right.

"Have you and Frank had words? I can see he's had rather a lot to drink again."

Sally explained about what had happened with Frank earlier, and how he wanted to take her to a hotel. "It's just that he can be so aggressive and unpredictable when he's like this."

"Look Sally, if you want my advise, I would take this William somewhere else if he shows up. Just to avoid any trouble. Take him to one of the coffee bars in town."

"Yes, that's a good idea. But I think he wanted to dance with me."

"That's not good. I mean with Frank on the scene. But, on the other hand, Frank wont even be able to stand up soon, if he has any more whiskey. Come on Sally, I thought I was the one who's meant to be miserable!"

The two women pushed their way through the crowd and headed back towards the table. They saw that Frank and Ken were still involved in their heated exchange, and decided to get them up dancing as quickly as possible.

However, as they neared the table, Sally noticed a girl, standing directly behind Frank, glaring at him. "Look at her, Lizzie. Now you don't have to worry too much about what you're wearing!"

Lizzie screeched with laughter.

"Oh my! What a revolting dress - it's absolutely hideous, and that awful scarf. What on earth was she thinking! Isn't she one of those silly girl's from the club?"

"Yes, her name's Pauline," replied Sally, now also beginning to giggle. "She works behind the bar sometimes, and she drinks, Tizer!"

They sat down, but still Pauline continued to lurk behind Frank. Sally noticed the wild look in her eyes, and it made her feel uncomfortable. She began to regret ridiculing her to Lizzie, even though her comments were purely made in jest.

Pauline became aware that Sally had noticed her, and the two women's eyes locked together. Sally felt a shiver run down her spine and quickly averted her gaze.

Lizzie, also sensed an ugly atmosphere developing and got Ken up to dance. She motioned Sally to do the same, and soon, both couples had lost themselves among the dozens of couples already dancing. Frank recognised the group singing, 'Rocking Around The Christmas Tree', as the Blue Jets, from the previous night at the hotel, but he had to close one eye to focus.

The rugby crowd began to make their presence felt, by holding a drinking competition. This involved competitors standing in a line, then downing a pint of ale. They would then balance the empty glass on top of their heads. Those who lost were required to drop their trousers and pants and have their backsides squirted with soda siphons. This was to the thunderous applause of the many onlookers, who cheered and made disparaging remarks about some of the genitalia on display. Eventually, the high-spirited antics had to be toned down when some of the female students complained, and Mr. Meredith had to step in.

Most of the faculty had by now, completed their obligations and a group, including the Dean, were heading towards the exit. Mr. Meredith had been assured by Jane, that in her five years of service at the university, there had never been any trouble at this particular event, despite the vast amounts of alcohol consumed by the guests. He swapped festive greetings and shook hands with several colleagues, while Jane fetched their coats. As he waited, he was approached for a dance by a young first-year, but had to decline and apologise on this occasion, even though it was a slow one. He wanted to go, and eagerly awaited Jane's return. He smiled as he saw her, and fidgeted with his car keys in anticipation of the drink they were going to have together, after leaving the function.

Jenny and Maureen looked around for prospective partners, as the Blue Jets played their *'Moon River'* number, but none came forward. A few moments later, they caught sight of Pauline again, and ran to her excitedly.

"Come on Pauline, they're playing your favourite tune. Guess what, Jenny just got turned down for a dance by Meredith!" Called out Maureen, laughing. But, Pauline just ignored her and walked off.

"Where's she going? not to get more drink I hope." Sighed, Jenny, concerned about her friend.

The young student was getting ready for bed when she thought she heard some activity from the along the corridor. She left her room, and tiptoed up to Lizzie's door in her bare feet. The message she had written out earlier was still attached to the door. The girl recalled how worried and desperate Lizzie's father had sounded on the telephone. She knew of Lizzie, and would acknowledge her if they met, but Lizzie was a bit too wacky for some tastes. However, the girl was still worried and thought about what she should do.

Returning to her room, she slipped on a jumper and some slacks, then, lifting her heavy duffle coat from the back of the door, she reluctantly headed over to the assembly hall.

It was a cold night, with light snow flakes already beginning to fall, as she pulled her hood up over her head, and hoped not to be recognised. Nearing the hall, she heard the steady beat of loud music, and the ear-piercing, drunken squeals of girls. There were several people milling around outside, saying farewells, or chatting to friends. She saw a group of local lads, no doubt about to try their luck gate crashing. No chance, she thought, especially dressed so casually. Then, she wondered how she would get in? There was still one of the porters checking tickets at the door. Perhaps, she could get someone else to deliver the message to Lizzie. Suddenly, the very idea of actually going inside was making her nervous. After all, she had never wanted to go in the first place, and get leered at and groped by all those drunks. The thought of it repulsed her. She was considering turning back, and just putting the message back on Lizzie's door, and forgetting the whole thing. It was then, that she came face-to-face with Mr. Meredith, and his secretary, as they were leaving.

"Hello, it's Karen isn't it? Remarked the Dean with a friendly smile. "I didn't see you at the dance tonight?"

Karen explained that she was packing, and told him about Lizzie's urgent message. Without hesitation, Meredith instructed the porter to allow Karen into the function. She thanked the Dean, and after wishing each other a merry Christmas, she entered the assembly hall with grave misgivings.

Despite Sally's negative feelings towards Frank, it did feel good to be back in his arms again. She closed her eyes and allowed him to lead her as they glided across the highly-waxed, parquet floor as one. Despite being more than a little drunk, he was still a highly accomplished dancer. He nuzzled her neck and teased her earlobes with his tongue. Sally thought about William, but had already given up hope of actually seeing him there at this stage. Perhaps, it was best if she didn't. Frank was in a strange, volatile mood, and who knows how he would react. She had learnt that when he had been drinking heavily, it was best to just give him a free rein, and keep the peace. However, Sally had reached a conclusion. Regardless of what might or might not happen with William Peddlescoombe, she was going to rid herself of Frank. It might not happen that evening, but she would certainly finish with him before the spring term commences.

As the dance progressed, Sally for some unknown reason began to feel very light-headed, and unusually for her, quite uninhibited. Her thoughts became bizarre and she started to giggle. She tried to recall how much she had drank, but it certainly wasn't very much. After a short while she began to feel herself getting aroused. Then, in total contradiction to her earlier decision, she moved in closer to Frank, and tightened her grip around him. She sensed a warm, glowing feeling down in the pit of her stomach and let her mind wander, visualising in her mind's eye, what sex would be like with him. Perhaps, she should sleep with Frank after all. Lizzie and Ken do it all the time, and probably so do many of the students on campus. Everyone, except her. No wonder Frank has been getting frustrated.

Sally let his hand settle discretely on her breast, and allowed her fantasy to continue unabated as they carried on dancing. However, no matter how much she tried to concentrate on Frank, it was William that kept appearing in her thoughts. It was he who was making love to her, and causing her to melt like this. Her thoughts were confusing her and she began to feel unsteady on her legs. Sally could never bear to be out of control, but now she could do nothing about it. Perhaps, it was the dope, Frank had secretly sprinkled over her meal earlier on, that was affecting her.

A sudden jolt by another merry couple quickly brought Sally back to reality. She heard Frank mouthing his usual vile expletives, and watched embarrassed as he began to square up drunkenly to the man. She turned and began to flee from the ugly altercation. But then, standing directly in front of her was William. Her eyes widened, and she heard herself gasp, as she found herself looking into his hazel eyes once again. He smiled at her, before he and his partner, Jenny, danced off, back into the crowd. Sally remembered his perfect smile, the same one that had captured her heart in the library, a few days earlier.

Frank returned, and tried to pick up where he had left off. But Sally pushed his hands away, and craned her neck to look around. But William had been swallowed up by the hordes, and was nowhere to be seen. He looked even better than Sally had imagined. He wore his dinner jacket unbuttoned, and his bow tie, loose around his neck, with a magnificent air of abandonment. His long, unruly hair adding a further wild, unconventional facet to his rebellious demeanour.

Frank belched loudly and glared at her. His eyes were now quite glazed and his pupils dilated. He staggered backwards, reaching into his inside pocket.

"Sally, I wanted to give you this. I got it for your birthday." Frank then opened the oblong box and took out the gold necklace.

Sally was stunned, it must have cost a fortune. Perhaps, he really did care for her after all. She beamed with pleasure, but immediately felt it wouldn't be right to accept such a gift, especially after the erotic thoughts she's just been having about William, not to mention her decision to finish with Frank.

However, it was too late. Frank was already placing the necklace around Sally's neck. A cheering crowd had now formed around them, and she had to keep very still, as he fumbled with the clasp. Then, with no warning, Frank suddenly lurched forward, almost knocking her off her feet.

Sally looked on in disbelief, hearing screams and the sound of glass breaking, as Frank crashed heavily through a couple of tables, before landing face down on the floor. There was an eerie silence, as he slowly lifted his dazed head. There were bits of fruit cocktail stuck in his hair, and his jacket was soaked with spilt alcohol. Sally followed his gaze, as he looked around to see who had been brave, or silly enough to shove him in the back so hard. She then noticed the look of astonishment on his face, as Frank recognised his attacker.

"Don't you dare ignore me, you bastard!" Screamed Pauline, the timid girl, who had been staring at Frank earlier. Then, rounding on Sally, she hissed, "So I'm not good enough - now you've got your little blonde whore with you!"

Shocked, Sally put her hands to her face, half expecting to be attacked by Pauline. But, before the other woman could make a move, William appeared at Sally's side. Moving quickly, and using his body as a shield, he put his arms about her and successfully managed to get her to safety. As they stood out of harm's way, William sensed he was standing on something. He moved his foot, and looked down to see the necklace lying in a pool of beer. He bent down and scooped it up with the intention of returning it to its owner, once all the commotion had died down.

The crowd were now enthralled at the grotesque, public display being acted out before them, and began to step aside, creating a make-shift arena for this impromptu parody of a Greek tragedy.

Pauline moved closer, with a crazed look in her eyes. The glass beneath her feet crunched as she inched closer to Frank. Sensing a further attack, he rose to his feet quickly and calmly began to step back, towards the exit.

"Pauline, Pauline, please listen to me," he implored. "I think you've had too much to drink. Now just stop all this and go back to your room."

Pauline just stared at him, never letting her eyes leave his, "You gave me that necklace, Frank. I thought I had lost it. I looked everywhere. They wouldn't let me back in the hotel to find it - but you had it all the time."

"I can explain, Pauline. You were being sick and I didn't want you to damage it, so I took it off." He sensed she was weakening and stopped retreating. He then heard Meredith's voice, and put his hand up to stop the Dean coming closer.

"I don't believe you, Frank. You just left me there. I could have died."

"Nonsense, come on, be quiet, and I'll take you back. You really should stick to your limits, Pauline."

With surprising speed, Pauline moved to attack Frank again, but as she did so, the chiffon scarf she was wearing came undone, revealing a disturbing array of bite marks to her neck and cleavage.

"No, I will not be quiet. You took me to that hotel, you got me drunk, gave me drugs and raped me. Then you left me for dead. I will not be quiet, and I will not be ignored by you, like I was just another piece of meat!"

Frank went pale and found himself on the retreat once more. He stepped back until he was brought to an abrupt halt as he reached the counter of the bar. Then, to his relief, Meredith stepped in between them.

"Gant, is this true, what this young lady is saying?" Demanded the Dean, looking from Frank, back to Pauline.

"No, she's lying. I was with Sally last night. It was her birthday." Frank looked around for Sally, and noticed William Peddlescoombe had his arm around her shoulder. "Sally, tell him I was with you last night."

Sally met Frank's pleading, desperate eyes. She then looked to Pauline, who she thought was quite mad and extremely dangerous. She hesitated, not quite knowing who she should be defending. She opened her mouth to speak, but no words came out. She felt sick, as she looked at the bites around Pauline's neck, they weren't just love bites, blood had been drawn. The grim reality of what Frank had in store for her began to manifest itself in her mind. She was wobbly on her legs and wanted to sit down, but a strong arm was supporting her and keeping her safe. She sensed William take her hand, and grip it tightly. She gazed up at him, and immediately felt stronger, with him next to her, willing her to make the right decision.

Sally looked the Dean of Students straight in the eye, took a deep breath, and before she could think too much about it, she answered the question.

"No, Mr. Meredith, Frank was not with me last night. I was with Lizzie in Gloucester."

Frank screamed abuse and threats at Sally, but as he did, he took his eyes off Pauline, for a moment too long. She reached across the bar for an empty pint glass, then lifting it above her head, she suddenly brought it crashing down onto the brass rail surrounding the bar. Frank watched in horror, but seemed transfixed, as she clutched the base of the glass and plunged the jagged end deep into the side of his face.

He screamed with pain and sank to his knees, holding the wound, as blood spurted through his fingers.

Pauline put the glass down and began to sob hysterically, as Meredith and a few others rushed to restrain her. Frank then rose to his feet unsteadily, and staggered towards the main doors, staining the dance floor red, as he made his exit.

It was a blessing in disguise for the three local men waiting outside. They never thought Frank would be out this early, and already injured. Job half done they laughed. They watched, as Frank pushed the handkerchief hard to the side of his face, to stem the heavy bleeding. They found it easy to follow him, and stalked their prey like animals going in for the kill.

Back inside the hall, Pauline had calmed sufficiently for Meredith to release her. He beckoned to the others to stand back and give her some space.

"Are you okay, young lady, it's, Pauline isn't it?" He inquired, but there was no reply. Meredith called for a chair, and asked Pauline, who was shaking uncontrollably, to sit. She obeyed his command, but wouldn't acknowledge him, and just stared down at her firmly gripped hands.

"It's been one hell of a nasty business, all this, Pauline." Continued, Meredith. "If, what you said was true, then I'll have to call the police. Do you understand?"

Pauline nodded, but still wouldn't look up.

Meredith called for another chair, and sat down beside her.

"It appears there's been an awful crime committed against you, and we must have this Frank chap arrested. He certainly wont be studying at this university again. I'll see to that personally. Do you hear me, Pauline?"

Again Pauline nodded, but said nothing.

"I can't condone you cutting him like that, do you understand. You could have killed him, or blinded him for life. What you did was wrong. I know under the circumstances you acted on impulse, but you could face charges too."

Pauline refused the water offered her and wouldn't even speak to Jenny or Maureen, who both stood nearby, looking terrified. It was as if Pauline had reverted back to her traumatised, child-like state once more.

Meredith, sighed, and realising he wasn't getting very far, called Jane over.

"See if you can get hold of a doctor, or the campus nurse. Perhaps, it might be best under the circumstances." Meredith shook his head in despair, "It's the last thing we need at Christmas."

Pauline then looked up, her face was drawn and ashen.

"I don't need a doctor, or a nurse," she said firmly. "Please don't call the police, Mr. Meredith, as I wont press any charges - not against Frank. He's my boyfriend, and you don't set the police on people you love."

The Dean's mouth dropped in amazement, as he watched Pauline calmly stand up, and walk out. He looked at the guests still remaining. They all stood silent, around the perimeter of the hall, as if expecting a grand finale, or an encore, but all they got was a drunk from outside stagger into the hall to proclaim, "It's snowing!"

With that, the students began to cheer loudly, as if the whole matter had been forgotten.

Meredith organised a caretaker to clean up the blood, before taking to the stage. Using the microphone, he apologised for the disruption and told the guests to carry on regardless. More cheers went up, and the Dean signalled to the band to start up again, before making his excuses, and going off to find his secretary.

"Jane, I want letters of expulsion sent out with immediate effect to both, Pauline Chater and Frank Gant. I will not tolerate this sort of behaviour going on at the university."

"Yes, Mr. Meredith. What about the police and the nurse?"

"Both Pauline and Gant have left the building. A great deal of alcohol has been consumed tonight, Jane. I think it best we leave matters until the morning. We don't know for sure, if Pauline was telling the truth. As for Gant, he got what he deserved. We'll expel them from the university, and let the police deal with it from there on."

One solitary guest however, had no desire to dance and cheer. In fact, Karen had literally only come over to deliver her message to Lizzie. She knew there was a good chance she would see Frank in the hall. It was something that she couldn't bear to think of. How would she react if he approached her? He may want to violate her again? Would she have the courage to challenge him, or would she simply break down and allow him to do as he wished.

At the time of her ordeal, there had been nobody to turn to, nobody would listen, or take her word against that of the captain of the rugby team. She could never bring shame on her family, after all, nice girls didn't get raped. It had happened a year ago, and right up until now, Karen had blamed herself for what Frank did to her. She was the one who accepted the drinks and got drunk, and she was the one who took the drugs he offered. It was asking for trouble. Karen had cursed herself for being so naive. Now she realised that locking herself away in her room day-after-day wasn't the way forward - she mustn't let the anger and self-hatred eat away at her anymore. Now, having witnessed the incident with Pauline, Karen knew she wasn't alone. She knew Frank had done the same to another, if not more. Although, what she had heard sickened her down to her soul, it also gave her something else - the courage to do something about it. Karen kept her head low, and watched as Mr. Meredith left. If he wasn't going to call in the police about Frank, then she would do it herself. She swallowed hard, went over to the telephone booth and lifted the receiver.

Sally looked down and realised she was still holding William's hand. She thought about letting go, but instead, found herself gripping him even tighter. He turned to her looking concerned.
"Are you alright, Sally? Things were getting a bit scary out there."

"Yes, I'm fine," she replied, her voice slightly quaking. "I was just very frightened. I'm glad it's all over now. Thank-you for helping me, William. I thought Pauline was going to kill me."

William let go of her hand, thinking he may be taking too much of a liberty.

"She would never have done that, not with me there. Besides, I think it was Frank, she had the problem with."

"Yes, you're right. She must be very disturbed. I can't believe Frank could have done such an awful thing."

"I can, Sally, he's pure evil."

She again heard the definite trace of an accent.

"Perhaps, I'll see you next term, William?"

He smiled, and feeling awkward, began to move away. However, he found he couldn't avert his gaze from her, and Sally wasn't making his departure any easier by staring up at him with those longing, deep-blue eyes.

The Blue Jets began to play, *'Sealed With A Kiss'*, and William instinctively stepped forward.

"Would you have this dance with me, Miss Carlington?"

Returning his smile, she took his hand and led him out to the dance floor.

"I would love to dance with you, Mr. Peddlescoombe!"

They had several dances together that evening, both of them just content to hold each other tightly, while the moment lasted. Sally, not only felt safe with William, she felt she belonged with him. The natural chemistry between them had been immediate. It had ignited a passion that day in the library, when they had first met.

It was Lizzie, who finally brought the lovesick couple back down to earth.

"Sally, I'm returning to Lloyd-Evans now, my father wants me to call him."

"Wait, Lizzie, I'll come with you."

Lizzie quickly gave Sally's new partner the once-over, and nodded her approval.

"So you must be the one my friend can't stop talking about!" Then, turning to a blushing Sally, she added, "No, I think you had better stay here with him!"

Later on, William volunteered to walk Sally back to Lloyd-Evans Hall, but as they stepped out on to a perfect, layer of newly fallen snow, Sally felt an enormous feeling of relief. The earlier incident had been extremely disturbing to her, but now she felt not only remorse, but also gratitude to Pauline for effectively saving her from a fate too horrendous to contemplate. It also automatically ended her relationship with Frank, without Sally even having to say a word.

"Look, William, isn't it so lovely, can we walk in the snow for a while?"

They followed the tracks towards the main gates, and walking with arms linked, headed out in the direction of the town. Falcondale now resembled a scene from a Christmas card, with the town's colourful Christmas tree lit up near the war memorial, and the pretty display of fairy lights stretching along both sides of the street. Most of the houses had smoking chimneys, with the glow of crackling fires, illuminating cosy front room windows.

"Is that a Scotch accent you have, William?" Asked Sally, inquisitively.

"Err, no, in fact it's half Welsh and half Canadian! Was that another blonde moment?" He laughed, "You should have said, Scottish!"

"Sorry, silly me!"

"Please don't apologise, Sally, I love your naivety!"

They took it in turns to ask each other about their lives and backgrounds. Sally found William to be the perfect companion, although he did seem to know everything under the sun. But unlike Frank, he wasn't obsessed with himself. He wanted to know all about her, and what she liked, what she believed in and what she thought about. To William, Sally's feelings and opinions were important and worth discussing. She had never come across this with a boy before, and found it quite refreshing.

As they slowly made their way along the deserted street, William explained how his parents lived in Ontario, but still retained his mother's house in town.

"David, my younger brother and I live there while we're at university. My mother, being Welsh loves Wales and visits regularly. She could never give up her home here."

The blizzard showed no signs of abating, and realising Sally was shivering, and only wearing a black evening dress under her coat, William decided to take her back to Lloyd-Evans Hall.

He ventured out towards the road, with Sally close behind, knowing from his childhood days, that the kerb was very steep in places. Everything around them was now covered in a thick layer of snow. As William inched forward cautiously, he found it difficult to sense where the pavement ended and the road began. However, he didn't have long to find out. For with his next step, his foot plunged down into the deep gutter, he lost his balance and fell heavily on to his backside, with arms flailing madly.

Fearing that he could have hurt himself, Sally tried to reach William as quickly as possible. She stepped into his footsteps and called out to him. Then, making exactly the same mistake as he had, she found herself falling ungracefully straight on top of him.

For a few moments they both lay perfectly still, half expecting to feel the pain from any injuries they may have sustained. William moved his head slightly to look up at her, "Did you hurt yourself?"

"No, but I may have ripped my dress. I'm just glad I had you for a soft landing!"

He laughed and brushed some snow from her face.

"Tell me, do you always end up in the gutter after a night out?"

Sally scooped up a handful of snow and plonked it down on William's head. He retaliated and did the same to her. Soon a mini snowball war was under way which lasted for several minutes. Once they were both sufficiently covered from head to toe in frozen ice, William raised his hands in mock surrender. He then took off his duffle coat, gave it a good shake, and went over and placed it around Sally's shoulders. She was touched by this and smiled up at him. He then reached into one of the pockets and retrieved the scarf she had left in the library. He led her over to a dimly-lit doorway and draped the scarf lightly around her neck. A drop of melted snow fell from Sally's damp hair and trickled down her cheek. William lowered his head and placed a kiss where it had landed.

Sally let out a sigh, and instinctively reached out to put her arms around him. William looked into her eyes, then glanced down to her lips. She opened her mouth, as if to speak, but no words came out. Still holding the ends of the scarf, he pulled her towards him. Sally responded, and allowed his lips to find hers. After a few moments, she pulled away, as if she couldn't quite trust herself. She then looked up at him once more, before letting herself fall into his arms again, and re-united her mouth with his.

The warm, tingling sensation deep down in her stomach, the same one she had experienced earlier, returned. William's coat slipped off her shoulders, and fell to the ground, but Sally didn't notice.

The strong aroma of freshly-made coffee then wound its way through the falling snowflakes, and was potent enough to bring a halt to the proceedings taking place in the doorway. William was the first to speak, as he knelt down to retrieve the coat and placed it back around his companion's shoulders.

"The coffee smells delicious, doesn't it? It comes from Pedro's, just up the street, " he indicated. "Sometimes, the air is thick with the smell of garlic too. Are you hungry!"

She shook her head, "No, but I'd love some coffee, and the chance to get warm."

Over the years, Pedro's had become extremely popular with students, faculty and townsfolk alike, not only because it stayed open late most evenings, but because of its Catalan owner, of the same name. Pedro was a very jovial, likeable eccentric, who had turned what was once a profit-losing bread and butter establishment into a smart, bohemian bistro. It was renowned for its excellent food, great coffee, and good service, and was now the principle meeting place in town. Pedro had succeeded in re-creating a distinctive, Mediterranean atmosphere in a small, Welsh town. The brightly painted exterior looked authentically rustic, and inviting, with its blue awning and candle-lit tables in the windows.

The restaurant was half full, and William and Sally sat themselves in a secluded corner. William ordered two large mugs of coffee, and a couple of shots of brandy, to warm them both up.

Pedro brought the drinks over, with a cheery smile, and lit the candle in the centre of the table. He also left a complimentary bowl of olives, along with a couple of tasty-looking hunks of French bread. He was a balding, weather-beaten man of about sixty, who, judging by the girth of his midriff, obviously enjoyed his food.

As they sipped their coffee, William sensed all was not right with Sally. He wondered if he'd taken things too quickly when he'd kissed her. A silence came over them, but eventually it was Sally who spoke first.

"William, please tell me more about your house. Is it nearby?"

He went on to tell her with great enthusiasm about the pretty farmhouse, where both he and David had been born. It was set in five acres of land, and was situated next to a vast orchard.

Sally nibbled at an olive, and listened intently as William described the layout of the old stone and timber-built house. She found herself longing to be there with him during the cold, winter evenings, all cuddled up warm and cosy by a roaring log fire. In her mind's eye, she visualised the rickety staircase, the vast collection of old books, and the ticking of a grandfather clock. To Sally, the house William was describing fulfilled her every dream of what a home should be like. It seemed like a million miles from the cold, stuffy existence she had been used to.

"I would love you to see the house one day, Sally. I'm sure you'll like it," continued, William, helping himself to some French bread. "Perhaps, you could come over for dinner some time, then you could meet David?"

"It sounds wonderful, I would love to," she replied, looking dewy-eyed. "So can you and David cook then?"

"Well, no, not exactly, but I'm sure we can cross that bridge when we come to it!"

"I can cook for both of you, I did domestic science at school, and advanced cookery. I can do a fantastic roast dinner!"

"Sally, you must be an angel, sent down from heaven. I can't wait." They both laughed, but again, the silence returned.

"Is there something wrong, Sally?" He asked concerned, "I'm sorry I kissed you. Maybe, I shouldn't have done that?"

She glanced at him affectionately, and went to speak, but she found herself embarrassed. She took a sip of her coffee, before gazing into his eyes, and completely taking him by surprise.

"William, please take me home with you - let me stay with you tonight?"

He took in a deep breath, and looked about him, feeling slightly awkward, in case anyone else had heard. He then looked back at her, "I'll go and get the coats."

As he went to stand up, Sally turned to him.

"I'm so scared of being on my own. I don't want to go back to my room." She glanced down and tried to hide the tears welling up in her eyes. "I'm terrified of Frank. He said such awful things about what he was going to do to me."

William cursed himself for being so ignorant. The events at the assembly hall earlier had been horrendous, and it was no wonder, Sally was terrified. More people began to arrive at Pedro's just as William and Sally were leaving, and they had to politely turn down invitations to stay from students who they recognised from the dance.

Outside, the snow had eased sufficiently for them to continue with their journey. They carried on down the street, before turning left into Orchard Lane, where William lived. The road was completely empty, with not even a car in sight. It looked quite picturesque, swathed in pure white, and appearing as if it went on forever, winding its way into the distance.

William pointed to a house about a hundred yards further on. It had a lantern shining out on the porch, and Sally could make out the faint glow of a Christmas tree in one of the downstairs windows. As they got closer, William reached into his pocket for his keys. Then, as he lifted them out, he found something else attached to them. Holding up the necklace, he stopped, and showed it to Sally.

"I picked it up, from the dance floor during the trouble. I totally forgot I still had it."

Sally looked at the necklace intensely, and paused for a moment, before speaking.

"I don't want it, William. If Frank did attack Pauline, like she said, then this necklace is associated with a horrid crime." She turned away, and backed off. "Frank wanted to take me to that hotel tonight. It scares me, William, please get rid of it."

Without another word, he pulled back his arm, and threw the gold necklace far out into the snow.

8. ORCHARD LANE

Ken gazed up at the window and immediately recognised Lizzie's silhouette as she drew the curtains. He was waiting for the right opportunity to gain access to Lloyd-Evans Hall. But now he was getting cold as he stood sheltering beneath the huge stone archway that led into the courtyard. Security at night had been relaxed a little now that the first-year students had finally settled into university life. But, because Lloyd-Evans was a female-only hall of residence, it was not the ideal place for Ken to be challenged, bearing in mind his association with Frank. He pulled up the collar of his dinner jacket to shield his neck from the biting wind and continued to wait for someone he knew to give him access. The icy vigil had at least sobered Ken up somewhat, and had brought home to him the reality of what had taken place that evening.

He had known at the time that he needed to make a decision, and that is exactly what he did. Now, Ken had realised it was the wrong decision. He reached into his pocket for his cigarettes, only to remember that he'd left them over at the assembly hall during all the excitement. Instead, and to take his mind off things, he tried to rehearse in his thoughts what he would say to Lizzie. But, his mind was troubled, and he kept going back to the events earlier, and the realisation, that he too, might be tarred by the same brush as Frank. He had to disassociate himself from his friend immediately, and in a way, Frank had already given him cause to do just that.

During the incident at the dance, Ken had merely looked on in total disbelief, much like everyone else. At first, he had even thought it was a prank, it certainly wouldn't be beyond the rugby team to try something like that. But even when reality had set in, there was nothing Ken could really do. It was a personal thing, and besides, Frank knew what he was doing, and would never allow himself to be intimidated, especially by a woman.

He had gasped in shock, to see Frank run away like that, and had half expected him to just re-appear. But when it became apparent to all, that he had fled like a frightened rabbit, Ken felt embarrassed, not only for Frank, but for himself too. After all, they were meant to be friends, and Frank's abrupt departure could only mean one thing, he was guilty, and perhaps, Pauline was telling the truth.

However, in an act of misguided loyalty, Ken had left the hall to go and look for his friend, totally ignoring Lizzie's pleas for him to come back.

At first he had been surprised by the sudden snowfall, and could only see a few yards ahead. He eventually caught up with Frank near the gatehouse. Frank had been in two minds where to go, he was bleeding profusely from the glass wound inflicted earlier by Pauline, but he also wanted to find somewhere to hide the large amount of cannabis he was carrying, in case he was arrested.

It was when Frank turned on him aggressively, that Ken realised he'd made a big mistake and should have stayed in the hall.

With one fist raised, and the other still clutching the bloodied handkerchief to the side of his face, Frank advanced on Ken, thinking it may be Meredith coming to apprehend him. But even after recognising his pursuer as his old friend, Frank still acted in a threatening manner.

"Frank, it's me, Ken, wait!"

The blow was powerful and would have caused considerable damage if it had connected to Ken's face. Fortunately, he was able to see it coming and managed to pull his head back, so that the punch just glanced off him.

"Where the hell were you?" Growled Frank, rounding on Ken once more. "You weren't there when I needed you. Look, see what that bitch did to me, you yellow bastard!"

Ken quaked under the onslaught and began to retreat, fearing Frank would start lashing out again.

"There was nothing I could do, Frank," pleaded Ken, raising his arms defensively. "What did you expect - me to come up and thump Pauline in front of everyone. I was just as surprised as you were."

A car came up beside them, and nearly ran into Ken as he stepped back, out of Frank's reach. The car's headlights lit up the fury emblazoned on Frank's bitter, twisted face as he scowled at the driver. Other people leaving the function on foot looked away and gave the pair a wide berth. A night-watchman came out of the gatehouse to see what all the commotion was about, only to quickly return following a torrent of abuse. Standing just across the road, waited the three local men, biding their time. It was Frank who they really wanted, but dishing out a sound beating to both these two could provide greater satisfaction.

The car seemed in no hurry to go, and eventually drove alongside the pair of students. Ken saw the window being lowered and found himself staring straight at the Dean of Students. It was then he realised that he now had a great chance to distance himself from Frank, and perhaps, come out of this with a bit of credit.

"Mr. Meredith, I'm glad you're here, look - I've caught him. Please help, I wont be able to hold him on my own."

John Meredith opened the door and got out of the car. He recognised Ken as being Frank's friend and seemed a little surprised at what he was hearing.

"Well done Kenneth, that's very commendable of you. Now be careful, I don't want anyone getting hurt." The Dean then came between Frank and Ken and beckoned them to step away from each other. "Go home Kenneth, this fellow will be dealt with through the proper channels, and no doubt by the police as well. Thank-you for what you tried to do."

Frank couldn't quite believe what he was hearing and cursed Ken further, for betraying him in such an underhand, and cowardly manner. He then turned unsteadily, and began to make his way along the High Street. The Dean waited until the warring factions had gone their separate ways, before returning to Jane, who was waiting in the warm car. As they drove past the lurching figure of Frank, the Dean called to him, "You had better get that cut seen to Gant, it looks bad!" The only reply he got was in the form of a two-fingered gesture.

After another few minutes of waiting, Ken decided to find a telephone and ring Lizzie. Burying his frozen fingers deep into his trouser pockets, he began to trudge back to the hall. He had only taken a few steps when he saw the lone figure coming towards him. At first, he couldn't see who it was, as the girl's face was obscured by the hood on her duffle coat. She was visibly startled and stepped aside fearfully when he came upon her so suddenly.

"Karen, is that you? It's okay, don't be scared - it's me, Ken!"

She walked in a half circle, trying to reach the door of Lloyd-Evans Hall without getting too close to him. Ken noticed the look of sheer terror in her eyes, as the building's entrance light began to envelope her. They both arrived at the door together, and Karen, even though she had her key ready in her hand, began to fumble and couldn't quite find the lock. She realised, that to open the door, she needed to take her eyes off Ken, if even just for a moment.

"Is he here with you?" She asked anxiously, looking around for any signs of Frank. "You're not going to hurt me are you?"

"No, Karen, of course I'm not. I need to see Lizzie, it's important. I'm alone, Frank isn't here. I don't know where he is, and I don't care. Look, I know what he did to you, and he's going to pay. I want nothing more to do with him."

Karen, her suspicions abating, gazed up at him, and nodded, as she finally got the door open. Ken followed her inside, and gently touched her on the shoulder.

"Please try to be strong Karen, Frank's time is well and truly up, he wont hurt anyone again."

"I wish I could believe that." She replied, locking the door.

Lizzie peered out of her room, half expecting it to be Sally. Her face displayed no real emotion at finding Ken there instead. He expected something from her, even if it was a mouthful of expletives, but there was nothing from Lizzie and Ken found this hard to fathom. He shook the snow from his jacket, and moved to enter the room.

"Come on Lizzie, what is it with the women around here? It's enough to give a guy a complex."

A short while earlier, Lizzie had learnt about the death of her 'mother', Margaret. However, Edward had still not told her that Pamela and the young soldier, he had tried to save during the war, were her real parents. Lizzie felt guilty, and somehow responsible for something that was inevitable. She should never have gone to the dance in view of the terrible argument she'd had with Edward and her sister, not to mention the awful episode with Pamela. Perhaps, Janice had been right all along about Lizzie's character being selfish and uncaring.

She had known immediately that the news would be bad, as soon as Karen had given her the message to call home. Sally, of course had offered to return to Lloyd-Evans Hall with her, but Lizzie had refused, she didn't want to burden her self anymore on her best friend. Instead, she hid behind her usual facade, and even fooled Sally into thinking everything was alright. Besides, at the time, Lizzie felt that in Ken, she did have someone to stand by her. He certainly didn't possess the emotional capacity of Sally, but he knew Lizzie just as well, and could be kind, gentle and understanding when the mood took him. Lizzie, however, would often resent him when Frank was around, as Ken always assumed a similar character to his vile, gloating friend. The Ken who Lizzie now needed was the same one that would hold her tightly after they had made love, who would brave refec early in the morning to smuggle her up breakfast in bed. Her Ken would lift her when she was down, he would make her laugh with his antics and build her confidence by telling her how great she was. But now, it was as if he had betrayed not only her, but womanhood in general. He had gone off after Frank, despite her pleading with him not to. She realised the powerful hold Frank could exert over people, but no matter how strong the influence, she could never forgive Ken for leaving her in favour of a an accused rapist and woman-hater. It became apparent to Lizzie that if Ken was so eager to follow a monster such as Frank, then he must condone his actions and therefore be of the same ilk.

"Lizzie, why didn't you wait for me, why did you come back alone?" Asked Ken, with the little-boy-lost expression on his face, but Lizzie wasn't prepared to accept any of it.

"Get the hell out of my room this instance!" She shouted, holding open the door.

Ken, looking hurt by her words, stepped towards her.

"Lizzie, what is it, what have I done to upset you? I was worried. Please let me stay, I'm freezing cold."

Lizzie stood glaring at him, her emotions going haywire.

"You just left me, for that creep, just when I needed you. I called you back, but you ignored me." Now tearful, Lizzie went to physically push Ken out of her room.

"I went to tell Frank just what I thought of him. It's only you who I care about."

She stared into Ken's eyes, and tried desperately to decipher the truth. She could see through his lies, and Ken knew it, and began to back away from her. He despised himself for thinking he could fool her so easily.

"I don't believe you. You're a liar and a user. I expect even Frank saw you for the cowardly toad that you are, and sent you packing - just like I'm doing now. It's over Ken, now just get out of my life."

Lizzie slumped down on the carpet and sat with her back against the door, absolutely drained. She had channelled all her pent up anger, sadness and frustration into one positive surge of energy. She had parted from Ken, which she would subsequently look upon as the correct course of action, bearing in mind his affinity with Frank. Sally had said a long time ago they were no good and they should look elsewhere, now it looked as if her friend had been proven right. She missed Sally, and wondered where she was and what she would be doing now. Closing her eyes, she sat perfectly still in her blue Cinderella evening dress, and listened out, just in case Sally came back.

As soon as William had opened the front door, he called out to David. There was no reply, but William knew his younger brother was at home, as his damp coat was hanging up in the hallway.

Sally now seemed somewhat hesitant about staying overnight at William's house, but what was the alternative - a night of fear, wondering what crazy thing Frank could do. William beckoned her to follow him inside. He then lifted the warm duffle coat from her shoulders and hung it up next to David's. Helping Sally off with her own coat, he led her into the warm sitting room. It was illuminated by a large standard lamp that gave off a soft, warm glow. The lamp was situated in what looked to be a reading corner, complete with an armchair and a well-stocked bookshelf. The open fire however, seemed to be on its last legs and was fading by the second. Sally stood in the centre of the room and immediately felt relaxed. She couldn't help noticing the colourful paintings depicting local scenes that adorned each wall.

"Who painted these, William? They're so beautiful."

"That'll be David, he's quite an accomplished artist. I've never really had the patience to do anything like that."

Sally then gazed around at the multitude of Toby jugs which took up every nook and cranny. Above her head was a haphazard assortment of copper pots and pans in rows, filling up all the available ceiling space. It was the most pretty and cosy house she had ever seen, but must be a nightmare to dust and clean she thought.

William opened a bottle of white wine, and watched her as he poured them two generous glasses. He saw the way her damp dress clung tightly to her hips, but then had to quickly avert his eyes when Sally turned unexpectedly to ask him about a perfect replica of an old Spanish galleon, made out of what looked like, thousands of matchsticks.

"My father made it. He taught himself to build with matches and tiny scraps of wood while a prisoner during the war. You'll find several of his creations scattered around the place."

Sally was amazed at the effort and eye for detail that had gone into making the ship, and she looked around eagerly for more examples of the intricate handiwork.

"I just love this house, William. It must be fantastic to live here."

"It would be, if it wasn't for all this old junk. It really needs to be sorted out." He replied, noticing she was shivering, despite the warmth. "Please Sally, come and sit by the fire, you're freezing. I'll go and get more wood. Can I get you a blanket or something?"

"No, I'll be fine. I'll dry off soon. Unless, of course if you happen to have a spare dress hanging in your wardrobe?"

William laughed, he enjoyed Sally's sense of humour, but he didn't like to see her cold and uncomfortable.

"No, sorry, I haven't got anything like that. What about one of my shirts? They're very long, and it would be just like a nightdress!"

"Yes, that's a good idea," replied, Sally, as she sat on the edge of her chair, gazing into the dying flames, while William tried in vain to poke more life into the fire.

"William, where exactly will I sleep?"

"That's no problem, you can sleep in my room. You'll feel safe there, its got a huge, heavy oak door, with big bolts, and I can light the fire too." He saw the look of concern still etched on her face. "You're still thinking about what happened with Frank, aren't you?"

Sally tried to smile, "You must think I'm a complete idiot, being too scared to go back to my own room?"

He knelt down beside her.

"Of course not. Frank is a psychopath. I certainly wouldn't trust him. Look, you can stay here until you go back home for Christmas if you want, we have spare rooms, and David wouldn't mind."

She took a sip of her wine, but there was still something preying on her mind.

"If I sleep in your room, where will you sleep?"

"The spare room of course! "He laughed. "Come upstairs and I'll show you my impressive shirt collection, and while you're getting changed, I'll get the wood."

Leading Sally upstairs to his bedroom, William cursed his brother for not attending to the fire in the living room, especially after David had returned home from the function before he did. For a moment, he was tempted to go into his room and wake him, but soon changed his mind after realising once his kid brother got a look at Sally, they would be stuck with him for the remainder of the evening.

While her host was out in the back yard, Sally couldn't resist having a crafty look around his room. It was certainly a room that had a good feel to it, and yes he was right, she did feel safe there. Although not the largest room in the house, it did overlook the orchard, and had French windows leading out onto a balcony. William had set aside an area for studying, but Sally couldn't see how anyone could ever study with so much clutter around. The mahogany desk was piled high with text books, encyclopaedia's and several dog-eared, dubious-looking novels. William seemed to share his father's passion for little curios, and Sally noticed there was a miniature globe, figurines and woodwork carvings in abundance. Many of these were of African or Indian origin, and if she didn't know any better, she could have mistaken the room as belonging to some intrepid explorer. One item that did catch her eye and spooked her out a little was a curious wooden mask. It had been cleverly adapted into a lamp, and blended in superbly with the rest of the other items, giving the room a certain exotic ambience. She noticed the Victorian fireplace that William had mentioned, and saw that it still contained ashes from when he had last used it. She felt like telling him not to go to all the trouble, since it was now getting so late, but William had been so insistent that she be made comfortable.

Sally looked at the shirts William had put out for her on the bed. After a few moments deliberation, she opted for a plain, white one that seemed to be the smallest, and was certainly in the best condition. She stood up and proceeded to take off her damp dress. Finding a hanger, she then inspected it for damage. There was a small tear just along one side, but nothing that couldn't be mended. The dress was the most expensive article of clothing she possessed, and it would take an eternity to scrape up the money to buy a new one.

As she walked back over to the bed, she thought she could hear voices. Standing completely still, she listened hard, trying to detect exactly where they were coming from. She heard a stifled giggle, it was definitely feminine, then there was a deeper, male voice. Then she heard what sounded like someone creeping around on the landing, and going off to the bathroom. Assuming it was David, Sally thought it best just to stand quietly to avoid any embarrassment. Besides, William would introduce them later.

However, this wasn't to be so. Sally gasped, and put her hands up to her mouth, as the bedroom door suddenly swung open, and in walked William's brother. It was difficult to say who was the most startled, Sally, standing there in her black silk, underwear, or David, clad only in his boxer shorts.

"Oh, I'm sorry, I thought you were William!" He exclaimed, looking Sally up and down, before adding; "Gosh, no, that's silly - you don't look anything like my brother!"

Sally quickly reached for the long-tailed shirt and held it up to hide her modesty.

"You obviously must be, David?"

"Yes, that's right," he replied, looking like he'd just seen a ghost. "So you must be, Sally. You look exactly like William described you."

"What, in my underwear! I hope I'm not too much of a disappointment to you!"

"I'm sorry, I just didn't expect you to be here." He then looked away and began to back out of the room.

"William's outside getting some logs for the fire," added Sally, feeling awkward.

David then turned and was whispering to someone behind him.

"I'm in a bit of a fix, Sally. I've got company and I didn't think William would be back so soon."

"There was trouble over at the hall, so we left earlier than expected. Then we got caught in the snow."

Yes, I heard about the situation at the hall. Nasty fellow that Frank Gant."

"So aren't you allowed to bring girls back here, David?"

He looked embarrassed and broke into a huge smile. David looked very much like William, with the same hazel eyes, only his complexion was fresher and younger looking.

"You see, William can be a bit old fashioned at times. He often gets a bit hot under the collar about things like this." He paused, as if waiting for a reaction. "But now you're here Sally, I guess it's okay for me to have Jenny here too."

She couldn't help returning his infectious smile, "Jenny? Yes, I think that would be fair. But in the meantime, your secret is safe with me."

"Thanks Sally, we'll pretend we haven't met yet." He said goodnight, but just as he was about to close the door, he poked his head back into the room.

"Sally?"

"Yes, David?"

"You're certainly not a disappointment!"

After waiting a few moments to see if there were going to be anymore interruptions, Sally continued to get undressed. Lifting one leg at a time, she placed her feet onto a chair and slowly rolled down her stockings, being careful not to snag them with her nails. These, she hung over the back of the chair with the rest of her garments. Wearing the expensive underwear had made her feel feminine and good about herself, and the feel of the silk against her skin was so sensual, it gave her goose bumps. Sally daren't admit it, but it had quite excited her when David suddenly came into the bedroom, and saw her so scantily clad. She shivered as she pulled on William's, white cotton shirt, before going over to the mirror to see how it looked.

Shortly after, there was a gentle knock on the door, it was William, clutching a bundle of kindling and a basket of logs. As soon as he'd got a good blaze going, he suggested they go back downstairs for another glass of wine, while the room warmed up.

"Yes, I'd like that," replied Sally, perching demurely on the edge of the bed.

"I must say, my shirt looks far better on you than it does on me!" He laughed.

"Flattery will get you everywhere, William Peddlescoombe!"

He opened the door to lead the way back downstairs, "Are you hungry, Sally? I've got some crumpets, they're delicious with butter and melted cheese."

"That sounds delicious, I'm starving!"

Downstairs, they laughed and joked, both revelling in each other's company. The wine had relaxed Sally, and she found herself thinking back to the passionate kiss they had shared, out in the snow. She felt herself longing for him to kiss her again, as she toyed with the stem of her glass.

"These are lovely, I've only ever had them with jam on," she said, helping herself to a second crumpet, glistening with melted cheddar.

"Yes, crumpets are my speciality, and staple diet. I put everything on them, even fish fingers and tartar sauce!" She laughed and watched, as he went over to the record player and stacked half a dozen 45s. Both of them instinctively put their glasses down and came together in the centre of the room.

William put on mostly slow songs, and Sally, being the much more experienced dancer, took the lead.

"Hold me tighter, William," she whispered while resting her head against his chest, for in her bare feet, he towered a good foot above her.

Their moment however was broken by a noise from upstairs and William went over to investigate. Fearing he might discover David's secret guest, Sally suddenly flung her arms up around his neck. She pulled him to her lips and kissed him hungrily. Sally could hear the feminine giggling again, and now William must have heard it too. But, if he had, he certainly wasn't too concerned about it now.

"What was that for?" He asked, surprised at Sally's raw passion.

"It's just for being you, William. Thank-you for all you've done for me."

He gently pushed a lock of blonde hair away from her eyes, and paused, looking at her longingly, before finally opening the door a few inches to listen out.

"My brother is sometimes his own worst enemy. He quite often needs protecting from himself."

"How do you mean, I don't understand?" She asked.

"I know he has a girl in his room tonight, and I know you've already met him. I heard you both talking when I came back inside."

Sally felt herself go red.

"I'm sorry, William, perhaps I should have said something to you. He has Jenny with him. She's a friend of Pauline's."

Putting his arm around her, they both went and sat on the rug by the fire.

"It's okay. Maybe I should explain. I just don't want you to think that I'm some sort of ogre where my kid brother is concerned."

"Of course I don't think that, and I'm sure David doesn't either. But I'm still not sure what you're getting at."

"Well, there was a fatal accident a few years ago that seriously affected David.

He's never really come to terms with it."

"How awful, poor David. What happened?" Asked Sally, looking concerned.

William stared intently at the fire, wondering if he should tell her about the incident that happened to his brother back in Canada. Sally cuddled up next to him and followed his gaze, as if looking into the flames was going to provide an answer.

She loved the sound of his voice, and listened with interest as William eventually found his words.

"It was the year before I started here at Falcondale. We were living in Niagara-on-the-Lake. David had this crush on a local girl called Amy, but wasn't making any headway with her. However, he got to know her little brother, who was a couple of years below him at high school. They both had a passion for fishing, like I do. One day, David was telling Martin about how he would go ice fishing during the winter, when the river and lakes would freeze over. The kid was enthralled by this, and kept pestering David to take him along the next time he went. But, my brother's a bit of a loner, and he always managed to avoid taking anyone fishing with him. Then one day, he bumped into Amy, and she asked him when he was going to take her little brother along. So, of course, David, seeing an opportunity to get into Amy's good books invited Martin ice fishing."

"Oh my god, I know what you're going to say," gasped, Sally. "Did Martin fall in?"

William paused for a few moments, before continuing; "Yes, he did, but he didn't fall into the hole they had just made, David was very safety conscious."

"So how did he fall?"

"He wanted to cut his own hole in the ice, and went out deeper onto the frozen river. David called him back, knowing it wasn't safe, but Martin either didn't hear him or didn't want to. David heard him shout, and saw his arms waving, as he fell through the surface. He went to try and pull him out, but he went under, and David lost sight of him."

"I can't believe it, I've never heard anything so sad. Did David get help?"

"No, not immediately, he was screaming Martin's name and went into the frozen water to see if he could find him. David was practically dead when a group of skaters eventually pulled him out."

"But there was no sign of Martin?" Asked Sally, putting her hands up to her face.

William shook his head, and took a gulp of his wine.

"He wasn't found until the next day. There was a massive police and rescue search. Martin was very popular, and David began to blame himself for his death. That winter changed David's outlook totally, and as a result, he became very reckless with his own life. He began to take unnecessary risks in many of the things he would do, believing that it should have been him who died that day, and not Martin."

"David must have felt so terrible, and he's still suffering."

"He took it real bad, and what made it worse was the attitude of some of the people. It's a sad fact of life that some folks always need someone to hate, and a defenceless, teenager seemed to fit the bill perfectly. Now David thinks he's living on borrowed time, and does the most crazy and dangerous things imaginable. Just a few days ago he was drunk and got up onto the roof. He said he could fly, and began prancing around trying to balance on the chimney." He turned to face Sally, "That's what I mean about having to protect him from himself. I never know what he's going to do next."

"But surely, if he's with Jenny, he wont do anything silly?" Replied, Sally trying to be re-assuring.

"Well yes, you would have thought so, but quite often he'll show off in front of girls, and few of them want to get involved after seeing some of his antics."

Sally went quiet and thought about what William had told her. She couldn't help thinking that he was going about things in totally the wrong way. David needed to get out and meet people, yes, he may be immature, but that wont last. He obviously lacks confidence, and wants to be accepted. That can only come by being praised, and by being with other people. However, she didn't dare tell William her opinion.

"What about Martin's family, did they blame David for what happened?"

"No, not in the least. They accepted that it was a very tragic accident, and one that could have been avoided. But obviously Amy wanted nothing more to do with him."

"What happened to David after that?"

"My parents sent him off to stay with relatives in another state until things had calmed down, but he proved to be too much of a problem for them."

"So he came here, to Falcondale, under the protective and calming influence of his big brother?"

"Yes, how did you know that?"

"Just feminine intuition!"

"David is studying Theology here, but he rarely goes to any of the lectures, or does any work, so I don't know if he'll get kicked out or just leave."

"That's interesting. So does David want to be a priest?"

"Heavens no. Some fool told him Theology was the easy option. David is very spiritual, but in reality, he doesn't know what he wants to do."

"So he's literally a free spirit, how sad, not knowing what you want out of life."

William sipped his wine and lay down on the rug, just gazing at the ceiling, while Sally propped herself up on her elbows next to him. She studied him for a while, then looked over towards the door.

"You've got me worried now, shall I go and see if David and Jenny are alright?"

Before William could answer, she was up and walking across the room. She opened the door quietly, and bent forward to poke her head out into the hallway, listening for any signs of misbehaviour. Sally was concentrating so hard, she didn't realise that William was now right up behind her. He looked down and took in her fine curves, revealed so superbly as the cotton shirt hung forward, hugging her shapely hips.

She wriggled slightly to gain a better footing, and as she did so, William brought his hands up quickly, and tickled her boisterously under the arms. Sally let out a shriek and reared back, giggling into William's arms. He felt the sides of her breasts brush past his hands, and as he ran his fingers further down her body, he realised she was naked beneath the shirt he had lent her.

Sally regained her composure and stood perfectly still in William's arms, while they both waited in silence to hear if her little outburst had provoked any response.

There was no noise apart from the two of them trying to stifle their giggles. He nuzzled her neck and noticed how she only had one clip holding her hair up in position.

It was then that they heard the noise from upstairs. First it was no more than a soft sigh, then a long moan. It gradually increased in both tempo and volume, until Jenny's cries of ecstasy became so intense and high-pitched that William and Sally could only stare at each other in disbelief and embarrassment.

"I don't think we need to worry about David tonight!" Smirked Sally.

William smiled and whispered; "I don't think we have to worry about Jenny either!"

He closed the door and turned the key in the lock, as Dion's *'Runaround Sue'* began to play.

Their lips came together immediately, writhing and dancing in unison. Sally knew things were rapidly getting out of hand. She had never felt like this with Frank, and wondered where it was all going to lead. Part of her wanted it to stop, knowing that somehow, she should break away and return to her own room back at Lloyd-Evans. It was madness. She thought she knew herself, her emotions, her physical likes and dislikes. There were no more surprises, at least, not until now. It was as if she had become a totally different woman, one that had gone from being the mistress of her own destiny, to one that was merely a slave to her recently awakened desires. Discovering these new secrets about herself, both surprised and shocked her. But now, as William began to undo the buttons on her shirt, she found they excited her too. Sally stopped him, and pulled away, she looked up and searched into his eyes, where something told her this was the man she was going to spend her life with. He seemed to sense it also, it was like an unspoken language had developed between them in the short time they had known each other.

They had both reached the point of no return, and Sally did nothing to stop him, when William undid her final button. Her breath came in short gasps, as she stretched up, arching her back, and pulled out the clip that released her long tresses. He then slipped the shirt over her shoulders, and watched, as it fell away from her body, and dropped silently to the floor. He gazed at her naked beauty, while awkwardly trying to remove his own clothes.

"Sally, can I ask you something?"

She smiled back at him, "I think I know what you're going to ask, William, and the answer is no, I didn't sleep with Frank. You're the first."

He then pulled off his jumper, shirt and vest in one quick manoeuvre, as Sally glimpsed his firm physique, and moved closer to touch him.

She had never been naked in front of a man before, let alone be this intimate. She held him close and kissed his toned chest, while William ran his fingers through her glossy hair and nibbled at her ear lobe.

Their eyes locked on to each other's, and their mouths came together, tongues eagerly exploring. Sally felt she was about to burst, as every hormone, every sense and every nerve ending all came into play as one.

His hands moved around to caress her back, her shoulders, and finally down to her buttocks. She sensed how his breathing was shallower and more intense. After a few moments, he pulled away, before leading her over to the fur rug, next to the fire. Sally followed, her delicate feet barely making a sound as she tiptoed alongside him.

They knelt down, facing each other. He let his gaze drop to survey her flawless skin, so beautifully pale, so beautifully soft. Reaching out, he grasped her breasts, and saw how her pink nipples immediately responded to his touch. Lowering his head, William kissed and licked both of Sally's breasts, making her moan and lean back to give him greater access. She realised for the first time just how sensual it was to be kissed there.

He beckoned her to lie down, and as she did so, he removed the rest of his clothes. She looked away, still slightly embarrassed, until he returned, now naked like her. The log fire felt warm, and this, combined with the drinks she'd had earlier, made her remaining inhibitions fall away. It was as if making love with William, was the most natural thing in the world.

Laying side-by-side, William's free arm skimmed across her hips and down over her legs. Slowly, he found his way to the inside of her thighs. She sensed immediately what he was about to do and moved onto her back, as his hand continued its journey. She opened her legs just enough for him to come into contact with her trimmed mound. Again, and again he allowed his hand to pass over her, each time, lingering that bit longer. Eventually, he inserted one finger, then two inside, making her writhe and moan in ecstasy at this new and unbelievable sensation. He felt how wet she was, and it made his formidable erection grow even larger.

He shifted position slightly, so that his manhood was now touching her skin. She tingled with pleasure, and began to let her hands explore him. She felt the broad shoulders, and the long, muscular arms as she ran her hands across him and down towards his narrow waist. His stomach muscles were firm and tight, as he moaned in expectation.

She was hesitant for a few moments, but then moved down further, to give her curiosity full rein. She took William's hard penis firmly, and ran her fingers up and down its length before starting to massage him, in a slow, rhythmic motion. He gasped and moved his hips in time with her, as she stroked him more vigorously with each movement. After a few moments, she sensed he was about to explode. She removed her hand and lay back down, placing her arms behind her head.

William kissed and licked her stomach, and down below her navel. He went lower, until he could feel her soft triangle against his chin. Sally opened her legs in anticipation of what he might do. Moving his head down further, he ran his tongue along her inner thighs, before letting it find its way inside her. She cried out, and grasped his hair, as William's probing tongue tasted her juices and brought her to the edge of losing control.

He continued to hungrily devour her, for what seemed like an eternity. She couldn't contain herself any longer, and cried out, grabbing hold of him, as the most intense, powerful orgasm shook her to the very core. William let it run its course before moving up beside her. She kissed him passionately, smelling her feminine odour on his face, and tasting her own essence on his lips.

Wanting to give him pleasure, Sally got up on her knees and took hold of his penis once more. She pulled the skin back over the head, and saw clear fluid oozing from the small hole at the top. She reached down and touched William's testicles, gently exploring their size, shape and how they felt under her kneading fingers.

Sally felt so liberated, so modern, and so utterly audacious. She glanced at William, and he smiled, as if he were using telepathy to tell her what he wanted. She lowered her head, and slowly guided his penis into her mouth.

She immediately tasted the sticky, sweet liquid that was leaking out onto her tongue. It made her feel quite powerful, and incredibly erotic, and she wondered if Lizzie had ever done this to Ken. She began to move her head back and forth, so that with each movement, she took more of him into her mouth, it felt huge and she gagged a couple of times. William was running his fingers through her lush, blonde hair and breathing heavy, as he thrust his hips in time with her.

He soon found himself on the edge of climaxing. He couldn't last any longer, and groaned loudly as he pulled down hard on her hair, and pumped a huge jet of sperm deep into her mouth. Sally squealed in surprise, and flashed her eyes up at him. She then sat upright, and swallowed hard, licking her lips with a mischievous grin, amazed at what she had just done.

She cuddled up next to him, and they both just lay there, listening to the crackle of the fire, and the steady ticking of the grandfather clock. There was no more sound from David and Jenny, and Sally prayed they were asleep, she couldn't bear to think they might have heard her.

It didn't take long before William began to touch her body once more.

"I think it's getting hard again!" She giggled, after their brief interlude.

"Sally, you are just so amazing! What should we do with it?"

"Stand out in the snow for a while!"

William laughed and turned to face her.

"I think I have a better idea for it!" He grinned, going up onto his elbows. He then trailed kisses along her curves, only stopping when he had positioned himself exactly as he wanted. He placed a finger inside her, and found she was still wanting. He eased her legs apart, and lowering himself down, he began to push himself inside her. It felt so big, and she whimpered at the pain, wondering if she could take it all. Then, as she became more accustomed to this new pleasure, she closed her eyes, and the familiar sensations from earlier returned. William started to increase the tempo, and soon they were moving in unison. He was rougher this time and thrust hard, making her cry out and bite into his flesh. They both began to reach their peak together. Sally couldn't help screaming out, as the massive orgasm engulfed her body. William, then spurted a fresh load of his seed inside her, as he gnawed at her porcelain neck.

Both were glistening in sweat when he finally rolled off and lay panting by her side. She put her head on his chest, and heard him murmuring something about having more crumpets, but that was the last she heard, as they were both asleep within minutes.

Sally wasn't sure if it was a sudden noise from outside, the drop in room temperature, or a combination of both that had shaken her out of the beginnings of a blissful sleep. She sat up, a little startled and looked around the room. It was now only illuminated by the dying embers of the fire that William had rescued earlier. It still let out the odd crackle of defiance, as if it could roar back into life at the merest stimulation. She wondered if the noise she had heard, could have been the fire after all. She looked down at William's sleeping face, and admired his handsome looks in the dim light, before pulling up the blanket over his shoulders.

Sally wanted to snuggle up to him again, and try to rejoin where she had left off, but the wind must have shifted direction as a chilly breeze was now blowing in from the top of the window, even though it was only open a couple of inches. Sally couldn't bear to be cold and knew that it would be impossible for her to get back to sleep while the draft prevailed. In desperation, she called out in a hushed voice to William, but he just groaned, turned over onto his back and began to snore. It was then that she realised she would have to get up and go and close the window herself. Straining her eyes, she gazed around the room once more, trying to spot the shirt William had lent her. It was no good, she thought, there was only one thing for it, she would have to make a dash, close the window, and jump back into their makeshift bed as quickly as she could.

As she tiptoed naked across the room, she felt William's seed dripping out of her and running down the inside of her leg. Her handbag was still on the table where she had left it, so she delved into it for some tissues. As she wiped herself, she noticed there was also a small amount blood, a sign of her now-lost virginity. It was then she noticed the shirt, lying on the carpet, exactly where it had fallen a little earlier. She thought about putting it back on, but decided that once she was back in bed she would soon warm up, besides, she quite liked the feel of William's bare flesh touching her own.

Goose bumps broke out over her skin as she reached up to full stretch and made a grab for the window. It was very stiff, and she had to move in closer to gain better leverage. After taking a deep breath, she decided to give it one hard shove. and hope it would be enough to finally close it. That seemed to do the trick and the top of the window slammed firmly shut. However, Sally now felt an even stronger draft cut straight across her midriff. It blew in wafts of snow, and made the curtains flap wildly. She let out a gasp, as the icy snow flakes settled on her warm skin, only to rapidly melt and trickle down her body. She looked around to see where this sudden gush of freezing air was coming from, and found herself staring straight into Frank's bloodied face.

He had wrenched up the lower window, just as Sally had closed the top. Now he just gazed with cold, dead eyes at her nakedness, as if he were daring her to do something rash, that she might regret.

She thought she would have screamed out of pure instinct when she brought her hands up to her face, but nothing came out. The abject terror of her predicament had made her temporarily mute. She then watched in horror as Frank slowly began to pull himself through the open window, like some vile snake-like creature she had seen in an old Hollywood film. His piggish eyes never left hers as they stared out from a grotesquely swollen face, after the beating he had taken from Carol's father and brothers earlier that night. The cut on his left cheek still oozed blood following Pauline's glass attack on him at the function. Despite her terror, Sally felt for a moment in her confused state, that she should be trying to help him. She rapidly dismissed the thought and retreated, unable to think clearly. She then stumbled on something behind her and couldn't stop herself from falling. Her eyes were now accustomed to the dim light from the fire, which cast a horrific glow over Frank's deranged face, as he towered over her, clutching a knife.

Sally's mouth dropped as she saw him smile his all-too familiar grin, but now it was just an ugly, terrifying, caricature that chilled her to the bone. She noticed his once pure white teeth were now bloodied and animal-like. She saw the wet, matted hair stuck fast to his forehead, as he sunk to his knees and inched closer towards her.

She heard William stir, and call out something. What it was, she never knew, for now Frank was running the cold blade up and down her trembling, naked body.

Sally's scream, when it finally came, even startled Frank, who staggered to his feet in an attempt to distance himself from the ear-piercing, nerve-shattering cry.

William was out of bed in a shot, and immediately felt the chill air on his skin, as his eyes searched the dim room for Sally. He saw a dark, hulking shape to the right of him, and a gut-wrenching feeling in the pit of his stomach warned of the very real danger about to descend on him.

The punch hit William with a sickening thud, making him fall back heavily. He tried to get up, fearing more blows, but Frank crashed down heavily on top of him, completely knocking the wind out of William.

"I want my property, Peddlescoombe. Give me the necklace, you can keep the whore!"

William looked up in horror at the face that was now staring down, inches from his own.

"Where's the necklace? I saw you pick it up at the hall. Tell me, or I'll cut your throat." Cursed Frank, as blood from a knocked out tooth socket dripped onto William's face.

"I haven't got it. I threw it out into the lane somewhere."

"You're about to die, Peddlescoombe, you lying bastard. I'll teach you to cross me."

With that, Frank grabbed a clump of William's hair, and thrust the knife up close to his neck.

William desperately needed to know if Sally was alive before he had his throat slit, and screamed out her name.

Sally then appeared at his side and yelled hysterically, as she desperately hit out at Frank.

"I'll deal with you later, bitch!" Shouted Frank, letting go of William and pushing Sally so hard that she fell backwards.

"For gods sake Sally, forget about me, save yourself!" Shouted out William, as he tried to struggle free from the dead weight on top of him. He felt the knife bite into his flesh, and knew his time had come.

Frank glared down at him.

"You're pathetic, Peddlescoombe. You'll never be able to satisfy a woman like her - she needs a real man!" Then, leering at Sally's naked body, he added icily; "On second thoughts, maybe I'll have her after I've finished with you. Now, for the last time - where's the..."

Frank never got the chance to finish his threat, as the poker hit the side of his head. David's blow wasn't enough to completely knock Frank out, but it was enough to stun him and allow William the chance to get out from underneath. Frank, albeit, dazed and unsteady, even managed to stagger to his feet. He reeled menacingly towards David, but was now too injured to be a real threat. David, still gripping the poker from the fireplace, raised it once more, expecting an attack, but Frank, using what little strength he had left, just stumbled past and headed towards the front door. He then fell out into the snow, and like a wounded animal, started to crawl away.

David followed close behind, but William, called him back, and told him to bolt the front door, relieved that Frank was finally out of the house.

Sally retrieved William's shirt, and hastily pulled it on, before bursting into tears. William rushed to her side, his lip swollen and bleeding.

"Sally, what a heroine you are. I really thought I was going to die!"

"I certainly don't feel like a heroine, I've never been so terrified in all my life."

William, placed a protective arm around her, and called to his brother, "David, keep an eye on him from the window, while I call the police."

Turning back to Sally, he asked her if she was alright. She looked at her shaking hands, and forced a smile, "Nothing broken, just a bit bruised, where I fell. But please, William - call the police straight away. It's not safe with Frank at large."

They then heard someone in the hallway, and glanced at each other in dread. The door opened and in walked Jenny, looking somewhat bedraggled and swamped in David's dressing gown.

"Why are you all staring at me? It's the middle of the night, why aren't you all in bed!"

Pauline knew they would come to her room. She had been drifting in and out of sleep for a few hours now, her mind constantly flashing back to the events in the hall.

She heard loud male voices, then footsteps - footsteps that grew louder as they got closer to her door.

When the knock came, it was a hard, masculine sound, not the gentle tap, tap that Jenny or Maureen would make. She was still dressed in the clothes she had worn to the dance, but now they were creased and soiled with spilt alcohol, and splashes of Frank's blood. When she finally undid the lock and opened the door, the bright light from the corridor dazzled her and made her squint.

The policeman asked her name, to which she replied in a non-descript child-like, manner. She noticed Karen was standing directly behind him, along with Mr. Meredith and Jane.

"Can we come in, Pauline, we have a few questions to ask you?"

Pauline switched on the light, and stepped back a few paces to allow them access.

The policeman was shocked to see the state of Pauline's room. Clothes had been ripped to shreds, pictures had been torn from the walls and the furniture had been turned over.

"I've seen Mr. Meredith already, I've got nothing further to say," said Pauline nervously.

Hesitantly, the police officer beckoned Karen into the room, along with Jane, while Meredith stood in the doorway.

"Now, young lady, I'm Constable Price, and this is, Karen, and Mrs. Parker, but I expect you all know each other."

Pauline shook her head, not acknowledging her fellow student.

"Okay then, let's carry on. Please listen to what I have to say, Pauline. Karen has made a very serious accusation regarding a male student here, who goes by the name of Frank Gant. Do you know him?"

Pauline nodded affirmatively, realising that this wasn't about her attacking Frank.

"Karen has made a statement to the effect that Gant drugged her, got her drunk, then raped her." Karen began getting anxious, prompting Jane to take the student's hand and grip it reassuringly.

"Okay, my girl, now listen here. Karen also said, he did the same to you. Is that correct Pauline?"

"No, of course it isn't. Stupid girl, she just wants the attention. Why would he do that? He's my boyfriend - I'm the one he loves, not her."

Constable Price exhaled sharply.

"According to my information, Pauline, you accused Gant of exactly the same thing, over at the hall, and in front of several hundred people. What's more, you then put a glass into his face. Is that true?"

"No, it's not, well not the first bit. He didn't rape me, I was drunk. I wont press charges."

"I think you owe it to young Karen here, to get him convicted. By all accounts, he's a very dangerous man and should be locked up. Besides, he could have attacked more women."

"Has Frank accused me of cutting him with the glass?"

"No, he hasn't, Pauline, but we haven't found him yet. Do you know where he is?"

"No, I don't. If there's nothing more to say, then please leave me alone." Scowled Pauline, her voice aggravated.

As they turned to leave, another policeman arrived outside the room, asking for his colleague. There was a short discussion in the corridor, and Price walked back into Pauline's room.

"I'm afraid things are a bit more serious now, Pauline. This so-called boyfriend of yours has apparently broken into a house and attacked the occupants with a knife." Price then wrote a telephone number down on a slip of paper and handed it to Pauline. "If you change your mind, or know anything else, please contact us.

We will protect you - this man has to be found."

Once they had gone, Pauline pulled on her coat and boots and went out into the snowy night to look for Frank. She decided to try his room at the Old Building first. It was obvious the police would have checked there earlier, but now they were heading to Orchard Lane, where he was last sighted.

It was easy to gain access to Frank's hall of residence since security wasn't so much of an issue as with the female residences, and more often than not, the front door would be left unlocked. She checked the list of residents in the lobby and made her way to his room. After knocking several times and getting no reply, she trudged back out into the snow. She began to head for the main gate, but couldn't quite see where the path ended and the grass verge began, as the snow was so thick in places. She reached the end of the building, and must have strayed off the path as she had arrived at another, smaller door. There was a light on in the lobby, and Pauline wondered if Frank ever used this instead of the main entrance. Walking over towards the door, she noticed long marks, and irregular foot prints in the snow, as if someone had fallen over and had then struggled to get up and walk. It was then, that she saw drops of blood in the snow and instinctively knew Frank was nearby. She stood still, and called out his name, but the strong breeze muffled the sound of her voice. She began following the tracks, which seemed to lead to a small coppice close by. Then, as she got nearer, she saw him. He was lying face down, literally just twenty feet from the back door of the building. She ran towards him, calling his name, but there was no movement or response. Placing her hands on his shoulders, she tried to turn him. He was frozen through and still wearing his dinner suit. He was heavy and a dead weight, but with all her strength, she managed to half turn him and pull his face from the snow. She was horrified to see the awful wound on his cheek that she had inflicted earlier. It was no longer bleeding, probably due to the cold conditions, but it looked ugly, and so permanent. In fact, Frank's facial wound probably saved him from a more severe beating from Carol's father and brothers, who had limited their attack to mostly just punching him about the body and kicking him once he was down. There was another wound on the top of his head, where David had hit him with the poker. The blood had trickled down his neck, to stain the white collar of his expensive shirt, just like the blood from the cut, had stained the front.

Again, she called his name, again there was no response. Pauline thought he was dead, and she had played a major part in killing him.

"I'm so sorry, Frank. Please forgive me." She sobbed, "I was just so jealous when I saw you with Sally. It was too painful to bear. Please don't leave me."

The tears streamed down Pauline's face, as she buried her head in her hands. After a few moments, she removed her coat and placed it over Frank. She then cuddled up next to him and held him tight, crying into his cold body. Now they were one, and she would follow him wherever, even to the grave.

She didn't know how long she and Frank stayed there, out in the snow, minutes or hours, but it was the voices that roused her from a semi-conscious state. She felt strong arms lifting her up and putting her onto a stretcher. She was confused and not sure if she had died or not. Opening her eyes, she saw ambulance men lifting Frank. He was still lifeless, and being such a large man, the two police officers were called upon to help get him into the ambulance.

"I didn't mean to kill him!" Cried Pauline, sitting up and throwing the blankets off.

"He's not dead, love," replied one of the men, "He should be dead, by the look of him, but I'd say you saved him. The heat from your body just about kept him alive."

Pauline let out a long sigh of relief, and got off the stretcher. She walked over to where Frank was lying and kissed his battered face. She then retrieved her coat, and started to walk away. He was alive, and now she would make it up to him, for in Pauline's eyes, Frank was her man, and she would lay down her life for him.

One of the ambulance men went to bring her back, but Constable Price stopped him.

"Let her be. She needs more help than we can ever give her."

9. THE REUNION

It was Wednesday, 19th December, when Pamela drove into Falcondale. She stopped briefly near the clock tower to consult her atlas, before driving the short distance into the car park at the rear of the High Street.

It was busy in town, not only with the regular shoppers, but with those desperate to stock up on supplies due to the recent spell of unpredictable weather. The snow storms had brought the harsh reality of winter to many of Falcondale's sheep farmers trying to eke out what living they could. The impending winter of 1963 would go down in British history as one of the worst in living memory.

After finding a parking place, Pamela was at first reluctant to leave the warmth of her car. She smoked a cigarette, before finally opening the door and venturing out towards an inviting looking cafe that she had noticed on the way in.

The Market Cafe seemed more like an English tea shop, with its quaint charm and chintz curtains, and Pamela, weary from such a long drive was more than ready for a nice hot cup of tea, and perhaps a morsel of cake. It was quite full inside, but she managed to find herself a seat over by the window, and watched the busy shoppers go about their business as she waited to be served.

Pamela had liked the town immediately, but she was uncertain about how welcome she might be in view of what had happened recently, with Lizzie and Janice.

She sipped her tea, and slowly went over the events in her mind. Edward had contacted her with the news of Margaret's death, and things now couldn't be left the way they were. Lizzie had to be told the truth. She had already been informed about Margaret, but Edward desperately wanted his family around him at this sad time. He was quite concerned however, about Lizzie driving back alone, he wasn't sure how everything may have affected her. He had told Lizzie, that he would come and collect her personally, but it had been Pamela's idea that she went in place of him.

"Please, Edward, it would give me the perfect opportunity to speak to Lizzie, and in a neutral environment. We'll both come back safely, I promise."

Pamela's thoughts were distracted by the chattering of two elderly women seated at the table next to hers. She tried to ignore the women and concentrate on what she would say to Lizzie, but couldn't help listening in on some of the conversation.

"It's beautiful, Nancy, and looks like a real pearl," said Doreen, closely examining the gold necklace. "So you found it in Orchard Lane, just lying in the snow?"

"Yes, that's right, I was there to do some cleaning for the Peddlescoombe's."

"Of course, I remember you telling me. How are William and David, they're such lovely boys?"

"They're not as innocent as they make out, Doreen. They've had girls at the house. I'm sure William has one sleeping in his room with him!"

"That's disgusting, Nancy. It wouldn't have happened in our day."

"That's very true, although I do recall you having a bit of a reputation when your Gilbert was away fighting at the front."

"Don't bring all that up again, Nancy. Now tell me more about the necklace." Replied Doreen, looking a little embarrassed.

"There's not much more to say really. I asked the boys about it, and none of them knew who's it was. I thought it may belong to one of their girlfriends, but apparently not."

"What a windfall and just before Christmas too. Are you going to keep it?"

"I don't know. Someone must be missing it by now, so I asked Constable Price what I should do. He wasn't very concerned, and since nobody had reported losing a necklace, he said to hang on to it."

Doreen wasn't surprised. "He's not one for paper work, that Constable Price. Well, I hope you get to keep it, Nancy.

"Thank-you Doreen, but I've always believed that honesty is the best policy, so I've put a small ad in the lost and found column of the Gazette." Replied Nancy, before looking around and whispering; "I also took it to the Jeweller's to get it valued, and you'll never guess what?"

"Tell me," replied, Doreen, moving her head a little closer.

"It's a Cartier necklace, and is worth a good thousand pounds!"

"Oh my word! A Cartier necklace in Falcondale, whatever next?" Exclaimed Doreen, putting her hand up to her mouth.

Nancy looked down to admire the piece once more, "But if no-one claims it, I wont keep it for myself - I'll give it to Carol. I think something like this needs to be worn by a much younger woman."

"You must be so proud, Nancy, having a grand-daughter like her?"

"Yes, the poor lass works so hard, but you never hear her complain, and she deserves a bit of luck - especially after losing her job because of that nasty, Frank Gant chap."

Pamela couldn't help smiling at the old ladies, as she finished her tea and placed the cup down on the delicate china saucer. It didn't take long before she was chatting away to them as if they were long-lost friends. Obviously the women were keen to know what Pamela's business was in town, as it was rare to see strangers passing through, especially dressed as elegantly as Pamela. After several minutes had passed she asked the waitress where the telephone was, and lit up a cigarette, before taking out her purse and venturing over to make her call. Pamela scolded herself for getting so worked up about things and decided to simply come out with the truth. Yes, that was it, she decided, just be honest. After all, she had nothing to hide or be ashamed of, and it's what Lizzie would expect.

Pamela listened to the continuous ringing tone for a couple of minutes, before hanging up. She then took a pull from her cigarette, and tried the number once more.

Sally was sitting quietly in Lizzie's room, watching her friend iron clothes on a sheet laid out on the carpet. Lizzie was a meticulous ironer and would handle her expensive clothes as if they might suddenly break and shatter. She carefully folded her blouses and skirts into neat squares, before placing them into a large suitcase on the bed.

"So how was the dreaded seminar this morning?" Asked Lizzie, breaking the silence.

"Not half as bad as I expected. My tutor had a stinking cold and just wanted to get home as soon as possible. I was a bit annoyed, especially after all the work, I'd put in."

"Don't you mean all the work William put in!" Teased Lizzie, before adding; "Never mind, I'm glad you went, I can't have you fussing around me all the time." Lizzie, then suddenly stopped packing and went and sat on the edge of the bed.

"Lizzie, are you okay?"

"Yes, of course, but it just doesn't seem real, Sally. I mean, I should be hysterical shouldn't I? My mother has just died and here I am, ironing away as cool as a cucumber."

"You knew it had to come, Lizzie. Perhaps, subconsciously you had already prepared yourself for the inevitable."

"Yes, you could be right, but I can't help feeling that it's not all over yet. It just hasn't sunk in, perhaps the mind isn't programmed to acknowledge shocks like this immediately. It could be, that its all just building up to hit me later, when I least expect it." Lizzie closed her eyes for a few moments, then added; "You will come to the funeral, wont you, Sally? Mum would have wanted my best friend there."

"Of course I will Lizzie, and we'll phone each other all over Christmas. Now come on, keep yourself busy, your father will be here soon.

Lizzie nodded and went over to the wardrobe, where she began removing her dresses.

"I'm sorry, Sally, for everything. For ruining your birthday, for making you witness those awful rows. Then, to cap it all, you discover your boyfriend is a rapist and a psychopath who tries to murder you - and here I am, feeling sorry for myself!"

"Lizzie, please, I'm sure you would have acted just the same if I had troubles at home. As for Frank, I hope I never see him again. I'm sure he'll go to prison, but I wont be looking forward to going to court." Sally then paused, as she heard the telephone ringing.

She was quite glad to leave Lizzie's room for a few moments. She did want to help her friend through her grief, but hated it when Lizzie went through one of her feeling guilty phases, and started apologising profusely. Besides, what happened at William's house, with Frank, had affected her greatly, and like Lizzie, she was in a void, as she struggled to process such disturbing information. She felt tearful, and was glad the caller had rung off when they did. Since that night, Sally had been terrified of being on her own, and had practically abandoned her room, choosing to stay with William and David instead. She would have told her friend how she had lost her virginity to William, and how wonderful it was to actually do it at long last. But what happened after with Frank had somehow taken the gloss off, what should have been such a memorable occasion. Besides, in view of Lizzie's mother passing away, it just didn't seem appropriate to even think of discussing such things at the moment.

Sally turned and started to head back to Lizzie's room, when she heard the telephone ring again. Picking up the receiver, she hoped it may be William, who she had arranged to meet later that day. However, the female caller asked for Lizzie Marchmont. She had a soft, well-spoken voice, and one that Sally had certainly heard before.

"Hello, It's Sally, Lizzie's friend. I'm sorry, she isn't taking any calls today. May I take a message?"

"Sally - I'm glad it's you." Replied the caller anxiously. "Please don't hang up until you've heard what I have to say. I'm sure you remember me, we met last week at Lizzie's house, my name is Pamela Cartwright."

Sally remained on the line while Pamela briefly explained why she had come to collect Lizzie and not Edward.

"You see, I'm Lizzie's real mother, not Margaret."

Sally was shocked, and went quiet for a few moments, as she tried to make sense of what she had just heard.

"Of course, it's clear now, you both look so much alike and have similar mannerisms. I should have known immediately."

"Can I rely on you to get Lizzie to come over to the cafe, Sally, so I can explain?"

"I'll get her there if I have to carry her myself," replied, Sally, feeling her heart lifting.

Returning to Lizzie's room, she had to quell a tear drop welling up in her eye. She stopped and took in a few deep breaths to regain her composure, before opening the door. Lizzie had just about finished and was in the process of sitting on her case, trying to close it.

"Sally, quick, help me with this damned case, I knew I'd packed too much!"

"Forget the case for now Lizzie, put your coat on, we're going out to tea!"

"But I don't understand. What if I miss father? He wont wait you know. I really don't know why I can't just drive myself anyway?"

"He obviously didn't know how you would take the news about your mother, and besides there's more snow on the way. He cares for you Lizzie. Now, just shut up for a moment, you wont miss him. Please, stop asking questions, and just trust me. Okay?"

"Alright, you win, where are we going?"

"To the Market Cafe, and bring an umbrella, it's starting to sleet."

"But it's full of old ladies drinking tea!"

"Lizzie, just do as you're told, and get your coat!"

It was a mixture of drizzle and sleet, but in a way it was a godsend, as it meant the expected heavy snow wasn't about to arrive just yet. Sally quickly scribbled a note for William to meet her at the cafe, and left it at the gate lodge.

Most of the snow from the blizzard of a few days ago had now turned to a dirty, grey slush, and the two women made the short distance into town trying to avoid filthy puddles and being splashed by passing traffic.

Despite Lizzie's promise not to ask anymore questions, Sally had to continually re-assure her about this unusual and unexpected trip out to the cafe.

They eventually reached their destination, but before going inside, Lizzie put her hand on Sally's arm, as she shook her wet umbrella.

"I think it's wonderful, Sally - so dramatic, and so downright romantic!"

Sally looked at her friend with a puzzled expression, "What on earth are you going on about, Lizzie?"

"You, Sally, I'm talking about you! First, you lose the man you thought you loved, only to discover, and just in time, that he was a rat. Then you find love again, and they fight over you, but real love conquers and you live happily ever after! Don't you think it's great, Sally?"

"Real life is not quite as straight forward as that Lizzie, I think you've been reading too many cheap romances!" Uttered Sally, as she opened the door, "Now it's time you had some happiness, do you remember what I said about trusting me on the way over?"

"Yes, of course, I do trust you, Sally." Replied Lizzie, cautiously.

"Good, then let's go inside, and Lizzie - keep an open mind."

The bell above the cafe door gave off a delicate little tinkle as Sally and Lizzie entered. They wiped their shoes on the mat and proceeded to take off their coats. It felt nice and warm inside due to a couple of wall-mounted electric fires, that were turned on full. A middle-aged waitress came over and was about to show the two women to a table. However, she seemed quite shocked at the sight of Lizzie's hair, and her tight, leopard-skin design slacks. Normally, Lizzie would glare back, and more often than not, would make a sarcastic comment. Today though, she chose to ignore the woman's keen interest and simply just gazed around, wondering why Sally had brought her to such a drab place.

"Hello, Lizzie. It's lovely to see you again." Said Pamela, wearing a somewhat apprehensive expression. "I'm so glad you came. Please come over and join me. I've taken the liberty of ordering coffee for you, as I know you prefer it." She then smiled warmly at Sally, and motioned for them to be seated. Sally was immediately aware that Lizzie was glaring daggers at her, wanting an explanation. The atmosphere was anything but congenial, and she began to pray there wouldn't be an argument. However, it was Lizzie who spoke first.

"Look, I don't hate you, Pamela, nor have I ever done. I was just appalled that you could live with my father, in our house, while my mother was dying upstairs in a spare room. Now she's dead, and you're here, for what reason I don't know, but if it's to apologise, then just do it, and go."

Pamela sat back in her chair and picked up the packet of cigarettes. She offered one to Lizzie, who declined - preferring to smoke one of her own. An awkward silence prevailed, as Lizzie refused to look at Pamela and fixed her gaze on some inanimate object on the far side of the cafe.

While the two women sat in silence, Sally took the opportunity to look for similarities in their faces and mannerisms. She watched intently as Pamela stubbed out her cigarette with half of it still remaining - a practice often shared by Lizzie.

Pamela's discomfort eased when the two elderly ladies got up to leave. At least now she could try and talk to Lizzie in relative privacy. The old ladies both stared at Lizzie, before smiling at Pamela and bidding her goodbye. The waitress helped the women with their coats and scarves, and went over to open the door for them. One of the ladies, Doreen, stepped out into the rain, and made a comment about the ghastly weather. But her friend didn't hear, for she had gone back to Pamela's table.

"It was lovely to pass the time of day with you dear," said Nancy politely, before looking down to scrutinize Lizzie. "I'm so glad you met up with your daughter at last, why, she looks just like you."

"Thank-you," replied Pamela, squirming in her chair, "I do hope your grand daughter likes that lovely necklace!"

Sally was slightly puzzled by the exchange going on around her, but her attention was now drawn towards Lizzie, who was looking totally bewildered. Both Sally and Pamela held their breath and weren't exactly sure how Lizzie would react to what she had just heard.

"What's going on? I don't understand. Why did that woman refer to me as your daughter?" Demanded, Lizzie, facing Pamela full on.

"Because, it's true, Lizzie - you are my daughter. Look at you, your appearance, the way you smoke, the way you drink your coffee, the way you smile, the way you cry, and the way you care." Said Pamela, sitting back to wait for the reaction.

"I don't believe you. But even if it were true, that would mean that you and my father were having an affair nearly twenty years ago."

"Edward is not your father."

"What!" Exclaimed Lizzie, raising her voice and attracting an audience. "Why are you doing this, Pamela, don't you think I've suffered enough?"

"Please, Lizzie don't be like that. Listen to what I have to say. Then you can judge me."

"Let's hear it then, but I'm losing my patience with you. You're trying to turn me away from Dad aren't you?"

"No, I swear I'm not," replied Pamela, her voice full of emotion. "I lost my husband, your real father during the war. I had nowhere to go and nobody to turn to. Edward and Margaret took me in and gave me a roof over my head and a job. I have never forgotten what they did."

"So he's not my father, oh my god, I just can't take all of this in. Why was it a secret? Why wasn't I told before?"

"It wasn't really a secret, Lizzie. Times were hard just after the war. I was a widow, our home had been bombed, I had no job and no money. Edward and Margaret were a similar age to me, and it just seemed easier to get you into a decent school, and get you looked after properly if you came from an established family. Nobody asked questions, and we all gained from it. I did mean to tell you, but Edward and Margaret grew to love you, and it just didn't seem right to upset everything. Please forgive me, Lizzie. I have never stopped loving you as a daughter, and I'm so proud of you." Pamela began to sob, and Lizzie, fighting back tears herself, moved closer to her mother.

"So, I've lost a mother, but gained another one, lost a dad, but gained another, and now I've lost him too?"

"No, Lizzie, you're wrong, you haven't lost him. Edward may not be your natural father, but he is your Dad, and always will be. He loves you from the bottom of his heart. I know, because he always tells me so."

Lizzie sat back in her chair, trying to take all this in. But her demeanour had changed, and she had a much softer expression on her face. "I'm sorry, Pamela, it must have been so hard for you. I can't imagine what you went through."

"There were many people in the same boat, Lizzie. Good people who had lost loved ones and everything they cared about. But at least I still had you. I can't find the words to tell you what it meant to me, to see you growing up. I remember when I gave birth to you, I literally thought I was going to die. But Thomas was there with me, holding my hand, mopping my brow and giving me strength."

"So, that was my Dad's name, Thomas?"

"Yes, Lizzie, that was your father's name. You were crying and wouldn't feed at first, so he picked you up and went out into the garden with you. Holding you tightly in his arms, he showed you the blue sky, and the clouds, and let you feel the rays of the sun on your tiny face. I remember how your little fingers were grasping his when he brought you back to me. You were so peaceful and calm. I often think back to you as a baby, your first milk teeth, and when you took your first steps. I can remember the first doll you played with, and your tears when I had to take you to school for the first time." Pamela then hesitated, and glanced away. "I can also remember my own tears when you called Margaret, 'Mum' for the first time. That was when I had to stop cuddling you."

Lizzie felt a lump in her throat and went quiet, thinking about what Pamela had just said. "What about Janice, does she know the truth?"

"No, she doesn't," sighed Pamela. "You can tell her if you want. But I'm afraid, Janice will still hate me, whether she knows or not."

Both women were now highly emotional, and as they turned to face each other, Lizzie reached across and hugged Pamela. Sally was now rapidly getting through her supply of tissues, and she too went around the table and joined in the Marchmont family reunion.

Once outside, Lizzie linked arms with Pamela, "I should have known all along really - we're two of a kind," she smiled. "So, do I still call you, Pamela, or Mum?"

Pamela laughed and gripped Lizzie's hand as they walked to the car. "I'll leave that up to you. Come on, let's get you back to Gloucester, we have so much to catch up on."

After a few steps, Lizzie stopped.

"Will you tell me all about my Dad when we get home, my real Dad?"

"I'll do more than that, Lizzie, darling," replied Pamela, beaming with pride, "I'll show you all the pictures I've got of him, and the letters he sent me from the war. He was such a wonderful, handsome man. In fact I still go to France every year and lay flowers at his grave."

"I can't wait to see the photographs and read the letters. I wish I had got to know him."

"So do I, Lizzie, I still miss him so much."

They got into Pamela's car and set off back to Lloyd-Evans to collect Lizzie's luggage. There was a brief silence as both women reflected on all that had been said. But it was Lizzie who continued the conversation.

"What about the thing you had with Edward, will you continue your relationship now the truth's out?"

"Probably not. I respect the feelings of Margaret too much, and I think your sister put paid to that. Anyway I still have the memories of your father to cherish."

Lizzie glanced at Pamela, and smiled warmly. "Can I come with you
to France, the next time you go?"

"Yes, of course you can my sweet, I'll be glad of the company."

"Thanks, Mum, I'll look forward to that," replied Lizzie, her words causing
Pamela's heart to leap with joy, and making her the happiest woman alive.

The taxi ground to a halt outside the entrance to a secluded private drive. The
driver waited for his next instructions, but finding them not forthcoming, he turned
around and slid open the dividing glass. The young female passenger seemed
oblivious to the fact that they had stopped, and just continued to stare blankly out
of the window.

Pauline clutched the letter she had received from the Dean of Students,
informing her that she had been expelled from the university forthwith. The
gravity of her predicament hadn't fully sunk in yet, and in disbelief, she kept
reading the letter over and over again, as if it were just some awful mistake. It was
in direct contrast to the day, a year earlier when she had received a letter from the
Dean, telling her of the place she had won. Like today, she had repeatedly read
that letter too, but then it was out of sheer pride and amazement that she had
actually been accepted.

It had been hard for Pauline to say goodbye to Jenny and Maureen. They had
promised to keep in touch, but in reality, Pauline knew it would never be so. Her
two friends had acted differently to her since the night of the dance, and who could
blame them. It was perfectly clear they wanted to distance themselves from a
woman, who was now known around the campus as a female psychopath.

She had arranged for her luggage to be sent home separately, and had then
checked the timetable for train services to Bristol. Pauline, up until then had never
thought of herself as an impulsive person. But the fact that she had now brought a
ticket to see the man who had previously raped her, surprised even herself.

"We're here Miss. This is it, Cedar Avenue. That'll be ten bob please." Asked
the driver matter-of-factly.

She delved into her purse and paid him, then clutching a carrier bag, climbed
out of the taxi and furtively walked up the tree-lined driveway towards the house.
It had taken her the best part of a day to travel from Falcondale to Bristol, and now
she had finally arrived, her stomach was in knots.

It hadn't been difficult to look up Frank's address in the telephone directory.
She knew his father was a prominent surgeon, that had been the easy part. But now
that she had arrived, she began to wonder what it was she hoped to achieve, and
what reception she would get. Pauline had tried to imagine exactly how Frank
would react, when she turned up, uninvited on his doorstep. But then of course, the
problem was, she didn't actually know him. She had built him up in her mind, and
to a certain extent her feelings for him had been confused by the horrific
experience in the hotel suite. Pauline, out of a subconscious, defensive reflex
action had changed Frank's malevolent character into something her fragile,
emotional psyche could deal with. To her, Frank's behaviour only meant one thing,
he must want her. This resulted in a misinformed deduction that meant Frank must

actually care, and in his own way, love her, and that was all she needed.

Pauline had certainly got her revenge on him, but that was never what she had intended. It wasn't premeditated in any shape or form, and as it turned out, it was a high price to pay. She just wanted to be acknowledged by him, and she had even begun convincing herself that she had been responsible for what had happened at the hotel, that night. But no, he chose to ignore her, and flirt with Sally, after he'd said it was all over between them. Then, what really made her snap, was the moment he went to put the necklace around Sally's neck, the same necklace he had placed on her, just the evening before. In Pauline's eyes, the necklace was a physical symbol of her relationship with Frank, and god help anyone who tries to undermine that. It was only in the cold light of day that Pauline had come to realise just how severe her retribution had been. Frank, with his scarred face would certainly find it hard to get another partner, or even a job, once he gets out of prison. That's where Pauline hoped to fit in. She had wanted to be his girlfriend next term, just like Sally was, but now all that had changed.

It said in the letter that she could appeal, but in her mind, the Dean's decision was final. The university would never back her if she refused to press charges against Frank, and they certainly didn't want all the negative publicity connected to the case. Pauline, like Frank had become an embarrassment, a liability that had to be removed as soon as possible. Besides, how could she ever face anyone again, after behaving in such a manner. She knew the Dean had made the correct decision, but how would her parents take it, especially after they had been so proud that she had managed to get to university in the first place. She had closed her eyes on the train, and hoped it was just an awful nightmare, and when she awoke, everything would be back to normal, but alas, that was not to be.

As Pauline turned into a slight bend she came face-to-face with a large, imposing mansion. This was it. Feeling totally overawed by the sheer size of Frank's home, she slowed her step as she neared the huge iron gates. They opened by themselves, as if by magic and she found herself venturing further inside. She looked around to see if there was any sign of the E-type Jaguar that Frank had driven her to the hotel in, but there was only his Ford Consul and a Mini parked outside.

Pauline noticed a curtain move, and thought she saw a face at the window. She gripped the handle of her bag tighter and felt her breathing go shallow. She thought about turning back, but no - she had to see him again, if he was there of course. Trying to think positive and banish the self doubts that kept entering her mind, Pauline tried to re-assure herself that it would be alright. She convinced herself that he wouldn't dare do anything crazy, not here, not at his own home.

The crunch from the gravel drive seemed to get louder as Pauline stepped into the porch, and up to the wood-panelled front door. She heard dogs barking, large dogs by the sound of them, and she swallowed hard, as the door opened before she had the chance to ring the chimes.

"If you're another reporter, I'm warning you now - I'll set the dogs on you. What do you want?"

Pauline was taken aback by the coldness of the woman standing in front of her, and was puzzled to be mistaken for a reporter.

"I've come to see Frank. My name's Pauline. I'm from the university. He may have mentioned me?"

The woman narrowed her eyes and studied the young female suspiciously.

"No he didn't mention you, and besides, he's not here. What's your business with him anyway?"

As Pauline looked closer, she noticed the woman had similar features to Frank, and assumed she was his mother. However, despite the woman's hostility, she was clearly distressed and looked like she didn't want to be disturbed.

"But he should be expecting me. I'm his girlfriend!" Replied Pauline, shocked by her own dishonesty.

The woman's jaw dropped in surprise, and she found herself inviting the visitor into the house.

Although reasonably well-dressed, Pauline felt distinctly scruffy and cheap as she sunk down into the soft, creaky leather settee.

Mrs. Irene Gant, to get over the shock of what she's just heard, went over to the cocktail cabinet and poured herself a glass of sherry. Pauline guessed she had poured herself quite a few in the past, judging by the woman's trembling hands.

The drawing room was large and airy, with an impressive collection of deadly-looking swords and shields from the middle ages adorning two of the walls. High up on the back wall, rifles and bayonets from later conflicts were exhibited in long, neat rows. These were mounted above a massive, gothic-style fireplace, that looked like it was made out of marble, and was the main focal point of the room. At each end, stood tall, potted plants, which helped soften the room somewhat, and added a much-needed feminine touch.

Irene, continued to scrutinize her guest in great detail.

"I wouldn't have thought you'd be Frank's type. He usually goes for blondes, you know - the more extrovert type. How long did you say you've been seeing him for?" She asked, before adding; "I'm sorry, I seem to have forgotten your name."

Pauline cleared her throat, before going on to tell further lies about her relationship with Frank.

"It's Pauline, Mrs. Gant. Well, you could say we've been close since October - that's when I first saw Frank at Falcondale."

Irene's limited response was to stroke an overweight Persian cat that had suddenly appeared by her side.

"So tell me, what do you know about all this dreadful business that's been going on, Pauline - are you involved too?"

"I don't quite follow you Mrs. Gant," replied Pauline sheepishly. "I've come to see Frank. Look, I've brought his suit jacket with me. He left it behind when we were out, having dinner. Will he be back soon?"

"You mean to tell me you don't know where he is!" Barked Irene angrily, causing the cat to leap in fear. "Either you're taking me for a fool young lady, or you're bloody naive. He's in jail! There's been enough reporters around here for the whole world to know." Irene got up abruptly and stormed off back to the cocktail cabinet.

There was a brief silence, until Pauline dared ask; "What's happened, why is he in jail?"

Irene turned and inhaled sharply, before lighting a cigarette.

"We had a call from the police, last weekend. He was arrested for attempted murder, breaking and entering, possession of a knife, rape - you bloody well name it, and there's more."

"I can't believe it - Frank would never do those things." Replied Pauline, acting innocent.

"They had to take him to hospital first, he'd been badly beaten up by local thugs. They must have slashed his face too - he has a terrible wound. The police then searched his room and found money, I mean lots of money, nearly £5000. Worst still, it was in a post office bag, and apparently the small sub post office in Falcondale had been robbed of a similar amount."

"Yes, I heard about the robbery, and the woman who ran the post office died of a heart attack, but I don't think she was at the scene." Replied Pauline, relieved that Irene wasn't aware that she had in fact slashed her son's face.

"It's dreadful. I know Frank can be bad at times, but not this?"

"I'm sure he didn't do any of it, Mrs. Gant. I expect we'll know the truth soon enough"

"The police came here and searched his room, they found drugs - you know that dope they all smoke these days. Drugs! In our house! Then they were asking about the robbery and this poor girl he's supposed to have attacked." Irene sat down heavily and took a large mouthful of the whiskey she had now poured.

Pauline was shocked, but offered a ray of hope.

"It's alright, Mrs. Gant - it was me. I'm the girl Frank was supposed to have attacked. We just had too much to drink, it was just a misunderstanding that's all. I haven't said anything to the police. They wont be able to do anything if I don't press charges."

Irene went pale and glared at Pauline, before demanding she tell her the whole story. Pauline then drew in a deep breath and began to relate the events at the hotel the week earlier. As she did so, Irene listened intently, never taking her eyes off the younger woman until she had finished. "When did you say you started at the university, Pauline?"

"Last October, Mrs. Gant. But why?"

"The attack on this other girl was before then, long before. No Pauline, you're wrong. Someone else has gone to the police."

Pauline, realising the implications, tried to be helpful.

"Surely Frank could fight it. He might even be able to get bail, and with a good solicitor, he..."

Irene rudely interrupted; "Listen, my husband is a respected surgeon, and is very well known around here. Mr. Gant sits on all sorts of committee's, do you realise that he's trying to be elected as a local Conservative Member of Parliament. Now all this adverse publicity will ruin him."

"But Frank might be innocent!" Exclaimed Pauline, naively.

"Yes, and pigs might fly!" Snapped Irene. "My husband was about to find the best lawyer money could buy, until he heard from the university that Frank had been expelled. He has completely washed his hands of him now. Mr. Gant wont stand bail for him, and wont even have him back in the house again. Frank has brought nothing but shame on this family, and to be perfectly honest, young lady, I don't think you're entirely blameless yourself. Now get out of my house."

As Pauline got up to leave, she had one last trick up her sleeve.

"I'm pregnant, Mrs. Gant, and Frank is the father."

Irene's jaw dropped, and she glared at Pauline, willing herself not to believe it.

"I've told you to get out of my house, you lying, manipulative creature."

"I'm sorry you don't believe me, but you'll find out soon enough!" As Pauline was about to slam the front door behind her, Irene called her back.

"One more thing, do you know anything about a necklace my son may have had?"

Pauline felt her face redden, "No, Mrs. Gant. I don't. But why do you ask?"

"I'm missing a very expensive Cartier necklace my husband brought for me on our twenty fifth wedding anniversary. I'm not saying Frank has taken it, but it just seems like too much of a coincidence. It has a single pearl, set in in an eagle's claw."

"I'm sorry, I can't help you."

Pauline was seething with anger by the time she reached the station. So it must have been Sally, or that weak-willed Karen who had gone to the police. She gritted her teeth, if she could love so intensely, then she could hate with an equal passion too.

She was going to wait for Frank. Now that he had nobody, she would be needed. She was going to stand by him, no matter what the consequences were. She would wait, and be there for him when he finally came out. It was important that they stand together and be counted. They had each other, even though Frank wasn't to know that yet.

She watched as the train approached, and thought back to how rude Irene had been to her. She then rubbed her belly, it was early days yet, but Pauline put it down to feminine intuition - Frank was going to be a father.

William, despite using all his strength struggled with the heavy suitcase, as he cautiously navigated a route down the staircase at Lloyd-Evans Hall. When he finally reached the bottom, Lizzie was there to kindly open the main door for him.

"I think that's everything," he said, somewhat relieved.

"I'm not so sure!" Added Sally, as she followed him down laden with assorted carrier bags.

Lizzie went over and helped her friend carry the bags out to Pamela's waiting car.

"I'm glad we're using Pamela's car and not mine," remarked Lizzie, her mood brighter than of late. "At least now I'll be able to bring a lot more stuff down, if Pamela drives me back."

"What sort of stuff?" Asked Sally.

"Oh, there's lots of things really. There's my record collection, my sewing machine - I can make clothes you know! What else, oh yes, I have one of those sit-under hair dryers you can use for perms. We can have so much fun next term, Sally!" Exclaimed Lizzie, excitedly, before stopping to think. "I've forgotten my vanity case, and oh yes, I've got your Christmas present upstairs too."

"Thanks for reminding me, I've got yours in my room." Called out Sally, as she followed her friend up the stairs once more.

"What's wrong with William, he seems a bit grumpy?"

"I really don't know," sighed Sally, "I'll ask him later, perhaps everything that's happened recently is taking its toll on him."

Lizzie stopped, and put her small case down.

"I think it's because you're going home for Christmas, and he'll miss you. That's what's wrong with your William!"

"Do you really think so?" Replied Sally, before adding; "I might not go home. The snow's coming and Mr. Meredith has said that any students worried about travelling can stay here over Christmas."

"Sally - you can't stay here over the holidays. It'll be so boring. No, I wont have it, you can come back with Pamela and myself."

"I wouldn't dream of it, Lizzie. You've got a lot of things to talk over with your father when you get home. I'll be fine here. Besides, I think staying on campus will be a hundred times better than going home to my parents."

"I'm sorry to hear that. But it's your decision, and if you change your mind, just ring me. I suppose you could always go and stay with William, since you've practically lived there for the last few days?"

"Yes, I suppose I could," said Sally, a little guardedly.

Lizzie burst out laughing, "You've got it all planned, haven't you, that's exactly what you're going to do isn't it? You scheming little mare!"

"Okay, I admit it," giggled Sally, "But keep your voice down, or he'll hear you."

"So, William is blissfully unaware that you're planning to spend Christmas with him? I would put him out of his misery ASAP, and then he might cheer up."

"His parents are due to come over anytime, and I'm a bit worried about meeting them - you know, first impressions etc. Plus they'll find out about all that business with Frank, and the police. They'll think I'm a bad influence on William."

"Nonsense, Sally, you are a warm, sensitive, and loving person. They will soon see that. Just tell the truth. Frank was the bad influence, not you."

"Yes, you're right, Lizzie."

"Sally, you know me, I'm always right!"

There was a sudden beep of a car horn sounding, and the two women knew it would be Pamela, anxious to get going before they were snowed in.

"See you next term Lizzie, I'll ring you, bye. Bye Pamela," called out Sally, sad to see her friend departing.

"Bye, happy Christmas, bye, William - and you take good care of Sally, not like that Frank, otherwise you'll have me to contend with!"

That was it, Lizzie had gone. Sally and William continued waving until the car was no longer in sight.

"Come on, let's go to Pedro's for a coffee." Suggested William.

"I had some in the cafe with Lizzie and Pamela. I saw you outside, why didn't you come in?" Asked Sally, intrigued.

"Not likely," he exclaimed, "You should have seen the state of you three when you came out. It looked like you'd been to a wake!"

Sally couldn't help laughing. "I'm so glad at the way it turned out for Lizzie. Come on then, let's go to Pedro's. I'll have a tea this time. Besides, there's something I want to ask you."

"Is there? Nothing bad I hope. There's something I want to ask you too."

"No, it's nothing bad, William. I'm curious to know what you want to ask me!"

Falcondale had become a hive of activity, with departing students saying their goodbyes, and parents, concerned about the weather, clogging up the town's narrow roads with their cars. Added to this were the panic shoppers, and farmers busy ferrying their sheep and livestock around. However, for the moment, they only had light sleet to contend with.

It was warm in Pedro's, and as Sally sat at a table, William ordered their drinks, along with a couple of fresh cream donuts he'd spied on the counter.

"You first," he said, taking a sip from his frothy coffee.

Sally hesitated, as she thought about how to phrase what she was going to ask him.

"Well, there's two things really," she said, pouring her tea into a floral-patterned cup and saucer. "Firstly, why have you been so down today, is it something I've said or done?"

"No, of course not," came the rapid reply. "Being with you, makes me happy," he smiled, "But I had hoped you wouldn't have noticed."

"William, I've been more intimate with you in the last week, than I have been with anyone before. Believe me, I noticed. So, what's bothering you? Perhaps, I can help."

He glanced around the room, and fiddled with a teaspoon, before answering Sally's question.

"Well, it's my parents. I got a telegram - they're not coming over this year."

"Oh William, I'm so sorry. I didn't think to ask. Is it due to the weather?"

He nodded, as he offered Sally one of the donuts.

"Not to worry, David and I will be okay. We'll get plenty of logs in, and it can't be that hard to cook a turkey?"

Sally took a bite of her donut, and squealed as the cream squirted out.

William couldn't help laughing, and passed her a serviette.

"So, what's the second thing, you wanted to ask me?"

Sally got her composure back, and licking the cream from her lips, continued.

"I don't want to go home for Christmas, William. I want to be with you. Now that your parents aren't coming, can I stay with you, and David?"

William broke into a huge smile, and lent across to remove a bit of cream she had missed.

"Sally, that's music to my ears, you've made my day. But what about your folks, wont they mind?"

"They wouldn't even miss me. In fact, when I rang home yesterday, my father even suggested I remain here."

"Maybe he's right. It's a big risk travelling at the moment. We had better go shopping. We'll need lots of things, lots of crumpets!"

"You and your crumpets, William Peddlescoombe! We'll definitely need a turkey though, and all the trimmings."

"Will you cook it for us, Sally?"

"Yes, William, of course I will. Now, finish your donut, I want to see you make a fool of yourself like I did!"

William grinned and did as he was told. "Yummy! This is absolutely delicious, and look - not a bit of mess!"

With that, Sally, took the remainder of her donut and rubbed it into William's face.

"There, that's for being too smart for your own good!"

William quickly responded, and within seconds, both of them were covered in cream and strawberry jam.

"Children! Children! please, I have other customers. Please behave yourselves!" Called over an irritated Pedro, from behind the counter.

They made their apologies and offered to clear up the mess they had made, before walking back along the high street again. William told Sally he kept a van in the garage back at home, which they could use for the shopping, and to bring a few things Sally might need from her room at Lloyd-Evans.

"Do you think your parents would mind me staying for Christmas?" She asked, putting up her umbrella.

"No, of course not. They've rented the house out to students in the past, so that wouldn't be a problem. In fact, it was something related to that, what I wanted to ask you."

They slowed their pace as they neared the gate-lodge. Several students were checking with the porters about the latest weather updates, and from where William and Sally were standing, it didn't sound good.

"Look, there's David and Jenny, shall we call them over?"

"Yes, in a moment," replied William, "Listen, Sally - I wanted to ask, if you fancied moving into the house permanently with David and I next term?"

Sally was quite surprised at this, and didn't quite know how to answer.

"I'm aware it's nearly 1963, William, but people will talk. I know I've been staying with you, but for us to live like husband and wife, well, we'd get kicked out of university."

"You're right, but I've thought of that. We have a spare room, so you could keep all your things in there. It would be your room. Then you wouldn't have to pay accommodation fees to the university. Think of all the money you would save, Sally."

"Gosh, that would be wonderful, so I would live there all official. But I would have to pay something?"

"Only a bit towards food and costs. The house is all paid for. My parents wouldn't ask you for any money. Please say you will, Sally. We can go and get your stuff before Christmas!"

"William! I don't know what to say. What about Lizzie?"

"You'll still see her, Lloyd-Evans is only ten minutes walk away."

"Okay, it's a deal - you've got a new housemate!"

With that, William scooped Sally up in his arms and twisted her around until they were both dizzy. "We can celebrate tonight. We can get some wine, and ask

Pedro to cook us something to take away."

David and Jenny then came over to enquire what all the excitement was about.

"Sally's going to move in with us, David, isn't it wonderful?"

David glanced over towards Sally, and couldn't help smiling at her.

"Really! What wonderful news. I can't wait. Welcome to the Peddlescoombe household, Sally!"

Jenny glanced disapprovingly at David.

"Don't you start getting any funny ideas."

David blushed and laughed it off, as he turned to his brother, "We've just been to see Meredith and asked if Jenny can stay on campus over Christmas. She's stranded. It's already snowing quite bad up north, and they're cancelling trains."

"So, what you're saying is, Jenny's going to join us for Christmas?" Asked William.

"If that's okay?"

"Of course it is, the more the merrier. Sally's going to cook the turkey for us!"

"I can cook too you know!" Remarked Jenny, darting a cold look in her rival's direction.

Sally couldn't believe the change that come over Falcondale during the Christmas break. She had been so used to the town being taken over by groups of noisy students, but now the streets were quiet in comparison. The dreaded snow, to everyone's relief had still not arrived, despite several days of oppressive dark, grey skies. There was still a bit of hustle and bustle, but it was mostly townsfolk going about their business as usual. The post office had reopened, following the robbery, and the death of Mrs. Davies. Now it was run by a couple, and new security measures had been put in place to combat the changing face of society. Two of the cafes, and a few of the shops, that mainly catered for students had closed until next term. Sally didn't exactly find the town depressing, but she was beginning to appreciate the life and soul the students brought to the community in general, and she began to look forward to the coming term, and of course, seeing Lizzie again. She had telephoned her from William's house on Christmas Eve, and was pleased to hear that she had patched things up with her adopted father, and Pamela was starting to visit regularly again, despite Janice's protestations.

Christmas had been interesting with William, David and his new girlfriend, Jenny all at the house together. Although Jenny seemed sociable enough, Sally felt a certain undercurrent of hostility emanating from her. Sally couldn't quite put her finger on it, but she suspected it was born out of jealousy, either because of how well she got on with David, or it was because of her looks, dare she admit it.

With her shoulder-length, mousy hair and engaging smile, Jenny could be described as reasonably pretty. She was very short, had expressive grey eyes, and a curvaceous figure, but she didn't make the most of her looks, and tended to dress rather drably. Sally wondered what the attraction was for David, there didn't seem any obvious connection and they certainly didn't study the same subjects. Maybe they met through one of the societies, she thought. Sally was curious, but knew she'd have to wait to find out.

William had suggested going to Aberystwyth to do the Christmas shopping, and Sally had leapt at the chance to go with him. He had charged up the battery on the old Morris Minor van, earlier that morning and let the engine run for a while to warm it up, before they headed off for their little adventure. It made a wonderful change to see another town, go into different shops, and most importantly, to see the sea. It was cloudy and bitterly cold, but Sally loved walking along the windswept beach, arm-in-arm with William. The trip did them both good to get away from Falcondale, even if it was just for a day.

The van was laden with Christmas goodies by the time they got back, and the house looked wonderfully festive and inviting, with the tree and fairy lights all glittering to add to the joyous atmosphere.

Once they had put everything away, Sally made an excuse to go back to Lloyd-Evans to get something she had left behind, but in reality she had brought presents for William, David and even something for Jenny to open. She had brought William a new fishing jumper, to replace his old threadbare one. It was a glorious royal blue, and much more jolly. She promptly wrapped the jumper, added a tag and placed it into her holdall, before starting on David's gift. This was an attractive maroon and dark blue, paisley-style, silk tie. Unlike William, who tended to dress scruffily, David often wore a collar and tie beneath his sweaters. The ties he chose though were usually very plain and dated, and Sally believed the one thing David lacked in life was colour. For Jenny, she had brought her a box of assorted bubble baths. They smelt divine, and Sally would often use them herself. Once all the wrapping was done, she had a final glance around her room. She had hated it last October, when she first arrived at Falcondale. She smiled as she recalled the first time she met Lizzie, when the outlandish student appeared at her door, sporting the biggest beehive she had ever seen! They had then gone on a pub crawl around town with a few of the others, and had remained the best of friends ever since.

Sally picked up the beautifully-wrapped present Lizzie had given her, just before she had left, and wondered what it was. It rattled, and was probably something hugely expensive knowing Lizzie. She suddenly felt a little embarrassed knowing she had brought Lizzie a set of heated rollers for her hair. But then, that's what Lizzie said she wanted.

Back at William's house, Christmas Eve was probably the most memorable day. A few of the other students who had decided to remain on campus came over, and an impromptu party started, with the record player coming out and a dancing contest taking place, which Sally won hands down.

David and Jenny cut up several French sticks they had managed to get from the baker's and put out crisps, nuts, a selection of cheese, and some ham for the guests. However, the food all seemed to get eaten within the first hour, but still, everyone appeared to enjoy themselves.

A bit later in the evening, Sally noticed that David had drunk a little too much, and was showing off. She remembered what William had said about his behaviour, but now she was seeing it first hand. She actually had to ask William to stop David at one stage, as she feared he might injure himself. He had got hold of a sharp kitchen knife and had placed his palm flat against a table, and was stabbing between his splayed fingers at a very fast rate. Some of the other guests looked on fascinated, but a few of them, like Sally couldn't bear to watch.

"Why did you stop my fun, Sally?" Asked David, his speech slurred.

"It's obvious, I didn't want to see you hurting yourself, especially after you've been drinking."

"Who are you, his mum?" Laughed Jenny, but Sally noticed the bitchy tone in her voice.

Sally was up early on a bitterly cold Christmas Day. She was sharing William's room, but her clothes and belongings were stored in the spare room, just to keep things above board, in case the nosey Nancy started snooping. She glanced down at the sleeping William, and wanted to wake him, just to wish him a happy Christmas, but he looked so serene, lying there, flat out and gently snoring. She kissed him on the cheek, then grabbed his dressing gown and tiptoed downstairs. She wanted to get the turkey prepared, then peel and chop the vegetables, ready for lunchtime. As she reached the bottom of the stairs she heard activity, and the smell of cooking coming from the kitchen. Opening the door, she was surprised to see Jenny working away, peeling potatoes.

"Good morning, Sally, happy Christmas," said Jenny cheerily. "There's a fresh pot of tea on the stove."

"Thank-you, Jenny, and happy Christmas to you." Sally glanced around and noticed Jenny had already done the carrots, parsnips, and shelled the peas. It looked as if she'd even made a start on the stuffing too.

"You didn't have to get up early and do all this, Jenny. I told William, I'd cook Christmas lunch."

Jenny put down the potato she was peeling, "It's okay, I'm used to cooking big meals. I come from a large family, and I'm always helping my mother."

"Well, alright, as long as you know what you're doing, I'll keep out." Replied Sally, a little disappointed. She went over to the stove to pour herself a cup of tea and noticed the oven was already turned on.

"So you've already put the turkey in the oven, Jenny?"

"Yes, everything's all under control, so there's not a great deal you can do, Sally. Just put your feet up, and take it easy."

"But you haven't put the stuffing in yet? Did you baste the turkey, and take the giblets out?"

"Oh, I'll do that later," replied Jenny, going slightly red. "Look, if you want to help, Sally - there's still some clearing up to do in the front room. I've done in here."

Sally felt like she was going to explode, and marched into the front room to get away from Jenny, before she said something she might regret. She had been so looking forward to spending Christmas with William and David, just the three of them. She wanted to cook them a lovely lunch, give them their presents and have both brothers to herself for a few days. Now, Jenny was on the scene, and seemed to be determined to take over Sally's role.

"Something smells nice!" Yawned David, as he came down the stairs, hair slightly bedraggled and dressed in customary shirt and tie.

"It's your Christmas lunch, David. Jenny kindly volunteered to cook it, still with the giblets inside!" Replied Sally, unable to contain herself anymore.

David started laughing, as he went over to one of the kitchen cabinets.

"That's my girl! Gosh, I need some aspirin - my head's pounding!"

Sally then took William up a cup of tea, a glass of water, and a Beecham's powder.

"I think I'm dying," he groaned, downing the Beecham's in one. "It was a damned good night though. You're really quite a dancer, Sally, much better than me!"

"You're not so bad yourself," she replied, sliding back into bed, next to him.

They lay together for several minutes, smooching and cuddling up, before hearing the sound of pots and pans clattering, and a few expletives being muttered.

"What on earth's going on downstairs?" Asked William, sitting up and reaching for his tea.

"That's what I need to talk to you about. Jenny has started cooking lunch, but I don't think she has a clue what she's doing."

"But I thought you were cooking lunch?"

"Yes, so did I, until little Miss Giblets got involved!"

William couldn't help laughing. "What do you mean?"

"I'll tell you what I mean - she's gone and put the turkey in the oven, without basting it, without the stuffing, and without removing the giblets!"

"Oh, crikey! It's going to be a disaster isn't it?"

"Yes, William it is, but David is down there now, helping her. I'm just a guest, I don't want to cause a row."

"David's there too? It'll be more than a disaster! Leave it to me, I'll go and have a word with them." Said William, leaping out of bed.

"Okay, but do it diplomatically, old giblet features has got it in for me!"

"You have my word on it," replied, William grabbing his trousers to go downstairs.

The Christmas lunch was rescued, Jenny was demoted to desserts, and Sally turned a near-disaster into a mouth-watering victory, utilizing her exceptional, cookery and domestic science skills.

William, to make up for the inevitable delay, prepared a wonderful, if somewhat un-festive starter of hummus, taramasalata, mixed olives and pitta bread, all courtesy of Pedro's of course. This was later followed by Sally's butter-basted turkey, complimented by pigs-in-blankets, sausage, apricot and chestnut stuffing, roast potatoes cooked in goose fat, peas, parsnips and carrots. However, to add a Welsh flavour, and to both William and David's delight, Sally also added a dish of locally-grown leeks, which she served with bacon and mushrooms.

The wine flowed freely and the four students amused themselves by clowning around and doing impersonations of various members of the university staff. William's impression of Mr. Meredith, had them all in hoots of laughter, with even Jenny finding it hysterical.

"I will not tolerate any lewd, drunken or foul-mouthed behaviour in my university!" He mimicked, balancing somewhat unsteadily on a chair. "Now, Jane, sober up, and get your bloody clothes off, we've got important university business to catch up on!"

Now it was Jenny's turn to shine and Sally had to bite her tongue as her culinary rival managed to produce a delicious sherry trifle topped with thick custard and lashings of double cream.

"Don't worry, Sally, we'll save some room for your lovely Christmas pudding later on, after the charades," groaned, William, rubbing his stomach.

After a boisterous cracker-pulling session, they sat back on the easy chairs and began to open their presents. William and David were delighted with Sally's gifts and eagerly tried them on, much to the annoyance of Jenny, who had to do a last-minute shopping dash, and on very limited funds.

"Wow thanks, Jenny, we can open this tomorrow," grinned David, pleased with the bottle of claret that Jenny had brought for him. William got the same, and he too appeared to appreciate his gift. Jenny, in return, got lavender bath salts from David, and a box of dates from William. If Jenny was disappointed, then she did a wonderful job disguising it. Sally also got the bath salts from David, and a pair of pretty gold earrings from William. However, not expecting anything from Jenny, she was quite surprised when she peeled off the wrapping paper to find she had given her a cheap, garish lipstick!

"I'm so sorry, Sally. The shops were closing, and I had to make a quick decision!" Blurted out, Jenny, feeling rather embarrassed.

"It's the thought that counts!" Laughed Sally, "Don't worry, It'll be put to good use!"

As the afternoon progressed, David became noticeably more withdrawn. Sally just put it down to last night's lingering hangover, and having eaten too much, but William later told her, it was typical of his brother's mood swings. Shortly after this, David went out to chop some wood, and the two girls began clearing the table. It was when they were both alone in the kitchen that Sally decided to ask Jenny what the problem was.

"I don't really have an issue with you now, Sally, as I've got to know you a little bit better. But yourself and Lizzie did have quite a reputation as being the 'fun' girls of the campus. Because you were seeing Frank, everyone became rather wary of you."

"I'm sorry, Jenny, I didn't realise - that's awful," replied, Sally, scraping some leftovers into the bin.

"Then it turned nasty with Frank, and you started seeing William. Well, it was like you could just have all the best-looking boys whenever you wanted them."

Sally was very shocked by this, and had to stop what she was doing.

"No, Jenny, it wasn't anything like that."

"Then, when you started flirting with David, I thought you were going to take him as well."

"Flirting with David?" Sally was dumbfounded, and turned to face Jenny. "What on earth are you insinuating? I'm seeing William!"

"Oh come on Sally, don't try and fool me. I've seen the way you and David look at each other. I'm not blonde and beautiful like you, but I felt that David and I had something special going on, that's until you dug your claws in."

"Jenny, please - I can assure you I've got no interest in David, he's William's brother, and yes, we do get on well together, but that's all it is."

"Are you telling me the truth, Sally? I know you could take him away from me with just a flick of your eyelashes."

"It's the truth, Jenny. Now, enough of this nonsense." Demanded Sally, feeling guilty, and beginning to go red.

After that, things between the two women, continued to be a little tense. William and David even noticed there was a certain degree of rivalry between them, but thought it best not to get involved.

Jenny, however, only stayed at the house Christmas Eve and Christmas night, choosing instead, to return to her room at Lloyd-Evans. This came as a welcome relief to Sally, and she found she could relax more without Jenny watching her every move. Sally couldn't quite work out though, if Jenny had left because of her, or if it had been due to David's continued low mood. However, Jenny was expected back over on New Year's Eve, and Sally decided to try and get along with her for everyone's sake.

On Boxing Day, the weather predictions were proved correct. A heavy blanket of snow lay over Falcondale, and more was on the way. The snow and blizzards of winter 1962-63 was one of the severest on record. It cut off communities, brought down power lines, halted train services and flights, and caused massive disruption to practically every aspect of life. The bitter conditions would last well into early March and effected most parts of England and Wales.

The four students opted to celebrate the arrival of the new year at the Black Lion in town. Many of the locals were there, and compared to student nights, the evening appeared to be quite subdued. The constant snow falls had made people downcast, and wary of celebrating what the future may have in store for them. However, in true community spirit they managed to sing, dance and join in Auld Lang Syne as the whole pub hugged, kissed, shook hands and patted each other on the back. It was only Sally and William though, who finally took the plunge and joined in the conga. David and Jenny left shortly after this, and trudged back holding hands in silence.

On New Year's Day, Sally and William went outside to frolic and throw snowballs, even Jenny came out and joined in the fun for a while, but there was no sign of David. Later that afternoon, after a lunch of cold meats, salad and pickles, he put on his coat and announced he was going for a walk. William insisted on washing up the dishes, before practising on his guitar, and surprisingly, Jenny also volunteered to help. Sally sat down by the dying fire and thought about Lizzie. She wanted to chat with her friend, and decided to phone her that evening, providing the phone lines were still intact. She sat back and allowed herself to be serenaded by the distant sound of William's playing. It was a relaxing romantic, Spanish piece, and it gave her a few precious moments to gather her thoughts and to reflect. However, after a few more minutes, she really felt the temperature drop, and noticed the fire had practically gone out. The logs had all been used up, and not wanting to bother William, she put on her coat, picked up the basket and headed off outside. Her Wellington boots made deep tracks in the fresh snow, as she made her way towards the shed, where the logs were kept. As she pulled up the hood on her coat, to keep out the chill, she noticed, David. He had cleared the snow from a circular seat at the base of a tree, just near the end of the orchard. He must be frozen sitting down there all on his own, she thought, putting the basket down.

"David, are you alright? Aren't you cold?" She asked, sitting down next to him.

He looked up at her, half smiled and shook his head. "I'm fine. Please don't concern yourself about me, Sally."

"But I do, David, I know what happened when you went ice fishing. William told me, I hope you don't mind?"

He looked out across the field opposite, his eyes red and damp from both the tears, and the cold.

"The snow, the cold, the winter, Sally - it all makes me sad. Sometimes, I wish I could forget, but it wont let me."

Sally followed his gaze, thinking over what he'd said.

"You can never forget something like that, David. I think you have to learn to live with it, learn to accept it, and understand that it was a tragic accident, beyond your control."

"He was just a kid, with so much to look forward to."

"I know he was, David. Please don't be so hard on yourself. You're a kind and wonderful person, and you can do a lot of good in the world."

He turned to face her, wiping away a tear, with his handkerchief.

"I love your way with words, Sally. It's so comforting."

"Please come inside, David. William and Jenny care for you so much, and don't want to see you sad."

They both stood up, facing each other.

"Jenny doesn't know, does she?"

"No, David, it'll be our secret."

"Do you care for me, Sally?"

The question took her by surprise, and Sally had to be careful with her answer.

"Yes, David, of course I care for you. I want to help you."

"You already have, Sally."

She then took David's handkerchief, and began gently dabbing away his teardrops.

"Come, on lets go inside," she smiled, reaching out for his hand.

Almost at once, they kissed. It was only a fleeting kiss between two friends, lasting mere seconds, but the intensity of it surged through both of them like a bolt of lightening. Sally immediately pulled away, but as she did, she heard William calling her name. She turned and looked, feeling her heart drop to the floor, as she saw him standing there watching, pain etched deep into his face. Jenny was beside him, clutching logs for the fire. She let them fall from her arms, turned and stormed back into the house, stopping briefly to collect her few things, before returning to Lloyd-Evans House.

"I can explain, William, it wasn't how it looked."

"How was it then Sally, you tell me?"

"David was upset, I just went to help him, that's all."

William didn't answer, but went back inside, put on his duffle coat and left the house also. David, meanwhile, went up to his room, locked the door, and didn't say another word.

It dawned on Sally, that it just wouldn't work, living here with the two brothers. Things were just too intense, and a certain invisible barrier had now been crossed. She couldn't put the clock back and began to pack, before lugging not only her case, but her heavy heart, out into the snow.

10. THE LAKE

Frank looked into the bathroom mirror and ran his finger along the length of the scar running down the left side of his face. It was about three inches long and had an angry, purplish, red hue to it. He had lost over two pints of blood and needed stitches following the events of the Christmas Dinner and Dance. The doctor at the hospital told him, if he had been out in the cold for just a couple of minutes longer, he would have died. Frank had also been told that a young woman, called Pauline had come to his aid, kept him warm, and had ultimately saved his life. Frank, however, dismissed this, as he had other things on his mind. He had also suffered a couple of broken ribs, plus extensive bruising, following the attack by Carol's family. He wanted revenge on Pauline for scarring him, like he wanted revenge on Sally for not backing up his story, when Pauline had accused him of rape. But that wasn't so important now, since he had learnt she wasn't going to press charges. He wanted revenge on William, for taking his woman and stealing the necklace, and revenge on his stupid, confused brother for hitting him with a poker. But it would all have to wait. The scar was healing, and the bruises had gone, but the pain from his ribs still made him wince as he reached up to continue shaving.

Frank's father, Hugh had reluctantly agreed to stand bail for his youngest son, after initially refusing point blank. It had been Frank's mother who had beseeched, begged, and finally threatened to leave him, if he didn't put up the money and hire a lawyer for Frank. Whether it had been out of a mother's love for her wayward, disfigured son, or Pauline's disclosure that she was carrying Frank's child, no-one would ever know.

Now, Frank was back home in the bosom of his family, fearfully awaiting his upcoming trial. To say he was jittery about it would be an understatement. If it went badly, he could end up going to prison for a considerable time. Of the cases against him, the attempted murder of William and Sally were the most serious. Next came the robbery of the Falcondale sub post office, and lastly, but no less serious - the alleged rape of the student, Karen. The thought of spending his life behind bars filled Frank with utter dread. It was bad enough getting thrown out of university before taking his finals, and having to own up to his mother that he had taken her best necklace, just to seduce a girl.

Hugh Gant, under pressure from his wife had hired the best lawyer money could find, and eagerly paced the drawing room waiting for Duncan Fraser to arrive.

"Is that parasite out of the bathroom yet?" He called to Irene. "This damned lawyer, for all the good he can do, will be here at any time."

Irene ran up the stairs, and knocked hard on the bathroom door, imploring Frank to hurry up. Since his arrest, Frank's father couldn't even bear to speak to him, for bringing such disgrace on the family, and used Irene as a go-between. The injuries Frank had received and the appalling cut to his face, had been more than enough to bring out the maternal instincts in his mother. Eventually, Frank sauntered down, and tentatively made his way into the drawing room.

"Frank, this is Mr. Fraser, who'll be representing you in court."

Frank greeted the middle-aged, balding man and shook his hand. He was an ugly-looking character, short and stocky, with a large nose and wearing thick spectacles. Scrutinising the lawyer, Frank wondered how on earth this chap could ever be considered the best.

"Sit down Frank, we need to go over a few things." Said Frazer, in a surprisingly, deep and authoritative, Edinburgh accent. "I've been looking over your case notes, and I'm very confident I can get you off every charge. How does that sound?"

Frank was taken aback, and glanced at his father.

"Impossible!" Boomed Hugh, "You mean you can get my son cleared of attempted murder, robbery and rape?"

Frazer, spent a moment weighing up both father and son, before carefully removing his spectacles. "Yes, that's what I said, Mr. Gant. I can get him cleared of everything."

"Every charge?" Butted in Frank.

"Every charge," replied Frazer, opening his briefcase and taking out some papers. "Now, in order for me to do this, I need to go through all of the charges. But first tell me what happened with Pauline chater."

"Well, I can't remember much, I'd been drinking all day!" Grinned Frank, reclining back in his chair. "Ruined a damned good night, that bloody Pauline!"

Frank's dialogue was brought to a halt by Frazer's fist slamming down noisily onto the table.

"Now, you listen here, you ignorant young oaf. I couldn't care less if they hung, drawn and quartered you at Tyburn, or beheaded you at the Tower of London," shouted the lawyer, glaring at Frank, with piercing, grey eyes. "Your father has paid good money to get you the best representation. You will give me the respect I deserve, or you can find someone else. Do I make myself clear?"

Frank was shaken by the small man's ferocity, and answered back immediately.

"Yes, Mr. Fraser, you have made yourself very clear."

"Good, now let's get down to work."

It was March, and the last remnants of the winter snow had finally disappeared. It cheered Sally's heart to see daffodils growing around the campus, and the sound of birdsong in the spring air.

The final few days of the Christmas break had been mind numbingly long and boring. Sally had even tried to patch things up with Jenny, but the wronged student wouldn't even acknowledge her, let alone open her door. Now, for Sally, it came as a great relief to eventually see the familiar faces of the returning students, and life on campus getting back to normality.

Lizzie had arrived back, all bright-eyed and optimistic, and Sally made them both a coffee, and told her about the disastrous events at William's house.

"There always a drama in your life, Sally? Why can't you just be like me, and live a normal, quiet existence! I'm sure he'll come running back to you, with his tail between his legs."

Lizzie's sense of humour and light-hearted approach to life made Sally feel better about things, and she was glad to have her friend back at long last. Lizzie told her all the news from home, how her mother, Pamela, was getting back with Edward again, and how Janice and Graham had to accept it. Bobby, Lizzie's little brother had also returned home, along with the family dog. It was all so uplifting, after the distressing times Sally had gone through, first with Frank, then the misunderstanding at William's house. One regret, Sally did have, was not being able to attend Margaret's funeral. Lizzie was very understanding though, since most of the country had ground to a virtual standstill during the bad weather.

Sally's relationship with Lizzie on campus, never returned to how it was. Lizzie somehow had changed. Even her style of dress was now toned down and very conventional in comparison. But more surprisingly, she had become very studious, and now attended all her lectures and seminars, putting the average student to shame.

Much to Sally's surprise, Lizzie also started seeing Ken again. Both he and Frank's court case was still pending, but Ken had miraculously survived being kicked out of the university. Now, seemingly he had seen the error of his ways, and he too was actually getting down to some hard work. Without Frank's influence, he had become much more cordial, and like Lizzie, was dressing in a more conservative manner.

Once again the student's club, along with the various pubs and cafe's were all busy with young people, their grants topped up, and looking forward to the coming of warmer weather. Sally was bored, so taking a leaf out of Lizzie's book, she buried herself into her studies. Last October, everything seemed so promising, it was all so new and waiting to be explored, now her life seemed so empty and desolate. She missed William desperately, and dare she admit it, missed David too. She thought she may have seen them around campus, being that Falcondale wasn't a large university by any means. But nothing, it was so strange, like they had just disappeared off the planet. She had been to the library, a favourite haunt of William's on several occasions, and had asked the staff if they had seen him, but alas, none had. She had even tried to write a letter to him, explaining the misunderstanding about kissing David, and how sorry she was, but each time she finished the letter, she tore it up, and threw it in the bin.

One morning, following yet another restless night, Sally had got up early, showered, washed her hair and had gone over to the post room, prior to attending a lecture. She had completed all her assignments for the ancient Greek element of her course, and it was now the turn of the Romans, in particular, the Augustan age. She had tried unsuccessfully to get books from the library on the subject, it seemed everyone else in her group were doing the same thing. Her thoughts turned once more to William, and how he had helped her with an earlier seminar. She wished her gallant knight on a charger was around now, to help her in her hour of need. Checking through the mail, she found a letter from her parents, an official-looking envelope, she didn't like the look of, and a note from the library about some overdue books. Returning to her room, she searched high and low for the books, before realising they could be at William's house. She then opened the letter from home, it was from her mother, saying how much they missed her over Christmas, and how bad the weather had been etc. Her father had been ill with a cold, so didn't fully indulge in the festivities, but had managed to lose several pounds of weight in the process, not that he was particularly overweight in the first place. Enclosed with the letter was a cheque for £100, which delighted Sally and made her immediately think about what she could spend it on. Lastly, she picked up the remaining letter, and eyed it suspiciously, it had her full name and address at the campus, typed out to perfection in chilling detail. She took the letter and went to sit on her bed. It was what she had been expecting, her worst nightmare confirmed. It was the letter summoning her to testify at Crown Court. She felt herself start to tremble, as her thoughts returned to that terrifying night. It had started as such a beautiful, surreal experience to sleep with William, then lie in his arms, and blissfully fall asleep. But almost without warning, that magical moment had been violated and shattered into a million pieces. Sally recalled Frank's bloodied face leering at her, like some grotesque devil. She quickly put the letter back in its envelope, and locked her door. She searched under the bed, and looked inside the wardrobe, her ears alert to every sound, petrified that Frank may be lying in wait for her. With her lecture forgotten, she hid herself under the eiderdown, recalling how Frank had threatened her, and said how he'd cut William's throat. Her blue eyes welled up, and she sobbed, fearful of seeing his face again.

She must have fallen asleep, as she was startled by someone tapping the door. To her relief, she immediately recognised Lizzie's familiar voice.

"Hi, Sally, darling, we haven't seen much of each other lately?" Chirped Lizzie, "Are you alright, you look as if you've been crying, you poor thing, what's up?"

"Nothing, it's okay. I just had a headache and went back to bed."

"I think you've been overdoing it. Ken and I are off to the cinema - Lawrence of Arabia is showing at the Odeon, do you want to come with us? Peter O'Toole's starring in it!"

Sally couldn't bear the thought of sitting for three or more hours in a cinema playing gooseberry to the loved-up, Lizzie and the now, whiter-than-white, Ken.

"I'm sorry, Lizzie, I'm not feeling so great. Perhaps, another time?"

As soon as Lizzie had gone, Sally locked the door again, and buried herself back beneath her bed covers. She didn't know if the tears she shed that day, were for William, or for having to attend Frank's trial.

Fraser was as good as his word, within five minutes of taking the stand, Karen had broken down, and the judge had to order a temporary halt in the proceedings, while the frightened student regained her composure.

Fraser, meanwhile consulted his notes until Karen was ready to take the stand again. The courtroom was claustrophobic and smelt official. It was devoid of windows, with dark wood panelling around the walls, and rows of benches located in the centre. There were separate tables for the prosecution, defence and court officials.

"If the young lady has recovered, you may proceed, Mr. Fraser," instructed the solemn-looking, grey-haired judge, as he spoke from behind a large desk.

"So, Miss Clarke, we have already established that you had a keen interest in my client," continued the lawyer, resuming his predatory stance. "The court is also aware that you willingly smuggled Mr. Gant into your room at the university, got drunk and consented to sexual intercourse with him. Is that correct too?"

It was horrific to watch, and Sally had to sit in silence, dreading when it would be her turn, as Fraser destroyed Karen's feeble defence with clinical efficiency. He had ingeniously made out Frank to be a respected son of an eminent surgeon, embarking on a course of formal study, only to be pursued and seduced by a wanton, manipulative female, seeking to enhance her social standing.

"No, it's not true. He raped me!" Pleaded Karen, her voice barely audible. "I told him no. I had the bruises to prove it. I couldn't leave my room for fear of seeing him again."

"Nonsense!" Replied Fraser, looking her straight in the eye. "If that were the case, why didn't you report it at the time?"

Karen, visibly shaking, couldn't bear the intense scrutiny, and dropped her gaze, as Frank leered at her from across the court.

"I was too ashamed."

"Speak up, girl, the court can't hear you," ordered the judge, peering over his horn-rimmed spectacles.

"I was too ashamed," repeated Karen, forcing herself to speak louder.

"Too ashamed?" Shouted Fraser, sensing an easy victory. "You weren't ashamed at all. You had successfully snared this unsuspecting, respectable young man into your sordid web of deceit. You seduced him, to forward your own ends. Then, when he no longer showed you any interest, you bided your time and waited for an opportunity to kick him when he was down. Isn't that right, Miss Clarke?"

Karen was no longer able to continue and the jury were later to return a verdict of not guilty.

Sally felt she was about to vomit, as her name was called out. She had chosen not to say anything to her parents, and instead, accepted the support Mr. Meredith had offered. Lizzie, to her credit had also volunteered to help, and drive Sally to the Crown Court, but she declined, not wanting to get her friend involved. Besides, Sally didn't know how long the case would last, and felt Lizzie would prove too much of an emotional drain on her.

As Sally waited, she discreetly scanned the courtroom, looking for William. She briefly recalled how he had led her to safety when Pauline was running amok in the assembly hall, and how they had danced together as the snow began to fall. She tried to remember the song that had been playing, when he had held her in his arms.

"Would Miss Sally Mary Carlington please take the stand."

Sally's daydream was brought to an abrupt halt. She felt her legs go weak, as she stepped up to take her place on the stand. It was then, that she looked down and noticed what looked like, a pool of Karen's urine around her feet. Her heart bled for the poor girl and the ordeal she had just been through. Sally however, couldn't bring herself to put Karen through any more humiliation and torment, and said her oath, as if nothing were amiss. She then stood motionless as Fraser eyed her from where he was sitting. He made a couple of comments on a sheet of paper, before striding up to face her. He had piggish, bloodshot eyes that bored into her, making her feel guilty before the questions had even started. Already, she felt tearful, and urged herself not to crack under the strain.

"Miss Carlington, am I right in believing that you had a romantic attachment with the accused?"

"Yes, I suppose I did," replied Sally, surprised at how confident and loud her voice actually was.

Fraser narrowed his eyes, but continued his full-on stare.

"There's nothing to suppose about it, either you did or you didn't. Please answer the question."

Fraser's aggression intimidated her, but she was determined not to quake under his onslaught as easily as Karen had.

"Yes, I did have a romantic attachment with him, if that's how you want to put it."

"Were you still in this relationship when Mr. Gant was attacked in the assembly hall and was seriously injured?"

"Yes, I was," replied Sally, unsure where this was heading.

"Did you try to help him in any way?"

"No, I couldn't, it all happened so quickly."

"Were you still in this relationship when Mr. Gant came to William Peddlescoombe's house and found you naked, with that same person?"

Sally struggled to get her breath, "Yes, I was - but it wasn't like that. You don't understand."

"Just answer yes, or no to the question, Miss Carlington."

"Yes," said Sally, and like Karen, her voice was barely audible.

"Why do you think my client came to William Peddlescoombe's house that night, bearing in mind he had just been glassed in the face and beaten up?"

"I'm not really sure, to get me, I think. He had made horrible threats to hurt me."

"I'll tell you why Frank Gant went to Peddlescoombe's house that night. It was because he loved you, Miss Carlington, and wanted to make sure you were safe. He also wanted to show how much he loved you, by giving you an expensive necklace. Is that true?"

"I don't know why he came," replied Sally, her voice emotional. "Yes, he did try to give me a necklace."

"Frank didn't come to hurt you that night. He was injured, he was scared, he was confused. But above all, he was worried about the girl he loved. He was also worried about the necklace he had misplaced. He needed help, Miss Carlington, in his hour of need, but you didn't give him any help, did you?"

"I was scared, he was attacking William."

"Attacking William indeed. The man was half dead, and bleeding profusely. Why didn't you help him? Why didn't you at least call an ambulance? Why did you just go off and have casual sex with another man?"

"Stop! Stop!" Cried out Sally, tears streaming down her face. "You don't understand!"

"I understand perfectly, Miss Carlington. You were caught in a compromising situation with William Peddlescoombe, and he, along with his brother chose to attack a defenceless, wounded man. Is that true?"

"No, it's not!" Screamed Sally, losing control. "He had a knife, he was going to kill us all!"

There followed a scuffle and raised voices, as she heard William's voice calling her. Turning around, she saw him. He looked back at her and she could see the pain in his eyes, as he was being restrained.

"Be strong Sally, you can do it. I love you!"

The judge brought the hammer down with frightening force.

"Young man! I'll have you tried for contempt of court if there's another outburst. Do I make myself clear?"

"Yes, your honour, I'm sorry," shouted back William defiantly. "But how can you allow this type of questioning, you saw what he did to the last girl, now he's doing the same to Sally?"

"I will remind you one last time to be quiet, or you'll be taken to the cells."

William had to sit back down, but managed to look over at Sally once more. She returned his glance, and was heartened by his display of gallantry, but she was shocked by his last three words. Did he really say, he loved her?

"Frank Gant was in no position to kill anyone," continued the lawyer, moving in for the kill. "Miss Carlington, please pay attention, this is a court of law, I'll have you know. I think it more likely you and your partners in crime were trying to kill him, after he had found you out. That's the truth, isn't it?"

"No, it's not the truth, I will not be bullied by you, Mr. Fraser. I think you're the one who needs to pay attention!"

To the dismay of the judge, a couple of cheers went up, along with the sound of someone clapping, as Fraser indicated that he had no more questions. Sally was more than relieved to return to her seat, next to Meredith and Jane. The case had not gone as she had expected, and the vile, cunning Fraser had managed to make her, as he did Karen, look no more than a conniving, cheap slut. It was then, as she was wiping the tears from her eyes, she heard William's name being called out.

"William Bradley Peddlescoombe, please take the stand."

Sally's heart jumped as she saw the familiar, lean figure walk confidently up to take his place. She noticed he looked a lot thinner, and possibly even a little gaunt. But despite his recent self neglect, he still cut a good figure of a man, dressed in his smartest suit.

As William awaited a similar fate, he glanced around, and again, his eyes met Sally's. He had wanted to go to her, to protect her during the horrendous ordeal at the hands of Fraser. He gazed into her eyes, and noticed how her usually, perfectly-applied make-up had been smudged during her one-sided battle with the callous lawyer. She attempted a smile, but thought better of it, William knew she was there in spirit for him, willing him on to see justice done.

He met Fraser's stare head on, and returned it unflinchingly.

"So, Mr. Peddlescoombe, please tell the court how you came to meet Miss Carlington."

William, speaking confidently, answered the question, describing how he had first met, and first spoke to Sally in the library.

"Did you know Miss Carlington was already in a relationship with Mr. Gant?"

"Yes, I did know."

"So obviously that didn't bother a person like you, who steals other men's women, and come to think of it, steals other men's property too."

"If you're referring to Frank Gant, then I can say categorically that the man is a womanizer, a drunk, a thief, and a charlatan."

"Please confine yourself to the questions, Mr. Peddlescoombe. I will not have my client slandered in this manner."

"No, it didn't bother me that Sally was seeing Gant. I wanted to get her away from him. I'd seen him hurt too many other girls in the past."

"Indeed." Replied Fraser, eyeing William like a hawk. "Well, a fine job you made of it. Bedding her, the night my client intended to profess his love for Miss Carlington, and you speak of womanizing!"

William hung his head in shame, as Sally buried her face in her hands.

"It wasn't like that."

"Wasn't it? Now tell the court if you are still in a relationship with Miss Carlington."

William looked over at Sally, unsure what to say.

"No, we aren't in a relationship any longer."

"Why is that? Mr. Peddlescoombe."

William looked down, choosing not to answer the question.

"May I remind you that you're on oath. Answer the question please."

"I saw her kissing my brother." Snapped William, immediately regretting what he'd said.

Sally was mortified, and wished the ground would open up, and swallow her alive.

"Kissing your brother? What a den of iniquity we've stumbled across here - and you have the nerve to criticize my client?"

At that point the judge intervened, "Mr. Fraser, I don't think this line of questioning is particularly relevant. Please pursue an alternative avenue."

Fraser, was momentarily humbled, but quickly followed a different line of questioning.

"So, back to this necklace. Am I right in assuming that you stole it?"

"I didn't steal it!" Replied William, shifting uncomfortably. "It fell to the ground in the hall, I just automatically scooped it up, when I was getting Sally out of harm's way."

"Very convenient. Now please tell the court what your income is." Asked Fraser, now tasting blood.

"It's just my student grant, that's all. But why?"

"May I remind you, Mr. Peddlescoombe, that I'm the one asking the questions. So, am I correct in saying that you exist on a very limited amount of money?"

"Yes, I do."

"If, I were to suggest that you purposely stole my client's necklace, with a view to selling it, would that be correct?"

"No, it wouldn't, how dare you suggest such a thing." Shouted, William, losing his temper.

"I think we've hit a raw nerve. I put it to you, William Peddlescoombe, that, because you couldn't compete with Mr. Gant on a financial scale, you stole and proposed to sell the necklace in order to woo my client's girlfriend. Can you confirm that please."

As much as he tried, William knew he couldn't get the better of Fraser, and sensed he would go the same way as Karen and Sally.

"Let me tell you, and the court something, Mr. Fraser." Continued William, taking a deep breath and trying desperately to remain calm. "Sally is a student, like me. She is the most genuine, caring, considerate and loving person you could ever wish to meet. Sally doesn't have a malicious bone in her body. Now you come along, and twist things around making it look like Frank Gant is the real victim, and Karen, Sally and myself are manipulative, criminals out to make a quick buck. Well, you are wrong, and if the jury are honest, true people, they will see through you, and realise what you are trying to do."

"Very nicely put, Mr. Peddlescoombe. Now, back to the matter in hand. Where is the necklace you stole from my client?"

"I don't know. I threw it out into the snow."

Fraser took a step back, and roaring with laughter, he turned to the jury.

"He threw it out into the snow! He threw a valuable Cartier necklace out into the snow! I think Mr. Peddlescoombe is trying to take us for fools, ladies and gentlemen!"

William knew Frank had won, and cursed himself for letting Fraser beat him so easily. Frank also knew he was on course for victory, by smirking and making gestures to his few supporters and family in the gallery. He also began smiling at a pretty juror, which didn't go down well with the judge and caused him to voice his disapproval.

All that was left now was the robbery at the sub post office, and even Frank doubted if the veteran lawyer could really get him off that. All Frank and Ken had to do was answer questions exactly the way Fraser had instructed them, and they would walk out of the court free men.

Fraser opened the defence by cleverly claiming the robbery was merely a student prank, carried out by two bored young men, towards the end of term. He pointed out that no-one had been hurt in the so-called robbery and most of the money had been recovered. To Frank's relief there was no mention of Mrs. Davies' death following the splashing incident in the car. Besides, as she had died from natural causes, and away from the scene of the robbery, it would have been difficult to lay the blame on him and Ken.

As the case drew to a close, Frank, again began smiling at, and flirting with the female juror.

"Mr. Gant, may I remind you that this is a court of law, and not a speakeasy where one picks up women. Any more transgressions and you will be dealt with accordingly. Is that clear?"

Frank, guffawed, and loosening his tie, sat back grinning in his chair. Ken meanwhile, sat like a frightened rabbit, and feared the worse.

"Sit up! Don't ruin it now, you imbecile!" Hissed Fraser, seeing all his hard work about to be wasted, as the judge again scrutinised Frank with disdain.

When the jury returned with their verdict, the whole court waited with bated breath.

"We the jury, find the defendant, not guilty of the charge of rape. Further more, we find the defendant not guilty of attempted murder."

Frank leapt out of his seat as he punched the air, and looked up to his parents triumphantly. However, Fraser had to scold him again for jumping the gun, and now wondered if the jury's verdict had a sting in its tail.

"With regard to the charge of robbery, we the jury, find the defendant guilty as charged."

There was a hushed silence, only broken by the sound of Frank swearing profusely.

The judge ordered the accused to stand, and looked at him as he would a piece of dogs mess on his shoe.

"I sentence you, Francis Gant, with the power vested in me, to three years imprisonment, to be served at her majesty's pleasure." Then turning to the guards, he ordered; "That will be all, take the prisoner down."

As Frank was led away, he snarled at William, "You, her and that cretin of a brother of yours will pay for this." Frank then began making pig noises at Sally, "I'll come, and huff and puff, and blow your house down, with you three little piggy's inside."

Frank's cold eyes, and disturbing threats sent a dark shiver down Sally's spine, and she hurried out of the court house as quickly as she could. A part of her had died that day, and she wondered if she could ever have faith in William, or the justice system ever again.

Meanwhile, William sat back in his chair, drained of energy, both physically and emotionally, and watched the court empty. What a fool he'd been. Now, he'd blown his chances for good, and humiliated Sally in public. He stood up and glanced over to where she had been sitting, but all that remained was an empty seat, and her black and amber university scarf.

It was about a week after Frank's court case, and William was desperately trying to get his life back on track. The case had badly affected him emotionally, and had caused him immense grief, to have witnessed the appalling suffering of both, Karen and Sally at the hands of the unscrupulous, Duncan Fraser.

It was a fine sunny day in early April, and William had been to see Mr. Meredith. He had promised to buckle down and get back to work, what with his finals coming up shortly. Meredith had been very sympathetic towards William, having watched the whole court scene unfold himself.

"Have you seen Sally since the case?" Asked Meredith, concerned.

"No, I haven't. I've been very low and haven't been on campus much."

"Well, I'm sure you'll see her, now you're about to get back into the thick of things, and attend lectures again. You're a good student, William, it would be a catastrophe if you threw it all away. Sally's a truly remarkable girl. You'll not find many like her around."

William thought about what the Dean had just said, and gazed out of the window. He focussed on a group of rugby players practicing taking conversion kicks.

"Big game on Saturday, do you think they can do it?"

"Changing the subject are we, William?" Grinned Meredith. "Yes, the team have a good chance this year. It's been a while since we last got to the final, and anything can happen in a one-off game."

Turning back to the Dean, William looked serious.

"I've wrecked my chances with Sally. I told the court she kissed my brother. I can't expect her to forgive me for that."

"Yes, I know you did, William. I was there when you said it. You can't put the clock back. But maybe, you should go and see her, and apologise."

"Do you really think that would work?"

"I've no idea, but it's better than doing nothing. You do want her back, don't you?"

"Yes, I do - more than anything I've ever wanted in my life." He replied, reaching into his pocket, to take comfort from the feel of Sally's scarf.

"Well, what are you waiting for - go and find her!"

The fine weather was set to last well into the month, and William was heartened to inhale the wonderful smell of freshly-mown grass as he made his way past the rugby pitch. As he neared the main campus area, he again checked his schedule, and re-confirmed that Sally's lecture, on the Emperor Tiberius was due to end in the next few minutes.

He waited patiently outside the Classics department, as the students began to emerge, his heart jumping whenever he saw a blonde, female student. There was no sign of her, so he decided to venture inside.

"Hello, sorry to disturb you, but I'm looking for Sally Carlington. I thought she may have been here?"

Miss Thornton, put down her notes, and stood up from the desk.

"No, I haven't seen Sally today. Is anything wrong?"

"No, it's okay, thank-you," he replied, walking out with an air of urgency. William immediately checked the library, knowing she would often spend time there, but again, no-one had seen her. As a last resort, he decided to try Lloyd-Evans Hall. He felt uncomfortable going into an all-female hall of residence, but it was daytime, so he wouldn't have any trouble gaining access.

Fortunately, it was quiet in the building, as most of the students were attending classes or just enjoying being out in the sunshine. As he reached her room, he heard banging noises and wondered what was going on. He knocked and anxiously waited for her to appear. Sally opened the door almost immediately. She had her long, blonde hair tied in a loose ponytail, and wore a clingy, pink, V-neck sweater, with equally clingy black slacks. Her dark eye make-up was the icing on the cake, and made her look incredibly erotic. He may have been mistaken, but he could have sworn, she briefly smiled, before quickly reverting back to a more solemn facade.

"Oh, I thought you were Lizzie," she said, looking rather surprised.

He was about to act smart and make comparisons about Lizzie and himself, but thought better of it.

"No, sorry, I'm afraid not. I was looking around campus for you." He replied, somewhat awkwardly.

"Well, I've been in here, packing."

"Packing? Why, are you changing rooms?"

"No, William, I'm leaving. I can't bear the humiliation of staying anymore. I'm going back home."

"Sally, please. What about your degree? What about us?"

She looked even more surprised.

"My degree is the last thing on my mind. I'll do hairdressing or become a waitress, anything to get me out of here." She then hesitated, "What do you mean, us? You certainly made your position clear about that in the courtroom."

William heard voices coming along the corridor and asked to be let inside.

"I've brought your scarf back," he uttered, glancing around at the assortment of boxes and suitcases. "You left it in the courtroom."

"Thank-you," she replied, bending forward to move a box out of the way.

William's gaze immediately fixed itself on Sally's cleavage, and he felt himself desperately wanting her. A lock of her hair had worked its way loose and hung seductively over her eyes.

"You seem to make a habit of finding my scarf," she said, glancing back up at him, "But you needn't have bothered, as I wont be needing it now."

He sat down on her bed, "Sally, I've come to say, I'm sorry."

"I don't want to hear it William. Not after you shouted out in court that you loved me, only then to tell the whole world you caught me kissing your brother. How could you do that?"

"I didn't mean to, Sally. I wish I had never said it."

She sat down on the bed next to him, her eyes full of pain.

"Why did you say it then?"

William hesitated for a few moments.

"I think it was two reasons. I just wasn't thinking straight. When Fraser asked if we were still seeing each other, I thought he must have known about you kissing David somehow."

"How would he have known about that?" She demanded.

"I know it's absurd, but at the time, he was tricking me into answering exactly what he wanted. I'm sorry."

Sally let her anger relax a little.

"He certainly ran rings around us. And yes, you're right, it was hard to think straight, having all those questions coming at you." She turned to face him again, "What was the other reason?"

William inhaled sharply, and shifted position.

"Well, the truth is, I was still angry with you Sally."

"I thought it may have been that." She stood up, placed her hands on her hips, and glared at him.

"I told you William, the kiss wasn't sexual. Your brother is a wonderful, sensitive, and damaged person. He needs lots of love and re-assurance. One day, I hope you'll understand that."

"Please don't make me out to be a monster, Sally. I do understand, but my feelings for you just got in the way." He pleaded, moving towards her.

"No, William, you don't understand. You hurt me badly, and I don't know if I can ever forgive you for that." She pushed him away, and went to open the door.

"Please go. I've got lots of packing to do."

William went back out into the corridor, looking totally dejected.

"Sally, you know the other thing I said in the courtroom? That was true, I did mean it."

"What was that, William? You said a lot of things in the courtroom."

"When I said I loved you Sally, I meant it. I do love you. I never stop thinking about you, I dream about you. Your eyes, your hair, your face, your skin, your wit, your compassion, I adore everything about you. I love holding you, the feel of you, kissing you, having you there with me. I even talk to you when you're not around. I can't bear to be without you." He then tried to put his arms around her, but she pushed him off again and began to close the door.

"Please, William - I've been to hell and back recently. I just don't think I can take anymore."

He glanced around, not quite knowing how to respond.

"I guess this is it then. I don't suppose, I'll ever see you again?"

"No, William, perhaps not. Look, I've got to call my father to come and collect me."

"I expect he wasn't very pleased to hear you're quitting?"

"I haven't told my parents yet."

There was an awkward silence, and William turned to leave, but as she was about to close the door, she called out to him.

"Where have you been William, why have I never seen you?"

He put his hands in his pockets and shrugged.

"I was just at home mainly. I did go to the lake fishing a few times in my boat. I like it there, it gives me the chance to think about things."

"Well, goodbye, William. I'll leave you to get back to your fishing and your thinking." She then shut the door and went inside. William made his way back down the corridor, and as he did so, he heard huge sobs of despair coming from Sally's room, and wished he could hold her in his arms once again.

Jane Parker walked into Mr. Meredith's office, the epitome of office efficiency. She wore a tight navy, pencil skirt, cream blouse and had her auburn locks just off her shoulders. At forty two, she looked as stunning as ever.

"I've got the address for you, Mr. Meredith, we did still have it on record."

"Excellent, Jane," replied the Dean, stopping what he was doing to run his eye over his prized secretary. "I'll just finish off drafting this letter, and we can be on our way."

"I'll get the cash out of the safe. Two hundred pounds, wasn't it?" She asked politely.

"Yes, that should be enough. Money doesn't go far these days." He shrugged, "Perhaps, we could get a bite of lunch, and have a drink after?"

"Yes, Mr. Meredith, that would be nice. We missed out over Christmas, what with all that happened."

"We did indeed, Jane, but it's Friday, and I'm sure we can push the boat out a little."

He continued drafting his letter, and when he had finished, he brought it out for Jane to type up. She was a very competent typist, and the letter was completed, and placed into an official, university envelope in less than five minutes.

"Very impressive, Mrs. Parker, if I may say so."

"You may, and thank-you, Mr. Meredith. I've had many years of experience."

He laughed and put his jacket on, resisting the temptation to come out with innuendo.

As they got into his car, Meredith couldn't help noticing the wonderful fragrance of her perfume and the way she looked. A change had come over Jane recently, which he couldn't quite understand.

"Do you know where you're going, Mr. Meredith?" She asked with a wry smile.

He wasn't at all sure how to take her last comment, and couldn't work out if she was guilty of using innuendo herself.

"I don't think I do Jane, I'm in a bit of a quandary, and need guidance. Do you know where we're going?"

"I should hope so!" She laughed. "I've lived in Falcondale for ten years now. It's number 20, Bank Street."

"That'll be near to the bank, I'd imagine?"

"Yes, that's very good for a Dean of Students!"

"I do believe you're mocking me, Mrs. Parker?"

"Not in the least, Mr. Meredith, I could never do that to my boss."

He smiled, and headed off down the drive.

"Jane, may I ask you a personal question?"

There was a moment of silence, as she considered his odd request.

"It depends how personal it is?"

"Well, I can't help noticing," he hesitated, and had to re-think his words. "I've noticed you look different these days, and you seem, well, happier - please don't misunderstand me when I say that, Jane. I'm certainly not saying that you were miserable in any way, but you've definitely changed."

"That's a very roundabout way of putting it," she added.

"But, am I right in noticing that?"

"Yes you are, and I don't mind telling you, it's not really any big secret - my divorce has been finalised. My ex is living with another woman."

"Oh, dear, I'm so sorry," exclaimed Meredith, feeling rather embarrassed. "I should mind my own business. I've really put my foot in it now, haven't I?"

"No, of course you haven't, Mr. Meredith, it is 1963 you know!" She giggled, reassuringly. "In fact, him leaving like he did, is the best thing that could have happened."

"Please Jane - call me, John. But, I don't understand. Your husband has left you, and you're happy about it?"

"Yes, in fact, I'm delighted! He wasn't a particularly pleasant man, a drinker and a womanizer - a bit like someone else we know. I met him, thought I loved him, then stupidly got married when I was in my teens. I've regretted it ever since."

"Well, I never. Jane, you've shocked me. But why didn't you leave him earlier?"

"We had a son, so I just stayed because of him really. I didn't want to disrupt his schooling, or his life in general. But, Adam's old enough to look after himself now."

Meredith was silent for a few moments.

"You are quite a remarkable woman, Mrs. Parker. I would never have guessed."

"Thank-you, Mr. Meredith, sorry, I mean, John. I think you are quite remarkable too. But please, I don't look upon myself as Mrs. parker now - just call me, Jane."

"Well, I've never been called remarkable before, thank-you for the compliment, Mrs. Parker, err, I mean Jane!"

As they arrived at their destination, Meredith took the initiative, and went around to open the door for his secretary.

"So what will you do now?"

"Well, I'm going to get the house decorated, and I may even sell it and move on. But initially, I just want the dust to settle, and see what transpires. You never know, Mr. Right may come along!"

Meredith opened the gate and they made their way up the path, and knocked on the door. It was a small, but pleasant unassuming terraced house, located just to the rear of the main street.

"Hello, Mrs. Matthews, how are you today?"

"I'm well, thank you, Mr. Meredith, please come inside. Do you want a cup of tea?"

"That would be lovely, thank-you. So is Carol here?"

"Yes, she's in the back room, looking at wedding dresses in a catalogue."

Mrs. Matthews, knew they were coming to see Carol, and led them through to the living room.

"Carol, love - we've got visitors."

Carol looked more than a bit surprised to see the Dean of Students, and his secretary in her family's modest home.

"Oh, hello Sir, I wasn't expecting you to be here?"

"Hello Carol, lovely to see you. You know Jane, don't you?"

Carol nodded shyly, and beckoned them to take a seat at the dining table.

"So what brings you, Mr. Meredith?" She asked anxiously.

"It's nothing to worry about, Carol. In fact, I hope we've brought you some good news." He replied, sitting at the table and removing the two envelopes from his inside pocket.

"I don't understand?"

"Just listen to what, Mr. Meredith has to say," added, Jane taking a seat next to him.

"Thank-you, Jane. Now, Carol, I'm sure you've heard about the recent court case involving, Frank Gant, or you've read about it in the local papers?"

Carol nodded, but the mere mention of Frank's name made her blood run cold.

"Yes, the whole town's talking about it. He should have got longer. But why does it concern me?"

"I'll tell you why it concerns you, Carol. You see the court case has brought it home to everyone, including the university governors, what a despicable, horrendous monster, Gant, was. Not only is he in prison, but he's also been expelled from the university."

"I still don't understand, Mr. Meredith?" Uttered Carol, looking nervous.

"Alright, I'll get to the point. I know you suffered at the hands of Frank Gant, and lost your job at the campus, because of him."

Carol nodded once more, "He tried to attack me, but luckily he was stopped in time. I had to attend a meeting, and no-one believed me. They thought I led him on. But I didn't, and I lost my job."

"Yes, I know that happened to you, and it put a stain on your character. Falcondale is a very small community and some people don't forget."

"Well, I don't let them upset me anymore. But I was sad to lose my job, I did love it there at the university. That's all in the past now - I've got a job as a chambermaid at the hotel now."

"Carol, I've had a meeting with the board of governors and they all agree that you were treated harshly and should never have lost your job."

"It's all a bit late now, Mr. Meredith," added Mrs. Matthews, putting the tray of tea down onto the table.

"No, not at all," he smiled. "I have a letter here, from the university, offering you, your old job back, and with a higher wage."

Carol looked shocked, and glanced up at her mother.

"I really don't know what to say."

"It's simple, young lady, just say yes, and you can start back on Monday, or the Monday after that. In fact, you can come back whenever you want."

Carol looked thrilled, and put her hands up to her face.

"Thank-you, Mr. Meredith, I'm a little overcome."

"There's more, Carol, the governors have decided that in view of all the torment you had to endure, they've agreed to give you an award!"

"Oh, I see, what like a certificate, or a medal?"

"No, Carol," laughed Meredith, "It's a cash award, two hundred pounds to be exact!"

He then passed her both envelopes, and took a sip of his tea.

Carol couldn't quite believe what was happening, and eagerly opened the envelopes, expecting it all to be some kind of joke. She read through the letter, and putting the cash back, she looked up at Meredith.

"I've never seen so much money. Can I talk to my mum in private?"

"Of course you can, and while you're at it, I think I'll pour myself another cup of your mother's excellent tea!"

Carol returned about five minutes later, and took her seat back at the table. Her mother, meanwhile stood hovering, and listening intently.

"I've thought about your kind offer, Mr. Meredith, and I have to say, no. I've moved on now, and I'm happy working at the hotel. I've even met a lad who works there, and he's asked me to marry him!"

"That's wonderful news, Carol, but I'm sad you wont be coming back to the university. At least take the money, you deserve it."

"No, Mr. Meredith, I couldn't possibly. I wouldn't know what to do with so much cash."

Meredith, looked disappointedly towards Jane, and they both stood up to go.

"Carol, your mother mentioned that you were looking at wedding dresses, is that right?"

"Yes, we're hoping to get married next summer, when we've saved enough money."

"They get married young around here, don't they, Mrs. Matthews?"

"It must be the Falcondale air!" She laughed, "Mind you, some of them these days, don't even bother to get married!"

"Indeed, Mrs. Matthews, you're quite right." He then, turned to Carol again, "Listen, my love, I don't know how much wedding dresses cost these days, or even weddings come to think of it. But I want you to take the money. It's yours to spend as you wish. I want you to be the prettiest bride in all of Wales. Now, please don't feel guilty about taking it."

He then picked up the envelope, gave Carol a kiss on the cheek, and put the money into her hand.

"Thank-you Mr. Meredith, and you, Jane. I'll never forget your kindness, but if I accept the money, there's something I'd like you to do for me," replied Carol, her voice full of emotion.

"Anything at all, just say it." Said Meredith, a little intrigued.

"Wait here, I'll be back in a moment."

She returned carrying a small velvet bag.

"I have been reading about the court case, and I couldn't help feeling so sad that Frank had stolen his mother's necklace. That poor woman, what an awful thing to do."

"Yes, do go on Carol," interrupted Meredith, wondering where this was going.

"Well, my Gran found a necklace a little while ago. She thought it may be valuable so she asked Constable Price about it and he said, to hang on to it as no-one had reported one missing."

"So does your Gran still have it, Carol?"

"No, she gave it me. I have it here." With that, Carol opened the bag and retrieved Irene's necklace.

"Gran also put an ad in the paper's lost and found column, but nobody ever replied."

"My, word, it's lovely. Are you sure this is it?" He asked, picking up the piece to examine it.

"Yes, it's Cartier all right, we've had it valued. It's worth a thousand pounds."

"So what do you want me to do, Carol?"

"I could never wear anything as beautiful as that, and it wouldn't be right, knowing it belongs to someone else. I'm sure Mrs. Gant would like to have it back. Could you return it to her please, Mr. Meredith?"

"Of course, I will, it would be a pleasure. What a remarkable young woman you are. I seem to keep meeting remarkable women these days!" He put the necklace safely into his jacket pocket, before saying goodbye to them both.

"Don't forget to invite Jane and myself to the wedding, will you?" He called back, as they returned to the car.

Meredith then drove to the top of the road, but instead of heading back towards the campus, he turned, and went in the opposite direction.

"Are you leading me astray, John?" Asked Jane, wondering where they were going.

"I'm taking you to the Falconbury Hotel, Jane. We're going to have lunch there."

"What a marvellous idea, how sweet of you," she replied. "I think it went very well with Carol?"

"Yes, I do too." He then reached into his pocket and handed the necklace over to her. "I think, you had better hang on to this, and put it in the safe on Monday."

"It's so beautiful, Mrs. Gant will be delighted to have it back."

"She will indeed, and Carol's a very honest person to return it." He then went silent for a moment, deep in thought.

"A penny for them?"

"Sorry, what's that," he replied.

"Your thoughts, silly. You were miles away."

"Do you know what Jane, I'm going to call Mrs. Gant and tell her the wonderful news. I'm also going to ask her to send Carol a sizeable reward."

"How wonderful, they'll both be happy." Smiled Jane, as the car turned into the Falconbury car park. She then turned to face him; "Can I ask you a personal question, John?"

"It depends how personal it is?"

"You're playing me at my own game, aren't you?"

"Never! So what do you want to know?"

Jane looked serious, and searched for the right words.

"I know your wife died some time ago, but why haven't you ever re-married? I'm sorry, perhaps, I shouldn't have asked that?"

He wound up the car's window, and pondered his answer.

"No, it's alright. You were very candid with me, and I shall be the same. Mrs. Meredith was one in a million, and I loved her dearly. Like yourself, we married young, and losing her has been the biggest tragedy of my life. But, I appreciate, I do have to move on. I would certainly consider another relationship, even marriage perhaps. But, again like you, I'm just waiting for the right person to come along - Miss Right, as it were."

They both sat quietly for a few moments, none really prepared to take the plunge.

"You shouldn't mix business with pleasure, you know!"

"Very true, Jane, but it depends which way you look at it. I say you should never mix pleasure with business. That's why, we're taking the rest of the day off."

"So that's the reason you said to put the necklace in the safe on Monday?"

"It is indeed, Jane - now let's go and have some lunch, I'm famished."

At Last, the first signs of day break began to filter into William's room. Shafts of light shone through the cracks in the thick curtains, willing him to get up and face another day. It had been a bad night, tossing and turning, putting his bedside lamp on to read, then turning it off, only to put it back on, and wander downstairs to strum on his guitar. It had gone painfully wrong with Sally, and he mulled over in his mind, if he could have said or done anymore to have made things better. Frank's court case was put on the backburner, as the very real possibility of losing Sally and never seeing her again filled his mind with the utmost despair. He wondered if she had already left the campus, and was now at home, back to her everyday life, back to her old routines. It hurt him to think of her being sad, and not blessing the world with her beautiful, radiant smile. He thought about getting in his van and going over to Lloyd-Evans Hall and trying once more to win back her heart. The idea spurred him on, and he drew back the curtains and gazed out over the vast orchard below. It had the makings of a pleasant, sunny Saturday in early April, and he considered making himself a cup of coffee and sitting out at the same bench, under the same apple tree, where David used to sit. He quickly dismissed the thought, recalling seeing Sally, kissing his brother there. It was just an innocent kiss, as she had so rightly pointed out, and he simply had to accept it.

Pulling on his jeans, jumper and hiking boots, he went downstairs. He sighed at the disgusting mess that greeted him, dirty plates, cups, old newspapers and beer bottles were strewn everywhere, the very sight of it depressed him greatly. He decided to put his boat on the trailer, and attach it to the van. If Sally wasn't there, or if she rejected him again, he would go to the lake, fishing. He couldn't bear the thought of coming back to the desolate house and being lonely again. Not only that, the house now harboured memories of Sally from the Christmas they had spent together. The kitchen where she had cooked them all such a wonderful lunch, the dining room, where they pulled crackers and opened their gifts. William even managed a hint of a smile when he recalled Sally's surprised face as she opened her gift from Jenny - the cheap, bright red lipstick! Then there was the living room, where they held the impromptu party on Christmas Eve. Where Sally had shown them all up with her dancing skills, beating everyone fair and square in that silly contest they had held. She belonged there, in his house, with him, it was meant to be. He looked in the mirror in the hallway, and combed his unruly, long hair. As he gazed at his morose reflection, he tried to will himself to find her and win her back. He can't give up.

The boat wasn't particularly heavy, just awkward, and he soon managed to get it rigged up to the trailer, which he now attached to the van. It was when he was bringing out his nets and tackle, that he thought he heard the sound of someone around at the entrance of the house. He put his keep net down and went to the front door. Opening it, he glanced around but couldn't see anyone. then, as he went to close the door, he inhaled her perfume, it was electrifying, and he felt the hairs on his neck stand on end.

That same morning, Sally, had searched through her wardrobe, looking for something suitable to put on. She wanted to look good, possibly even sexy, but she didn't want it to look as if she'd dressed up on purpose to go and see him. Eventually, she opted for a dark purple, tweed skirt, her black, high-neck sweater and black high-heeled shoes. She decided to wear her hair down for a change, then applied her make-up, before setting off on the familiar route to Orchard Lane. Although, she did feel a little nervous, she tried to go over in her mind what she would say to William, if she got the chance to see him.

It was pleasantly warm, and Sally stopped to browse in the windows of one or two of the shops as she made her way along the busy street. She swapped pleasantries with several of the townsfolk, she was even getting to know a few of them now. She then walked past the Black Lion pub, but had to step out into the road as they were having a rather substantial beer delivery. She came to Pedro's and stopped, reading the sign in the window;

SATURDAY NIGHT IS PAELLA NIGHT! 8PM - MIDNIGHT. PRICE INCLUDES THREE COURSES, PLUS A FREE BOTTLE OF HOUSE WINE!

Already the notice was getting plenty of attention, and Sally guessed there would be many takers that evening. She recalled how William had once mentioned the paella at Pedro's.

She slowed her pace as she neared his house, remembering that Nancy would often clean there at weekends. She waited a few moments, and sensing no-one was around, she raised the heavy brass knocker and tapped hesitantly on the front door. Getting no reply, she knocked again, but still no answer. She peered through a downstairs window, the place looked a mess, but there didn't seem to be any sign of life. After knocking a third time without success, she walked around to the rear of the house. She heard some activity and noticed William's van, with a boat on a trailer attached to it. The back door was open, so she knew either William or David had to be there. The ground was uneven, and she realised that wearing high heels in rural Wales probably wasn't such a good idea. As she neared the door, she saw William.

"Sally, is that you?" He called out, feeling his heart racing. He couldn't quite believe it, here she was, standing before him, her beautiful hair catching the sun's rays so exquisitely, as it gently blew in the light breeze.

"Yes, William, it's me," she replied, noticing his unshaven face light up.

"I didn't think I'd ever see you again, Sally. In fact, I was about to call by on my way fishing, to see if you were alright."

"Thank-you William, I'm here for the same reason. I was worried about you also, and didn't sleep very well."

"That makes two of us," he smiled back. "So when is your father coming to collect you?"

"I don't really know, I still haven't told him yet."

"I see," said William, sensing that she might not be going today after all. "Do you want some coffee? I've just made some, it's the real stuff, I got it from the deli."

"Yes, that would be nice," she replied, returning his smile. "I didn't know you had a boat?"

"It's not really much of a boat. My father used to go fishing in it."

"I would like to meet your father one day, and your mother."

"Would you Sally, really?" He beamed back.

She nodded and went over to look at the boat.

"William, will you take me fishing with you?"

He looked surprised, "I thought you'd never ask!"

"We'll have to stop off at Lloyd-Evans first though, I'll have to change."

"It's a deal, I can't wait!"

"Come on, I'm still waiting for my coffee."

William led her into the living room. The mess was appalling and he felt embarrassed.

"I've been neglecting it a bit."

"You've been neglecting yourself too," she replied, looking him up down. "I noticed that you've lost quite a bit of weight. How long have you been living like this?"

He put his head down, feeling ashamed; "About three weeks."

"Oh, William, what shall we do with you?"

He glanced up at her with his hazel eyes. "You've lost weight as well, Sally. Have you been sad like me?"

She looked down at herself, and nodded.

"William. I want to explain."

"There's no need," he interrupted, "I do understand. I know what David's like."

"He needed someone there with him."

"I realise that now. I wanted to tell you, but I just got it in my head that you preferred him to me."

"No, William, that's not true. I've been living and breathing you since we first met, I've missed you so much."

"I've missed you too, Sally."

"We need to give it some time, William. We both did stupid things, and we need to forgive each other."

"I would forgive you for anything."

"Thank-you." She took her coffee and sat at the table. "You said, you were here on your own, so where's David?"

"He's gone. Went about two weeks ago. He just took off and didn't say a word." He replied, joining her at the table.

"I'm so sorry, it's all my fault."

"No, it isn't. It's typical David, that's what he does, he's very unpredictable."

"But, where's he gone?"

"I don't know for sure, but he may have gone to the states. We've got some family and friends over there."

"I feel so awful that he's given up on his degree," sighed Sally, putting her cup down.

"He hasn't, he saw Meredith and managed to get a sabbatical."

She looked relieved, and reached out to touch his arm.

"You must have been so lonely here?"

"Yes, I was a bit," he replied, grasping her hand, "I kept thinking of you, and what you were doing, all alone too, at Lloyd-Evans Hall."

"Well, at least I had Lizzie for company, when she wasn't with Ken that is."

"You could have come back?" He whispered.

She avoided his question and got up to take her cup over to the sink.

"What about that Nancy woman, doesn't she clean here at the weekends?"

"No, not at the moment. She was getting far too nosey and was moaning all the time, so I gave her a sabbatical!"

"That's terrible, William - jobs are hard to come by."

"Don't worry, she'll be back next week."

"Finish your coffee. I'm going to help you clean this place up. It wont take long, then we'll go out on your boat."

Sally had never been on a boat before, and for that matter, she had never been fishing either. As they headed out towards the centre of the lake, she marvelled in its tranquillity, and immediately understood why William spent so much time here. They had the lake to themselves, apart from a few anglers much further away, on the bank. She watched, as he reached for a rod, and methodically began to check the line, before attaching the weights. He then used an oar to turn the boat so that they weren't directly facing the sun.

"How do you steer it, William, does it have a rudder?"

"No, it's just a simple rowing boat. I steer it with the oars," he smiled back.

"It wont sink will it?"

"No, of course not, if you keep still."

"What do you do with the fish when you catch them?"

"I just throw them back, unless they're very large, then I'll measure and weigh them. But I only do that when I'm fishing from the bank."

"It's all very technical. So, why don't you just fish from the bank, like those people are doing?"

"I do a lot of the time, but carp can grow quite big, and it's very exciting catching them from the boat. It can be a real battle with the big ones - like shark fishing!"

Sally went quiet, and looked about her.

"Just how big do they grow?"

"Sometimes, up to four feet, and they can weigh about sixty pounds, but that's rare."

"Maybe we should fish from the bank, William. I didn't realise they grew that big, I just thought they'd be like sardines!"

He laughed and tossed her a can of sweet corn, and a can opener.

"Here, make yourself useful, open this!"

Sally looked at the can with a puzzled expression.

"Is this our lunch?"

"No, silly, it's for the fish, it's bait!"

"You feed the fish sweet corn?"

"Yes, they love it, well most of the time they do. But you can never tell with carp."

"I suppose you've brought a little barbeque as well, to cook them chicken or sausages to go with their sweet corn!"

"You're not taking this seriously are you, Sally?" He remarked, putting a few pieces of corn on to the hook.

"I'm enjoying watching a master at work," she replied a little sarcastically. "So how many will the great fisherman catch?"

"It's hard to say really, I've been out here the whole day before, and not caught a thing!"

"I'll catch one, here, let me hold the rod." She asked, as she tried to stand up. The whole boat then rocked violently from side to side.

"No, no, stay still or we'll capsize, I'll pass it to you."

Sally decided that William was right and she stayed put while he cast out the line a few feet, before giving her the rod.

"What happens if one bites?"

"Well, you'll feel one or two gentle tugs. Then, if it's a big one, that's when the battle starts, and you'll have to fight it until it gets tired, but try not to let it go under the boat."

"If I end up in the lake as fish food, William Peddlescoombe, I'll hold you fully responsible!"

"Okay, now keep quiet, they like calm."

"Oh, do they indeed. Whatever next, a brandy and a cigar perhaps!"

"Women and fishing - not a great combination!" He laughed, sitting back to watch her.

After a bout ten minutes had passed, Sally felt the rod being tugged.

"William quick! I think I've caught something!"

"Okay, now stay calm and start to raise the rod up towards the sky, but hold it tight!"

Sally did as she was told, and like William had said, the carp was starting to put up a fight. It went this way and that, and round in circles, as it pulled violently at the line. This went on for a couple of minutes, before the fish began to tire.

"What do I do now, William?"

"Keep reeling it in, but gently and keep the rod up."

There was an almighty jerk, and William quickly lent across to help Sally. He gripped the rod and kept it upright, while they attempted to reel the carp in together. With the boat tilting from side-to-side, Sally lost her footing and couldn't help herself falling back onto William. As she did so, the carp came out of the water, and writhed precariously above their heads, for what seemed like an eternity.

"Put the rod out towards the water again, quickly!" Shouted William, as Sally began to panic.

It was too late. She let go of the reel completely, and the carp came hurtling down into the boat. It wasn't a big fish by any means, but it landed on Sally's lap and struggled fiercely.

Screaming, she begged William to save her from the wriggling fish.

"Please, before it eats me alive!"

He grabbed the carp as if it were second nature, removed the hook, and tossed it over the side.

"Are you okay, Sally?" He asked, looking concerned.

"No, I'm not okay! Look at me, I'm soaked through!"

"You still look gorgeous to me!"

"What, smelling of fish!"

"I love it when you smell of fish, Miss Carlington!"

"Get me off this boat now, William, I need a bath! Who's stupid idea was it to go fishing in the first place?"

William burst out laughing, but thought it best not to answer that question.

It was twilight by the time they got back to William's house, it was starting to turn distinctly chilly as the evening drew in. They had stopped off at Lloyd-Evans for Sally to change again, but they had both noticed how noisy and rowdy the town had become. Saturday evenings were usually the busiest night, but tonight seemed more wild and crazy than normal.

While Sally made them tea, William lit the downstairs fire, before going up to light the one in his bedroom. While he was upstairs, he began to run her a hot bath. The bath was a huge, cast iron, Victorian affair, which took forever to fill. This gave William the opportunity to add some of the scented oil that Sally had left behind over Christmas, and as an added touch, he placed a dozen lighted candles around the edge of the bath, and up on any free ledges he could find. It looked incredibly inviting, and he stood for a moment admiring his handiwork, hoping he might get the chance to enjoy it himself.

He called down to Sally when it was ready, and eagerly awaited her response. She handed William a cup of the strong tea he liked, and eagerly opened the bathroom door.

"William, it looks fantastic - I can't wait to get in!" She exclaimed, beaming up at him.

He then led her into his bedroom, so she could get undressed and offered her the same shirt she'd worn the night they first made love.

"I've lent you this before, I recall."

"How could I ever forget!" She replied. "Although, there's a part of that evening, I don't need reminding of."

"You mean Frank?"

She nodded and looked away, before ushering him out of his own room.

William had only been gone a couple of minutes, when he heard her calling down to him.

"I'll need a towel!"

"There's some in the airing cupboard on the landing," he called back.

There was a brief moment of silence.

"But William, I don't have any clothes on!"

His mouth went dry at the thought of her naked, and as he climbed the stairs, he felt the familiar bulge in his trousers returning.

After finding her a towel, he pushed the bedroom door open. He thought Sally would have heard him, but she was just standing there, staring out of the window. She was a curvaceous, size ten, and he stood transfixed, staring at her exquisitely-shaped rear. She had the most soft, responsive skin he had ever touched, and now he longed to touch her once again. He tried to speak, but no words came out.

She turned, and his eyes fell on her firm breasts, her nipples pink, and pointing slightly upwards. She gasped, and looked surprised before reaching across to retrieve the shirt.

"William, you were quick, I didn't hear you."

"I'm sorry," he muttered, finally managing to find some words.

"What were you looking at?"

She quickly pulled the shirt around her body.

"I was just admiring the orchards, before it got too dark. It's such a beautiful view."

He knew she was looking at the tree with the circular bench around it, which David used to sit under.

William then reached out and pulled her towards him, kissing her hungrily.

Sally didn't respond the way he had expected her to, there was something holding her back, preventing her from submitting to his desires.

"Please, William, stop! I don't want this, not now." Her voice was decisive, but pained, and she pulled herself away from his grip.

"But Sally, you don't know what you're doing to me."

"I want things to be as they were. I want to love you, but I can't forget that you hurt me."

"Sally, please forgive me!" He pleaded, his voice full of emotion.

"You humiliated me in public, how could you do that?" She shouted, hammering at William's chest with her fists. "You hurt me so much!"

He let her pound away, until she grew tired, and the blows became little more than touches. He then took her in his arms and held her in silence, as if he were draining all the power from the demons that had consumed her soul.

"You are so wonderful and brave Sally, and you are so loved. Nobody will ever hurt you again."

He heard her sob his name into his chest, and felt her arms go about him.

William kissed her forehead and led her towards the bathroom. He closed the door, and took his clothes off. He then stepped into the bath, before taking her hand and helping her in next to him. He lifted the shirt over her head, and tossed it onto a chair. She was shaking, and felt cold to touch.

"I'm so sorry," she whispered.

"Sally, you never have to say sorry to me. You are in my heart forever."

"We all have to say sorry sometimes, William."

He sat back in the steaming tub, his arms and legs draped tightly around her body, keeping her safe. Together, they lay in the soothing, cleansing water, their sadness and despair ebbing away under the light of a dozen flickering candles. She reached down to take his hand and rested her head on his chest, listening to the sound of his beating heart.

"William?"

"Yes, Sally?"

She glanced up at him, her deep blue eyes, still wet with tears.

"You are forgiven."

Lizzie, sat grim-faced in the student's clubhouse. She was sitting at a table with several other girls who were with players, but unlike them, she wasn't showing the slightest bit of enthusiasm about the celebrations. Mayhem was going on all around her, and the beer was flying, as it had been for most of the afternoon.

The university had won the Welsh College's Shield, and to top it, Ken had been the player to score the winning try. As with tradition, he was now required to drink the concoction known as Dai's Death. Dai was the legendary rugby player who scored the winning try when Falcondale last won the shield, over forty years earlier. During this monumental win, he had the tip of his nose bitten off. This, was later recovered and preserved in alcohol, and left lying in state at the student's club.

The bottle was opened to rapturous applause, and Ken, standing at the bar, legs akimbo, and still clad in his black and amber rugby kit, surveyed the contents with a look of grave concern.

Slowly, the chant of Dai! Dai! Dai! began to increase in volume, until it reached ear-shattering intensity. Ken reached for the bottle, put it to his lips, and drained every last drop, leaving only the tip of Dai's nose for the next winning try scorer. He was then cheered and raised aloft by the rest of the highly animated team. Balancing high on their shoulders, he proudly lifted the shield and presented it to the excited audience. There was more singing and more cheers, before he was eventually put back down, to make his speech.

He glanced over at Lizzie, who was sitting behind a vast array of bottles, glasses and over-flowing ashtrays.

"Lizzie, I dedicate this win to you, the love of my life!" He staggered backwards, but just managed to grab hold of the bar rail to steady himself." You must have another drink to celebrate!" The crowd then cheered their support, but Lizzie wasn't having any of it.

"If this is how you behave every time you win a match, then you can keep your damned rugby!"

Ken laughed, "Shall I get you some wine?"

"I'll have Chablis, not that vile muck they serve in here."

"They don't have it here, Lizzie." He called back in a slurred voice, "It's only a student's bar. What about some beer instead?"

She cringed with embarrassment, and felt her face redden.

"No, I don't want beer! I'll have a Babycham!"

Again the cheer went up, and within moments, a dozen bottles of Babycham appeared on the table.

"They're from the team!" Beamed Ken, proudly.

"Sit down, before you fall down!" She ordered, pointing to an empty chair.

Ken, managed all of two steps, before collapsing into a drunken heap on the floor.

"You lot got him into this state, so you can take care of him!" Shouted Lizzie to the team, as she scooped up the Babycham's and headed towards the door. "I'm going back to Lloyd-Evans to see Sally," she said to the other girls. "I expect she's hard at it, cramming for her exams."

She left the clubhouse to the sound of the team chanting ringing in her ears. She was desperate to tell Sally, to go and see William, and make things up. Lizzie hated seeing her friend miserable, and wanted her back, the way she was.

It was the rumbling of William's stomach that woke Sally up. They both must have drifted off to sleep, as some of the candles had gone out, and the temperature of the water had dropped somewhat.

"I think your tummy's trying to tell you something!"

He stirred, and changed his position slightly, before continuing to cuddle her.

"Yes, you're right, I'm famished, aren't you?"

"Crumpets?"

"No, sorry, run out of those. What about getting done up and going to the Falconbury Hotel?"

"No, certainly not after what Frank did to Pauline there," she replied sternly.

"There's some fresh eggs in the fridge, we could do scrambled eggs on toast with lots of Worcester sauce, yummy!" Suggested William eagerly.

"It'll be me cooking it, wont it?" Sally said, before adding; "What about Pedro's, they're having a 'Paella night', with free wine?"

"Have you ever been to a Pedro's Paella night?"

Sally shook her head.

"It can't be that bad?"

"We'd be lucky to get a table, they'll be lining up outside."

"Fish and chips?" She mentioned, "Maybe not, on second thoughts, I've had enough of fish for one day."

"Leave it to me, I'll give Pedro's a call."

Sally applied her pink lipstick, black eyeliner and mascara, before attending to her hair. She then checked herself in the mirror, and decided to wear it up in a beehive for a change. The effect on William was immediate. He gazed at her in total awe, as she made her way downstairs, trying not to trip in her high-heels.

"I can't take you anywhere dressed like that, Sally!"

"Oh, William, I knew this sweater was too tight. Do I look stupid?"

"I think you'll get quite a bit of attention. You're going to make the men drool!"

"Well, as long as I make you drool!" She smiled.

"I am already!" He replied proudly, passing her a glass of wine. "I've actually managed to book us a table at Pedro's. I didn't think we'd stand a chance, but he said the place was nearly empty."

Sally looked at him with a puzzled expression.

"That's odd, I wonder why that is. Perhaps students don't like paella?"

"Not sure really, he said most of them were over at the clubhouse."

"Must be some sort of function," she replied, sipping her drink. "Just think, we can have Pedro's all to ourselves!"

He nodded and turned towards her, "Sally, there's something I've been meaning to ask you."

"What might that be, Mr. Peddlescoombe?"

He hesitated for a moment, before looking into her eyes.

"Will you come back and live here? It's been so empty without you."

She moved a stray lock of hair away from her face, before glancing down to his lips.

"I'm here, aren't I?" She whispered, before adding; "There's something I want to ask you as well, William."

He looked intrigued. "What might that be, Miss Carlington?"

"Will you light the candles again tonight, they were so lovely?"

"Yes, of course. I'll bring them down to the front room when we get back."

"I wasn't exactly thinking of the front room," she smiled, craning her neck to kiss him.

They emerged a couple of minutes later and walked, arm-arm into Falcondale, with William wearing nearly as much lipstick as Sally.

COMPENDIUM OF THE SOUL

BOOK TWO

11. PAULINE AND FRANK

Pauline had been right about her pregnancy. She gave birth to a baby girl on the 15th August, 1963, and named the child, Tina Frances. However, the baby had been born several weeks premature, and was not expected to survive. Pauline was distraught, and looked on helplessly as her daughter was placed in an incubator, with her tiny life in the balance.

Whether it was Pauline's love for a life born out of rape, or the child's own determined will to live, or a combination of both, nothing short of a miracle happened. Little Tina Frances survived.

She had fought valiantly against all the odds, and had clung on desperately to a life, so fragile, so delicate and so weighted against her, that very few had given her even the slightest chance of pulling through. Pauline felt it was divine intervention, that Frank, baby Tina and herself were meant to be.

Pauline had also kept her promise to wait for Frank. He was finally released from jail three years later, after serving time for the robbery of the sub post office at Falcondale.

At first, Frank had spurned Pauline, and refused to acknowledge the lengthy letters she would send him while he was in prison. It was only after she had got up the courage to actually visit him in person, that he came around to her way of thinking, or so she thought.

Irene Gant, Frank's mother had turned out to be an unexpected, and much-needed ally to Pauline's cause. Although Frank's father, Hugh, still wanted nothing to do with him, Irene's stance had softened somewhat following the birth of Tina. She began to make regular trips from Bristol to West London, to see her new granddaughter, and would ensure Pauline had enough money to keep herself and the baby provided for. It wasn't as if Pauline's own parents weren't there to help out. They did all they could, not necessarily in monetary terms, but in kind. They would always look after the baby when Pauline went to her night club job, and would bring over bits of old furniture and household items to the modest, ground floor flat Pauline was renting just off the Fulham Palace Road in Hammersmith.

Irene, was a link to another world, another way of life. She represented everything Pauline strived for, money, the nice home, fancy cars, and a lifestyle way beyond her means. But more importantly, she was Frank's mother, and Pauline could use this to her advantage.

Irene had put her marriage in jeopardy with her visits to see Pauline. However, unbeknown to her husband, Irene was also in contact with Frank. If anyone could get through to the reasoning side of her son, it was Irene. She had constantly begged Hugh to relent and not to be so harsh with Frank. He was a bad apple, there was no denying that, but Irene liked to believe everybody had a good side to them. Even when she pleaded with her husband, reinforcing the fact that they now had a grand child, Hugh remained resolute.

"I'll not have bastards in my family, nor will I have drug-peddling robbers and rapists under my roof. I'll hear no more of it, do you understand, Irene!"

Irene grew to despise her husband for his overbearing, intolerant attitude, and found her cloak and dagger actions now fully justifiable under the circumstances.

It was only a few weeks prior to Frank's release that his father, suddenly took an active interest in his son's welfare. He instructed his solicitors to make it known to Frank that an undisclosed sum of money had been made available to him. This however, was no more than a bribe to keep Frank and his indiscretions as far away from the Gant family home as possible. The money was to be paid three quarterly, and came with certain conditions, the main ones being; Frank must not set foot in Bristol. He must not try to contact members of his family. He must marry Pauline Chater. He must bring up the child to the best of his ability and provide for her.

Frank had seethed with resentment when he heard about the conditions, and at first, refused to have anything to do with his father's bizarre scheme. It was only when Irene had managed to talk to him and explain in no uncertain terms that he literally had nothing, and nowhere to go, that he finally accepted the proposal. Irene had also pleaded Pauline's case admirably. She put it to Frank, that at least now, he would have a home to come out to, a ready-made family, and an income, provided he stick to the terms of the agreement.

"Can't that gutless swine come here and tell me himself!" Shouted Frank, angrily.

"Please, you mustn't speak of your father like that. It's a very good offer." Replied Irene, disheartened.

"He just wants me out of the way. I'm an embarrassment to him. Haven't I suffered enough?"

Frank reluctantly read through the contract, and put his signature to the document. But, he couldn't see anything in the small print that said he had to actually like his new family. He decided to go along with it for the moment, since he had no other options available to him at the present time.

Pauline worked her fingers to the bone, what with working all available hours at the club, and having to juggle looking after Tina, with painting and decorating the flat. She was pleased, however with the end result and now, all it needed was Frank, to be the last part of the jigsaw. She had put up a calendar, and excitedly marked off the days until his release. She even taught Tina how to say his name. Pauline was certain that Frank would love his daughter, their new home, and most importantly, her. Pauline had never got the figure back, she had dieted so hard to achieve, before the birth of Tina. Although, determined not to let her weight creep back up to her pre-university days, she was happy to remain a curvy, size twelve. Pauline was proud of her full, shapely bust and enjoyed likening herself to the actress, Jane Russell. She was also one of the most popular hostesses at the club, with her innocent looks and long, raven hair.

It had been Irene, who persuaded Frank to agree to a visit from Pauline and Tina, very near to the end of his sentence. She had wisely thought that letting him see Pauline with his daughter, would get him used to the idea of becoming a family man, rather than have him frightened off at an early stage. All Irene wanted was for her son to become a better person, and if he found himself at the opposite end of the table, with family responsibilities, it might just provide the impetus he needed to get his life into perspective.

Frank's transformation into family life was no easy thing. He married Pauline under protest, refusing anymore than the bare minimum of guests present. There was no reception, and certainly no honeymoon. Pauline was understandably devastated by Frank's actions and found herself in tears on her wedding day. Even Irene had to question if this was indeed, the right course of action.

"Listen Pauline, I've supported you trying to make a life for yourself and Tina with my son, but having watched the debacle of your wedding, I can only have sympathy for you. I would certainly back you up, if you left him immediately."

Pauline, holding Tina in one arm, and trying to wipe her tears away with the other, thanked Irene.

"It was meant to be the happiest day of my life, but I'll survive, I always do. I'll see things through with Frank, It certainly can't get any worse."

The subsequent days were no better. Frank had little time for Tina, and despite Pauline cooking for him, and tending to all his needs, he remained ungrateful and simply viewed her as little more than a servant. He rarely spoke, except to swear if she'd done something to upset him, which turned out to be all too often.

"Frank, I've cooked you a pie, it's one of your favourites." Called out Pauline, one day as she proudly placed Frank's dinner on the table.

He came out of the shower five minutes later in a red polo shirt and jeans. He had his fair hair cropped these days, and looked trim and muscular from working out during his time inside. The faded scar on the left side of his face, however still gave him a menacing and somewhat imposing appearance. He didn't even bother to sit at the table, he just picked up the plate of food, and hurled it at the wall.

"It's bad enough having to live here in this shit hole with you - but I'll not eat shit as well." He put his jacket on and stormed out, leaving Pauline beside herself, as she looked up at the ruined wall, which she had only recently finished wallpapering.

Pauline, eventually worked out her own routine with Frank. She prepared his meals early and kept them warm in the oven, never knowing when he would appear. He would usually be out drinking all hours with so-called friends, but he was still a meticulously, smart and fussy dresser, so as long as his shirts were ironed to perfection and she gave him space, Pauline found it possible to survive in, what was an intimidating and hostile environment. Frank was also frequently violent when drunk, so Pauline learnt to keep quiet, keep out of the way and simply act as the dutiful wife. He would only ever have sex with her when he was drunk, and these were the times Pauline feared the most. The beatings she took during the early days, could be considered mild, compared to what they would be like in the future. Quite often, especially after sex, she would go and sleep in with Tina. She found cuddling her little daughter a welcome relief from the cold brutality of Frank's regime.

But things did begin to change a few months later. At a loss for something to do, Frank began to act as an unofficial driver to some of the more wealthy clientele who would frequent Lake's, the club, where Pauline worked part-time. It was an exclusive gentleman's club in Curzon Street, Mayfair. It could be described as both shabby and smart at the same time, and had an old-fashioned aura about it. The shabbiness came from the fact, that the old Georgian building was in great need of refurbishment. It always amused Pauline to see customers arriving at weekends, dressed in evening wear, and having their meal in a dining room covered in cracks and damp, peeling wall paper. But the club was popular with its own distinctive atmosphere, and Pauline found working there very fulfilling. She felt she was quite lucky to get the job, since several applicants were called for interview, but there was something about Pauline's innocence that swayed the job in her favour. The owner's wife had seen the candidates personally, and for Pauline it felt as if she had applied for a modelling job, rather than as a club hostess.

"I can see that you're polite, and well turned out, Pauline, I like that." Said, Mrs. Lake, running a keen eye over Pauline. "Lots of girls come into this type of work with the wrong attitude. In order to gain respect, you have to earn it. I shall expect you to be courteous and civil to the clients at all times, is that clear?"

"Yes, Mrs. Lake, I have had some experience working behind the bar at the student's club."

Mrs. Lake couldn't help laughing. "Pauline, nothing could be more different! But I can see something in you. When can you start?"

At thirty five, Claire Lake saw herself as a good judge of character, especially when it came to hiring new hostesses. She could spot the freeloaders from a mile off, and prided herself on the honesty and integrity of her girls. Her husband, Walter, an alcoholic had now taken a back seat in managing the club, and was more than happy to leave things in the hands of his capable wife, even though the club had been losing money lately, and had slipped down the pecking order in favour of some of its rivals.

Claire was a tall, attractive woman, with a short black bob. Her slender, toned, figure was a testament to keeping herself in good shape, despite the many temptations to enjoy the rich food, and fine wine which were always readily available on the premises.

Frank hadn't realised at the time, that by undertaking these menial driving jobs, he was on the brink of starting one of London's most successful mini-cab companies.

Pauline would usually act as an intermediary, and would arrange for her husband to ferry the clients home, or to restaurants, especially after they'd had a few drinks too many. They soon became used to Frank, and started to trust him with other duties, like running business errands, or driving their wives around on shopping trips. Frank soon found that his charm was working wonders, and he was able to treat himself to a couple of new hand-stitched suits.

Claire had been suitably impressed with Frank, and had given her permission for him to continue on a trial basis, to see how things worked out. His relationship with Pauline had also softened significantly by this stage, and he actually began to treat her as a human being at times. Maybe it was because he now appeared to have a purpose, or it was because he had just grown used to Pauline being around. Frank even started to take an interest in his daughter. He began taking Tina out to the park, and would often bring her toys and dolls home to play with. Pauline was delighted and looked forward to the future with optimism, now she was finally turning things around with her newly-acquired husband.

In a comparatively short space of time, Frank had made enough cash to trade in his ageing car, and buy a white Mercedes Benz. From then on, he never looked back, but still he was impatient and longed to buy more cars, employ more drivers, and get out of the cramped flat they were living in. This was where Mr. Bloom entered the equation.

Having narrowly escaped the Nazis during the second world war, with most of his wealth intact, Abraham Bloom played his hand cautiously. He had opened a modest jewellery shop in Golders Green, where he specialised in buying and selling unusual pieces from around the world for those that could afford them. He had a reliable network of contacts, and could supply his clients with anything, from a sapphire engagement ring to a diamond-studded, platinum tiara. Much of his business was concluded away from the shop, often during the evenings at his client's homes, or in local hotels. For reasons of his own, Bloom preferred to deal only in cash, and trusted very few.

One evening each week, the elderly man would make a habit of coming into the club, whether he had business or not. He never encouraged any of the hostesses to socialise with him, and would sit alone, at a secluded table, smoking a cigar and consuming several large cognacs before setting off to visit a mysterious lady friend.

Pauline knew he must have been well tipsy by the time he left, but he certainly never showed it, and always behaved impeccably. As the months passed, Mr. Bloom became quite fond of Pauline, and would look out for her to serve him. Pauline found she enjoyed the pleasant and enlightening conversation of the well-educated old Jewish gentleman, and they soon became friends. In fact, he had developed quite a crush on Pauline, who was now in her early twenties, and would give her little items of jewellery from the case, which was always at his side. The gifts were certainly not anything of particularly high value, but they were different, and far more interesting than anything she had seen in the shops. Sometimes, when there was no-one around, he would open the case and show her some of his finest pieces, and tell her how they could all belong to her - if she became his wife.

"Abraham, you are so sweet, but I love my husband. Anyway, don't you already have a lady friend?"

The old man chuckled, and upon leaving would often produce a crisp, £5 note from his bulging wallet, and present it to Pauline, as a tip, which was more than generous in 1966.

During these times, when Frank's rages were not quite so much of a problem, Pauline liked to see if there were any signs of jealousy from her husband.

"At least my boyfriend at the club likes me enough to give me presents!" She remarked, admiring the pretty gold earrings in the mirror.

Frank would usually just sneer, and generally treat her with contempt. It was only after she had mentioned the old gentleman's wealth, and the fact that he carried much of it around in his case, that finally, Frank began to take a keen interest.

"So what's actually in this case, your decomposing friend carries around with him?" He asked one evening, with a calculating glint in his eye.

"Several thousand pounds, I'd say, but the jewellery is probably worth much more. I'll see if I can get him to use your car service. I'm sure he'd agree, if I recommended you, Frank." Beamed Pauline, delighted that she was finally helping her husband into meaningful employment.

It didn't turn out be a difficult thing to arrange. The following week, Mr. Bloom had arrived at the club in high spirits. He insisted on buying Pauline a drink, which was acceptable in those days, and excitedly began to tell her how he had just sold an antique diamond ring to a very discerning client. The old man was glowing, and Pauline listened intently as he described the magnificent house where he had conducted his lucrative deal.

"It's been a fantastic week, my petal. I'm sure it's you who brings me such good fortune, you are my lucky omen, Pauline!" Laughed the experienced jeweller, as he downed another cognac.

"No, Mr. Bloom, on the contrary, you create your own fortune. You must be a very talented salesman!"

He smiled warmly, and reached across to take her hand, which he examined in great detail, noticing its general lack of adornments.

"What's this, such beautiful, delicate hands, and nothing to compliment them? I want you to come to my shop. You can choose anything I have. Pauline, please say you will, it'll make a foolish old man very happy."

Pauline was quite taken aback by this show of generosity.

"I've never met such a kind, good-hearted man as you, Mr. Bloom. But, I think it would be wrong of me to accept." She replied, trying her best to be diplomatic. "However, there is something I did want to ask you?"

He agreed immediately to allow Frank to drive him, and Pauline was delighted. Some time later, as she took a tray out to the kitchen with a broad smile on her face, Claire cornered her when there was no-one else around.

"I've been watching you and Mr. Bloom." She said, backing Pauline up against a wall. "Don't forget what I told you when you first came here, Pauline."

"It's purely innocent, Mrs. Lake. I wont disappoint you."

"No, that's right, Pauline, you certainly wont disappoint me." Smirked the older woman, as she suddenly kissed Pauline on the side of her neck, and ran her hand over her breast.

Pauline was aghast, and quickly pulled herself away, before going back out into the public area of the club. However, she struggled to concentrate on her work, and made an excuse to leave early.

Even Abraham Bloom was impressed when he saw Frank, dressed immaculately in a dark suit and standing next to the gleaming, white Mercedes.

"You have a wonderful, charming and beautiful wife, young man, I hope you appreciate her?" He remarked, easing himself into the back of Frank's car. "Do you know Battersea Bridge, the Chelsea side?"

"Yes, I know it well," replied Frank casually, immediately taking a dislike to his passenger.

"Good, then, let's be on our way. I'll show you exactly where to drop me when we get closer."

However, Mr. Bloom, never reached where he was going. He was found early the next morning, face-down in the River Thames, just a half mile from his destination.

It had been a profitable night's work for Frank, even though he had ruined his suit and a perfectly good pair of shoes during the proceedings. He had been surprised by the old man's reluctance to meet his maker, and even after a savage blow to the head with a brick, Mr. Bloom still managed to twitch a fair bit. The only downside to the evening was Bloom's missing keys. Frank must have searched every pocket for them, as he waded knee-deep in the water and mud at the river's edge. He finally had to assume that they had somehow ended up at the bottom of the river during the struggle. It was a big disappointment to Frank, now he would have to settle with just the jeweller's case, and not the contents of his shop, as he had hoped.

He waited for Pauline to get back first, so that she could send her mother home after babysitting. He was pleased to find that she was in the shower, as he crept in through the house. After quickly changing out of his damp suit, he poured himself a large whiskey to calm his nerves, before forcing open the case.

Pauline came down ten minutes later, with her newly-washed hair swathed in a towel. She had been troubled by Claire's approach, but put it behind her once she was back home. The first thing she saw as she walked into the living room was Mr. Bloom's case on the table.

"What have you done?" She screamed at Frank.

"There was a bit of an accident, that's all. These things happen. Don't worry the police wont come around here."

"What do you mean, an accident? That's Mr. Bloom's case you're trying to force open. Answer me, Frank. What have you done?"

He ignored her, and putting the drill down, took up a crow bar, which he used to violently wrench the lock open.

"He's dead. He had a fall, but now we're rich!"

"You killed him didn't you? You've murdered that harmless, little old man." Gasped Pauline.

"Listen, there's plenty more old people around. Besides, he would have wanted you to have all this, Pauline. He liked you, remember!"

She put her hands up to her face, no longer able to look at the bundles of cash and jewellery, sitting there on the living room table.

"He trusted me, Frank." She wept, "He trusted me."

"Well, that just goes to show, you shouldn't go around trusting women who work in nightclubs!" He smirked, examining an emerald brooch.

"We've got to go to the police, Frank. We must hand all this over. You can still say it was a tragic accident."

"Listen, I dropped him off where he wanted. He was drunk and must have fallen into the river. That's my story, and I'm sticking to it."

"No, Frank, I don't believe you, you're lying."

Frank picked up the drill, and moved menacingly towards Pauline. She backed away, terrified of what he might do. He reached around and grabbed the towel at the back of her head, then, pulling her down, he thrust the drill bit into her mouth.

"You're in this too, you bitch!" He snarled, "Let's not forget that it was you who set it up in the first place." Removing the drill, he then pushed her violently to the floor, where he kicked her hard in the abdomen.

Fearing further violence, and in excruciating pain, Pauline somehow summoned the strength to crawl towards the door. It was then, she felt hands touching her shoulders, but they were gentle, soft hands, and so tiny that Pauline dared reach up to hold them. She opened her eyes, and looked up to see her daughter standing before her.

"Tina, please - you must go back to bed. Mummy will be up soon to tuck you in." Pleaded Pauline, desperate to keep the child out of harm's way.

"Look, Tina, lot's of toys - come and see!" Called out Frank, scooping up a handful of glittering jewellery.

Tina immediately left her mother and ran excitedly over to the table.

As she stood on a chair, not knowing which item to touch first, Frank placed the old man's personal effects, and anything of no apparent value, back inside the damaged case, which he would dispose of later that evening.

Sally was ecstatic when William had given her the news. She immediately bundled the children into the car, and went to have a look herself.
"I can't believe it William, it's finally up for sale!" She gasped, gazing up at the empty house excitedly. "We had better put in an offer straight away!"
"Don't worry, I've already done it," he replied, smiling. "It's been accepted!"

It was the autumn of 1967, when Sally and William moved into The Birches, following the birth of their second daughter, Penny, during the so-called, summer of love. They had moved to Sally's home town of Twickenham, after she had sat her finals, and left Falcondale with a first class, joint honours degree in English and Classics. William was very impressed, since he had only just managed to pass with a second in his chosen subjects. Possibly, having to attend Frank's court case so close to sitting his finals, and the temporary break up with Sally may have affected him. But surprisingly, William was unconcerned, and had been more than eager to move to London, where he felt there would be numerous opportunities for him to make a name for himself.

Initially, the couple had rented a modest two-bedroom flat in East Twickenham, just a short distance from Richmond Ice Rink. At the time renting seemed a sensible idea, rather than leap straight in and buy a place, not quite knowing where their future incomes were going to come from.

William teamed up with a childhood friend from Canada, called Jeremy, who had recently moved to England. They began to buy up dilapidated old shops in prominent areas of London, gave them a bit of a psychedelic face lift, then converted them into profit-making souvenir shops. It wasn't exactly what William had planned to do, but he found the challenge each property presented to his artistic capabilities, very exhilarating. Added to this, Jeremy appeared to have the Midas touch where it came to getting funds to invest in the renovation of the numerous properties. They soon found they were making a substantial living, and after a while, no longer needed help from the banks, even though their careers could be considered precarious.

At the time, Carnaby Street was rapidly becoming the fashion centre of the world, and was attracting millions of visitors each year. One small shop, they had opened, in the centre of the street was already bringing in more profit in one day, than some of the other shops could make in a week.

While William had been reaping the benefits of full-blown capitalism, Sally had been on the verge of a nervous breakdown. Nothing could have prepared her for the task of looking after a baby and two toddlers, hell-bent on getting into as much mischief as possible. During those early days, help wasn't exactly forthcoming. Certainly, Sally's parents looked in, but their visits were few and far-between, and would never involve the offer of assistance in any shape or form. It was similar to her own childhood days, when she had felt unloved and was only born in the first place out of some misguided sense of duty. Although, they would never admit it, Sally's parents had hoped their only daughter could have gone on to meet someone of considerable status, possibly even titled. Now, to see her at such a young age, stretched to the limit and surrounded by chaos, only served to remind them, that perhaps, they had failed somewhere along the line themselves. Soon Sally began to dread the visits, feeling she was obliged to have the flat looking completely spotless, and totally devoid of any signs of habitation by young children.

Sally also had quite a strained relationship with William's parents, especially his mother Joan. Although, William's mother was always civil to Sally, and had been more than generous in the past, there was an invisible barrier between the two women, which neither of them seemed prepared to cross. Sally had always assumed this was due entirely to her short engagement to William, along with the conception of their first child, Jonathan before the wedding date. However, there were other reasons. William had married Sally without asking for his parent's blessing, and worse still, they had gone ahead with the small, unassuming ceremony in a registry office without inviting them, or indeed, Sally's parents. Both, William and Sally did apologise profusely later, when they realised how much sadness their selfish actions had caused. They were forgiven of course, but by then the damage had been done. Joan's resentment at being deprived of attending her oldest son's wedding would never truly disappear. It was only after Sally had borne a child that she began to understand about the special bond that exists between a mother and her first born child.

Lizzie, however, would drive down from Gloucester on a frequent basis, and stay over. It was these visits that Sally looked forward to the most. They gave her the chance to talk to another woman on her own wavelength, but more importantly, Lizzie's visits kept her sane. Once Jonathan and Laura were potty trained, Sally began to send them to nursery. At first, she missed them desperately, and wondered how she could fill these new expanses of time that were appearing in her life. It was an innocent remark, she made to Lizzie one day, about being bored that ultimately led to a dramatic change, not only in Sally's life, but in William's and Lizzie's too.

"Look at you, Lizzie, always so elegant, always dressed to turn heads. You must be doing so well in your job. I envy you sometimes and wish I had something more."

"I don't believe what I've just heard!" Exclaimed Lizzie. "I would swap places with you any day! What more do you need? You have a lovely house, you've brought three gorgeous children into the world, you have an adoring husband to look after you, and you seem okay for money."

"Yes, I know you're right, Lizzie. I don't want to sound ungrateful. William does earn a good income, but it all goes on the mortgage, the cars and bills etc. I don't bring anything in, and that's the problem, I miss my independence, and want to wear nice clothes again. Can you understand that?"

Lizzie sighed, and went to light a cigarette. Then, thinking twice about it, in view of the children, she returned the packet to her bag.

"Listen Sally, the truth is, I work as a typist, nothing more, despite what you may think, and maybe what I've implied. I detest my job, but in about ten years, I may be good enough to become a private secretary to some boring old fart, but it's not what I want." Confessed Lizzie, taking a sip of her Chablis. "Do you really think, I could afford to buy these clothes? No, of course not. I make them myself!"

Sally glared in amazement at Lizzie's eye-catching black and white, flared trouser suit. It was perfectly cut, with unusual, swirling patterns, and large, circular holes cut out in the top half, to reveal Lizzie's slim, midriff.

"Lizzie, are you telling me you made that outfit?"

"Of course I did. Do you like it, it's not too daring is it?"

"It looks fabulous! I would never have guessed." Gasped Sally excitedly. "But who taught you to make clothes?"

"My mother, she learnt dressmaking during the war. She made all her own clothes too."

"Lizzie, can you do something for me?"

"As long as it's not going to cost me!"

"Can you teach me to make clothes?"

Within a few short months, and under Lizzie's expert guidance, Sally was creating her own distinctive wardrobe. Initially, she stuck to simple dresses and skirts, but as her confidence grew and her dressmaking skills improved, she found she could tackle much more complex designs on a wider variety of materials. Although her creations were by no means quite as bizarre as some of Lizzie's, they did exude a certain glamour in an era setting new boundaries in women's fashion.

Unwittingly, Sally and Lizzie now found themselves at the forefront of establishing their own clothing label. At first, the women were simply supplying their own circle of friends and contacts, who were desperate to be the first to wear these exciting, innovative creations. Word soon got around, and within a year they were supplying several well-known retailers in and around central London on a regular basis. The opening of, Scarlet's boutique, in Richmond was a natural progression, once William and Jeremy had found suitable premises. Subsequently, Lizzie moved closer, and a workshop was set up in the rear of the building, so that garments could be produced on the premises, rather than at Sally's home. Because of Sally's family commitments, it was Lizzie who automatically became the principle partner in the venture. This was an arrangement that suited them both, and resulted in the business becoming a highly successful concern. A short time later they had to hire their first employee, as business was becoming so brisk.

Once William was satisfied that his wife's enterprise was bearing enough fruit, he sold out entirely to Jeremy, and extricated himself completely from the buying and selling side of things. Instead, William moved into the field of interior design.

Jeremy on the other hand found himself getting more involved with Scarlet's, from providing essential maintenance work to the building, to running errands and delivering stock. However, it was soon to become apparent that his interests were something a little more than business-related.

12. MAYFAIR

Pauline checked herself in the full-length mirror before taking the Piccadilly line tube from Hammersmith to Hyde Park Corner for her evening shift at Lake's. She would then walk the short distance along Park Lane, before turning right into Curzon Street. It was a pre-requisite of the job that hostesses looked immaculate at all times. Pauline had grown quite accustomed now to getting ready and being at her best in a short space of time. Mrs. Lake had even taken the trouble to take Pauline aside, during her first week to give her a crash course in choosing and applying the correct make-up to achieve the greatest effect.

Pauline was very jumpy, she had it in her mind that the police were going to come and arrest her at any moment, after she had unwittingly set up Mr. Bloom for Frank to murder. It was the evening following her husband's atrocious act, and the last thing Pauline felt like was going in to work. She knew there would be questions, especially as it had been her who had last seen the old man leave the club. Pauline had even considered taking a few days off sick until the dust had settled, but Frank had told her to go into work, and just act normal as if she didn't know anything about it. She knew he was right but she didn't possess his ruthlessness, and found it difficult to distance herself from the appalling events of the night before.

It was busy, Saturday nights always were. Inside, the atmosphere was dark, and smoke-filled. She could hear the rich, deep tones of Yvette, a cabaret singer, who was a regular performer at the club. She was belting out a Shirley Bassey number, and from the applause she received, the audience were certainly impressed. Pauline made her way to the staff changing rooms and hoped she would be put in the poker room. There were often high-stakes games held at the club during the weekends. These were probably illegal, but no less popular, and tens of thousands had been won and lost over the years. Pauline preferred the poker room as the men were so involved with the game, they had little time for flirting and trying to touch up the young hostesses. Although Lake's was supposed to be exclusively for men, more and more women were now frequenting the club, mainly at weekends as a result of the changing times. There were even a few highly talented women players who would regularly play at the poker tables, Claire Lake being one of them. Claire had made a mini fortune by using skill and guile to outwit her male opponents. She knew most of them would be fairly drunk by late evening, and those that weren't, she'd order champagne on the house for. Claire was on a winner. She would often lose a few hands on purpose, then as her rivals grew in confidence, she would wait until she had an unbeatable hand, before moving in for the kill. Being the only player sober, she found it always worked with maximum effect. Frank was also an avid poker player, and was probably one of the very few to notice what Claire was doing. He made a habit of watching her play, and vowed to go in there one day, pretending to be drunk, and take her for every penny.

Pauline greeted the five other girls coming on duty, and with practised efficiency, put on her black mini skirt, frilly white blouse, and tiny black apron, as was the customary uniform for hostesses at the club. Stockings and suspenders were also obligatory, but like the other girls, Pauline would wear them under her every day clothes to save time hooking them up once she'd arrived.

"Pauline, I'm glad you're here, it's been hectic tonight." Exclaimed Claire, looking unusually flustered. "Can you attend to tables, six through to twelve, with two of the other girls. We've got a Conservative MP sitting at table six, and I'd like you to look after him."

"Yes, Claire, I'll go immediately."

"Thank-you, Pauline, and before I forget, can you please see to Yvette." Added Claire, surveying the young hostess in her uniform. "She has a half-hour break to get changed after her next song. She likes a thinly-cut smoked salmon sandwich, and a flute of champagne." She then waited for Pauline's reply. "Are you with us tonight, or was I talking to myself?"

"Yes, sorry Claire, I was deep in thought." Replied Pauline, uneasily.

"Perhaps, I've been working you too hard? We'll have a little drink together tonight, when we close. I think you deserve it." Claire then moved in close to Pauline, almost kissing her on the lips, before the younger woman managed to move aside.

"I would love to, but I have to get back home for the babysitter."

"I'm sure we can get around that, Pauline." Smiled Claire, I'll get one of the girls to go. I take it, your Frank is out for the night again?"

Pauline nodded, before she was summoned into the main kitchen to help carry plates of food through to the hungry clientele. She then had to rush back as Yvette finished her song. Fortunately, the sandwiches had already been prepared, and finished off with a salad garnish, so all Pauline had to do was pour the singer a glass of champagne.

The dressing rooms were in the basement, twelve in total, six being on each side of the damp, cold corridor. Like the rest of the club, the rooms had seen better days and needed a vast amount of money spent on them. Pauline hated going to the basement. She had seen a mouse scurrying around down there once, and now looked around anxiously, in case it might return. Stepping over a puddle of water on the concrete floor, she arrived at Yvette's dressing room. The door was ajar, but Pauline still knocked.

"Come in, come in, I don't have much time!" Was the terse reply from inside.

"Hello, you must be Yvette? Claire asked me to bring you this." Said Pauline, as she placed the tray on a side table.

"Thank-you," replied the singer with a slow, but distinct French accent. "So you must be Pauline?"

Pauline was shocked to discover that Yvette was naked, apart from what looked to be, a huge, extravagant blonde wig. She was standing next to a rail of sequined dresses and smoking a strong-smelling, foreign cigarette.

"Yes, I'm Pauline," Came back the nervous response, but she couldn't help being amazed at the aura the professionally-trained singer was exuding. "Will there be anything else, Yvette?" She gasped, feeling herself go red, as she stole a glance at Yvette's body.

"Yes, I want you to zip me up." Yvette then selected a glittering, gold number from the rail, and proceeded to take it off the hanger.

"Come now, Pauline, don't be shy. I'm sure you've seen a naked woman before. I have nothing that you don't have. Besides, I always go naked under my stage costumes, as I don't want the lights to pick up a panty line."

Pauline watched in silence as Yvette pulled off the garish blonde wig, to reveal short platinum blonde hair underneath.

"I'm sorry, you took me by surprise, that's all!" Came Pauline's muted reply.

"When I take you, young lady, it wont be by surprise, I can tell you that now." Purred Yvette, running her tongue around the rim of her champagne glass. Before adding; "If you feel uncomfortable, you can send in one of the other girls?"

Pauline looked away, feeling embarrassed.

"No, I'll be fine," she answered, not wanting to come across as naive and foolish.

Yvette, like Claire was in her mid thirties, and had a lithe, supple dancer's body, with small, pert breasts. She moved with a cat-like grace, that made Pauline feel a little clumsy.

"Claire speaks very highly of you, Pauline." Smiled Yvette, as she pulled on the magnificent dress.

"Does she really? That's surprising, it's nice to be appreciated!"

"Oh, yes, Claire appreciates you, my dear."

"So are you and Claire friends?"

"Yes, we are great friends. We trained together at stage school in Paris, back in the fifties."

"How wonderful. I've loved your performance so far tonight. You are so talented."

"Thank-you, Pauline, that's a very kind thing to say, but you haven't seen anything yet." Smirked Yvette stubbing her cigarette out, and not taking her eyes off Pauline. "I understand you're going to stay back, and join Claire and I for a drink later?"

Pauline gulped as she zipped up the back of Yvette's dress.

"No, I'm sorry, I can't tonight. Perhaps another time."

Yvette turned, and selected another wig from her dressing table.

"I think you should reconsider, Pauline. Claire really looks after the girls who please her, and you don't want to disappoint your boss, do you? Now off you go and get back to your duties."

Pauline had been back out on the club floor for just five minutes when Claire came looking for her, followed by two plain-clothes detectives. She knew immediately what it was about, and felt her legs turn to jelly.

"Pauline, can you please come to my office, these two policemen would like to ask you a few questions."

Claire's office adjoined a plush penthouse apartment at the top of the building, which had panoramic views over Central London. As Pauline followed her employer, she felt she would crack under any questioning, and this was even before anything had been said.

"What's it about Claire, I don't understand?" She asked, trying to act as innocent as possible.

"I've just had some very disturbing news, Pauline." Replied, Claire motioning her to sit. "Poor Mr. Bloom has been found dead. It looks like he fell into the river."

Pauline feigned shock, and put her hands up to her face.

"I can't believe it, not that nice old man. He was very drunk last night though. Was it an accident?"

"That's what we're still trying to establish." Said one of the detectives, a tall, balding man in his fifties. "I'm DCI Miller, and this is DS Brookes," he continued, introducing his colleague, who was a much younger man, with sandy-coloured hair, and an intense, staring face. "So you saw Mr. Bloom, last night, Mrs. Gant?"

Pauline hesitated, she had to be very careful what she said. But even being put on a spot, she felt it odd, and even a little flattering to be referred to as 'Mrs. Gant', especially as her marriage was little more than a sham.

"Yes, I saw him frequently during the evening, I even went and sat with him."

"I see," continued, the Inspector. "So, you say he was drunk?"

"Yes, he was. He'd drank rather a lot of cognac."

"How did he get home, did he drive, or walk, or get a lift?" Butted in the younger officer, with an arrogant air about him.

Pauline felt her face was about to betray her, and began to stutter.

"Please, you must realise that Pauline knew the old man, and was his favourite hostess - all this is a big shock to her." Said Claire, coming to Pauline's rescue.

"Thank-you, Claire," replied Pauline, gratefully, before turning to the younger detective. "No, he never drove, he would always get a taxi."

Claire was watching intently. She knew Pauline was trying to hide something, and was aware her husband, Frank had driven the old man. Now, she could use this to her advantage, when it came to seducing the younger woman.

"Did you call for the taxi, or did you see the driver, Mrs. Gant?" Asked the supercilious policeman, moving closer to Pauline.

"No, she didn't!" Interrupted Claire, "She was helping me. I imagine Mr. Bloom rang a taxi himself, he often did. There's plenty of telephones out in the lobby, all with taxi numbers attached to them."

"Did, Mr. Bloom have any enemies here, or do you know of anyone who would wish him harm?" Asked the Inspector, taking over the questioning.

"Nobody that I'm aware of." Replied Pauline, growing in confidence.

"Is there anything else?" Muttered Claire, irritably.

"Just one other question, did the deceased have a case with him?"

"Yes, he did." Blurted out Pauline, back on the defensive again. "He always carried a case with him."

The two officers glanced at each other.

"Maybe it's at the bottom of the Thames, Inspector?"

"Yes, it's possible, or the tide has taken it away. That's not discounting that a third party has it, of course." Replied the older man, turning to Pauline. "That's all for the time being, we'll be continuing with our investigations. But if you should recall anything, please get in touch. Thank-you ladies." With that, the two police officers took their leave.

"Stay here Pauline, while I show the gentlemen out." Ordered Claire, giving

Pauline a wry smile.

While she was gone, Pauline checked herself in one of several huge mirrors in Claire's sumptuously decorated office. She took a few deep breaths and tried to calm herself back down, but inwardly, she was relieved it had all gone so painlessly.

Pauline looked around the office, all of the furniture was in black, apart from the cream carpet. There was a large desk, with a leather chair located back towards the wall, and to one side was another circular table, with several other chairs placed around it, presumably for meetings. Then, right over in the corner was a soft seating area with a black leather sofa, and two more armchairs. Claire's office also contained a bar, boasting an impressive selection of spirits, mixers and wines in a glass-fronted fridge. Pauline certainly wasn't a drinker, but now she could have downed whatever was put in front of her.

Claire returned a few minutes later, and closed the office door.

"So what are you hiding?" She asked directly.

Pauline felt herself squirming again.

"Nothing, I was just nervous that's all, and couldn't think straight."

"Good reply, but I'm still not convinced. That's why I helped you."

"Thank-you, Claire. Frank did drive him, but said he dropped Mr. Bloom off at his destination, and left him there. So, he must have stumbled, and fell into the river after that."

"Yes, Pauline and pigs might fly!" Retorted Claire, pouring herself a vodka and tonic. She then poured one for Pauline, before eyeing her employee suspiciously. "I did it for you, Pauline. I can see good in you, but what are you doing with a man like Frank? He's bloody psychotic!"

Pauline took a long gulp of her drink.

"He's my husband, Claire, that's why." She replied in a none-too convincing tone.

"Then you are very misguided, that's all I can say. Get rid of him now, Pauline, before he totally destroys your life."

"I appreciate you helping me, Claire. I don't know how I'll ever repay you." Said Pauline, changing the subject and finishing her drink.

Claire put her glass down, and placed her hands on the wall, either side of Pauline.

"I know how you can repay me, Pauline." She then pulled the younger woman towards her and kissed her passionately on the lips. Pauline did nothing to stop her, and found herself responding.

"I'll see you up here, when we close tonight." Said Claire, releasing her prey.

Pauline was breathing in gasps, as she straightened her uniform, and opened the door.

"Yes, Mrs. Lake." She replied, in a hushed whisper.

Pauline chose to take the stairs, rather than the lift, thinking it gave her more time to change her mind about what she was about to do. It was as if, someone else had possessed her mind and body, and was making decisions on her behalf, willing her to submit to a yearning she never knew existed. Her mouth was dry and she was trembling, as at last she reached Claire's office. The door was ajar, and she heard laughter coming from within.

Now, her nerve was deserting her, and she was about to run back downstairs, and get the taxi home that the club provided. As she turned to flee, she heard Claire's voice calling out her name.

"Pauline, there you are. I'm glad you didn't change your mind." She smiled, clutching a flute of champagne in one hand, and one of Yvette's cigarettes in the other. "Come in, we've been expecting you!"

Yvette was sitting like a curled-up cat on the leather sofa. She had changed out of her glitzy stage dress, and was now wearing a long, satin robe.

"How wonderful of you to join us, Pauline. Did you enjoy the rest of the show?"

"Yes, I thought you were brilliant, Yvette," replied Pauline, overawed by the French singer.

"Thank-you, how sweet. Come and sit here, next to me, while Claire fixes you a drink."

Pauline did as she was told, and took her place next to Yvette. The atmosphere was soft and relaxed, but Pauline was tense, and at a loss for words.

"Our Pauline is a very shy girl, Yvette. We'll have to be gentle with her at first." Laughed Claire, eyeing Pauline like a hunter watching its prey.

"Yes, but only at first!" Replied Yvette, placing her hand on Pauline's thigh. "I can't believe you are that shy Pauline?"

She let Yvette's hand run up to her stocking tops, where she stroked the tantalising expanse of bare flesh.

Claire, brought Pauline's champagne over, and sat the other side of her. Within moments, she was caressing Pauline's breasts through her white blouse.

"I designed these uniforms, just for my girls. They're so erotic aren't they?"

Pauline could only nod, she was speechless, and at the same time, longing to be kissed again by Claire. She could feel her nipples hardening beneath her bra, and slid down the sofa, slightly parting her legs, intuitively knowing where Yvette's hand was going to go next.

Claire began to undo Pauline's buttons, as Yvette slid her hand across the girl's lap, and began to gently stoke the inside of her thighs.

Upon reaching the final button, Claire pulled Pauline's blouse open. She kissed her deeply, never taking her hand off the younger woman's, firm breasts. Pulling the blouse off Pauline's shoulders, Claire indicated with her eyes that she wanted the bra off.

Pauline reached around behind her and undid the hooks, before slowly peeling the straps, down along her arms.

Claire gasped with pleasure, as Pauline's size 36C breasts were finally unfettered, and were hers for the taking. She took each one in her hands, running her fingers over the hard, sensitive nipples, before moving her mouth down to hungrily devour them.

Yvette then slid her hand down into Pauline's knickers, sensing the damp patch on the gusset. She had a soft, silky mound, that was wet and yielding, and Yvette's fingers eased purposely inside her.

"Claire, this little minx is drenched, I want to taste her!" Exclaimed Yvette, fingering Pauline more vigorously.

"You can after me, Yvette, she's mine, remember!" Garbled Claire, riled at having to take her mouth away from Pauline's nipple.

"She is so inexperienced!" Laughed Yvette.

"In that case, we had better show her how to satisfy a woman." Was Claire's reply, as she moved across towards Yvette.

The singer removed her fingers from Pauline, licking each one, before undoing her robe, and reclining back on the sofa. She was naked underneath, and beckoned Claire between her parted legs.

"Eat me!" She begged, offering her womanhood to the nightclub boss. Claire needed no further encouragement, and delved her tongue into Yvette's waiting dampness. Both women moaned with pleasure, and Pauline watched with a mixture of shock and pure elation.

Within moments, Yvette was on the edge of climaxing, and began bucking her hips, as Claire's lapping tongue showed no mercy.

Pauline could take no more, and put her hand down to feel herself. She, too was on the verge of exploding.

Yvette, let out a loud gasp, then a long moan, as she came hard on Claire's tongue, before laying back panting, as the older woman now turned her attention back to Pauline.

"I think you'll come quicker than Yvette!" She drawled, stripping off her clothes, to reveal a trim, unblemished body.

Pauline pulled off her knickers, wriggled out of her short skirt, and waited expectantly on the leather sofa, clad only in her stockings and suspenders. When Claire's tongue found its way inside her, fresh from Yvette, it took her by surprise. To be consumed and enjoyed like this by another woman was exquisite, and Pauline found herself pulling down hard on the back of Claire's neck, and wrapping her legs tightly around her.

"She's delicious!" Uttered Claire, coming up to breathe, as Pauline squirmed and writhed in ecstasy.

Yvette came across, and joined them. She sat astride Pauline, giving her the first ever experience of tasting another woman. Pauline was an eager student, and went about her work with amazing enthusiasm. She felt Yvette's juices oozing into her mouth, and in seconds, both women came simultaneously.

Pauline was flowing like never before. Claire was possessing her, devouring her, swallowing her essence. She came hard, and screamed as the powerful orgasm ripped through her body. It was mind shattering and all-engulfing, and she knew she'd now chosen a route, she'd never return from.

13. THREE KINGS

SPRING 1968

Sally, to her delight, had finally lost her baby weight, and was once again able to wear some of her favourite clothes. Caring for the three children was still not getting any easier. Penny had milk teeth coming through, and her continual crying throughout the night was taking its toll on both Sally and William. Jonathan and Laura didn't seem to have suffered too much, although Jonathan was prone to ear infections, which kept him up on many an occasion. Penny, however, had the loudest cry out of all of the children, and demanded attention immediately.

It was a pleasant, mild and sunny Saturday morning. Sally had got Jonathan and Laura washed and dressed, and was about to give them their breakfast. Penny was thankfully in a deep sleep, after getting some relief from the small amount of painkiller the doctor has prescribed for her. Sally had put this in her feed, having recently given up breast-feeding. The two older children were sitting at the table drinking milky tea, when there was a knock at the front door. William was still sleeping, and Sally hoped it hadn't disturbed him. She was used to the postman calling, what with deliveries of dress-making materials and samples, and just assumed it would be him. She was still in her dressing gown, and didn't have any make-up on, when she opened the door to David.

It had been over five years since that Christmas, when William had seen them kissing at the bench beneath the tree in Falcondale. David had guiltily slunk off to his room, William and David's girlfriend, Jenny had stormed off, and Sally had packed her things and moved out, back into Lloyd-Evans Hall. David had later gone on a sabbatical from his studies, and no-one had seen or heard from him since. Now he was here, on Sally's doorstep, looking like nothing had ever happened.

He looked lean and tanned, his hair was much longer than Sally remembered, and seemed fairer.

"Hello, Sally."

"David!" She gasped, feeling a tingle run up her spine.

"I hope I haven't surprised you too much?" He said, breaking into that same mischievous smile that always set her heart a flutter.

"No, no, not at all," she replied totally in shock, pulling her gown together, and trying to bring her hair under control. "It's so wonderful to see you again. I just wasn't expecting you, that's all!"

"That's understandable, I was going to write, but you know, I just never got around to it!"

"You look well, David, and so tanned, but please, you must come in." She smiled, leading him into the hallway.

"Thank-you, and you look no different to the last time I saw you. I understand you have three children now?"

"Yes, we do, and it's very hard work I can tell you. In fact, you're just in time to have breakfast with them, I hope you like scrambled eggs?"

"Sally, there's two things I can never forget about you, and one of those is your fantastic cooking!"

"I wont ask what the other thing is," she laughed, taking him through to the large kitchen, where Jonathan and Laura were seated at a breakfast bar, making a huge mess.

"Children, this is your Uncle!"

David was quite overcome, and immediately went over to the two little ones and started pulling funny faces and acting silly.

"They're wonderful Sally, and Laura is a mini version of you! It must have been tough studying and taking your finals, being pregnant?"

"It was more than tough, but we had plenty of help. A girl from town helped me, she used to be a cleaner at the university, then worked at the hotel, her name is Carol."

"Yes, I think I remember her. I imagine you needed all the help you could get." He grinned, helping to cut Laura's toast. He then glanced up to Sally, who was bringing over his breakfast. Their eyes met, and locked on to each other for perhaps, a little too long.

"William is upstairs, he's sleeping," added Sally, not wanting David to say anything that might incriminate them. Penny, our youngest has been keeping us awake at night. But I'll go and call him, he'll want to see you."

"No, please don't do that on my behalf, Sally. I don't want to be an inconvenience." He replied, looking a little uncomfortable.

No sooner had he finished his sentence, when William walked in, all puffy-eyed. Sally became anxious, she didn't know how this unexpected meeting would turn out. William and David had always been close, but the kissing incident had obviously caused a massive rift between them. She needn't have been too concerned. William broke into a huge smile, and went across to hug his brother fondly. The two of them then sat together and ate breakfast, while Sally attended to the children. David spoke of how he'd returned to Falcondale and had managed to complete the rest of his Theology degree, after spending time in the states, drinking, gambling and doing menial jobs. He apparently needed this time in his life to try and come to terms with the torment of his youth.

"So where did you stay in Falcondale, David, I thought mother had rented the house out?" Asked William, intrigued, as he took a sip from his coffee.

"I stayed in the Old Building - I probably had Frank's old room!"

"Please don't go there, David." Replied William, not appreciating his brother's sense of humour. "Sally still has the most awful nightmares about that night."

"I'm sorry, I wont mention it again," said David, touching his brother on the shoulder affectionately.

William sat back, deep in thought. The events of that night, when Frank came to the house had disturbed him too, and like Sally, he tried to bury them deep in his sub-conscious, where he hoped they would remain.

"Listen, David, about that Christmas we spent together." He said eventually, his face still serious.

"What, you mean, Sally and I at the bench?"

"Yes, that's exactly what I mean," continued William, a little awkwardly. "It was just something innocent, we all over-reacted. Let's just forget it, and start over, after all it was a long time ago."

"Thank-you, William, it's been eating away at me. That's why I told mother not to tell you I was back at Falcondale, I felt so ashamed, like I'd hurt you so bad."

"David, you're too sensitive," replied William, with a hint of a smile on his face. "So that explains why mother's been quiet, she knew more than she was letting on."

"William, perhaps we could go out tonight, the three of us and have a few drinks and a meal?"

"Sounds great, but only if we can find someone daft enough to baby-sit three young children!"

The meal was a welcome relief to both Sally and William, they hadn't been out for such a while. Sally looked absolutely ravishing, in a flower-patterned mini-dress, with her blue eyes sparkling, and her glorious, blonde hair loose about her shoulders. Both brothers were mesmerised, but David had to hide his admiration, not wanting to destroy all the good work that had just been done.

If Sally did give David the odd glance it was very discreet, and she certainly didn't give anything away, she was a happily married woman who was in love with her husband, and that's how things had to stay. They drove across the river into Richmond, after Sally had eventually found a baby sitter. William had booked a table at a charming Italian-themed, riverside restaurant he'd always wanted to try, called Vesuvius. They opted for the three-course menu, William was ravenous, and soon got through his Parma ham and melon starter, before demolishing a sirloin steak. Sally and David both had minestrone soup, followed by chicken breast stuffed with stilton, and wrapped in bacon. To follow, they all had home-made Italian ice cream sundaes.

It was during the dessert, when the wine was flowing freely between William and David, that the latter, released his bombshell.

"So what are you planning to do now, David, will you move to London?" Asked William, wiping his lips with a serviette.

David waited until the waiter had replenished their glasses.

"Well, no - not exactly, I'm going out to the far east."

"How exciting," exclaimed Sally, "Is it relief work, to do with your Theology studies?"

"No, Sally, it's nothing like that. I've been accepted by the US army, I'm going to Vietnam."

Sally's face dropped as much as William's, and there was a loud clatter as her spoon fell onto her plate. But it was William who spoke first.

"David, you're a Canadian citizen, I'm sure it's illegal to join a foreign army and fight against a friendly nation."

"Yes, you're right, William, but the US have found a loophole, and hundreds of Canadians are joining already."

Sally then interrupted, "But why? I thought you were a man of peace?" She pleaded, her eyes full of emotion. "There were demonstrations at Grosvenor

Square last year about Vietnam. Lots of police got injured and there were many arrests. The people don't want it, David."

"It's a question of standing for what you believe is right. I can't abide oppression, and I want to do my duty. We have to stand alongside America on this."

"But Canada still views North Vietnam as a friendly nation, David." Remarked William.

"Canada has been secretly supporting and supplying the US, not directly to South Vietnam, but via America itself." Continued David, getting animated. "Anyway, the US is taking foreign volunteers, and I've been accepted. I report for training in two weeks."

Sally was motionless, and deep in thought.

"It sounds as if it's all finalised, like you've already made up your mind to go?"

"I have Sally," stated David, resolutely.

Both William and Sally glanced at each other, aware that David saw this as an ideal opportunity to die with honour, and find release from the wounds to his troubled mind. Neither of them, however, made these views known to him.

"Why can't you come and work with me in interior design, or maybe, Sally and Lizzie could find something for you in the rag trade?" William knew he was wasting his breath, he had come up against the stubborn trait present in all Peddlescoombe's. They just couldn't sit back and watch what they perceived as an injustice being done.

David stayed over that night in one of the spare rooms, but the light-heartedness, and the joy of seeing him soon evaporated, as the realisation that the war in Vietnam was escalating, came home to both William and Sally, in different ways.

Sally was up just after 5 am. Penny was crying and wanting her milk. She scooped the baby up in her arms and carried her downstairs to the kitchen. Although it wasn't cold, she felt a draft, and noticed the back door was open and the kitchen light was already on. Sally guessed it was David and strapped Penny into her high chair, before warming up her feed. Poking her head out into the garden, she noticed David sitting on one of the patio chairs, smoking a cigarette and drinking coffee. He didn't notice her, and she was able to enjoy a few precious moments, simply admiring him. She loved William with a passion, and would happily marry him again, if that were to be the case, but with David, she saw a troubled soul, an unknown entity. He was a free spirit, she couldn't obtain. He was like her, the forbidden fruit.

Penny began to cry and David looked around and saw Sally standing in the doorway. She looked so sensual, her hair all in a mess, and still wearing the remnants of last night's make-up. He wanted to tell her how much he loved her, and how he had longed for her, and how he envied his brother, and how it could never be. She smiled warmly at him, and he saw the sensual eyes, the passion, and the love in the heart of the woman, who was the mother of his brother's children.

"David, why are you up so early?"

It took him a moment to stop marvelling at her beauty, and try to construct a sentence.

"I like being up this early, it gives me time to think," was his reply, as he took a long pull on his cigarette.

"Same old David, I see," she sighed, "Perhaps, you do a little too much thinking?"

"Yes, maybe you're right Sally, but much of my thinking is about you."

"Please stop it, David. I'm married to your brother."

"I'm sorry, but can I just say one thing?"

"Of course you can, but please don't torture yourself," she said, sitting down next to him.

"Seeing you again Sally, even for these few valuable moments has filled my soul. I will never forget how you looked last night. You've stolen my heart, and I'm powerless to prevent it."

"David, if you think so much of me, you wouldn't hurt me by going off to fight in a war that doesn't concern you. Please stay, I'm sure you'll find something fulfilling here to do with your life." She hesitated, before finally finishing her sentence, "And maybe you'll find a woman who deserves to be loved by someone as wonderful as you."

David bent down and picked up his holdall.

"It's got to be like this, Sally. The more I'm around you, the worse it'll get. I would just undermine your marriage. I would be like a parasite, waiting for my chance, waiting to destroy everyone's happiness. I have to go, do you understand?"

She stood up and nodded, feeling a tear welling up in her eye. He moved closer to kiss her, she went instinctively into his arms. However, the kiss never took place. They both knew it would be so wrong. For a few short moments, they held each other, wondering about what could have been.

"David, please don't go."

He kissed her gently on the cheek, before burying his face into her hair, breathing in her intoxicating feminine scent.

"Say goodbye to William for me, he'll understand." David then turned and left, without looking back.

Sally un-strapped Penny from her chair, and took her out into the garden, where the birds were still singing their dawn chorus. She cuddled her baby daughter tightly, and let out a sigh, as Penny put out a chubby little hand, and wiped away a tear from her mother's face.

It had been a couple of months now since Pauline's intimacy with Claire and Yvette. The French singer however had bookings in both the UK and Europe, and would only appear at Lake's a couple of times a year. But Claire's passion for Pauline continued unabated, and seemed to be warmly welcomed by the younger woman. Claire had even promoted Pauline to act as manager in her absence, and used this to her advantage. It meant that Pauline now had more responsibilities and other duties to perform. In reality, it just meant Claire and Pauline could spend more time together, especially when the club had closed or during mid-week when it wasn't quite as busy.

Pauline found she enjoyed being the feminine half of her relationship with Claire, and revelled in the knowledge that she was desirable once again. Although sex with Claire could occasionally get quite playful, and did involve bondage and the use of handcuffs and whips, Claire was never rough nor did she act in a threatening manner, which Pauline frequently got from Frank. Claire knew exactly how to please her, and knew the limits, and vice versa. To Pauline it was all new and uncharted territory, and of course she was getting back at her husband, and rebelling against him in her own way. Had Frank treated her better and respected her not only as a woman, but also as his wife, and the mother of their daughter, it's debatable whether Pauline's relationship with Claire would have blossomed as it did.

Frank, on the other hand was no fool, and suspected something was going on. He had gained quite a reputation at the club, and was often used as an unofficial bouncer when things occasionally got rough, and this did cause him to wonder who could be so foolish as to mess around with his woman. It wasn't only Frank's frightening physical presence that got him noticed. He had an air of arrogance about him, and had gained respect for his business acumen and entrepreneurial spirit. Frank would simply get things done when most others just thought about it.

Frank and Pauline had also moved out of their cramped flat after he'd secured a brand new, state of the art house in Kew, half a mile from his office. The interior was full of modern works of art, and the general decor of the house wasn't to most people's tastes. But Frank didn't care about that, he was only concerned at the further social standing it had brought him.

He decided to leave things as they were regarding Pauline. Her frequent nights of having to work late, always meant that Claire would send one of her girls in a taxi, to take over the baby sitting of Tina. Frank had already seduced two of Claire's staff, and now had his eye on a petite blonde, called Anne. He quickly realised Anne called for a little more hard work and determination on his part, as she represented a far more tantalising proposition. Anne had baby sat three times now. On her first visit, she seemed more interested in doing a good job and getting into Claire's good books, rather than be too impressed with Frank's often basic line of seduction. Undeterred, he was delighted to see her return the following week, this time she seemed a lot more relaxed and even accepted a glass of wine when he offered it to her.

Anne was wearing the Lake's uniform of short black skirt, and tight white blouse which was always highly effective in raising Frank's blood pressure. He ran his eyes along her lean thighs, as he lent over her to place the drink on a side table. She smelt delicious, and obviously took her appearance seriously. In fact all of Claire's girls were turned out beautifully, but some of them had to be taught how to apply their make-up, to dress, to act, and even how to walk. But with Anne, all this seemed to come naturally. Frank knew she was a rising star at the club, and could probably command a fortune sitting with the well-heeled clientele, ensuring they were drinking only the best champagne money could buy. She had rebuffed his earlier crude attempts to grope her, and had told him in no uncertain terms that she was engaged to be married. She had put up a seemingly impregnable barrier against Frank's efforts to seduce her, but this was only making him more determined. He realised, to bed Anne, he had to come up with a different approach. She was young, intelligent, pretty and going by the conversations he'd had with her, was highly ambitious too.

The beginning of a plan was manifesting itself in Frank's mind, but he didn't quite know how to put it into action until the following Friday. Anne had already told him she would be baby sitting again as there was a big poker game taking place at the club. Claire would be playing along with some of her wealthier clients, and Frank decided he would try a few hands himself.

He sat opposite Claire with £100 at his disposal. She removed her sunglasses and welcomed him to the game.

"The blinds are £5 and £10, is that a little too much for you Frank?" She grinned, before adding, "You can play for smaller stakes in the next room." The blinds were the small initial bets players had to make at the start of the round. Obviously, as the game progresses the bets could get considerably higher.

"Five and ten are fine with me, Claire." He replied, noticing the sarcasm in her voice. He was angry that she'd just humiliated him in front of the other players in the knowledge that it would affect his play.

Two of the other four players were drunk and lost their money to Claire fairly early in the game. She was playing her usual way, bluffing and going in with large bets. Frank declined champagne and instead ordered a cold beer. He put on his sunglasses, but was still raging inside over Claire's comments. He looked down at his two cards and saw he had two tens. He waited patiently for the 'Flop', where three cards are dealt upturned for all to see, and used to improve their original two cards. It didn't help him, and Claire raised immediately. The other two players folded, leaving just Frank and Claire to battle it out. The 'Turn', where another upturned card is dealt brought Frank the third ten he was waiting for. Claire raised, and Frank went with her. The 'River', the last upturned card brought an ace. Claire went all in, causing Frank to fold his three tens. She then sat back in her chair, taking a sip of her champagne. He had lost the hundred he started with, and felt his fists clenching under the table, as he desperately tried to control his anger.

"Are you playing again Frank, or am I a bit too good for you?" She smirked, like a cat who'd just had the cream.

"I think a break is called for. I need half an hour," he replied determined not to let Claire see him so out of control. Frank got up to leave the table, as Claire continued to play. He looked around for Pauline but was surprised not to see her, as she would often host at the card tables when Claire was playing. He had to get out, to clear his head. He needed time to think, time to have a drink, then he would come back for Claire. He knew it was a bad idea to play poker in his current state of mind, but he couldn't let her get away with it.

Standing in the upstairs lobby, he pressed the button to summon the lift, and waited impatiently. He glanced at himself in the enormous mirror and admired his reflection. Tall and deceptively handsome, he looked immaculate in his black dinner suit and bow tie, the scar running down his left cheek giving him a somewhat dangerous appeal. He was flushed, but put that down more to being angry, rather than the alcohol. The lift was showing no signs of arriving, so he decided to take the stairs instead. It was as he passed Claire's office, that he heard the sound of a glass breaking, and went across to listen outside the door. He just assumed it to be her drunken husband, Walter, since Claire was still involved in the poker game, and decided to go in and investigate.

He gave a little tap, then opened the door quietly. He saw that the office was in semi-darkness. He then noticed another door, which he'd never seen before. It was built to blend in with the bookcase, and unless opened, would never have been detected. The door was ajar and emitting a soft glow. He walked across, and pushed it further open. Even Frank was surprised with what he saw. It was a large room, just like a dungeon, lit with several candles, and smelling of incense. Each of the four walls had exposed brickwork, and on one side he saw manacles attached to the wall. On the opposite side was an enormous wheel-like device with securing straps, then to the left of this, was a metal cage, like one in which you would keep a wild animal incarcerated. He moved closer, and saw a huge, sinister-looking wooden table in the centre of the so-called dungeon. It was heavy and dark with a naked girl tied spread-eagle on its surface. Her ankles were secured by leather straps. The girl's arms were tied above her head in a similar fashion. The brunette had a shapely body, and a pair of magnificent breasts, which Frank had seen before.

Pauline was gagged, and tried to move as soon as she saw her husband. Her eyes were filled with fear as to what he might do. He saw the broken glass on the floor, which she had somehow knocked over, while waiting for her mistress to return.

Frank looked about him and gazed into an open, leather case containing various whips, and a cat o' nine tails. Beside it were two other cases, one with assorted dildos and strap-ons of varying size, while the other case boasted an impressive array of handcuffs, nipple clamps and other devices designed to inflict pain.

Frank should have been incensed seeing his wife like this, but the sight of her naked, bound and gagged, and about to be used as another woman's plaything turned him on in the extreme. He was failing to contain himself, and pulled the gag from Pauline's mouth. She stared up at him, terrified, unable to move, and expecting the worst. He placed his hands on her body, and ran them across her breasts, feeling her nipples harden immediately. Running his hand lower, he skimmed it across her belly, and down to her inner thighs. Inserting a finger inside her, his suspicions were confirmed, she was wet and waiting, but obviously not for him. How long she had been bound like this, he had no idea, but he was determined to take her there and then, and really give Claire something to savour when she would later devour his wife's juices.

Frank was just about to enter her, when he heard the door open. The light from the corridor illuminated his face and erect penis as he stood with his trousers and boxers around his ankles. It was a bizarre situation, and one couldn't say who was the most surprised, Frank or Claire.

"So you've found my secret office have you, Gant?" Shouted Claire, as she walked in clutching the wad of cash she'd just won. "How dare you come in here. Get out!"

"What are you doing with my wife?" Replied Frank, threateningly.

Claire couldn't help being impressed by Frank's manhood, as he casually pulled up his trousers, but there wasn't a hint of this on her stony, hard stare.

"I make her happy, and know how to satisfy her, unlike you, Frank. Your marriage is a shambles. Pauline only stays with you because of Tina."

The remarks cut into Frank like a knife. He felt his anger rising again, but was determined to get the upper hand.

"You're nothing but a filthy parasite, Claire. You think you can just walk in and destroy a marriage, and one where there's a child involved. If you were a man, I'd break every bone in your scrawny body."

"That's typical, coming from you, Frank. I've seen the marks on Pauline's body where you've beaten her. You being released from jail was the worse thing for both her and Tina. You're no better than an animal. Women such as Pauline need protection from the likes of you."

"Look who's talking," came back Frank. "You're no better than me, in fact you're just a female version, and a fucking ugly one at that!"

"How dare you compare yourself to me. The very sight of you repulses me. Now get out of my office!" Screamed Claire, throwing the money down onto a side table, her eyes blazing.

"I'm not leaving until you've been made to pay for what you've done. How can Pauline and myself live as man and wife, as father and mother to our daughter after this? You didn't even keep it private, you're gutter trash and will be treated as such." With that, Frank pulled out a flick knife from the inside of his jacket, and moved menacingly towards Claire. "I want my pound of flesh, bitch!"

Fearing for her life, Claire began back-stepping until she bumped against the wall.

"Frank, please don't do anything stupid." She gasped, her voice trembling. "Look, you can take back the money you lost tonight and a bit more, please Frank, don't!"

"A hundred pounds, is that all our marriage is worth? You mouthy trollop." He sneered, moving up to put his face into hers.

"What do you want Frank, I can't obviously fight you like a man?"

Frank, grinned and moved away, before walking back over to where his wife was still tethered to the table. He cut the straps that bound her with athletic ease and watched as she sat up with a surprised look on her face. Hearing Frank speaking so gallantly had surprised her, and now he was like her knight in shining armour, come to rescue her, but at what price, she thought.

"Get dressed, I'll deal with you later, you're an embarrassment." He snarled, as Pauline scuttled around searching for her clothes.

"I want Pauline to stay, Frank. She is on duty for the rest of the evening, and we are getting busy." Added Claire, trying to diffuse the tense atmosphere.

Frank clicked the knife shut, and returned it to his pocket.

"So having sex with a rug-muncher is in my wife's job description is it?" He asked threateningly, still wanting Claire to realise he was far from happy with the situation.

"Well, we can't do pistols at dawn so how do you want to settle it?" Snapped, Claire, going to Pauline's side.

"I'll not rest until I see you destroyed." Was Frank's terse reply.

"I would suggest poker?" Replied Claire, "So how much is your damaged ego worth, Gant, a thousand, five, ten? Just name your price."

What Claire suggested was exactly what Frank wanted to hear. He could have suggested it himself, but having just lost to her at poker, he thought she might smell a rat. Now he had her where he wanted her.

"Don't try and belittle me, Claire. I want you dead and buried - we'll play for the lot, your club against my cab company, along with all my cars, accounts, premises, and my house."

Claire couldn't hide the smirk on her face, now she had Frank just where she wanted him, or so she thought.

"What about Pauline?" She asked, watching his wife putting her bra back on.

"Pauline too!" He grinned, "Winner take all - tomorrow night!"

"It's a deal!" Hissed Claire, "It'll be a pleasure!"

Frank nodded, pleased with how things had worked out, but tried hard not to show it.

"I'll have my lawyer come over first thing tomorrow to check over both sets of assets and draw up a contract."

"You're a bigger fool than I imagined, Frank. I'll take you for everything, and leave you homeless in the street where you belong."

As Frank made his departure, he scooped up the wad of cash Claire had put down, it must have been at least a thousand pounds.

"I'll hang on to this as a deposit, and to show you're as good as your word."

"Get out!" Shouted Claire, before turning her attentions back to Pauline.

"I think we have some unfinished business, Mrs. Gant, to the victor, the spoils, so they say."

"But you haven't won yet, Claire," replied Pauline, hesitantly taking off the clothes she'd only just put back on.

"Oh, I think I have, Pauline. I always get what I want."

Frank punched the air as he left Claire's office. It was a situation that suited him. He had a strategy he was going to employ against his rival the following evening. She was so confident of beating him, but now he was equally, if not more confident he'd turn the tables on her. He helped himself to a bottle of Champagne as he left the club. He had one more pressing engagement that evening, the final seduction of Anne.

It was around 1am when Frank arrived home. He let himself in with his key, took his jacket off, undid his bow tie and swaggered into the lounge. Anne was watching a late-night movie and drinking a coke. She looked hot in her sexy, black uniform. Although Frank despised Claire with a vengeance, he couldn't fault her when it came to designing uniforms for her female staff. The champagne was still chilled, and Frank deftly uncorked it, before pouring them both a glass each.

"What's the occasion, Frank - you seem very pleased tonight?" Asked Anne, as she sat up to take her drink.

She had a couple of buttons undone on her blouse, and Frank leered hungrily at her pert breasts.

"I'm celebrating because Lake's nightclub will be mine this time tomorrow night!"

Anne looked surprised, and put her drink down.

"Really? I don't quite understand, Frank. Should I be pleased about that?" She asked, a little concerned. "Will I still keep my job?"

"Let's just say that Claire and I have come to an arrangement, and she'll be vacating the club very soon."

"I can't say I'll be sorry to see her go." Continued Anne, eyes wide with curiosity. "Did you know she regularly seduces her female staff?"

"Yes, I heard that," smiled Frank, inching closer towards her on the settee. "Did she ever get anywhere with you?"

Anne went quiet, and Frank guessed something had happened.

"Only once," she replied eventually. "I try to keep out of her way, but she says to get promotion or references for work at another club, you have to be 'nice' to her. She wears the girls down with her demands, and threatens them with losing their jobs to get what she wants."

"Did she have you in her secret office?"

Anne hesitated, before confirming what Frank suspected.

"Yes, I was put blindfolded into the cage, before being manacled to the wall."

So did you enjoy sex with Claire?" Asked Frank, feeling his erection practically bursting through his trousers.

Anne knew he was getting excited.

"She whipped and violated me, but it was my first time with another woman, and when Claire wants something, she usually gets it. But, yes I suppose I did enjoy it, she certainly knows how to please a woman, and I have to say, it was very different."

"I know how to please a woman too." He replied with a mischievous grin, before adding; "Listen, I'll need someone who I can trust, someone who'll be loyal. I see those qualities in you, Anne."

"I'm very flattered, but what about your wife, she's second only to Claire now?"

"There's room for two, Anne. Besides I'm not sure if Pauline will be staying."

"So I take it you know about Claire and your wife?"

"Yes, of course I know," replied Frank, not wanting to sound like he was the last person on the planet to know his wife was having a fling with her boss.

"So, it didn't bother you?"

"I have other, more important concerns Anne, and right now, you're one of them."

"I knew there would be a catch, so really it'll just be the same as with Claire, except you're a man?"

"I would have thought you would have preferred that?"

"I've already told you Frank, I'm engaged to be married. I don't see letting Claire have her way with me occasionally as cheating, I see it more as a means to an end."

"So you would view having sex with another man as cheating?"

"Yes, I would," she replied, going a little red, "It's all about penetration you see."

Frank laughed, "I think Claire would have ways of penetrating you, if she hasn't done already!"

Anne giggled, and let him re-fill her glass.

"So what would my job be, and would I get more pay?"

Frank stood up and went to fetch his jacket. He reached inside and took out the wad of cash he'd taken from Claire earlier. He counted out £200, and handed it to Anne. She was shocked, and a little disgusted that he was taking her as a prostitute. Frank saw this immediately, and moved to rectify the situation.

"Anne, you would be a valued employee, a manager, and in order to carry out your duties effectively and command the respect you deserve from the other staff, you'll need a clothing allowance, so here is this month's."

"But Frank, this is nearly two month's salary, I don't know what to say."

"Just say yes, Anne," he smirked, "Besides, the uniform you're wearing will have to be replaced."

"Why's that, it's practically new?"

"I'll show you why!"

With that, he lunged at Anne, and ripped apart her blouse. She tried to fight him off, but he was a huge powerful man, and she was little more than eight stone in weight. As he yanked off her bra, she fell backwards onto the settee, and Frank came down next to her, his hands all over her body. She felt him pulling off her skirt, then tearing at her knickers and was powerless to stop him. Within seconds she was naked apart from her black stockings and suspenders. She smelt divine, as he drooled over her, before kissing her on the lips forcibly. She felt his tongue invade her mouth, and for a moment she thought about biting him, but something stopped her, and she found herself kissing him back. She felt herself getting wet, and began to tug at his shirt. He responded by pulling it off, over his shoulders, before gripping her firmly and sucking at her hard nipples. She was panting and wanted him inside her. She reached down and felt his huge penis, straining to be set free.

"Frank, I want you," she pleaded.

He didn't reply, but swept off his remaining clothes as fast as he could, and before she realised what was happening, his penis was entering her mouth.

She sucked at it hard, savouring the fluid oozing onto her tongue. This only lasted a few moments, before he pushed her back onto the settee and began to lick roughly between her legs.

She was swimming in juices and came rapidly, digging her nails into his broad back, as she screamed out his name loudly.

Sweat was pouring from him, as he then pulled her across his lap, and began to beat her buttocks loudly, they turned red immediately and he bent his head down to kiss each one, before spanking her vigorously again.

Between blows, he managed to bring one hand beneath her hips and started to finger her, as he continued his assault on her shapely bottom.

She came a second time, with Frank's fingers buried deep inside her, and felt her body go into spasm as it betrayed her, and all that she had said earlier.

Anne then surprised Frank, by getting up off his lap, and sitting astride him.

She took hold of his manhood, and guided it inside herself, while beginning to rock up and down on top of him.

"You're not getting it all you own way," she grinned, as he watched her youthful breasts bobbing in unison with each of her thrusts. Her blonde hair was flowing with abandon, as she rode him violently, like a stallion. With each of her actions she was getting more of him inside her body.

She was moaning and gasping, and practically falling off with every animated move. They climaxed simultaneously, with Frank grasping her hips, and holding her steady, as he came powerfully inside her.

The poker game was set to start at 8pm, and Claire was already sitting at the table when Frank arrived. She was dressed in a tight figure-hugging black dress and wore a pair of designer sunglasses. Despite her many years of showing no emotion on her face during poker matches, Claire found it hard not to break into a grin when she saw Frank stagger as he entered the room. She knew he would have been drinking before the game, and gloated in the fact that he would be easy prey.

Frank looked the part, in a dark blue suit, silk tie and expensive Italian-made loafers. He was accompanied by a huge, bearded brute, known as Mark, who was his right-hand man in the cab business, next came the wheelchair-bound, Linda, Frank's secretary, then a couple of square-jawed types in suits, obviously as back-up.

Frank took his seat at the table, and Mark placed a bottle of single-malt whiskey down next to him, further to his opponent's delight.

"Are you sure you want to go through with this Claire?" He asked impassively, his speech seeming slightly slurred. "If you want to chicken out, I'll understand."

Claire was heartened by this and saw it as a sign of weakness on Frank's part. Obviously, he wanted her to back out, as he was scared of losing in the cold light of day, she assured herself.

"I'm going to take your business, your home, and your woman, Gant. I'm going to chew you up, and spit you out, like the vermin you are."

Claire's words angered Frank, but he had succeeded in doing what he had intended, by giving her false hope, and making her believe he wanted out. Mark opened the scotch, and poured Frank a good-sized shot.

Linda, a stern-looking woman in her forties, manoeuvred her wheelchair up to the poker table and placed two contracts down for both parties to sign. She had been there earlier to meet Claire's lawyer, and together they had listed both sets of assets and drawn up the paperwork. She had informed Frank that what they were doing probably wouldn't stand up in court if Frank won, and took everything from Claire, or vice versa. This gave Frank a certain degree of re-assurance, just in case he did lose. Once the forms had been signed, Linda placed them in her case, and pushed herself back into the shadows with the two henchmen to await the start of the game. She had been a lifelong polio sufferer, and now spent practically all of her life confined to a wheelchair. She had been recommended by Duncan Fraser, who represented Frank at his trial a few years earlier, and ever since taking her on, Frank had been more than impressed with Linda's vast legal knowledge and sharp, articulate wit.

They decided to play with chips to the value of 1000 each, winner take all. The atmosphere was tense and smoke-filled. Claire had her entourage sitting close behind her. This included her husband, Walter, her own lawyer, and a couple of the regular doormen. Pauline, meanwhile seemed uncertain where to nail her colours and flitted around nervously, to Frank's annoyance.

A croupier dealt the first cards, two apiece and face down. Frank folded. The same thing happened in the next round, with Claire doing the same thing. On the third game she went in with a hundred. Frank followed and raised after the 'Flop', where three cards are dealt face up. Claire raised again and Frank folded. It continued with Claire seemingly having the upper hand, bluffing and placing high bets.

Frank knew it would be like this and played into it. In the next game he got a king and queen of diamonds. He didn't raise however, and let Claire carry on in her set pattern.

She went in with a hundred again, and Frank followed, after hesitating. When the flop came, the cards were kind to Frank, a three and a ten of diamonds, plus the king of hearts. He just needed one more diamond for a flush. But even if he didn't get the hand he wanted, he was still holding a formidable pair of kings, and with the possibility of getting another.

The 'turn' came which featured an ace of clubs. This made Frank nervous. He saw her shift in her chair, and take a drink. He suspected she had a pair of aces - not good for him. The situation got more tense, and Frank felt himself sweating, which he was pleased about, as it would give Claire the impression he was under pressure. He gulped at his whiskey, and looked to be like he was stalling.

Meanwhile, Claire glanced around at her husband, and gave him a knowing smile, before sitting back in her chair.

Frank had been right, she was holding a pair of aces, and still with another card to come, she was smug and confident, and enjoying seeing Frank squirming.

Had she been the judge of character, she thought she was, she would have seen through Frank's trickery, and would have known he was feigning drunkenness. In fact, the so-called whiskey he was drinking was nothing more than cold tea that he had prepared earlier. He was completely sober, and hadn't had a drink at all that day. It was all part of his rouse to lead Claire into a false sense of security, but Frank was by no means home and dry yet. Unknown to him, he needed to improve his hand, as at the moment, his pair of kings wouldn't beat Claire's pair of aces.

He nodded to the dealer, who then dealt the 'river', and final card.

He swallowed hard as the card was turned upwards on the green baize table for all to see. Claire gulped, and felt her heart racing. It was unbearable, and she wanted to finish it while she had the chance. She went 'all-in', her hand hadn't been improved by the last card, but she still sensed her pair of aces would be more than enough to destroy Frank.

There was another delay as Frank assessed the situation he was in. The final card had been the king of spades, which now meant he had three kings - good enough to beat Claire. He got up and paced the floor, much to Claire's enjoyment. He would join her shortly, and go all-in, but he wanted to prolong her suffering by making her believe he was beaten.

"Take your time Frank, a bit scared are we? Poor Frankie boy!" She laughed loudly.

Everyone's eyes were now back on Frank, who was still acting like he was dead and buried. All of Claire's chips were on the table, goading him into taking action - if he dare.

Frank eventually sat back down, poured himself another large 'whiskey' and downed it in one.

"All-in!" He suddenly called out, with an air of authority, while glaring straight at Claire, both their eyes still hidden behind dark glasses. He then pushed his remaining chips into the centre of the table, and sat back to await his fate.

"You're a bloody loser, Gant!" She grinned, fingering her two cards confidently.

"There's only one loser here, you bitch, and it's certainly not me." He hissed, laying his two cards down for all to see.

The dealer looked up at Frank, before turning to Claire, who now showed her hand.

"Three kings beats two aces," said the dealer, with no expression on his face.

There was a moment of silence as Claire let the reality of what had just happened slowly sink in. She had just lost her nightclub to Frank in one single poker game. It was surreal, and she couldn't quite take it on board. Walter moved forward to comfort his wife, while the two doorman, expecting trouble took a few steps closer.

Frank motioned for his own men to make their presence felt, and indicated to Linda, to bring the two contracts. As this was happening, they heard a loud, gut-wrenching scream, and looked on in silence as Claire slumped forward, her head cradled in her hands. She was now making a low sobbing sound, and seemed to be gasping for breath.

Walter placed his arm around his wife, and was about to sit down beside her, when Claire suddenly leapt up, pushed him away violently, and turned to Frank.

"Ok, Frank - you've had your little game. Now let's all have a drink. I'm sure we can come to some sort of arrangement about this."

Frank took the contracts from Linda, and removed his sunglasses. Claire noticed how clear and steely blue his eyes were, and immediately realised he was sober, and she had been duped.

Ignoring Claire, Frank turned to Mark, "Get me a real drink, it's time to celebrate. I've never owned a nightclub before!"

Claire took off her glasses, and now moved towards Frank, she hated to be ignored.

"You can't be serious, Frank? It was all just a bit off fun."

"You signed the contract Claire." Replied Frank, sarcastically, taking out a huge cigar from his inside pocket. "If you had won, you wouldn't have shown me any mercy - so, I'll show you none."

"Frank, please, let's talk. This is our income, our home. It's all we've got." Begged Claire, clasping her hands together. I'll do whatever you want."

"Will you Claire?" He smirked, before blowing a cloud of cigar smoke into her face. "Well, I'll tell you what you can do, you can take your arsehole of a husband,

and get out of my nightclub - now!"

"But Frank, this is our life, we can't just move out overnight, like it was a bed and breakfast?" Claire began to sob harder, and the tears could clearly be seen streaming down her face.

Frank moved up close, and put his face into hers.

"I said I want you out. Are you fucking deaf as well as ugly?" He then turned to Pauline, who was skulking in the shadows. "It's decision time. You go with her, or stay with me. Personally, I don't give a shit."

It was Linda who finally butted in.

"Frank, please - leave the details to me. I'll sort everything out, besides there's still some issues I need to talk over with Claire."

Frank seemed happy with that, and began to walk towards the door with an arrogant swagger. He was looking forward to some unfinished business with Anne, but first he wanted to celebrate.

"Come on boys, let's go down to the club and I'll introduce you to your new female colleagues. We're in the nightclub business now!"

14. SCARLET'S

1971

It was a chilly January morning, and Lizzie had been the first to arrive at the boutique. Business had been going well recently meaning she now had to arrive that much earlier to prepare, check and ensure orders went out on time. Sally would arrive a little later, once she'd got the two older children off to school and had dropped off Penny at the childminder's.

Although she was wearing a maxi-skirt, boots and a tight woollen sweater, it felt freezing, and Lizzie immediately went into the small kitchen area to make herself a cup of coffee. She then went out to the workshop, where most of the dressmaking took place and put on the electric fire. The main shop was equally cold, but as she wouldn't be opening until nine, it could remain like that for the time being.

The current style for many young women during those days were Trevira skirts and suits, with knee-length platform boots. Lizzie absolutely hated the Trevira range with a vengeance, simply because she was working with polyester. However, she persevered with the order hoping to get a foothold, then perhaps later she could present the client with something a little more in keeping with her own creative style.

She began inspecting the garments on the rails and hoped to have them ready for Jeremy to collect at 08.30. Jeremy, William's former business partner regularly volunteered his services to the boutique by delivering orders to local customers. He never charged anything to do this, and Sally always felt it was because he had a crush on Lizzie, who would often receive a single red rose in the post, delivered to the shop. It was always anonymous, and simply signed with three kisses in the form of X's. However, for reasons of his own, Jeremy never seemed to take things a step further which mystified Sally. Lizzie seemed totally oblivious to any attention Jeremy showed her, and dismissed Sally's theory out of hand.

She had practically finished checking the last of the skirts when Jeremy arrived. He was a good six inches shorter than William, and showed signs of premature balding. Jeremy would be the first to admit that he never turned heads where women were concerned. But, he did possess an easy-going nature which many found agreeable.

"Lizzie, I've got you alone at last!" He laughed as she led him into the back room.

"I warn you now, Jeremy - I'm not a morning person, so don't expect too much of me!" Came the curt reply. Lizzie could be moody and opinionated, and when she didn't like something or someone, she soon made her feelings known. But, Jeremy's effervescent character and disarming smile soon had her softening her stance.

"A cup of that coffee would be nice. It'll only take a few minutes to load these rails." He replied chirpily, as he cast his eye over the shapely brunette.

Sally had been right about Jeremy's crush on Lizzie. He had fallen for her the first time they had met, but Jeremy was engaged to be married at the time. Lizzie certainly hadn't been short of boyfriends during those days, and they were all handsome, debonair and rich, but nothing had ever lasted more than a few months.

Although Jeremy knew how to make money, he was always conscious that he was somewhat lacking in the looks department and this held him back from making a move on Lizzie. He also felt a little out of his depth with her, as she could on occasion, be quite extravagant and rather over the top. It was as if he was forever deciding if they were compatible, and whether he could actually make her happy.

Just as Lizzie had finished making his coffee, the postman arrived with a bundle of mail. She sorted through the letters, which were mostly bills, and circulars until she came to one particular envelope with a London postmark. She quickly tore it open and read the contents, hoping it to be a positive reply from a leading chain of women's fashion shops she'd been in contact with. The company had sent a buyer just before Christmas to look at some of the boutique's stock. Although the woman had been very shrewd and astute, Lizzie felt she was quite taken with one particular range of garments. These were light, cotton smock dresses that Lizzie had designed for the summer. They were cool, airy and tantalisingly see through.

"A thousand smocks!" Gasped Lizzie in total shock. "Jeremy, come here, quickly!"

Jeremy thought there had been some sort of accident, and came rushing in from the van.

"Lizzie, are you alright. What's happened?"

"They've ordered a thousand of those smock tops, that's what's happened!" She then grabbed Jeremy and planted a huge kiss on the surprised Canadian.

"Wow, Lizzie! I should be around more often when you get orders!" He exclaimed excitedly with a red lipstick mark on his cheek.

"Wait, there's more," she gasped again. "They want us to model some of those awful Trevira suits. There's no accounting for taste! This is big Jeremy!"

He had never seen Lizzie so exuberant before, and it excited him.

"I think this calls for a celebration!"

"I'll say," replied Lizzie, still unable to quite take in what she had just read.

Sally was equally shocked when she arrived at the boutique a short while later.

"Gosh, we're going to have our work cut out making up all these tops."

"Yes, I know. I think we may have to get some extra help." Replied Lizzie misty eyed. "Oh and before I forget, we must buy something for Jeremy. He's just taken that last order into town for us. He's been so good."

Sally broke into a grin. Lizzie could be very naive about certain things, despite her often scary business-like persona.

"Jeremy likes you Lizzie, that's why he helps out."

"Nonsense," Lizzie said, immediately dismissing Sally's observation. "He's an up and coming property developer, what would he want with a half-crazed clothes designer?"

"Lizzie, you're as bad as me at putting yourself down!"

It took a little over a month to prepare the order of a thousand smock dresses of assorted sizes and patterns. It meant long hours working into the night and every weekend. They hired an extra seamstress and between them the mountain was soon reduced. As a bi product, both Sally and Lizzie lost weight. It wasn't that they needed to in any way. It was simply because they were so focussed on making a success of Scarlet's, that they put themselves second, and that meant skipping meals.

The modelling session was booked in for early March, and Sally and Lizzie decided to don the garments and do the modelling themselves. They already had a stockpile of the Trevira range and decided not to make any more just in case an order wasn't forthcoming.

Both women dazzled. They were natural models. William just gazed with pride at seeing his wife strut her stuff with such abandon. When Lizzie took to the catwalk, Jeremy simply couldn't take his eyes off her, which didn't go unnoticed by more or less everyone present.

"Honestly, how can a man get so excited at seeing a woman in polyester?" Exclaimed Lizzie a bit later on in the changing room.

"I don't think it was the outfit he was looking at Lizzie. You had him mesmerised!"

"Okay, Mrs. know it all, so why doesn't he do anything about it then?"

"I think I might have a little chat with our Jeremy."

"Don't you dare, Sally Peddlescoombe. There are some things you just have to leave to fate."

But Sally did take it upon herself to find out what was going on with Jeremy. It was one afternoon in the shop a few days later. Lizzie had gone out to see a client, and Sally was busy running up some of the dreaded Trevira outfits to be used as staff uniforms.

"So you're a bit taken with Lizzie are you Jeremy?" Sally blurted out as he came in to fetch some stock.

"Who told you that?" He replied defensively.

"Oh, come on, it's the worst-kept secret in the world. You can't keep your eyes off her."

"Is it that obvious, Sally?"

"Yes, I'm afraid so! Why don't you just ask her out?"

He scratched his head and sat down alongside her, watching intently as she went about stitching a hem using the sewing machine.

"I'm scared Sally."

"Scared? But you're a successful business man Jeremy?"

"Well, I don't know about that, but look at me, I'm balding, short and not the most attractive man on the planet!"

"So, you're afraid Lizzie will turn you down, is that it?"

"Yes, in a nutshell." He replied, looking anxious.

"Don't you have anyone in your life at the moment, Jeremy?"

"I was engaged to a girl back in Canada, but it all went wrong."

Sally stopped sewing, and turned to face him.

"How do you mean, what, she got cold feet?"

Jeremy sighed and looked away.

"No, not in the least, she found someone else and ditched me."

"Oh that's awful. But from the way I see it, perhaps you're better off without her. So did you know who she went off with?"

"Yeah, he was like a guy I used to work with. Handsome devil, all the girls liked him."

"I see, so that knocked your confidence a bit where women are concerned?"

"You've got it dead right Sally. There's no keeping secrets from you is there?"

She laughed, and turned her attention back to her sewing.

"If I were you Jeremy, I would ask Lizzie out, while there's still an opportunity."

"Do you think there's a possibility she might say yes?"

"I wouldn't be telling you this, if I didn't think you stood a chance."

"Thank-you, Sally. That's just what I needed to know. Valentine's Day is coming up soon, I think I might just send her a card."

"Don't forget the roses Jeremy, you're known for your roses!"

"So you know about those too, do you?"

"It's pretty obvious it's you, but Lizzie doesn't seem to realise it!"

A week later Sally and Lizzie went into the Orange Tree pub, next door to the boutique for a drink after work. It was Lizzie's idea, as she had something preying on her mind and seemed a bit jumpy.

Sally sat at an empty table, while Lizzie went to the bar to order the drinks.

"It's been so hectic, lately Sally," Remarked Lizzie, returning and taking a seat beside her friend. "My fingers are actually getting calloused from all the stitching I'm doing!"

"Mine too, but we're over the worst now, and it's exciting seeing Scarlet's taking off like this." Sally then took a sip of her wine, before adding; "So what is it you wanted to tell me, I'm intrigued?"

Lizzie coughed and nearly choked on her wine, as her eyes darted around the crowded pub.

"You know this mystery chap who sends me the red roses?"

"Yes, it's so strange." Laughed Sally. "So has he sent you another one?"

"Well, yes he has, but a dozen this time, and he sent me a Valentine's card too!"

"You're lucky. William totally forgot about Valentine's Day!"

"Most men do, once they've snared you!" Replied Lizzie dryly as she lit a cigarette. "He wrote in the card to meet him here for a drink, in exactly five minutes time!"

"Oh, my god, that's at seven o'clock, how romantic." Gasped Sally, pretending to be surprised. "Who do you think it is?"

"I'm not sure. There's one or two buyers who have shown an interest, and I did think it could be Jeremy at one time, but he's far too shy."

"Well, it's all very mysterious, so how will you know him?"

"He said he'll be wearing a flower, Silly!"

"Yes, of course!" Giggled Sally. "This is so exciting, why didn't you tell me earlier?"

"Oh, I don't know, it all seemed a bit weird, and as you know, I don't do weird."

"So, Lizzie Marchmont doesn't do weird? Pull the other one!"

At dead on seven, Jeremy strolled in, looking a little sheepish. Lizzie put him under scrutiny, but he didn't appear to be wearing a flower.

"Hello, ladies, can I get you another drink?" He asked politely.

"Yes, I'll have a glass of Chablis." Replied Lizzie, finishing her drink. Sally declined and started to think about leaving, in order to give Jeremy some space.

He sat down and joined them, chatting about how they were getting through the huge order. Lizzie, however, seemed pre-occupied and kept glancing up whenever someone walked into the pub.

There was a roaring log fire on one side of the bar, which was throwing out a considerable amount of heat.

"It's rather warm in here, I think I'll take my coat off," remarked Jeremy, as he rose to his feet. Lizzie wasn't really paying any attention, but when he sat back down again, she couldn't help noticing that he was wearing a T-shirt with a distinctive red rose design on the front. She gasped, nudging Sally, and the two women stared at Jeremy's garment in amazement.

"That's a very unusual T-shirt? Remarked Lizzie, grinning. "I never took you to be the type to show your feminine side, Jeremy?"

"Do you like it?" He asked. "We're offering a T-shirt printing service in one of the shops in London. You can have whatever you want printed on them."

"Whatever next!" Replied Lizzie. "That's fascinating, what a good idea."

"Yes, they're selling like hotcakes. We also print customer's names on fake newspapers and posters, that kind of thing."

"You're very innovative, Jeremy. I like that in a man."

Sally couldn't help smiling. Lizzie and Jeremy were getting along like a house on fire. Lizzie loved extravagance and was very tuned into those who displayed extrovert tendencies.

Jeremy finished his lager, and asked if he could replenish the women's glasses. Sally refused, and said she had to be going as William would be struggling looking after the children, but Lizzie never turned a drink down and readily accepted Jeremy's offer.

As he returned to the bar, a bit of a commotion seemed to break out. People were looking and commenting on what was written on the back of Jeremy's T-shirt.

Sally and Lizzie glanced over to see what the excitement was all about, and were shocked to read; 'LIZZIE, IF I ASK YOU OUT, WILL YOU SAY YES?' written in bright red capital letters on Jeremy's back.

"I think that's a cue for me to be off!" Said Sally, putting on her coat. "I'll leave you two lovebirds to it!"

Jeremy tried to laugh it off, but he was clearly embarrassed. He hadn't planned on the whole pub knowing his intentions. It was just then, that the landlord came over to the table. He was a portly, red-faced man, who obviously enjoyed his work.

"Could you please tell me, which one of you would be Lizzie?" He asked in a jovial manner.

"That would be me." Replied Lizzie, going slightly red.

"Well perhaps you ought to give this poor chap an answer, and put the rest of us out of our misery!"

The pub went quiet, and now all eyes were on Lizzie and Jeremy.

Lizzie took a sip of her wine and tried to maintain her composure.

"Most certainly!" She replied in a confident tone. "I do believe the answer is a very positive, yes!"

A cheer went up from the other customers, and Jeremy brought the whole pub a round of drinks. As he went to sit back down, a chorus of Kiss! Kiss! Kiss! could be heard, and Lizzie and Jeremy, not wanting to disappoint, duly obliged.

Lizzie then became rather overwhelmed by it all and had to rush off to the ladies room to touch up her make-up. While she was gone, Jeremy looked up to Sally.

"Before you go, Sally, I just wanted to say thanks for giving me such good advice. You certainly weren't wrong."

"That's quite alright, Jeremy. I'm never wrong about things like that. Just you take good care of my friend, and don't keep her out late - she's got lots of work to do!"

"I'll try not to, Sally but there's a nightclub in Mayfair everybody's talking about. I'm hoping to take Lizzie there."

"Oh, really," replied Sally, "What's it called?"

"It's called, Lake's. Have you ever heard of it?"

"No, I can't say I have." Was Sally's reply.

1981

The smoke was everywhere, and William didn't know what to do next. He pulled out the grill pan, and rescued what was left of the bacon, meanwhile, the toast had popped up, and the sausages were burning.

Opening the back door to let some air inside, he tried to re-gain his composure. The frying pan was bubbling, and this too was beginning to smoke as he removed it from the heat, before attempting to crack more eggs. The last two efforts had resulted in both the yolks breaking upon impact. He had then placed the damaged eggs onto a plate, which would eventually form part of the breakfast he would eat.

William then realised he'd forgotten, not only the mushrooms, but the tomatoes as well. He delved into the fridge, and quickly prepared the mushrooms, before putting them into the pan where the sausages had been.

Giving up on the tomatoes, he then searched in the larder for the tinned variety, just as the doorbell rang. Suspecting who it could be, William called up to Sally and the others, saying he would answer the door.

He was right, it was Sally's bouquet, and very impressive it looked. He checked that the attached card was correct and gave the driver his payment, before returning to the battlefield that was the kitchen. Perhaps, he should have just done scrambled eggs after all, he thought with a sigh, as he tried to persevere.

It was May 18th, and the day of William and Sally's eighteenth wedding anniversary. William knew his wife wouldn't eat all the full-English breakfast he'd just cooked, because of the calorie content, but felt he had to make the effort. He placed the plate of food on a tray, along with the toast, fresh orange juice and a pot of Earl Grey tea, and proudly carried it upstairs to the waiting Sally.

Business was brisk at Scarlet's and orders were coming in thick and fast. As Sally was needed at the boutique, and it being a Monday, they had decided to go into London later that afternoon, check into a hotel, have a meal, then see a show.

"William, how delicious, and you didn't break the yolks - I'm very impressed!"

William smiled, and ran back down to collect the bouquet and the card, before presenting them to Sally with a flourish, and kissing her passionately on the cheek.

"Happy anniversary, darling!"

"Oh, William, they're lovely. You shouldn't have!"

"You wouldn't be saying that, if I had forgotten!"

"True, but you didn't, you remembered!" Replied, Sally affectionately, taking a bite from her toast. "Eighteen years! Did you still think we would be together all this time?"

"When I first saw you in the library all those years ago, I knew you were the only one for me. I married you for life, Sally, and I'll never ever leave you. So, yes, I knew we'd still be together."

"How sweet," she replied, returning his kiss.

William gazed into her blue eyes.

"Did you think we'd still be together, Sally?"

"Of course I did, silly! After all, I did come back to you, didn't I? Do you remember when you took me out fishing in your boat?"

"How could I ever forget, you nearly got us both drowned!"

They were both in fits of laughter recalling the day when Sally had tumbled back in the boat, with the carp falling down on top of her, when they heard the telephone ringing. William ran down to answer it, but Laura had already beaten him to it.

"It's for Mum," she said, passing the phone to her father, and going off into the kitchen to make herself a coffee.

Sally put on her dressing gown and came down to take her call.

"Who is it?" She asked, but William shrugged his shoulders and handed her the phone.

"Hello, It's Sally speaking, can I help you?"

"Yes, I hope so, Mrs. Peddlescoombe. My name is Sarah Clifton, and I'm a reporter for Entrepreneur's Weekly. Have you seen it on TV?"

"Yes, I have many times." Replied Sally, a little puzzled. "In fact, it's one of my favourite shows."

"That's just what I wanted to hear, Mrs. Peddlescoombe. We've been hearing some wonderful things about Scarlet's Boutique, and would really like to feature you on next week's programme."

"Really?" Exclaimed Sally excitedly. "When, and what will it involve?"

"Obviously we'd like to do it as soon as possible, and we'd bring along a camera crew. We would like all of your staff present, and Lizzie Marchmont of course."

"Yes, I'm sure we can arrange that. What about the questions?"

"Don't worry about the questions, Sally. We'll give you a list of them well in advance so you can prepare your answers. Can you all wear something designed by the boutique, it's for the viewers you understand?"

"Yes certainly!" Said Sally, smiling at William. "We can do it either late afternoon tomorrow or Wednesday?"

It was arranged for the Wednesday, and Sally flung her arms around William.

"We're going to be on TV! Scarlet's is going to be on the Entrepreneur's Weekly!"

William was delighted and called the rest of the family to tell them of the news.

"I'd better get ready and go along to the boutique," said Sally rushing back upstairs. "I can't wait to tell Lizzie! We'll have to give the place a thorough clean and make sure all the lines are organised on rails."

Sally was like an excited child, and flew into the bathroom to shower. William, meanwhile stared at the full plate of food, as he carried it back downstairs. He was reluctantly about to start, when Jonathan strolled into the kitchen, rubbing his eyes.

"What's all this about the boutique being on TV?" He asked, before noticing the full English breakfast going to waste. "I can help you with that Dad, if you don't want it?"

By the early eighties, Frank's mini-cab and nightclub ventures were thriving. He had installed both Pauline and Anne to take over the general running of the club, and Frank himself would only put in an appearance during the evenings. This was usually to drink with his cronies, gamble and have his way with the female staff. It was tolerated only due to the fact that most of the women preferred Frank as the owner. He was very generous at times, and despite his fearsome reputation, he actually let the girls get away with a lot. All they had to do was smile at him, wiggle their bottoms, and they would get a bonus, or some extra time off. Although there was discreet prostitution at the club during Claire's time, it was now rife, with Frank demanding his share of the takings, supplying rooms and pimping girls to the clients.

Frank also had over a hundred drivers working for him, with most of those hiring their cabs directly from the company. By using this method, Frank would be assured of a regular income regardless of how poor business was. He would provide a vehicle with a valid MOT certificate and a tax disc, but it was up to the individual driver to insure, maintain and put in their own petrol and oil. Many drivers new to this type of work were attracted by the vast amounts of money that could potentially be earned, and thought this to be a fantastic opportunity. All they had to do was earn enough each month to pay for the hire of their car, and apart from running costs, the rest of the money they earned was theirs to keep. It was good in theory, but in reality, very few drivers made enough to live on. There were busy times, especially evenings at the weekend and over Christmas, but only the most dedicated drivers were willing to work these hours. Many left after a few weeks, with the reality of their predicament hitting home when they found they still had the rest of their car hire contract to honour, and Frank was meticulous about making sure they kept their payments up. The situation led to many dissatisfied workers, and to many heated arguments. However, some did earn a good living, and these were always the professional, collar and tie drivers who took their work seriously. They all owned their own vehicles, and maintained them to a high standard. As they had newer and better quality cars, they could vary their work from the bread and butter local trips, to airport and VIP work, and many of the larger companies who had accounts with Frank preferred to use these drivers.

It was one afternoon in late May, and Frank had just returned from a trip to the airport. It had been a busy day, and finding all his available drivers out, Frank decided to use one of the Mercs and take the job himself. The traffic was appalling, and he didn't return to the office until after 5 pm. He was hungry, thirsty and irritable. Walking over to a local burger bar he treated himself to a quarter pounder, fries and a drink. Calls were still coming through to the control room, so he took his food into his office, where he could have some privacy. Turning on the TV to catch the news, he hungrily devoured the huge bacon burger. Frank was about to switch channels, when a local news story came on about aspiring entrepreneurs. What he then saw took him completely by surprise.

"So what do you owe your success with Scarlet's Boutique to?" Asked the smiley, red-headed presenter.

"Vision, lot's of hard work, determination and a bit of good luck." Replied Sally, looking every inch the business woman in her tailored suit.

"Would you say the rag trade was an ideal career for a school-leaver to enter into?" The presenter, then asked Laura.

"Yes, I would highly recommend it, if that's what they wanted to do. There's certainly plenty of variety. I'm now more involved in the marketing side of the business, after initially starting out in the back, sewing!" Replied Laura confidently.

The presenter laughed, and now directing her next question to both Sally and Laura, continued.

"So is it true that Laura will soon be leaving Scarlet's to take up nursing?"

"Yes, she will," smiled Sally proudly. "My daughter has been offered a place at Westminster later this year."

The presenter turned back to Sally's eldest daughter.

"I'm sure you wont have to make your own uniforms there, Laura? So does that mean there'll be a vacancy coming up at Scarlet's?"

"Yes, my mother, and her partner, Lizzie will be interviewing candidates very soon." She added, smiling over to where her father was standing.

Frank watched intently. Laura was the spitting image of her mother nearly two decades earlier, the same glorious blonde hair, the same deep blue eyes, and the same smile that could melt any male heart. Glancing at Sally, his memories of what were, and what could have been came flooding back. His emotions however, were split between jealousy, lust and hatred. He eyed Sally, as the presenter talked to the ever flamboyant, Lizzie about her ground-breaking designs. Sally oozed elegance and style, and still looked stunning, despite being at least thirty seven now. It was amazing to see both mother and daughter together, and Frank not only wanted them both, he wanted to get into the rag trade too.

As the programme finished he noticed William Peddlescoombe grinning contentedly in the background, and his face turned into a grimace as he recalled that night back in December 1962, when Pauline had glassed him at the dinner and dance, and how he had tried to murder William Peddlescoombe for stealing his girl, only to end up behind bars for his trouble. He still had a debt to settle with Peddlescoombe and now seemed like a good time to exact payment. Frank liked what he saw, a thriving business that attracted beautiful women, and better still, was run by beautiful women. With visions of catwalks in Paris and Milan going through his mind, he finished off his meal, and decided to take a drive over to Scarlet's Boutique and have a look for himself.

Frank eventually arrived home around 7 pm, took a shower and poured himself a whiskey. He had entertained the thought of going to the gym, but he'd already been four times that week and now just fancied having a few drinks, a meal out, and going along to the club to play some poker. He shouted out to Pauline, and since there was no reply, he assumed she was already at Lake's. Pop music was blaring from Tina's room, as he made his way up the stairs and knocked loudly on her door.

Tina's bedroom was always locked. She had been fearful of Frank since childhood, and could never forget just how brutal her father could be. The music was suddenly turned off, and Tina waited nervously behind her closed door.

"Tina, it's Dad. Open up, I want to speak to you."

Tina felt her heart drop, and anxiously looked around her room for a weapon. She knew her mother wasn't there, and the thought of being alone in the house with her father filled her with dread.

"What do you want? Go away." She called out, feeling herself beginning to shake.

"I just want to chat, that's all. What are you doing?"

"I'm practicing my dance moves." She replied, hesitantly opening the door. She knew she had no other option. It wouldn't be beyond Frank to break the door down, he'd done it in the past.

"So you still want to be a dancer, Tina?"

"Yes, I do, but why are you asking?" The eighteen-year old was confused by his interest, but he appeared sober. He could sometimes be trusted when he hadn't been drinking.

"It's just that I have a friend whose daughter is about to start training as a nurse. Wouldn't you like to be a nurse, Tina? It's a very rewarding profession."

"I've never really thought about it." She replied, puzzled.

"Just think, you could be at Westminster Hospital, in London, saving all those lives, and doing good. I think you would make a fantastic nurse, Tina."

"What about my dancing?"

"You can still dance. But think of all those dashing doctors, in their white coats, and the excitement of being in an operating theatre, or being in charge of a ward, saving lives."

It worked. within the space of a few months, Tina had been offered a place at Westminster Hospital as a student nurse, just like Sally's daughter, Laura.

However, it wasn't Frank going on about doctors and saving lives that eventually swayed her, as she was a very caring person in general, it was the knowledge that she could have a room in the nurses' home, and finally be away from her abusive father.

William drained the last dregs of his coffee before picking up his holdall and heading out to the garage. It was 4 am and he intended to make an early start on the motorway before the traffic began to build up. He wanted to wake Sally and kiss her goodbye, but she was sleeping so soundly, he decided not to disturb her. As he went to open the front door, he remembered the packed lunch in the fridge that Sally had made up for him. He then wrote her a note telling her he would call once he'd arrived at Falcondale, and how he loved her and was missing her already.

Although it was still dark he could just about make out where he was going and didn't bother to turn on the light in the garage. The car responded immediately, and the Ford's three litre engine roared into life. The streets were empty and William made rapid progress along the Chertsey Road, which would eventually lead him towards the M4 motorway, and then a straight run into Wales, via the Severn Bridge. The rain was coming in sheets, so he put on the wipers and listened to the radio. Blondie was playing, and listening to the song made him smile, as he recalled Penny dancing away, oblivious to the world, and playing the same tune. He stopped at some lights near Sunbury and waited as a convoy of assorted trucks turned left and looked as if they were heading the same way as he was. William noticed the brakes didn't seem very effective and moved his seat forward, remembering he had moved its position to vacuum the car the day earlier. It was then that he noticed the red roses he had brought for Sally, laying on the back seat, along with the card. He cursed himself for forgetting to leave them for her, and decided to bring her something back when he returned in a couple of days.

The house his parents owned was about to undergo some essential repair work. There were leaks and cracks, plus damp had started to appear on some of the walls, causing a foul smell to be ever present in the property. David was still absent, where, nobody knew, and William's parents weren't able to make the trip from Canada, due to his father having a heart condition. So, it was left to William to return to Falcondale and meet the builders to go through a plan of repair. He knew the company, and once a price had been agreed, he would leave the keys and let them get on with it. Besides, a local woman called Carol would look in and make sure the house was all in order. Carol was now the Housekeeper at the nearby, Falconhurst Hotel. She was well known in the town and had gained promotion after the previous housekeeper had retired.

The lights turned green at long last, and William looked forward to a long stretch of motorway. He soon passed the trucks and swung back into the inside lane. At last he saw a sign for the M4 and put his foot down on the accelerator. The road was clear apart from another truck in the distance which he was quickly gaining on. Indicating right, he moved out into the middle lane. However, the truck also began to move out into the same lane. It had been overtaking another slower moving vehicle in front of it, and the driver hadn't noticed William approaching. William then had to take evasive action, and seeing there was nothing behind him, he swung out into the third, outside lane. It was then that he saw the startled face of a terrified young deer, just a few yards ahead if him. Thinking he had got clear of the truck on the left of him, William swerved back over into the centre lane. The car went into a skid and William, in an effort to straighten up, slammed on the brakes. He was shocked to find they weren't working, and the car, still skidding was careering off the motorway. William desperately pulled at the handbrake, and twisted the steering wheel around, but it was too late, it flipped over several times and went across the barrier, crashing down a slope into woodland.

The last thing he recalled was the terrible crushing feeling, the heat, and seeing flames all about him. He shouted out Sally's name, as the car came to halt against a tree, with William trapped inside.

Sally woke with a start around 05.30. She could no longer sleep, and sat up anxiously. She glanced over to William's side of the bed, and wished he'd woke her before he'd left for Wales. She put her hand under the covers to see if it was still warm, where he had been sleeping. But it was cold, and she felt herself shiver, and went over to open the curtains. None of the children were awake, so she decided to go and make herself a drink, before waking them for school.

Sally had just got to the bottom of the stairs when she heard the telephone ringing.

"Hello, is that Mrs. Peddlescoombe?" The voice was pleasant enough, but distant and official.

"Yes, this is she, who am I speaking to?"

"Sergeant Harris, Metropolitan Police. Are you related to William Peddlescoombe?"

Sally felt her heart drop as soon as she heard William's name mentioned.

"Yes, he's my husband, but why, is there something wrong?" She replied, with a gut-wrenching feeling of sickness in the pit of her stomach.

"I'm sorry to inform you, Mrs. Peddlescoombe, but there's been a traffic accident involving your husband."

Sally arrived at the hospital an hour later, accompanied by Lizzie. She had called her friend immediately, and sobbing down the phone had told her the news. Lizzie, not wanting Sally to drive, came over straight away, and leaving the children to their own devices, set off following the same route William had taken just a few hours earlier.

"William Peddlescoombe - I was told he was here? I'm his wife." Blurted out Sally, as she rushed into reception.

"Just a moment, Mrs. Peddlescoombe, I'll go and check with the rapid response team." Replied the West Indian staff nurse, in a calm and re-assuring manner.

Sally began pacing the corridor. The whiteness, the sterility, the smell of the hospital, was all feeding into her anxiety. Lizzie was doing her best in a difficult situation, and was trying desperately to keep her friend in one piece. Suddenly Sally turned and looked in the direction of where the nurse had gone, and decided to follow her into the accident and emergency unit.

There were around ten cubicles, with three being occupied, two of them by elderly patients, one with an oxygen mask strapped to her face and receiving treatment, for what looked like a fractured neck of femur. The third cubicle had the curtains drawn around. Sally could see there was quite a bit of activity going on inside and began to walk across. She was challenged by the nurse from earlier.

"Please, Mrs. Peddlescoombe, you shouldn't be in here."

"He's here somewhere, my husband, isn't he?" Sally pleaded, her voice full of emotion.

A doctor then appeared in blue scrubs, just as Lizzie found her friend.

"I'll talk to Mrs. Peddlescoombe, thank-you nurse." Said the young-looking, Australian registrar. He then ushered both Sally and Lizzie into an adjoining cubicle. "I'm Doctor Irving. I'm sorry, Mrs. Peddlescoombe, I don't know how much you've heard, but your husband's car came off the motorway about five miles from here. No other vehicles were involved."

"Please, is he alright?" Begged Sally, reaching for the doctors arm. "You must tell me, I have to go to him."

There was an awkward silence before the registrar spoke again.

"I'm sorry, we did all we could."

What do you mean, did all you could?" Sally yelled back at him, her eyes filled with a terror she couldn't comprehend.

"Your husband died a short while ago."

"Died? William dead? No, it's not true, it can't be - he's my husband, he's on his way to Wales. It must be some kind of mistake?"

"I'm sorry, Mrs. Peddlescoombe. We have some of his personal; effects." The doctor then pointed to William's holdall, and a plastic NHS bag containing his watch, wallet, loose change and his wedding ring. Beside these were the roses he had brought Sally, along with a scorched envelope containing a card.

Sally walked over and picked up the flowers, they seemed unaffected by the accident. She stared at them lovingly, before putting them up to her face and inhaling the fragrance.

"William always gets me flowers on a Friday." She whispered, her mind and body both in deep shock. "I want to see my husband doctor, where is he?"

"I don't think that's a good idea. He was very badly injured. If you could give us a few minutes, we could..."

"I want to see my husband now." Demanded Sally, clutching the roses to her breast.

Dr. Irving nodded to a nurse who was standing by, and she went into the cubicle where William lay, in order to quickly cover his body, and turn his eyelids down. Dr. Irving then led Sally and Lizzie through to see William.

The first thing that Sally saw, was a lifeless corpse laying beneath a white sheet. Monitors were still attached to him, but they were no longer making any sound. The smell of charred flesh caught in the back of her throat. She went over to him, and pulled back the sheet covering his face.

It didn't look like William, it had to be somebody else, not her husband, not the father of her children. Her mouth was dry and she tried to swallow. Then she began to recognise his features, the remnants of his hair, his dimples, the way he looked when he was asleep.

"William! William!" She cried out. "Wake up, please, it's me, Sally."

She put her arm beneath his neck, avoiding a large, soiled dressing that was covering the left side of his face, and bent down to kiss him. She noticed he was still warm to touch, so she climbed up alongside him, still clutching her red roses, and put her head on his chest, just like she had always done.

"William, please wake up, we have to get back home to wake Penny up for school. It's her sports day, and she's such a fast runner."

The nurse was about to intervene, but the doctor motioned for her to wait.

Sally reached for William's blackened hand, and gripped it tightly.

"Look, he's not dead, he can't be."

Dr. Irving shook his head, his face distraught.

"Please, Mrs. Peddlescoombe, you must leave your husband now."

"I can't leave him, I'll never leave him." Sobbed Sally, "Look, he's clutching my hand. I told you he wasn't dead. Not William - we said we would never leave each other."

Both the doctor and the nurse glanced over at the monitor. It was still switched on, but there was no movement, the line was flat.

Sally began to wail uncontrollably into William's chest. It was a cry of such anguish, and one they had never heard before, or wanted to hear again. It was a cry that touched their very souls.

Lizzie, forcing herself to stay in control, thanked the doctor, as he and the nurse left. She then went over to Sally, who was still cuddling William, the roses, now crushed between their bodies. Lizzie put her arm around Sally, and placed her head on her friend's shoulder. She then wept huge tears of grief for the woman she had known for half her life, and for the man who had been her husband.

The cowgirl was absolutely stunning. Dressed in a rhinestone bikini and Stetson, she took to the stage accompanied by the sound of Roxy Music's *'Love Is The Drug'*. The mainly male audience were in raptures, and cheering her on wildly.

Flicking her mane of Barbie-doll blonde hair, she caressed the pole, and gyrated her shapely hips as if she had done it a million times. Half-way through the song she unclipped her bikini top and tossed it to a lucky customer in the audience.

The volume of the music was turned up and the atmosphere at Billy Joe's Bar and Grill grew in intensity.

David was simply trying to leave. He was unsteady, and feeling the effects of several day's drinking. The exit sign was just a blur on the wall, as he pushed his way through the heaving crowd to make his way back to the motel.

"Hey, cowboy, don't you like my dancing?" Shouted Ellie from the stage, as she writhed her curvy body back and forth.

The crowd laughed and jeered as they turned their attention to the limping Vietnam veteran.

"I gotta go," he called back, desperate to find freedom.

"Hey, that's downright rude." Continued Ellie." I need someone to help me get my boots off!"

It didn't take long for the other customers to take the initiative and push the drunken David forward towards the stage. Giggling, Ellie pulled up a chair, and sat back, presenting a cowboy-booted foot to David. With the spotlights shining brightly, and not wanting to disappoint or cause a scene, David staggered forward and took hold of Ellie's boot. The crowd roared him on as he struggled and eventually pulled the boot from the dancer's dainty foot. She then presented him with her other boot, and he duly began to oblige. However, that last shot of bourbon must have really hit home, for he began to see stars and lurched forward, plunging into the bare-breasted Ellie, sending her tumbling back onto the floor, with him coming down hard on top of her.

Within seconds, two burly doormen were dragging David outside. He tried to protest his innocence, but his words fell on deaf ears.

"Listen buddy, you know the rules - no touching the girls, got it?" Shouted one of the men aggressively.

"I didn't mean to, I fell." Muttered David, his speech slurred.

"It didn't look like that from where I was standing, pal."

"Please take your hands off me, I'm disabled."

"Disabled, my ass! Are you gonna go quietly, or do we have to get rough?" Replied the doorman, taking David by the lapels of his jacket.

"You can't treat me like this. I want to speak to the manager."

"Well, the manager don't wanna speak to you, and I'll treat you any way I want, you flea-bitten bum." With that, the man hit David hard in the stomach with his fist, and watched grinning as his victim dropped to the floor. It was only when the doorman went to kick David while he was down, that he noticed the injured man's artificial leg.

Somehow David managed to eventually stagger back to his room in a nearby cheap motel, where he downed the remains of a bottle of scotch, before passing out on his bed.

He woke early and paced the room. He was broke and desperate for another drink. The demons were taunting him for being so weak, telling him to work, beg, steal or borrow, whatever it took to get the liquor he needed to blot out reality, and drift through another day of unrelenting oblivion. The truth be, he had exhausted all the employment opportunities in the small town. He had wandered from bar to restaurant washing pots, clearing garbage, anything to buy drink. Then, when he was either too drunk or hung-over to work, he was fired.

Finding some small change in his jacket pocket, he went to call his mother. He hadn't been in touch with her for several weeks, unable to bear the ranting about his shortcomings from a woman who loved her son and wanted him home.

"David, is that you?" Called out his mother in a surprised voice.

"Yes, Mum, it's me. I want to come home."

There was a long silence at the other end of the line. It wasn't like his mother not to speak.

"Mum, is there something wrong?" But all he could hear was his mother weeping. "Please, Mum, what's happened, is it Dad?"

"No David, your father is still sick, but he's here with me."

"Mum, can you send me some money to get back? I'm in South Carolina."

"David, I've been trying to contact you, but nobody knew where you had gone."

"Please tell me what's wrong?"

There was another pause before his mother managed to find the words.

"It's William. There was an accident. He was killed."

David let out a heart-wrenching cry and slumped against the wall.

"What about Sally, is Sally alright?"

"Sally wasn't involved." Sobbed Joan Peddlescoombe. "William was alone when it happened. The funeral is in two days. I'm flying out tomorrow. There's no time for you to come home David."

This time it was David who couldn't speak, but when he did, it was more than his mother could bear.

"I killed William, Mum. I kissed Sally, I wanted her for myself, I fell in love with her. I hurt William so badly. It was me who killed him."

"Please, David, you mustn't say that. William died in a car accident. It wasn't your fault. You aren't being rational, you didn't kill him."

"Please forgive me, Mum."

"David, there's nothing to forgive. Please be strong. Now give me the details of where you're staying and I'll send you enough money to book a flight to London, get a room and buy a suit."

"I can't go Mum. It wouldn't be right."

"William was your brother, and he loved you David. I expect to see you at the service on Wednesday."

David went into the bathroom and looked at himself in the mirror. He was under-weight, unshaven and gaunt-looking. What had he become. His hands were shaking as he turned on the shower and stood under the refreshing stream of warm water. He washed his face, his hair and his body, and let the tears he shed for his brother, fall from his eyes, and mingle with the trickling water.

Hardly a word was said in the Peddlescoombe household. It was eerily silent and depressing. Sally had been the first to get up from her lonely bed. She hadn't slept well, in fact she had survived on the bare minimum of sleep since learning of her husband's death. She didn't want to wake the girls or Jonathan. She couldn't bear to see their sad faces, or talk to them. She had no energy left. She couldn't explain to them what or why it had happened. All of them were in a daze, in shock, unable to understand the reality of what had occurred.

Sally went to her wardrobe and took out the three black dresses that Lizzie had made for her and the two girls, along with the suit she had made for Jonathan. The dresses were beautifully put together and looked classy, but Sally felt abhorred at the very thought at having to wear one. For some reason she hadn't been able to leave such symbols of the frailty of human life in the children's bedrooms. She preferred to wait until the morning of William's funeral, and give them out then.

Sally showered and washed her hair, before going down to the kitchen in her dressing gown to try and force at least, a cup of coffee inside herself. Her weight had plummeted, as with the girls and Jonathan in the past week. She felt weak, frail and emotionally unable to cope with the demands of the day ahead of her.

As it happened, the children were all awake, and like their mother, unable to sleep. Penny had made her own wreath for her father, using brightly-coloured paper flowers, along with leaves and twigs she had collected from the garden. Laura was probably coping the best out of all of them, maybe it was her staunch character, her nurse training, or maybe it was just a brave face she was presenting to the world, time would tell. Jonathan, like Penny needed constant re-assurance and seemed to be having difficulty coming to terms with the fact that he would never see his father again.

A little after eight, the doorbell began ringing, as flowers and tributes started to arrive in a continual stream. After reading the attached condolence cards, Sally placed them in the front room, and by ten o'clock the whole of the table, and carpet were a sea of floral colour.

One-by-one, the children appeared, looking sombre in their black outfits. Sally tried to insist that they eat breakfast, but like her, no-one could touch a thing. During mid-morning the telephone had rang twice, but the caller couldn't or wouldn't speak. Sally wondered who it might be and tried to coax the person to talk, but to no avail.

At midday Lizzie and Jeremy arrived. Sally was more than glad to have the support of her old friend, and greeted her as warmly as she could.

"We're all going to get through this, Sally, you, the girls, Jonathan and myself." Said Lizzie as she gave Sally a much-needed hug.

"I just feel dead inside, Lizzie. I keep thinking that William will just walk in, and I'll wake up from the worst nightmare I've ever had."

"I know Sally, I feel the same. How are the girls and Jonathan coping?"

"Every day is different with them, but they are mostly very subdued and deep in their thoughts. But I do hear them crying in their rooms, especially Penny."

"The poor love. I'll speak to them. Sometimes it's good to talk these things through with someone whose not quite so involved."

"Perhaps you're right. I do try to chat to them, but they are keeping their grief to themselves at the moment. I don't feel like I'm helping at all." Replied Sally, her voice full of emotion.

"Has there been any word from David?" Asked Lizzie, changing the subject.

"No, not directly. Joan rang me and said she had spoken to him, and that he was coming over."

Lizzie didn't want to push matters further regarding William's brother and took it upon herself to gather everyone around to see what kind of mental state they were in.

At twelve thirty the funeral cortege arrived. It consisted of a magnificent Rolls Royce hearse, bedecked with bouquets of all shaped and sizes. This was followed by a stretch limousine, with another smaller one bringing up the rear.

The immaculately attired Funeral Director was courteous and respectful, as he and two bearers came into the house to collect the tributes from the front room. These, they placed inside the hearse around William's coffin, and attached the rest to the roof of the vehicle.

The journey to the cemetery would take about twenty five minutes from Sally's home, and Lizzie and Jeremy would travel in the same limousine as Sally and her family. It was a grey cloudy day, with a slight breeze, but no rain had been forecast.

There were a little over a hundred mourners for William's funeral, and Sally tried her best to greet as many of them as possible, while fighting desperately to keep her emotions in check.

Sally, Laura, Penny, and Jonathan took the pews at the front of the chapel, along with Lizzie, Jeremy and William's mother, Joan, while the other mourners filed in behind them. The atmosphere was surreal and Sally, and the children searched each other's eyes looking for comfort, solace and answers to so many unanswered questions. Sally gulped and felt her heart drop as the sound of organ music filled the chapel. Along with the others she then rose to her feet when her husband's wicker coffin was carried in by four bearers. The whole exercise was carried out in a smooth, quiet and calm manner overseen by the director himself. Sally and the children stood together, and reached out to grasp each others hands as they watched the coffin being placed on the bier. The priest conducting the memorial service then motioned for everyone to stand as he consulted his notes before commencing the funeral oration. The words he spoke brought a certain degree of comfort to Sally, the girls and Jonathan, especially when he told of how William had worked relentless to provide for his family and was looked upon as a pillar of the community, respected and loved by all those he met.

Sally glanced across to where Joan was sitting. She was tearful beneath her veil as she looked into Sally's eyes. But there was no sign of David, which disheartened both Sally and Joan alike.

David had got a flight into Heathrow soon after speaking to his mother. It was a night flight that saw him in London by noon the next day. He made his way to Richmond and booked into a small hotel near the green. His mind was working on auto pilot, as he tried to think about what he needed to do. His brother's funeral was for the following day and he had to buy an appropriate suit, make contact with his mother, and lastly and most importantly, he had to see, or at least speak to Sally. The mere thought of seeing her again, hearing her voice and being captivated by her smile lifted his heavy heart.

The black suit he brought in a town centre shop certainly wasn't the most expensive, but it looked smart and made him appear more confident and focussed than he could really admit to.

With shaking hands he rang the hotel in London where his mother had chosen to stay. She had travelled alone due to her husband's ill health, and desperately wanted to see her last remaining son.

"David, is that you, are you in England?"

She sounded old and her voice weak, trying to speak to her only added to his distress even more.

"Yes, Mum - I'm in Richmond."

"That's good. Did you manage to get something to wear?"

"Yes, I got a suit today. How's my father?"

"He's not good, David. The doctor said he has angina and has to take things easy. To be honest, I think this could finish him."

David hated what his mother had just said. She was known for speaking her mind, but she was right. Parents aren't supposed to outlive their children, and his father would have to have a strong constitution to overcome the death of his eldest son.

"I'm coming home to be with you both after this, Mum."

"That's good David. Perhaps we could fly back together. I want to see you before the funeral. I feel so alone."

David knew he should go to her. It was his duty as a son, but he was desperate to see Sally, and put his mother off.

"I'll be there early tomorrow Mum, I'll see you then."

"Yes, alright David, but how will you get to the cemetery?"

"I don't know yet," he replied in need of a drink. "I'll get a taxi I suppose."

It was early evening and David had to get out of his small, claustrophobic hotel room. He walked along the towpath and went into a pub called The Old Ship. He had tried to avoid drinking, knowing that it was his enemy, knowing that it destroyed every decent thought and emotion in his head, but he needed the drink to numb his pain. He couldn't live with it, but he couldn't live without it. At first, he just stuck to beer, but soon moved on to whiskey. There was a payphone in the pub, and he thought about calling Sally. What would he say to her? How would she react? He decided to have another drink before calling, then another, and another until he was too incoherent to speak. He felt ashamed for letting himself down again, and trudged miserably back to the hotel. He consoled himself that he would call her in the morning, and would see her later at the funeral. He would be alright by then, the alcohol would have worn off, but he would need more. He switched the light off, and lay back in bed, the demons returned to haunt him. The young boy's face, when David had agreed to let him go ice fishing with him, the soldier under his command who died in Vietnam, the mine that blew his leg off. He was only half a man now. What would Sally want with him, a screwed up, drunken cripple who once had designs on his brother's wife. But now his brother was out of the way, deep down he knew he could never match up to William or step into his shoes. David allowed his demons to torment him, he no longer had the strength to fight them off. Pessimism had won over optimism, loathing over pride, and worthlessness over his feelings for Sally.

The morning was no better for David. Although, he'd sobered up somewhat, the mere thought of actually seeing his mother, Sally and the rest of her family brought him out in a cold sweat. He tried to call Sally that morning, but when she answered the telephone and he heard her voice, he failed miserably to even speak to her.

The taxi took him directly to the cemetery, where he asked the driver to pull over away from the others. He saw them all dressed in black, some crying, some shaking each other's hands and offering condolences. He felt a few drops of rain on his face as he alighted from the taxi and tentatively began to walk towards the large group of mourners beside William's grave.

He saw Sally standing between her daughters. They were sobbing and holding onto each other for support. Lizzie and Jeremy were also there, standing close by, their faces drawn and ashen. He could barely make out the words the priest was saying, but knew them to be poignant, emotional and comforting. It was then that he noticed his mother. Someone had found her a chair, and she sat composed and regal-looking, never letting her demeanor drop. Although her face was veiled, David recognised her immediately, and she him. At first, she lifted her arm, as if to beckon him over. But then she hesitated, and lifted her veil slightly so he could just about make out her tear-filled eyes. She must have seen the look of torment etched into his face, the pain, the anguish, but she didn't motion for him to come closer. For Joan understood her son, and was just relieved to see him there. The knowledge that she wasn't alone gave her the hope, strength and impetus to come through the worst ordeal a mother could ever face.

The rain got decidedly heavier, and David went to stand beneath a large oak tree. He was now quite obscured from Sally, and he fought hard to hold back his tears, as he saw the bearers move towards his brother's coffin. It had been placed on the ground, sitting on horizontal beams. Ropes had been threaded beneath the casket at either end. Now, two bearers stood at either side and awaited a sign from the director to take them up and lower the deceased down into his grave. He saw Sally surge forward and throw herself onto William's coffin. She was crying hysterically and clung to the casket knowing she would never be so physically close to him again. Lizzie came forward with Jeremy to console her, to re-assure her, to be with her, but she pushed them away. Laura and Penny stood close, holding each other for support while Jonathan remained directly behind them, clutching his face in his hands.

Do not stand at my grave and weep.
I am not there.
I do not sleep.
I am a thousand winds that blow.
I am the diamond glints on snow.
I am the sunlight on ripened grain.
I am the gentle autumn's rain.
When you awaken in the morning's hush, I am the swift uplifting rush of quiet birds in circled flight.
I am the soft stars that shine at night.
Do not stand at my grave and cry;
I am not there.
I did not die.
(Mary Frye).

Lizzie and Jeremy drew back to give Sally her last moments with her husband. The rain was now coming down in heavy sheets, as the mourners opened their umbrella's and retreated in amongst the trees. Only Sally was left, her hair drenched, her clothes sodden and soiled with mud. She clamped her arms tightly around the coffin and called out his name. She needed to be held, to be cuddled, to be loved. She needed David there to take care of her and bring her out of the nightmare she was trapped in. But he had already left, and was back in the taxi and heading to his hotel. It was left to her son, Jonathan to come to his mother's aid. He bent down in the mud beside her, and pulled her close against him. She turned to look up at Jonathan's face, and reached out her arms to hold him. He held, and embraced his mother, warming her with the heat from his body. He then took off his jacket and draped it around her shoulders, just like his father had once done, when he and Sally had shared their first kiss, during the fierce snow storm back at Falcondale. With their tears combining, mother and son stood up as one, and together they remained solid and proud, as William was finally laid to rest.

After the funeral was over, several of the mourners came back to Sally's house. Lizzie had to act as temporary host until her friend was able to face people once again. It lifted Lizzie's heart to see William's mother Joan speaking so amiably to the two girls and Jonathan.

Sally and William had married in secret, back in the early sixties when she was pregnant with Jonathan. Joan had never forgiven her for that, and the relationship between the two women had remained strained since that day.

"Where's Sally? I wanted to see her before I leave." Asked Joan, placing her empty tea cup on the table.

"She's in her room. The doctor gave her a sedative and told her to rest." Replied Lizzie.

"Well, not to worry. Perhaps I'll call her when I get back to Canada."

Lizzie nodded, but felt distinctly uncomfortable under the older woman's gaze.

It was then that Sally appeared in the doorway. She had got changed into a conservative-looking skirt and sweater. She was puffy around the eyes from where she had been crying, but now seemed a lot more in control of her emotions.

"Hello, Joan. I'm sorry I've been such a bad host. I let things get to me a bit."

It was odd, under the circumstances to see Joan smile, but smile she did, and it lit up the whole of her face, as if she had seen enlightenment.

"Sally, I'm very proud at the way you and your family coped. I can see you loved my son with all of your heart."

"I can't put into words how I felt about William. He was my world, my life, my love." Replied Sally, demurely.

"You have been a fantastic wife to William, Sally, and have given him the most beautiful children, and myself, the most wonderful grandchildren. I'm indebted to you for making my son so happy."

"Thank-you Joan, you don't know what that means to me."

Joan nodded, and got up to take her leave.

"My taxi should be here shortly, Sally, but before I go I want to apologise to you for being such an awful mother-in-law."

Sally couldn't bear to become tearful again, and reached for a tissue.

"You have nothing to apologise for, Joan. If I could turn back the clock, things would have been different."

"Thank-you, Sally," replied Joan, as she reached out to embrace her daughter-in-law. "I'm going to make a promise to see more of you and your lovely children. Maybe, you could all come over to Niagara-on-the-Lake soon. After all, we are a family, and need to be together."

Just hearing Joan's words gave Sally the lift she had been needing, but there was still something else deeply troubling her.

"I looked for David. I hoped he would have been there today?"

Joan paused for a moment, and looked into Sally's eyes.

"David still has his problems, but he's coming home for a while and we'll see if we can patch him up a bit." Joan then reached for her coat, and as Sally helped her put it on, she turned and said; "David was there today."

"He was?" Gasped Sally, her eyes widening.

"Yes, I saw him standing under an oak tree."

Joan noticed the spark in Sally's blue eyes immediately, and smiled warmly at her.

"You never know what lies ahead. Just reach out, Sally and follow your heart."

After Joan had left, Sally called Jonathan, Laura, and Penny together in the front room.

"Today is the start of a wonderful adventure for all of us. Yesterday has gone, now it's all new beginnings. We must all be strong and meet whatever life throws at us. We are a family, and we will grow and continue. We will recover from this and get stronger. We will never forgot your father, and the love he gave us, but now we only have his memory and we have to move on." Sally then went and kissed each of her children on the cheek, before turning back to her youngest.

"Penny, pour everyone a glass of wine. I think we need one."

15. LAURA

1983

Laura breathed a sigh of relief as she pushed the wheelchair into the centre of the ward, applied the brakes then placed a blanket over the elderly gentleman's knees. She had only two more patients to get washed, dressed and ready to attend clinic appointments before she could go for a well-earned coffee break and relax for twenty minutes or so.

That morning had been especially busy on Lister ward for the elderly, where Laura was currently allocated. Two new student nurses had just started and were still trying to familiarise themselves with everything, then one of the trained staff had called in sick, and to top that, a patient had died! It wasn't a good start to the day, and Sister Wilcox wasn't amused.

Laura returned to Ivy, and poking her head through the curtains, asked the old lady if she had finished on the commode.

"No, I haven't. It's all rush, rush, rush with you girls nowadays. Come back in five minutes!"

Laura apologised and went to help one of the new students who she was working alongside, to lift a patient out of the bath. Another nurse was calling for help at the far end of the ward, while the telephone rang continuously in the empty office.

"Laura, the porter is here to take Daisy over to X-ray. Is she ready yet?" Called out Sister, as she replaced an over-flowing laundry sack.

"Almost, but we seem to have run out of pads!" Replied Laura.

"Oh, not again!" Cursed Sister, struggling with the heavy sack. "Can you go down to Remington-Hobbs Ward, and ask if we can borrow some. I would send one of the new girls, but they'd probably get lost!"

"Yes, I'll go straight away," replied Laura, removing her starched, white apron. She then hurried down the stairs to the next floor, feeling quite relieved to finally get away from the unbearably warm ward, even if it was just for a few minutes. As she waited for the pads, Laura noticed a girl from her training group wave and begin to walk towards her.

"Hello Laura, I thought it was you on the coach this morning, which ward are you on?" Asked Tina, looking pleased to see her colleague.

"I'm up on Lister, I've just come for some incontinence pads. So when did you start down here?"

"Only a few days ago. I didn't realise geriatric nursing was such hard work!"

"Yes, it can be back-breaking, but it's just as bad upstairs." Laughed Laura, before whispering; "You're lucky, at least you haven't got Sister Wilcox down here to contend with."

"Oh, I've heard about her, is she really that bad?" Asked Tina, turning to go back to her work. "You can tell me over coffee, besides, there's something I wanted to ask you. I'll see you in the canteen."

Laura wondered what it was that she wanted to ask her, as she stepped out of the lift, struggling with the enormous box of pads. It was then that she heard a voice.

"You want to come with me?"

"I'm sorry, replied Laura, a little mystified.

"X-ray - you want to come too?" Repeated the porter, as he stood staring at her in tight, leather trousers.

"No, Roberto, I'll send one of the new girls," Interrupted sister. "You can show her where X-ray is, if you would be so kind."

"Yes, I can show her, that's no problem." Replied the porter in a thick Spanish accent, trying to hide his disappointment at not having the pretty blonde to accompany him.

"Don't be getting up to any of your little tricks, Roberto!" Glared Sister Wilcox sternly, before going over to help Laura with the box.

Between them, they carried the pads into the sluice, where Sister quite surprised Laura with what she was about to say.

"You've done wonders with Ivy since you've been here, Laura. The poor old soul wouldn't speak to anyone at first, let alone have someone to help feed and dress her."

"I'm sure she would have, given enough time," replied Laura modestly.

"No, I don't think so. You're a very good nurse. I can see it in you, but you can get even better. There are two important rules in nursing, that you'd do well to adhere to. Firstly, you must learn to prioritise, secondly, you must never make patients totally dependent on you. That second rule doesn't apply quite so much in this type of nursing, but it's something you should always be aware of."

"Yes, Sister, I'll bear that in mind."

"You'll make mistakes sure enough, it's inevitable, just like I did when I was a student nurse like you. I went and mixed everybody's false teeth together in a bowl! Just make sure none of your mistakes are fatal ones. Check everything a second time, and don't take everything your colleagues say as the truth. Double check. Do you understand?"

"Thank-you, Sister," beamed Laura. She was beginning to get attached to the formidable nurse. Although she was one of the old school, and had a fearsome reputation for being a bit of a dragon, she was very fair and did possess a sharp, and often crude sense of humour.

"Now, off you go and enjoy a well-earned break." Smiled the woman with over thirty years of nursing experience etched into her face. Laura thanked her again, but as she was about to go, Sister called her back; "Don't worry about Ivy, I've already taken her off the commode - priorities Nurse Peddlescoombe, remember!"

The canteen was only a couple of minutes walk away from the ward, and involved a short detour through the hospital's beautifully maintained gardens. Here, during the warmer weather, patients, and staff on their lunch-breaks could sit out and enjoy the tranquil surroundings, and forget they were in the centre of a bustling city.

As Laura made her way along the narrow path, she noticed a porter ahead of her, returning a breakfast trolley to the kitchen. She increased her pace and stepped out onto the grass in order to pass him. As she did so, one of the trolley's side panels flew open, and out fell several bowls of half-eaten porridge. One of the bowls landed at her feet, bounced erratically, before emptying its contents over Laura's shoes.

The young porter was very apologetic, and immediately bent down with a paper towel, and tried to remove as much porridge as he could.

"I'm really sorry, I can't believe I just did that." He said, staring into the nurse's deep blue eyes. "It's the path you see, it's too bumpy!" He exclaimed, looking quite embarrassed.

"It's alright, if it were only porridge that landed on my shoes while I was here, I'd be quite pleased!" Replied, Laura, seeing the funny side of the situation.

He returned her cheery smile, and allowed her to continue, before scooping up the rest of the bowls and shoving them back into the trolley.

The canteen was an uninspiring flat, rectangular building containing several rows of fixed tables and chairs. It was all self-service and customers could sit where they wished. Laura looked around for anybody she might know, and as she was about to sit at an empty table, a hand suddenly waved over from the corner, and she immediately recognised the short black hair of Tina, sitting alone.

"A moment on the lips, a lifetime on the hips!" She remarked, seeing the donut on Laura's plate.

Laura put her tray down and sat opposite her colleague.

"I'm sure I'll soon work it off on the ward! Looks like you need a few of these, have you lost weight, Tina?"

"My weight fluctuates. My mother was fat when she was young, so I really watch what I eat. But you're lucky, Laura, you've got the film star looks, the hair, the great figure. I'm just plain skinny."

Laura sensed a pang of jealousy and changed the subject to what had just happened outside.

"Oh, that's so funny. I bet you were annoyed though?" Giggled Tina.

"Yes, I was bit at first, but having cold porridge spilt over me was fairly typical of the day I've been having so far!"

"What did you say to him?"

"Nothing really, I needed a new pair of shoes anyway, and I suppose this was a good reminder. But he seemed quite a nice chap, and not bad looking either!" Laura, then turned, and glanced over at another table. "Look, that's him sitting down with that seedy-looking bloke in the leather trousers."

"Yes, I see what you mean, he is rather handsome isn't he?" Gawped Tina, open-mouthed, before suddenly averting her eyes, and quickly looking back to Laura.

"What is it Tina, what's the matter?"

"Don't look over, but that funny-looking one saw me staring, and now he's blowing kisses at me!"

Laura laughed, and took a sip of her coffee.

"So what was it that you wanted to ask me?"

"Oh, it's nothing really, I just wanted to ask what your home telephone number was, that's all."

Laura looked puzzled. They were colleagues certainly, and both were student nurses training at the same hospital, albeit in different sets, but they could not be classified as friends.

"Do you mean my home number in Twickenham, Tina?"

"That's right, it's for my mother, Pauline. Do you remember that conversation we had a while ago about universities?"

"Oh, yes, that's right. We found out that both our mothers went to the same university, twenty odd years ago." Replied Laura, warily.

"Well my mother now keeps going on about meeting yours. They must have been really good friends back in those days?"

Laura was beginning to regret telling Tina where she lived. It was not that she didn't like her colleague, but it was more out of some hidden sense of duty to protect her mother. It was becoming clear to Laura that no good would come of this.

It was common knowledge that Tina had psychological problems. What they were, nobody knew, but at times it had been a major struggle for her to get through her course. She was frequently off sick, and her terrible screaming and nightmares had caused several of the other residents in the nurses' home to put in formal complaints.

Laura had once tried to befriend Tina, when they had worked on a medical ward together, but she had found it too much of a strain. In many cases, people who have suffered severe trauma will seek out caring professions, like nursing, and Laura, still coming to terms with her father's death, felt that she may be able to talk to Tina about her difficulties. However, Tina had been rather off-hand with her, and in not so many words had told Laura to mind her own business. Since then, they had only really chatted together, just the once, and that must have been the time, Tina meant.

"Look, Tina, I'll have to ask my mother first. She hasn't been very well lately, and I don't want to add to her problems, if you can understand that?" Said Laura, hoping this would satisfy Tina, and the matter would be dropped.

At last the clock reached a quarter to five, and Laura was finally able to go off duty. It had been a frantic day, and she longed for a nice, relaxing soak in a cool bath. Her mind hadn't been fully on her work since the chat with Tina, and now she just wanted to get out of the hospital as quickly as possible. Hurrying into the small, stuffy cupboard, that was known as the locker room, Laura kicked off her scuffed black shoes with a determined effort, and put them into a carrier bag. Then, changing into a light, cotton dress and brushing her hair, she applied a token gesture of make-up. She was almost ready, there was just her sandals, which she pulled out from her handbag, before stuffing her pale, blue nurse's dress in with her shoes, and fleeing out into the warm, spring sunlight. Laura didn't have a locker, since these were for the regular staff on the ward, and being a student, passing through, she didn't qualify.

Laura had completed eighteen months of her three-year nursing course, and was based at London's prestigious, Westminster Hospital. Like the other nurses in her group, she was moved around to various other hospitals within the health authority to complete certain aspects of her training. Laura was now into her third week at St. Mary Abbot's Hospital, in Kensington, which specialised in the care of the elderly. However, before the recent health cuts by the government, the hospital had been able to provide several more facilities, like a bone marrow laboratory, an X-ray department, and a hearing-aid unit.

There was something special about Kensington, which Laura loved, and after the initial shock of the back-breaking work, and the endless rigours of washing, feeding and toileting the patients, she soon developed a soft spot for the friendly, old hospital. Probably, the busy High Street, with its wide variety of shops, wine bars and restaurants, also helped contribute to Laura's love of the area.

That afternoon she hadn't planned to return to the nurses' home with the other girls on the coach. Instead, she had arranged to meet her brother, Jonathan. Being away at university, she didn't get to see him very often, but the row between Jonathan and their mother, Sally last Sunday, just couldn't be swept under the table. Laura had to talk to him, and try to clear the air.

Once free of the hospital, Laura slowed her pace, and her mood lifted somewhat. She wasn't due to meet Jonathan until five thirty, which gave her a chance to browse in some of the shops. She desperately needed a new pair of shoes. She had been putting this off for weeks, but now, it would seem, she'd have to bow to the inevitable, especially after the porridge incident earlier that morning.

Stopping at one shop, Laura gazed longingly at the beautiful shoes on display, then, after noticing the price tags, she sighed, and swallowing her pride, walked towards a more modestly priced establishment. The bored-looking assistant gave Laura a well-practised smile, as she returned from the back room, with a pair of plain, black shoes, and watched disinterested while Laura paced up and down, testing out her new work wear. The assistant began to smirk, and Laura realised what a sight she must look, in her light cotton dress, and wearing such ugly shoes. Finally, with her mind made up, she begrudgingly took out her cheque book and guarantee card. The area health authority did not provide for nurse's shoes, and the twenty five pounds she had to pay would leave quite a dent in Laura's meagre salary for the month.

"I just can't believe you've got a hangover, Jonathan - it's five thirty in the afternoon!" Exclaimed Laura, staring in amazement at her dishevelled brother, whom she had now met.

With thirsty gulps, he quickly downed the can of coke he'd brought on route to Holland Park.

"Coke's supposed to be good for hangovers, you know!" He said, burping loudly and throwing the empty can in a bin. "Plenty of fluids and plenty of sugar, that's what the body needs!"

"Vitamin C is also quite handy," replied Laura, somewhat sarcastically. It annoyed her when Jonathan was like this, and the fact that he knew he was getting on her nerves, just made him act even worse.

They stopped at a cafe, and Laura waited until their cappuccino's had been served, before launching into the subject of why she was angry with him.

"I want you to apologise to mum, Jonathan, you had no right to speak to her the way you did."

He fiddled with the teaspoon on his saucer, as he tried to think of an adequate reply.

"Did you know that on the continent they drink cappuccino's in the morning, like a breakfast drink, rather than at other times."

"I don't believe you sometimes, Jonathan. How many A levels have you got?" Replied Laura, with a hint of anger in her voice.

Jonathan apologised, before taking on a more serious tone.

"Listen, Mum has no right to sell our home, it's not what Dad would have wanted, besides, she didn't even ask our opinions - she just went ahead and made the decision. It's our home Laura, it's our memories, it's all we've got to keep us together. Anyway, where would we go?"

Laura sipped her coffee.

"I feel as strongly about it as you do, but there are ways of thinking this thing through, without losing your head. You know how we've all suffered. Don't forget, we nearly lost Mum at one stage, you have to be patient with her."

Jonathan produced a packet of cigarettes, lit one, coughed, then immediately stubbed it out using the heel of his Dr. Martens boot.

"Why on earth does she want to go back and study in Wales again anyway, I thought she had already done the degree thing? I sometimes think that Dad's death has seriously affected her powers of reasoning."

Laura felt her anger building up again.

"Haven't I just said that, Jonathan, in not so many words. Of course its affected her, you idiot! Falcondale is where Mum and Dad first met. I suppose she feels a certain affinity with the place. If she thinks you're against her, it might really push her over the edge."

He lit another cigarette, and turned to face his sister.

"I know I can be an utter moron at times, and I think this is one of them. I know I speak out before I've had time to think, it's something I inherited from Dad."

Laura smiled at him, Jonathan reminded her of her father so much, with his tall, leggy build and craggy complexion. He even had William's hazel eyes, and unkempt dark hair.

"The last thing I want is to be cross with you, Jonathan. I'll tell you what, if you make it up to Mum, I'll have a word with her about selling the house. She's got her interview in Wales coming up soon, and she's asked me to go with her. Perhaps, just being back at Falcondale, for a day or so might just get it out of her system, and anyway, we've always got Lizzie as a secret weapon!"

"You're a genius, maybe you should be the one at university?"

"No, Jonathan, I'm just a woman!" Replied Laura, laughing. "Now, the very least I expect you to give her, is a decent box of chocolates and some nice flowers, and Jonathan - do it soon!"

Laura was amazed she had managed to get through to him so easily, and wondered what the catch might be. She didn't have to wait long to find out.

"Listen sis, what's the chance of me crashing out in your room tonight. I don't feel up to apologising and all that just at the moment."

As they waited for the Circle Line train at High Street Kensington, Laura couldn't help thinking about what Tina had said earlier that morning. It had gone from something merely preying on her mind, to something that was now deeply disturbing her. The last thing she wanted were ghosts from the past suddenly turning up, and causing her mother further, unnecessary distress. Perhaps, she should say something to Jonathan about it, but what would be the point? He wouldn't do anything and would just think she was being paranoid. Besides, Tina's request was perfectly innocent and harmless. Laura decided in the end to mention it to her mother on the trip to Wales, and if there was a problem, then she could always explain the situation to Tina.

Tina thanked the girl on the other end of the line, but declined to leave a message. It had been the third time, she had tried to contact Laura that evening, she just had to tell someone the good news. There were others who Tina spoke to, but these were few and far between. One girl, Sonia, who lived on the same floor as Tina in the nurses' home, would always pass the time of day with her, and would wake Tina if her nightmares began to disturb the others. Sonia, however, was still working that evening, and probably wouldn't get back until some time after nine o'clock. Walking back down the corridor to her room, Tina was still far too excited to settle, and get to work on the written assignments, she needed to complete in order to catch up with the other students in her set.

Still dressed in her uniform, she decided to get changed and go to the off-licence to buy something to celebrate with. Surely, Laura would be back soon, Tina re-assured herself, then she could walk the short distance over to Vincent Square, and tell her the news personally, over a glass or two of wine. If Laura wasn't too tired, she might even agree to what Tina had in mind.

She wasn't much of a drinker, but on this occasion, Tina had spent her hard-earned money on two bottles of sweet German wine, a large bottle of strong cider, and several packets of crisps and nuts to accompany the drinks.

As it was still only eight thirty, she decided to phone her mother, Pauline, since she hadn't spoken to her for some time. At least this would then give her the chance to tell someone about what had happened that afternoon.

The telephone rang for some time, and Tina was just about to replace the receiver, when her mother finally answered.

Pauline Gant sounded distant, and said very little, but Tina was used to her mother's frequent bouts of depression.

"Mum, I've got Laura's mother's telephone number. Remember, that woman who you said you went to university with." Shouted Tina, eagerly down the line. "And, you'll never guess what?"

"What's that?" Replied Pauline, sombrely.

"I got asked out on a date this afternoon, by this handsome young porter at the hospital. I think he's Spanish, or Italian!" There was nothing but silence on the other end, and Tina soon realised what was wrong. "Mum, are you still there, is Dad with you?"

"No, he's gone out, Tina - I don't know where. He can rot in hell for all I care."

"What's happened?" Called out Tina, loudly. "Has he hurt you again? Please, Mum, say something. I need to know if you're okay?"

There was a long pause, before Pauline did at last reply.

"It's alright, Tina - it wasn't quite so bad this time. Please, you mustn't worry about me."

"I'm going to tell the police. I know I've threatened to before, but this time, I'm really going to do it. I hate him!" Screamed Tina tearfully.

"No, Tina, just keep out of it. You're free from him now."

"I wont. He's got to be stopped before he kills you. Why do you let him get away with it?" Tina closed her eyes, and gripped the telephone tightly, as she tried to summoned up the strength of her convictions. "This time, I'm going to tell them everything, all about Mr. Bloom too. We're shielding a murderer. We can't go on like this Mum, it's insane."

Tina was wasting her breath. Pauline had already hung up the phone. Back in her room, her elation had quickly evaporated into despair. She opened the cider, and poured herself a tumbler. She downed this immediately, then poured herself another, and another. Tina knew what her father's beatings were like, always brutal, and always after he'd been drinking. Usually, it was Pauline who bore the brunt of Frank's savagery. He would only start on Tina, if she started screaming, or happened to get in the way. As he rained blows down on his wife and daughter, Frank would shout obscenities, and tell them how much he hated them for making him a prisoner. In Tina's younger years, the beatings were often so severe, she had to take weeks off school at a time. During those years, Pauline became very adept at hiding her husband's brutality. She found she could come up with the most imaginative of excuses to explain the mass of bruises covering both her daughter, and herself.

Finally, when she was old enough, Tina left home. This was even with her father's blessing, for it was he, who had suggested she take up nursing, and now, to her great relief, she found she could be independent, and live a more meaningful life. She would become a nurse, and have nothing more to do with him ever again. She had begged her mother to leave Frank, and go to the police, but Pauline would always stay loyal, and stick by the man, she claimed to love.

It had turned rather chilly now as Tina closed the door and stepped out onto the street. She breathed in the cool, night air, in an attempt to clear her fuzzy head.

She was in two minds as to whether she should confide in Laura about her father, or just simply mention about her forthcoming date with the young man at the hospital. However, by the time she had reached her destination, her mind was already made up. Tina was determined to put on a brave face in front of Laura, after all, it was a trait, she had got from her mother.

The main door to Empire Nurses' Home, where Laura lived was open. It usually was, despite there being an intercom system in operation. Tina went over and pressed the button to summon the antiquated lift in the centre of the lobby.

The noisy contraption stopped abruptly on the third floor, startling Tina, and making her lose her balance and crash the bottles against the sliding door. Fortunately, there didn't seem to be anyone around, and she crept along the corridor towards Laura's room without any further ado. Knocking lightly, Tina stepped back, expecting her friend to open the door.

"Oh, I'm sorry, I was looking for Laura, I didn't realise she had company," remarked Tina shyly, not knowing where to look.

"It's okay, she wont be long, Laura has just gone for a bath. Why don't you come in and wait for her?" Replied, the bare-chested man standing in the doorway.

"No, I wouldn't want to disturb you, I'll see her tomorrow. Just say, Tina called." With that, she turned to leave, but the slim, dark-haired man called her back.

"Please, it's not what you think - I'm Laura's brother, Jonathan. She's letting me crash on her floor tonight!"

He had a kind, understanding face that appealed to Tina, and she immediately felt relaxed by his laid-back attitude.

"Yes, alright, I will come in and wait, if you don't mind?"

Jonathan smiled, and kicked the sleeping bag, he'd just laid out under Laura's bed, before pulling on his T-shirt.

"Is that booze, you've brought with you Tina?"

Jonathan could tell by the look on Laura's face that she wasn't at all impressed. "I don't believe it, I go for a quick bath, only to come back and find that my brother is holding a party in my room!"

Tina couldn't help laughing, and temporarily forgot about her earlier telephone conversation with her mother. She then poured Laura some wine, before producing the packets of crisps from her carrier bag.

Laura took the glass and went to sit on the floor next to her brother. She found it hard to be angry, since Tina was so obviously enjoying Jonathan's company, and had lost much of her usual shyness.

As the drink took its effect on Tina, she once again found her mind in turmoil. She didn't know whether to laugh or cry, as she fought to curtail the sadness that ate away at her heart.

"Laura, I have some news," she blurted out eventually, taking her mind off her problems. "Plus, there's something I wanted to ask you."

Laura inhaled deeply. She had heard this before, and hoped it didn't involve her mother again. Trying to put her off track, she studied the other girl critically before remarking;

"Are you drunk, Tina?" That seemed to have the desired effect, and suddenly Tina began to giggle hysterically.

"Why, yes, I do believe I am!" The more Tina tried to control her speech, the more she seemed to slur her words.

"Maybe you should go back to your room and sleep it off?" Said Laura, finishing her wine.

"No, I can't tonight, I'm far too excited!" Tina then proceeded to tell Laura about how she was asked out earlier that afternoon by the young chap in the canteen.

Laura listened intently, and felt a pang of jealousy, when she realised it sounded like the porter who had spilt the porridge over her. She helped herself to more of Tina's wine, as her colleague continued with her story.

"So, you've agreed to go out with him on condition that I, and one of his friends make it a foursome?"

"Yes, I have," replied Tina, looking a bit uncomfortable. "He sounds very nice though, Mediterranean, I think. I'm sure he'll bring someone nice for you too!"

Laura was a bit bewildered. The chap who she had the incident with earlier, was English, and certainly didn't speak with a foreign accent.

"Look, Tina, why can't you just see him by yourself, and not involve me?"

"I did want to, but I'm not very experienced with men, and I get quite shy. Please, Laura."

"Go on Laura, it sounds like a bit of a laugh!" Added Jonathan, trying to help Tina.

Laura found herself reluctantly agreeing to go, after seeing how much it meant to Tina. But, there was one condition she insisted upon.

"You've got to be there, Jonathan, to rescue us, if things go wrong!"

Jonathan later volunteered to walk Tina back, as she was now quite tipsy. However, she would only let him escort her part of the way, which made him wonder if there was anything wrong.

"Don't worry, I'll be okay, please don't come any further." She then turned, and took a few steps, before looking back to where he was standing. "I really did enjoy myself tonight, and thanks for helping me."

Jonathan smiled, and watched as she walked away.

"So did I Tina, I'll see you on Friday, for your big date, but I'll keep out of the way, I promise!"

If he were to admit it, there was something in her naivety, and innocence that not only intrigued him, but excited him as well. Jonathan waited a few moments until she was some way off in the distance, then, noticing her enter a building, he became curious, and started to follow in her tracks. He stopped when he reached the point, he had last seen her, and seemed puzzled by the fact she had gone into Rochester Row Police Station. Unbeknown to Jonathan, Tina was going to stand by her decision, and tell the police everything about her father, Frank Gant.

16. NICK

The alarm shrieked through Nick's ears, to totally obliterate the remnants of a pleasant dream. He looked sleepily at the luminous numbers on the clock, not quite believing that he really had to get up, and so disgustingly early. It was 05.30, and he was due to be back at the hospital in an hour. Pulling himself up to a sitting position, he sighed deeply. Outside the beginnings of daylight were taking the place of night. Once he was up and about, however, he found that he actually rather enjoyed seeing the whole of the day through. It seemed to give him long peaceful moments in which to reflect, and catch up on the more simple pleasures of life, like browsing through a newspaper, or just having a normal conversation with someone, who wasn't connected with anything vaguely academic. He wandered down to the communal bathrooms at the end of the corridor - at least they were always empty at this time of the morning, he consoled himself.

As he ran the disposable razor across his stubbly chin, Nick wondered if he would see the young nurse again. He tried to picture her smile in his mind's eye, but only succeeded in nicking himself, as his face broke into a broad grin, thinking about the porridge incident.

Nick was a twenty-eight year old 'mature' student, in his third-year, at Central Kensington College. He resided in Prince's House, a ghastly, monstrous tower block, situated right bang in the centre of the college. It was grey, drab and depressing, but Nick did have a choice - he didn't have to live there.

It had been six months since he had moved out of the matrimonial home. He was still very much on speaking terms with Sandra, his wife of five years. But, they had both changed during their married years, and had more or less, swapped roles.

Nick and Sandra had met through their work. This was during the mid-seventies, when both of them were employed by the Star Insurance Company. They were very committed to their jobs and were earning, what could be described as a decent living. The company however, was losing out to more aggressive rivals, and was eventually taken over by one of them. The inevitable changes occurred, and the company, although still retaining its name, changed its image dramatically.

During this time, Nick became increasingly despondent with the new cut and thrust policies the company was employing. He resented being pressurised into pestering regular clients to buy more insurance, while having to winkle out new ones by using dubious means. Sandra though, seemed to thrive in this new environment, and would think nothing of opening the telephone directory to literally cold call potential customers. She soon linked up with other like-minded employees, and chose to work by commission-only, as the rewards could be far higher. Nick refused to have anything to do with door-knocking, and came to the decision that aggressive selling wasn't for him.

The money they had both made before Nick's abrupt change of direction was still sufficient to pay a substantial deposit for a semi-detached house in the leafy suburb of Osterley in West London, with its magnificent park, a mere stone's throw away.

The couple's relationship at the end of the seventies was still very solid, and Sandra was in total agreement that Nick should try his hand at something else.

"I just want you to be happy," she said, reclining on the sofa, dressed in a designer-label dress, after making yet another kill in the corporate insurance market. "I can make more than enough to pay the mortgage, so you can just take some time off and see what you want to do."

She was an attractive woman, the same age as he, with confident, expressive brown eyes, and shoulder-length bottle-blonde hair, styled to make it look slightly tousled.

One day, after much deliberation, Nick decided to take Sandra up on her word.

"I've been offered a place at university." He exclaimed excitedly, showing her the envelope.

Sandra put down her wine and studied the letter in great detail.

"But it's for three years, and why archaeology?"

"Sandra, it's what we agreed," replied Nick, "It's something I've always wanted to study. I love anything to do with history."

Sandra took a sip of her red wine and lit a cigarette.

"Okay, you go ahead and do it Nick - if that's what you want. I just thought you would do something that led to a decent living, that's all?"

Nick started his course the same year in defiance of Sandra, who true to her word, took over the role of breadwinner. Since the Piccadilly Line went straight to South Kensington, Nick decided to become a commuting student, and for the time being, the arrangement seemed to work.

Over the next few months, Nick noticed that Sandra even seemed to enjoy the fact that she now had a student for a husband. It was a good talking point and made her feel younger. She began to tease him about his newly-acquired bohemian look, what with the pixie boots and baggy sweaters.

"I expect he'll be wearing a donkey jacket soon and demonstrating at Trafalgar Square!" She remarked sarcastically to friends at a dinner party.

Craig, one of the guests, immediately took up the baiting.

"Don't start throwing flour bombs at Mrs. Thatcher will you, Nick? We mustn't bite the hand that feeds us!"

Bored, Nick got up to leave the table, it was then that he noticed the glance Sandra gave to Craig. It was the same glance she had once given him.

"Nick, come back, I'm sorry, but I find it all so amusing." Said Craig smirking. "But why all this culture stuff, I mean, where's it going to take you?"

Nick had disliked the smarmy Craig, since the old days at Star Insurance, and now felt his anger rising.

"We're not all hedonistic materialists like you Craig. There are other things important in life, besides money." Nick was just getting into a rhythm, when he was rudely interrupted by the giggling Sandra.

"He's off to Hollywood Craig, that's where the culture's taking him. I expect he'll be the next Indiana Jones, and all that!" The whole table then erupted with laughter at Nick's expense.

The agreement initially was for Nick to take a room in the college's halls of residence and only return to the house at weekends. This seemed to work fine for the first month, but after a while, Nick began to see less and less of Sandra, as she reaped the rewards of her industrious activities. She now seemed happy to spend her free time out with friends or colleagues from work. Shortly after this, he applied to become a full-time live-in student.

Nick had funded his course of study himself, but now, what with having to pay accommodation fees as well, his bank balance soon started to shrink at an alarming rate. The crunch really came when his car needed repair work that ran into several hundreds of pounds. This, he also paid for himself, rather than ask his wife for the money. Eventually, he decided to look for part-time work in Kensington, just to keep him afloat. He didn't want anything too exciting or difficult, but at the same time it had to be rewarding and worthwhile.

Looking through the pages of the Evening Standard, there seemed plenty of opportunities; bar work, waiting at tables, security, hotels, building sites. He telephoned a few, and on more than one occasion was shocked to learn just how low the hourly rate of pay was. There was one advertisement, however, that caught his attention, the hours were just right, and it was literally about half a mile from the college. Picking up the telephone, he was amazed to get an interview immediately.

Mr. Watts, the Head Porter was aged about sixty, thin and wiry with a full head of thick grey hair, some of which was tinged a dark yellow colour. This had been brought about by some thirty years of writing out portering rosters while sitting hunched over a desk, with his head being supported by the same hand that held his cigarette. In fact, the whole of Mr. Watts' small office was a shrine totally dedicated to smoking. The ceiling was almost a deep saffron, and was dotted with dark amber-coloured globules of nicotine that perfectly matched the yellow-streaked net curtains. On the orderly desk was a large, but spotlessly clean pub-type, glass ashtray, which contained a pipe, and a box of Swan Vesta matches. While at the other end, was another ashtray, this was a more battle-hardened veteran. Made of aluminium, it boasted 'Player's Navy Cut' proudly around its rim. It obviously hadn't been emptied for some time, judging by the twenty or so, assorted dog-ends nestling at its base.

Mr. Watts studied Nick's application form for some time, flicking from page to page in deep concentration. Eventually, he turned his swivel chair around to face him. His eyes, for such a heavy smoker were surprisingly clear and seemed a little out of place against his flushed and somewhat ruddy complexion.

"Student eh, ever done this sort of work before?"

"No, I haven't Mr. Watt's," replied Nick, trying to shake off his distinct middle class accent. "But, I'm a quick learner, and don't mind getting stuck in."

Mr. Watts then reached over and picked up the telephone. As he did so, Nick stared nonchalantly at some saucy postcards pinned to a board containing health and safety notices.

"Harry, do us a favour, and bring me along a cup of tea, with plenty of sugar!"

Said Mr. Watts amiably to the voice on the other end of the line. Then, returning to Nick, he picked up his pipe, lit it and sat back comfortably in his chair.

"We've had a few students here in the past, some good, others not so good. As long as you do your work, and turn up on time, I'll keep off your back. St. Mary Abbot's isn't a particularly busy hospital, the government cuts have seen to that, and I don't mind if you study when it's quiet." The Head Porter then paused, as if he was trying to weigh up whether he'd made the right decision or not. He took a few puffs from his pipe, before adding; "Can you start on Monday?"

"Yes, Mr. Watts, I can. Thank-you, I'll look forward to it."

"That's alright, son, you can call me, Reg from now on. I'll get someone to show you around the hospital." They both then stood up and shook hands. "Just a word of warning before you start."

"A word of warning?"

"I don't want to catch you in the pub across the road when you're on duty, and another thing - mind yourself with the girls."

"Girls, Mr. Watts?"

"Yes, girls. Some of my lads think they're Romeo's and chase after the young nurses. Being married doesn't seem to make the slightest bit of difference to most them either!"

"I understand, Mr. Watts."

"I hope so son, a big strong lad like you, just be careful, it's easy to get led astray here. I've got a grandson at university, who wanted to work here during the summer holidays. Not on your life, I told him, so you mark my words."

There was a loud knock at the door, and with that, Mr. Watts patted Nick on the shoulder and ushered him out of the office.

Nick was quite amazed at the sight which welcomed him as he stepped out into the corridor. For standing in front of him was a man of average height, and possibly of Mediterranean, or South American appearance. It was difficult to put an age to him, maybe it was the thick, black curly hair, stiff with gel, which made him look younger. He could have been in his forties, or even fifties, if one looked closer. The man had long, skinny legs, and was wearing the most unflattering tight, black leather jeans and cowboy boots. His light blue porter's shirt was undone to the waist, revealing a hairless chest, festooned with a an abundance of gold chains of every type and size. He couldn't be described as being overweight, but he was blessed with a magnificently rounded beer-belly that protruded proudly over the top of a thick belt. It seemed absurd to Nick, that a man so obviously vain, could flaunt an appendage like this with so much abandon.

"Nick, this is Roberto, or Colombian Bob, as he's sometimes called." Said the Head Porter, "He'll show you around the hospital."

Sally began to run the bath, she had already passed the vacuum cleaner over the main rooms and hallway, then had to mop the kitchen floor after Pepys, the dog had trampled in mud from the garden. It was a large house to keep clean and tidy, but usually Penny would help out, mostly at weekends when she could. Despite protestations from Laura and Lizzie, Sally flatly refused to accept anyone in to help. To have a complete stranger going through all the rooms, touching things - William's things, was totally unthinkable.

"But, they wouldn't be a stranger for long, Sally. Come on, it's far too much for you to manage." Remarked Lizzie one day, trying to be helpful.

"Lizzie, I know you have my best intentions at heart, but I really don't mind doing the housework, and Penny has never complained. Besides, it keeps me from thinking about things."

However, that was back in the past, this was now, and Sally was selling the house. The estate agent had telephoned the day earlier to ask if he could bring over a prospective buyer. Two families had already viewed the house, and one of them seemed quite intent on taking things a step further, but Sally had heard no more.

Lizzie was due to come over later, but Sally didn't want her friend there at the same time as a possible buyer. Lizzie had made her views very clear that she was against the sale of the house. Perhaps she had been talking to Jonathan and Laura behind her back.

Sally sighed as she thought back to the row she'd had with her son. She thought about contacting him at the university, but no, she would do as Laura had suggested and let her try and talk some sense into him. Sometimes a mediator is quite useful in these type of matters.

Sally stood in the bathroom and looked along the shelf at the line of coloured bottles. After a few moments deliberation, she eventually picked one out, and gave it a sniff, before pouring some of the contents into the water. She gazed into the mirror, while waiting for the bath to fill, and wondered if the clothes she had chosen to wear were suitable. She then turned off the taps and went into the bedroom to get undressed.

Sally was just in the process of selecting a more appropriate outfit, when she was disturbed by the door bell ringing.

"Okay, I'm coming, please be patient!" She muttered under her breath, as it rang a second time, while she was hurrying to tie the sash on her dressing gown. She padded down to the front door in her bare feet, ready to vent her anger on whoever had so rudely interrupted her long-awaited soak. However, Sally's irritation disappeared immediately as a courier thrust a magnificent bouquet of flowers into her arms. Going back inside, she opened the attached envelope and beamed with pleasure as she read Jonathan's touching apology. Smiling, she put the flowers in a vase and went back upstairs to enjoy her bath. No sooner had she reached the top of the stairs, when the door bell rang again. This time it was another courier, who asked her to sign for a parcel.

Sally gasped as she unwrapped the huge box of expensive Belgian chocolates. What a silly boy you are Jonathan, she thought, as she stared at the mouth-watering sight in front of her. There were over two dozen chocolates in the box, and she wondered how on earth he could have possibly afforded them.

As Sally went back upstairs, a definite aroma drifted under her nostrils. It was unmistakably scent, like a man's aftershave lotion. It certainly wasn't anything she would ever wear, it was far too masculine, but at the same time it was overpoweringly sweet and sickly. She thought she had smelt it earlier, and subconsciously thought it must have come from one of the couriers, but no, that was absurd. Perhaps it had just drifted in from outside?

For some unknown reason she went towards Penny's room, but when she reached the door, she realised how late it was getting, and decided to go back to the bathroom. It was now going to be a very quick dip, rather than the lovely, long soak she had planned for herself.

Twenty minutes later the estate agent arrived, exactly on time.

"Hello, Mrs.Peddlescoombe, it's nice to see you again." Stewart Marsh was a pleasant young man, in his early twenties, and always cheerful and polite. Sally had even thought he would make an ideal partner for Laura, but she had since discovered that the fresh-faced trainee was already married.

"Please come straight through," smiled Sally, as she held the front door open.

"May I introduce, Mr. Frank Gant." Said Stewart, in a pleasant, but business-like manner.

Sally stepped back, her eyes locked onto Frank's. She swallowed hard and couldn't quite get her breath. She stumbled back into a small table in the hallway, almost knocking it over.

"Hello, Sally, it's wonderful to see you again, and after so long." Said Frank, moving forward to offer a gold-embellished hand. "I must say, you look great - the years have been kind to you."

Sally stopped dead in her tracks, her mind unable to fathom what was happening. Again she found herself inhaling the sweet, sickly aroma of Frank's aftershave lotion. It was exactly like the smell she had detected earlier.

"What do you want?" She asked, her voice mirroring her terror.

"I've come to view your house. I'm very interested in buying it." Frank replied, with a cool air about him, giving Sally a smile that immediately disarmed her.

"Is everything okay here, Mrs. Peddlescoombe?" Asked Stewart, seeing Sally's discomfort. "Perhaps, we ought to come back another time?"

It was Frank who replied for Sally.

"Mrs. Peddlescoombe and I used to know each other many, many years ago. It's just the shock of seeing me again. That's right isn't it, Sally?"

Looking first to Frank's mocking face, then back to Stewart, Sally suddenly felt foolish, like Frank was trying to intimidate her. She didn't want to come across as weak and timid, and willed herself to stand her ground, besides, Frank wouldn't do anything with Stewart there.

"It's fine, Mr. Marsh. I'm sorry, I've had a lot on my mind lately." Replied Sally, sounding more confident.

Frank smiled at her again, then turned to Stewart.

"Listen, as Mrs. Peddlescoombe and I are such old friends, would you mind giving us five minutes alone?"

Stewart looked across at Sally, who hesitated for a moment, before nodding.

"Yes, very well, I'll go and wait out the front."

"That's a good chap, Stewart. I'll recommend you highly when we get back to your office to complete the deal."

A wide grin appeared on the young man's face as he obeyed Frank's request, and headed outside.

Sally was now very nervous again, and moved away from Frank.

"I still don't understand. Did you know I lived here?" She asked, trying to sound braver than she actually was.

"Sally, please relax. No, I didn't know you lived here, it's just a coincidence." He lied convincingly. "I've not come here to do you any harm. I'm just interested in seeing, and possibly buying your house. That's all. So there's really no need to be afraid."

Sally eyed him warily. He looked very dashing in his dark grey business suit, open-neck white shirt and suntan. She could see when he smiled at her why she had taken a fancy to him all those years ago.

"I'm sorry Frank. I'm just not good with surprises, especially not this type." She replied tensely. "You said some very horrible things. It was a long time ago, but it did scare me, and still does."

"That's totally understandable," he reasoned, gazing at her with his steely blue eyes. "I didn't mean to spook you out. Look Sally, I've changed. I'm not the same man I was. I'm sorry about the things I said. It was done in the heat of the moment."

She took in his powerful frame, the short, sandy-coloured hair, and the faded scar running down his left cheek.

"Life changes us all, Frank, in one way or another." She replied, forcing herself to smile.

Frank was highly excited that things had been so easy, he hadn't lost the old charm. He ran his eyes over Sally's body, taking in her feminine curves and womanly fragrance. He had to keep himself in check, he couldn't blow it, the situation still required a certain amount of patience and guile. He called Stewart back in, and Sally proceeded to lead them around her home.

The beautiful, mock Tudor house was certainly very different to Frank's garish, modern abode in Kew. He liked Sally's style and the way she had arranged things. Even the furniture was tastefully understated and classy, so different to the leather themed layout he was so used to.

They came to the kitchen, and as they entered, Sally noticed the back door was still open. She had left it like that to allow the floor to dry. Pepys was excited and jumped at Frank, leaving a muddy paw mark on his jacket. This seemed very odd to Sally, as Pepys was normally wary of strangers. Then, as Sally was apologising, Frank made a casual remark.

"I hope you don't mind, but I arrived about ten minutes early, and couldn't resist a look at the garden. So, Pepys and I already know each other."

"Err, no that's quite alright." Replied Sally, wondering why she hadn't heard Pepys barking. "I hope you liked the garden, is it what you're looking for? My late husband did most of the landscaping himself."

"You mean William?" Asked Frank, pretending not to know her husband was dead, after he had murdered him by cutting the brake pipes in his car.

Sally nodded, and seemed upset even by the mere mention of William's name.

Frank decided not to pursue the matter.

"It looks absolutely perfect. I've got two dogs myself, they'd just love the garden. Do you know I've really liked what I've seen today, and could feel very much at home here."

Sally was quite relaxed now, and even rather pleased that she may have found a buyer for the house. They eventually came to the lounge, and Stewart checked his watch.

"Thank-you, Mrs. Peddlescoombe. You really do have a lovely house, and I'll be in touch if there's anymore viewings."

Sally thanked him and led them both towards the front door, but Frank hung back.

"Pity, I couldn't have stayed for a coffee, it smells delicious!" He said.

"I'm sorry, how rude of me," replied Sally, remembering the pot of fresh coffee she had made earlier.

They saw Stewart out and went back to the kitchen, where Frank seated himself at the breakfast bar.

"I've been well informed that you're a very successful business woman in the rag trade, Sally?" He asked leaning back casually.

Sally's nerves had come rushing back, now she found herself alone with Frank.

"I was a couple of years ago," she said, looking away from his constant gaze. "I just help out a bit part-time now."

"Really? Sometimes in business, you have to keep venturing forward, especially when times are good."

"Yes, I'm sure you're right, but losing my husband a couple of years ago, had quite a negative effect on me."

Frank was silent for a moment, before standing up and walking over towards her.

"I did want to ask about William earlier, I'm so sorry."

"It's all right, you don't have to apologise, how could you have known?"

"I admire you so much Sally. You've come through this, not only supporting your family, but running a business, and a beautiful home. You really are quite a woman."

It was a magnificent point scored for Frank, and he even noticed Sally blushing.

"Thank-you, that's very kind," she said, again backing away from him.

But Frank reached out and put his hand on hers.

"I really am sorry for what happened in the past, Sally. Maybe you could find it in your heart to forgive me?"

"I do look for the good in people, rather than the bad. But, I think we should just stick with the business in hand, Frank."

"That's a very good perspective to have Sally, and yes, I quite understand."

"You look like you've done very well for yourself, Frank. What is it that you do?" She asked, eager to change the subject.

"I own one of London's largest mini-cab and haulage companies, and I have a nightclub in Mayfair." He remarked, in a matter-of-fact manner.

"Okay, I'm impressed." She replied, taking a sip of her coffee.

"Well, it's like anything - you have a dream, and then work hard at it. There's really no reason why it can't happen."

"You're very focussed, Frank. Maybe you should talk to my son, Jonathan. He could certainly do with a bit of your motivation."

They continued chatting for another half an hour, mostly about Sally and Lizzie's business. This was safe ground for Frank, who true to form, was still reluctant to speak about himself.

"It's been a pleasure, Sally. I do hope we can see more of each other, and I'd love to see Lizzie again." Smiled Frank as he finally got up to leave.

But Sally was still very suspicious of him, despite the new benevolent change of character, and was quite relieved that he was finally going.

"Thank-you, Frank. So do you think you'll buy the house?"

"It's very likely, but I'll talk with my lawyer, and I'll probably have to come back and see it again. Perhaps, you could give me your number, Sally?"

"Frank Gant!" Exclaimed Lizzie. "Frank Gant!" She gasped a second time.

"Yes, Lizzie, he was here this afternoon looking around the house."

"I can't believe it, not after all these years. My goodness, but Sally dear, why on earth didn't you ring me for support?"

"He was only looking around the house, Lizzie. Besides, the estate agent was here too."

Intrigued, Lizzie pulled deeply on her cigarette, and turned her perfectly coiffured head sideways to emit the smoke. Eyes wide, she sat forward, hungry for more information.

"It's very weird about the aftershave smell, Sally. So do you think it just wafted in while he was nosing around your back garden?"

"Well, yes, that's the only logical solution I can think of. Mind you, it was rather strong and smelt absolutely vile, so it probably wouldn't have taken very much." Sally laughed and poured herself another coffee. "It was that strong I could have smelt him coming from Richmond Bridge!"

"Sally, you should have detained him here under false pretences, I would have loved to have seen him again. Is he still good-looking?"

"Yes, I suppose he is, in an Oliver Reed sort of way. Very intense, light blue eyes, short cropped hair, big and muscular, and extremely dangerous-looking. In fact, rather scary, I'd say. You certainly wouldn't want to meet him on a dark night!" Sally put her cup down, and poured Lizzie another glass of wine.

"Frank always did have that menacing look about him, but I did rather like him when we were at university, and still wonder if he should have been locked up, or that Pauline?"

"Yes, good point. He says he's changed now, and seems to have done very well with his businesses."

"I knew Frank would do well, whether within the confines of the law, I don't know. Sounds like he's still very much into you, Sally?"

"If you want the honest truth, Lizzie, he scared me." Replied, Sally, opening the box of chocolates that had arrived earlier.

"Maybe he thinks you come with the house. How strange and what a funny coincidence?"

"That's what I thought, but he says that's all it was, just a coincidence." Continued Sally, taking a chocolate, and pushing the box towards Lizzie.

"Do you realise, Frank might be the answer to all of your problems. If he's changed as he says he has, he could be the perfect partner for you?"

Sally wouldn't be drawn into what Lizzie was suggesting, and reached for another chocolate.

"Gosh these are delicious, Lizzie, have another one!"

"I think I will. Where did they come from, my word, they're Belgian and the best."

"I presumed Jonathan sent them, along with the flowers - but there wasn't a card."

"How strange?" Said Lizzie, examining the box in more detail. "These would have cost a fortune, much more than Jonathan could afford?"

"Yes, you're right. I think I'd better ask him."

"I bet it wasn't Jonathan. It's blatantly obvious Frank sent them anonymously." Stated Lizzie picking up her wine.

Sally sat back, deep in thought, staring at the chocolates.

"No, of course Frank didn't send them. That's absurd."

"Your naivety never ceases to amaze me Sally!" Laughed Lizzie, gazing at her friend affectionately.

Sally was still quiet, and seemed to have something on her mind.

"Lizzie, I know you've been talking to Jonathan and Laura behind my back. But you're wasting your time. I've come to a decision, and I'm selling the house, and it doesn't matter who buys it."

However, Lizzie, taking another chocolate was determined to have her say.

"I've known you for many years, Sally darling, and I think you're making a big mistake. Will you please listen to what your family are trying to say to you."

Sally looked seriously at her friend.

"Penny will be home from school soon, and I don't want her to see us arguing about this when she comes in."

"But that's just it for heaven's sake - you'll be uprooting Penny from school, from all of her friends, and everything she's familiar with. This is her home. You say this place is like a shrine to William, but going back to Falcondale, where you first met him would be foolhardy. I don't understand you at times, Sally. It's like you're trying to rewind a tape of your life. William won't be there. You must stop trying to find him!"

"No, that's not true," replied Sally unconvincingly.

But Lizzie was right, and Sally knew her friend wouldn't give up without a fight.

"Listen, I know William's insurance has paid off your mortgage, and you've still got plenty of money to last you a few years. Take the children off on holiday, and re-build some bridges. Then, when you come back you could get more involved in the business again. There'll always be a place for you, and it'll give you something positive to focus on."

"I'll think about it, Lizzie, but I've already told you, my mind is made up."

"Sally Peddlescoombe, you can be a head-strong mare at times, but please, keep the house, and give up this Wales thing. No good will come of it, believe me."

17. THE VOYEUR

Penny turned into Oxford Park and deliberately slowed her pace. Normally, she would walk home part of the way with one or two of her school friends. If the weather was mild they would look in some of the shops in nearby Richmond, and then go and sit on the green, just chatting, mostly about boys and music. Penny particularly liked Buck's Fizz, Duran Duran and ABC, and today the girls had been keen to buy records, but on this occasion, Penny had been told by her mother to return straight home.

Penny would often think how lucky she was to have a mother like Sally. She was given much more freedom than most girls of her age, and more importantly, Penny was treated as an adult. Sally valued her youngest daughter's opinions and at times, they both looked upon each other more as close friends, rather than mother and daughter. This relationship had really only come about after Laura had gained her place to study nursing at Westminster Hospital. Subsequently, this meant Laura had to move into one of the hospital's nurses' homes in London. This was a tough decision to make, even though Twickenham wasn't a great distance from the capital, it was still too far for her to travel between shifts, and that wasn't even taking into consideration the cost of fares on a student nurse's pay.

So, in her older sister's absence, Penny was promoted to the role of her mother's chief confidante, and sounding board, as well as a much-needed emotional support.

Penny was similar in looks to both her mother and Laura, with the same strawberry blonde hair, only Penny wore hers much longer, and had green eyes, rather than the deep blue of Sally and her sister. Although, it had been said that Penny, with her thinner face was not as stunningly pretty as Laura, she certainly had the potential to match her sister's looks when she begins to mature. Even now at fifteen, Penny's once, stick-like figure had filled out to a shapely 32C-22-34.

As Penny's house came into view she hesitated. Like her brother and sister, and of course, Lizzie, she was totally against the idea of selling up. Twickenham was Penny's home town, and yes she would miss her friends if she moved away, but apart from that, she loved her home, even without her father being there to watch her grow into womanhood.

Now that things were starting to happen, and people were actually coming to see the property, Penny was beginning to get scared. She knew she would have to eventually tell Sally the truth, and now that Lizzie had spoken to them all to gain support for a counter move against her mother, Penny would have to come clean.

She would tell Sally today, she decided, as she went around the back of the house to let herself in. She would say that two of her friends had set their minds on becoming interpreters, and would be off to university straight after their A-levels, which was indeed quite true. Penny would then say, she wanted to join them, and train to become an interpreter as well. This part wasn't strictly true, since Penny had always wanted to work with animals, perhaps, as a veterinary surgeon. However, that wasn't important right now, but the fact that she needed to stay settled in order to pass her exams was. She could also point out to her mother that by staying in Twickenham she would be much closer to many of the London universities and colleges, which would help prevent all the family being split up and having to live apart.

Penny felt rather pleased with herself and was confident that her argument would help win her mother over, especially if Lizzie was backing her up as well. However, she also realised just how important going back to Wales was for her mother. It was as if there was something more to it than simply selling up, and making a new start by heading west to become a student all over again. She was also quite intrigued at the prospect of actually seeing the place where her parents had first met, and had even volunteered to go to Wales with Laura for Sally's preliminary entrance interview. Penny added the finishing touches to her plan. She would go to Falcondale, just literally to see it, then she would tell her mother that she didn't want to move there. That seemed far better than the alternative, which was staying with Lizzie while her mother was away. Although Penny loved Lizzie like an aunt, she couldn't bear to watch her downing vast quantities of wine, and go off incessantly about her bizarre fashion creations from the sixties.

Penny could hear Lizzie's loud voice as soon as she reached the back door. She was greeted by an excited Pepys, and stroked him affectionately before dumping her bag, and taking off her school blazer.

Both Sally and Lizzie were laughing. It was strange to hear her mother laugh these days, and it made Penny feel relieved that finally she was showing positive signs of healing after the loss of William.

"Your Mum's got a secret admirer!" Giggled Lizzie, clutching the obligatory glass of white wine and a cigarette in the same hand. "Come over and have a drink with me, Penny, darling, seeing as your mother has gone teetotal!"

"No, Lizzie. I don't want her drinking at fifteen." Protested Sally. "Besides, she'll have homework to do."

"Suit yourself!" Slurred Lizzie. "I used to drink at a much younger age than that. Never did me any harm, just as long as you know your limits."

Penny defied her mother and poured herself a glass of Sauvignon Blanc and joined the two older women at the kitchen table to learn more about this mystery man. However, Penny's heart sank when she discovered he had viewed the house and liked it, despite her room being in such a mess.

The telephone rang and cut short Sally's story of Frank's visit. While her friend was out of the room, Lizzie took the opportunity to re-assure the teenager that the war of attrition was showing good signs. Now it may only need Penny's support to bring about a change of heart on Sally's behalf.

While her mother was talking on the telephone, Penny went upstairs to get changed. As she entered her room, she thought she could smell the hint of a strange odour in the air. It was hard to ascertain exactly what it was, but it seemed to have a sweet essence. Picking up items of clothing from the carpet, she thought for a moment that the smell could be coming from these, especially from her underwear. However, the more she tried to detect the smell, the more her senses became over familiar with it, and the aroma faded. She dismissed it from her mind and continued hanging garments in her wardrobe, before switching on her stereo, and flopping down on the bed.

She couldn't hear her mother calling her over the *Flock Of Seagulls* cassette she was playing. It was only the loud knocking at the door that finally made her turn the music down, as Sally entered with an astonished look on her face.

"Penny, you know that man, I was telling you about earlier?"

"Yes, that Frank, chap?" Asked Penny, looking just as surprised.

"That was him calling just now."

"Oh, no, please don't say he wants to buy the house?"

"Well no, not exactly. He wants to discuss the purchase privately with me, over dinner!"

"So what did you say?"

"I said, yes!"

Penny got up and went over to hug her mother, knowing she needed re-assurance about what she was going to do.

"Mum, I don't mind, honestly. I just want to see you happy again."

Sally looked lovingly at her daughter, and smiled.

"I feel just like a teenager again, going on a first date. Isn't that silly? Do you think Jonathan and Laura would be upset?"

Before Penny could answer, Lizzie burst into the room, holding up a slinky, tight-fitting black dress, she had just found in Sally's wardrobe.

"Sally, for once in your life, will you stop trying to please other people. Just go and enjoy yourself!" Ordered Lizzie firmly. "Look, you could wear this - you'll be a sensation!"

That night, Sally found it hard to sleep. She kept going over events in her mind. There was something different about Frank. It made her feel both frightened and a little curious. But deep down, it made her feel excited. She felt her spine tingling, as she tried to remember just how it felt to be held by a man once again.

The drive to Frank's office would normally have only taken about twenty minutes, but now the late afternoon rush hour had started, and Frank found himself stuck in thick traffic. He fiddled with the radio, changing channels, only to eventually turn it off as he found the constant DJ chatter an irritation. Despite being stationary, he felt pleased with himself, and longed to put the next part of his strategy into action. He was like a wild animal about to move in for the kill, following a period of prolonged stalking.

Feeling himself growing hard, as he thought back to earlier that afternoon, he refused to allow the image of Sally's naked body to fade from his mind's eye.

Frank grinned as he marvelled at his own audacity for entering Sally's house so easily, and the most remarkable thing was, he got so close to her without being detected. Getting hot, he wound the window down, checked his sunglasses in the rear-view mirror and lit a cigarette. Usually, Frank would smoke cigars, which he believed reflected his lifestyle, but driving he found cigarettes far less cumbersome.

It had actually been true, what he said to Sally, about arriving early to look around the house. However, he failed to mention that it was over an hour too early. He had driven up and down Oxford Park several times, before getting out of his car to stretch his legs. Then, after seeing Sally's Volvo estate parked in the drive, he had gone closer to have a look at the exterior of the house, after all, he did have a valid reason for being there. Not seeing any sign of movement at the front, he had looked around warily, before opening the unlocked back gate, and wandering into the rear garden. He knew the back of the house quite well, but had not seen the garden in daylight before. He walked boldly across the well-kept lawn towards the tree-house. It was here, that he'd spent many a night recently, armed with his high-powered binoculars, peering into the many rooms. He felt he knew the contours of Sally's body rather well, even if it was from a distance. He noticed how brightly-coloured the tree-house was painted, and for a moment thought about building one for his own son, Jamie. Looking closer, Frank had immediately dismissed this idea, after realising how much time and effort had gone into building such a structure. Besides, Jamie would be able to have this one, if everything went to plan.

Gazing at the rear of the house, he noticed that the kitchen door was ajar. He casually strolled towards it, the only sound he could hear was the creak of his expensive leather loafers. It was then, that he saw Pepys come trotting out to investigate. After a token bark, more of affection rather than malice, the Border Collie wagged his tail, and came over to lick Frank's hand.

"Hello, boy," he whispered, as Pepys sniffed at his clothes. "I haven't got anything for you today, so you run along."

Pepys had now become used to Frank's nocturnal visits and got excited when he saw him, especially when a nice treat was the reward. Frank quickly pushed the dog away, as he finally heard some activity coming from inside the house. He knew it would be Sally, and looked up as she opened the bathroom window a few inches. Frank entered the house, and peered at the gleaming, wet kitchen floor. He could distinctly hear Sally running a bath. He then heard a door close, and now could only hear the feint rumble of running water.

He walked through Sally's pristine kitchen, being careful not to make any marks on the classic-themed tiled floor. Upon reaching the staircase, he stood dead still, trying to listen out for any further movement. If someone else was in the house, it could only be Laura, the student nurse. Frank knew Penny was at school, Jonathan was at university, and Lizzie would always park in the drive. After a few moments, and feeling his mouth go dry, he began to creep up the stairs.

It was a large house, but Frank through his observations, had a good idea of where all the rooms were located. He heard the unmistakable sound of splashing and was satisfied Sally would be a little longer in the bathroom. Sneaking along the upstairs hallway, he went past several closed doors, until he arrived at one which was open. Upon entering, Frank found himself in Sally's bedroom.

He stared at the king-size bed and her designer clothes carefully laid out across the satin bedspread. Gazing around, he saw several framed photographs of Sally and William. He picked one up from a bedside table, and saw Sally as he used to remember her. She was obviously much younger then, and looked fit and tanned in a skimpy bikini, laying on a sandy beach somewhere exotic.

Noticing her huge collection of perfumes and cosmetics on the dressing table, he opened a bottle and deeply inhaled its aroma. Reaching down to one of the drawers, he was just about to pull it open, when he heard the sound of a door being closed. He froze for a few seconds listening to the sound of delicate footsteps as they got increasingly closer. Then, he heard her mutter something and go back to the bathroom. She had obviously forgotten something, and this gave him a few more precious moments. He looked across at what he guessed was a walk-in wardrobe, and moved hastily towards it. It was a job, but he managed to squeeze his substantial frame in among the rails of Sally's clothes.

Within moments Sally was back in the bedroom. She sniffed the air, and looked about her, somewhat bewildered. Her hair was swathed in a towel, and she was wearing a long black silky robe, that clung to her hips perfectly. Frank watched intensely, as Sally undid the sash, before slipping the robe off, and hanging it on the back of the door. She was now naked, and Frank, breathing heavily, couldn't take his eyes off her full, shapely breasts, and large pink nipples, hard due to the change in room temperature. He admired her delicious, rounded buttocks, as she stood in front of the full-length mirror admiring her body, without even realising he was there.

After a few moments, she turned and walked with her distinctive sway of the hips, towards the walk-in wardrobe. Frank's heart was pumping wildly, and he knew he was about to be discovered. He didn't care. He had made his mind up, he would have her there and then. He sighed as she got closer, and let his eyes dart from her breasts, to her firm belly, and down to her beautifully trimmed mound.

Sally flicked through the clothes as if she knew exactly what she was looking for. Frank could hear her breathing as she got closer to him, and at one stage her left breast was literally just inches from his mouth.

Frank was very uncomfortable, bent over in a half crouching position, and longed to straighten himself up. Part of him wanted her to find him, but the longer the situation went on, the more confident he felt about getting away with it undetected.

Miraculously, Sally didn't see him in the closet, she was far too pre-occupied with what she was going to wear. It was vital that any potential buyer should see her in the best possible light, after all, first impressions are so important.

Sally snatched down a hanger supporting a very conservative mid-length skirt, complete with a matching blouse, before hanging up the clothes she had laid out on the bed earlier. Frank was sweating profusely now, as he watched her bending and stretching naked. He wouldn't be able to contain himself for much longer, and was about to burst out from where he was hiding, when the sharp intrusive ring of the doorbell startled them both. Frank breathed a sigh of relief as Sally slipped her robe back on and headed off downstairs to see who it was. Unable to get a proper footing because of her shoes being in the way, he started to lurch forward and reached up to grab a rail that might prevent him falling, but the rail couldn't hold his weight and collapsed, bringing down several dresses on top of him. Surely she must have heard that, even from downstairs, he thought, but she didn't. Frank's luck was still holding out, as the noise was largely stifled by the doorbell being rung a second time. Frank crept out of his lair, and stood hesitating in the centre of Sally's bedroom, deciding his next course of action. Feeling confident that she wouldn't return in the next few seconds, he moved out onto the landing, where he crouched, listening and watching. Sally was chatting to someone at the door who wanted a signature for whatever it was they were delivering, and within moments she looked like she was about to come back up the stairs. He could see her admiring a bunch of flowers, so he sneaked into another bedroom. It was smaller than Sally's and very untidy, with clothes and cassettes strewn everywhere. The walls were adorned with posters of pop stars, and in one corner stood a unit of shelves which was home to at least a hundred teddy bears of all shapes and sizes. Frank sat on Penny's bed, until he finally heard Sally return to her room, then he silently sneaked back downstairs and left via the same way he had arrived.

At last the traffic began to move, bringing Frank back from his recollections of earlier that day. He finally got clear of the road works that were causing the delay, and putting his foot down hard on the accelerator, he felt an exhilarating surge of power as the large Mercedes Benz effortlessly overtook another car from the inside lane. The other driver sounded his horn angrily as Frank dangerously cut in front of him, in order to turn right at the next roundabout.

Both cars then had to fall in behind yet another line of slow-moving traffic, and the driver of the other car took the opportunity to swing into the inside lane, so that he could pull up alongside Frank. The man stared at him from an open window before directing a stream of obscenities at the driver of the Mercedes.

Frank removed his sunglasses with an air of silent menace, and wound down the passenger side electric window. He then slowly glanced sideways until he was looking directly into the face of the other driver.

The man felt uncomfortable under Frank's cold, intimidating gaze. Sensing danger, he averted his eyes, and looked about him to see if he could manoeuvre his vehicle out of what looked like an ugly situation. There was a small gap in another lane, and as the man slipped the gear stick into first, a large globule of saliva came hurtling through his window, and struck the steering wheel, before splattering over the dashboard, like a heavy deposit of bird droppings. He then heard the sound of an irate car horn, as he himself cut in front of another car, only to feel his heart sink, as the big Mercedes suddenly appeared directly behind him in his rear view mirror. Those same crazy eyes were now boring into the back of his head as the man prayed for the traffic to move. It seemed to take forever, as they drove the few yards bumper to bumper, until thankfully, the Mercedes veered off and turned into another street.

Frank eased into his designated space in the car park at the rear of the offices belonging to The Gant Carriage Company. As usual he entered through the back door, thus having to pass through the driver's waiting room to get to his office. It amused him when the chatter always came to an abrupt halt as soon as he made an appearance. On some occasions he would catch snippets of conversation, usually derogatory, either about him, or his company, and Frank would then be on hand to set matters right. Sometimes, Frank would speak if he felt like it, but this was usually in the form of a grunt, just to acknowledge someone. To be addressed on first name terms by Frank was a great honour indeed, and this would often result in the driver responding by offering to make Frank some tea, or by running an errand for him. But to achieve this status, one would have to be with the company for at least two months, but in truth, few were.

"Good afternoon gentlemen, I trust we're all raking the money in, on such a fine and pleasant day?" Called out Frank, in an unusually friendly manner as he headed to his office.

"I've been here since seven this morning, and I've made twelve pounds. I don't call that raking in the money, Frank."

Frank stopped and hesitated for a moment, before turning around to see who had just addressed him. Some of the other drivers buried their heads in newspapers, and two actually left the waiting room.

"What's your name?" Asked Frank, as he stepped towards the balding, middle-aged man.

"Tony!" Came back the deadpan reply.

"So, what is it you're saying to me, Tony - you're not making any money?" Demanded Frank, looking the man up and down with a critical eye.

"Yes, that's what I'm saying Frank. None of us here today have made any real money. We don't get enough jobs."

"Well, let me tell you something, Tony. If I was a fare-paying passenger, and you came to collect me - I would tell you to fuck off! Do you know what I'm saying?"

"Look Frank, it's a genuine grievance. You don't have to take that line." Replied the driver, taking a step back.

"It's quite obvious to me why you're not making any money, Tony. Just look at the state of you. To me, you look like a dosser. We all wear jackets and ties here, a suit if you own one. It's what makes us stand out from the crowd, and makes us the top cab company in West London."

All the men nodded in agreement, and looked down at their clothes. Tony, however still wasn't convinced.

"That's nothing to do with it, I'm just a cab driver, not a dinner companion."

"Don't try and be funny with me - it could be a big mistake." Snarled Frank, walking over to inspect what the rest of the men were wearing. "I built this fucking company up from nothing. There's no secret to what I did. I just dressed smart, and was civil to the punters. Then, as they paid their fare, I asked them to use me again. I even gave them a business card. That's all you have to do, it's not difficult."

Tony shook his head and began to walk away, but not before Frank had bundled him up against the wall.

"The next time I see you, pal - you'll be wearing a collar and tie. Do you understand, you loser?"

The man nodded and Frank let him go, before turning back to the others.

"That goes for all of you, if you want to work for the best, you've got to be the best. Now, where's Mark? I want him in my office immediately."

Mark had been with Frank since the early days, and was one of the first drivers to join the business. He was thirty eight, and was now Frank's right-hand man, ruling with an iron fist in the owner's absence. At six feet two, he was as tall as Frank, and just as imposing, with his stocky build and short-trimmed black hair and beard.

Frank reclined in his swivel chair, lit a cigar and took a healthy swig from a vodka and tonic.

"Come in Mark, here pour yourself a drink." Said Frank amiably, "There's a little job I want you to do for me."

Mark opened a fridge next to the cocktail cabinet and took out a can of cold lager, before seating himself opposite Frank.

"Is it Tony - do you want him taken care of?"

Frank laughed, he was usually very well spoken, but when talking to Mark, or any of the drivers, he tended to adopt a more localised accent.

"No, forget Tony. He's just a wanker. I don't think he'll be coming back. Just make sure he doesn't owe me any money."

"Take it as done. What else did you want me to do?" Replied Mark, downing his lager in one.

"I want you to visit an estate agent's office in Twickenham, and speak to a young chap called Stewart. Tell him I sent you, and just say I don't want anyone looking at the house I went to see recently in Oxford Park. He'll know which one." Frank then took two hundred pounds from his wallet and threw it on the desk. "Give him that, and say Frank will be in touch."

"So you are going to buy it then?" Asked Mark, scooping up the cash.

"Maybe, as an investment. House prices will rocket soon. But the club is draining me of every available penny. There's always work to be done. It's a bloody new roof now. I think it would have closed down if Claire hadn't lost it to me in that poker game."

"Can't you sell it Frank, and get out while the going's good?"

"Maybe I will, once the roof's done. Listen Mark, take on another twenty drivers, and make sure they use company cars."

"I'll get right onto it boss." Mark got up to leave, but Frank called him back.

"How's Pauline?" He asked in a direct manner, staring straight into the other man's eyes.

"What do you mean, Frank?" Replied Mark, warily.

"Exactly what I said. How's my wife? After all, you chauffeur her around most of the time, don't you?"

"She's fine Frank. But I still don't know what you're getting at?"

"What I'm getting at is this, if she told you something, something about me, you would tell me wouldn't you?" Frank took a long pull on his cigar, before adding; "I mean you wouldn't keep secrets from me would you?"

"No, of course not, Frank. She never talks about you." Replied Mark, feeling distinctly uncomfortable with the questions.

After dismissing him, Frank leafed through a motorcycle magazine. It was his son, Jamie's eleventh birthday soon, and he was planning a big surprise for him. Nothing too big and powerful, just something that Jamie could churn up the mud with. He saw one that fitted the bill perfectly, and phoned through his order. With a bit of work here and there, he thought Sally's back garden would make an ideal circuit for Jamie to practice his riding skills.

Frank had been pleased with the day's events, now there just remained a couple more things on the agenda. He had seen Sally's home, and like her body and mind, he wanted to possess it. It hadn't been difficult to track her down, after seeing the television programme on Scarlet's boutique. Now the audacity of what he was planning looked like it could bear fruit. Not only could he have Sally, and the house, but also the business, Laura, and possibly, even Penny too. He licked his lips at the endless possibilities, money, property, women, and of course, hours of fun in the secret office.

It intrigued him to think that both, his daughter Tina, and Laura were student nurses together in London. In fact, ever since William's untimely death, Frank had known not only Sally's whereabouts, but also the movements of her whole family. Now the moment was right. She'd had time to mourn, and his re-appearance at this stage wouldn't be viewed as suspicious, just a coincidence that's all.

Frank however, did have to raise money. He needed a lump sum. The mini cab business was thriving, but much of the proceeds were being ploughed into endless repair work on the club, and most of his other cash was tied up in fancy cars, contracts and investments. He thought about trying to raise the cash himself, but it would take too long, and besides, he wanted it now. He decided that someone else would put up the cash for him, or at least part of it.

As with Sally, Frank knew the complete whereabouts of Albert Chater. He knew exactly what time the old man took his meals, and what time he went to bed. But more importantly, Frank knew where he kept his cheque book. Frank had visited Albert before on several occasions, and why not, he was after all family now.

Unlike Pauline's parents, who lived a somewhat Spartan existence, her grandfather was rather well off. Like many who had spent their lives in honest toil and had learnt from the harsh realities of two world wars, Albert knew the importance of thrift. He had stayed loyal to the banking industry for all his working life, and never boasted of his wealth. Starting out as a messenger for the Bank of England, the young Albert soon showed promise and rose through the ranks to eventually become manager of one of the high street banks in his local town. Retiring due to ill health, Albert hoped he had enough years left to enjoy some of the things that he and his wife, Lillian had deprived themselves of for so many years. But, despite Albert's good intentions, his thriftiness remained as strong as ever, and his most ambitious act of self-indulgence was to take his partner for a two-week break to the Isle of Skye. Then, just a year ago, his beloved Lillian passed away. It was to surprise him, as much as it would grieve him, since Albert had always expected to be the one who went first.

Lillian's death affected Albert in the most uncharacteristic manner. He began to give his money away, albeit, this was in relatively small amounts compared to what Frank wanted now, and of course it was only given away to his immediate family. Albert had decided he was far too old and ill to spend it, and why should the likes of, Pauline, Tina and Jamie have to wait until he was dead to enjoy the benefit of the money. After all, he had proved the doctors wrong, and could perhaps, live for another ten or so years.

That had been like music to Frank's ears. Immediately he set about parting Albert from his money as quickly as possible.

Frank poured himself another drink and decided to pay a personal visit to

Pauline's grandfather. He couldn't see the problem, this was no different from before, it just involved a lot more money that's all.

His mind darted back to Sally. He stood up, went across to the mirror, practised his smile, before stubbing out a cigar and finishing his drink. If he had read the signs correctly, and Sally had been out with him before, there was no reason why she wouldn't be adverse to re-kindling their little fling from two decades earlier.

Sally sauntered in to the front room, she felt good about herself and couldn't resist doing a little twirl. She had decided not to wear the slightly revealing dress that Lizzie had recommended. The slinky, black velvet number was certainly something she would have worn a few years ago, but now it just filled a space in her wardrobe. A part of her simply wouldn't allow the dress to be thrown out, it was a reminder of what used to be, and discarding it would be like severing a part of her life that she wasn't quite ready to relinquish.

Instead, Sally chose a somewhat conservative, silk three-quarter length dress in navy blue. It had tiny white polka dots, and was something that not only flattered her figure, but was comfortable and cool to wear.

"Well, what do you think?" She asked, tossing her head back in glamour-model fashion.

"You look great Mum!" Exclaimed Penny, amazed to actually see her mother out of jeans for a change.

Turning to Jonathan, Sally went over and peeped around the Socialist Worker he was reading.

"What about you Jonathan? After having me eat practically all those chocolates, do you think your mother can still look the part?"

Jonathan laughed, he was confused about the chocolates, but was clearly taken aback by his mother's transformation.

"Penny's right, Mum - you look absolutely stunning. Why not forget this Frank bloke, and let me take you out instead?"

"Don't push your luck, Jonathan Peddlescoombe!" Joked Sally. "You're not quite off the hook just yet, I can't be bribed that easily!"

"Come on Mum, I've seen the light, you'll see a new, caring, responsible side to my character. With determination, I too shall become a respected pillar of the community."

"Shut up, Jonathan - you talk such a load of old crap at times!" Shouted Penny at her big brother.

"Penny, who on earth teaches you to speak like that? It's not very becoming for a girl of your age." Remarked Sally, as she checked her lipstick in the mirror above the fireplace.

"It's nearly eight, and Mum's getting edgy!" Replied Penny, cheekily.

"Don't be silly, of course I'm not getting edgy." Said Sally, before asking Jonathan what time it was for the fourth time.

"Mum! There's a huge car pulling up outside!" Squealed Penny, peering out of the window. "It must be him! Isn't it romantic?"

"Quick, Jonathan - go and let him in!" Flapped Sally, not knowing which way to turn. "Penny, do you think my lipstick is the right colour?"

Jonathan heard the crunch of gravel beneath expensive shoes, as Frank got out of the car, and walked towards the front door.

"Hello, you must be Frank?" He asked, putting out his hand.

"You must be Jonathan?" Laughed Frank, taking the younger man's hand in a vice-like grip, and automatically stepping into the house. "Here, perhaps you could give these to your mother?" With that he thrust a bouquet of red roses into Jonathan's arms.

Penny couldn't resist coming out into the hallway to get a glimpse of her mother's date.

"Mum won't be long, she's just gone upstairs to change her dress!"

18. THE DOUBLE DATE

The journey seemed to take ages. First there was the long wait for the train. It always meant bad news when the train indicator simply read 'District and Circle Lines' rather than giving the time of arrival in minutes. Then, after they had boarded, there was an unexplained stoppage between South Kensington and Gloucester Road. Tina got very anxious during this time, she hated being stuck in confined spaces, and the carriage being full to bursting point certainly didn't help matters.

"Do you know anything about these so-called dates, or where they're planning to take us?" Asked Laura, trying to take her companion's mind off the journey.

"No, I'm sorry. I didn't think to ask. He just said to meet at the Devonshire Arms, opposite the hospital." Replied, Tina, her face somewhat pale, and voice nervous.

"Well, this truly is a blind date then?" Added Laura, with a hint of reservation.

"I haven't had much experience with boys, Laura. Perhaps, I should have found out a bit more. But you said yourself how nice he was?"

As the train pulled into High Street Kensington tube station, Laura was beginning to have pangs of regret about getting involved in the first place. She decided to telephone Jonathan at the first opportunity, and see if she could be rescued sooner rather than later.

Tina was probably the first person off the train, and she immediately looked and sounded much better as soon as she was safely on the platform.

"Come on, Laura - we're only ten minutes late, that's not bad considering the time it took you to get ready."

Laura was a bit irritated with Tina's remark, but decided to let it go.

"You've just learnt the first rule of dating, Tina. It's always the woman's prerogative to be late. Now slow down!"

It quite surprised Laura that someone had actually rang Tina on the ward, and asked her out. It wasn't that she was unattractive or anything like that. In fact, Tina was very pretty in her own elf-like sort of way. Even though she looked under weight, it seemed to suit her. She had a pointed, almost child-like face, framed by jet black, shoulder-length hair, which she normally wore in a pony tail. Tonight, however, she had decided to have it loose around her shoulders, which matched her black camisole top, blue jeans and leg-warmers.

Laura felt ashamed of herself for thinking such a thought, and began to feel a little protective over Tina. But something didn't seem to add up, and Laura was having misgivings of what might lay ahead of them.

As they neared the rendezvous point, Laura, realised that she might just be jealous of Tina. Yes, that had to be the reason, she surmised. Just because Tina was so unassuming and seemed to take a back seat in life, didn't mean that men wouldn't find her attractive.

"Tina, I'm sorry if I don't sound too enthusiastic about all of this."

"No, Laura - please don't apologise. I didn't think anything of the sort. In fact, it's me who's got the problem about tonight." Replied Tina, the worried look reappearing on her face.

Laura stopped and turning to her colleague, decided to try a more open approach with her new friend.

"Look, I know you didn't appreciate it too much before, when I tried to help you. It was rather thoughtless of me to think you would just confide in a stranger. Anyway, the offer is still there, if you want to talk. You know about my father being killed in a car accident, so you see, Tina - I too know something about pain."

"Thank-you, I'll remember that. I was sorry to hear about your father. Sometimes it's not to easy to talk. Talking can bring back far too many memories, ones that are best left well alone." Replied Tina, with a hint of emotion in her voice. "Now, it's my turn to apologise. You see, I feel like I've bamboozled you into coming with me tonight. But I am grateful, Laura. I couldn't have come on my own."

"I think we're both a bit fragile, Tina. Come on, let's see if we can make the best of it."

It was a Friday night, and the Devonshire Arms was busy, judging by the noise coming from inside. It was a popular pub, situated along Marloes Road, which connected the Cromwell Road to High Street Kensington, and was conveniently sited directly opposite St. Mary Abbot's where both Laura and Tina were currently deployed. Outside was a pleasant, well-maintained beer garden, complete with cascading hanging baskets, and tables bearing brightly-coloured sun-shades. As the two women passed by, Laura immediately recognised a few familiar faces from the hospital, and hoped she wouldn't be recognised out of uniform.

"Listen Tina, you can wait here if you don't want to come inside? I'll go in and see if I can see them."

"No, it'll be okay, Laura. Just give me a few seconds. I wonder where the toilets are?"

Laura poked her head in through the open doors and saw a sign pointing to upstairs.

"They're up there, Tina. You go up, and I'll get us some drinks, and meet you back out in the garden, alright?"

Tina nodded and scurried like a frightened rabbit through the thong of customers, and disappeared up the staircase. 'Do You Really Want To Hurt Me' by Culture Club was playing on the jukebox as Laura squeezed through to the bar. It was smoky inside, and she couldn't help feeling slightly nervous herself, as she hummed along to the song while waiting to be served.

"Have your shoes dried out yet?" Inquired the friendly male voice behind her.

Turning around, Laura found herself staring straight into the brown eyes of the young porter who had spilt the porridge over her.

"Oh those? No, I threw them out in the end." She replied, noticing how different he looked out of his blue porter's outfit.

"Really? That's terrible. Look, it was my fault - you must let me replace them."

"Don't worry, they were old, and besides, I had another accident with a bedpan later that morning, so I had to buy a new pair anyway." Said Laura, realising what a pathetic conversation they were having.

"Well, at least let me buy you a drink then." Smiled the young man, captivated by the blonde's sparkling blue eyes. "Are you here for this double date thing?"

"Blind date, you mean!" Replied Laura, returning his smile.

"Yes, that's more like it. So is Tina with you?"

"She's just using the washroom."

He allowed his eyes to roam up and down Laura's body, and liked what he saw. Like Tina, Laura was wearing tight jeans, and an equally tight blue Gingham check shirt.

"So does your friend realise what she's letting herself in for with Roberto?"

"Roberto!" Remarked Laura, surprised. "Are you saying that Tina is here to meet, who I think you mean?"

"Yes, that's right," replied the porter. "I'm a little surprised myself. But Roberto is very excited about it. Look, he's over there. Shall I call him?"

Laura couldn't quite believe her eyes as she looked to the far end of the bar, and saw Roberto. He was dressed in a light brown, cowboy-style buckskin jacket, with fringes and a leather Stetson to match. Beneath the jacket, he sported a black lace shirt, unbuttoned to the navel, his customary leather trousers, and the usual array of necklaces and medallions.

Roberto was totally immersed in a game of spoof for drinks, with some very unsavoury-looking characters. The game involves each player having three coins in their hand, then presenting a closed fist. Inside the fist would be either none, one, two or three of the coins. Taking turns, each player then has to guess the total number of coins held in all of the participates fists to win the game. Roberto, or Colombian Bob, as he was affectionately known was very adept at this and had in the past, won lots of money, and got extremely drunk as a result of his finely honed skills.

Fortunately for Laura, he was far too pre-occupied to notice her, and his colleague's attempts to gain his attention.

"Wait!" Called out Laura, reaching up to stop him waving. "There's obviously been some sort of mistake. Tina thinks she's here to see you, whatever your name is?"

"Oh, I'm sorry, my name's Nick." Replied the young man. "I don't understand. It was definitely Tina who Roberto spoke to on the telephone. I know because I was there when he made the call."

"Well, Tina obviously thought it was you." Exclaimed Laura, as the thought began to dawn on her, that she could end up as Colombian Bob's date herself.

"Oh shit!" Muttered Nick under his breath. "What an awful mess, and you still haven't told me your name yet?"

Laura sensed someone immediately behind her.

"Nick, this is Tina, and I'm Laura. Nice to meet you."

Frank was dressed immaculately in a dark suit, just as Sally had imagined him to be. Like a perfect gentleman, he escorted her over to the car, and opened the door for her.

"Sally, before you get in, I just have to say that you look stunning tonight."

Sally felt embarrassed and was lost for words. It had been a long time since she'd been complimented by a man.

"Thank-you, Frank, how sweet of you. You look very dashing yourself." She replied, thinking that may have been a bit too forward. Frank laughed, and made sure she was safely inside the car before closing the door.

The sounds of the outside world were barely audible as she sunk back in the sumptuous, soft, doe-skin seat and allowed herself to be chauffeured in style to an unknown destination. Frank was quiet as they drove, and Sally, believing he preferred this in order to concentrate on the road, remained silent too.

The journey only took about half an hour, before Frank pulled up in a side street in Chelsea. He turned off the engine but left the ignition on, so they could still hear the music from the car's speakers.

"Sally, you always struck me as a very cultured person, a woman who enjoys the finer things in life. Am I right?" He asked, turning to face her.

"Well, yes, I suppose you could say that. But I'm sad to say that I've become a little bit boring these past couple of years. In fact, this is the first time I've been out in recent memory."

Frank moved closer towards her to inhale her delicious fragrance.

"Nonsense. You mustn't say such things. Tonight, I want you to have the time of your life. That's why I've brought you here. You deserve it Sally, after all that you've been through. I want to make you happy."

"Thank-you, Frank. What a lovely thing to say. But where are we?"

"It's a club I'm thinking of buying. Let's go inside, I bet you've never been here before?" With that, Frank got out of the car, and went around to open Sally's door. They walked about twenty five yards, before coming to a grand-looking building, manned by a doorman with a top hat.

"What is this place?" Asked Sally, like an excited schoolgirl, as Frank led her up the steps, past two stone pillars, and into a plush, marble-floored lobby.

"This is Swann's. I'm sure you'll like it," he replied, grinning proudly.

The doorman welcomed the couple, and took Sally's coat, before leading them through into the main area of the club.

Swann's was one of the most exclusive clubs in London, and according to Frank's information, was just about to come onto the market. It was a gold mine, and the prestige of owning such an establishment made Frank drool with pleasure. He would need to come up with at least a million deposit to be taken seriously. That's where Sally might come in handy, if Frank wormed his way back into her life, he could delay buying her home, and wait for another buyer. If that went to plan he would begin to manipulate Scarlet's boutique, selling his own home, the mini-cab business, and Lake's in the process. Bringing Sally here was the first stage. He knew she would be impressed, and tempting her to get involved with it would be that much easier.

Sally felt quite overawed by the luxurious surroundings. Magnificent, huge chandeliers hung from the high ceilings, and situated around the perimeter of the spacious, main hall were tall arches that led into cosy, candle-lit alcoves, each with its own elaborate winding staircase. Everywhere the eye could see were hand-sculptured statues and busts intermingling and complimenting intricate balustrades.

It certainly must have been very exclusive, as Sally had never heard of Swann's before, nor had she ever heard Lizzie mention it. Perhaps the two of them were just out of touch, she thought, feeling old.

In the centre of the main hall were about twenty tables arranged around a dance floor and a stage area. Over to one side was a long bar and service area, where several scantily-clad waitresses stood, eagerly waiting to avail themselves.

The Head Waiter, who seemed familiar with Frank was immediately on hand and led them over to their table, where he lit the candelabra and clicked his fingers towards one of the waitresses.

Sally was more than pleased that she'd taken Lizzie's advice in the end, and had opted to wear the more elegant, black velvet number, even if it was more daring. A white-jacketed jazz quartet was playing on stage, and although Sally preferred classical music, she felt it blended in superbly with the plush surroundings.

Frank summoned over the waiter by his first name and whispered something Sally, couldn't quite make out. Pierre then went off, only to return five minutes later with a trolley upon which stood an ice bucket containing a bottle of the very best champagne.

"Sir, may I present, Monique." Said Pierre, turning to a pretty, young waitress standing behind him. She will be here to cater for all of your requirements." With that, Pierre opened the bottle with a flourish and proceeded to fill their glasses.

"Thank-you, Pierre," purred Frank, lighting a cigar, and passing a keen eye over Monique, as she smilingly handed each of them a menu.

"So Frank, you must tell me more about yourself, and why you want to buy not only my house, but this place?" Asked Sally, still very much overawed by the surroundings.

Frank laughed and took a healthy sip of his champagne. He then sat back deep in thought, as if searching for the right words.

"I had nothing, Sally when I came out of prison." He said in a husky whisper. "I literally had to start from scratch. In a short space of time, and by sheer hard work and determination I built up one of London's biggest mini-cab companies. Nobody helped me, I did it on my own. That's why I appreciate what you and Lizzie have done with Scarlet's."

"What you did was amazing, Frank. But I can't see how that compares with what Lizzie and I did. We had support, it was easier."

"It's refreshing to hear your modesty, Sally, but Scarlet's is becoming a word-wide brand now, and still growing."

"Like I said, Frank, I haven't had a lot to do with the business since William died. Poor Lizzie has been managing it in my absence."

"Sally, you inspire me so much, I can imagine you rising up like the proverbial phoenix out of the flames and onwards to glory. A woman like you thrives on the cut and thrust, and the excitement of the business world."

"Are you talking about the right person?" She laughed. "I've got as much cut and thrust as a damp squib. You haven't told me about your club, Frank?" She quickly added, trying to get the conversation away from herself.

Again Frank laughed, and Sally guiltily found herself enjoying his company.

"I acquired Lake's way back in the sixties. At the time I had no experience of running a club, but as with the cab business, I made it my priority to learn. I found I loved it, Sally. I love the glamour, the glitz, the personalities, the prestige. I could never imagine myself not running a club. But it wasn't the goldmine I hoped it would be."

Sally saw a hint of sadness in his pale blue eyes.

"But it's in Mayfair isn't it. I couldn't think of a better place for a club?" She remarked.

"Yes, that's true, but there's lots of clubs in the area, bigger and better than mine, but the main problem was the building. The repairs are on-going, you see the building is listed and that causes more problems. It still needs so much doing to it. I want to sell both the club, and the cab business, and buy Swann's." As Frank said the last sentence, Sally saw the excitement in his eyes, like a small boy wanting his first bike or his first air rifle.

"I'm sure you could do it, Frank. You certainly seem to have a knack when it comes to business."

"Yes, I'm sure I could, but I don't want to do it alone. I need someone to help me, someone who I can trust, someone who has the balls to get involved, someone with grit and determination. Someone like you, Sally."

Sally couldn't help coughing on her champagne. She wasn't sure if he was serious or just joking.

"Frank I'm flattered, but I have no experience with nightclubs. I think you've overestimated me?"

"Sally, look at the bigger picture, have a look around you. Look at what the waitresses and the other staff are wearing? Scarlet's could design and provide glamorous uniforms for the whole club. But more importantly look at the space in here. Just imagine a fashion show, put on by Scarlet's and attracting all the top models and fashion houses. That's what you need to be thinking."

It worked, Sally went quiet for a few moments, and was gazing about her, mulling over all the possibilities in her mind.

"I must say, you have amazing insight, Frank. Lizzie would love to meet you again." She said, coming back to reality.

"I've given you food for thought, Sally. By all means talk to Lizzie. Nothing will happen for a while anyway."

Sally studied her menu, and couldn't help noticing the incredibly high cost for each dish. She thought perhaps she should be polite and select the cheapest, which on this occasion was Dover sole. She put her menu back down and glanced at Frank. She couldn't help feeling that perhaps everyone had got him wrong, and he really was a good person.

"So did you ever marry, Frank?"

Frank didn't want these questions, but he knew they would come eventually, and he was ready for them.

"Yes, I married when I came out of prison, but I'm separated now. She was unfaithful to me."

"Oh, Frank, that's terrible. I'm so sorry, and do you have children?"

"I have a grown up daughter who's working in London, and a son who's about to turn eleven, and lives with my wife."

Sally then heard loud laughter coming from a table off to her left, and by the sound of it, one of the women in the party seemed to be rather drunk. Ignoring the frivolities, Sally turned her attention back to Frank.

"It must have been so difficult for you under the circumstances?"

"Well, we all have our crosses to bear, Sally. But life must go on. Anyway, that's enough about me. Let's talk about you, and why you're selling such a beautiful house?"

Sally spoke again about losing William, and the dreadful loss she still felt. She then told Frank how she wanted to return to Falcondale and take up her studies once more.

"So like you Frank, I need a fresh start too," she said, her voice betraying the sadness that still lurked below the surface.

Frank had felt very uneasy when Sally had mentioned the suspicious nature surrounding William's death, and how the case was still open. He took a pull on his cigar and looked down at the menu.

"Come on, let's eat. They do a an excellent Chateaubriande here!"

But Sally didn't hear him, she had been too concerned by the drunken woman who had been staring at her since they had first arrived. She didn't know the woman with the short bob, but something about her was disturbing, and it made Sally feel distinctly uncomfortable.

"Sorry, Frank. I didn't hear you, I was miles away."

A short distance across London, Tina stared up and looked into Nick's eyes. She felt herself go red with embarrassment and appeared quite lost for words. Nick, certainly didn't look too comfortable with the situation either.

"Tina, I'm very glad you could make it. I wasn't sure what you wanted to drink?" He said eventually, trying to break the ice.

"Bacardi and coke please!" Replied, Tina with a girlish giggle, as Nick attempted to attract the barman's attention.

Laura caught Tina's eye and saw the unmistakeable smile of pure happiness on her friend's face. She knew it would break the girl's heart to tell her there had been a mix up, and Nick wasn't her date tonight.

Handing Tina her drink, Nick sensed there was something amiss.

"What is it Tina, you look a bit bewildered?"

"You're not Spanish are you?" She exclaimed, taking him completely by surprise. "On the telephone you were speaking with a Spanish accent."

"Err, no, I'm not Spanish. I'm English. Anglo-Saxon to be exact." Replied Nick, looking to Laura for help.

"Nick was just telling me that he was so shy about asking you out, he had to get his friend, Roberto to do it for him!" Added Laura, trying to smooth the situation. "You see the effect you have on men, Tina!"

"Yes, that's right, Tina. I've always been a bit shy. I hope you don't mind?"

Tina giggled again and took a mouthful of her drink.

"No, of course not. I think it was a very romantic gesture. So did you bring a friend for Laura?"

Nick almost choked.

"Err, yes, I did. He's over there. I'll go and get him."

Explaining the situation to Roberto was the easy part, especially after the Colombian had got a glimpse of his new companion for the evening.

Laura squirmed as the decrepit old porter staggered towards her in his cowboy boots, and began to slobber over her hand, as he muttered sweet nothings in his native dialect. Roberto, then turned to address the three of them.

"I want the very best for my senoritas - come! We go to Conchita's!"

"What's Conchita's?" Asked Laura, looking around to Nick.

"Your guess is as good as mine!" Was the reply, as he hailed down a passing taxi.

Roberto was warmly welcomed in the small, squalid Hispanic club near Earl's Court. He generously paid the five pounds entrance fee for each of them, before proudly leading the hesitant group into the smoke-filled claustrophobic atmosphere.

After finding them a table, the animated Colombian ordered drinks all around. He seemed to know most of the other guests, and was making it blatantly obvious that Laura was with him.

Within minutes of them taking their seats, Conchita - the owner of the club appeared. She was a voluptuous, raven-haired woman of about forty, whose clothes and style adequately reflected her Romany origins. She seemed very excited to see Roberto, and made herself comfortable upon his knee. His three companions could only look on in total amazement as Conchita, with a somewhat theatrical flourish, swept the long tresses away from her face, and proceeded to writhe her body on Roberto's lap in a highly erotic manner. The old Colombian wallowed in the attention he was getting, as Conchita ran her fingers though his thick hair and kissed him passionately on both cheeks.

"Eh, Conchita, pretty little thing you are!" He called out, desperately trying to kiss her on the lips.

Mockingly, the woman replied with a stream of insults, before sliding off his lap and daring him to get up and dance.

Rising to the occasion, Roberto stood in the centre of the small dance floor. He began to gyrate his hips and tap the heels of his boots on the floor in tune to the flamenco-style music. Then, upping the tempo, he turned sideways onto Conchita, and with stomach wobbling, began to clap and stamp his feet loudly. The crowd also started to clap and cheer, but this was really for Conchita. She was a professional dancer and soon began circling Roberto, laughing and urging him forward as if she were baiting a bull.

"Why is he just standing there tapping his feet, why wont he dance?" Asked Tina naively.

"He'll fall over if he tries anything more energetic, especially after the amount he's drunk tonight." Replied Nick.

Eventually, Colombian Bob found his rhythm, and began to thrust his hips back and forth, while taking small pigeon steps towards his partner. As he got to within a few feet of her, his tongue began to flick in and out of his mouth in a highly suggestive manner.

Conchita swore again, before spinning her body around in one flowing, graceful movement so that she was now right behind him. The crowd were lapping it up and were cheering and applauding even more loudly than before.

The dance ended, and the beat of the music suddenly changed to the 'Rumba'. Roberto then turned to face her and reverted back to a more socially acceptable kind of routine, as Conchita let out a screeching whoop, and oozed closer towards him. With her slim, lithe body, and skirts flowing she teased and tantalised the Colombian, but never allowed him to touch her body on the dance floor.

Soon, the whole club was up and dancing, apart that is, from Roberto's three guests, who felt distinctly left out.

After a short while, Conchita came over to their table and beckoned the apprehensive trio to dance. Tina by this stage was really quite drunk, and she led Nick off to a separate corner of the room. Laura breathed a sigh of relief, since her supposed partner was still occupied with the effervescent Conchita, or so she thought.

Out, through a thong of dancers, emerged Roberto, sweating profusely and moving his hips like pistons. He bore down on her, wearing his all-too familiar drunken grin. Laura squirmed on her seat, looking this way and that, before resigning herself to her fate.

Unlike Nick and Tina, who appeared to be dancing in a crumpled heap, Laura soon found herself on the retreat as Roberto attempted to show off his dancing prowess. The Colombian drove his drink sodden body to new limits, writhing in front of his pretty, young partner like a man suffering the effects of chronic diarrhoea.

Holding Laura by the hips, he demonstrated in animated fashion, exactly how she should move to the rhythm. Then, as she tried to copy the steps, he moved his damp, matted head close to hers and began to nuzzle her.

On the other side of the club, Nick was becoming increasingly embarrassed by Tina's behaviour. She was bending over and charging at him mimicking a bull, shouting, Ole! Ole! at the top of her voice. Most of the other guests were far too busy enjoying themselves to be concerned with Tina's antics, but after she had staggered into several other dancers and knocked some drinks over, Nick urged her to take a breather and successfully returned Tina to her seat.

It was Conchita who finally came to Laura's rescue. However the wily old bird wasn't about to relinquish his prey that easily. Holding Laura close to him and panting breathlessly, he whispered in her ear.

"Now that I have tasted a glass of you, Laura - I want the whole bottle!"

"Is that all you think about, drink!" Replied, Laura turning her head to escape his rancid breath. She noticed he had been distracted, and a loud cheer went up as all eyes again turned to Conchita, as she slapped a pound coin down on the edge of a table.

The audience chanted Roberto's name, and it wasn't long before the bow-legged hospital porter rose to the challenge. With his eyes fixed on Conchita, he muttered obscenities as he slowly unbuckled his thick leather belt and strode confidently towards her. Conchita screamed with delight, before joining with the crowd to make a half circle around him.

They roared their approval enthusiastically as the Colombian first slid the tight leather trousers, then a pair of skimpy black briefs over his pale knees. Both garments settled on the tops of his boots, as he then backed unsteadily towards the table and began to vie for position. The music was drowned out by the cheering and clapping as Roberto made his first sortie over the corner of the table.

The noise was deafening, and both Nick and Laura had to stand on their chairs to see exactly what was going on.

"I think it may be some sort of ritual by the look of it." Exclaimed Nick, as Roberto clasped his hands behind his neck for extra balance, before proceeding to manoeuvre his small hairy buttocks directly over the coin. Then, using what can only be described as a clenching movement, he gazed up to the ceiling with a pained expression on his face, before bending and successfully snatching up the coin with the cheeks of his bare behind.

"I've seen enough," gasped Laura in shock. "I've never seen anything so disgusting in my entire life!"

The crowd were in raptures as Colombian Bob then passed his hand between his legs, relaxed his muscles and watched with pure satisfaction, as the coin dropped into the palm of his hand.

All around the club came the unmistakable sound of more coins being slapped onto tables in eager anticipation. Roberto kept every coin he managed to pick up, and insisted that the loser also buy him the drink of his choice. Roberto was to drink a lot of tequila that night.

Nick and Laura were both equally stunned by Roberto's talents and stared at each other with muted looks on their faces. Tina however, had gone very quiet, and looked a deathly shade of pale. Laura went over to sit next to her and see if she was alright, but returned to Nick after a few moments.

"She's blind drunk! Can you keep an eye on her for a minute while I call my brother to come and pick us up?"

Nick nodded and sat down next to Tina.

"Why don't I just get you a taxi. Westminster isn't too far?"

"No, I have to get back home to Twickenham. I'm going to Wales for a couple of days with my mother." Replied Laura gratefully.

Colombian Bob reached across the table to steady himself, while lifting his leg in order to get some leverage. The young couple who were sitting at the table certainly weren't impressed by the display going on before them. The woman took a mouthful of pizza, only to hold it in her mouth, fearful that she may be sick at any moment. Her companion put down his knife and fork and stared in amazement as Roberto fumbled drunkenly for the elusive coin. But it was one coin too many. The last few drinks had really hit their target, and Roberto felt the world closing in on him. He opened and closed his cheeks a couple more times in a last ditch attempt to avoid failure. His supporting hand then seemed to slip in a pool of spilt beer, and since his trousers and briefs were now firmly anchored around his ankles for better purchase, Roberto was unable to stop himself from falling.

He saw a few laughing faces flash past on his descent, and the lights temporarily dazzled his bleary eyes. A full ashtray also accompanied him, as he crashed through the adjoining table almost in slow motion. There was the inevitable sound of breaking glass, and a couple of half-hearted screams, before a short eerie silence pervaded. The guests soon went back to what they were doing as an over-turned bottle of San Miguel beer span around a few times, before coming to rest at the edge of the table, where it discharged its contents onto Roberto's up-turned, grinning face.

"No, no, leave him there!" Shouted Conchita to a small group of onlookers, who were about to go to the Colombian's aid. "I'll put a blanket over him later. It wont be the first time!"

When Laura returned from phoning Jonathan, Tina was shouting hysterically at Nick. Nobody else seemed remotely interested in the rumpus, but Laura couldn't help feeling protective towards her vulnerable friend.

"Tina! Tina! For heaven's sake stop shouting, you'll get us thrown out of here. What's the matter with you anyway?"

Tina stopped shouting, but then aimed a blow at Nick;

"He's married, the cheat is married! How could you do it, ask me out, knowing you're married?"

Laura looked to Nick for an answer.

"Is that true, have you got a wife, Nick?"

He looked into her blue eyes and nodded, and Laura felt her heart sink. She turned sullenly to her friend and tried to help her up.

"Come on Tina, my brother is on his way to collect us, we can wait in the foyer."

Nick tried to help get Tina up, but Laura pushed him away.

"She's had a lot to drink, are you sure you can manage, Laura?"

"We'll be fine thank-you, and you can thank your friend Roberto for such an entertaining evening. He sure knows how to give a girl a good time." Replied Laura coldly, as she glanced over to Roberto, who was laying unconscious in a puddle of beer and cigarette ends, his small genitalia on full display.

A few miles away, Frank clicked his fingers and Pierre came running.

"We'll both have the Chateaubriande, and make sure it's nice and rare."

"Does Sir not require a starter?" Replied Pierre, unable to resist a glimpse at Sally's cleavage as she studied her menu.

"We'll both have the crab and avocado," retorted Frank, with a hint of irritation in his voice.

"Wine Sir?"

"Vintage Bordeaux." Glared Frank, before adding; "And Pierre, make sure the cork is still in the bottle. We don't want you swapping it for supermarket plonk!"

Pierre chose to ignore Frank's last remark, and raised his eyebrows to Monique, before leaving the table with an abrupt turn.

"He'll be one of the first to go." Sneered Frank, "He's so up his own arse, it makes me sick."

Sally laughed, thinking Frank was joking.

"I couldn't imagine you being nasty to your staff, Frank?"

"No, you're perfectly right Sally. I'm very good to my staff, especially those I like!"

Sally resigned herself to the fact that the Dover sole wasn't going to happen, and not being a big meat-eater, she was going to choose the minestrone soup starter. But since Frank seemed to know exactly what he was doing, she decided just to go along with him and hope to get the opportunity to select her own dessert.

The quartet began to play *'Petite Fleur'* and Frank invited Sally up to dance. The feel of her in his arms brought memories flooding back into his mind. She still moved with a grace and elegance few women of her age could ever match. He smiled to himself as he recalled how he used to teach her to twist and jive at the Black Lion in Falcondale, all those years ago.

Sally half closed her eyes and allowed Frank to lead her as they glided effortlessly across the floor, almost as one. She was quite surprised that for such a large and powerful man, he could move so well, and she too allowed herself to be whisked back in time, to days that had long since passed.

The dancing had relaxed Sally somewhat, and for the moment she was able to put the drunken, staring woman out of her mind. The band played a few more tunes from the sixties and several more couples got up to join Sally and Frank on the dance floor.

Eventually Monique came over to tell the happy couple that their starters were being served, and Frank, now perspiring heavily took the opportunity to go and freshen up in the washrooms.

Despite the club only being about half full on that particular night, Sally began to sense her anxiety building up again, as she waited for Frank to return. She was aware that eyes were on her, and had been for much of the evening. Out of the corner of her eye she noticed the loud woman from the other table stand up and begin to walk over to her. She heard another voice calling out to the woman.

"Claire! Claire! Please come back, he's not worth the trouble." But Claire didn't want to hear.

Monique refreshed their glasses, and had just left the table when the woman struck. Sally had guessed she was extremely drunk, and now she was to be proved correct.

"So you're his new whore are you?"

At first Sally couldn't quite believe that this crazy woman was addressing her. Passing off the remark, Sally continued to stare straight ahead.

"I'm speaking to you trollop, how dare you ignore me!"

Sally felt the sickening feeling of fear well up in her stomach. For some reason it reminded her of the Pauline incident, when she attacked Frank at the Christmas Dance. She swallowed hard, and knew she had to turn and face this person with so much anger in their heart.

The woman was of equal size and proportion to Sally, but looked to be in her fifties. She looked very glamorous in in a shimmering gold dress and sun-tanned complexion. Her face, however was hard, and bore the ravages of many years of hard drinking.

"Look, I don't know who you are, or what you want, but I do feel there's been some mistake." Replied Sally, surprised by the firmness in her tone.

For a few moments their eyes met, it was Sally who averted her eyes first, and how she regretted it. For, as she turned, the woman grabbed the untouched crab and avocado cocktail and threw the contents over the front of Sally's dress.

Sally was up in an instant, she had never known anger to possess her as it did now. In a move that still surprises her to this day, she brought her right hand up and slapped her aggressor as hard as she could across the side of the face. The woman crashed to the floor screaming loudly, as her companions and staff rushed to her aid.

"Ladies! Ladies! Please, what is happening?" Shouted Pierre, his arms waving uncontrollably.

"That tart, that whore who Frank Gant brought in, just attacked me!" Yelled Claire, clutching her face.

Pierre went to Claire immediately and helped her to stand, before leading the distraught woman back to her table. He then went back to Sally, who was just standing there in her ruined dress, still in a state of shock.

"Madam, please return to your seat, I think the excitement is over now."

"But wait, that woman threw my starter over me for no apparent reason. I don't even know her. You must throw her out!" Demanded Sally, now close to tears.

"Madam, you are talking about Claire Lake, one of our most valued guests. The matter must end here."

"I'm not staying here another second. You're a disgrace!" She said angrily to Pierre, before storming out to the lobby." Tell Mr. Gant, I'll be waiting outside!"

Retrieving her coat, Sally fled out into the night. Unable to control her tears, she hurried past a group of giggling girls, until she finally arrived back to where Frank's car was parked. She could hear some sort of commotion going on behind her, and wondered if it was Frank's voice she could hear shouting in the distance.

"I'm so sorry, I think I've ruined your evening. Some crazy woman attacked me and I just had to get out of there." She said as Frank appeared.

"Don't worry," replied Frank putting a protective arm around her. "We can go somewhere else. Besides I like women with a bit of spirit in them!"

"Frank, I feel so awful about tonight. I shouldn't have over-reacted like that."

Frank reached down and took Sally's hand.

"Listen, I was only upset about not getting my steak. Shall we go to this little Chinese place I know?"

"That's very nice of you to offer, but no thanks. I've somehow lost my appetite. Besides, look at the state of my dress, it's ruined."

Frank smiled and opened the door for her, taking the opportunity to glance sidelong at her full bosom. He could remember every detail of her naked body, from the time he came to see her house, and had hidden in the walk-in wardrobe.

"Don't worry about the dress. I'll take you shopping and we'll buy you a new one."

"Thank-you Frank, but there's no need for you to do that. Would you mind taking me home please." Replied Sally, still a little jumpy from the incident.

Frank had seen the commotion when he was coming out of the restrooms, and when he saw Claire, he thought it best not to get involved, especially in front of Sally. He realised Claire was drunk and wasn't sure what she would say. He didn't want all the hard work he'd put in with Sally going to pot, and certainly didn't want Sally knowing he was married to Pauline, and that she'd had a lesbian affair with Claire. It also intrigued Frank why Claire was there in the first place and he wondered if she too was planning to put in a bid for Swann's.

"I'll take you home on one condition Sally - you invite me in for a coffee?"

"I'm sure I can agree to that Frank. But there's one question I have." She asked, turning to face him. "Who on earth was that woman back at the club, and did you know her?"

There was a long pause as Frank searched for a plausible answer.

"She was just someone from the past with a grudge, that's all. Unfortunately it happens in my line of business."

There was something in the tone of his voice that told her not ask any more questions, and like the outward journey, a silence developed between them. Sally just assumed he was brooding about what had happened back at Swann's. Frank however was more concerned about his loss of control. He had probably broken Pierre's nose after hitting the waiter while leaving the club. The last thing Frank wanted at the moment was the police calling around to see him again, so soon after their unexpected visit a few days ago, regarding his suspected sexual abuse of his daughter, Tina.

Only the porch and landing lights were on when they arrived back, and Sally assumed that Jonathan and Penny were already in bed. Frank, as before insisted on opening the car door for Sally, and as she stepped out, she heard herself ask him in for his cup of coffee.

19. TINA

It had taken Jonathan the best part of an hour to finally reach Conchita's. By then, Nick had already left. His presence only seemed to aggravate Tina, who still felt totally humiliated by the situation. She just couldn't bear to think that it had been Roberto who had asked her out, and not Nick, as she had originally thought, and to rub salt into the wound, Roberto had sounded really nice on the telephone.

"Well you're a welcome sight, what kept you?" Called out Laura as her brother walked into the club's foyer.

"Come on, it's not like Earl's Court is just up the road - the traffic was horrendous. Why couldn't you just get a taxi back home?"

"Stop your moaning Jonathan, you know the pittance I earn. In fact, I don't even think I could afford the bus fare back home!" Replied Laura, sounding a little fed up. "You can give me a hand with Tina, she's had a bit too much to drink!"

"What again?" Asked Jonathan surprised. "Your friend certainly knows how to enjoy herself."

Together, they woke Tina and bundled her into the back of Sally's Volvo estate. Laura, however was very concerned about the girl's safety, and decided to take Tina back to Twickenham with them.

"We can't just dump her back in the nurses' home Jonathan, it's dangerous if someone is drifting in and out of consciousness. Do you think Mum would mind if we let Tina sleep in the spare room?"

Jonathan shook his head, "No, mum's very liberal about things like that. Anyway, she might not be back from her date with this Frank bloke yet?"

"I know you're still not very happy about Mum seeing other men, but please don't make it so obvious in front of her." Said Laura as they sped westward along the Cromwell Road.

"I just can't help it. I don't want to see her hurt, that's all." Replied Jonathan, turning down the radio.

"So, what's this Frank like?" Inquired Laura.

"Very big, and quite scary looking. Not what I would really call Mum's type. I didn't take to him, but then, no-one listens to me anyway. Apparently he and Mum went to university together years ago."

"Really? That's interesting. That's where she met Dad."

"So how did your date go?" Asked Jonathan, changing the subject. "Love at first sight was it?"

"If I told you what my date was like, Jonathan - you wouldn't believe it, not in a million years!"

While Tina seemed quite content to remain asleep in the back, Laura between giggles, proceeded to tell her brother about the strange evening she'd had in the company of a certain character of Colombian extraction.

"Sounds nice, this Colombian Bob!" Joked Jonathan, pulling into the drive. "So, has he got a sister for me!"

Laura laughed, but as she wound up her window, she noticed a huge, white limousine parked directly in front of them, and where Sally would normally park her car. Jonathan squeezed in beside it and glanced around to Laura.

"As you can see, he's a bit on the flash side!"

Tina appeared sufficiently sober enough to bear some of her own weight, and being supported either side by Jonathan and Laura, was led around the back of the house and in through the kitchen. After pouring a cup of black coffee into the inebriated girl, they managed to get her up to the spare room with the minimum of fuss, and without waking Penny. With her brother's help, Laura removed Tina's coat and together they lifted her onto the bed.

"Jonathan, I'm starving. Why don't you go down and make us some toast, while I try and get Tina undressed?"

He nodded, and left the room diplomatically as Laura began to pull Tina's pixie boots off. However, on the way to the kitchen, Jonathan couldn't resist having a listen outside the lounge door, where inside, his mother was entertaining Frank. He smirked as he tried to make out what the hushed voices were saying, above the laughing and the Diana Ross album playing in the background.

As the four slices of hot toast popped up, Jonathan decided to scoff a couple of them there and then. He spread the butter thickly, and searched in the larder for a suitable topping. At first he reached straight for the cinnamon, but then realised he was at home now, and didn't have to resort to such poverty-stricken measures like at university.

The toasted cheese tasted good, and the aroma soon woke Pepys, bringing the little dog trotting into the kitchen, in the hope of a morsel.

No sooner had Jonathan taken a bite out of the second slice, when he was shocked out of his senses by a loud, ear-piercing scream. Thinking it was his mother in some kind of trouble, he rushed out of the kitchen and headed straight for the lounge. However, on hearing the scream again, he soon realised it was coming from upstairs.

"What on earth is happening?" Called out Sally, as she sped out of the lounge with Frank right behind her.

"I think it might be Laura's friend, Tina - she's drunk." Shouted back Jonathan as he took the stairs two-at-a-time, with Sally right on his heels.

Frank stayed discreetly downstairs upon hearing Tina's name being mentioned. Sally had spoke earlier about her daughter going out on a double date with a friend, but he was sure Sally said they would be staying back at the nurses' home in London. He recognised his own daughter's screams and wondered what she might have said. Frank was now certain it had been Tina who had gone to the police about him sexually abusing her. Pauline wouldn't be stupid or brave enough to do anything like that, unless of course Tina had put her up to it. He dismissed any thought of betrayal by his wife, and had questioned Mark earlier, but discounted him almost immediately. As the commotion was still continuing upstairs, Frank crept back into the lounge to collect his jacket.

Jonathan and Sally burst into the spare room, to find a distraught Laura trying unsuccessfully to calm Tina down.

"What is it, what's wrong with her?" Called out Sally, going to her daughter's aid.

"I don't know, I was taking some of Tina's clothes off, to put her to bed, when she just started screaming. It was awful, like she thought I was trying to hurt her."

Sally, Laura and Jonathan all stared helplessly, as Tina, clad only in her underwear writhed to the top of the bed in a disturbing state of torment. She curled herself into a ball, fearful in case they move any closer. There were countless lines of scar tissue on Tina's body. They were from several years of self-harming, and were far too abundant for the girl to hide. It was a painful sight, and Laura, her face a mask of shock, gradually inched closer, calling Tina's name, desperately trying to bring her new friend safely back from whatever hell she was trapped in.

"Jonathan, you try!" Said Laura in desperation, after failing to get any response. "Tina seemed to like you."

Jonathan sat next to his sister on the edge of the bed, and at first, just softly called Tina's name.

"It's Jonathan. Please come back to us, Tina. No-one is going to hurt you, I promise."

After a few moments had lapsed, Tina's hysteria seemed to abate, and Jonathan was able to reach out and touch her hand.

"It's like she's in some sort of trance," he whispered. "Like she's re-living something terrible that had happened to her."

"Keep talking to her, Jonathan," said Sally. "I'll go and fetch some cold water and a flannel, the poor girl looks very hot."

The water treatment seemed to work wonders, and they managed to get Tina to lay down, before covering her modesty with a light blanket. Not wanting her to feel embarrassed by his presence, Jonathan urged Laura to take over, and he quietly left the room. He noticed Penny was awake and waiting out in the hallway, curious to see what had been going on.

Recognising Laura's voice, Tina dared open her eyes. She was still trembling and looked about her, like a frightened deer.

"Laura, please don't let him hurt me again. Don't let him do those things to me. Please promise me." Gasped Tina, struggling to catch her breath.

"You're safe here, Tina. You're at my home in Twickenham. Jonathan and I brought you back, remember?" Replied Laura in a re-assuring manner, mopping Tina's face with the cold flannel.

Sally looked anxiously across at her daughter.

"Are you sure, it's only drink she's had. She's not on any medication is she?"

"Yes, I'm sure it was just the drink. I was there with her." Said Laura with a puzzled expression.

"Well, if that's the case, I think your friend needs urgent help." Remarked Sally, solemnly.

Tina sat bolt upright and looked first to Sally, then back to Laura, before glancing hesitantly around the room.

"I have some tablets, they're in my bag," said Tina nervously. "It's here, isn't it, my bag, or have I lost it?"

"Don't worry Tina, your bag is here. I really don't think you should be taking tablets though, not after having drank so much." Replied Laura, motioning her to lay back down.

Slowly, Tina began to get her breath back and pulled the blanket up around herself. She then apologised to both Sally and Laura for causing such a scene, and told the women she would now be okay.

Sally wasn't convinced however, and remembered she'd left Frank waiting downstairs.

"It's alright, Penny, you can go back to bed now. The excitement seems to be over for one night!" She said to her youngest daughter, who was hovering outside. "Heaven knows what Frank will make of all this. What with the incident earlier, I doubt if he'll want to see me again, or even buy the house for that matter."

When they were alone, Laura began to hang up Tina's clothes. She then went over to the dressing table and produced a plain, cotton nightdress from one the drawers.

"I think my mother was right, Tina. You really do need proper help." She said, passing the garment.

For a few moments, Tina just stared at the nightdress, aware that some sort of explanation was expected.

"Laura, do you recall what you said earlier in the evening about wanting to help me?"

Laura nodded, and went back to sit on the edge of the bed.

"If you want me to help you Tina, you must tell me what happened to you."

"I can't Laura. It's too awful. I just know that he's going to kill me for going to the police. But I didn't tell them everything, only what he did to me, and the beatings he gave to my mother. I didn't tell them about the old Jewish man." Sobbed Tina, starting to tremble once more. "Maybe I should have told them, but I didn't want him to think it was my mother. Now he might take it out on her, because of what I've done."

"What are you talking about Tina, you're not making any sense. Who is going to kill you?"

Tina began shaking violently, and drew in a deep breath, as she tried to stop her voice from faltering. She then turned and looked up at Laura.

"My father wants to kill me."

Painstakingly, Tina told of some of the horrific crimes Frank had committed against her. What Laura heard in those few minutes was to remain with her for the rest of her life. The disclosures sickened her down to the depths of her very soul, and try as she might, her mind just refused to comprehend that a person could act in such a way towards another human being, let alone their own flesh and blood. Laura felt ashamed of herself. Not because she was guilty of anything, but because she could do nothing to help, she could do nothing to ease Tina's pain, all she could do was listen.

"What about all those scars on your body, did he do that?"

"No, he didn't, well not directly anyway. It's hard to explain." Replied Tina, closing her eyes in anguish.

"Please try to tell me, Tina. I do want to help." Said Laura, wiping a tear from her eye.

Tina took a drink from the glass of water on the bedside table, and held Laura's hand.

"You see, sometimes I become dissociated, it's like someone else has taken over my mind and is thinking evil thoughts. I feel evil inside, my blood isn't clean, it's contaminated, and I have to get it out of my body. So by cutting myself, I can ease some of the tension. I find it easier to deal with physical, rather than emotional pain, and to me, cutting serves as a useful avoidance tactic. Can you understand that, Laura? I did tell you it was hard to explain."

"I'm trying to understand, Tina." Laura moved closer, and reached out to put her arms tightly around her friend. "You don't have to say anymore, not now, not tonight."

"I can't keep it in any more, the pain is too much to bear. I had to tell someone, Laura. I don't know how much longer I can go on living like this." Cried out Tina, her face drained of colour.

"But if you're already on medication, you must have spoken to someone about it?" Added Laura.

Tina paused for a few moments before answering.

"They're just tablets for depression, that's all. I could never tell anyone what my father did to me. I've spent nearly two years in and out of psychiatric hospitals, but I've never been held against my will, its always been a voluntary thing. I'm not mad you know."

"No, Tina, I know you're not mad." Laura then stood up and paused for a few seconds. "When I was taking your clothes off earlier, did you think I was your father, come to do horrible things to you?"

Tina was unable to answer, and turned her head away in shame. A steady trickle of tears ran down her face and onto the nightdress she was still clutching.

"I think I'm going to be sick."

Laura hoisted Tina up, and practically frog-marched her out into the hallway, and along towards the toilet. As they passed the landing and reached the bathroom door, Tina suddenly stopped and froze in terror. She had heard her father's voice coming from downstairs. It was unmistakeable, Frank's voice had its own distinctive, eloquent tone, always confident, always rising above other voices, each syllable always perfectly executed. Like a scythe, her father's voice cut through Tina, and chilled her to the bone. She panicked, and with surprising strength, broke free from Laura's grip, and fled back towards the spare room. Leaping onto the bed, Tina wrenched back the curtains and began to open the window, aware that Laura would be right behind her.

"Tina, what are you doing? You'll fall!" Screamed Laura as the petrified girl lent dangerously out on the ledge.

"It was all a trap wasn't it? You're with him, I should have known. That's why you brought me back here, isn't it?" Yelled Tina, her face contorted with fear and rage.

"Please, Tina, I don't know what you mean. This is crazy." With that, Laura shouted desperately for her mother to come and help her.

By now, Tina had got her top half completely out of the window, and was preparing to jump, when she saw her father's gleaming white Mercedes parked directly below. Pulling herself back inside, she glared intently at Laura.

"Please don't let him kill me!"

Tina then charged forward, knocking Laura to one side, in her desperation to get out of the room. She ran back out onto the landing, and into the bathroom, before slamming the door shut, and locking herself inside.

"Laura, this girl has gone totally mad. I'm going to call the police!" Gasped Sally. "I'm sorry, but it's the only way. What is she doing now?"

"I really don't know." Replied Laura, visibly shaken. "She's convinced that Frank is her father and he's going to kill her, and we're all part of it. She's so paranoid, she just flipped when she heard his voice."

"That's absurd. Frank's a lovely man, and besides, she doesn't even know him. Anyway, he's gone now. Whatever next!" Sighed Sally, wearily as she began to hammer on the bathroom door, calling out Tina's name.

The only noise Sally and Laura could hear however, was the rumble of water running. They both shouted frantically, but there was still no answer.

"Mum, she was going to jump out of the spare room window. She might try the same in here?"

"No, it's not big enough to get out of," replied Sally. "I think we'll have to force the door open. Where's Jonathan?"

Jonathan barged the door several times without success, and even with the combined pressure of the three of them pushing, the door still wouldn't give. Eventually, Jonathan had to get a crowbar from the shed, and using this, attempted to wrench open the solid pine door. Penny had now joined her mother and sister, and together the three women waited patiently for Jonathan to gain access.

"It's coming, just one more shove and we'll be in!" He called out, as the heavy metal bar gouged out large splinters of wood from the door frame. Then, as he drew back to apply his weight for the last time, part of the lock fell away, and the door just seemed to swing open by itself.

"Penny, you stay out here." Ordered Sally as she hesitantly followed Jonathan and Laura into the deathly-quiet bathroom.

Although Laura had eighteen months nursing experience under her belt, nothing could have prepared her for what she was about to witness.

Tina was sitting motionless in the empty bath. In a hideous sort of way, she even looked quite relaxed and serene, with her head resting nonchalantly over to one side. Both her elbows were casually resting on the edge of the bath, her slashed wrists oozing their crimson discharge down onto the sparkling, white enamel. The flow passed down, along her legs, to briefly merge with the running water, before being sucked into a spiralling void.

For what seemed like an eternity, Sally, Jonathan and Laura could only just stare in a state of shocked disbelief. It was Laura who eventually showed initiative and sprang into some sort of activity. She reached down to Tina's neck and began to desperately feel for her carotid pulse. Jonathan and Sally seemed to be panicking, and making it that much harder for Laura to detect any sign of life. She found she couldn't think straight, it was the early hours of the morning, she was tired and by her own admission, had consumed quite a few drinks herself during the course of the evening.

"Penny, quick! Run down and phone for an ambulance - hurry!" Shouted Laura in despair, before telling Jonathan to find something to act as a tourniquet on

Tina's arms.

Closing her eyes, Laura willed herself to concentrate. For a moment, she thought she could feel a distant and very feeble beat, but then it was gone, she had lost it.

"Mum, can you see if she's breathing. I can't seem to get a pulse."

Sally reached down and placed a hand over Tina's chest, but there was nothing. She then tried listening around Tina's nose and mouth, but it seemed to all be in vain.

"I can't tell if she's breathing or not!" Screamed Sally, her panic still very much in evidence.

Although Tina hadn't been alone in the bathroom any longer than ten minutes, it would have been impossible to estimate accurately how much blood she could have lost. The injuries to her wrists were life-threatening, especially her left arm, where the wound was gaping. Tina's life appeared to be ebbing away from her at an alarming rate.

"Jonathan, what are you doing, hurry up!" Yelled Laura, as her brother wasted valuable time foraging in a cupboard, searching for bandages. "She could already be dead. Mum, quick hold up her left arm, and press a towel onto the wound."

Sally took the initiative and began applying pressure to Tina's other arm, while Laura now started to think seriously about giving artificial respiration. Penny then bounded into the bathroom as Laura was trying one last time to detect Tina's elusive pulse.

"It's coming, I got through to the ambulance, and look, I've found some bandages!"

"Well done, Penny. Can you put them tightly on Tina's wrists. Mum and Jonathan will hold them up for you."

It was while the others were doing this, that Laura sensed the tiny, feeble beat once again. She felt it once more, equally just as weak. She waited for a third one - it was feint, but definitely a pulse.

"She's alive!" Exclaimed Laura, greatly relieved. "Come on, let's get her out of here."

The four of them now attempted to lift Tina out of the bath. She was still breathing, albeit very shallow, but they didn't know how long she could hold on for. They managed to sit her on a chair, and Laura tried to clean her up the best she could.

"Penny, go and get Tina's clothes and hand-bag, before the ambulance gets here."

Cleaning blood from someone is not easy, and it was Jonathan, who suggested that he and Sally hold Tina up in the shower so Laura could wash her down properly.

Tina let out a pained groan as they pulled her to her feet, and sat her on the edge of the bath, before swinging her legs in and standing her up. However, despite the tight bandaging, the blood still kept appearing.

"Can anyone see any more cuts. She's still bleeding heavily from somewhere?" Said Laura desperately.

Before Sally had a chance to have a good look around, Laura discovered to her horror that the blood was coming from between Tina's legs. She glanced down at the floor and noticed there were two empty razor blade wrappers, but only one discarded blade.

"What is it, Laura?" Asked Sally, aware that Laura had noticed something very disturbing.

"Oh my god, she's got the other razor blade inside her, it must have cut her to ribbons when we moved her. For god's sake keep her very still." Yelled Laura, putting her hands up to her face in despair.

"Can't we pull it out with tweezers or a pair of pliers?" Asked Jonathan, anxiously.

"No, we could do even more damage." Replied Laura, reaching for another towel.

As much as Laura soaked up the blood, more kept coming. Penny ran to the airing cupboard and brought back a fresh supply of towels for her sister to use. Tina had suffered severe internal damage, and her life was now hanging in the balance.

There weren't many dishes and cups to clear, and once he got going, it wouldn't take long. It was a wonderful spring morning, and with the back door open, David Peddlescoombe could gaze out over the orchards adjoining his home.

He put the kettle on for another cup of coffee, before starting to dry up the last few remaining items of crockery left over from the day before. David was fiercely independent and didn't want his visitor to think that he needed the slightest bit of looking after.

He had enjoyed a marvellous meal on the Thursday evening, after arriving back at Falcondale. It was a huge plate of home-made pasta over at Pedro's. It was good to see the old Catalonian again after so long, although these days Pedro tended to spend more time drinking wine and chatting to his customers than he did in the kitchen, preferring now to leave that part of the business to his daughter and son-in-law. Then, last night, David couldn't resist bringing home a delicious fish supper, which he enjoyed with a hunk of bread and butter and a few cold bottles of beer.

Sipping his coffee, David stepped out and breathed in the fresh, morning air. Being back at Falcondale brought warmth to his heart, and he began to wonder why he had not come back sooner. He didn't really have any plans for the rest of the day, and was content to just have a drive around to get the feel of the place again. He could then finally accept that he was at last, back at his spiritual and true home.

The house hadn't changed much at all in the years he'd been away. It had been rented out to students and sometimes to holiday makers, but for the most part it had remained unoccupied. There had of course been the yearly visits by David's elderly parents, which had lasted up until about five years ago. Plus, when William's children had been young, he and Sally would bring them for a sentimental holiday back to his family's old home. But that had all been some time ago. Since then, a local woman had been coming in, just to do some light housework and to keep an eye on the place. Now, the woman had agreed to come in three times a week, and more if necessary to make sure David was well looked after. His mother, Joan, had originally wanted someone to be with her son on a daily basis, but eventually after David's insistence, they had come to a compromise.

Perhaps, losing his leg during the war in Vietnam was the best thing that happened to him. For up until then, David had been on a one-man self-destruct mission. He had never got over the death, many years ago of his young school friend in the tragic ice fishing accident, and felt responsible for the boy's death. Then, there was the disturbing incident involving Frank Gant trying to break into the house just before Christmas, back in 1962. Things then seemed to be on an even keel, until he found himself falling in love with William's girlfriend, Sally. Then he was caught by his brother kissing her under the tree in the garden. This, and the trauma of attending Frank's court case eventually caused the break up of William's relationship with Sally. Although, they did subsequently get back together again, it did raise a question mark, and David found himself taking the blame for this also.

David had been glad to be accepted into the US Army, even though he was a Canadian, and turned out to be one of the bravest soldiers his commanding officer had ever come across. However, this didn't hide the fact that he was reckless with his life, and as a Lieutenant, very few of his men were willing to go on missions with him, fearing his do-or-die attitude would end in misery.

The unfortunate meeting with the land mine had effectively put David out of the war. It had come at a time, when the possibility of him dying from a bullet fired by one of his own side was becoming an increasing possibility.

Although there were protests about the war in Vietnam, many servicemen did return to a hero's welcome back in their own communities in the states. But this wasn't the case in Canada. Many returning Canadian soldiers who had fought for the US, came home to be largely ignored in their country, and for David, this was no different.

Returning to live temporarily with his parents back in Niagara-on-the-Lake, David was then about to be embroiled in another war, the war against himself. At the time, David felt he had been cheated out of a hero's death. He should have been killed, but instead, it was a job only half done. It was after he had been fitted with an artificial leg, and was learning how to walk again, when further damage was inflicted. David received a copy of a letter of complaint sent to the US Army, from the parents of a soldier who had fallen while serving in David's platoon. In the letter, they mentioned that they were aware of David's reputation as a hothead, and felt he should never have been allowed to lead men into battle. Nothing more was done or said about the matter, but another seed of doubt had now been planted into an already, fragile state of mind.

David, then returned to the US during the seventies, wandering state-to-state, doing any low-paid, menial jobs offered him. He soon turned to drink and drugs to ease the torment he was going through. It was only after he was found almost frozen to death in an alleyway, that he finally got the treatment he needed and deserved to help him overcome the demons that ravaged his mind. Although, he probably didn't know it at the time, due to his alcohol and drug problem, David was suffering from the acute effects of what is now known as Post Traumatic Stress Disorder, which was increasingly becoming recognised at the time.

David was one of the lucky ones to be selected to join an exclusive programme of rehabilitation. It certainly wasn't easy, and at one point, he actually dropped out, only to end up back on the streets again. However, before he degenerated too far, David realised that the programme represented his only chance, and with determination, was able to walk back through the doors of the clinic and resume.

"I'm not saying we can cure you," said Doctor Werner, upon David's return. "This is something you'll have to live with, but we can teach you how to cope with it."

After completing the programme, David felt more alive and focussed than he had for years. He began to accept that the boy's death, and that of the soldier were from no fault of his own. By losing a leg, David had paid a high enough price, and now it was time to think about himself and his future, instead of dwelling on events from the past that he was powerless to change.

Developing a passion for History and in particular, warfare and its causes, David was to return to full-time study. In 1980 he was finally granted his doctorate, but then took a sabbatical, and soon found himself falling into bad habits once again.

David stepped into the kitchen and washed up his coffee cup, before putting it back into one of the cupboards. He then went over to sit at the large oak table in the living room, and let his mind wander. He heard the laughter once more, he could clearly remember it as if it were yesterday. In his mind's eye, he visualised William, Sally and himself all sitting around the very same table. He remembered the countless bottles of wine, the records, playing charades, and Sally, it always came back to Sally. He couldn't stop thinking about her, and recalled how jealous he felt after he learnt she was pregnant with her first child, Jonathan.

Still with Sally in his thoughts, he turned to gaze at a framed picture of her, which adorned one of the walls. William had painted it on a hot day, back in the summer of 1963. Sally, not wanting to miss a moment of the brilliant sunshine had decided to change into her bikini and sunbathe out in the garden. She looked more stunning than ever during those early days of pregnancy, it was as if she had a sort of radiance about her. William could only stare in admiration at the woman who would soon become his wife and bear his children, as she laid back, soaking up the sun, her glorious, blonde tresses hanging loosely around her shoulders. He just had to capture her and that special moment on canvas, and it took him the best part of the week to perfect it. William had liked it so much, he insisted it be framed and hung on the wall for all to see and admire.

David was so taken aback by the painting, that he had to go over and take a closer look at it. He was amazed how William had added so much detail. It was exactly how she used to look. He looked at her face, her eyes, her lips, her curves, and couldn't help running his fingers gently over the painting's fine lines. He began to utter her name, wanting her, needing her there with him, but alas, he was rudely jolted out of his reflective mood by a loud knocking at the door.

"I'm coming, I'm coming, hold your horses!" He called out, as the visitor knocked again.

Although he would always have a very pronounced limp, David could over short distances walk just as fast as anyone else, and this was one of those occasions when he did just that, as the confounded knocking continued.

"Hello, you must be Mr. Peddlescoombe?" Asked the breathless woman, standing in the porch. "Sorry, I'm so late, but I had to stop off at the shops to get a few bits and pieces for you."

"You must be Mrs. Owen?" Asked David in return, as the woman walked straight past him and into the house.

"Yes, that's right, I thought I'd better knock rather than use the key?"

"No, that's fine, Mrs. Owen, please use the key in future, I really don't mind." He followed the woman into the kitchen and watched as she took off her coat and began to unpack the shopping.

"I've got some lunch for you, Mr. Peddlescoombe. I'll see to that first. You do like home cooking don't you?"

"Yes, yes, I do, but Mrs. Owen, I wanted to talk to you first, please sit down for a moment."

The woman looked concerned.

"The devil makes work for idle hands, Mr. Peddlescoombe. There's nothing wrong is there?"

"No, of course not. I'm sorry, I didn't want to alarm you." David looked at her for a few moments, with a puzzled expression on his face. "Do I know you from somewhere. You seem very familiar?"

She smiled and got back up to continue her duties.

"I'm probably familiar, because I've lived in Falcondale all of my life, and I expect you've seen me around? My grandmother, Nancy, god rest her soul used to clean this house for more years than I can remember. In fact, you're quite familiar too, Mr. Peddlescoombe, I can recall you as a cocky young student some twenty years or so ago."

"Really? That's wonderful!" Laughed David. "I want to know all the news about Falcondale, Mrs. Owen, everything, since I've been away."

"You don't ask for much do you?" Replied the slim, motherly-looking woman with a broad grin. "But first we can start with you calling me by my first name, which is, Carol."

"It's a deal, Carol, but only if you call me David?"

"We'll have to see about that. But I can't be standing around here yapping all day, not while I'm being paid to work." She replied, placing a covered dish in the oven.

"That was superb, absolutely delicious!" Exclaimed David, a little later and somewhat enthusiastically, having just demolished a second helping of chicken casserole. Carol enjoyed being praised for her cooking, although her own family never let a single scrap go to waste, they rarely, if ever complimented her on her culinary skills, that she'd learnt over the years.

"Is it true that you'll be taking over from old Mr. Meredith?" Asked Carol, clearing the table.

"Yes, that's right. Mr. Meredith becomes Professor Emeritus, while I take over as Dean of Students."

"So, you'll be helping the new one's to settle in then?"

"That's right, but it's only a small part of my job." Replied David, intrigued by her interest.

"In that case, you'll be seeing my lad, Gareth. He starts in the Autumn term." Said Carol, her face beaming. "We're so proud of him. We've never had anyone go to university from my family before."

"That's wonderful news, Carol, I'll certainly look out for your Gareth among the freshers."

Carol stayed an hour longer than she should have done, and was able to tell David of all the comings and goings that had occurred in the town during his absence. But she never once sat down, and just carried on with her work as she spoke. David enjoyed her pleasant, down-to-earth company and found he was uplifted by her cheerful manner and often sarcastic sense of humour.

As Carol put on her coat to leave, she turned to David, as if she had forgotten something.

"Didn't you say earlier, you wanted to talk to me?"

Carol was right, he had wanted to talk to her earlier. He was going to tell her he didn't need anyone fussing around him, cooking meals and cleaning up. He was, after all, by his own admission, entirely self-sufficient.

He thought back to that delicious lunch Carol had brought him. He thought about the warm tales she had told him, tales that reflected a local person's perspective on the town and the college community.

"It was nothing, Carol, nothing of any importance." Replied David in a re-assuring tone. "Can you drop by again tomorrow?"

Jonathan could hear the noise, the loud banging, the clattering, but for a few moments his mind just couldn't work out exactly where he was. He tried to will his eyes open, but they adamantly refused his feeble demands, and remained firmly shut. Although it was lunchtime, Jonathan didn't feel at all hungry. This was probably quite a good thing, since he seemed to have enough trouble just trying to deal with his overwhelming tiredness. The porters removed the remaining metal food trolleys from the lift and loaded them onto a trailer attached to an electric tug. As the odd-looking vehicle moved further away into the distance, there remained only the more familiar hospital sounds to disrupt his desperate attempts to sleep. For most of the morning, the corridor had been a hive of activity, and before the weariness had eventually overtaken him, Jonathan had seen the early-morning cleaners arrive, who seemed to chat incessantly as they went about mopping the floor and polishing it to an impressive sheen with an electric buffing machine. A little later he had seen the nurses on the early shift arriving in their dark-coloured capes, and some wearing different uniforms to reflect their status in the nursing hierarchy. As the morning grew older, so the corridor became busier, white-coated doctors, physiotherapists, and radiographers pushing cumbersome X-ray machines all appeared going about their various duties in a calm, professional manner. He heard the confident, assured voices and the click of expensive shoes as the consultants began their rounds, with clusters of youthful insubordinates following anxiously in their wake. Everyone seemed to be carrying a bleeper, some of which appeared only to evoke minor irritation, while others screeched and wailed demanding immediate attention.

Sometime after nine, there was a constant stream of patients being taken to and from the suites of operating theatres situated further along the corridor. The patients came and went in varying modes of transportation, from wheelchairs, stretcher-trolleys, to whole beds, complete with drip-stands, monitors and oxygen cylinders.

Every half-hour or so, Jonathan would wander into the Intensive Care Unit to ask if there was any further news of Tina's condition. Getting little information he would amble back out and return to the torn and battered bench seat in the corridor. It must have been around ten thirty when he finally succumbed, and drifted off into a much-needed sleep. He could vaguely remember asking the woman pushing the WRVS trolley what time it was, after he had brought a couple of cans of coke, but everything else seemed quite hazy after that.

"Mr. Peddlescoombe, can you hear me?" Called out the chirpy female voice. Getting no response, the staff nurse tapped Jonathan lightly on the shoulder.

With a concerted effort, he forced his eyes open a few centimetres and noticed the woman who had been a little off hand with him earlier.

"Yes, yes, I'm awake. Is Tina alright?"

"It's far too early to say just yet." Replied the staff nurse, in a direct manner. "I'm going to the theatre now to collect the young lady. You may as well go home, you wont be able to see her."

"Thank-you, but I'd rather wait." Came Jonathan's reply.

Waiting was exactly what Jonathan had been doing since the ambulance had brought Tina into the Accident and Emergency Unit at West Middlesex Hospital. It was around four in the morning when Tina had arrived, and following a blood transfusion and major surgery, her life still remained very much at risk.

According to Jonathan's calculations, Tina had been on the operating table for at least six hours. What he didn't know was that two separate surgical procedures had taken place at the same time. One team had been working to save Tina's left hand. Apart from arterial and nerve damage, the tendon was found to have been completely severed. Another, gynaecological team were desperately trying to halt the unrelenting haemorrhage caused by the razor blade that Tina had inserted into her vagina. To accomplish this, the surgeons had to make a further abdominal incision in order to gain access to the damaged areas. In all, Tina had required thirteen units of blood, taken from the hospital's limited reserves. This situation, certainly didn't go down well with those who would have preferred to keep the blood for a more just and deserving cause.

The disturbing reality of the situation was brought into sharp perspective as Jonathan watched Tina being brought back to intensive care from the operating theatre. She was laying unconscious on a bed, with a respirator carrying out her breathing for her. In the background were the unmistakeable blips from a heart monitor. Swinging precariously above her head was a unit of blood. It was raised high, to allow the dark-red fluid to run down along a transparent tube, and return life to Tina, a life that she had earlier tried so hard to extinguish. As the nurse, anaesthetist and porter rushed past him with their assorted paraphernalia, Jonathan got a glimpse of the side of Tina's face. He didn't recognise her at all, it could have been anyone.

After opening his remaining can of coke, Jonathan lit a cigarette. There were numerous 'No Smoking' signs displayed on the walls, and normally he would have obeyed these, but now Jonathan was far too tired to care. He then checked his pockets for change, before trudging along to the line of payphones at the far end of the corridor.

"Jonathan, thank god it's you! We were so worried. Are you still at the hospital?" Asked Sally, concerned.

"Yes, but I'm coming back soon. Tina has only just come back from surgery."

"Is she going to be alright, Jonathan?"

"They wont tell me, Mum. It's because I'm not a relative, and couldn't give them any information about her."

"Please come back, Jonathan. You've done all you can."

"Is Laura and Penny, ok?"

"Penny has gone riding, but Laura was quite shaken up when you left. She's sleeping now. Listen, Jonathan, we've decided to set off for Wales on Monday instead - in view of all that's happened."

Jonathan returned to the bench and took up his vigil once more. He must have got his second wind now, for he didn't feel nearly so tired as he had earlier. The activity inside the intensive care unit had lessened somewhat, and the theatre team had since left. Jonathan was pensive, he was in two minds about going in again. He was genuinely concerned for Tina's welfare, but at the same time, he didn't want to interrupt the nurses when they might be busy. He was also very much aware of the suspicion he would be arousing in view of Tina's appalling injuries. Perhaps, they thought he had something to do with it? That would explain why they seemed so distant towards him. Jonathan cringed at the thought, and realised his tiredness may be affecting the clarity of his thinking. After another cigarette, he decided just to bide his time, and wait for another half-hour.

Flicking through an old copy of Reader's Digest, he became aware of someone coming out of the unit. It was the same nurse that had collected Tina from the theatre.

"Mr. Peddlescoombe, I thought you would have gone home by now. There's really no change."

"What do you mean, no change? Please stop all this pretence and tell me the truth."

The nurse saw the desperation in the young man's eyes, and sat down next to him.

"I think she'll pull through, given time, but only if she wants to. We're not sure about Tina's hand. There was a great deal of nerve damage, and she may need more specialist surgery." The nurse was about to say more, but paused.

"What? What is it? Please tell me." Pleaded Jonathan.

The nurse waited until a group of visitors had passed by, before turning back to him.

"The surgeon who operated on Tina said she will never be able to bear children. I'm sorry Mr. Peddlescoombe, she means something to you, doesn't she?"

Jonathan swallowed hard and felt his eyes begin to moisten. "Yes, I do believe she does."

20. THE BLACK LION

The incident during the early hours of Saturday morning hadn't affected Penny in any way, and if it did, she certainly wasn't showing it. Perhaps, it was because she was too young, and blissfully unaware of the circumstances that could cause a young woman to take such drastic action.

During the first part of the journey to Wales, along the busy M4 motorway, Penny had been the only one inclined to try and make conversation, but had to concede defeat after getting little response from either Sally or Laura. Both Penny's mother and older sister had been left completely numbed by the experience with Tina, and had only made the trip after being assured by Jonathan that she would pull through. They had talked over the matter a dozen times amongst themselves, anxious to know if their actions at the time had been right. Now they were both quiet and alone in their thoughts, trying to make sense of the insensible, searching for a suitable recess deep in their psyche where they could file the memory of such a traumatic event.

It had been Laura who finally broke the ice, when they pulled over at a service station to get some coffee and stretch their legs.

"So how have you left things with this Frank chap, Mum, are you going to see him again?"

"Yes, I think I might." Replied Sally trying to sound enthusiastic. "In fact, I've invited him over for dinner at the weekend - well, it's the least I could do under the circumstances."

"I'm sure he'll love your cooking, and you wont have to worry about me being in the way, I'll be back on duty then." Added Laura, surprised her mother was still prepared to see Frank.

They finished their coffee and returned to the car feeling refreshed and in far better humour, having at least uttered a few words to each other. It was a grey, murky day that threatened heavy rain. This had yet to materialise, but the dark, depressing conditions did add time to their journey. The conversation again petered out, and died a natural death, so Sally switched on the car's stereo and listened to Radio Two, while Laura and Penny seemed content to doze.

It was four in the afternoon when they finally reached Falcondale. Almost out of instinct, the two girls woke, and like their mother, took in the environs of the town with a quiet interest. The High Street looked practically empty, apart from a couple of vans making deliveries, as Sally turned into the car park and drove to the rear of the Black Lion Public House.

"So what's the plan, Mum?" Called out Penny in elated mood, as she reached into the back of the car for her overnight bag.

Sally exhaled deeply and switched off the engine.

"Well, poppet, I think we'll have a cup of tea, a short nap, followed by a shower, then, if we have time, we can have a quick look around town, and finally dinner. How about that?"

"Sounds good to me." Said Laura, stifling a yawn.

After checking in, the three women went upstairs to inspect their rooms. Sally had decided on a single room, while Laura and Penny seemed happy to share.

Both rooms overlooked Falcondale High Street, and before doing anything else, Sally couldn't resist abandoning her case in the middle of the floor to pull back the lace curtains and gaze reflectively out of the window.

It had been many years since she had last been back to Falcondale, and she wasn't quite sure how it would all affect her, being there at the place where she had first met William, and so soon after his death. The melancholic mood was still very much with Sally, and now William was at the forefront of her thoughts. She sensed he was very near, she felt the warm glow of his love, and knew that somewhere he was watching over her and the children, keeping them all safe.

The fatigue from the journey just seemed to wear off by itself, and after tea, Sally took the opportunity to get showered before hanging up her things, and deciding what to wear for dinner. In the next room she could hear Laura and Penny arguing about which bed they were going to sleep in. Smiling to herself, she felt grateful to be blessed with such a loving and supportive family.

The heavy rain that had been imminent finally kept its promise and roared down in sheets. The three of them would now have to be content with an early dinner and a cosy evening spent within the confines of the Black Lion.

To Sally's delight, the hotel looked pretty much the same as it had during her student days. Of the other rooms available, only two were actually occupied. Both, it would seem by older applicants, like Sally who had arrived to be interviewed the following day. One of the other students, a woman of similar age to Sally told her that Mr. Meredith was about to retire as the Dean, and a new, younger man was about to take his place. It had been Mr. Meredith who had originally sent out Sally's interview letter a few weeks ago, and she had immediately remembered him on seeing his familiar name at the foot of the page.

Laura was pleased to see her mother chatting away happily to the woman in the guest lounge. Hopefully it meant she had put the Tina episode behind her for the time being. There was a lull in the rain, so Laura and Penny decided to go out for a walk along the High Street. Penny was now beginning to wish that she had stayed at Lizzie's after all. First of all it was her mother who was down in the dumps for most of the journey. Now it was Laura's turn to become sullen, she had clammed up on her for no apparent reason whatsoever. Penny let her sister wallow in silence as she glanced in at some of the shop windows they passed. A couple of local boys appeared next to them and one made comments and smiled at Penny. She was flattered and smiled back, but she couldn't quite understand the lad's broad Welsh accent.

"He said he wants you to meet him tonight at the war memorial, you stupid girl!" Sneered Laura.

"Really, is that what he said?" Asked Penny excitedly. "I thought you were away with the fairies?"

"Actually, I was thinking about something," replied Laura testily. "Don't you go getting any funny ideas, Penny. We're having dinner with Mum later, just the three of us."

"Laura, you can be such a spoilsport at times. You must have been young once!" Giggled Penny.

Laura glared at her sister, but refused to let the remark antagonise her.

"Come on let's get back. I think it's starting to rain again."

Penny, however didn't move and glanced back at her sister, with a defiant expression on her face.

"What on earth is the matter with you, Laura, is it the time of the month?"

Laura had to laugh at Penny's dry sense of humour, and after pausing for a few moments, decided to confide in her about the problem that was causing her so much concern.

As they reached the doors of the Black Lion, the heavens opened once more, and the two girls quickly stepped inside. They looked through into the lounge and saw their mother was still engrossed in conversation with her fellow mature student.

"Don't say anything, Penny, will you? Demanded Laura. "I'll tell Mum myself tonight, after dinner."

Sally had just finished her lemon sorbet when the bombshell hit her. In one way she should have been grateful, since Laura at least had the courtesy to wait until her mother had finished her main course before blurting out her revelation.

Laura's disclosure had chilled Sally to the bone. But somewhere amid all the madness that had recently occurred there appeared something that did answer one, if not all of her questions. Sally put her wine glass down on the table gently, as she couldn't quite trust her hands to hold it any longer. In the recent past, she had become rather an expert at hiding her true emotions, now this was one of those moments when she needed to put her skills into practice. Flicking up her clear blue eyes, she gazed at Laura intently.

"You mean, you're telling me that Tina is the daughter of Pauline from university, all those years ago?"

Laura nodded.

"Mother, you look like you've just seen a ghost!"

For a while, Sally seemed unable to speak, it was as if her voice had become paralysed by fear. Her mind went racing back to December, 1962, and the events that led up to the expulsions of both Pauline and Frank from university. She could recall with frightening clarity the moment Pauline caused such a terrifying scene at the Christmas Dance when she attacked Frank, cutting him with a broken glass after accusing him of raping her on Sally's birthday. She also recalled how the crazed Pauline had turned on her, with those freaky, staring eyes, and uttering vile threats. If it had not been for William allowing Sally to stay with him, she would probably have packed up her things, and fled back home for good.

Focussing her attention back to Laura, Sally reached across and took hold of her daughter's arm. Finding her voice, she spoke with an air of urgency.

"You should have told me this before, Laura. This poor girl has a psychopath for a mother. It's no wonder she has problems."

"It sounds like she has a psychopath for a father too. I'm sorry, Mum, I was just trying to protect you from the past. Tina told me her dad had done terrible things to her, and wanted to kill her."

"Laura, listen carefully, this is important." Whispered Sally, glancing around to see if anyone was within earshot. "That night when Tina tried to kill herself, she said something about Frank being her father?"

"Yes, that's right, but I don't think she was thinking straight."

Sally gulped at her wine and sat back in her seat, deep in thought.

"Something very disturbing has come to mind, Laura, and I can't bear to even think that it could be true." She then told Laura about the alleged rape of Pauline, by Frank.

"Oh my god, so you think Frank could be Tina's father, and she was telling the truth?"

"I don't know what to think, Laura. It's just too awful to comprehend. Frank seemed such a nice chap, when I went out with him. I know he had his bad points, but surely he could never sexually assault his own daughter?"

"What are you going to do, Mum - it all seems too much of a coincidence?"

"I think I want out of it, Laura. I don't need all of this in my life right now."

"But what about Tina? We can't just abandon her?" Replied, Laura, concerned.

Sally went quiet again, thinking about what she should do.

"I'll give him the benefit of the doubt. Frank did say he was separated from his wife, as she had been unfaithful to him, and he mentioned a grown-up daughter working in London. But it all seems very odd now. Perhaps I should just stick to the business in hand, which is the sale of the house."

Laura didn't want to hear anything about selling the house, and brought the subject back to Friday.

"I feel so sorry for Tina, she's been to hell and back. She told me the most awful things, that's really why I've been so quiet during the trip."

"Laura, you tried to be her friend, which I don't think for one moment was easy. You did far more than most people would have done. Tina, as a result of what's happened to her, is a very damaged person. Let's just hope that her drastic actions have drawn attention to that, and she's able to get the professional help she so desperately needs." Sally gave her daughter a re-assuring smile, before calling over the waiter. "Can we have some coffee please."

Penny, who had pretended not to be listening, suddenly interrupted.

"Not for me, please Mum, can I go out for a walk in the town?"

"Yes, of course you can, darling," replied Sally somewhat mystified, as Penny left the table.

Laura waited until her sister had gone, before turning hesitantly back to her mother.

"Mum, there's something else I need to tell you."

"Go on," said Sally, bracing herself for more shocks.

"Since Tina discovered that you knew her mother at university, this Pauline has been anxious to get in contact with you, and knows where we live. I wish I hadn't said anything now."

"I see," replied Sally, appearing distressed.

"Apparently this Pauline wants to apologise."

Sally then told her daughter how she had first met Frank during her initial week at Falcondale, and how the situation with Pauline descended into such a hideous spectacle. She then spoke of William, and how he came into her life all those years ago. Over an hour and two more coffee's passed, before Sally realised that Penny had been away for some time.

"Don't worry about her, Mum. I know exactly where she is," said Laura, glancing out of the window towards the wooden bench seat at the war memorial.

"So both Frank and Pauline blamed you for getting them kicked out of university?"

"Yes, I suppose they did. Frank, because I didn't give him an alibi, and Pauline, because of jealousy. I was just glad I was never to bump into them again. Now, I've been out on a date with Frank, met his deeply disturbed daughter, and now his wife wants to meet me!"

"It's weird about Pauline. There was a mix up over the double dates last Friday and Tina caused quite a stir, in fact it was very embarrassing."

"Well, if she takes after Frank and Pauline, that's hardly surprising," added Sally, coldly.

"I take it then, you don't want to speak to Pauline?"

"I don't think so, Laura. There's nothing that Pauline and I need to discuss."

The sky had cleared sufficiently for Sally to risk going out to get some fresh air. She wanted to be alone for a while, just to gather her thoughts, and try to focus her mind on the interview the following day. Although what Laura had told her at the dinner table was upsetting, Sally was determined not to let it affect her. It was still fairly early in the evening, and she headed off in the general direction of the university. It wouldn't be dark for an another hour or so, and Sally felt compelled to wander around the grounds. As she reached the war memorial, she noticed Penny sitting with a young man. She knew immediately by her youngest daughter's suspicious actions that she had been smoking, but decided not to say anything on this occasion to show her up. It was Penny, who spoke first, probably thinking her mother was there to tell her to come back to the hotel.

"Mum, this is Peter, I said it would be okay if I went for a coffee with him, just to that cafe up the road, you know, Pedro's?"

"Yes, I suppose so, Penny," replied Sally, giving the lad the once-over. "Just call in and tell Laura where you're going."

As Sally neared the main gates of the campus, she thought she could detect the unmistakable smell of curry coming from somewhere. Glancing across the road, she was amazed to see that the quaint little tea shop, where Lizzie had discovered that Pamela was her real mother, had now turned into an Indian restaurant. It was a good thing Jonathan wasn't with them, otherwise he would have been straining at the leash to devour a red-hot curry.

She looked in at the gate house, but didn't recognise the middle-aged man, who was too engrossed watching a portable television to notice her. Then, turning left, she followed the perimeter road in the direction of the halls of residence. Feeling her heart begin to beat a little faster, and her mouth start to get dry, Sally quickened her pace a little in anticipation of what, she didn't know. She passed a small group of female students and noticed a couple of them were wearing the distinctive black and gold scarves, just like Sally used to wear herself. She made up her mind to go up into the attic when she got back home and dig out her own college scarf, ready to wear proudly, come early October.

Walking another twenty yards or so, she caught sight of the grand arch that stood at the entrance of Lloyd-Evans Hall. Sally slowed her pace so that she could take it all in, and wondered if the building was still the same as when she had lived there. It certainly looked no different, and for a few brief moments she was transported back to a time over twenty years earlier. Gazing up at the rows of windows, she counted along from the end, until her eyes settled on one in particular - it was her old room. The light was switched on, and she noticed that someone had at last got rid of those awful, tacky curtains, and had now replaced them with something a little more acceptable. Looking along to the next window, she smiled, knowing she was looking up at what was Lizzie's room. Sally recalled the first time she ever set eyes on her best friend, and now wished she had taken a picture of her standing there in the doorway, with her magnificent beehive hairdo, that practically touched the ceiling. Straining her eyes a little, Sally thought she could make out a milk carton, and what looked like, several cans of beer sitting precariously on the ledge. In fact, as she looked around at the other rooms, she saw that most of the students appeared to be using the outer window ledges as makeshift fridges. This certainly wasn't allowed in Sally's time, and they even employed someone during those days, whose specific job was to walk around the campus and report back to the Dean anyone placing food or drink outside their windows.

Sally turned and continued her journey, veering off from the perimeter road, before crossing the little bridge that spanned the river Teifi, which ran a course directly through the campus. She heard the familiar sounds of merriment emanating from the social club, however, the old Nissan hut that served as the main social centre for the whole of the college community stood in abject darkness. Now used as a storeroom, its doors were locked firmly with a stout chain and padlock. The hut looked smaller than she had remembered and seemed somewhat gloomy and antiquated, compared to the brightly-coloured, purpose-built clubhouse, which stood alongside it. Sally chose not to venture inside, and instead wandered past the administrative offices in the direction of the library. The college library seemed to hold a special place in her heart. In fact, Sally had always liked libraries and could often be found just sitting reading or browsing among the shelves at both those at Richmond and Twickenham. She was tempted to have a quick peek inside, and that would be it, she would make her way back to the Black Lion to have an early night.

The library had grown considerably since the sixties, and not only in terms of the books it had acquired. Within the last five years, a new annexe had been added to re-house the language laboratories and the recently established, Department of Computer Studies. Like the student's clubhouse, the building was ugly, soul-less and looked distinctly out of place, with its hideous fluorescent lighting and cold, uninspiring architecture. Sally was appalled that the college authorities could ever allow such a monstrosity to mar the landscape. Why couldn't they build something more in keeping with the style of the main building she thought, with its magnificent columns, friezes and aesthetically-perfect lines. She pushed through the new turnstile entry system, and wondered if she was becoming far too sentimental and a little stuck in her ways. The university was probably strapped for money, and the new buildings, as ugly as they might be, offered marvellous facilities for the benefit of students and staff alike, much more so than was available in Sally's day. Times were changing, and money, or the lack of it had to be the deciding factor in all situations like this.

Once inside, the layout of the library was very much as Sally had remembered it - just as imposing, and still retaining that familiar smell of musty old books. She thought she recognised the librarian as she made her way past the counter, and went down towards the bowels of the building, where the specialist books were kept.

As if being drawn by a magnet, Sally made her way straight towards the Classics section, and pulled out a selection of books. From the ancient Greek era, she picked Aristophanes, the comic playwright, and Euripides, the tragedian. Then, from the Roman shelves, she selected Virgil's, 'The Aenid' and 'The Histories' by Tacitus. Clutching the books as if they held special meaning to her, Sally went over and sat alone at a desk, where one-by-one, she flicked though the ancient works of literature, taking time to read salient passages. It was as if, she were subconsciously expecting the pages to cast some sort of magical spell, and conjure up someone who could come to her rescue, and ask if she needed help, someone like, William.

Sally felt her eyes begin to moisten, and slammed the book shut. She stood up abruptly, asking herself what she was doing, what did she hope to achieve by putting herself through this, or by even coming here? She put the book down and hurried from the library, before her tears came in full flow.

Outside, Sally stood in the porch, knowing it was where William had left her the note all those years ago. She felt angry with herself for allowing her emotions to creep up on her again. It was meant to be all over and done, the crying was supposed to be finished. She would never forget William, but she had to learn to live without him, she must.

Pulling a tissue from her bag, she dabbed her eyes before slowly walking down the stone steps. She passed by the assembly hall, which was being used by the Karate Society. The sound of terrifying shouts and screams coming from within was unnerving and caused her to quicken her pace. As she came around the side of the administration building she was relieved to see the main gate not too far in the distance. A little way ahead a door slammed shut. It startled Sally, and she instinctively looked over and saw in the descending darkness, what looked to be the dim figure of a man. He appeared to be fumbling with a bunch of keys, it was probably one of the college porters doing their security rounds she consoled herself. The man turned away from the door and began to walk towards her. As he got closer, she noticed he was quite tall, and walked with a pronounced limp. However, there was something else about him, something strangely familiar.

Sally's mouth dropped open as her eyes searched the man's face, not quite believing what she was seeing. She could remember calling out his name, and reaching out to touch him, before her legs betrayed her, and a sudden darkness overcame her senses, causing her to fall limply into the man's outstretched arms.

Sally came around a few minutes later, and found herself slumped in a comfortable armchair in a cluttered, dimly-lit office. It wasn't the sound of the huge, mounted wooden clock that woke her, but the sound of David's gentle voice.

"Sally, wake up, it's alright, you're safe, please open your eyes."

"David, is it really you, I'm not going mad am I?" Asked Sally in desperation, as she tried to get to her feet.

"Hey, steady on now. Have a few deep breaths first, and a good swig of this." Replied David, placing a glass of brandy in her hand. "We don't want you falling over again."

Sally sipped the brandy, and not liking the taste immediately passed the glass back to her brother-in-law.

"Thank-you. I think I'm alright now. I feel so foolish, I've never fainted before."

"I'm just glad I was there to catch you in time. I'm not quite as fast as I used to be!" He smiled warmly, and reaching for another chair, sat down beside her. "Sally, what were you doing? You looked as if you'd seen a ghost."

"I was just having a look around. I'm here for an interview tomorrow - it's for a place at the university. Then I saw you, and thought it was William."

"That's what I thought. I'm sorry if I gave you a shock." He then looked into her face intensely and added; "You're still in so much pain, Sally. It hurts me to see it in your eyes."

"You seem to read me like a book, David, but yes, you're right - it hurts like nothing on earth. I've been kidding myself that I'm over William's death. I even came back to Falcondale thinking things would be different, that everything would be alright."

"You thought you would see him again, didn't you, Sally?"

"Yes, I suppose I did."

"Perhaps, we both did." He replied, his voice full of feeling.

"Please forgive me, David. Sometimes I forget that other people suffer too. Grief can be such a selfish emotion."

"We've both come back, Sally, back to the past, looking to change what's impossible to change. It's all part of the grieving process."

"It's re-assuring knowing that. I'm glad you can share it with me, David."

"It's wonderful to see you again, Sally." He replied, changing the subject.

"It's nice to see you too. It's been such a long time. You look well, and I know you've been through a lot yourself, but I thought you were living back in Canada?"

"Yes, I did go home for a while, after William's funeral, but something was missing. You see, much of what I've been through has been self-imposed." He said, glancing down to his artificial leg. "I've learnt a lot about myself these past years. But there has to come a time when the madness and suffering stops. I've rid myself of the devils that tormented me for so long. I've come home now, Sally. I've had enough." He then reached across and affectionately placed his hand on hers.

"I'm so pleased you've decided to come back and live in Falcondale, David. But what are your plans, will you work?"

"Yes, I will, in fact I'm going to be the next Dean of Students, but I don't officially start until next term. I'm sort of learning the ropes from old Meredith at the moment. This will be my office."

"You wont be interviewing me will you, David?"

"No, I don't think so," he smiled. "But I'll have to discipline you when you get drunk and misbehave!"

"I feel as if I'm drunk now," she replied, rising to her feet.

"Please, Sally - you must come back and stay at the house tonight, we have so much to talk about."

"I would love to David, but Laura and Penny are with me, we're staying at the Black Lion. It's all been arranged."

"Well, I'll come by and have dinner with you if that would be okay?"

"Yes, that will be fine," replied Sally. Her expression then became one of sadness as she added; "I looked for you at the funeral, David?"

He looked uncomfortable.

"I was there Sally, I really was."

"Yes, I know you were there, David, your mother told me."

"I can explain..."

She put her finger up to his lips, "There's no need to explain, I understand." She then got up to leave. "I'll see you later tonight."

Jonathan delved deeply into his rucksack and began to pull out the contents, which he then placed on the bed. Other visitors, bored with small talk had long since turned their attentions to the scruffily-dressed, long-haired young man as he went about his ritual.

"It's here Tina, I know it is, I'm sure I put it in." He said, producing a tatty tobacco roll-up tin, and placing it with the rest of the items.

There was no reply from Tina. She was conscious and had now come off the danger list, but she was still very weak. She had been transferred from intensive care to the ward only the day before, and considering the amount of blood she had lost, looked surprisingly well. However, there were still grave concerns about whether she would regain full use of her hand, which remained heavily bandaged.

"Well, at least I've found the Walkman, and here's a copy of Time Out to read." He muttered, still engrossed in his search. "Damn! It's such a pity, I know you would have loved Led Zeppelin."

Tina continued to lay in silence as her visitor then began to return his assortment of dog-eared books, study notes and music cassettes back into the bag. When he had finished, he brushed small particles of tobacco, and what looked like biscuit crumbs from the clean counterpane, and sat back in his chair, not quite knowing what to say.

Since realising her suicide attempt had failed, Tina had descended into a dark spiral of gloom. She felt cheated and humiliated, but above all, she felt fear, fear from the knowledge that the threat from her father, was still very real. She doubted if anyone would take her views seriously, especially with her past history. She had tried to remember exactly what she had told Laura, but most of that evening was now just a blur. As Jonathan tried to make conversation, Tina wondered if he knew the full extent of the truth.

"Tina, can you hear me?" He whispered, getting up to put on his jacket. "I'll let you rest now, but I'll come back and see you tomorrow. Would you like me to switch the Walkman on?" Getting no reply, he gathered up his rucksack and turned to leave, just as a nurse came over to the bed.

"Tina, your mum and little brother are here to see you. I'll send them over."

Jonathan saw a look of deep anguish appear on Tina's already pained face. As he was about to go, he heard her say something. Her voice was so weak, that he couldn't quite make out what she was saying, and had to crouch down and put his head close to hers.

"You will come back tomorrow, wont you, Jonathan?" Tina asked, in a hushed tone.

"Yes, of course I will." He smiled, "I promise."

Tina's bed wasn't far from the ward office, and while Jonathan was walking the short distance to the exit, he saw who he thought was her mother speaking to the sister in charge.

The facial similarity was striking, it was just like seeing an older version of Tina. However, there was one exception, Pauline was a lot curvier than her daughter. He also noticed a chubby, surly-looking boy aged about ten. The lad was obviously bored with being in the hospital and was fiddling with a cardiac arrest machine situated nearby.

Seeing Tina's mother and the boy though, were of little importance to Jonathan. He was more interested in the third member of the party. Standing just outside the office and within earshot of the conversation, stood a tall, powerful man, who looked as if he could handle himself in any situation that might arise. The man didn't notice Jonathan's hate-filled eyes boring into him, as the young student passed him and went out into the corridor.

As the sister explained Tina's condition to her mother, she couldn't help noticing the remnants of a black eye, and the yellowing signs of bruising around Pauline's face.

"Please don't expect too much, Mrs. Gant. Tina is very lucky to be alive. Even the young man who's been visiting can't get her to speak."

"I see, thank-you sister, you've been very helpful." Replied Pauline, her speech slightly slurred. "When do you think she'll be able to come home?"

The sister looked concerned and asked Pauline to sit down.

"It might not be quite as simple as that, Mrs. Gant. When Tina is well enough, she will have to undergo a psychiatric assessment. I understand she's had problems in the past?"

"She's been a voluntary patient in a mental hospital, if that's what you mean, but Tina's over all that now."

"Possibly not, Mrs. Gant. You must accept that it's very likely Tina will be detained, most probably in a secure unit where she wont be able to harm herself. Do you understand that?"

"Yes, I think so," replied, Pauline tearfully. "Now can I see my daughter please?"

Out in the corridor, Jonathan paced to and fro, allowing his anger and thirst for retribution to well up and poison his heart. Part of his mind was still thinking rationally, but it was only a very small part, and now this too was becoming consumed by his all-conquering hatred. Jonathan was by no means a violent person, nor had he ever been, but the suffering and pain that Tina had endured throughout her short life at the hands of her monstrous father couldn't go unanswered. He didn't know what he was going to do, but he realised he'd never get another chance like this one. He thought about going back into the ward and shouting to everyone that a dangerous child abuser was in their midst. He wondered if Tina would be safe, with him so close to her. His rational side kept telling him that nothing would happen to her in a full hospital ward, and especially not at visiting time with so many potential witnesses. But how could he be sure?

Going up to the double doors, he peered through the glass and down into the ward, but could only see the ends of the beds on either side. He noticed the boy and the woman standing either side of Tina's bed, but where was her father? Jonathan closed his eyes tightly, and clenching his fists tried desperately to think what he should do. He would wait, yes, that was the answer. Wait until he came out, then get him outside somewhere, maybe the car park. Perhaps he ought to go and find some sort of weapon, after all the brute was quite a size.

As Jonathan opened his eyes, he gazed in terror as he saw the man who he mistakenly believed was Tina's father just a couple of feet away and heading straight for him. For a moment he was completely overawed by the towering figure in front of him, and instinctively took a step back. In retrospect, it was probably the best thing to do, for it gave Jonathan sufficient space to launch the hardest punch his skinny body could muster. The punch took the man totally by surprise, and caught him on the side of the head. He staggered under the impact, but to his credit, didn't go down as Jonathan hoped he would.

With arms flailing wildly, Jonathan moved in for another attack. He heard shouting and screaming going on around him, as both staff and visitors witnessed the ugly assault with horror.

"You scum, I'll kill you, if you ever touch Tina again!" Screamed Jonathan, surprised by not only his own bravery but also by the pure savagery of his actions. In his blind fury he didn't know how many of his punches were on target, but just kept hitting out with every ounce of strength he possessed.

In the end it wasn't the onlookers who stopped Jonathan, but a massive blow to the solar plexus, as his victim hit back with frightening power. The punch, an upper cut, lifted Jonathan several inches off the floor and sent him crashing into a pile of oxygen cylinders. Before he had even hit the ground, the man was towering over him, and with thick brogues was kicking Jonathan senseless.

Severely winded and unable to breath, Jonathan raised his arms in a vain attempt to protect himself from the vicious kicks that slammed into his body. He glanced up and tried to shout to his attacker that he'd had enough, but no words came from his mouth. To his right, he saw the gloating face of the boy leering down at him and egging the man on to further violence.

"Kill him, Mark - go on kick his head in!"

"Stop it, he's had enough!" Yelled Pauline, trying to pull Mark away. As she did so, the boy rushed in and kicked out at Jonathan himself, while the young student lay bruised and bleeding on the cold floor.

"It was him, he just attacked me for no reason." Exclaimed Mark, trying to regain his breath. "Reckons it was me who hurt Tina."

"He thought you were Frank, that's why he attacked you, Mark." Cried out Pauline, grabbing the driver's arm and leading him away from the scene.

Back in the car Jamie was quite excited about the incident. He was at an age where violence and aggression held great fascination for him. Mark, however seemed rather disturbed about what had happened, even though he had lost control himself, and had gone in far harder than was absolutely necessary. But he refused to be drawn further on the subject by Jamie, and was relieved when Pauline asked him to stop the car so that the boy could go into a takeaway and get a burger for his supper.

"That young lad was obviously the one the ward sister spoke of." Said Mark, finally breaking the silence. "So what new atrocity has Frank committed now?"

"It's best you don't know, Mark." Replied Pauline from the back seat. "Tina wouldn't speak to me, but when I spoke to her last, she said she was going to the police about him. Perhaps it's something to do with that."

"That bastard, Frank needs shooting, and even that would be too good for him. How many more beatings can you take, and god knows what he's done to Tina?" Said Mark angrily, as he turned around to face her.

"Don't ask me to leave him, Mark. I can't, and I wont, so don't bring it up again."

"Listen to me, Pauline - Frank doesn't love you or Tina, and never will. It'll end up with one, or even both of you getting killed. You've got to get out while you can, while you're still young enough, while there's still hope."

"I'd certainly end up dead if I did that. You don't know what Frank is capable of."

"I think I do, Pauline. I know exactly what Frank's capable of. Please, leave him. Bring Tina and Jamie with you, it's not too late."

"He would kill us both."

"We would cross that bridge when we come to it." Replied Mark sombrely. "It's now or never, Pauline."

She leant forward and allowed her lips to meet his. It was a tender, meaningful kiss, shared by two people who had known and trusted each other for a good many years. It was as much a kiss of companionship and unity, than of lovers, but whether the watching Jamie would interpret it that way was another matter.

21. ST. MARY ABBOT'S

Percy, the storekeeper just stood there, arms on hips and legs akimbo looking amazed. He had told the porter several minutes earlier to lay the new lockers down flat when loading them onto the trailer. The porter had even agreed with him and admitted himself that the grey metal boxes would fall over at the first pot hole or gust of wind encountered. There were about thirty new staff lockers to be delivered to the wards that day. They weren't particularly heavy, just awkward and difficult to manoeuvre. On any ordinary day, Nick would have had no problems loading them onto the trailer attached to the electric trolley. But today, Nick's mind certainly wasn't on his work.

It was therefore, no surprise to Percy that several lockers toppled over and crashed noisily to the ground the moment Nick moved off.

"Out on the beer with old Colombian Bob were you last night then, Nick?" Inquired the man somewhat sarcastically as he observed the chaotic scene.

Nick emerged from the cab, sighed and looked up to the heavens wearily.

"No, as a matter of fact, I wasn't, but perhaps I should have been - at least then I would have had a reason to call in sick, for all the good I seem to be doing today."

"Must be women on your mind then!" Laughed the storekeeper, trying to wind Nick up.

They younger man made no reply and instead began to re-arrange the load so that all the lockers would be lying flat, as was originally suggested to him.

Feeling guilty, Percy decided to lend a hand, and together they went about clearing up the carnage.

Ready, once again, Nick climbed back inside the cab and was about to move off when his pager sounded. Going into the stores to answer it, he glanced at his watch - it was almost lunchtime and Reg, the Head Porter had told him earlier that he had to finish loading the lockers early.

The voice on the other end of the telephone informed him that the patient's meal trolleys were now ready at the main kitchens to go off to the wards. Nick sighed again and trudged off, leaving the lockers in the light drizzle until later that afternoon. He felt tired and wondered if Reg would have a go at him for not being quicker. He began to think of excuses before his mind started to wander again, until it settled on something a lot more pressing, his university finals.

Nick was due to sit exams in less than a month, and he should really be back at college revising, not humping lockers around the hospital. Up until recently, his part-time job had fitted in perfectly with his studies. He had even been able to change some of his shifts to attend important seminars. But now it was different, he had underestimated the enormity of what he faced and now needed more time to prepare, valuable time that was slowly ebbing away.

It was simple, all he had to do was give in his notice with immediate effect, if Reg would agree to it. There was no other way. He couldn't allow all the hard work he'd done just to be thrown away.

As he headed towards the kitchens, he thought about the letter he'd received the day earlier from his estranged wife, Sandra. It was a letter that demanded a reply, and this was now preying on Nick's mind. He had grown quite indifferent to Sandra during the last few months and resented her arrogant attitude. He knew she had been seeing the loathsome Craig and that soon her hedonistic lifestyle would wreak its revenge, but as he was no longer living at the matrimonial home, he couldn't be affected by his wife's escapades. The letter had now changed all that. When Sandra wanted something, she usually got it, and her manipulation of his easy-going nature remained fresh in Nick's mind.

He used to love watching her in action, especially if he were the object of her devious machinations. He loved the subtle build-up, the attention lavished upon him, the teasing, and then - his eventual ensnarement. Seeing Sandra expose her raw, passionate desires so skilfully and unashamedly not only evoked feelings of revulsion from him, but excitement too.

Now he was to discover that Sandra could use her manipulative power to equal effect even when putting pen to paper. It was a long letter. Despite Sandra's obvious faults, she was a very emotional woman, who would always speak her mind over anything she felt strongly about. Nick could even imagine her writing it, sitting up late into the night, face pack on, and wine glass in hand, exuding elegant puffs of expensive cigarette smoke. She told him the inevitable, the news he knew would have to come. Sandra had lost her job over some minor indiscretion, as she put it. Along with the job, she had lost Craig and the rest of the fickle, parasitical crowd of hangers-on that cling like leeches to those scaling the heady heights of success.

Sandra's downfall had been the drink. She had always had a weakness for it, but like everything else, she believed it was firmly under her control. Indeed, she had even utilised alcohol as an ally in her ascendancy up the corporate ladder. She felt that its effects made her witty, sexy and liberated from convention, and in the beginning she may have been right. But Sandra never stopped to think that these were attributes that she already possessed. In fact, for much of their married life there had been an uneasy truce between Sandra and the alcohol. Now it seemed there had been a shift of power, with the forces of addiction gaining a foothold in what was to be, a slow but decisive victory.

Now she wanted Nick back, she needed him, only he could understand the true extent of her suffering and torment. She massaged his ego like nobody else could ever do, and immediately sowed the seeds of yearning and lust in Nick's vulnerable, lonely heart.

Nick heard the familiar sound of metal meal trolleys being pulled across the hospital's uneven pathways. In the distance he could make out the distinctive figure of Reg doing his fair share of the work. Again, he began to wonder how he should put the news of his impending departure to a man he had grown to both admire and respect. However, there was still something preventing Nick from coming straight out with it, he knew what the problem was, but just couldn't seem to accept that something as base and primeval as love could undermine the fruits of nearly three years of hard study.

He heard footsteps behind him, and the sound of feminine voices. Turning, he saw a dozen or more student nurses hurrying past, in order to get to the dining room for a quick cup of coffee and a chat before their afternoon shift began.

The coach had delivered the nurses early from Westminster Hospital, where they were based, meaning they still had a good twenty minutes left before they were due to start work.

His eyes eagerly searched through the group, hoping to see Laura once more. But they all looked so similar with their hair tied up, and wearing the same light blue dresses and black capes. He had assumed he would recognise her immediately, but now he was beginning to think that perhaps she wasn't among the group after all. It had been over a week since that disastrous night at the club, where Roberto had made such a fool of himself.

It was then, that he saw her, the cause of his uncertainty, the embodiment of the strange, potent force that defied the laws of logic. That same force that rode rough shod over his plans and academic aspirations. For there, in front of him, stood Laura, the reason for his indecision.

He recognised her straight away, the glorious blonde hair - sadly, but meticulously pinned back, the delicate shape of her neck, her unmistakeable profile. But, she wouldn't acknowledge him. In his mind he willed her to turn around. He couldn't bear to think she was purposely ignoring him.

He waited until it was time for the nurses to go to their respective wards. They filed out of the dining room with Nick walking just behind the group. Any moment now they would go their separate ways. There was a delay, it was a miracle. One of Nick's colleagues was trying to push past the girls with another of the meal trolleys. The nurses stopped and let the porter through, and it was then that Laura looked towards Nick. For a few moments, their eyes were firmly fixed on each others. He hesitated, before realising that at the very least he should smile or say something, even if it was just hello, but by then the moment was already lost, and the girls had moved outside. Nick knew he had to act quickly, and seeing that Laura was now walking on her own, he increased his pace and moved up alongside her.

"Laura, I'm so glad to see you at last. I've been wondering what happened to you?"

Looking a little startled, she stopped and glanced around to face him.

"Oh, it's you," she replied stiffly, before continuing to walk ahead. "I had some time off, I went to Wales with my mother and little sister."

The atmosphere was frosty to say the least, and Nick felt lost for words.

"Listen, Laura - I need to talk to you, perhaps later and somewhere in private. There's something I need to explain."

Laura stared at him coldly.

"There's nothing we could possibly talk about Nick. You seem to have a short memory, like asking my friend out when you were married."

"Laura, please, just give me the chance to tell you the truth." Nick never got to continue, as Laura quickened her pace and stepped into the building where her ward was located. He remained outside, while she pressed the button for the lift. She was trembling and felt tearful. She hadn't meant to be so awful to him, it must have been all her anguish and frustrations over the recent events reaching a peak. She could see him from the corner of her eye slowly turning to leave. Once she was sure he had his back to her, she turned her head and watched him go, while waiting for the lift to descend.

Sister Wilcox sighed and tried unsuccessfully to stifle a yawn as she finally reached the end of a thick pile of patient's medical notes she had been reading. There had been another new admission on the ward earlier that day, the fourth in the same week. No sooner had a patient died, when another appeared ready to take their bed.

She rolled her neck from side-to-side and arched her spine as she felt a twinge of pain in her lower back, the legacy of a lifetime devoted to the care of the elderly. Glancing over towards the packet of cigarettes sticking out of her cardigan pocket, she thought about popping out onto the fire escape stairs for a breath of air and a few drags of her only vice.

Sister Wilcox could have left nursing and retired some years ago, after her husband had passed away. The mortgage had been paid off with quite a tidy sum left over, the children were all grown up with families of their own. So what was it that kept her there? It certainly wasn't the back-breaking, constant lifting of patients or the endless stream of bedpans that kept her in the job. It was the company. Just listening to the chatter of the other nurses on the ward, especially the young students doing their geriatric stints kept the veteran nurse on the payroll. She loved to hear of their escapades, mainly where men were involved, and would always be on hand to offer expert and much-needed advice. Hearing tales of lusty males being smuggled into the nurses quarters, or terrifying confrontations with haughty matrons reminded Sister Wilcox of her own youth, and indeed how she eventually came to meet the man she would marry.

She reached for her navy blue cardigan, and glanced through the glass partition out onto the ward. It was getting near afternoon break time, and most of the nurses, not wanting to disturb sister were keeping busy talking to the patients, or finding odd jobs to do.

The afternoons were certainly nowhere near as busy as the mornings. Many of the patients would be over at the rehabilitation hall, either playing bingo, or being subjected to a singer whisking them off on some sentimental musical odyssey back through time. Some of course, were far too frail or ill to attend, and would remain on the ward in bed, or dozing in the day room.

As sister opened the office door, she noticed Laura emerge from behind the curtains drawn around the new patient's bed. She waved and beckoned the student nurse to come over.

"It's ok, Laura, don't rush. It's nothing important - I'm just going out onto the stairs for a quick cigarette. Ask Staff Nurse Mullins and one of the other girls to go for their breaks, and just be around the office for me, in case the phone rings. Thank-you, I wont be too long."

The sister was glad to have Laura back on the ward after she had taken time off recently. She instinctively knew the girl had what it took to be a good nurse, and felt more than comfortable leaving her in charge of things.

Usually, they would have found a few moments to talk, either while making the beds or hauling some poor soul out of a nice hot bath. But today, that had not happened, and Sister Wilcox knew something was troubling Laura. Although the pretty young nurse was always totally efficient, the warm smile and the sparkle in her eyes seemed to be missing. It wasn't like her just to bury her head in her work, and avoid chatting to her colleagues. Something must have happened during her time off, deduced the sister as she took a long pull of her cigarette and surveyed the outlook from the fire escape stairs.

Perhaps, she ought to ask Laura into the office for a talk, after all, it could well be work-related. She thought about this for a moment, then changed her mind, it was far too formal. She would simply just have a chat to her in the dining room, once the others came back.

She was then disturbed from her thought process by someone coughing just down below her. Taking a step back, she tried to be as quiet as possible, in case she was seen smoking, not only in uniform, but out on the fire escape to make matters worse. After a short while, a smile appeared on the sister's face, and she stepped forward to lean over the railings.

"Why, is that you lurking around down there, Mr. Watts?"

"That sounds remarkably like that naughty Sister Wilcox sneaking a crafty cigarette, if I'm not mistaken!" Laughed the Head Porter, who was seated on a wooden bench just beneath her.

"Don't be hard on me Reg, it's been one of those days, the patients are dropping like flies."

A grinning Mr. Watts then appeared in her line of vision.

"I'll join you in a smoke, if I may, Sylvia. I haven't seen you in ages?"

"You would if you emerged from your office once in a while," replied the sister mockingly, before adding; "No, save your legs, Reg - I'll come down there."

"Now it's your turn to be hard on me is it? Look, I'm out of my office and working like one of the lads!"

"Well, we are honoured indeed! So what's the occasion?"

"My, my, you never change lass," laughed Reg, as he led her over to the bench and proceeded to fumble in his pockets for his cigarettes.

She watched as he first produced a pipe from the top pocket of his navy serge jacket, then a tin of hand-rolling tobacco from one of the side pockets, and then, a packet of tipped cigarettes from somewhere else.

"Here, have one of mine," the sister remarked. "You seem totally incapable of making a decision this afternoon!"

"Aye, you're right lass, do you know, I just can't make up my mind what to smoke, I really can't!"

"I expect you've probably got a few cigars tucked away somewhere too?"

"I have actually, now let me see, where are they?" He replied, starting the search all over again. "Nah, I think I'll just have a roll-up." He decided at long last. "Would you like one, Sylvia? I know you can roll 'em just as good as me."

"Thank-you Reg, yes I think I will. I haven't had a roll-up for months, well not since the last time I sat out here with you!"

Back up in the ward, a brilliant ray of warm sunlight poured in through the narrow sash-cord window. The stream of light illuminated tiny particles of dust in its wake as it settled nonchalantly on the old woman's gaunt face. The sun had finally carried out its threat and penetrated through the thick, sullen grey cloud that had blanketed much of London, and the South East of England for the last few days.

Its soothing warmth somehow managed to breathe further life into a tired, worn-out body, a body that had survived the rigours of life few could imagine. From tending to the sick and dying of the muddy, rat-infested trenches of the Somme, to miraculously surviving Hitler's bombing of London during the blitz. Violet Cummings never knew when to stop fighting, whether it be for the lives of the young servicemen during her youth, or trying to eke out a meagre living from her state pension.

She remembered being in London one day during the summer of 1918. It had been shortly after her George had finally been discharged from, not only the hospital, but from the army too. He had been hit by machine gun fire which had shattered his right shoulder and penetrated his steel helmet. The surgeons had managed to piece most of his shoulder back together, but couldn't save his right eye.

It had been a warm, but cloudy day in the capital and wanting to be alone they had ventured into Hyde Park, where they were to come across their own secluded, private paradise. It was a small, shaded patch of grass, close to the Serpentine, lying beneath the long tendril-like branches of a Willow tree.

They carried with them a picnic of fresh crusty bread, ripe tomatoes and a hunk of tender home-cooked ham. To compliment this and celebrate their new lives together, they shared a bottle of vintage claret, that George had been saving for an occasion just as this.

When they had eaten their fill, George rolled up his jacket to act as a pillow, and they both lay down together giggling like school children, drinking in each other's company, making up for the long periods of separation they had endured.

After a while, there was a silence between them, George could hear her gentle breathing, and reached out to place his arm around her shoulders. Violet, in turn, moved slightly onto her side and rested her head against his chest, listening to the strong, rhythmic beats of his heart.

They lay like this, not uttering a word until a stream of sunlight broke through the slender branches to bathe them in a sea of gold, as if it were mother nature herself giving them her blessing. George pulled her closer to him, and Violet, closing her eyes to savour the moment she had dreamt of for so long snuggled into him contentedly.

"George, what was it you wanted to ask me?" She whispered.

The old woman had called out his name, over and over again in her delirium. Sensing he was near to her, calling her, she felt the warmth of his love, and reached out to touch him.
"You've come for me, George, my love, I knew you would. Take my hand, show me where to go."

The lift stopped abruptly, causing Nick to quickly try and steady the half-dozen new lockers he was taking up to Laura's ward. As the doors crashed open noisily, for some reason he assumed her just to be there waiting, as if she was expecting him. The ward however, was uncannily quiet as he popped his head out and looked for someone to assist. After a few moments of waiting, he used a special key to place the lift on 'hold' and began to take the lockers out, one-by-one.

"What have we done to deserve these then?" Called out a cheery feminine voice behind him.

He turned to see Betty, one of the auxiliary nurses already staking a claim to one of the lockers.

"All of the wards are getting them. Apparently, there's been a few thefts recently." Replied Nick, trying to be helpful.

"It wont work you know," said Betty, placing her hands on her generous hips. "The keys will get lost and we'll be back to stage one again."

"Yes, you're probably right," was Nick's rather impatient answer. "Where shall I put them?"

"In the changing room I suppose, I'll go and let the boss know." Since Sister Wilcox was still off the ward, Betty called out to Laura, who was busy changing a dressing.

"Just tell him to leave them in the changing room, Betty." Said Laura, slightly peeved at being interrupted.

"I already did, but he needs a signature for his requisition book."

"Well since Staff Nurse Mullins is on her break, I'll have to sign it, I suppose. Can you finish the dressing on Peggy's bed sores please?"

As Laura made her way to the changing rooms, Betty saw her stop at a sink to wash her hands. She then noticed Laura peer into the mirror to check her appearance, and put right the few wisps of blonde hair that had gone astray from beneath her starched, white nurse's cap. She then walked purposely into the changing room.

About twenty feet away, Violet rose up from her bed and looked about her. She pulled back the sheets, and with a determined effort, swung her legs over the side and managed to sit herself up. The sun was still shining relentlessly into her face as she lurched forward unsteadily and grasped the back of a chair for support. Her eyesight was very poor, and she had to feel her way down the ward, past the other beds, and towards the staircase next to the lift.

"Can I help you?" Asked Laura, in a direct manner.

Nick, turned and fixed a smile on her.

"Well, yes, I've been sent to deliver these. I'll come by and collect the old ones if you leave them out." He replied, realising his smile was having little effect.

"Fine, okay. I understand you want me to sign something?"

Nick passed Laura his requisition book and watched intently as she tried to decipher the near-ineligible writing.

"Laura, please. I only want a chance to explain. It's not what you might think."

She signed the book, and practically threw it back to him.

"You're married Nick, and you led poor Tina along, that's what I think. Perhaps hurting someone like that doesn't mean an awful lot to someone like you does it?"

"Laura, please listen. My wife and I are separated. She lives in the other side of London, and I live about ten minutes from here, in college digs. Our marriage is finished."

"Why should I believe you, and why should I care, come to that?"

"Because it's the truth, you can ask Roberto, he'll tell you."

"What! Ask that revolting old Spanish pervert!" Retorted Laura, angrily. "I think not!"

"Roberto's Colombian actually, and a bloody nice bloke if you take the time to get to know him."

"He's a dirty, old, malingering alcoholic, and I wouldn't be surprised if he were skulking around here somewhere, up to no good?"

"That's a bit harsh, Laura. But no, he's not here today. He's off sick."

"There, I rest my case. Now, if you don't mind, I've got work to do."

"Well, I'm sorry I bothered you, I can see that you're very bitter. At least tell me when Tina is on next. Perhaps, she would be polite enough to accept a genuine apology." Said Nick, feeling slightly aggrieved.

The mention of Tina's name seemed to hit Laura like a thunderbolt, and Nick sensed he'd touched on a raw nerve.

"What is it, is there something wrong?"

Laura quickly tried to regain her composure, but her mind was flashing back to that wretched bathroom scene.

"Tina is ill. In fact, she's very ill." There was no more anger in Laura's voice, only emotion. As she struggled to complete her sentence, Nick felt a strong compulsion to reach out and comfort her.

"Tell me what happened?"

She turned away from him, putting her hands up to her face, trying to summon up the words.

"She attempted to kill herself at my home, and very nearly succeeded. She's been in hospital ever since. My brother, Jonathan has seen her and says she's still in danger. I'm hoping to go and see her myself soon."

"Was it because of me being married?" Gasped Nick, his face drawn.

Laura inhaled sharply and dabbed her eyes with a tissue.

"No, Nick - it wasn't because of you. It was something else." She then opened the door and stepped back out onto the ward, feeling the pain of an unhealed wound being violently re-opened. She saw Betty rushing around, looking anxious.

"Betty, is everything okay?"

"I can't seem to find Violet, I've looked everywhere."

It was Nick who saw her first, a tiny, frail old lady feeling her way along the corridor with a look of the utmost determination on her face. He called to her a couple of times, but there was no response. Not wanting to scare the elderly woman, he approached cautiously, allowing her to see and hear him as he came up beside her.

"Hello, Miss, can I help you?" He blurted out, not quite sure how to address her. "I think you may have got a little lost."

The old woman stopped and looked around slightly confused. It took her a few moments before she finally focussed on the tall, dark-haired young man standing beside her.

"Don't leave me George! Look, I'm still wearing it, the ring you gave me." Pleaded the woman anxiously.

For what seemed an eternity Nick stood in the corridor with the old lady, trying to convince her that he wasn't George. Eventually, he let her win and was able to take her hand and lead her back to the ward. They looked quite the couple, casually strolling in, with Violet smiling broadly, and her arm linked tightly through his.

Sister Wilcox saw the pair approaching and hurried from the office to meet them.

"Thank-you, young man, you've just saved my bacon!" She then turned to Laura, and added somewhat sourly; "If some of my nurses had been a little more observant, this would never have happened."

"Sister, please," interrupted Nick. "Look, I think it was my fault. I took Laura away from her duties to sign for some lockers I had delivered. Please don't blame her."

Sister Wilcox looked at both of them, with a knowing frown on her face.

"I'll be the judge of that, if you don't mind." She replied sharply. "However, that was a very commendable gesture, and one I hope you appreciate, Nurse Peddlescoombe. Now, let's put an end to the matter. Violet is back and seemingly no worse for wear after her little adventure." She then turned her attention back to Laura. "You can go off for your break now, nurse."

Without a second glance at Nick, Laura turned and headed towards the changing rooms to remove her white apron and collect her cape. She had never felt so low in her life, and now wished she had never taken up nursing in the first place.

She left the ward as quickly as possible and marched across the green towards the dining room. She brought a coffee and gazed around for an empty table. From the corner of her eye she noticed a couple of girls from her training group trying to catch her attention. When one of them actually called out her name, Laura felt that she couldn't just ignore the girl, but she surprised herself by simply flashing a false smile, and then walking off to a table over in the far corner, to sit with her back to everyone.

Laura thought she might cry, purely out of frustration, but it was only her fierce pride that prevented her from doing so. She felt angry, not only with herself, but how she had been spoken to by Sister Wilcox. She wanted to scream and let the old bag know just how insulted she had been. The woman had no right to address her like that, in front of someone else, it was humiliating to say the least. If the sister hadn't of sneaked off herself for a cigarette, none of this would have happened in the first place.

She closed her eyes for a few seconds trying to quell her anger. She breathed in deeply, and let out a long sigh, before opening her eyes again and deciding to confront the sister when she returns to the ward. It was then that she became aware of a figure standing over her.

"Laura, please don't be annoyed with me. I want to apologise. Can I sit down, just for a few minutes?"

She didn't reply, as she looked up at Nick's handsome, pleading face. He took her silence as a cue to be seated, and placed his coffee on the table opposite hers.

They both soon noticed how silent the dining room had become, as Laura's colleagues glanced over, eager to know why the young porter had joined their solitary friend at her table.

The silence seemed to break the ice as both of them now looked straight at each other, aware they were the main focal point in the room.

It was Laura who spoke first, feeling that perhaps she had been too hard on him earlier on. In fact, the more she thought about it, the more she began to realise that she had probably just chosen Nick to manifest all her pent-up anguish upon. Her mind was a whirlpool of mixed up thoughts and emotions, her father's death, her mother selling the house and planning to move back to Wales, now all this grief with Tina. It would take Laura a good while to process everything that had happened recently and finally come to terms with it all.

"Maybe it should be me who apologises, Nick. I've been very rude to you." She took a sip of her coffee, and softened her demeanour; "It was very good of you to try and take the blame back on the ward, but I can stick up for myself you know."

He smiled and sat back in his chair, gracefully acknowledging her last remark. There was another silence, and Laura, feeling uncomfortable, glanced at her fob watch.

"I'd better be getting back, or I'll have sister to contend with again."

He nodded, knowing full well that she still had plenty of time left, time enough to hear what he wanted to say to her.

"Laura, about the other night. I never meant for Tina to get hurt, you must realise there was a genuine misunderstanding about the date. Please, at least give me the chance to make amends. Perhaps, even over a quiet drink or a meal somewhere nice - you certainly look like you deserve one!"

"I'm sorry, Nick but the answer is no. Besides, it wouldn't be fair on Tina. She liked you."

He stared at her open-mouthed.

"Please tell me what happened, Laura. I remember her being blind drunk, and you both getting into a car with your brother. But earlier, you said Tina tried to kill herself. I don't understand. She must be very troubled."

Laura began to explain about the horrendous events of that night, but then noticed Sister Wilcox enter the dining room.

"I can't tell you anymore, I really need to go." With that, she left her coffee and began to get up.

He implored her to wait while he searched in his pockets for a pen and a piece of scrap paper. He then quickly scribbled his number down, while Laura waited nervously.

"Laura, call me - if you change your mind. I'll be waiting."

She hurriedly shoved the piece of paper into her pocket just as the sister arrived at the table, with a cup of tea in one hand, and a rather tasty-looking slice of chocolate gateaux in the other.

"I do hope I'm not interrupting anything?" She asked, somewhat sarcastically, sitting herself down on the other vacant chair opposite Laura.

"No, not at all, Sister." Blushed Laura. "In fact, I was just on my way back to the ward."

"Nonsense," said the sister firmly. "Why, you've got plenty of time left. Besides, I want a word with you."

Nick decided that now was probably a good time to finish his locker deliveries, and drained his coffee in one. He said his goodbyes to the women, smiled at Laura and took his leave.

"What a charming young man," remarked Sister Wilcox, as she and Laura both watched Nick leave the dining room. "He's a student you know, and a very hard worker, so Mr. Watts was telling me. But I expect you know that?"

"Sorry, Sister, I don't quite know what you mean?" Replied the student nurse awkwardly, and feeling her anger returning.

But the sister just started laughing, her earlier foul temper gone as quickly as it had came.

"You can't fool me Laura, I've seen it all before, a hundred times over." She said, before taking a bite out of her chocolate cake. "But that's not what I want to talk about."

"Am I in trouble Sister?"

"No, my dear, of course you're not. I've already told you, you're one of the best nurses I've got, and I'll give you a damned good report when you go. But good nurses can only be good if they've got other good nurses working alongside them. It's all about teamwork, Laura and communication. You'll be wise to remember that."

"Thank-you, Sister, that means a lot to me. In fact it was the last thing I was expecting to hear - especially after losing a patient." Replied Laura, a little surprised and knowing full well that the wily older woman had successfully avoided a confrontation taking place.

"These things happen with confused patients. We're not a prison, and I expect you'll lose a few more before your career's over - I certainly have!"

"I hope not," smiled Laura, pleased to be back on talking terms with her mentor. "Thank-you again, Sister. I really needed a boost to my confidence."

"Let's just put it behind us, shall we? Now, having got that out of the way, I've been in touch with Violet's husband, George," Continued sister, changing the subject. "I've told him to come and visit her as soon as possible."

"You mean, he's not dead?" Exclaimed Laura, quite surprised.

"Good gracious no! He's a lovely old man, but for health reasons he can't get to visit very often. Apparently, after Violet began to deteriorate, poor old George just couldn't manage anymore, and that's where we came in."

"Perhaps, I could get Violet all dressed and ready for him when he arrives!" Replied Laura, eagerly.

"I think there's only one person who'll be getting dressed up around here, and that's you, Laura! So when are you going out with this young Nick, fellow, or have you been seeing him already?"

Laura nearly choked on her coffee. She still couldn't get used to Sister Wilcox's habit of firing direct questions, especially those of a personal nature.

"It's something that would take far too long to explain, sister. It's complicated."

"Well, we're both on duty until nine. I knew there was something bothering you." With that, she gently touched Laura's arm, before adding; "You know my door is always open if ever you want to talk."

"Thank-you, Sister, I'll bear that in mind. But I have to think things over first."

"Well, Laura, don't think about things for too long, especially where young Nick is concerned. I'd snap him up now if I were you."

It was nearly ten in the evening when Laura finally got back to her room at the nurses' home. She kicked off her shoes and threw her cape over a chair, before collapsing onto the bed. It had worn her out, explaining to Sister Wilcox about Tina earlier in her office. When she had finished, the older woman sat quietly for a few moments before asking Laura if she could do anything to help. Laura declined the offer but deep down, she had been glad of the chance to tell someone else, someone outside of her own family circle. Now it was like a heavy burden had been lifted from her shoulders, and she could draw strength enough to move on.

As Laura was undressing to take a shower, she realised there was one more thing she needed to do. Reaching into the pocket of her discarded uniform, she retrieved the scrap of paper containing Nick's number.

What she was about to do was in total contradiction to the person that had been so sharp in their manner towards the young, studious porter earlier that day. Even then, when her mind was greatly troubled, she did at least have the courage of her convictions, and was able to say no him. Now it was like the virtuous facets of her personality, which had taken the moral high ground, had now simply chosen to switch themselves off. There were no thoughts of Tina, when she poured herself a glass of chilled white wine. She took a couple of sips then clutching a handful of coins, she padded out along the corridor towards the payphones to call Nick, and say yes to his invitation to go out.

The next morning both Frank and Pauline were up early, and for very different reasons. Today was the day of Frank's visit to Albert, Pauline's grandfather. Of course, she was to know nothing of this, and besides, she had plans of her own, to go and visit an old friend, called Sally from her university days.

Usually Pauline would avoid Frank at all costs in the morning. Her presence only served to irritate him. But now, after many years of bruising encounters, she had finally learnt to use the art of plain common sense. Today, she had braved his wrath simply by intuition. It seemed that his mind had been somewhere else recently, and this distraction whatever it was had the effect of blunting Frank's usual displays of blatant savagery. Pauline had a vague idea it probably involved another woman, however, she choose to block the thought from her mind. This was something she had grown rather adept at over the years with Frank. It served no valid purpose to torture herself further, and besides, he always came back when he got bored with his extra-marital activities.

Ignoring his wife's attempts at making conversation, Frank poured himself a mug of coffee and lit a cigarette. He was surprised she was up so early, and watched her with contempt as she went about her business in a grubby dressing gown and worn slippers, busy clearing away the evidence from another of her frequent drinking binges.

Frank had recently begun to sleep in one of the spare rooms. It appalled him to have Pauline's body in such close proximity as his. He found her a depressing eyesore, an unworthy, sick embarrassment.

As he pulled deeply on his cigarette, he went over in his mind what he would say to Albert, and how it would need to sound convincing. After all, this was going to be a big one, and he wanted to make sure nothing went wrong. Getting money out of the old fool had never been particularly difficult, it was covering his tracks that was the problem. In the early days, when Frank used to send Pauline with the begging bowl, he had been amazed at her success rate. However, the sums involved had always been quite meagre, and before long he began to grow frustrated. It was then that he started visiting Albert himself, unbeknown to Pauline, of course.

Giving the old boy tales of impending business doom and a future of poverty and hardship for his wife and children, Frank soon began to reap the rewards of his labours. As Albert's health deteriorated further and his thoughts became confused, Frank would forge the old man's signature and simply write out cheques to himself. After a while however, the bank became suspicious of these transactions and Frank had to temporarily curtail his activities.

Now he was about to ask for a loan, saying he and Pauline needed it until they sold their home. It would probably mean Frank would have to take Albert to the bank personally to get the cheque approved. He would use guilt as a weapon, and tell Albert that Swann's would soon be snapped up without his help. It was a simple ruse, and Frank cursed himself for not trying it earlier to raise capital.

"You'll not get another penny out of me, you blood-sucking parasite!" Scowled Albert, reaching for his walking stick.

"What are you talking about Albert? It's for your family, your own flesh and blood - think of it as an investment. We'll give you interest." Replied Frank, somewhat surprised by the hostile response.

Although Frank's large frame was little more than a blur, the old man stared at him with eyes burning with hatred and fear.

"It was a black day in hell when she married you, Gant. Now be off with you, get out of my home and never darken my door again."

"You'll regret this you bloody old fool. Can't you see how this will hurt Pauline?"

"It's you who's hurting her, you bloody charlatan. All I regret is not seeing through you earlier. Now get out, or do I have to take my stick to you."

"You piss-ridden old swine," snarled Frank as he lunged at Albert, grabbing him by the collar and pulling the pensioner's scrawny body off the chair, until their faces almost touched. "I'll break that stick over your fucking head, you decrepit pile of shit!"

Frank pushed the old man violently back onto the chair, and went to the table, where he began picking up the photographs of Sally's house that he'd showed him.

However, with surprising speed and agility, Albert pushed himself back up from the seat and moved towards Frank, who was now standing with his back to him. Albert knew he would only get one chance, so with every ounce of strength left in his tired body, he raised the stick and brought it down hard.

Perhaps, it was his poor eyesight, or the dimness of the room that caused him to miss, but that's exactly what he did. He lost his footing and instead of hitting the back of Frank's head, the blow just caught the younger man's shoulder.

With frightening brutality, Frank turned, pulled back his fist and sent it crashing into the side of Albert's head. It connected with a bone-shattering thud and Albert was knocked several feet across the room.

An eerie silence pervaded, there wasn't even a groan. Frank, now breathing hard and perspiring inched closer to the crumpled body. He saw blood trickling from Albert's ear, and bent down to see if he was still alive. A decision had to be made there and then. Perhaps, this was a better solution, he thought. Pauline would stand to get the money in Albert's will, but it would just take longer, but at least it would be legitimate, in a sense.

Lifting up the old man's body, Frank carried him like a baby to the top of the staircase, where he then stood Albert up, supporting him under the arms. As they swayed on the landing, the old man's head lulled back and forth. Frank was then taken aback as Albert emitted a long groan, and looked up slowly. For a moment, their eyes met, as they stood face-to-face once more.

Then, with alarming coolness, Frank gave Albert the gentlest of shoves, and watched as the old man fell backwards down the steep staircase.

Wiping his brow, Frank stepped slowly towards him. He could see a vast pool of blood forming on the hard tiled floor below.

Kneeling down, he checked to see if Albert still had a pulse. He felt around for nearly a minute, until he was finally satisfied the old man was dead. Frank, then calmly stepped over his grandfather-in law's body and let himself out of the front door, pleased that things had gone so smoothly.

22. THE VISIT

The drive back from the supermarket had taken nearly forty five minutes. Road works and heavy traffic had conspired to add half an hour to a journey that Sally would normally have completed in ten minutes.

She checked her watch, it was almost one in the afternoon. Lizzie was dropping by with some champagne and caviar that she had brought a couple of days ago while on a trip to France, and to make matters worse, Sally had arranged to have her hair trimmed later that afternoon.

As she lugged the shopping bags out from the back of the car, she wondered if she had chosen the right thing for dinner with Frank later that evening, at least there wouldn't be too much to prepare she consoled herself. But, there was still the dreaded housework. This remained a bone of contention, and Sally would simply just do it herself, except on the days when Penny was good enough to help out. Today, however Penny wouldn't be back from school. She was going to a friend's birthday party and had arranged to stay overnight with another girl who had also been invited. It worried Sally a little, and she probably wouldn't have let Penny go until she had spoken with the friend's mother and received adequate assurances that everything would be above board. Thankfully, Penny was a thoughtful girl and understood her mother's fears, plus she had promised to telephone during the evening and be back by lunchtime the following day.

Sally was still putting away the month's groceries when Pepys began barking and wagging his tail excitedly. She was pleased to see Lizzie's familiar smile at the back door. Having not seen her friend for some time, Sally felt she needed to sit down and have a good heart-to-heart chat with someone she knew well and trusted. She had of course spoken with Lizzie on the telephone about the Tina incident, but still had the need to discuss it on a more personal level.

"Sally darling, you have got yourself behind with things haven't you? Look, you haven't even done the washing up from last night, you are slipping!" Remarked Lizzie, puffing as she placed a heavy box on the kitchen table.

"It's not funny, Lizzie. I've still got so much to do, and get my hair done later."

"Your hair looks just fine as it is, silly woman. Why go and waste good money for nothing. It's pretty obvious the effect Frank is having on you. Besides, you should have used my hairdresser, she would have come out to you, she brings all her own stuff you know."

"Now you tell me. Maybe I should save myself all this work and give her a call, then just order a Chinese take-away instead!"

"Don't worry, it'll be worth it, Sally. The cooking is half the excitement of it all. I'm sure Frank will love it. So what are you going to cook him anyway?"

"Well, it was a bit of a problem. As you know, I rarely eat meat, but Frank is quite a carnivore. So I'm going to compromise and cook him a fillet steak."

"Oh, right, so that's it?" Replied Lizzie tartly. "Well, I suppose that's simple enough. He likes steak does he?"

"Yes, he loves it. Anyway, the supermarket was so full, I just got flustered and had to get out. So I didn't have much chance to really look around. I can't seem to cope with crowds these days, but I'm sure he'll like it."

"I expect so," said Lizzie, a little concerned. "Sally, I do believe all this Tina business has set you back a bit?"

"Maybe you're right, it has, but there's more." Sally suddenly looked very distressed and agitated.

"What is it, Sally?" Asked Lizzie, concerned.

"I think Frank may be Tina's father."

"Oh my god. You mean when he raped Pauline?"

"Yes, I'm not a hundred per cent sure, but I'm going to try and get it out of him tonight."

"Sally, what on earth are you getting yourself into. Have nothing more to do with him, say you're keeping the house. Do anything, but just get out of this mess."

"I need to find out, if only for Tina's sake. I was foolish to think he had changed."

"I would cancel tonight. We can go out, just the two of us. There's a new wine bar that has opened in Richmond, I've heard it's very nice." Implored Lizzie.

"I owe it to Tina. You should have seen the poor girl. It was so dreadful." Sally sighed, and went over to put the kettle on. "After William, I didn't think that anything would ever shock or hurt me again. I suppose I've just been putting up some sort of facade, a very fragile facade that has just shattered, and shown me as I really am, just teetering on the brink."

"Don't speak like that Sally, you were doing so well. Look, we all put on an act. I do it all the time. How else are we able to cope? Okay, it was a terrible thing to have happened in your home, but Tina isn't dead is she? In time she'll get over it, and so will you. Just see it for what it was, Sally - a step backwards, that's all."

For the first time in their long friendship, Sally wanted to shout at her friend. She detected a callousness in Lizzie's words. She had always been renowned for her sarcasm, but this was different. The cynicism upset Sally, as it appeared like Lizzie was belittling what had happened with Tina. However, she chose to ignore her friend's remarks on this occasion.

"I see you've brought the champers and caviar?" Asked Sally, changing the subject.

"Certainly have, and that's not all. Here, I've got you some Chanel perfume, a nice hunk of brie, and a few bottles of Chablis. So you can forget the coffee and bring a couple of glasses instead."

"No, Lizzie I'm having coffee. I need to have a clear head in order to get the truth out of Frank tonight."

"Be it on your head, Sally Peddlescoombe."

Pauline had spent considerable time earlier that day trying to make herself look her best. After much deliberation she finally chose the outfit for her visit. She wanted a smart, casual combination, but it had to be something that exuded a certain style and finesse. The problem was, Pauline had piled on a few extra pounds recently, and most of her clothes were not particularly flattering to her fuller figure. She then noticed the silk blouse hidden away at the back of the wardrobe. It had been covered by a polythene dry-cleaning wrapper for over eleven years, and now she felt herself grow excited about seeing it again.

It was decided. She would wear the black and purple striped blouse over her black slacks. She tried it on and stood in front of the bedroom mirror, gazing at herself from different angles. It was a tight fit now, but she didn't think anyone would notice, especially if she wore her thick, patent leather belt over the top. Her mind drifted off, and she recalled the last time she had worn the blouse, and how lucky she was to still have it. Although, it held a mixture of both good and bad memories for Pauline, she was determined not to allow her emotions to get in the way today. There was however, nothing she could do to prevent herself from thinking of Mark. Was it really that long ago she had a fling with him?

As Pauline turned into the drive and walked beneath the canopy of overhanging trees, that led to Sally's house, she became aware of the clicking sound her shoes were making. It was a noise she detested, as it made her feel so self conscious, and made the choice of footwear she had chosen play on her mind. Noticing the small, wooden gate that would lead her right up to the front door, Pauline could feel herself tensing up. She slowed her pace, and out of desperation, began to practice her breathing exercises, the ones she had been taught for moments exactly like this.

The situation reminded her of a trip she had made to Bristol some twenty years or so ago. It was the trip she had made to Frank's parent's home, shortly after they had both been expelled from university back in early 1963. She had been nervous then, probably even more so than now. She recalled lying to Mrs. Gant about her relationship with Frank. Irene Gant had appeared as a terrifying figure to Pauline on that occasion, and even to this day, she wondered how on earth she had managed to pull off such a deception. However, it had proved to be a very worthwhile visit, for in the years following Tina's birth, Pauline had to rely on Irene's help many times over, even if it had been in total defiance to her husband's wishes.

There were two cars in the drive, a Volvo estate, and a sleek-looking BMW. Pauline guessed that Sally had company, and maybe she should abandon her surprise visit and come back another time. However, Pauline knew she was just subconsciously looking for a reason to back out, and began to urge herself forward, determined not to be intimidated.

Why had she come here, was it really just to thank Sally and her family for helping her daughter in her hour of need? Her feelings were confused, yes she had been jealous of Sally when she used to go out with Frank. Yes, her jealousy had grown so intense that it bordered on hatred, and she could have quite easily killed her rival in love. Pauline gritted her teeth as her mind unwittingly flashed back to that evening in the hall, when Frank had placed the necklace on Sally. But now, years after she had won Frank, she could even admit to spells of remorse, for not only having treated Sally so badly, but wishing her harm as well. Now she believed that to feel sorry for Sally was not only a humble act, but a gesture to be admired. After all, Pauline was the better woman - the voices she was hearing in her head were telling her so.

Pauline had only been made aware of Sally's existence, and the loss of her husband, William by Tina, who of course was on the same nurse training programme as Sally's daughter, Laura. It was quite a coincidence thought Pauline at the time, unaware of Frank's involvement in bringing this about. She began to wonder, out of sheer curiosity just what it would be like to meet Sally again after so long. She would be able to tell her that she was Frank's woman, and even offer Sally a belated apology, after all, at least she still had a man.

Now though, the situation had changed a little. Pauline was in the position of having to feel obliged, to thank Sally for saving Tina's wretched life on that ghastly night a few weeks earlier.

As she stepped into the porch, she got a whiff of freshly-made coffee. It made her mouth water and she imagined being warmly invited in as an old friend and sitting down to chat with Sally and her kin. But rather than comfort her troubled mind, Pauline's vision only served to fill her with further hatred and contempt. She looked about her at the homely porch. It was nicely painted, it was clean, in fact it was totally spotless, even the Wellington boots showed no signs of wear and tear. There were shelves on both sides, housing pots of colourful plants. The double-glazed windows sparkled and the tiled floor shone, even the door mat had not a blemish on it.

As Pauline rang the bell, she heard its easy-on-the-ear chime, then hearing a dog barking and scratching at the inside of the front door, she stepped back a couple of feet, feeling her heart beating madly.

When Sally opened the door, Pauline recognised her immediately. She took in all of her features, and couldn't help noticing how Sally had managed to keep her curvaceous figure despite having three children. Sally was still the strikingly attractive woman Pauline had known at university, and apart from having her hair shorter now, didn't really look any different. It was because Pauline was so distracted by this vision of perfection in front of her, she hadn't even noticed the look of complete shock on Sally's face.

Sally had simply froze in the doorway. Alarm bells were ringing wildly in her head, but age, experience and breeding had long taught her to remain calm.

It was Sally who spoke first, as she gazed into the puffy, bloodshot, yet frighteningly familiar eyes of her uninvited visitor.

Some people seem to keep the same appearance throughout their lives, a look that never bends or submits to the vagaries of time and changing fashion, no matter how pathetic they appear. Sally saw that Pauline was one of these people.

"Can I help you?" Asked Sally, politely but firmly.

"Hello, Sally - I knew it was you straight away." Replied Pauline, smiling awkwardly.

"I'm sorry, but do I know you?" Stuttered Sally, knowing full well who Pauline was.

"Yes, I'm from your past. I'm Pauline, remember? We were both at Falcondale in the sixties."

Sally felt as if she had been kicked in the pit of her stomach, and swallowed hard as she gripped the door frame for support. She probably would have just slammed the door shut and fled back inside the house if it wasn't for Lizzie coming up to stand behind her.

"Pauline you say, well this is a surprise. I don't think I understand?" Replied Sally, her voice faltering.

"Sally, please - I don't mean you any harm. I'm not here to cause you trouble." Said Pauline, moving closer.

Sally's recollection of Pauline was now disturbingly vivid. She stepped back, scanning the visitor's face, noting the hurriedly-applied lipstick, the pale, plump cheeks and sagging neck. Then she gazed up into those haunting, eyes encased in black eyeliner.

"Who is it Sally, not a salesman is it?" Called out Lizzie.

"No, it's Pauline, you know from Falcondale, remember?"

There was a silence as the reality of the situation began to dawn on Lizzie.

"Oh, what a pleasant surprise. Pauline, is that really you?" Gasped Lizzie, craning her neck to look over Sally's shoulder.

Pauline nodded, she wasn't expecting Lizzie to be there, and now felt a little overawed as the two women stared down at her from inside the house.

"Look, I'm sorry, perhaps it was a mistake coming here," uttered Pauline, turning to leave.

"Wait, Pauline - don't go, look you're here now, so why not come in for a coffee?" Suggested Sally, glancing to Lizzie for support. It was a rash decision inviting Pauline into her home, but Sally's curiosity had got the better of her on this occasion.

Pauline, like many women, believed her home to be special and unique in its own particular way. But now seeing the beautiful and homely residence where Sally lived, she was quickly brought down to earth and suddenly realised the house she shared with Frank was in fact, a true reflection of herself. It was cold, clinical and boring. It lacked even the slightest evidence of imaginative, artistic creativity, despite Frank's efforts in bringing in his interpretation of works of modern art. This discovery upset her greatly, and to a large extent deflected her from the real reason she was there.

Her mind was momentarily transported back to when the three of them were all so much younger, when Sally and Lizzie had so much going for them, and Pauline could only watch from the sidelines. A plump, forlorn figure, eaten away by envy and self-loathing. She recalled how she tried to be like them, witty and alluring. Then came the crash diet and the new clothes she brought herself. She even found herself a job in the student's clubhouse, just so she could meet people and be just like Sally and Lizzie. Now Pauline felt like that once more. The two women scrutinising her had weathered the ravages of time remarkably well. It was as if they had some sort of aura around them, they shimmered and shined, and felt comfortable in their roles.

"Pauline, please do have a biscuit, they are rather nice." Interrupted Sally, sensing hostility building up between Lizzie and their unexpected visitor.

Pauline reached into the tin and helped herself to a couple of the expensive-looking chocolate biscuits, before reclining back on the settee. Sally offered her a plate and racked her mind for something to say that might break the ice. Pauline appeared to be lacking social skills and looked extremely uncomfortable.

"Sally, thank-you for being so kind and inviting me into your lovely home." She whispered, almost solemnly as she placed the empty plate next to her cup and saucer. "Especially after I had been so horrible to you at the Christmas Dance?"

"It was all a long time ago, Pauline. Why, I'd completely forgotten about it." Replied Sally, hating herself for lying so blatantly.

"I felt awful afterwards, and hoped that one day I would get the chance to apologise. You see, in life you only get one chance, and Frank was my chance. I wasn't going to let anyone stand in the way. I saw what I wanted, went after it, and got my wish. I became Frank's wife. Perhaps, if it were William, you might have acted in a similar way?"

Sally nearly choked on her coffee, and had to put the cup down quickly.

"You mean to tell me that you married Frank, after accusing him of raping you?"

"Yes, I did Sally, but why does that surprise you? He's a wonderful man, difficult at times, but yes, truly wonderful."

"But, Pauline, he went to prison!"

"Yes, he did, and Tina and myself waited for him."

Sally looked to Lizzie in amazement, and saw that she was just as shocked as she was.

"So let me get this correct, Pauline. Tina is Frank's daughter as a result of him raping you?"

"Please don't say he raped me. Frank is Frank, besides I must have led him on."

"Well, yes we all do stupid things when we're immature," continued Sally. "But you had marks on your body, I saw them, and you attacked him with that broken glass?"

"Are you saying I caused a scene because I was immature?" Demanded Pauline, glaring intently at Sally.

"No, Pauline, of course I'm not," replied Sally, sensing Pauline's rising anger. "I just didn't understand that's all."

"I've been horrible to Frank too, Sally. Sometimes I have to let him know that he can't just treat me like dirt whenever he has the inclination."

"I see. How is Frank these days?" Asked Sally, feeling her blood freeze over, in the knowledge that she had been out on a date with him, and he was coming over to her house for dinner later that evening.

"He's certainly not the easiest of men to live with, not by a long chalk." Smiled Pauline, proud to speak of her husband. "We've been together as a family since he came out of prison," she continued dreamily.

"He must really love you?" Interrupted Lizzie in a somewhat mocking tone, before getting up to go and fetch some wine.

Fortunately, Pauline seemed totally oblivious to Lizzie's sarcasm and continued happily speaking of the love she shared with her partner. It was only the sound of a large glass of wine being put down heavily in front of her that shook Pauline out of her trance-like state.

"He gave me a wonderful daughter, so yes, Lizzie in answer to your question, I suppose he does love me." Then turning her attention back to Sally, Pauline continued; "That's the main reason why I'm here. It's because of Tina, and what you did to help her. Sally, you and your family saved her life, and for that reason alone, I have come here to thank you personally."

Sally noticed that Pauline looked quite tearful now, and went over to sit next to her.

"How is Tina, Pauline?"

"She's off the danger list now, if that's what you mean. But she'll never be able to have children or even finish her nurse training. How she'll cope, I just don't know."

"I'm sorry, Pauline, poor Tina, that's so awful. I can't bear to think about it. If there's anything I can do - anything at all, just ask."

"Thank-you Sally, you're being so nice to me," replied Pauline with a concerned look on her face. It was a look that unnerved Sally, and had her wondering if it was a look of contempt or simply the face of a woman trying her best to contain the obvious torment she was going through.

"There is something you could do. Please thank Jonathan for me. He's been wonderful, visiting Tina every day. I think it's seeing him, that's given her the will to go on."

"I'll certainly do that, Pauline. I think my Jonathan has taken quite a liking to Tina. He speaks very highly of her."

"I'm glad someone does," remarked Pauline sourly. "But they do seem suited, it's such a pity he wont be able to see so much of her."

"What do you mean?" Asked Sally, a little surprised.

"Tina is going to be assessed for Section Three of the Mental Health Act, that's what I mean."

"Section Three? I'm sorry, I still don't follow you, Pauline."

"It means, Tina will be locked up in a psychiatric hospital." Butted in Lizzie, getting up to refill Pauline's glass.

"Yes, that's right, if you put it that way," was Pauline's slow reply. "When she's fit enough to travel, she'll be taken to Greenfields - it's a secure unit, full of poor souls like my Tina."

"But Pauline, that's terrible. What on earth has happened to make her be like this?" Blurted out Sally, before realising that she may have over stepped the mark.

If Sally's forthrightness had bothered Pauline in any way, she didn't show it. She picked up the replenished glass of wine, and brought it up unsteadily to her flushed face. There was a pause as she took a couple of large mouthfuls, before settling back on the settee.

"Tina has always lived a life of fantasy. When she was young she used to make up the most unbelievable stories. Then, if she wasn't taken seriously she would fly into the most violent of rages. She even accused her father of interfering with her sexually."

"You mean, Frank?" Gasped Sally, shocked.

"Yes, that's right. She was obviously trying to wreck our marriage for some unknown reason. But I know all of her tricks now, and what she's capable of doing. In fact, going to Greenfields may be the best thing for her."

"You can't really mean that, Pauline?"

"I do, Sally. I can't guarantee her safety if she's at home, and she's far too much of a risk living in the nurses' quarters. Tina needs treatment, and if that means being sectioned, then so be it."

"Maybe the best thing for her is to be heard, to be listened to. If what she said was true, then action needs to be taken." Remarked Lizzie bluntly.

"You don't know what you're saying. Frank would never do anything like that, not to his own daughter. How dare you." Hissed Pauline, glaring at Lizzie.

"But there must be something in it, Pauline, if things have got this bad?" Exclaimed Sally, trying to take the attention away from Lizzie.

Pauline realised she was being unreasonable, and softened her stance.

"Look, I've already said that Frank is not an easy man to live with. He used to beat me, and sometimes Tina, if she got in the way. She wanted her father away from us. That's why I think she accused him of assaulting her."

Sally and Lizzie stared at each other in total shock, unable to believe what they had heard.

"But Pauline, but why did you stay, why didn't you just take Tina and leave him?" Asked Sally, after a brief moment of silence.

"Frank is my husband, and I will stand by him, no matter what he's done."

Sally realised she was dealing with a very disturbed woman, and decided not to press her any further. She felt uncomfortable and wanted Pauline out of her house, but she couldn't help thinking how Tina had suffered so badly, and how she had been so let down by those who were supposed to love and protect her.

Lizzie glanced up to the clock, and turned to her friend.

"Sally, look - it's getting on for three, don't forget your hair appointment!"

"Oh no, what shall I do? I completely forgot!" Exclaimed Sally, frantically.

"Shall I call them and cancel it for you?" Asked Lizzie, trying to be helpful.

"Yes, will you, thanks. My hair is of little consequence after hearing of Pauline's troubles."

"Sally, look I'd better leave. I'm sorry if I've caused so much disruption. I didn't realise you had an appointment." Said Pauline, finishing her wine, and getting up to go.

"It's fine, no problem, I'll see you out." Replied Sally, leading her visitor towards the door.

As they walked out into the hallway, Pauline suddenly stopped. "Could I just use your phone to call for a mini-cab?"

Sally waited patiently as Pauline dialled the number that had been ingrained in her mind for so many years. It was then that she noticed Sally's own number displayed on the dial and quickly made a note of it. Ten minutes later, they heard a car pull up outside and the tooting of a horn. Both Sally and Lizzie went to the front door to see Pauline out.

"Sally, you remember a little earlier, you said if there was anything you could do for me?"

"Yes, Pauline, of course I remember - what is it?"

"Well, I've thought of something else. I'd like us to become friends. Will you promise you'll come over for tea at my house soon?"

"Of course, Pauline, I'm sure we could arrange something." Replied Sally, trying her best to sound sincere.

Once Pauline had finally gone, Sally and Lizzie went back into the house. But it was Lizzie who was the most concerned about the visit.

"She's totally crazy, and I hope you're not going to take her up on the offer of tea?"

"No, of course not, I just wanted her to leave."

"Listen, Sally, you've got to call Frank and cancel tonight. You can't have a suspected wife-beater and child molester in your home."

"He's very interested in buying the house, Lizzie and I don't want to do anything to threaten that. Besides, there's always two sides to every story. I just can't believe he would do that to his own family."

"Just say you're not selling, and tell that crazy Pauline where to go. Doesn't it seem odd to you that she didn't appear to know anything about Frank buying your house? Isn't that something a husband would normally discuss with his wife?"

"Lizzie, there are times when I don't understand you. You just heard what she said about Tina. How could I possibly be rude to her, after all she's been through. Besides, I genuinely believe she feels remorse about the incident at Falcondale."

"Well, I'll let you be the judge of that. But please, look at the facts; Pauline is crazy, she proved that when she attacked Frank, and we could both see that she's still got problems. Then, to confound things, you are seeing her husband tonight. Plus, we already know Frank was a robber, rapist and all-round villain, and now we have these other atrocities which he may have committed. On top of that, we've got Tina, their daughter, who is also showing signs of being totally insane. Doesn't all that say something to you, like stay away?"

Sally looked directly at her friend and nodded.

"Yes, you're right Lizzie, I'll let Frank come over tonight, and tell him I can't see him anymore because of the circumstances. Then, I'll tell him that the house sale has to go through the proper channels."

Pauline was pleased to finally get out of Sally's home. Although, she was an alcoholic, her drinking was something she preferred to do at home, and always alone. Getting drunk in front of others, only increased her agitation and paranoia. Had she remained any longer, then it would only have been a matter of time before she reacted to Lizzie's sarcasm, and who knows what might have happened.

Mark knew she had been drinking, and chose to keep silent as he drove her back.

"You're very quiet Mark, had another row with Frank?" Asked Pauline curtly, after a few moments.

"No, Pauline. I just know better than to try and talk to you after you've been drinking. Sometimes, it's like the whole world is your enemy."

"How dare you! I'm not drunk, certainly not after a few glasses of wine. If you think that, then you don't know much about me after all these years?"

"See, that's exactly what I mean, you should listen to yourself, always paranoid and looking for a fight. Anyway, where have you been, I've never picked you up from there before?"

"I've been to visit an old friend from university. It was someone I used to hate." Replied Pauline, searching through a diary she had produced from her bag.

There was a silence as Mark tried to make sense out of Pauline's last remark.

"I don't understand, what do you mean?"

"She was Frank's girlfriend once. Until I came along." Replied Pauline, with a cold chill in her voice.

"So why go and see her, the past has gone, why re-live it? Haven't you got enough pain in your life at the moment?"

"She helped save Tina's life. That was the house where my daughter tried to kill herself. I had to see Sally again, if only just to say thanks. She's also..." Pauline stopped as her voice filled with emotion.

"She's also what?" Asked Mark.

Pauline grimaced as she compared Sally's phone number to the one she had found in Frank's pocket, and had copied into her diary.

"If you must know, she's the woman Frank is having an affair with. In fact, I think he's going around there tonight."

Mark was shocked and had to stop the car.

"Are you sure, Pauline, how do you know?"

"You know as well as I do that Frank is always seeing other women. I can't stop him, it's just something I have to live with."

"But how did you know he was seeing this Sally, then?"

"Women's intuition, and a phone call from Claire, she told me that Frank was at Swann's recently with some new tart."

Mark reached across and put his arm around Pauline, who was staring expression-less through the windscreen in front of her.

"I'm sorry, Pauline. It must have been hard for you seeing her again after all this time?"

"I wanted to confront her there and then, but she wasn't alone, her bitch friend was there too. In fact, it was Lizzie who I started to detest the most after a while."

"Pauline, please, I'm asking you again - leave Frank. Do it now, before it's too late. Putting yourself through all of this is doing you no good. I could give you and Jamie a decent life."

"What about Tina, can you give her a good life too?"

"It's too late for Tina, but you, Jamie and I could go abroad, Spain, perhaps?"

"I don't want to hear all that now, Mark. I can't even think straight at the moment."

As the car pulled up outside the house that Pauline shared with Frank, Mark looked around warily, before kissing his boss's wife affectionately on the cheek. Pauline didn't respond, and opened the door to get out. As she did so, she turned to him and said in a low, direct tone;

"Do you remember this blouse, Mark?"

He gazed at the tight-fitting garment for a few moments.

"No, why, should I remember it?"

"You see, that's what I mean. You don't know me, you don't understand me. This was the blouse I was wearing that day, surely even you can remember 'that' day, Mark?"

With that, she slammed the door hard, and walked towards the house without once looking back.

Mark shook his head and put the Ford Grenada's gear lever into drive, before speeding off down the road. He thought Pauline was being unreasonable about the blouse, it only served to highlight even more, her deteriorating mental state. If the day she was referring to was the one and only time they had slept together, how could she really expect him to recall what she was wearing over a decade earlier.

The day in question was a September afternoon back in 1972. Frank had returned home early, and was in high spirits. He had just won a new contract with a large international company that had established its main headquarters in London. It would mean a lot of work for his drivers, and the opportunity of lucrative overseas courier work. Frank was understandably excited.

He uncorked some champagne and set up the garden furniture under the canopy they had recently attached to the rear of the house. There had even been talk of a swimming pool at one stage, but Pauline never mentioned this unless Frank spoke about it first. She was happy because he was happy, and for a while they seemed the perfect couple, chatting away and giggling together out on the patio celebrating Frank's new success.

"Go and get your gear on, let's hit town!" Said Frank straight out of the blue, as he poured the last of the champagne into their glasses.

"You mean go into London, just the two of us?" Replied, Pauline beaming with excitement.

"Yes, just the two of us. It'll be fun, we can have a meal, then go on to a casino."

"But what about Tina, she'll be back soon."

"Don't worry about Tina, she's a big girl now. Just leave her a note. I'll book us a table."

"That's a good idea, Frank. Yes, Tina wont mind being on her own. Besides, there's plenty of food in the fridge."

Pauline rushed off to get changed. If she was going to a restaurant and a casino in London, she would want to look her best. After much deliberation, she opted for a black and purple silk blouse which accentuated her figure perfectly. It was one that she had recently brought, and would go well with her black skirt and platform shoes. It was while she was upstairs changing that she heard the telephone ringing. It rang for some time, before she eventually picked up the extension on Frank's bedside table, presuming him to still be out on the patio finishing his drink. However, Frank must have answered it from downstairs at the same time. Pauline listened discreetly as her husband chatted to a well-spoken woman on the other end of the line. At first she thought it was a business call, and she was about to hang up, but there was something about the over-familiarity of the conversation that aroused her suspicions, so she listened intently to the rest of Frank's phone call;

MARION: "I'm sorry, Frank. I know I shouldn't have called you at home, but I was excited. It's wonderful news isn't it?"

FRANK: "Marion, you did it, you got me the contract, I thought I'd blown my chances. I just can't believe it!"

MARION: "Well, it certainly wasn't all plain sailing, but you're right you did nearly blow it, in fact you were bloody awful at the meeting, not convincing at all. After you had left, the MD was about to go for the North London company, they had far more experience. I really had to sell him your firm, Frank. I just hope you live up to my expectations."

FRANK: "I have done so far, Marion!"

MARION: "How about meeting up tonight, Frankie boy? We could touch on a few points not covered at the meeting!"

FRANK: "If you put it like that, Marion, how can I refuse! Oddly enough, I've already booked us a table for tonight."

Pauline replaced the receiver and sat on the bed, she decided to try and keep calm, and after a short while went downstairs to see how Frank would handle things.

"Listen Pauline, something's cropped up, there's a problem with the new contract. I'm afraid we'll have to give tonight a miss."

Pauline remembered screaming at Frank. She couldn't recall quite what she said, but she certainly remembered the blows. She was lucky they weren't punches, as these probably would have killed her, coming from such a powerful man. Frank used his open hands to beat her viciously about the head and body. As Pauline slumped to the floor, he slammed his knee hard into her face with terrifying effect. She fell back heavily, her head swimming and her nose gushing blood.

After he had got bored with the assault, he went over to the cocktail cabinet. Pauline saw her opportunity and took it. She hauled herself up, and grabbing her handbag, ran to the front door and fled out into the street.

Making sure he wasn't coming after her, Pauline made her way to a telephone kiosk at the top of the road. Delving into her bag, she found some tissues to soak up the blood that was still streaming down her face. She waited a few moments before she felt calm enough to press a coin into the slot and speak to someone at the mini-cab office.

Fortunately, the small vanity mirror situated inside the kiosk hadn't been vandalised, and she was able to do a quick clean up job on her face as she waited for her cab.

The car was there within minutes, and Pauline was pleased to see that Mark was the driver. He looked horrified as she got into the car beside him.

"Pauline, what the hell has happened to you, are you alright?"

"Yes, I think so, Mark. Let's just get out of here in case he comes to look for me. Go to my mother's house?"

"I think I'd better take you to a hospital, Pauline."

"No, Mark, nothing's broken, just put your foot down."

He nodded and muttered something derogatory about Frank, before obeying Pauline's instructions and setting off to drive her to her parent's home.

As they neared their destination, Pauline suddenly ordered Mark to stop the car.

"What is it, what's the matter?" He asked, braking abruptly.

"I can't let my parent's see me like this. Oh, I don't know, just drive around for a while, I don't care." She blurted out, close to tears.

"Look, I'm taking you to my place," replied Mark decisively. "You can have a nice long bath and time to think. If we hurry, we might even be able to save your expensive blouse."

Ignoring Pauline's objections, he turned the '69 Vauxhall Victor around, and headed of in the direction of his own home.

What happened at Mark's home was a combination of several things. Mark has never made a secret of his feelings for his boss's wife, and like now, always seemed to be on hand when things went wrong for her. As for Frank, Mark did admire his business acumen, but this however was in direct contrast to his feelings for him as a husband to Pauline. Although, he was never in awe of Frank, deep down, Mark knew that the day of reckoning had already appeared on the horizon.

Pauline on the other hand needed to be loved, right there and then. For a few hours she allowed herself to despise Frank and all that he stood for. To her, this was her vengeance, just like when she humiliated him at the Christmas Dance when they were students, like when she allowed herself to be seduced by Claire and Yvette. On this occasion, what happened between her and Mark would remain their secret, a secret, until Pauline decides that it should stay that way no longer.

Her mind, already troubled by Frank's betrayal and the savage beating she had taken was made worse by the alcohol she had consumed, and of course by Mark's subtle advances.

They only made love once, and on that September night, Jamie was conceived. Pauline quickly had to find an opportunity to sleep with Frank to avoid any suspicions regarding her pregnancy. It was later automatically assumed by both men that Frank was the rightful father of the child.

Now, having reached home after her visit to see Sally, Pauline was beginning to re-consider Mark's approaches in a different light. Perhaps, it was getting near the time to relinquish her secret after all.

23. THE SINGING BAMBOO

It was only a five minute walk to Westminster Cathedral from Empire House, the nurses' home where Laura lived. At first she was rather pleased about this as it meant she would have that much more time to get ready and wouldn't have to rush in order to meet Nick. That was the theory behind it anyway, but of course Laura ended up rushing.

She had a good-size room with an impressive view over Vincent Square, but she had been fortunate to have acquired the room in the first place. Initially, when she had started her training, Laura had been housed along with the rest of her group at Queen Mary's Nurses' Home. This was mainly for the younger, first-year students, and was thought to be more of an open prison than an accommodation block. It was located immediately behind Westminster Hospital, over-looking a pretty rectangular flower garden. The main entrance to QM, as it was known was manned by porters on a twenty-four hour basis, and Miss Sharp, the Home Warden, a stern lady in her mid fifties, always kept a tight rein on any nocturnal activities.

During their second year, the vast majority of the students were desperate to escape from Miss Sharp's oppressive regime, and either moved out to less stricter homes, or if they could afford it, moved into private flat shares. For Laura, it had been a case of being in the right place at the right time. A friend had told her that a room had just become available in one of the highly sought-after buildings around Vincent Square. She immediately contacted the accommodation officer, only to be told that the room had already gone. Dismayed, Laura returned to QM and put the matter out of her mind. However, two weeks later she received an unexpected letter in the internal post telling her to call the accommodation office as soon as possible. It was then that she learnt that the other girl had caused a disturbance, what with late-night parties and entertaining men in her room, and was asked to vacate forthwith. Laura couldn't believe her luck when she finally got to see the room, and accepted it immediately after promising there wouldn't be a repeat of the last person's antics. It suited her to stay there for the time being, after all, it was right in the centre of London, close to work, and the rules were lapse, provided a little discretion was used. Besides, several of Laura's friends had in the past, given up the security of the nurses' home for rented accommodation, only to find they couldn't afford it and had to ask for their rooms back again.

It was a clear, pleasant evening with just a hint of a cool breeze in the air. Laura checked her watch, and immediately quickened her pace. She was only a few minutes late, but didn't want Nick to leave and think she had stood him up. She eventually reached the top of Thirlby Road, but instead of turning left into Ashley Place, which would have led her straight to the cathedral, she hesitated a little and continued along Victoria Street. She felt slightly nervous, and began to think about her mother, as if to take her mind off her impending date. However, she couldn't help smiling as it seemed they were both having dates as it were on the same night. More absurd was the fact that a similar arrangement had happened a couple of weeks earlier. Laura quickly stopped the more unpleasant aspects of that evening from entering her train of thought. She began to wonder where Nick would take her, and what they would talk about, but above all she found herself pondering over whether she was doing the right thing in view of Tina. There were several places locally they could go, if he was only planning to take her for a drink. However, she had decided to go out on an empty stomach, just in case they did end up going for a meal after all. Laura wasn't due back on duty until the following afternoon, so at least she could relax, have a couple of drinks and just try to enjoy herself, after all, she deserved it, as Nick had pointed out.

Laura had deliberately dressed down. She was wearing a faded denim shirt tucked into a pair of equally faded tight jeans, and over her arm she carried a short jacket in case it turned chilly. Her mother had told her a long time ago that she must never expect her boyfriends to be loaded with money and to pay for everything. One sure method of avoiding unnecessary embarrassment by going to a restaurant that was too expensive was to dress down and just plead ignorance.

Laura felt her heart beat faster and deliberately slowed her pace as she neared the meeting place. Her earlier nerves had returned, and she delved into her bag for some chewing gum. She heard a group of people coming up behind her, and the sound of male laughter. Instinctively she moved over to one side to allow them to pass.

"Hello, gorgeous - you've got a lovely arse!" Shouted one of the group. Another one stopped and uttered something obscene. Laura thought he was going to approach her, but the young man seemed to hesitate and lose his nerve as the others got further away. She breathed a sigh of relief once they were out of sight, and veered left as the cathedral came into view. She could do nothing to prevent herself from feeling slightly flattered, even though the compliments were a little on the crude side. Outside the cathedral, there were several people milling around, obviously meeting others just as Laura was. She scanned the figures through the fading light, but it was Nick who saw her first. He waved and came towards her. She was pleased to see that he too was dressed casually in fawn-coloured chino's and a baggy jumper. Laura was also relieved to see he wasn't wearing his jumper tucked into his trousers, which was becoming the trend during those days.

"Laura, you made it!" He said, looking more than a little surprised.

"Of course. Why, did you think I'd stand you up then?"

"Well, I wasn't sure," he replied awkwardly.

"I always keep promises. Besides, it was me who rang you, remember!"

"I'm glad you did, Laura. Are you hungry?"

"I could be tempted by a morsel, but it depends on what you've got in mind. I'm not dressed to go to Buckingham Palace!"

"Let's go and have a drink first," he laughed.

They walked along Victoria Street and crossed over to go into the Duke Of York pub. It was busy inside, but they managed to find an empty table, where Laura sat as Nick went to the bar to get the drinks. During the short time since they had met, an invisible barrier seemed to have gone up between them. Nick wasn't sure if it was due to shyness with it being their first date, or if it was due to other reasons, like him being married, or the Tina incident. These were bound to make the situation awkward.

"Have you been in here before, Laura?" He asked, after a few moments of silence.

"Yes, a few times, but just passing through - you know, girls' nights out, that sort of thing."

He nodded and took a sip from his beer, but it was Nick who had to initiate most of the conversation. It wasn't that Laura was shy in any way, she was merely testing the water and tactfully trying to remain a little reserved. The talk at first was predictably superficial, with Nick inquiring about her family, and why she had chosen to go into nursing. They were both consciously trying to avoid certain subjects like, Nick's marriage and Laura's friendship with Tina.

They finished their drinks perhaps a bit too quickly, making Nick have to return to the bar once again. Laura felt uncomfortable sitting alone at the table in such a crowded pub. Nick seemed to be taking forever, and now the pretty blonde was getting some unwanted attention from one or two of the other customers. A few feet from where she was sitting, Laura noticed a wall-mounted jukebox, and decided to put some music on. She selected a couple of records, and had one selection remaining, however, she couldn't make up her mind to go for *'Atomic',* by Blondie, or Spandau Ballet's *'True'.* So in the end, she put more money in and picked them both.

Nick returned, put the drinks on the table and went to stand behind her. He couldn't resist letting his eyes wander up and down her shapely figure, as she stood with her back towards him, clad in skin-tight blue jeans.

"What music do you like, Nick?" She asked, turning unexpectedly, and catching him leering at her bottom.

"Oh, I'm not really that fussy," he babbled back, looking embarrassed.

"Come on, there's still another two selections - you choose."

He moved in closer behind her, deeply inhaling her rich, heady scent and glorious, lush hair. He was tempted to place his arm around Laura's waist, but resisted, even though she may not have objected, he realised he still had some way to go.

"I've booked us a table at the Singing Bamboo, do you know it?" Asked Nick, as they sat back down, and moved a little closer to each other.

"Isn't that the one near the Devonshire Arms?"

"Yes, that's right, but there's no hurry, we can go by taxi."

It was fortunate that Nick had taken the trouble to book a table. The restaurant was popular at the best of times, and it happened to be exceptionally busy that evening. They passed at least a dozen people waiting on the stairs and in the lobby, hoping to get in.

The waiter led them over to a table, which overlooked the street below. The Singing Bamboo was somewhere Laura had wanted to go since she first started her secondment at St. Mary Abbot's. Indeed, when she came off duty after a late shift and went out to catch the coach back to Westminster, she would always look up at the restaurant's softly lit windows and wonder what it would be like to go inside. One girl in Laura's group had actually been there and was still raving about it.

It was very unique inside with beautiful, exotic plants bordering the tables to give a certain degree of privacy. Huge murals adorned the walls and delicate-looking Chinese lanterns gave the restaurant its distinctive, inviting reddish glow.

Laura was very excited and gazed about her, taking in the wonderful decor, and soaking up the rich atmosphere, with all its hustle and bustle. Nick was delighted his partner was so impressed with the eatery he had chosen for her.

As the powerful limousine slowly glided into Sally's drive, Frank glanced at the interior clock, it was a little after 8pm.

He alighted from the car, bringing with him a bottle of expensive champagne. The earlier incident at Albert's hadn't affected his mood in the slightest. In fact, he felt rather satisfied with himself. The only drawback Frank had was a dull, aching pain in his left shoulder, where the old man had caught him with his walking stick. Frank even admired Albert's audacity, as he briefly mulled over the events in his mind. At least, the old bugger hadn't got him on the other shoulder, for that could have had a serious effect on his drinking arm. Frank rang the doorbell, unbeknown to him that his wife, Pauline had visited earlier that day.

He heard the familiar sound of Pepys' bark and cleared his throat as Sally opened the front door.

After exchanging pleasantries, she invited him inside, and led him through to the large kitchen area, that doubled as a living room. Sally looked stunning in a short, clingy, black dress, and Frank was immediately aware that she wasn't wearing a bra.

Without asking he went straight over to the freezer, and pushed some of Sally's frozen goods to one side in order to make space for the champagne. He carried out this exercise in a tender and loving manner, as if he were tucking up a small child into bed.

"I see you've come prepared Frank," said Sally jokingly. "I didn't realise you had such a fondness for champagne, I've got some in the fridge, and what's more - it's chilled!"

"But is it a decent brand?" He replied icily. "I only drink the best."

Sally's champagne wasn't Dom Perignon, like Frank had brought, but all the same it was still good quality. She felt rather annoyed by Frank's remark, but let the comment pass, thinking that perhaps it was just his way of having a joke.

"Well, fussy, let's have a glass of wine instead!" With that, Sally poured them both a glass of the Chablis Lizzie had brought over that afternoon.

Frank finished his drink almost immediately, and reached for the bottle to help himself. Sally declined a refill, she was more interested in finding out a bit more about him and if there was any truth in Tina's disclosure, about him sexually assaulting her. However, it was a very sensitive subject and she needed to proceed with caution.

She asked Frank more about his work, owning a successful mini-cab business, along with a Mayfair nightclub. He seemed happy enough to tell her about the day-to-day running of the business, but wasn't so forthcoming about the club. She eased off a bit, and once she had things under control in the kitchen, she manoeuvred Frank into the lounge. Although he was quite entertaining in his own, often crude way, she began after a short while to find his presence a little oppressive.

"I can't help noticing you seem more interested in your transport business, Frank?"

"Yes, I built it up from scratch into a multi-million pound empire. It's my baby." He replied, proudly. The club doesn't bring in as much income as you would expect. There's lots of overheads, insurance, costly repairs, staff to keep happy, licensing rules, fire regulations, the list goes on. I've had to carry out extensive rebuilding work since I took it over, and to be honest, if the right offer came in, I'd sell it straight away."

"Well, I must say it all sounds very glamorous."

"Yes, possibly, but I don't even think about that now, it just comes with the territory."

There was a lull in the conversation, and Sally decided this was a good a time as any.

"Pauline was here today, Frank."

The effect was immediate. It takes a lot to shock Frank, but Sally's chosen words hit their target with devastating accuracy.

"Pauline? But, what do you mean, I don't understand?" He gasped, jaw dropping.

"Why on earth didn't you tell me you married her and that Tina was your daughter?"

Frank put his glass down gently, and sat back on the sofa. He was well used to being in uncomfortable situations, and was an expert at bluffing his way out of them.

"Sally, please listen to me. I had my reasons," he replied, staring directly at her. "So how was she, drunk I imagine?"

"Well, she wasn't when she arrived, but yes, I suppose she was quite drunk by the time she left. But, I have to say, it was rather an emotional occasion for her, as it was for myself and Lizzie."

"So why was she here, was it about me?" Frank asked defensively.

"No, it wasn't actually. She was here because she wanted to thank me for helping your daughter. Tina tried to kill herself here, Frank, while you were sitting downstairs. Did you know that?"

"No, I didn't know it was here at your house, Sally. I'm grateful for all you did to help her." He replied, unconvincingly

"It wasn't just me. In fact, my daughter, Laura did more to help, and of course, my son, Jonathan has been visiting Tina in hospital."

"You have a wonderful family Sally. You must be very proud of them?"

"Frank, please, I went out on a date with you, after you had told me you were separated from your wife." Remarked Sally, in a heated tone. "You put me in a very awkward and compromising situation, which I'm not happy about. I think you owe me an explanation."

Frank sighed and finished his wine, before pouring the remainder of the Chablis into his glass. He then unloosened his tie and sat forward.

"Sally, listen to me. Pauline is very sick. She has mental health problems, which she has passed onto Tina. I try my very best with her, but every day is a challenge. Surely you must have noticed there was something troubling about her?"

Sally hesitated, and took a sip of her wine, unsure that you could simply just pass on mental health problems like you could a cold.

"Yes, I suppose she did seem odd, but I just put that down to nerves. So what is your relationship with her now?"

Frank was getting increasingly uncomfortable with Sally's questions.

"I have to endure a lot with Pauline. I even married her when I found out she was pregnant with Tina." He replied warily, before realising that he could yet turn this to his advantage. However, he had to be careful not to say anything about being forced by his father to marry Pauline or be ostracized by his family and cut off financially.

"That was an honourable thing to do, Frank." Remarked, Sally softening her stance.

"It was the very least I could do. You see, it was never rape. Pauline and I made love, that's all. We were both drunk, but I wanted you, and you stood me up, Sally - remember?"

"Please don't go there Frank." Begged Sally, feeling herself becoming emotional. "So do you both live as husband and wife?"

"We share the same house, but I sleep in another room. You see, several years ago, Pauline had an affair, it was with another woman."

"I don't believe you. Pauline said she loved you."

"What Pauline says and does are two different things. She had an affair with the owner of the night club I took over. At the time, Claire was Pauline's boss. In fact, I believe you met her at Swann's, when we went out."

"Oh my god," gasped Sally. "So Claire must have thought you were cheating on Pauline?"

"Yes, I suppose so. I was very hurt at the time, but I forgave Pauline and stuck by her when Claire sold out and just dumped her."

"I'm sorry, Frank, I didn't know."

"Pauline is also an alcoholic, and I suspect she may be having an affair with one of my senior drivers."

"Frank, that's terrible. But why have you never left her?"

"I've tried in the past, but she threatens suicide. I stay purely for Tina and my son, Jamie."

"I have something to ask you, Frank." Continued Sally, drawing in her breath. "It's something that's been playing on my mind."

Frank was calm and relaxed now. He was in control and was successfully trashing Pauline while making himself look like he was the victim.

"Ask me anything, Sally. I've got no secrets, especially from you."

Sally again hesitated, and finished her wine, before summoning up the courage to stare Frank fully in the eye.

"I can never forget the night Tina was here. In fact it was the one of the worst of my life. I can't even bear to think about it."

"Sally, don't torture yourself. You helped save my daughter's life. If it wasn't for you..."

"Frank, please listen to what I have to say." Interrupted Sally, "Tina said she tried to kill herself because of what you did to her." Her words hit Frank like sharpened arrows. "She told Laura that you abused her, that you sexually assaulted your own daughter. Please tell me that's not true, you are her father."

Frank bided his time, thinking over how he could give her an adequate answer. He glanced down, noticing a few specks of Albert's blood still on his shoes. Sally spoke again.

"Frank, are you alright? Look at me, tell me the truth."

Frank didn't quite know how he did it, but his eyes began to water just at the right time. He now looked up to face Sally.

"Look, I know I've never been an angel, but I really have changed now. I would never hurt a fly. I'm just a family man who has suffered. Pauline has poisoned my own daughter against me. It's a cross I've had to bear for years now. I've done my very best for both of them, but they need help and just treat me with contempt."

"So you didn't touch her?"

"No Sally, of course I didn't," he lied.

She went over and sat next to him on the sofa.

"I'm sorry I doubted you Frank."

"It's alright, thank-you for being a friend. It's so nice to have someone on my side rather than against me."

"Oh my god!" Shrieked Sally, jumping to her feet. "I think I may have left the cooker on, something's burning!" As she rushed off into the kitchen, Frank calmly reached into his pocket, pulled out a cigar and sat back to light it up. He smiled contently as he rolled the smoke around in his mouth. Life was looking good.

A few minutes later Sally served up the first course. She went into the lounge to find Frank going through her record collection. It annoyed her slightly, like the champagne in the freezer incident. All he need do was ask. Among the collection were several records she had enjoyed listening to with William, and these held special memories for her.

"So you're a bit of an Elvis fan are you, Sally? I would never have guessed."

"They belonged to my husband. I prefer listening to classical music personally. Would you like to listen to some while we eat?"

To Sally's relief, Frank didn't pursue the matter regarding William, and they ate their starter to the sound of Beethoven's *'Violin Sonatas'*. Sally knew he hated it, but she was determined to force just a smattering of culture into Frank's boorish life.

Returning to the kitchen, she wasn't surprised to hear that Frank had changed Beethoven to the Rolling Stones. Educating him may take longer than she first anticipated, she surmised. But it didn't really matter, as she had no intention of seeing him again. She naively believed the story he had spun her, but she didn't want to get involved, she would just stick to the job in hand, which was getting Frank to buy the house.

The garlic mushrooms were smelling divine, the French fries, petit pois and grilled tomatoes were practically done, and now there was only the fillet steak left to cook.

The tender meat sizzled as soon as it hit the hot grill pan. Timing was crucial, as Frank insisted that his steaks were always rare. The mere sight of the blood was enough to put Sally off, and it made her wonder how anyone could ever eat their food so raw. She was concentrating so hard that she had no idea Frank was standing directly behind her as she went about her work. It was only when he placed his hands on her hips, causing her to nearly jump out of her skin that she became aware of his presence.

"Hey, easy now, you're jumpy tonight!"

Sally froze for a moment, before instinctively stepping to the side, and pushing away a lock of hair from her eyes. No man had ever touched her in that manner since her husband, William.

"I'm sorry, Frank, you startled me. Were you getting lonely in the lounge all by yourself?"

"Well, yes, that's right. In fact, I came out to get a re-fill. The Dom Perignon must be cold enough by now?"

"Frank, please don't open your champagne on my account, I'm not much of a drinker, so it would be a waste. I still have plenty of wine already chilled."

She wasn't sure if he simply didn't hear her, or whether he was just being bloody-minded, but whatever, he took the bottle from the freezer and proceeded to uncork it. He then casually walked over to the cabinet and took out two of Sally's best crystal glasses, and filled them to the top.

"Here, let's have a toast!"

"No, Frank, not for me, I've had enough." Was her cautious reply, as she quickly turned the peas off.

Putting the glasses back down, he again placed his hands on Sally's hips, only this time facing her.

"You look absolutely beautiful tonight Sally, I mean it. You are stunning, simply sensational."

She gazed into his familiar light blue eyes and began to giggle.

"You haven't changed from the Frank of old have you?"

He laughed, and drew her closer towards him.

"Look, I'm sorry about prying into your record collection, I didn't mean to upset you."

She pulled away from him.

"So you noticed I was upset then? It's okay, I forgive you."

"I notice everything about you, Sally, your moods, your appearance, your smile, your laugh. I have never forgotten you, or got over you for that matter." He offered her the glass once more. "Here, have some, it's the best."

"No, Frank, I'd better not, otherwise you'll end up having to do the cooking by yourself."

"Well, if you don't want to celebrate me buying your house, then I'll have to celebrate alone."

Sally looked amazed and gave him her full attention.

"Really, Frank - do you mean it, you're actually going to buy this house?"

"That's what I said, here take this." After successfully getting her to take the champagne, he calmly took a seat at the table, with Sally desperate to join him.

"This is fantastic news, I was starting to wonder."

"That's the trouble with you women, you're too impatient," he replied smugly. "I concluded a transaction a little earlier today. It was very much to my advantage, and I expect to reap the benefits in the very near future, so yes, buying your house is now a reality."

"That's very impressive, Frank," she exclaimed, quite in awe of her guest's business prowess.

"So, to the house then!" Laughed Frank, raising his glass to clink it with hers.

He insisted she finish her drink, and subsequently re-filled both glasses. By this time he had noticed that Sally's eyes were distinctly starting to glaze over.

He went on to tell her he had been in contact with his solicitors and had given them instructions to begin the purchase process. Sally certainly hadn't been expecting this news so soon, but deep down she felt her heart sinking.

The first course was absolutely delicious. Laura, had eaten Chinese food on countless occasions before. But this, she discovered was a totally different experience altogether.

"I believe they specialise in the 'Peking' style of cuisine, it's much nicer than Cantonese." Said Nick, as he helped himself to another crispy wan-ton.

In all, there were seven courses, but even by the third, the crispy aromatic duck, Laura was feeling quite full. She had loved the evening so far, and didn't want it to end. Nick was excellent company and she soon found herself growing rather fond of him.

As the waiter came over, Laura was laughing and trying unsuccessfully to feed Nick with chopsticks. They quickly re-gained their composure and Nick ordered another bottle of rose wine, along with their desserts.

Nick found it quite arousing to see Laura tipsy and losing her inhibitions. He was now seeing another side to her, a side that was liberated, carefree and perhaps, a little wild.

Laura wasn't enjoying her lychees, so Nick asked her if she wanted to share his dessert instead. Now, it was his turn to feed her. There was a definite stirring in his loins as he reached over with a spoonful of vanilla ice-cream, only to drop some down the front of her shirt. She let out a sexy squeal, and undid one of her buttons as she picked up a serviette and dabbed the sticky mess from the top of her bra.

Nick was immediately apologising and offering his help, but he couldn't help glancing down at her pert breasts and shapely thighs. Laura looked up, and for a moment their eyes locked together and seemed to speak their own language.

The waiter returned to clear the table and inquired if they wanted coffee. Again, Nick and Laura's eyes met, searching for signs, meanings, a signal to go a stage further. It was Laura who spoke first.

"You can always come back to the nurses' home for a coffee?"

Nick gulped, and seemed a little taken aback.

"Yes, I'd like that," he replied. "Are you sure it's okay, what about the home warden?"

"She finishes at five o'clock." Smiled Laura, finishing her wine. "It's just the porters to get past!"

It was the telephone ringing that finally interrupted Frank's drawn-out tirade about all the magical things he was going to do to improve Sally's home once he'd brought it. The telephone was situated in the hallway, and Frank could just about make out what the conversation was about. He knew Sally had a daughter who was a nurse, and then there was the layabout son, but judging by the tone of Sally's voice, and what she was saying, he presumed she must have been talking to her youngest daughter. This was later confirmed when he heard Penny's name being mentioned. Frank, again topped up the glasses, as he listened to Sally telling her daughter to be careful, and not to be too late coming back the next morning. He smiled as he heard Sally telling Penny how nice he was and what a wonderful evening she was having. But more importantly, he was relieved to hear Sally saying that he was entirely innocent of assaulting Tina. So obviously, the whole family must be aware of Tina's disclosure, he assumed. However, nothing was said of the proposed purchase of the house.

As Frank craned his neck by the doorway, the distinct smell of burning again wafted in from the kitchen. It wasn't long before Sally noticed it too and quickly had to end her conversation with Penny. He grinned as he heard Sally rush into the kitchen and mutter some unexpected expletives after discovering she had burnt the steak to a cinder. She sighed deeply as she turned off both the oven and the grill pan, and sat down on a stool clutching her head in her hands.

"Look, Sally, it's really not a problem. That's why I always have my steak in a restaurant, they usually get it perfect. Cooking steak at home doesn't normally work."

"Oh, Frank, but your last steak was ruined when we went to Swann's. That was my fault too."

"Don't worry. Honestly, I'm having a wonderful time, just being here with you is enough."

"Frank, you're so understanding. I'm really sorry about tonight."

"Hey, stop being so silly. We could always get a takeaway?"

Sally studied the Indian menu she found in the kitchen drawer and finally made her selection.

"But, Frank, it shouldn't come to this. I feel like an absolute failure. First I get drunk, now I've ruined your supper. I just feel so awful."

He put his arms around her and held her tightly. Her yielding, feminine body felt good, as he gently ran his hands down along her waist and over the contours of her hips. Either, she didn't notice, or didn't mind when his hands then slid further and began to caress her buttocks.

Frank was gone about twenty minutes collecting the takeaway, which gave Sally the chance to feed the steak to Pepys, and touch up her make-up a little. While in the bathroom she thought about him, and although she hated to admit it, she had rather enjoyed the sheer closeness of his masculine body pushing up hard against her own.

Frank's vindaloo made Sally's vegetable biriani seem quite tame in comparison, and she had to keep taking sips of champagne to cool her mouth after being foolish enough to try some. Although she did enjoy curry, it wasn't something she would eat on a regular basis, probably due to the high calorie content. Tonight's meal however, was exceptional, and soon her mood began to lift.

Frank's humour was extremely blue, as he told her of some of his mini-cab driving exploits, before going on to share with her, a few of his vast repertoire of dirty jokes. On a couple of occasions, Sally found herself laughing quite uncontrollably, which was very odd for her.

"I'm sorry, Frank, I don't know what's got into me. I don't usually make a fool of myself like this?"

He grinned, and poured out even more champagne, knowing full well it was the cannabis resin he had managed to sprinkle over her food that had got into her.

"I'm pleased to see you're enjoying yourself, Sally. It's just what you needed. I think it's what we both needed."

They continued sitting at the table being absolutely silly for a little longer, until Sally felt she was about to pass out. Frank immediately went to her assistance, scooped her up in his arms and carried her over to the sofa. She was limp to hold, and the thought of having such a helpless, submissive woman at his mercy made him grow excited. His plan had worked perfectly, as it usually did. He knew she might be sick, many were who weren't used to cannabis and drink combined. But, he was determined to have her that night, whatever the consequences.

Nick felt distinctly uncomfortable being smuggled into the nurses' home by Laura, even though he probably wasn't the only unauthorised guest that night.

Although Laura had made her room look as nice as she probably could, it was still very basic. The walls were painted a uniform magnolia, but most of this was covered by her extensive collection of photos, prints and posters. Over to one side, and pushed up against the wall was a single bed. At the end of this, stood a small sink with a couple of shelves either side. These were completely full of Laura's wide array of shampoo's, moisturisers and perfumes. Opposite was a desk-come dressing table with a portable black and white television and hi-fi taking up practically all of the space on top. An armchair draped with a nursing uniform sat in the corner of the room, next to a plain and uninspiring wardrobe.

Nick gazed out over Vincent Square, illuminated by streetlights, while Laura put on a Roxy Music album. Like most of the other residents in the building, she had a tiny refrigerator next to her bed, which doubled up as a handy bedside table. From this, Laura produced an already-open bottle of white wine and poured them both a drink.

Thinking it inappropriate, Nick chose not to sit on the bed, but instead perched on the edge of the armchair. She apologised and removed her uniform from the chair, dropping a bra down onto Nick's lap by mistake. Giggling with embarrassment, she then threw the garments into the wardrobe, before sitting on the bed opposite him, holding her drink.

As Sally lay motionless on the sofa, Frank put on a Diana Ross album. He recalled Sally playing this when he was there before - the time he was so rudely interrupted by his daughter's hysterical antics.

"Sally, come on now, you're not being a very good hostess are you, falling asleep in front of your guest like this."

"Frank, I can't move, my head is spinning. I feel really weird," gasped Sally, trying to force her eyes open.

"Well, if you're in no fit state to entertain me, then I'll have to do it myself." He replied with a hint of menace in his voice.

Sally tried to stir, but her limbs failed her and she just rolled over onto her side.

"I'm sorry, Frank," she murmured incoherently. "I just want to sleep."

"You've been a very naughty girl, Sally. You've misbehaved, and for that, you'll have to go to bed early."

Frank began to run his fingers through her tousled hair, and moved his face closer to hers. Kissing her lightly on the cheek, he ran his arm beneath her and reached across to grasp her shoulder. He then kissed her passionately on the lips. Initially, there was no response, but Frank didn't mind this, and even expected it.

After a few moments, Sally opened her eyes wide, and stared at him blankly. She pulled away from him, gasping for breath. Frank however, was back kissing her almost immediately, only this time, Sally had reached up to put her arms around him, and returned his kiss with equal passion. This was all Frank needed, it was the green light he'd been waiting for.

Once more, he scooped her up in his arms, and leaving the record to play itself out, carried her upstairs and into her bedroom.

He staggered a little as he banged her head against the wall, while attempting to lay her limp body on the bed. Sally groaned, but offered no resistance as he pulled off her one remaining shoe, and flipped her over onto her stomach. He then turned his attention to the zip at the back of her dress.

His fingers worked clumsily, but gradually he peeled the garment away. He pulled each of her arms out of the sleeves, and slowly eased the dress down past her hips and thighs. Sally only had her black knickers left to cover her modesty, but these too were soon yanked off, to leave her naked and at his mercy. He belched loudly, and threw her clothes into the corner of the room. Leering at her nudity, he started to remove his own clothes, slowly at first, then quicker, as his breathing became heavier. When he was ready, he crept onto the bed, inching closer and closer, never taking his eyes off her.

He ran his hands down the length of her body. There was no response, so he turned her over, and gazed at her full breasts, before mauling them and running his tongue hungrily across her nipples.

He then pushed his hand down, and placed it roughly between her legs. She had a beautiful, dark blonde, silky mound, trimmed to a neat triangle. With a piston-like motion, he began to work his fingers inside her. She was damp, but not damp enough, which annoyed him. But he persisted until he managed to get all four fingers deep within her. She stirred and groaned a few times, but didn't make things easy for him. He continued for a little longer, only stopping when she finally clamped her legs firmly shut.

"No, please, not now, I can't..." She muttered sleepily, before rolling onto her side.

Frank reared up on his knees, his eyes blazing with fury, as he glared down at the sleeping woman lying before him.

"I'll teach you to go to sleep on me, you fucking bitch!" He cursed under his breath. He then pulled her back over onto her front, forcing her legs apart with his knees. He began to position himself, but as he came down to penetrate her, he felt himself shrinking. He swore, and punched the pillow violently. As with most men, this had happened before, and always after heavy drinking. He wiped beads of sweat from his brow, and lay down beside her. He would rest for a few minutes, he thought and then try again. The drink however, had taken its toll on Frank that night, for as soon as he closed his eyes, he was asleep and snoring loud enough to wake the dead.

Nick sat back on the chair and glanced around Laura's room. He was a little lost for words and was starting to feel somewhat awkward.

"I think you've done an amazing job, Laura," he said finally. "Your room has a really good feel to it."

"Well, it's just a home from home really, but I do try to make it cosy." She smiled back.

He finished his drink and sat forward on the edge of the seat.

"Nice wine, anymore left?"

"Sorry, that's it, I'm afraid. I've got a bottle of red, if you think you can manage it?"

"No, that's okay," he replied, looking anxiously at his watch. "It's getting late, perhaps I ought to go."

For a moment, he thought he detected a hint of disappointment in Laura's face, as she put her glass down and turned to look up at him.

"You don't have to rush off, Nick. I don't bite!" She suddenly heard herself blurt out.

"But don't you have to work tomorrow?"

"Well, yes I do, but that's not until the afternoon." She replied hesitantly, before adding; "You can always sleep on the floor if you want, I don't mind."

Laura produced a sleeping bag from under her bed, and gave him a pillow. She then draped a silk scarf over the bedside lamp, giving the room a dim, sensual glow. Again there was a hint of hesitancy in the air, until Nick finally took the initiative and stripped down to his boxer shorts, before climbing into the hard, chilly makeshift bed.

Laura stood in the centre of the room with her back towards him, and began to unbutton her denim shirt. This, she hung over the chair, before undoing her jeans. He watched intently as she struggled to wriggle free of them, before sliding them down to her ankles and casually kicking them off.

Nick felt himself grow hard, as his eyes followed her, tip-toeing back over towards the chair. As she lent over, his eyes darted to her breasts. They dangled enticingly, looking as if they were about to burst out of the low-cut, black bra that contained them. He drooled at the contours of her body, flicking his eyes down past her narrow waist. His gaze settled on her curvaceous bottom, before inching its way along to her firm thighs, and finally down to her exquisite long legs. He wondered how he would get through the night with her sleeping up on the bed alongside him.

With the lamp still switched on, Laura slid into bed.

"Are you still awake?"

"Yes," he replied, after a pause.

"Well, good night, Nick, and thanks again for such a wonderful evening."

"I'm glad you enjoyed it. Good night, Laura."

They both lay on their backs, staring at the ceiling, and listening to the usual laughing and door-banging that went on late into the night in establishments like these. They remained like this for several minutes, each one knowing that the other was still awake. It was Nick who spoke first.

"Laura, are you still awake?"

"Yes, I can't seem to sleep," came her hushed reply.

"It's cold down here."

There was a delay in her answer, which seemed to Nick like an eternity. Even the noise from the corridors had stopped as if in anticipation of what Laura was about to say. Her throat felt ticklish, and her heart raced, as she turned her head to where Nick was laying.

"You had better get in with me then, it'll be warmer." She whispered gently.

24. GREENFIELDS

Penny stopped and hesitated for a few moments in front of the house. It was the sight of Frank's car in the drive, and the still-drawn curtains that had set alarm bells ringing in her head.

Last night's party had been rubbish. It had been ruined by a gang of youths who had gate-crashed. Because of this, Penny has left earlier than expected, but she had enjoyed staying over at her friend's house, so the evening wasn't entirely a disaster. She looked at the positive side of things. At least nothing had gone wrong, and her mother would have no reason not to allow her to stay over at a friend's house in the future.

She let herself in quietly, but was surprised that Pepys didn't make his usual fuss whenever someone came home. Immediately, her nostrils were assaulted by the smell of stale nicotine, and last night's curry. Going into the kitchen to make a drink, she saw the remnants of the meal her mother had tried so hard to cook. Glancing over to the table, she saw a couple of empty wine bottles, a dirty-looking ashtray, laden with cigar butts. A champagne bottle was laying inelegantly on the floor, amid the crumbs of a broken poppadom. Down where Pepys's food and water bowls were kept she noticed one of her mother's best china plates. Left-over curry had dripped over the side, making an ugly, brown stain on the expensive tiled floor. Obviously, Pepys hadn't been too impressed with the offerings given him.

The annoying, repetitious sound of a record stuck on a turntable distracted her, and prompted her to go to its aid. The lounge was in a similar condition. Fast food containers and grains of pilar rice littered the once-proud mahogany coffee table, and a cigar had burnt itself out on the mantelpiece. Picking up one of her mother's shoes, Penny began to make her way upstairs, with Pepys following close behind.

The landing creaked out a warning as she reached Sally's closed door. There was snoring, but it wasn't her mother's. Penny tapped lightly at the door, while Pepys rose up on his hind legs and waited expectantly. There was no reply, so Penny opened the door and followed the little dog inside. She smelt the familiar, vile aftershave lotion, and thought for a moment she preferred the smell of stale curry.

It wasn't like her mother to sleep in for this long. Through the semi-darkness, Penny made out two shapes in the bed. Sally was in a foetal position, with her back towards the huge figure of a man, who she assumed was the owner of the car outside.

"Mum, Mum, wake up! Can you hear me?"

Sally could only groan and bury her head back in the pillow. Frank, however, sat up and stared straight at Penny, as if defying her to shout again. The young girl ran around the bed to her mother's side and began to shake her violently.

"Mum, Mum, please wake up," pleaded Penny, becoming anxious.

Eventually, Sally forced her eyes open, and eased herself up. Realising she was naked, she grabbed the sheet and hoisted it up to cover herself.

"Please, Penny - there's no need to shout like that, I've got such a headache."

"I'm not surprised!" Screamed Penny, hysterically. "How could you do it, and in the same bed you shared with Dad?"

"Stop, please Penny - it's not what you think." Sally froze as she realised what she had just said, and turned horrified to look at Frank. Confused, she searched his eyes for answers, but found none. He smiled, and placed his arm protectively around her shoulders, before turning his attention back to Penny.

"Now you listen here young lady, where I come from behaviour like that gets a hard slap across the bottom." If Frank hadn't looked so menacing, Penny would have laughed at his words, thinking them to be a joke. "If I were you, I would apologise to your mother right now," he added, just as forcibly.

"I'll never speak to you again!" She screamed at Sally. "In fact, I never want to see you again either! I'm leaving!"

"Penny, wait, please don't go," begged Sally, in a concerned tone.

"Leave her, let her go and cool off for a while, she'll be okay." Added Frank, casually.

They heard crashing and banging from Penny's room, as she gave full vent to her anger. She emerged a few minutes later clutching a hold-all, and charged downstairs.

A bhagee thumped against Sally's bedroom door, splattering grease and slivers of onion against the pristine paintwork.

"Another thing!" Cursed Penny, fleeing from fear of retaliation, "Pepys doesn't like curry!"

"I'd better go after her," said Sally, leaping unglamorously from the bed, and pulling on her dressing gown.

"No, let me. It's just a teenage tantrum. I'll talk to her, I've got kids of my own remember. I know how to handle them." With that, Frank began to pull his clothes on, albeit in no particular hurry, and followed Sally downstairs. As he went to go past her, he noticed tears welling up in her eyes. He stopped and held her.

"Listen, nothing happened. We both had a bit too much to drink. We fooled around a little, but that was all."

She looked up at him, searching his face for any signs of doubt.

"Are you sure Frank? It's just that I can't seem to remember much about last night."

He kissed her on the forehead.

"Sally, please, what on earth must you think of me? I would never take advantage of a woman after she'd had too much to drink. Why, the very thought - it's despicable."

"I'm sorry. What an awful thing of me to suggest." She replied, before turning to face him again. "Did you remove my clothes, Frank?"

"Yes, Sally - I did. I didn't want you to be sick over them. I have seen a naked woman before you know!" He then smiled and gently squeezed her hand, before stepping out into the drizzle to find Penny.

He didn't have to search far. Just as Frank suspected, she was sitting up in the tree-house, feeling very sorry for herself.

As he pushed his large frame through the small door, Penny became quite disturbed by his presence, and shuffled further into the corner.

Frank was used to people fearing him, and he would often utilise this in order to gain a psychological hold over them. It worked well, both in his private life and in business, so there was no reason why he couldn't manipulate a fifteen-year old girl.

"Penny, listen, I know you're very upset at the moment, and the last thing you want is to talk to me."

There was no reply, so Frank moved closer, causing Penny to cringe and draw in her knees tightly.

"That's okay, Penny, if you don't want to speak, I understand. I wont come any closer, I promise."

Still no reply.

"Listen, Penny, I'm not your enemy. I just want to be your friend."

He moved even closer, making Penny respond like a trapped animal, and squeeze herself further into the corner.

"Your mother tells me you want to become a vet?"

Silence.

"I like animals too. In fact, I've got two dogs at home. Their names are Conan and Thor, and they're Bull Terriers. As long as they are handled right, they can be very affectionate. You'll have to meet them soon."

Penny continued to ignore him and began to sob.

"I don't know, you girls - always crying aren't you? Hey, I'm only joking! It's good to cry sometimes. When I was a child I did my fair share of crying. You see, I just wanted to be loved."

She still wouldn't respond, but at least the sobbing had now stopped. He glanced at his watch, before continuing. "I had nobody who really loved me. Except for Treacle that is. He was my teddy bear. I expect you've got a special teddy too, one that you love more than the others?"

Silence.

"You see, just like you, I was the youngest in my family. I was never listened to, always sent to bed early, always getting my brother's cast-offs. I was hated by my father and by my brother, Giles. My father wanted me to be just like Giles, a perfect little gentleman, someone he could be proud of. But I was a disappointment and he resented it and would ridicule and beat me for the slightest of reasons. The more I tried to be like Giles, the more I seemed to antagonise my father.

I remember one Sunday when we were having roast chicken for lunch. Our Sunday lunches were always detestable affairs, and as usual, I was the one being picked upon. When I was eventually dismissed from the table and sent to my room, I cried on my bed for ages, I wanted Treacle, but I couldn't find him. He always sat on my bed, that's where he lived. Losing him made me even more upset, and I cried harder. Then, a bit later on, Giles came into my room, he was holding Treacle. He called me a cry baby and hit me hard, before handing Treacle back. He said Treacle hated me, and was dying because I was such a horrible little boy.

In fact, that's exactly what did happen. After a day or so, Treacle really began to smell horrid, and his fur went all damp and putrid. My mother had to throw him away in the end because he stank the whole house out. Then, I found out what Giles had done to him. I was heart-broken and wouldn't eat for days."

Frank paused for a while, and fiddled with his fingers.

"Can you guess what he did, Penny?"

She tried to retain her indifference, but curiosity was getting the better of her. She chanced a half-glance at Frank.

"What did he do?" Was her barely audible whisper, as she darted her eyes away from him again.

"Giles had taken Treacle, and had slit his back open," continued Frank, also whispering. "He then took some of his stuffing out, and replaced it with the giblets from the chicken, and sewed him back up again."

Penny gulped, as she tried to imagine such a revolting scenario, and it was then that she thought she heard Frank sobbing. It was very stifled and not really much more than sniffing, but she was convinced he was actually crying.

"Yuk, that's horrible!" She said.

"It's okay, it was all a long time ago." He replied, wiping his eyes.

"It's got nothing to do with what's happened!" Called out Penny, angrily.

"That's where you're wrong. People who we love are often the first to hurt us. You mustn't blame your mother, think of all the good things she's done."

"Please go away."

"Okay, Penny, I'll go. I wanted to be your friend. Perhaps, that might still happen. You see, I'm planning on seeing a lot more of your mother, and you, of course."

"We don't want you!"

Frank reached around to his back pocket and pulled out a thick, leather wallet.

"Listen, Penny, I want you to take this money and go and buy your mother a present - not chocolates though, I don't want her getting fat. Perhaps, some nice perfume, or earrings, you must know the things she likes?"

He then put a wad of assorted notes on the floor next to her, and began to climb down from the tree-house.

Penny couldn't resist glancing at the money, she had never seen so much before, and hated herself for being tempted.

"I don't want your money. Take it away!"

Frank's head suddenly re-appeared through the door.

"Look, Penny, we will be friends. This is what friends do, they share things and make each other happy. You can always buy something for yourself with whatever's left over."

"So, that's what you do is it, buy people's friendship?"

"Never look a gift horse in the mouth, Penny. You sound like a spoilt brat, and it doesn't suit a pretty little thing like you." He muttered bitterly, as the situation began to bore him.

"Perhaps, I am!"

"Goodbye Penny. I expect you to come back inside soon." With that, he finally climbed down, then, as he started to walk towards the house, he turned and looked back towards the tree-house. "Don't forget to apologise to your mother, it's even more important than the present."

Penny heard his loud voice, but paid no attention to it, she was far too busy counting the money.

As Frank strode back into the kitchen, Sally handed him a cup of freshly-brewed coffee.

"Perhaps, I should go out there and speak to her?" She asked anxiously.

"No, I would just leave her alone right now. She'll soon come back inside, you mark my words."

"Whatever must you think of me, Frank? Whenever we've been together, there's always been some sort of drama."

"I told you last night, Sally - I think you are wonderful, and I like being with you. Plus, the body's not bad either!" He winked as he reached for his jacket.

"Frank, look I'm sorry to put a dampener on things, but what we're doing isn't right. You're married to Pauline, remember."

"Sally, I've told you, I don't sleep in the same bed as her, and as far as I'm concerned it's over between us, so stop worrying." He said, with a serious tone to his voice. "Look, I have to go. I'll ring you later, you never know, I might even have a little surprise for you!"

"Please, Frank, you've done enough. Anyway, I really don't think I deserve one."

He bent down and gave her a short, tender kiss before playfully slapping her bottom and heading for the door.

"Now, don't concern yourself about Penny, she'll come around, believe me, I know about these things."

Penny did buy something for her mother with Frank's money. She brought her two presents, both what Frank had suggested, a pair of beautiful, gold hoop earrings, and an expensive bottle of perfume. Sally, though, was more delighted to get an apology from her daughter, and the chance to explain a few important facts of life to her.

Frank was good to his word, and not only phoned, but came over again that evening. The surprise he spoke of was a weekend in Paris. Sally, of course protested.

"I can't Frank, it just wouldn't be right."

"It's exactly what you need, a couple of days away. It'll be wonderful, besides, I want to treat you to a few new outfits."

"What about Pauline, what about Penny?"

"Pauline is having an affair with Mark, one of my drivers. Don't worry about her." He then glanced over at the sulky teenager, who was sprawled out on the sofa engrossed in the TV. "I'll give Penny some money, I'm sure she could find another party to go to and someone to put her up. Or what about Lizzie? Couldn't she stay with her?"

"No, not Lizzie, please!" Came the teenager's reply. "I'll stay at a friend's, thanks, Frank!"

It seemed Frank had made a new friend after all.

It was well into August, David Owen had taken over as the leader of the SDP, and KC and The Sunshine Band was number one with *'Give it Up'*. None of it, however, meant anything to Jonathan. He had more on his mind what with Tina being transferred to Greenfields Psychiatric Hospital. He had known it was going to happen for some time, ever since Pauline had mentioned it, after they had met while visiting Tina. He had reacted by simply putting it out of his mind, and was content to believe that with his help, Tina would recover and there would no longer be a need for her to go into a secure unit.

It was probably Jonathan's fear of the unknown that disturbed him so much, and the fact that Greenfields was in deepest Sussex, which would make visiting Tina that much harder for him.

Jonathan's benevolent nature and laid-back attitude to life made it quite simple for him to make friends. These qualities had held him in good stead where Pauline was concerned, and gradually a delicate understanding began to develop between them. Despite her earlier doubts, Pauline couldn't help not liking the well-meaning young student. Jonathan was also able to make things up with Mark, who he'd mistaken for Tina's father and had attacked, only to come off second best. He was pleased the older man didn't hold any grudges towards him.

It had taken them two hours to reach the hospital. It wasn't the length of the journey that had been the problem for Jonathan, it was the atmosphere in the car. Pauline hardly said a word and just stared blankly out of the window from her seat in the back. Mark had tried to engage her in conversation, but had sensibly given up the struggle after being on the receiving end of quite an unsavoury rebuff. Jonathan had grown to like Mark. The large, bearded man, who was Frank's number two had a humorous layman's knowledge about almost every subject that mattered, and a few that didn't. Together, the two of them attempted to make the journey that much more bearable in view of the circumstances.

Greenfields was set in fifty acres of beautiful park land, and the main building was a grand Georgian structure spread over three floors. Much of it however, on closer inspection was crumbling and falling into decay. Landscaped gardens, complete with pretty flower beds and stone urns were located at the front and sides of the house, while a large, well-hidden car park was to be found at the rear. The whole complex was very impressive to look at, and seemed an ideal location for anyone out of sorts and trying to get their lives back into perspective again. The only residents to be seen were a group of youngsters kicking a football around, while being observed by bored-looking staff.

Mark parked the Granada, but chose to wait in the car as Pauline and Jonathan walked the short journey to the reception area. Jonathan couldn't help noticing Pauline's pale complexion and red, puffy eyes as she struggled to light a cigarette. He guessed she had been drinking heavily, and tried not to stare at her more than was necessary.

The receptionist asked them to sit in the lobby while she rang through to Tina's unit, and asked for a nurse to come and collect them.

"Hello, you've come to see Tina Gant have you?" Asked the young, efficient-looking male nurse.

"Yes, I'm Tina's mother, Pauline, and this is Jonathan, my daughter's boyfriend." Replied, Pauline, taking an instant dislike to the nurse.

Jonathan felt a tingle run down his spine when he heard Pauline referring to him as 'Tina's boyfriend'.

I'm delighted to meet you, my name is Angus, and I'm directly involved in Tina's day-to-day care." Said the nurse in a pleasant Scottish brogue. He then led them out of reception and into a long corridor with what looked like rooms running along either side.

"Is she alright, I mean, has Tina settled in okay?" Asked Pauline nervously.

"Well, that's something I need to speak to you about, Mrs. Gant. Let's go in here, and we can have a little chat." Angus then led them into a small, stuffy meeting room.

"Has something happened then?" Demanded Pauline.

"No, not exactly," responded Angus in a self-assured manner. "But we are extremely concerned about your daughter's safety. Enough to warrant putting a member of staff with her at all times."

"She's never had that before?"

"Believe me, Mrs. Gant, it is very necessary now. Tina will use any means and any implement available to harm herself. Although her hand is still heavily bandaged, she will try to remove it in order to inflict further damage."

"She's lucky to still have a hand, I would have thought she would have learned her lesson by now?"

"Yes, quite, but that's not all. Tina has been trying to open up her abdominal wound." Replied Angus gravely.

"It just get's worse," sighed Pauline. "Can we see her?"

"Of course you can, but the staff member will have to stay very close by."

As they got up to leave, Angus stood in front of them.

"I'm sorry, there's one other thing, I'll need to see exactly what you're bringing in for Tina."

"I thought this was a hospital, not a prison!" Uttered Pauline, abruptly.

"We're trying to keep Tina alive, and if that means searching your bags, so be it."

They were led through a maize of corridors with heavy security doors situated at each end. This was a long process, as each of these had to be opened separately from the huge bunch of keys that Angus was carrying with him. When they finally reached the corridor where Tina was housed, their hearts sank. It was dull, grey and depressing. The lack of windows only gave it an added air of oppression. Furniture, apparently confiscated from Tina's room, lined one side of the peeling, thick walls. The staff had been forced to move everything from the room for her own safety, leaving just a simple mattress on the floor.

Like the corridor, Tina's room was stark and grim. The only redeeming feature it had over the corridor, was the fact that it did have a window. However, it only looked out onto the back of the boiler house, and had been covered in perspex, making it impossible to open. There was a separate sink, shower and toilet unit in one corner, but this allowed no privacy, as the door had been removed for safety reasons.

There was a female nursing assistant present, a large, middle-aged lady with an aloof face and swollen ankles. She had been with Tina for several hours now, and was eagerly awaiting her break.

It was Pauline who went into Tina's room first, while Jonathan and the assistant waited outside, with the door open. Tina was highly agitated, and paced up and down refusing to speak.

After a few minutes of this, the nursing assistant poked her head through the doorway;

"There's a patient's lounge in the next corridor, if you want to take Tina for a cup of tea. She likes that."

Pauline stared icily at the woman, before glancing back to her daughter and the cold walls that incarcerated her.

"Yes, that's a good idea. It would make anyone go insane being stuck in here all day."

The lounge wasn't quite so depressing, just nondescript with tatty armchairs and sofa's placed around the perimeter. A table tennis table had been placed in the centre of the room. The net was worn and secured with sticky tape on one side. Its surface was chipped and stained were drinks had been spilt over it during the course of many years.

The assistant headed straight for the vending machine and dispensed herself an anaemic-looking cup of coffee, before slumping down into one of the armchairs, and lighting up a cigarette.

A thickset, violent-looking man sat two seats away from her. He was drooling at Tina, and after a short while, took his penis out and started to masturbate. Tina was unaware of the attention she was getting and simply curled herself up into a ball in another of the armchairs.

Jonathan, shocked at the man's actions, alerted the assistant, who casually glanced side-long at the patient.

"Put that bloody thing away, Eric. How many times do you have to be told!"

Eric turned towards the woman, grinning and showing a mouthful of rotting teeth.

"It's all mine you know, no cosmetic surgery down there!"

"Filthy beast! That's your next cigarette confiscated!"

Jonathan felt very depressed. At least at the general hospital, Tina seemed to be showing signs of improvement, or that's how he interpreted it. Here, Tina didn't show the slightest hint of recognition or interest in either Pauline or himself. This hurt Jonathan and made him long to be alone with her, to whisper things to her, and try again to build up her trust and their fragile relationship.

As he sat down opposite her, he noticed how much weight she had lost since the first time they had met in Laura's room several weeks ago. Although her eyes were clear, they lacked life, and her face had a gaunt, disturbed appearance about it.

He had brought her in a few cans of coke and several of the Mars bars, she seemed to like. However, the cans, along with a hairdryer and some cosmetic sprays that Pauline had brought were all taken away. He watched as Pauline half-heartedly fussed around Tina, trying in vain to get her to drink a cup of putrid vending-machine tea.

"Why wont she speak or drink anything?" Demanded Pauline.

"She will when it suits her," was the nursing assistant's curt response.

"Can't you get her to say anything? You seem to know her better than anyone else!" Replied Pauline sarcastically.

"It depends on what character she is."

"What do you mean?"

As the woman was about to explain, Angus appeared in the lounge with another man behind him.

"Brenda, I'm sorry it's taken so long," explained the Charge Nurse, walking over to her. "You can go for your break now." He then turned to Tina, "This is Alan, he's an agency nurse. We're a bit short staffed as usual. Alan will stay with you until Brenda gets back, Tina."

There was no response from Tina, so Alan went around to the side she was facing, and placed a hand on her arm, taking it upon himself to get acquainted with her.

The response was immediate. Tina wrenched her arm away, then let out an ear-piercing scream;

"Get away from me!"

Despite her abdominal wound, she leapt from the chair in one rapid movement and fled from the stranger who was invading her privacy and reminding her of the torment she had been through with her father. Rushing towards the door, she found Angus was already there and blocking her exit. She glared fiercely at him, trying to weigh up in her panic-stricken mind whether she could get past him or not.

"Tina, Tina, please stop! No-one is going to hurt you." Said Angus in a calming manner. "Even if you did get past me, there's nowhere to go, all the corridors are locked, remember."

Tina stood a mere foot away from him, her stance threatening and aggressive, but very different to the petrified creature of just a few moments ago.

"How dare you call me Tina! She's a weak-willed bitch, now get out of my way."

"Okay, Freddie, I didn't know it was you. The doors are locked, let's talk man-to-man?" Replied Angus, realising one of Tina's alter ego's had appeared.

"I'll kick them down, and you along with them, if you don't get out of my way, you stupid bastard."

"Sorry, Freddie, I have to stay put."

"In that case, there's going to be a storm."

'Freddie', Tina's alter ego, then swaggered over towards the drinks machine and began to pick up dirty cups from the tray beside it.

"Don't do it Freddie, you'll be restrained."

"Who by, You?"

Angus picked up an internal telephone which was near to where he was standing and rang the nursing office.

"Check Tina Gant's prescription card and see how much haloperidol she can have."

'Freddie' was by then hurling cups, not at any particular person, but up at the ceiling. Here, they smashed into pieces, raining down shards of china onto those below. Everyone except Angus covered their heads with their hands and literally battened down the hatches until the storm was over. Fortunately, there was only about a dozen cups on the tray at that time.

'Freddie' then flew headlong at Angus, but the experienced nurse easily prevented the patient from going anywhere by applying an effective-looking arm lock.

"You've done all you can now, Freddie. Tina is safe. Please get 'Cindy' - tell her I want to speak to her." Angus then led 'Freddie' back over to the chair and sat down alongside 'him'.

"What happened there?" Exclaimed Jonathan, to a shocked looking Pauline, as they emerged from beneath the table.

"Now, let's calm down. Everything is over and done with," said Angus in a gentle tone, as he tried to pacify Tina.

"I'll be the judge of that!" Came the sudden reply from Tina's lips. "I want to leave, I'm not a prisoner."

"Hello, Cindy, I'm glad you're here." Replied Angus, with a relieved look on his face.

Jonathan came over to Tina's side, totally bewildered by what was going on.

"Tina, listen, you have to stay here, just until you're better. I'll come and see you as much as I can, I promise."

"Who is this person, and why is he calling me Tina? My name is, Cindy'"

Jonathan's face dropped as he glanced at Angus, uncertain how to respond to this new facet of Tina's illness.

Footsteps were heard hurrying along the corridor, and seconds later Brenda appeared puffing heavily, carrying a small pot of medicine.

"Cindy, I need your help again." Said Angus to Tina's newest alter ego.

"I always try to help whenever I can. What do you want me to do?"

"I want you to take this medication, it's for Tina, she needs it."

Brenda handed over the pot, and together with Angus, watched with relief, as Tina calmly swallowed the tranquilliser.

Angus then turned to Jonathan and Pauline.

"We're taking Tina back to her room now. Would you mind returning to the meeting room, I'll join you in a few minutes."

"Will we be able to see her again before we go?" Pleaded Jonathan.

"No, it's not a good idea, she really needs to rest right now." Replied Angus, not taking his eyes off Tina.

"Well, can I leave this for her, she needs something?" Angus scrutinised the personal cassette player Jonathan produced from his jacket pocket.

"Okay, but she'll need to be supervised when she's listening to it, and I can't guarantee it wont get broken."

"Thanks, Angus, I understand. I think it'll mean a lot to her."

"Could I listen to it as well?" replied Tina in her 'Cindy' persona.

"Of course you can, my name is Jonathan, I'm Tina's boyfriend."

"Not bad, at least Tina has good taste in men!" Replied, Tina/Cindy with a mischievous grin.

"Will you tell Tina that I'm thinking of her, Cindy?"

"I think I could do that for you."

"Thank-you," smiled Jonathan.

It was over twenty minutes before Angus returned to the meeting room where Pauline and Jonathan were anxiously waiting.

"What's wrong with her, why does she keep reverting to those characters? It's so weird." Demanded Pauline, rudely.

"Mrs. Gant, it wont help if you let yourself get worked up. Please put those cigarettes away, you can't smoke in here."

"You think you're so bloody important don't you? Well, you're a bloody fascist!"

"Mrs. Gant, I think you've been drinking, and if you attempt to light that cigarette, I'll have you forcibly removed from the hospital. Now, do you want to discuss your daughter's welfare or am I simply wasting my time?"

Pauline glared in complete silence while Angus sighed and gazed out of the window for what seemed an eternity.

"I'm sorry, I've been under a lot of pressure lately. Will you please continue." She said, finally.

"Thank-you, Mrs. Gant. You must remember that Tina has only been with us a short while, and her consultant, Dr. Brown, hasn't formed an opinion about her as yet."

"So, you don't know what's wrong with her?"

"Your daughter is currently diagnosed as going through a situational crisis."

"A situational crises?" Remarked Pauline, blankly.

"It's a convenient term that can account for a number of conditions."

"So what about these 'Freddie' and 'Cindy' characters, where did they come from?"

Angus paused for a while and thought carefully about how he was going to answer Pauline's question.

"Dr. Brown has spent a number of years studying and conducting research in the United States. It was there that he begun working with patients diagnosed as suffering from MPD or Multiple Personality Disorder."

"What's that?"

"It's a split personality, have you ever heard of that before, Mrs. Gant?"

"That's ridiculous, I think your doctor has been watching far too many horror films." Exclaimed Pauline with a nervous giggle.

"MPD is a condition which is widely gaining acceptance in the states. It's relatively unheard of over here. However, some experts are now beginning to recognise it, but there are still many who remain sceptical."

"So is the doctor sure about this?"

"Well, he is a leading expert in his field." Replied Angus, with a knowing grin. "He's not usually wrong with his diagnosis. I expect you'll meet him soon."

"Can he make my daughter well? That's all I want to know."

"Please listen carefully. I'm not implying at this early stage that Tina has MPD, but she is certainly showing signs of it. I'm going to try and explain some facts as best I can."

Jonathan was unsure whether it was appropriate for him to remain, and began to get up to leave.

Pauline, however took his arm and beckoned him to sit back down.

"Please continue," she urged.

"Mrs. Gant, this condition has arisen in Tina because of her in-built will to survive. Her mind has created a complex system of so-called characters, who each appear to serve a particular purpose. Take 'Freddie' for example, he is a dominant male character and is perceived to be the strong protector of the system. 'Cindy', on the other hand is the one who copes. She is calm, sensible and articulate, although today was the first time I had ever seen her flirting. It was probably the 'Cindy' character who got Tina through most of her nurse training."

"Are there anymore of these personalities, and will they go away?" Asked Jonathan, quite shocked.

"A good point." Replied Angus, thoughtfully. "Yes, there are more personalities, rather a lot more, I'm afraid."

"Tell me this is not happening, please!" Uttered Pauline, her voice filled with emotion.

"I'm afraid there's worse to come, Mrs. Gant. There is one extremely malevolent character called, 'Lucinda' who poses an enormous threat to Tina's life. It's likely that 'Lucinda' was involved when Tina tried to take her own life recently."

"This is absolutely ridiculous!" Barked Pauline, desperate for a drink. "I've never heard so much nonsense in my entire life. Tina's not an actress, she's not appearing in the school play, what with all these different characters you speak of. Come on Jonathan, let's get out of here while we've still got our sanity."

"Please, let's just hear the rest of it," implored Jonathan. "We need to know, if we're going to help her."

Angus, irritated by Pauline's attitude, had to be further prompted by Jonathan to continue.

"There are also a number of child-like persona's. Each one appears to have their own separate identity and demands to be treated like an individual. They will often appear when Tina is relaxed and feels safe, it's as if they were literally coming out to play. Whereas other characters will emerge if Tina feels threatened, like earlier for example."

"What's caused all this?" Asked Jonathan, out of curiosity.

Angus looked directly at Pauline.

"That's the difficult part. From Dr. Brown's research in America, and from our own studies here, it would indicate that many of the sufferers of this condition have at some stage in their lives been subjected to severe trauma. This is often of a sexual nature and has taken place during childhood."

"Are you saying that my daughter has been interfered with?"

Angus drew in a deep breath.

"I would say it's a lot worse than being interfered with, Mrs. Gant."

"That little bitch has often accused her father of the most appalling things. She even went to the police recently and caused all sorts of problems for Frank."

"So you don't believe her, Mrs. Gant?"

"Of course not. She's always been a bit strange, attention-seeking, that sort of thing, always wanting her own way. She's spoilt that's all."

"I don't think you really understand the gravity of Tina's situation."

"Why, what has she been saying?"

"Nothing yet, well not to us anyway. Perhaps she will in time, but that's something she doesn't have too much of."

"What do you mean?" Demanded Pauline.

"Mrs. Gant, I can't remember ever having such a suicidal patient here before. Tina is gravely ill, she wants to die, and she's very determined."

"But this is a secure unit. She wont be able to do anything here?"

"Hopefully not," replied Angus, looking concerned. "But we all have a massive task on our hands to keep this young woman safe."

Brenda glanced at her watch, it was nearly seven in the evening. She called over to Tina, who was lying on the mattress in the middle of the floor. She seemed content listening to the personal cassette recorder that Jonathan had brought in for her.

"Tina, come on, I'm finishing soon. So if you want a bath, you'd better hurry as the night staff wont let you have one."

Tina seemed to have settled down quite significantly following the events of earlier that day. Brenda had been assigned to Tina since the patient had first arrived, and a certain measure of understanding had been reached between them. Brenda had nursed high-risk patients on a number of occasions during her fifteen years of service at the hospital and felt nothing could ever shock or surprise her anymore. It wasn't that she particularly trusted Tina in any way, Brenda was too long in the tooth for that. But she used her vast experience to her advantage, and could spot certain signs in her charge's behaviour. She did allow her patients one or two concessions, as long as they didn't give her a hard time. It was an unwritten arrangement that had worked well in the past.

"Are you going to take this away from me now?" Asked Tina, in what appeared to be a child-like voice.

"Yes, 'Polly' - it's getting near bedtime, and you really must have your bath!" Replied, Brenda, somewhat patronisingly.

"Will I get to listen to it, after my bath?"

"Only if 'Lucinda' doesn't appear. We want a nice quiet night, don't we?"

Brenda had nursed several patients with MPD and found that life was easier if she just went along with it, and addressed each character as a separate person. She hadn't fully formed an opinion if it was a true disorder of the mind, or if it was just another way patients could manipulate the system and get attention.

"Will you be watching me in the bath?" Asked the child-like, 'Polly'.

"Yes, of course, you're only a little girl, and we don't want you to drown, do we?"

"But I think Tina will be back soon. She's the one who wanted the bath, not me. I just want to play."

Brenda watched bemused as Tina's different personalities came and went, until finally, Tina herself arrived back on the scene.

"Welcome back to the land of the living! We were just about to go for a bath." Said Brenda, wearily.

One particular bathroom had been set aside for Tina's exclusive use. It was in an area scarcely used by anyone else, but more importantly, the smoke detector was faulty, which meant a crafty cigarette for Brenda.

"How are you feeling at the moment, Tina?"

"Fine, really - I'm just looking forward to a nice hot soak."

"Well, you go ahead. I'm not sitting in there with all that damp and steam."

"I'll be okay, Brenda."

"Leave the door open slightly, and I'll sit out here in the corridor." Yawned the nursing assistant, pulling out her packet of cigarettes.

'Lucinda' forced a smile, before switching on the light, and going over to run the water. However, after putting in the plug, it was only the hot tap that she actually turned on, thinking this would give her extra time, and would create more steam to disguise what she planned to do. She would still need to be very quick, as the bath would only take about four minutes to fill up, and Brenda would undoubtedly become suspicious if it took longer.

Reaching into her pocket, 'Lucinda' produced the tape that Jonathan had left in the cassette recorder. Then, as the steam filled the bathroom, and the sound of running water drowned out the noise, she pulled length after length of tape from the plastic casing. When she felt she had sufficient, she doubled it over as many times as she could to form a noose strong enough to hold her weight.

Attached to the wall, just above the bath were several old brackets, spaced at about three-foot intervals. They were once used to support old heating pipes that had since been removed. With measured movements, Lucinda/Tina climbed up onto the edge of the bath, and stretched up to loop the strands over one of the brackets. She felt an excruciating pain in her abdomen, and knew she had pulled the wound open. Gasping from the pain, she began to entwine the rest of the tape around her neck. The sound of a chair scraping the ground from out in the corridor alarmed her, and she expected to be caught at any moment.

"Is everything alright in there, Tina?" Called out Brenda.

"Yes, yes, I'm fine." Came the reply.

As Tina's alter ego, Lucinda, stared down at the half-full bath, she realised there wasn't anything else to do, just let go. This was what she had wanted for so long now, it had gradually crept up and overtaken her life, making everything else pale into insignificance. Her father, Frank would never be able to hurt her again. Freedom beckoned, and she felt ready to reach out and grab it, while she had the opportunity.

The bundles of tape were tight around Tina's neck, and she felt blood running down to her feet, making them slip on the edge of the bath. There was nothing except the crudely-tiled wall to stabilise her. She tried to grasp it with the flat palms of her hands, but still she felt herself slipping. Thoughts of Jonathan began to flick through her mind. She wanted him, she loved him. He had been the only beautiful thing to have happened in her life. Tina wanted it all to stop now, she wanted to get down, she wanted to scream out for Brenda to help her.

As she fell from the edge of the bath, she felt the makeshift noose suddenly tighten. It bit into her skin as she slid into the scorching hot water. Some of the strands of the tape snapped, and for a split second she thought they would all snap and she would end up plunging down below. She turned her body awkwardly, but her descent was halted by a sudden, violent jolt. It was violent enough to break Tina's neck. The strands had held firm.

Tina finally came to rest with the bottom half of her body submerged in the scalding bath, while her top half sat upright, like some grotesque marionette with its head dangling on a string.

Brenda had heard a dull thud, over the sound of the roaring water, and simply assumed it to be Tina climbing into the bath. She sat back in the chair she had found in the corridor and returned to her magazine. As she lit up her second cigarette, Brenda became concerned about the amount of steam coming out from behind the door.

"Is everything alright in there, Tina?"

Nothing.

"Tina, answer me!" Screamed Brenda, flinging open the door. Crimson water poured over the side of the bath, and as Brenda recoiled at the sight of Tina's agonised face, she slipped and fell heavily, hitting her head on the hard, tiled floor.

Brenda was found by the next nurse who came to relieve her. She recovered, but never returned to work again. For Tina, it was too late. She died on her forgotten, twentieth birthday, a far cry from the tiny, premature baby that had refused to give up hope, and had clung on so desperately to its fragile, wretched life. Lucinda had succeeded.

THE BLACK ANGEL

I drank from the cup of trust.
It scalded me.
I ate from the table of hope.
It poisoned me.
I yielded to the embodiment of love.
It violated me.
I embraced the Black Angel.
It loved me.

Rest in Peace
Tina Frances Gant
(15th August 1963 - 15th August 1983)

COMPENDIUM OF PASSION

Enter Lincoln Greene

BOOK THREE

25. LETTERS

1983.

David sat back in his chair and gazed out of the window. It was a pleasant, sunny day, hot but not unbearable. He marvelled at the rolling green hills in the distance and wished he was there, lost in thought, strolling across them. It was something he and William used to do when they were younger. They would just set off, wandering in no particular direction, but would always find themselves way up in the hills, exploring as young boys do. It was a sight he never tired of, and as he paused, pen in hand, he came to realise how difficult it would be to leave Falcondale again.

Returning to his letter, David was still not any wiser. Despite his new status of Dean of Students, he still didn't quite know what to say. Usually, when he wrote letters, he found it easy to express himself, much easier than talking to someone in person, or on the telephone.

He had written to Sally many times in the past, and would simply imagine she was there, listening to his words. He thought back to the night a few weeks earlier when he'd had dinner with her and her two daughters. He remembered her smile, her soft voice, and how much he missed her. There were lots of things he could tell Sally, if he had a mind to, but those words didn't come easy, in fact it seemed harder, the older he got.

David had already sent Sally out an official university letter, offering her a place at Falcondale come next semester. Inside the envelope, he had put his own short note, thanking her for that wonderful night, and asking her to write back as soon as she could. For two weeks he anxiously went through his mail, searching for an envelope bearing her handwriting. But nothing was forthcoming, and it hurt him.

David had thought about telephoning Sally with the news of her place, but when he had picked up the receiver, something stopped him, like it had in the past. He hated the phone, and would be the first to admit it, but this was different. A strong bond had always existed between them, but now, he believed it had gone that much deeper. He felt Sally realised it too, but it wasn't something quantifiable, or anything that could be easily discussed on the telephone. It was something that could only be nurtured through empathy and deep, close human contact. He knew they belonged together, but their dogged reticence, and feelings of guilt made it that much harder to take their relationship to the next level.

He picked up the half-written letter, tore it up and threw it into the waste paper bin. David then wrote another letter, only this time the words came straight into his head. He put the letter into an envelope and placed it into his jacket pocket, before glancing down to his watch, and heading back home for lunch.

Carol was expecting him, and seeing her warm, cheery smile soon lifted his spirits.

"How are you, this fine day, Carol?"

"You'll not find me complaining, Mr. Peddlescoombe." Replied David's part-time housekeeper.

"Good. Now listen Carol, I want to speak to you about something."

"There's not a problem is there, Mr. Peddlescoombe?" She asked, looking concerned.

"Lord no, nothing like that," he replied, taking a seat at the kitchen table.

"I've made you a mushroom omelette with some salad. I know you don't like anything too stodgy for lunch." Remarked Carol, trying to change the subject.

"Sounds wonderful, just what I need!"

As she put the plate down in front of him, she stood back a few paces and began fiddling with her thumbs, awaiting what her employer was going to say.

David eyed her warily before coming out with what was on his mind.

"I'm leaving Carol. It was the wrong decision to have ever taken this job in the first place."

"But, Mr. Peddlescoombe, you've only been here the flick of a lamb's tail."

"I know, it's my wandering heart. I just can't stay put in any one place for very long."

"I'll make us a nice cup of tea." Replied Carol, with a hint of sadness in her voice.

"I've already written out my resignation."

"I see."

"It wont affect you, Carol. I'll rent out the house, and you can still keep your job taking care of things."

"Please forgive me for speaking out of turn, Mr. Peddlescoombe, but I think you'll be making a big mistake."

"Speak as you find, Carol. You know I value your forthrightness."

She brought two cups of strong-looking tea over to the table, and sat down opposite David.

"This is your home. It's where you belong. We all need somewhere to go back to."

"I realise that, but there's nothing here for me anymore."

"I think you're suffering from the Falcondale lull."

"Whatever is that?"

"When the students go for the summer, it makes Falcondale a very lonely place. It's something you don't really experience unless you live here."

"Yes, it has become unbearably quiet, but that's not the reason."

"You're not a young man anymore, Mr. Peddlescoombe, you can't just go gallivanting off. Besides, where would you go?"

"I don't know. Abroad, somewhere sunny and warm - the South of France perhaps."

"You haven't given this any consideration at all have you? You're a typical man, just acting on impulse!"

David couldn't help laughing.

"Carol, you seem to know me better than I know myself!"

"Of course, I have a husband and sons of my own. There's not much I don't know about the male species!"

"I came back here looking for something, I thought I'd be closer to William. I thought I could recreate the happier times again."

"You can't wallow in the past, Mr. Peddlescoombe. You have to shape your own future and make your own happiness. Sometimes it's not easy."

"But Carol, my spirit is dying here. There's nothing to hold me anymore."

"There is, if you open your eyes. The grass isn't always greener on the other side. You have a lovely home, and your new job."

"But it's lonely and boring!"

"Boring? it's your future. Once the term gets started it'll be different, you'll be able to get much more involved. Besides, you have what it takes to become the university president one day."

"What? I think there's probably one or two in with a better chance than me."

"Nonsense. Everyone knows you're the man for the job. You've got it all going for you, just as long as you stick it out."

"I still need more." Replied David, glancing up at a portrait of Sally.

"Is that it?" Remarked Carol, following his gaze. "After all this, you just need a woman?"

"I don't know what I need anymore."

"But, she's coming isn't she, I thought you said Sally was going to be a mature student here next semester?"

"She hasn't replied to me. Perhaps, she's changed her mind. Maybe there's something wrong?"

"Perhaps, she's just too busy at the moment. Sally's got a family to look after hasn't she?"

"Sorry, you must think of me as a complete idiot, Carol?"

"No, of course I don't. But leave your decision for a bit longer, she'll come, don't worry."

"You're right, Carol. But I feel I have to do something."

"Then go to London and see her, if it'll make you feel any better."

David finished his omelette and took a sip of tea, before sitting back in his chair.

"Okay, you've convinced me. I'll give it another try."

"What about London?"

"I'll do that as well."

"That's the spirit, Mr. Peddlescoombe. Now make sure you come down to the Black Lion tonight. There's a talent contest on, and you might hear me singing!"

"Well, that'll be worth seeing, it's a date!"

David felt much better after his talk with Carol. He was the type of person that needed order and direction in his life, the problem was, he didn't yet know it, and Carol had acted as a steadying influence on him.

He was clearing some of William's belongings from the house, and had gone upstairs to continue. It was a depressing, pain-staking job, and David had thrown away practically nothing. He simply couldn't bear to discard any of his brother's possessions, preferring instead to just store everything in the attic, ready for the time when the wounds had healed sufficiently, and he was much more mentally prepared for such a gruelling chore.

Sitting at his brother's antique bureau, David furtively turned the key in the lock. Inside were papers, notes, sketches and poems that William had written. He read through a selection, before choosing some to give to Sally when he next saw her. David then came across an envelope, dated from 1963. He paid particular attention to it, as it had his name written on the front. The writing was beautifully neat and had been written by hand. However, in brackets it read; 'Only to be read in the event of my death.'

David felt his heart drop to the pit of his stomach, as he took a letter knife and carefully opened the envelope. Switching on the small lamp on top of the bureau, he inched forward, and began to read the contents.

My dearest, David,

I hoped that you would never have to read this letter, but the fact that you are, can only bring you a measure of comfort from my demise. David, I have never loved another soul like I have loved you, that is until Sally came along.

I was here to protect you and keep you out of trouble. It was a job that I loved doing. Seeing you growing up and maturing into a man gave me so much satisfaction, despite the difficulties you had to overcome. I know I must sound more like your Dad, than your brother, but I have always considered myself in Dad's absence, to be your surrogate father, and have found it to be an honour.

Before Sally, my whole life evolved around you, and what we did together. We are two of a kind, loyal, considerate, passionate and inseparable. I could list a thousand things that bring a smile to my face, when I think back about the experiences we've shared. I'm sure we've made Mum and Dad proud, and they've always spoken so highly of you, despite your shortfalls. I know, and they realise too, that you'll come good in the end. I've never stopped believing in you, David. So please be strong and get through this ordeal. Death is as natural as life. I've always seen it as the start to yet another, new adventure, albeit in a different time, a different place and on another plane. You will have your memories, as I do, but please don't spend your life dwelling on them, as they will drag you down. I want to be your inspiration and your motivation, not the mill stone around your neck.

Our strength is in you, David. You must look after Mum and Dad, and help them come through this. You are now their only son, and they love you dearly. I know you can do it. I have complete faith in you. Do not disappoint me, little brother.

Most importantly, you must look after Sally and any children I may have had with her. Sally was the reason I was born, the reason I lived, the reason I loved. She possessed my heart, my mind, and my soul. Without her, I was, and still am, nothing.

Sally will accept you, David, I know she will. Make her your wife. I know you love her, and if that's a mere fraction of the love I had for her, then I know it'll be enough. She will plead guilt and say it's not right, but tell her how I loved her, and now want her to be with you. I will look down on you both and give you my blessing. David, you, Sally and my unborn children are whom I cherish the most. I cannot bear to think of us being apart. Make me happy and let me rest in peace, knowing you are there for her.

David, thank-you for being my brother.

William.

David wiped a tear from his eye, and after placing the letter back in the envelope, he held it close to his heart, before putting it to his lips and kissing it tenderly. For the second time that day, following his talk with Carol, his soul had been lifted. He then looked upwards.

"Thank-you, William. I will look after Sally, and your children, and they will be loved. They deserve to be loved. Our hearts are re-united today."

As David strolled back to the university, he reached into his jacket pocket and pulled out the resignation he had written out earlier. He gazed at it for a while, and like his letter to Sally, he tore it up and threw it into a nearby bin.

For Sally, the unthinkable had happened. She had let Frank have sex with her. It had happened in Paris, just as he had planned. The occasion was probably as romantic as she could have hoped for. The Paris Ritz, a boat ride along the Sienne, a wonderful candle-lit meal, and of course, the champagne. There was always champagne with Frank. Sally had allowed herself to be seduced, both by the occasion and by a man used to getting his own way. She had looked magnificent that night, the long slinky dress he had bought her earlier, clung to her curves superbly.

As Frank led his beautiful partner into the crowded restaurant, every red-bloodied male turned to admire her, while every woman turned to envy her.

However, when Frank finally had his way with Sally, it was an experience that left her cold. She knew it was going to happen, it was inevitable. In a way, she wanted him to make love to her. She had to re-enter the world again and separate herself from the painful memories of the past.

The moment they returned to the plush hotel suite, a little after midnight, he embraced her forcefully. He had kissed her hungrily, like a wild animal trying to devour its prey. His large hands groped her body, ransacking the expensive dress, as he went about removing it in a hurried, business-like manner. Finally, after he had stripped her down to her underwear, he told her to stand in the centre of the room, while he calmly went over to the mini-bar and helped himself to a drink. Then, still dressed in his dinner suit, he put on some soft music and came towards her. They held each other, and danced, their movements fluid and precise. As they smooched and glided across the floor as one, Sally felt the thick, shag-pile carpet soft and sensual beneath her feet. She now found herself totally under his spell, and felt powerless to oppose him.

When he finally took her, it was down on the same carpet. Its gentle softness contrasted sharply with the rough manner in which he made love to her. He gorged himself on her body for the remainder of the night, before eventually taking her over to the bed and causing her to cry out in pain each time he penetrated her. She felt cheap and violated. He had succeeded in making her feel like nothing more than a prostitute. Yet still, Sally blamed herself. She put these negative emotions down to the fact that she was being unfaithful to William, and allowed the guilt associated with it to consume her. She was totally unaware that the man she had just had sex with, was the murderer of her husband.

The Paris trip was Frank's licence to practically move into Sally's home, and from here on, her life would never be the same. She was now sharing him with Pauline. He moved between the two women's lives with wanton abandon, coming and going whenever he chose. Sally soon learnt not to ask questions as he rode roughshod over her feelings with total disregard. The news of Tina's death had brought home how fragile life was, and how easy it could be snuffed out. Everything else now seemed to pale into insignificance in comparison.

Sally now channelled her energies into heavy drinking, and trying to get her son, Jonathan through his nightmare. He had been deeply affected by Tina's suicide, and was far too young to have to carry around such heavy emotional baggage. He had been smitten by Tina, but he had also known it was a relationship that promised nothing, except the potential for more sadness and grief. But to Jonathan's credit, he had been optimistic enough to stick it out with her, in the vain hope that one day he and Tina would be able to have the kind of relationship any young couple could expect to enjoy. However, it was the fact that Tina had used one of his cassettes to carry out the act that caused him such grave concern, and made him feel directly responsible for her actions that day.

Laura, on the other hand appeared to take the tragedy in her stride. Perhaps it was the fact that she was currently assigned to a ward specialising in the care of the elderly, and had become familiar with the spectre of death, or maybe she was simply distancing herself from events, and keeping her feelings private.

"Mum, Mum, wake up!" Called out Laura before having to resort to giving her mother a nudge.

"I'm sorry, I was miles away, I think I must have dozed off." Replied Sally distantly.

"Why don't you go up to your room and have a lay down. I'll bring you up a cup of hot chocolate if you like?"

"No, I think I'll have a gin and tonic. I deserve one."

"Looks like you've had a few already." Said Laura, with a hint of sarcasm in her voice.

"Be a darling and get it for me will you. I just don't feel like I have the strength."

The bottle in the drinks cabinet was empty, so Laura had to open another. She was surprised at this, as her mother usually only ever drank when Lizzie came over. Laura handed Sally the glass and went over to the bin, only to find it full of more bottles of every shape and size.

"Have you been having a party Mum?"

"Is it full again, can you empty it for me?"

"I'll be doing the vacuuming next! It's not like you to let things go to pot?" Said Laura, opening the back door for Jonathan.

"Oh bloody well leave it then, if it's such an effort for you." Called out Sally sourly.

Laura was quite taken aback by her mother's out-of-character attitude, but her attention was distracted by the sound of dogs barking, and seemingly very close by.

"Where's that barking coming from Mum, it sounds as if they're in our garden?"

"They are," replied Sally, taking a sip of her drink. "That's Conan and Thor, they belong to Frank. Hopefully, they're tied up."

"What are they doing here? They sound dangerous." Gasped Laura, going towards the window.

"They're bull terriers, horrid savage things. Frank left them here for a few days. Poor Pepys, he's terrified of them. I have to keep him inside."

"Is Frank coming back today?"

"I don't know. You can never tell with him." Replied Sally, yawning.

"Mum, will you please go up and have a lay down, Jonathan and I will tidy up."

"No, Laura. Jonathan has had a terrible setback. I want to stay down here with him."

Jonathan glanced across at his mother, "It's okay, Mum, you've done enough, I'll be fine. Anyway, it'll take my mind off things if I help Laura."

After Sally had finally gone, Laura and Jonathan made themselves a cup of coffee and sat at the table.

"She's drinking a lot isn't she?" Said Laura, anxiously.

"Yes, she been like this since she came back from Paris."

"It looks like she's drinking throughout the day. Have a peep in the cupboard, it's full of booze, hardly any food. Do you think Tina's death has affected her this much, Jonathan?"

"I don't know, but I'm glad to have a rest from her. She just keeps going on about Tina, and asking me if I'm okay. It just makes me feel worse."

"It's called love, Jonathan. Mum cares about you."

"Yeah, you're right, I shouldn't have said that. But something has made her like this?"

"It's Frank!" Called out Penny, as she ambled into the kitchen and proceeded to pour herself a glass of wine.

"Penny, what are you doing?" Exclaimed Laura in total disbelief.

"Having a glass of wine, what does it look like? Frank always lets me drink, and Mum does, sometimes."

"But, Penny, you're only fifteen!"

"I'm sixteen soon, and anyway, Frank lets me smoke. Frank and Mum are always getting drunk. He sleeps in her bed."

"He sounds absolutely awful. What on earth is happening to her?"

Jonathan didn't reply. He just stared down at his coffee, before lighting up another cigarette.

"I must admit, I don't really like him at all, he's very scary." Continued Penny, delighted to have a captive audience. "But he's good in other ways. Can I have one of those cigarettes, please Jonathan?"

"You had better have it in the garden, you know how Mum feels about you smoking." Replied Jonathan, throwing her the packet.

"She doesn't care anymore. I can't go outside, Frank's dogs are out there."

"I wish you would shut up about bloody Frank, and what did you mean when you said he's good in other ways?" Asked Laura angrily.

"Well, I caught him and Mum naked in bed once, and he gave me a hundred pounds after I had kicked up a fuss."

"A hundred pounds?"

"That's right, but he's given me more since then, and he was really upset about that Tina girl dying."

"I should damn well think so, she was his daughter." Replied Jonathan coldly.

"It was quite sad really," continued Penny, taking a mouthful of wine. "He started cuddling up to Mum, then he began to cry."

"I suppose he must have loved her despite the awful things we've heard." Said Laura.

"That's the second time I've seen him cry. It's weird to see a big bloke like him crying." Said Penny, stubbing out her cigarette and pouring herself more wine.

"But it seems like he's living here now?" Added Jonathan.

"He is, more or less, but you never know when he's going to appear. Sometimes it's two in the morning. Mum's already had the neighbours complaining." Replied Penny.

Laura had a serious expression on her face.

"I can't believe Mum would go for someone like him?"

"That's not all," continued Penny. "He wakes her up and gets her to cook him hot dinners."

"What, and this is the person who's supposed to be buying our house?"

"I haven't heard much about that recently. But apparently, his eleven-year son is coming to stay with us too."

"Frank's son, coming to live here?" Gasped Laura.

"That's right. He's called Jamie, and he's horrid. I think he's got a motorbike too." With that, Penny lost interest and went back into the lounge to watch television.

26. LINCOLN GREENE

The first sight to greet Laura when she arrived on the ward was Ivy. The elderly lady was looking very sorry for herself, slumped in a wheelchair, outside the nursing office. She had a bandaged head, and was covered in a blanket, as if she was about to go somewhere.

Returning to work that morning, Laura had to put the Tina and Frank business temporarily out of her mind as she suddenly found herself having to concentrate on her nursing duties.

"What's happened to Ivy?" She called out.

"She fell earlier this morning," replied the night nurse, sitting with her. "There's a laceration to her head, but she remained conscious, and she injured her arm, trying to stop herself falling. Sister wants her to go to Westminster for an X-ray and a check-up."

"Oh, Ivy, you do get in the wars, don't you?" Smiled Laura, crouching down next to the patient. "I can't leave you alone for five minutes!"

Ivy tried to smile, but it was obvious she was in a lot of pain. It was then, Laura realised the others were waiting for her in the office to take hand-over. Within ten minutes, she had been given the job of escorting the old lady the few miles across town to her appointment.

The ambulance arrived about twenty minutes later, and Laura, after collecting Ivy's notes took her down to the ground floor. The ambulance crew wanted to transfer Ivy into one of their own stretcher chairs for safety, and while they were doing this, Laura chatted to another student from her set.

"Are you off for a skive?" Joked Amanda cheerily.

"Yes, if you can call it that. Poor Ivy had a fall, so I'm taking her over to Westminster to get checked out."

"I don't think Ivy will be the only one getting checked out over there. Watch out for Dr Greene, he's working in A&E at the moment, and he just loves blondes!"

"I've never heard of him," giggled Laura. "Is he a bit of a Romeo then?"

"I'll say so, he's been with quite a few of the girls from our set." Amanda then moved across to whisper in Laura's ear; "He's meant to be very big down below, if you get what I mean!"

"Who's he been with, I'd love to know?" Inquired Laura, excitedly.

"There's no time to tell you now, look they're waiting to go." Replied Amanda, pointing to the ambulance. "But if he offers to show you the ropes, be it on your own head! Let's catch up soon, Laura, bye."

Laura waved goodbye to her friend and climbed into the back of the ambulance with Ivy. It was mid-morning by the time they arrived, but fortunately the Accident and Emergency Unit wasn't too busy at this time of day. Laura checked Ivy in, and was told to wait with her in a sterile-looking cubicle. The old lady was drifting in and out of sleep, and looked uncomfortable sat in the wheelchair, but she still managed the occasional smile, despite her fall. An hour passed before they were eventually taken into X-ray. They were only in there for a short time, before being told to wait back in the cubicle again. However, a friendly young nurse put her head around the curtain to tell them that, Dr. Greene would be along to see them soon, and did they need anything?

Laura couldn't help smiling at the mention of the doctor's name. I'll probably need a chastity belt if he's as bad as Amanda has made out, she thought!

Two minutes later, a tall, shaven-headed, black doctor arrived, looking dashing in his long white coat and wearing the obligatory stethoscope around his neck. He was very pleasant, and charmed Ivy immediately.

"I have good news for you, Mrs. Butler," he said, hanging up a set of X-rays over a screen. "There's no break, your arm is just badly bruised. We'll have to put it in a sling for you," he smiled.

"Thank-you doctor, that's good to know, but it's still very painful, and what about my head?" Asked Ivy, straining to hear him.

"It will be painful for a while, but I'll write you up for some pain-killers." He then glanced across at Laura, and asked for Ivy's prescription card. He wasn't disappointed in what he saw, and let his eyes linger on the pretty, blonde nurse.

Laura became a bit flustered, and dropped Ivy's notes on the floor. The doctor immediately bent down alongside her and helped to retrieve them. However, Ivy's drug card had slipped under a chair and Laura had to bend and stretch to reach it. Dr. Greene took the opportunity to survey her fine curves, noticeable even in her starched, blue nurse's dress.

"I haven't seen you around before?" He asked, glancing up at a stray lock of hair that had fallen across her face.

"I've been working over at St. Mary Abbot's," she replied, handing him the card and trying to re-gain her composure. "I don't come to A&E for another couple of months."

"That's a shame, I could have shown you the ropes!" He added, with a hint of an African accent.

Laura tried to stifle a giggle, but found herself flirting with the handsome doctor.

"Wont you be here then?" She asked, her courage returning.

"No, probably not. I have a locum job over in the states, so I'll be leaving soon."

"Oh, that's a shame," she replied, a little breathlessly, "You're very good with Ivy."

"Thank-you, Laura," he said, moving closer and reading her name badge. "A beautiful name, for a beautiful woman!"

Laura didn't quite know how to respond to that. She had never been complimented in such a way before.

"So what about Ivy's head?" She asked, trying to change the subject.

"Yes, of course, I'm sorry Ivy, I was distracted by your lovely, English rose nurse!" He said to the old lady, while keeping his eyes firmly on Laura. He then removed the bandage, and examined Ivy's head wound.

"Be careful, doctor, it hurts!" She winced in pain.

"I'm sorry, Mrs. Butler. I'll be as gentle as I can, but it can hurt sometimes," he added, turning his attention to Laura once again.

Feeling herself starting to blush, Laura took Ivy's hand and held it tightly as the doctor continued with his examination.

"It'll need a few stitches," he said finally, as he tossed the old bandages into a yellow bag. "But I think, we'll use Steri-Strips, as I don't want to cause Ivy any more pain. So where are you from Laura?" He asked, glancing down at her breasts.

"Twickenham, in West London," she replied shyly. "But, I'm staying in the nurses' home at the moment."

"That's interesting to know, which one?" He asked, turning to look into her blue eyes.

"Empire House, on Vincent Square. So where are you from?"

"Ghana, as a child, but I've lived in this country for most of my life. My father was a foreign diplomat."

"So did you do your training here, Dr. Greene?" She asked, meeting his dark, expressive eyes.

"Yes, I trained here in London, but please, call me, Lincoln."

"Lincoln Greene! What a wonderful name!" Laughed Laura, now becoming quite relaxed in his company.

"I'm glad you like it!" He laughed back, his pure white teeth, seeming even more brilliant against the darkness of his skin.

They were interrupted, as the nurse from earlier wheeled in a dressings trolley. She smirked, and immediately sensed the electrifying atmosphere between the white student nurse and the black doctor. She then flashed a knowing smile at Dr. Greene.

"Do you want me to assist?"

"No, I'll be okay, I'm sure Laura can look after me."

The nurse glared at Laura, before going back out, and pulling the curtains shut with one swift move.

As he was putting the final touches to Ivy's bandage, Dr. Greene's pager sounded. He finished off, then went out to made a call on the telephone in the corridor.

"I'm sorry, Laura but I have to go. It's been a pleasure to spend time with Ivy and yourself."

Laura felt quite disappointed as she thanked him and said goodbye.

"Perhaps, I'll see you around, we get on so well!" He said, turning her legs to jelly with his broad, piercing smile.

"Maybe," replied Laura awkwardly, "It's a small world."

Laura and Ivy had yet another wait. This time it was for the ambulance to take them back to St. Mary Abbot's, and Ivy was getting impatient. Laura wondered if she should go to the ambulance office and ask how much longer the delay would be.

Sighing, she glanced at her fob watch, it was now nearly three o'clock, and like Ivy, she was getting hungry and thirsty too. She looked in her bag for something to give the old lady, and found half a small bar of chocolate, then delving deeper, she found a packet of fruit gums, and helped herself to one. It was then that she heard Dr. Greene's familiar, deep, sensual voice.

"I thought, you'd be long gone by now?" He asked, concerned.

"No, we're still waiting for transport." Replied Laura, a little deflated.

"Leave it to me!" He said, "I'll go and see them in the office and say, Ivy's a priority case! You'll be back in Kensington in no time, and if not, I'll drive you myself."

He returned five minutes later with a triumphant smile on his face.

"The ambulance is on its way!" He exclaimed excitedly. "See what the power of the long white coat can do!"

Laura smiled, and her eyes latched onto his, perhaps lingering a little too long. She couldn't help noticing the powerful electricity erupting between them.

Lincoln was as good as his word, within minutes, an ambulance was there to collect them. Laura waited as the crew put Ivy on board and strapped her safely inside. Lincoln came over beside her, she could smell his strong, musky scent. It was manly, and very alluring.

"Laura, I was wondering if you'd do me the honour of having dinner with me?"

She was stunned, and felt her heart jump. She was about to answer yes immediately, despite what she'd heard about his reputation. She hesitated for what seemed like an eternity.

"I'm sorry, Lincoln, you've been so kind to Ivy and myself, I feel awful saying no, but I have a boyfriend."

He looked disappointed, but managed to put on a brave face.

"That's okay, Laura. I should have realised, a woman so exquisite, and so stunningly attractive as yourself would naturally have a boyfriend. I'm very jealous, but please, I'm the one who should be sorry, I didn't think."

"Perhaps, another time," she added, trying to bring him down gently.

"Yes, perhaps another time." With that, he turned to leave.

"He's going to end up bedding you, Laura!" Called out Ivy from inside the ambulance, and within earshot of the doctor.

"Ivy, you shouldn't have been listening!" Gasped Laura, her face crimson.

The car had been playing up again, so Nick had taken the Piccadilly Line from South Kensington to Osterley. It felt rather strange, returning to the matrimonial home after such a lengthy separation. Nick had responded to Sandra's letter, although it was more out of curiosity than anything else. He thought he knew all of her tricks and felt that he couldn't be manipulated by her anymore. The letter however, had left him completely miffed. Something strange was going on, and it was so totally unlike Sandra to have written it. Could she have really changed, he wondered, pressing the door bell.

Sandra looked radiant as she came to the door, casually dressed in jeans and baggy, pink T-shirt. She had recently had her hair done and her make-up looked immaculate. After giving him an affectionate hug, she took his hand, and like a teenager smuggling in her boyfriend, led him inside. Her perfume smelt divine, but not over-powering as was often the case with Sandra. Nick thought she had filled out a little since the last time he'd seen her, but the bit of extra weight seemed to suit her.

It had been quite a week for Nick. He had sat his finals, then had a boozy goodbye drink with his friends at the hospital. He had even managed to see Laura, but it didn't seem to go too well, because of the tragic news about Tina. That's what he assumed anyway. The thought that Laura may have been tiring of him did cross his mind, but he chose to dismiss it.

Now, it seemed odd, and a little sad that two chapters of his life had come to an end at the same time. He tried to convince himself that his experiences at both the college and the hospital were pretty hellish affairs, what with all the studying he had to do, and then having to live in a tiny, cold and noisy room. Then, there was the awful, mind-numbing 06.30 starts at the hospital, combined with having to endure low pay. If Nick were to describe this to anyone, they would have thought him mad. But the truth was, they were marvellous times, and he had loved it, both at the college and the hospital, after all, he had met Laura there. Now his heart felt heavy, for he hadn't told her he was leaving. Perhaps, it just didn't seem important what with Tina's death. He wasn't quite sure if he would ever see her again. They had arranged to meet in a cafe in Kensington in a couple of day's time, but she had seemed a little indifferent when he had first suggested it.

As soon as Nick stepped into the lounge, Sandra was upon him.

"Here you are, a small surprise gift. I'm so proud of you!"

"What is it?"

"Open it and see, come on, hurry up!" Exclaimed Sandra in an animated tone.

As Nick removed the wrapping paper and opened the small box, he was amazed to discover a spectacular and very unusual watch. The face was made up of Egyptian hieroglyphs, with the Sphinx, and pyramids set out on a dark blue background. He smiled and kissed his wife on the cheek.

"You seem so different Sandra, what's happened - have you had a lobotomy or something?"

"Damned cheek! I've changed, Nick, just like I said in my letter. I've started a new job, stopped drinking, and wait for it - I've got rid of Craig, and I've never felt better."

"But what happened, you and Craig seemed so suited?"

"Oh, come on, he was just a little shit. Anyway forget him. I've cooked us a lovely meal, come and sit down."

"It certainly smells pretty good, but I'm intrigued by your metamorphosis?" Replied Nick, still suspicious.

"Stop going on about it. Can't you just take something at face value? Besides, there's more surprises that I'll tell you about over dinner."

The chicken supreme was excellent, but cooking had never been one of Sandra's strong points and Nick felt it wasn't the time to start questioning if it was shop-brought.

"Come on then, what are these surprises. You haven't totally turned your back on capitalism and joined the labour party or anything like that have you?"

"No, not exactly, Nick." Cringed Sandra.

"You've turned into a lesbian?"

"Very funny! Now listen carefully, do you remember Willis from the insurance company?"

"Of course. I haven't seen him for years. Is he okay?"

"Yes, in fact he's more than okay. He's started up his own business in the city, and by all accounts, things are going extremely well. He deals with most of the contents and home insurance referrals I get. He wants you to go and work with him."

"I couldn't cope with all that again Sandra."

"It's not cold-calling or door-knocking. It's all referrals, and you just sit in a nice, air-conditioned office in London, it's as easy as that."

"But it's been such along time."

"Nonsense, you're just a bit rusty that's all. It's nothing you haven't done before - call him, you can start whenever you want."

Nick sat back and sipped his wine. He liked old Willis, he was an honest, hard-working sort, and would probably give him a very good deal.

"I must say, it sounds tempting." He replied.

"Think about it, while I go and get the desserts."

"I would probably need a bit of a break first." Shouted Nick through to Sandra in the kitchen.

"That's okay. You can start when we get back from Spain."

"Spain?"

"Yes, I knew you'd want a break, so I booked us a two-week holiday. It's a place called Llafranc."

"Llafranc?"

"It's a lovely little fishing village, completely unspoilt, and close to Barcelona. We can go sightseeing!"

"Sandra, stop babbling on. Are you mad? Whatever makes you think we can just act as if nothing has happened and simply go on holiday together?"

"Come on Nick, you wouldn't have come over tonight if you weren't still interested in me would you?"

"I was curious that's all."

"Okay, fine. But we both need a holiday, especially you. I think you deserve one."

"But I'm absolutely broke, I can't even get the car fixed."

"There's still plenty of money in our account."

"It's your money, Sandra."

"We're husband and wife, Nick, remember? Come on, please say yes."

"I don't know. I'd forgotten just how impulsive you could be."

"It would be wonderful to be a couple again, and in sunny Spain, it would be so romantic."

"Wait, just hold on a second." Replied Nick, a little puzzled. "So what exactly happened with you and Craig?"

"I don't want to talk about it. We're finished and that's all you need to know."

"Sandra, I know you only too well. Did he chuck you?"

"Yes, he chucked me, now are you satisfied?" She replied angrily.

"Was it because of your drinking?"

"No, it wasn't this time. It was because he caught me with another man, if you must know!"

"So, let's get this straight, you, a married woman, were two-timing Craig, he caught you out, and dumped you, is that what happened?"

"Yes, that's about it, how many times do I have to tell you!"

"God, Sandra, I just don't understand you at times. So now, you're lonely and want your little old hubby back?"

"Yes, I suppose so, but don't start playing the hurt innocent with me. You've been seeing someone else haven't you?"

"So what if I have. Laura and I have a very special kind of relationship - it's based on trust!"

"Have you slept with her?" Demanded Sandra, standing up to face him.

Nick poured himself another glass of wine and sat back at the table.

"Yes, I have slept with her."

"So that's your idea of trust is it?"

"I didn't come here to argue with you Sandra, perhaps I'd better leave."

"Don't be so dramatic, Nick. We're both adults. These things happen, none of us are perfect. Besides, where would you go, back to her? Stay here tonight, it's still half your house. You can always sleep in the spare room if you want to stay faithful to your precious, little Laura!"

She then went across to him and sat on his lap, running her well-manicured fingers through his hair.

"I knew you hadn't changed Sandra." He replied, pulling his wife down to ravish her.

It was a hot, sticky day and Laura had to wrench up the window as far as it would go in order to obtain even the slightest of breezes. The only noise she could hear was the distant hum of a cleaner's vacuum, somewhere on another corridor. There didn't appear to be anyone else at home on Laura's floor, had the sunshine lured them all off to nearby St. James's Park, she wondered. Laura was off for a couple of days, and had arranged to meet Nick later that afternoon, it was a date they had agreed upon a few days earlier. The idea of going back on the underground didn't appeal to her in the slightest, it just seemed to be getting hotter. Dressed in a light cotton sundress, and wearing sandals, she felt relieved to be rid of her dowdy blue uniform, with its restrictive high, cardboard collar and starched white apron. Eventually she decided to walk from the nurses' home the short distance into the park, she would then cross over into Green Park, and make her way up towards Knightsbridge, where she could catch a bus into Kensington.

It had taken that much longer, but the walk had given Laura some valuable time to be alone and think, which at the moment was something she felt she needed to do. Getting off the bus near the station at High Street Kensington, Laura glanced at her watch. There was still half an hour to go before she met Nick, and since the shops were there, she may as well put the time to good use and do some browsing therapy. She went into a department store and looked at the women's autumn range, but nothing seemed to catch her eye, so she tried a few of the more trendy boutique shops. Laura could of course get whatever clothes she needed from Scarlet's, but if the truth be known, she wasn't particularly keen on some of Lizzie's creations, and would often accept the garments offered her in order not to offend her mother's best friend. After much deliberation, Laura found a pair of culottes she liked and paid on her credit card. Realising the time, she began to make her way to Mario's. Fortunately, the cafe where she was meeting Nick, was down a nearby side street and opposite the library. It was a small, simple cafe, which served wonderful coffee. Nick and Laura had been there several times after spending afternoons sunbathing together. She sat up on one of the tall stools by the window, hoping to catch a glimpse of him as he approached. He had recently been spending time in the library, due to his exams, so she wasn't sure if he would appear from that direction, or come from the High Street.

Taking another sip of her coffee, Laura checked her watch again. He was ten minutes late, and she began to feel anxious. She recalled when they had arranged the date, she may not have been too responsive, due to Tina's death being at the forefront of her mind, but she definitely said yes to the time and place they agreed, she was clear about that.

Ordering a glass of water, Laura took out her compact. She had never been one for wearing masses of make-up, normally it would just be a little eyeliner, or mascara with a hint of blusher. Only if it was a special occasion, or if she was going out, would she wear lipstick and apply foundation.

"You look superb, Miss, as beautiful as ever!" Remarked the young waiter, as he brought the water over. "But where is your friend? I would never keep a lady like you waiting!"

Laura felt flattered by the attention and smiled, but now twenty minutes had passed and she was feeling rather self-conscious. The cafe was empty, and the waiters scrutinised her as they stood bored behind the counter.

Finishing her coffee, she went to the payphone across the road and called the hall of residence at the college. The number rang for several minutes as was often the case, before someone eventually answered.

"No, sorry, Nick's gone. He went a couple of days ago." Said the unknown student on the other end of the line.

"Do you know where?" Asked Laura desperately.

"No idea. He did his exams and just went."

"Thank-you," she replied politely and replaced the receiver. She sighed and glanced over towards the cafe again. The waiter who had served her gave her a lusty grin and waved, but Laura, feeling embarrassed and let down pretended not to notice, and quickly walked away.

After checking the library, she made her way back towards the High Street. There was one more place to try, but she was in two minds about it.

The beer garden at the Devonshire Arms was busy, mostly with tourists and office workers alike. Tight Fit's *'The Lion Sleeps Tonight'* was playing on the jukebox as she stepped through the door. But, in direct contrast, it seemed rather empty inside. Glancing around, Laura saw a few familiar faces from the hospital, but Nick's wasn't one of them.

"I love small breasts, they're much more responsive!" Came a Hispanic accent she recognised immediately. Fortunately the remarks were not directed at her.

Roberto was up to his old tricks again. This time it was with the new barmaid.

"Can you let go of my hand please, Roberto, I have a customer to serve!" Replied Chrissie, not at all fazed by the South American's advances.

"Just an orange juice please!" Said Laura, trying not to bring attention to herself. However, it was a bit too late for that. She soon felt Roberto's piggish, bloodshot eyes boring through the flimsy dress she had worn, and now she wished she had worn a bra.

"Hola! Yes, indeed hola!" Exclaimed Roberto, in a drawn out, throaty groan.

"Hello Roberto, it's lovely to see you again. Are you well?"

"Yes, Laura, I am positively throbbing now that you've come to me, I knew you would!"

"Actually, I'm here to see Nick. Have you seen him?"

Roberto stepped back a couple of paces, and in theatrical style admired the young nurse's curves.

"I cannot stand here and watch you drink that, Laura. It's for babies! No, you must have a real drink befitting a lady of your poise and beauty." He replied, having not listened to word she had said.

"No, Roberto, I don't need a drink. I just want to see Nick."

He took his eyes off Laura's breasts only long enough to summon Chrissie over.

"A cocktail for the lovely senorita, and one for you as well, Chrissie, as you are equally as lovely."

"Give it a rest Roberto," laughed the barmaid, before glancing over at Laura. "He's full of it, isn't he?"

Laura smiled back, as Roberto ushered her over to a table.

"First, we must eat. Then we go to a place I know, maybe a little music, yes?"

"No, Roberto." Replied Laura firmly. "Thanks for the offer of a drink, but I only came to see Nick, and I can see he's not here."

"Please, Laura - don't be in such a rush to go. You are a very a beautiful woman, and I only joke with you." He said with a hint of sadness in his voice.

"Do you know where he is Roberto? I was meant to meet him."

He shook his head, and sighed deeply.

"Nick has gone Laura."

"Gone? But where to?

"He's gone back to his wife, Sandra."

"But what about his job at the hospital?"

"He finished his exams, and left his job. I thought he would have told you he was leaving."

"I don't understand Roberto?"

"I'm sorry to give you such bad news Laura, perhaps I can make it up to you?" He stood up to go around and sit next to her, but as he did so, she leapt up, and with tears streaming down her face, ran from the pub.

It was quite noisy in the nurses' home that evening, it was Saturday night and lots of the girls were playing music and having a drink or two while they got ready to go out on the town. Laura, her eyes still watery from the tears she had shed, wearily trudged up the stairs to her room. It was then that she noticed a note pinned to her door.

MESSAGE FROM NICK,
SAY'S HE'S SORRY, BUT CAN'T DO TODAY. SAID HE'LL CALL ANOTHER TIME AND EXPLAIN.

"It's a bit late for that!" She muttered, screwing up the scrap of paper. She flopped down on her bed, her earlier good mood, now a distant memory. Laura eyed the bottle of red wine sitting on her dressing table, and considered drowning her sorrows. As she stood up to pour herself a glass, she went over to the mirror and studied her reflection. She then reached for her handbag, and began to do a hasty repair job on her make-up.

No, she thought defiantly. I've been stood up at the last minute, by that swine, but I'm still going out to have a good time. Damn him! Damn all bloody men!

She then went out into the corridor and called on some girls, who she knew would be going out.

"Yes, of course you can join us, the more the merrier!" Exclaimed Amanda, delighted. "Come in, we've got some wine!"

"Give me five minutes, I'm almost ready, I've just got to get changed," replied Laura excitedly. "I've got some drink too, I'll bring it along."

There were four girls in total, and they took the Circle Line from St. James's Park to Sloane Square. Two of the girls had apparently met members of a local band and had been told they would be in Drummond's, on the King's Road that evening. Drummond's was formerly known as The Chelsea Drugstore, but had now been turned into a trendy wine bar. It still however, retained the elaborate aluminium arches and circular windows from the sixties and early seventies.

Amanda wasn't too bothered about meeting the band, and doubted if they would even be there. She just wanted to get out and let her hair down for a bit. At twenty, she was the same age as Laura. She was very pretty, with sparkling green eyes, and long chestnut hair.

Both Laura and Amanda proved to be very popular, the blonde and the brunette as it were. Laura was wearing a risqué black, lacy see-through blouse along with her short skirt, which drew many admiring glances. Amanda, on the other hand wore a clingy, short white dress. They were hit on by several males and found neither of them had to buy a single drink during the whole evening. They eventually got chatting to a couple of young men, who claimed to play for Chelsea Football Club. They certainly had plenty of spare cash to blow, but the two girls weren't entirely convinced. Besides, the one coming onto Laura resembled Friar Tuck, rather than a professional footballer, as she had so deftly pointed out to Amanda.

Some time after this, the two girls who were meant to meet the band came over, looking rather disappointed. Obviously the band members had failed to materialise.

"We're going clubbing up the West end, if you two want to come?" Shouted one of them above the noise. Amanda, shook her head, and glanced across at Laura.

"You can go, but I don't feel like it. Besides, I'm on an early tomorrow. What about going to the Goat in Boots on the Fulham Road, there might be some dishy doctors there?"

"What about the SAA bar at Westminster, you get them there too, and we're dressed to kill!" Suggested Laura, her speech a little slurred.

"Laura, you're shameless, what about your boyfriend?" Giggled Amanda.

"He stood me up, so forget him!"

"Okay, let's go," agreed Amanda, finishing her drink. "The hospital club is a lot cheaper too, and if there's no doctors there, we can always get a Chinese and finish off the wine!"

On the tube going back, Laura told Amanda about her meeting with the notorious, Lincoln Greene. Amanda was in stitches when Laura mentioned that he actually said, he would show her the ropes!

"That's hilarious, he was certainly true to form!"

"Have you ever been with a black man, Amanda?" Asked Laura, discreetly on the crowded train.

"Why do you ask?" Exclaimed Amanda. "You're curious aren't you, innocent little Laura, now that you've met him!"

"Yes, I must admit, I have wondered what all the fuss is about!"

"So, I take it, you haven't gone black?"

"No, I haven't," replied Laura, going red, but you still haven't answered my question, Amanda!"

"Well okay, yes, I have. I had an ex who was black." Replied the brunette, as they got off the tube.

"But, surely it can't be that different from any other man?"

"It's different alright, trust me on that, Laura. In fact it's quite hard to explain. It just seems more erotic, more carnal, like you're rebelling or going against the system."

"You mean the taboo thing?"

"Yes, that's exactly what I mean. Even though it's 1983, there's still a lot of people out there who are horrified to see a white woman with a black man."

"That wouldn't bother me, I'd go out with someone if I liked them, no matter what colour they were."

"I'm the same," said Amanda, "But some women, once they've tried it, prefer black men."

"Yes, I suppose you're right, but why?"

"Well, for a start, a black man's skin feels different, so smooth, so velvety, and they seem much more masterful and dominant in the bedroom. It's lust in its purest form. When you give yourself to a black man, it feels so electrifying, so intense, and the contrasting colours of the skin is so erotic."

"You explain it very well." Replied Laura, more than a little intrigued. "So, is it true that they are quite big below?" She added, with a grin.

"I thought we might come to that! I think it's all a bit of a fallacy really. I've had white boyfriends who were very well endowed, but come to think of it, yes, my ex was quite big. But, listen, if you're so interested, then I suggest you try it, and see for yourself!" Laughed Amanda.

"Lincoln did seem very nice. Surely, he can't be that bad?"

"He's a man isn't he?" Added Amanda, pushing open the door of the SAA bar.

The Staff Amenities Association was half full inside, and quite dimly-lit. It was rather an uninspiring building, but the bar area was huge, with lots of tables and chairs, plus another raised level containing a pool table and slot machines.

"It's my round, what do you want to drink?" Asked Laura, reaching into her handbag.

"Do you know what, I still feel a bit tipsy. We must have had a hell of a lot tonight, but maybe a small white wine wont do any harm!"

As Laura stood at the bar to order the drinks, Amanda looked around for a free table.

"Two small glasses of dry white wine, and some change for the juke box please." Asked Laura politely.

"Hey, Laura, you'll never guess," remarked Amanda, nudging her in the ribs. "Your friend, Lincoln is here. Look, he's sitting over there!"

Laura glanced around, and indeed, Amanda was right. Lincoln was sat at a table, in his white coat, chatting to what looked like another doctor.

"Don't keep staring, he'll catch you, and it'll be embarrassing."

"He must be on call," Amanda, replied. "Why will it be embarrassing?"

"He asked me out, and I turned him down. I told him I had a boyfriend."

"Oh, Laura, but Nick's married isn't he? Look, I have to go to the ladies, I'll be back in a minute."

As Amanda left, Laura waited patiently for their drinks to arrive.

"That'll be £2.80 please." Said the barman, placing the two glasses of wine on a tray.

Before Laura could respond, Lincoln was towering over her. He was a good six feet two, and under any other circumstances, he could have been considered quite menacing, with his shaven head and broad shoulders.

"I'll get these, Laura, please, put your money away." With that, the doctor handed a five pound note to the barman. "Small world!" He smiled back at her.

"Thank-you, yes, it certainly is!" She replied, her voice nervous. "So are you on duty?"

"Yes, unfortunately, but only until 11.30. Please come and join us."

"No, I couldn't possibly, besides I'm with a friend."

"That's okay, your friend can come over as well." He answered, his dark, smouldering eyes burning into hers. "I must say, you look gorgeous, Laura. Have you been out with your boyfriend?"

Laura, looked solemn, and took a sip of her wine.

"No, I've been out with friends. My boyfriend stood me up."

A sad look appeared on Lincoln's face. He then glanced down noticing her lace blouse. "How could any man in their right mind possibly stand you up?"

"He's married!" She exclaimed, letting the drink do the talking, and immediately regretting what she'd just said.

Lincoln reached out to touch her hand. Laura felt her spine tingle, as his fingers entwined with hers. She recalled what Amanda had said about the effects of the contrasting skin colours.

"I'm sorry, I didn't realise." He remarked, squeezing her hand harder.

Before she had time to reply, Amanda returned.

"I see you two are getting acquainted!"

"Hello Amanda," smiled Lincoln, just as his pager sounded. He let go of Laura's hand, and walked to the end of the bar, to pick up the internal telephone.

"I'm sorry, I have to go." He said, returning almost straight away, as the pager interrupted a second time. "Listen, Laura - I'll be in my apartment by midnight, if you want to come up for a chat. It's number 102, in the doctor's quarters."

His eyes were on her again, taking in the whole of her body, glancing hungrily at her breasts, her legs, and back up to her eyes again. "Please, I'll expect you."

The two women glanced at each other and smirked, before taking their drinks to a nearby table.

However, Laura seemed distant, and deep in thought.

"You look sad. What's the matter?" Asked Amanda

"I'm sorry, I was just thinking about Nick. I've had a bit too much to drink."

"I wouldn't shed a tear over him, Laura, men aren't worth it. Come on, let's put some music on!"

A couple of minutes later, Kraftwerk's, *'The Model'* was playing over the club's sound system.

"Yes, you're right, Amanda, he's not worth it, but I really enjoyed tonight."

"So are you going then?"

"Going where?"

"Going to Lincoln's apartment!"

"No, of course not. Whatever gave you that idea. I'll finish my wine and probably go to bed." Replied Laura, defensively.

"Well, I'm going to get a takeaway. Don't you want one?"

"No, I'm not hungry anymore."

The two girls said their goodbyes, and promised to meet up again soon. Amanda went off to get her Chinese, while Laura began the short walk to Empire. When she got back to her room, she sat on her bed for a few moments, again deep in thought. She then checked herself in the mirror, and brushed her hair, before heading back out, and making her way to the doctor's quarters.

Lincoln was shirtless, and just wearing a pair of running shorts when he opened the door. He had a towel draped around his neck, and looked as if he'd just stepped out of the shower.

"I'm glad you could make it," he said, in his deep tone. "I haven't been back long myself. Please, come in." He made a sweeping gesture with a well-muscled arm, and Laura found herself hesitantly stepping inside. She again, caught the smell of expensive musky aftershave, and it set her hormones racing.

Lincoln had a one-bedroom apartment a couple of minutes away from the main hospital. It was fairly minimalist with cream and maroon walls, and a three-piece dark leather suite. Soft music was playing discretely in the background, as he took her denim jacket.

"This is nice, it's huge compared to my room at Empire."

"It keeps the rain off! Take a seat. Can I get you a drink?" He asked, seeing tantalising glimpses of white flesh through her blouse, and noticing she had a couple of buttons undone, showing the top of her low cut black bra.

"I'll have a coke, or whatever, if you're having one?" Replied Laura, nervously.

"Of course, I'll just put a shirt on, I certainly don't want you to think I'm a savage!"

Laura laughed and watched as he strode, with a confident swagger into the bedroom. She couldn't help noticing his athletic V-shaped torso, and pure dark, unblemished skin. He returned a few moments later in a tight black T-shirt, and wearing faded jeans. He was clutching two exotic-looking drinks.

"Sorry, totally out of coke, but try this, it's made from fresh pineapple and coconut juice."

Laura's mouth had suddenly gone very dry and she could feel her heart racing. Sitting back on the leather sofa, she tried to act calm, aware that he was standing over her, taking in every detail of her body.

"Did you have a busy night?" She asked, taking a sip of her drink, and trying to break the sexually charged tension.

Lincoln sat down beside her and put his drink down next to hers.

"We had a traffic accident, that's what dragged me away from you, but it was only a couple of broken bones."

His eyes dropped down to her legs, and he noticed that her skirt had ridden up, showing an alluring expanse of thigh. He felt himself getting harder by the second.

"So how come you got involved with a married man? I have to say, it did surprise me." He had moved closer and could inhale her intoxicating fragrance. He then placed his arm around the back of sofa, just above her shoulders.

"I didn't know he was married at first, but he told me it was all over between them."

Lincoln couldn't help laughing. He had a deep, masculine laugh that made Laura jump.

"Hey, you're nervous?" He said, reaching out to place his arm around her. "I'm sorry, I wasn't laughing at you, but that's what all married men say when they're playing the field."

"He's very nice, I'm sure he was telling me the truth."

"Yes, he sounds nice, cheating on his wife, lying to you, then standing you up. You don't deserve that Laura." He sensed he was home, and moved in for the kill. He pulled her onto to him, wrapping his strong arms around her body.

She felt the electric bolt surge between them again.

"What do I deserve?" She heard herself whisper.

"You deserve to be made love to, like the gorgeous, woman you are." He then lent over, and before she knew what was happening, he was kissing her. She responded. It was a passionate kiss, and he heard her moan, as he explored her mouth with his tongue. He was desperate for this white girl, and tonight he would have his way with her. He lunged at her neck, kissing and licking her passionately. Laura could hardly breathe, she was so excited, and when she did, her breath came in rapid gasps.

"I want you naked!" He released his grip, and sat back expectantly. He then beckoned her to stand before him, and disrobe.

Sade's *'Smooth Operator'* was playing as Laura, obeying his command, kicked off her shoes, and stood in front of him. It all felt very surreal, she didn't have time to think about what she was about to do, other than to please him.

She watched from a couple of feet away, as he pulled off his T-shirt, to reveal a smooth, toned torso, the colour of rich, dark chocolate. He then swept off his jeans, before turning his attention back to the young blonde nurse, about to strip for him.

Laura, could never consider herself a dancer, but she had a lithe, curvaceous body and moving her curves to the sensual rhythm wouldn't have been a problem for her.

Reaching up, and not taking her eyes off his, she began to unbutton her blouse. She noticed him licking his lips, and saw the huge tent pole appear in his crisp, white boxers.

As she reached the last button, she let the blouse fall away to the floor behind her. Next, she reached around, and unzipped the back of her denim skirt, and slowly peeled it down over her hips and thighs, until that too, dropped away to the floor.

She then casually kicked the skirt into the corner of the room. Lincoln's eyes were ablaze, and she saw him put a hand inside his shorts and begin to feel himself, as he watched her.

Now, wearing only her bra and knickers, she moved closer, revelling in the powerful knowledge that he desired her so much.

"Come to me." He said, moving to the edge of the sofa.

She moved within touching distance of him, every nerve ending she possessed was tingling in anticipation. He placed his hands on her hips and pulled her toward him. He drooled over her stomach, kissing and licking her navel, leaving her belly button wet with his saliva.

He stared up at her breasts, which were begging to be fondled and caressed by his large hands. She instinctively knew what he wanted, and reached up to unfasten her front-opening bra. He let out a long groan as he looked ravenously at her unfettered breasts. With his hands clasping her buttocks, he launched himself at her, nibbling and gnawing at her pink nipples. They immediately became stimulated, and grew to a size she'd never known before. She groaned and grabbed the back of his neck, twisting herself, she pushed each of her breasts into his waiting mouth.

Laura was now realising, that she knew so little about the wants and needs of her own body. Although she was certainly no virgin, this was different - she was being violated, and she was loving it.

Her bra joined her other clothes on the floor, and she threw her head back, as he continued to bite and chew on her bare flesh.

"I want to be inside you so much." He uttered, reaching down to her last garment of clothing.

"I want you inside me." She answered back, as he grasped her panties and eased them down over her long legs, before putting the damp gusset to his nose, and inhaling her essence. He leered at her greedily, before pulling her naked body down on top of him. He then made her kneel across him, as he let his hands run over her taught, white buttocks, and explore between her legs. There was a loud crack as he slapped her bottom hard and made her wince. She was wetter than she had ever been in her life, and felt herself oozing, as his long, dark fingers delved their way deep inside her.

It was one of the quickest orgasms she'd ever had. It came about so rapidly, so consuming. She let out a yelp, and gasped with ecstasy as she willingly gave up her body to him.

"Have you ever been with a black man before?" He asked, taking out his massive manhood.

Laura was still on all-fours, laying across him, her head buried in a cushion.

"No," She whimpered, "Have you ever been with a white woman before?" She knew it was a stupid question, but she wanted to hear his answer.

His smile and silence said it all. He eased her up, and taking her hand, placed it upon his erect penis.

She gripped it hard, and in her excitement, started to rub him vigorously.

"Easy, girl, you'll make me come too early, and I don't want to waste it." He uttered, sitting back and thrusting his hips forward.

Laura couldn't help herself, she sank to her knees and began to run her tongue up and down his full length, tasting the semen that was slowly dribbling out. She wanted his come in her mouth, and could have begged for it, but he made her stop.

"You'll get it in your beautiful mouth soon enough." He told her, before scooping her up roughly in his arms and carrying her through to the bedroom.

It was lit by a couple of sensual, low voltage lamps. She then felt the brief chill on her bare back, and sensed the silky texture of the duvet, as he dropped her down onto the king-sized bed. She had no time to notice anything else.

Lincoln grasped her arm, and producing a length of rope, he set about tying her wrist to the bedpost. Once she was tied securely, he did the same to her other wrist, and Laura did nothing to stop him.

With her arms, outstretched, and tied either side of her, he lowered himself down, and again began gnawing at her nipples before running his tongue slowly down her body, to the entrance of her womanhood.

She opened her legs, knowing what he wanted. It was bestial, the way he devoured her, lapping, sucking and draining the delicious, salty juices from her swollen lips. His fingers delved between her buttocks, it felt wrong, and debauched, but she yearned for him to continue, and opened her legs even wider. She had never been stimulated like this before, and the experience was mind blowing. He responded by licking her even more ferociously. She writhed and bucked her legs, as his onslaught continued.

She began to feel the massive build up once more. It was all consuming, and she could do nothing to prevent it happening. She screamed out, arching her back, pulling hard at the ropes that bound her.

"I'm going to have you every way possible." He grinned, before rolling onto his back, giving her a few moments respite.

Within moments, he was back on top of her. He brought her legs up high, so that the backs of her ankles were resting on his shoulders. He then positioned himself so he could penetrate her at his leisure.

"Slowly," she cried out, feeling his hugeness filling her. He began thrusting, slow at first, then much harder, and more forceful.

The sloshing sound of her wetness grew in intensity, as he went deeper inside. He was enormous, and it felt as if he were at the very gates of her uterus. Laura now fully understood what Amanda meant earlier, when she said it was so different - it was. So rebellious, so taboo, and so gloriously shameful.

"Harder!" She screamed, as Lincoln pounded her unmercifully.

"I'm going to cum inside you." He roared, thrusting even harder, so that it felt like his massive black penis would come out of her mouth.

"Please..." She begged, panting and unable to move her tethered arms.

She felt his body convulse, as he bit down hard on her breast, and filled her with what seemed like a gallon of sperm. She climaxed at the same time, her orgasm shaking the whole of her body. It was so intense, and like nothing she could ever describe. She could feel the dampness of the bed beneath her and feared she may have wet herself during her climax. He untied her, and she sat up, her nipples raw, and tingling.

"Don't worry," he laughed. "You've just had your first female ejaculation! I think some people refer to it as, 'squirting'!" He added proudly.

She looked up at him, a little shocked, before dropping back down exhausted.

Laura lay next to him for a few minutes, amused at the thought, that she was now black property, and Lincoln had been true to his word, and had literally shown her the ropes. She was amazed that his erection never seemed to go down. She eventually got up and went into the bathroom. Looking at herself in the mirror, she saw that her eye liner was smeared, and her hair looked as if she'd been pulled through a hedge backwards. She had to sit on the toilet, as Lincoln's semen continued to pour out of her.

Still naked, she padded back out to the bedroom. Lincoln had put his boxer shorts back on, and had brought in a jug of iced water, containing slices of lemon. He poured her a glass, and she downed it immediately.

He went over to her, and lowered his head to plant a soft kiss on each of her enlarged breasts.

"I'm Sorry if I was a bit too enthusiastic! But you were amazing, simply amazing!" He drooled.

"I'm glad you enjoyed it!" She replied. "I must say, it was quite amazing for me too!"

Laura went into the front room to retrieve her clothes, but Lincoln pulled her back.

"When you're here with me, you stay naked!"

"Do I take it, we haven't finished, Dr. Greene?"

"Certainly not, Student Nurse Peddlescoombe. I have unfinished business with you!" He drooled, giving her bottom another hard slap.

27. THE PARTY

The noise was infuriating and certainly wasn't the best start to a day Sally had been dreading. It was Penny's sixteenth birthday, and after much harassment, she had finally given in and consented to her daughter having the party in the house the following night.

"It has to be finished by ten, and I don't want any drinking or loud music. Is that clear?"

"What's the point of having it then? Come on Mum, all of my friends were given a certain amount of freedom to hold their parties, and things went okay." Pleaded Penny.

"Eleven then, and not a minute later. Do you understand young lady?"

"Listen Mum, I've got an idea. Why don't you come back at midnight, and I should have most of them out by then?"

"Come back at midnight? But I'm not even planning on going out!"

"Mum, I'll be sixteen! I already drink and smoke, well sometimes. Plus, you've let me stay over at my friend's before, so what's the difference? It'll be alright, so stop worrying."

"I don't know Penny. You certainly have a lot more freedom than I ever did at your age."

"Please Mum. All of my friend's parents went out on their birthdays. You don't get it, I'll lose all my credibility if they see you here."

"All right, you win. I'll go over and see Lizzie for a couple of hours, but don't forget, only let in people who you know, and I'll expect you to be up early in the morning. I'm not getting everything ready on my own."

So it was planned, and the dreaded day soon arrived.

Frank, snoring loudly was totally oblivious to the loud racket going on outside. Sally glanced at her bedside clock, it was just after seven in the morning. The noise wasn't going to go away, so wearily she got up and went over to pull the curtains back.

"No, No, stop! Don't do that!" She shouted, quickly opening the window. But Jamie didn't hear her.

"Frank wake up, please stop him!"

"Will you stop shouting, for fuck's sake!" Growled Frank, sitting up in bed.

"It's your son. He's riding a motorbike over my flower beds, and by the look of it, he's totally ruined my lawn! Frank, please go down and stop him."

"I said Jamie could ride his motorbike out there."

Sally couldn't quite believe what she was hearing.

"But, my beautiful flowers?"

"I'll be digging it all up anyway, when I buy the house, so it doesn't matter."

Sally was so angry that she stormed out of the bedroom and locked herself in the bathroom. She was feeling ghastly with a hangover, and looking at her reflection in the mirror certainly didn't improve things. For the first time in her life, Sally felt old and tired. She took a couple of tablets for her aching head and trudged downstairs.

Jamie was a spoilt brat, there was no other word for it. The TV was blaring, cups and dishes were strewn everywhere and breakfast cereal had been spilt over the mahogany coffee table. It was the school summer holidays and the thought of Jamie being there any length of time made Sally shudder. There was only one thing for it, to go out and speak to him herself.

Standing in the kitchen doorway, she called out several times, but he chose to ignore her.

Clutching her coffee, Sally gasped in horror as she walked across what was once a beautifully tended lawn. It was now crisscrossed with tyre marks and large holes, where clumps of turf had been churned up. Stepping over piles of dog mess, Sally shouted loudly, and noticed one or two of the neighbour's curtains twitching.

When Jamie finally came into view, it was a sight that terrified her. He was revving up his bike, and without any warning suddenly accelerated straight towards her, sending dirt and geraniums flying in his wake. Dropping her mug of coffee, Sally waved frantically for him to stop. Then, just as he was almost upon her, he swerved and doing a broad-slide, came right around behind her. He was grinning as he took off his helmet to expose his sweat-matted hair, and chubby red face.

"Jamie, what on earth possessed you to do that, you could have killed me!" Screamed Sally.

"Sorry!" He replied sarcastically. "I wasn't going that fast."

"Yes you bloody well were, look what you've done to my lovely garden. How dare you!"

"My Dad said I could ride my motorbike out here."

"I don't care what your Dad said. You've ruined my garden. Look at my flowers!"

"My Dad's buying this house. I can do what I like."

"Well, it's not his yet, and I would appreciate it if you would stop churning up my lawn."

Jamie just laughed and started revving up the engine again. The smoke was unbearable and Sally started to cough. With her eyes streaming, she put her hand up beckoning him to stop. However, Jamie laughed even louder and pointed a stubby, sausage finger at her. Sally glanced down and was horrified to see that the silk robe Frank had brought her in Paris was gaping open, revealing her naked body in all its splendour. Sally hurriedly pulled the robe together.

"You despicable little creature. You make me sick!" She shouted at him, before storming off back inside.

It took Sally and Penny the rest of the morning to tidy the house and most of the afternoon to get the drinks and prepare the necessary nibbles for the party.

Fortunately, Frank had taken Jamie out for the day and didn't return with him until later that afternoon. This gave Sally a chance to calm down and give her daughter the present she had asked for.

"Wow! Look at those speakers Mum, it's perfect!"

"Well, I certainly wouldn't have chosen a stereo myself, but if that's what you wanted?"

Penny immediately set up the stereo, and eagerly tested it with her ABC album. However, mother and daughter's harmony was soon shattered by the homecoming of Frank and Jamie, plus the dogs.

Jamie immediately invited himself into Penny's room and plonked himself down on her bed.

Frank, meanwhile stood in front of Sally with his hands behind his back.

"Come on Sally, I've brought a little present for Penny, so I had to get you something too!"

"Frank, don't think you can get around me with bribery." She remarked, coldly.

"I just want to help that's all. What's the harm in that?" He said, taking a beer from the fridge.

"You can help by buying more flowers for the garden and laying a new lawn. I can't forgive you for what you allowed Jamie to do. I'm so annoyed." She replied, still refusing to accept his gift.

"We'll talk about that later, Sally. Let me pay for Penny's party, it's the least I can do, besides Jamie and I brought a few more goodies while we were out, Mark's bringing them over shortly."

Frank was as good as his word. Half hour later Sally answered the door to a large, but pleasant bearded man, with the most warm, expressive brown eyes.

"Hello, you must be Mrs. Peddlescoombe?" He asked with a smile.

"Yes, that's right, can I help you?"

"It's Mark!" shouted Jamie from upstairs.

"Looks like we've already been introduced!" Laughed the visitor. "I'm Frank's right-hand man, and general dogs-body!"

"Poor you!" Smiled Sally, taking an instant liking to Mark.

Penny joined them, to get away from Jamie and couldn't believe her eyes when she saw what was in the back of Mark's car. There was cooked chicken, smoked salmon, several different cheeses, assorted pate's and pies and most importantly - drink!

"It's a children's party, Frank. I don't want them drinking." Protested Sally, angrily after they had brought the food and drink inside.

"Don't be so uptight. She's sixteen! You were young once. Besides, it's only beer and wine."

"And champagne!" Exclaimed Penny excitedly.

"I don't understand you sometimes Frank." Said Sally coldly.

"It'll be fine, besides, we'll be here to keep an eye on things."

"No Frank. It's Penny's party. She and her friends can run it without us being in the way. I'll be going over to Lizzie's."

"But Jamie can go, can't he?" Asked Frank, glancing across to Penny.

"I suppose so," she replied, trying to keep the peace. "He wont know anyone though, and he can be a little shy at times."

"You could have fooled me!" Remarked Sally dryly.

"I agree." Said Frank. "It'll be good for Penny to accept some responsibility, but I'll look in a bit later, just to make sure everything is okay."

"You really don't have to Frank. I can manage." Pleaded Penny.

"There might be gatecrashers, and if I'm buying this house, I certainly don't want any teenage yobs wrecking it, do I Penny?"

It was after 5 o'clock and Sally was just buttering the last of the French bread, when the telephone rang.

"It's for you Mum, it's the estate agents." Called out Penny.

"Hello Mrs. Peddlescoombe, It's just a call to say that we've finally got some good news."

"Really?" Asked Sally, intrigued, "What might that be?"

"A couple who looked around your house a few weeks ago want to put in an offer."

"But, there must be some sort of mistake. Frank Gant is buying the house, surely you knew that?"

"Yes, I do recall Mr. Gant coming to see your house, but he's not buying it, Mrs. Peddlescoombe."

"No, you must be wrong? I've accepted an offer from him. As far as I know, his solicitors are talking to your company about it."

"Are you dealing with another estate agent besides us Mrs. Peddlescoombe?"

"No," replied Sally slightly bewildered.

"I'm sorry, but I can assure you there are no negotiations going on with Mr. Gant, regarding your house, Mrs. Peddlescoombe."

Sally replaced the receiver and walked into the lounge, where Frank was watching a Rocky film with Jamie.

"You've been lying to me Frank, haven't you?"

"What the hell are you going on about now?"

"The house. You've got no plans to buy it, have you? You're just a fraud."

"Of course I'm buying it, my solicitors are on to it now."

"Don't lie to me anymore, you rat! I've just spoken to the estate agents and there aren't any negotiations going on at all. How do you explain that?"

"Are you calling me a liar, Sally?"

"Yes!"

"You fucking whore!"

Sally stepped back, shocked by the ferocity of Frank's verbal attack.

"I think you had better leave!" She replied, amazed with herself at being so confident.

"Look, Sally okay, I've had one or two problems with the business side of things. But I'm expecting some money to come through very soon. I'll tell my solicitors to get on to it right away."

"Please, Frank - don't say anymore. Just go."

"But Sally, I'm sorry. We've had some wonderful times together. Remember Paris? Come on, let's not spoil things, please give me another chance."

Sally sighed and paced across the room.

"I don't know. I really don't need all this in my life right now. You've practically moved in, your stuff is everywhere. It's like you already own the place. No Frank, things have moved too fast."

"Listen Sally, now is probably not a good time to talk. I'm sorry I lost my temper and swore at you, it's completely out of character."

"You frightened me Frank, I'm still shaking."

"I feel so ashamed. Look, I'm going to go out for a while. I'll book us a table at a restaurant you haven't been to before. You can get dressed up, and I'll even get one of the drivers to chauffeur us!"

"Just go Frank, I need some time on my own."

"Okay, Sally, if that's what you want. It's Penny's birthday, don't forget. We mustn't ruin it for her." With that, Frank picked up his jacket and walked out.

Sally, her nerves in tatters went into the kitchen and poured herself a stiff drink.

"Come on Mum, we've still got lots to do," said Penny, attempting to try and make everything normal again.

"Pour me another gin and tonic Penny, I'm going upstairs for a lay down." Replied Sally, desperately trying to hold back her tears.

"Is Frank coming back Mum?"

"Not if I can help it. I think we can do a hell of a lot better than that uncouth swine, don't you Penny?"

Frank took Jamie to a popular burger restaurant in the West end, it was a treat, but it was mainly to get them both out of the house. He had lost his temper with Sally, and realised his foolishness could have put his plans in severe jeopardy.

"Have what you want, son." Said Frank, eyeing the young waitress.

After studying the menu closely, Jamie chose an extra large bacon and cheese burger, while Frank was content just to have a coffee. He would eat later at the club, have a few drinks and play some poker before looking in at Penny's party.

"Wow, Dad! Look at the size of it!" Gasped Jamie, as the waitress placed the huge plate of food down in front of him.

"Just don't get too fat, Jamie. Girls aren't interested in fat guys, unless you're loaded with money of course. Just remember to keep yourself in shape."

Jamie glanced down at his stomach, which was protruding over his jeans.

"I want to start working out, like what you do, Dad. I want to be just like you."

"We'll have to stop your mother feeding you rubbish first. Just because she's looking like a sack of shit these days, doesn't mean you and Tina have to."

Jamie had to think about what Frank had just said, as he sank his teeth into the gigantic burger.

Frank realised he'd just mentioned his daughter's name as if she were still alive. It seemed absurd that he would never see her again, hear her voice, see her smile, or have her bow to his demands. He glanced at Jamie, who was totally unaware of his sister's death, and was relieved the youngster didn't press him further regarding her whereabouts.

"I'm only interested in one girl. But I don't think she likes me." Said Jamie, taking a slurp from his milkshake.

"I think I know who we're talking about." Grinned Frank. "It's Penny, isn't it?"

Jamie started to blush, and dropped his gaze.

"Yes, it's Penny," he admitted. "I want to ask her out, but she'll say I'm too young."

"She's certainly good looking. I admire your taste, Jamie. Have you made her laugh yet?"

"No, I don't think so," he replied, looking puzzled.

"That's part of the key, Jamie. Wear good clothes, smell nice, and make a woman laugh, and you're halfway in bed with them."

"Is that what you did with Sally and Mum?"

"Yes, I suppose so, plus I used a little charm, that always comes in handy. Listen, son, they're just women, they're not like us. You just have to take what you want."

"I don't understand?"

"It's simple," continued Frank. "You have to let a woman know you're in charge. It doesn't matter what age you are. Women respect power and strength. They like to be dominated, it's how nature intended things."

"So, you're saying I should just take Penny?"

"Well, yes, but you have to be a bit subtle, and use your imagination. Sometimes you have to be brutal. They appreciate it in the end. Is that clear?"

As Jamie tucked into his French fries, he scrutinised his father, not quite understanding what he was talking about, but wanting to emulate him. He liked the way Frank used his power to manipulate people and make them wary of him. When they were like that, they talked and made mistakes, which Frank picked up on, like an animal detecting the scent of a weaker prey. However, Frank's methods weren't always based on sheer brutality. His charm, manners, and the ability to say the right things at the right time also came into play, in what was the total, Frank Gant package.

"So why are we staying at Sally's? Why aren't we at home with Mum?"

"Aren't you enjoying it at Sally's, Jamie? It's more fun, and of course, you get to see Penny."

"Yes, I suppose so, but have you left Mum?"

Frank grinned and lit a cigar, much to the disgust of several other diners in the restaurant.

"No, I haven't left your mother. You have to understand that she's a sick, twisted woman. She's an alcoholic and can't be trusted. She's hurt me in the past, Jamie, hurt me a lot."

"I still don't understand, Dad?"

"I've left her alone for a while, so she can think about all the bad things she's done in her life. But, Sally, now that's different, Jamie. I'm on a sort of secret mission, and you're helping me"

"Wow, cool!" Exclaimed the eleven year-old, as he finally demolished his burger. "So, we're like secret agents?"

"Yes, in a way. Like I said, you have to help yourself to whatever you want in life. If you don't, someone else will. It's a simple rule of the jungle. Sally has a lifestyle, a home, and a business that excites me. It's something I want to get involved in, and you're helping me to achieve that, Jamie."

"Mum said you killed an old man once to get the money to start your cab business. Is that true Dad? What's it like to kill someone?"

"Keep your voice down." Cursed Frank, looking around to see who had heard.

"So she told you that did she, I bet she was drunk?"

"I don't know, I can't remember. How did you kill him Dad, did you shoot him, like in a gangster film?"

Frank laughed.

"Listen, son, he was an old man, a very rich old man, and he happened to have something I wanted, so I just took it. Besides, he was going to die soon anyway, I just helped him along."

"I think I'm getting to understand you, Dad. You're a bit like Al Capone. What did the old man have that you wanted so much?"

"Well, apart from the obvious wealth, he had style, class, and charisma, but more importantly, he had ambition and he was successful. We were poor at the time, and the old man was a means to an end. He had to go, Jamie. There was no other way, just like Sally's stupid husband."

"Wow! Did you kill him too, Dad?"

Frank was now revelling in his son's hero worship and making the grave mistake of divulging too much information.

"He was standing in the way of what I wanted, so like old Mr. Bloom, he had to go too!"

"Did you shoot him Dad?"

"No, son, I cut the brake pipes on his car. I'd seen it done in a movie, and it worked a treat!"

Jamie went quiet and looked into his father's steely blue eyes. He looked at the scar running down the left side of his face, the cropped haircut, the menacing stare and the terrifying aura that surrounded him, like some vile parody of a halo.

"Gosh, I can't believe you did that to Penny's father." He said after a few moments, with a hint of sadness in his voice.

"It got us where we are today, boy, into Sally's life, where we can take what we want." Frank watched as Jamie noisily drained the last few dregs of his milkshake through a straw. He was already beginning to regret his disclosure, and was glad he hadn't said anything about killing Pauline's grandfather, Albert. Frank, then reached into his jacket pocket and took out his wallet. It was made of Italian calf skin and was bulging with cash and credit cards. He coolly took out a hundred pounds and passed it to Jamie. The boy's face lit up as he fingered the crisp, twenty pound notes excitedly.

"Thanks, you're the best Dad in the whole, wide world!"

"It's your wages son. It's for helping me. We're a team, remember, and we always stick together. Do you understand?"

Jamie nodded, and placed the money into his pocket, before making a start on his hot apple pie and cream.

"That means I can buy a set of ramps now for my motorbike. I'm so glad we're staying at Sally's house, it's fun playing in her garden."

Frank finished his coffee and stubbed out his cigar in the saucer, before standing up to leave.

"Listen, Jamie, I've brought a new club, it's called Swann's. I'm going over there later, do you want to come and see it?"

"I would like to Dad, but another time. Can you drop me off at home so I can get some clothes for tonight, and go to the motorbike shop?"

Frank tried to act natural, but in truth, he didn't really want Jamie going back to Pauline, as he feared she might tell him in a drunken stupor, that his father was directly responsible for Tina's death.

"I suppose so Jamie, but don't go listening to any crap your mother comes out with. I'll pick you up in a couple of hours, okay?"

Jamie smiled with pride and hugged his father, causing Frank intense embarrassment.

"I'm going to take your advice and have a look in the shops for some cool clothes to buy."

As they walked out towards the car, Frank stopped, and turned to his son.

"Listen boy, everything I've told you is top secret, do you understand? Not a word to anyone."

But Jamie wasn't paying any attention, he was far too busy thinking about the motorbike ramps he was going to buy with his Dad's money.

Later that afternoon, Pauline sat in the office of Lake's nightclub in Mayfair. She was trying to contact casual staff to work during the evenings. She had heard rumours that a well-established rival club had been taken over and was due to re-open under new management. If this was true, then Pauline's assumption that some of her staff had been spirited away to work at the new club may well be justified.

She didn't particularly feel in the mood to sweet talk people into working as several issues were clouding her troubled mind. Coming to terms with the loss of her daughter, Tina was the main one. This was why she was here at the club. Just being away from home and things connected to Tina, and her short life, gave her the brief, but temporary respite she needed.

Getting up and walking through into the secret office, she felt angry with Sally for trying to steal Frank and was looking forward to having things out with her. Picking up a vicious-looking riding crop, she beat the palm of her hand with it. Pauline had a good idea of what she wanted to say and do, as she then brought the crop down hard on the bondage table in the centre of the darkened room. It was the same room where Claire had seduced her several years earlier, and where they continued to meet for mutual satisfaction, until Frank had discovered them. He then cheated Claire out of her club, in a highly dubious game of poker that still has people talking about it to this day.

The thought of those sensual moments with Claire sent a tingle along Pauline's spine and made her wonder what life would have been like if things had turned out differently. Her thoughts came back to the present, and that blonde bitch, Sally, along with her pretentious sidekick, Lizzie who both pretended to like and befriend her, knowing all the time that Sally was intent on taking away the man who meant the most to her.

Pauline was also disturbed by what her son, Jamie had disclosed earlier that afternoon. Frank had dropped him off without even calling in to see how she was coping. The boy had come bounding through the house full of positive vibes about his father, which made Pauline want to scream. She wanted to tell him that the bastard who thinks he's father of the year, is in fact a cold-blooded murderer, and a sexual predator that preyed on his own daughter. The fact that Frank had threatened to skin her alive if she told Jamie of Tina's death, only served to twist and distort the situation further.

Pauline didn't have the heart to tell Jamie how ridiculous he looked as he cavorted around gazing into every mirror, in a tight pair of jeans, and a shirt similar to what Frank would have worn. She asked him where he had been, but couldn't get a straight answer.

"Dad and me are gangsters. We take what we want and kill everyone who gets in our way." Was one of the replies she got back.

"That sounds like Frank. I'm glad he's been teaching you how to get on in life." She remarked dryly.

"I'm working for Dad now. He gave me £100."

"It sounds suspicious to me. If you follow in your father's footsteps you'll soon end up in prison or dead."

"That's what you think. I'm going to a party with him tonight, and I'm not telling you where it is."

"Just get out of my sight!" Screamed Pauline, at the end of her tether. Frank had obviously succeeded in turning Jamie against her, and this was the last straw after losing Tina.

"I'll go when Dad gets here. You don't frighten me, you're just a stupid woman. I could kill you and nobody would care."

"You mustn't speak to your mother like that! What on earth has your father been saying to you, Jamie?"

"You're no mother to me, Dad says you're a drunk. Sally's a better mother than you, I'm going to live there."

"Jamie, please stop, I can't bear it."

"Dad says he kills people who get in his way. He killed that old man and got loads of money, then he cut the brake pipes on Sally's husband's car. My Dad's a real gangster."

"So you've been at Sally's? I knew it."

"He told me not to say anything, you wont tell him I told you, will you Mum?"

Pauline couldn't believe what she had just heard, about William Peddlescoombe's murder, but knew it was probably true.

"Jamie, what you've just told me is very dangerous knowledge. I think it best we pretend we didn't have this talk for both our sakes."

Jamie looked frightened, and went across to put his arms around his mother.

"I shouldn't have told you, I knew I shouldn't have told you." He sobbed.

"I'm going to the club, Jamie. I don't want to be here when your father calls to collect you, I just can't bear to see him." Uttered Pauline, her face drawn and ashen.

That had been a couple of hours earlier. The conversation she'd had with Jamie was haunting her. She felt like a knife had been plunged through her heart. There were no limits to the atrocities Frank was capable of committing.

With her mind in turmoil, Pauline tried hard to concentrate on the present, and picked up the telephone to call one of the casuals, but she was disturbed by the intercom from downstairs.

"Hello, Mrs. Gant, I've got a lady here called Claire. She says she wants to speak with you urgently." Called out Anne, the duty manager, from the lobby.

Pauline paused for a few moments, in two minds what to do. Frank would surely kill her if she allowed Claire into the club.

"Okay, Anne send her up, she knows the way."

Claire had retained her lithe, dancer's figure, even though she was now in her mid fifties. Her dark bob was flecked with grey and noticeable crows feet had appeared around her eyes. However, she still possessed an air of confidence and strolled into her former office with athletic ease.

"I see you're lady of the manor!"

"What an unexpected surprise, Claire. It's nice to see you again after so long." Said Pauline getting up from the desk to greet her old lover. "I must say though, you're taking quite a risk. What if Frank's here?"

Claire gave a wry smile, as she sat down at the other side of the desk.

"I made it my business to make sure he wasn't here." She replied, glancing around at the office. "I see nothing's really changed, and you've still got the leather sofa!"

Pauline felt herself blush as her mind flashed back to when Claire and Yvette had enjoyed her on the sofa, back in the early days.

"Frank decided to keep it as it was, especially the secret office." Purred Pauline, feeling her senses coming to life.

"Ah, yes, my secret office! Well, at least he's got taste in one area." Replied Claire, with a smirk.

Pauline felt embarrassed about how she looked. She had been putting on weight recently, and knew the effects of the alcohol would be evident on her face.

"So what brings you here today, Claire?"

"Frank. That's what brings me here." Was her cold reply, as she edged closer towards Pauline." I recently had a bid accepted to buy a nightclub. It's called Swann's."

"I'm glad to hear things are on the up again." Said Pauline, standing up to go across to the bar.

"Well, things were, until I got gazumped. The sellers suddenly decided to take another offer."

"That's terrible, but what has Frank got to do with it?"

Claire went over to join Pauline at the bar.

"I heard a rumour from a good source that it had been Frank who had put in the offer."

"Well, that's news to me. He hasn't mentioned anything about buying another club. Besides, he hasn't got the funds. The repairs here have been very costly."

"Is there anyway you could find out, Pauline?"

Pauline took a large gulp from her vodka and tonic, and passed one to her visitor.

"You know what he's like. I daren't ask him."

"You don't have to, just call your bank."

"The business account is in Frank's name. They wont give me any information."

"What about your personal account, is it in both your names?"

"Yes, it's a joint account, but why?" Asked Pauline, looking anxious.

"Please, Pauline, just ring them and check your balance."

Pauline searched through her bag for her address book.

"I don't think this will help Claire, there certainly wouldn't be enough cash in our account for Frank to buy a nightclub."

"Perhaps not, but a deposit maybe?"

"Oh my god." Pauline's face suddenly dropped as she reached for the telephone.

"What is it, Pauline - you look so worried?"

Pauline slumped back in her chair, unable to take in what may have happened.

"My grandfather passed away recently. The inheritance money was paid in a couple of days ago."

"That's not good." Replied Claire, mirroring Pauline's concerned look.

Pauline was on the telephone to the bank for less than a minute.

"It's all gone Claire. Frank has taken every last penny of Albert's money."

"I'm sorry, Pauline. But I'm not surprised."

Pauline began to get tearful, and Claire went to comfort her.

"He's gone too far this time. He's stolen my money, caused the death of my daughter and he's seeing someone called Sally, who I went to university with."

"I know, I've seen her. I even threw a starter over her!"

"I don't know how much more I can take, Claire? He's slowly killing me, like he killed those other poor souls."

"What do you mean, Pauline?"

"He murdered an old Jewish man for his money. That's how he started up the cab business."

"Oh my word, Pauline. That was Mr. Bloom, wasn't it? I remember the police coming here and questioning you. So you've protected him ever since?"

"There's more. Apparently he also murdered Sally's husband, William. He cut the brake pipes on his car. He's probably killed more people that I don't even know about."

Claire put her arms around Pauline and soothed her as she wept her heart out. It was unusual for Pauline to cry like this.

"There, there, my darling, we'll get him."

Pauline glanced up at Claire, and held her tightly.

"I keep thinking about poor Tina, and my grandfather. Did Frank really murder him too?"

"Pauline, you've got to leave him, we must call the police. Frank has got to be stopped." Said Claire, as she wiped a tear from Pauline's cheek. "I'm here, I'll help you. Together, we can beat him."

Pauline managed to get a measure of composure and stood up to pace the office.

"I'll do it, Claire, I'll do it for all the people whose lives he's so cruelly taken away, the lives he's crushed and walked over, and destroyed. I'll do it for Albert, for Mr. Bloom, and for William Peddlescoombe, but ultimately, I'll do it for Tina. I owe her that. She was my daughter. I should have been a better mother to her. I should have protected her. I should have been there for her."

"And what about, Sally?"

"Don't worry about Sally, I've got some special plans for her."

Pauline hurried into the bathroom. Although she had just broken down in front of Claire, she hated showing signs of weakness, and cursed herself for letting it happen.

While Pauline was away, Claire finished her drink and decided what she would do. She couldn't trust Pauline to destroy Frank. No, she would have to do it herself. Once she was free from Pauline, she would inform the police that Frank Gant had murdered Abraham Bloom and William Peddlescoombe. That should stop him in his tracks for a while.

Penny was delighted so that so many of her friends could make the party. It meant a lot to Sally's youngest daughter, and she was determined to make sure it was a success. The only down side was the fact that Sally had removed the alcohol Frank had brought and had locked it away. But, all was not lost. Penny had been secretly hiding a supply of cider in her room for some time, and a few of the guests had brought alcoholic drinks with them.

Sally and Penny had only just finished setting up by the time the first partygoers started to arrive. The spread looked spectacular and Sally beamed with pleasure to see Penny so excited. She wasn't quite so pleased however, when she saw what her daughter had got changed into.

"I don't care if it's the latest fashion, I still think it looks absolutely ridiculous!"

"Mum, all of my friends will be wearing rah-rah skirts, I think they look pretty cool!"

"Well, it's your birthday Penny. But, I'm telling you, one day you'll look back at photographs of this and cringe. I know, I've been there!"

Their conversation was soon interrupted as more equally outrageous guests arrived, some of whom were sporting haircuts similar to the Flock Of Seagulls band.

"Hi Penny, happy birthday!" Said one friend as she handed Penny a gift-wrapped box and kissed her on the cheek.

"Gosh, what a lot of food, I've never seen anything like it!" Exclaimed Deborah, another friend, who seemed a little unsteady on her legs.

Sally smiled at Penny proudly.

"I'd better get a move on, I don't want to embarrass you in my old-fashioned clothes." she smiled, giving Penny a quick hug.

"Don't rush back, Mum!"

"And don't you push your luck young lady!"

Penny wasn't quite so sure about Jamie being there. He wasn't a particularly pleasant boy, and for the early part of the evening he just wandered around staring at the girls.

"Jamie, listen - I really need your help." Asked Penny, having just latched onto an idea.

"Do you want me to beat someone up?" He replied excitedly.

"No, not exactly. Can you be our DJ. We've got no-one to play the music. All the tapes and records are next to my new stereo."

"Wow! yeah!" He grunted, "Can I have some cider too?"

Penny brought him over a glass of the weakest cider she could find, before disappearing back into the crowd to mingle.

"Brilliant idea Penny. Jamie was really giving me a hard time." Said Deborah, beginning to slur her words.

"I'm not surprised Deborah, with you wearing that dress. It doesn't leave much to the imagination does it?"

"You're just jealous Penny, because I've got an eleven-year old boy after me!"

"Come on, let's get everyone dancing, if you can manage to walk that is!" Joked Penny as she sashayed out into the middle of the floor.

There was a dark-haired boy at the party called Kyle, who Penny rather liked. He went to a grammar school not far from Penny's. Although he had been looking over at Penny for much of the evening, he was very shy and hadn't yet spoken to her.

Jamie turned the music up loud and the whole house shook as most of the girls and a mere handful of boys began to dance. But after several more songs, Penny was disappointed there had still been no movement from Kyle.

"Jamie, here, put this one on. It's time for a slow one!" She called out to the chubby DJ. This time Penny would take matters into her own hands.

"Hi, your name's Kyle isn't it?"

"Yes, yes it is." He replied, a little shocked at Penny's boldness.

"Will you dance with me, Kyle, it's a slow one?"

She took her young man by the hand and led him out as Jamie played Spandau Ballet's *'True'*, which was Penny's favourite song at the time. As they danced together, the other guests couldn't help but notice how wonderful they looked entwined in each other's arms.

Jamie took a leaf out of Penny's book and made straight for the hapless Deborah, who was giggling hysterically at something and looked ready to pass out.

It was about this time that Frank arrived. For once he wasn't wearing his trademark suit, but trainers, jeans and a leather bomber jacket. Even though it was late evening, he kept his sunglasses on, and passed through the crowd drawing quite a bit of attention to himself. He laughed as he saw Jamie mauling the much-taller, teenage temptress as they swayed unsteadily to the music. Once the record had ended, Frank called for silence and took up position in the front room, like some dignitary about to make a speech.

"Hello everyone, I hope you're all enjoying the party?"

This was answered by loud cheering and whistling.

"Good, that's what I wanted to hear. Now, I want you all to join me in singing, 'Happy Birthday' to the most beautiful girl here tonight, which is Penny of course!"

This was followed by more cheering and hooting.

"When we've done that," continued Frank, "We're all going to have some champagne! Now, come on, let's hear it for Penny!"

The house was in uproar, and Penny didn't know whether to laugh or cry with embarrassment, as Frank hoisted her up onto his shoulders.

As the melee died down, Frank put Penny back on her feet and led her into the kitchen, saying he had a surprise for her. He sat her down on his lap, and poured her a glass of champagne.

"Here, this is for you!" He then placed a small, beautifully wrapped parcel down on the table in front of her.

"But what is it? Gosh, it's so exciting, I love presents!" Giggled Penny, trying to control her hiccups.

"Open and see!" Replied Frank, running his hand along the sixteen-year old's thigh.

Penny's face lit up, as she peeled away the wrapping and opened the box.

"Oh wow! Thank-you, Frank, it's a necklace!"

Frank laughed at her exuberance.

"What, just a necklace?"

"It's real gold isn't it?" Gasped Penny.

"Certainly is!" He grinned.

"But there's a stone attached to it, it's very pretty."

"What, just a stone?" He laughed again.

"No, it can't be. Is it really a diamond, Frank - for me?"

"Just for you Penny. A pretty diamond for an even prettier girl!"

She put her arms around him and hugged him tightly, before giving him a sloppy kiss on the cheek.

"You'll have to do better than that!" He laughed, putting his hand on her waist.

"Thanks Frank!" She replied, between hiccups. "Oops! I think I'm a bit tipsy! Can I wear it now?"

"Of course, here let me help you."

"I can't wait to show it off, I've never had a diamond necklace before."

As Frank went around behind her to put the necklace on, Deborah staggered into the kitchen, with Jamie hot on her heels. She slumped down at the table, uttered something incomprehensible and began to fall asleep.

"She's in no fit state to go home." Said Frank, removing a cigarette from between the drunk girl's fingers.

"She can stay in Laura's old room. Mum wont mind. I'd better ring her parents." Added Penny.

"Jamie, and Penny, come and give me a hand to get her upstairs." Ordered Frank.

The three of them then bundled Deborah upstairs and laid her out on Laura's bed. As they went to go back downstairs, Frank stopped Penny on the landing.

"Penny, wait - let's go into your room for a moment, I've got another surprise for you." Frank then produced a pre-rolled joint from his jacket pocket and proceeded to light it.

"So that's the funny smell I've noticed recently. Does Mum know you smoke those?" She asked.

Frank shrugged his shoulders.

"I don't really care! Does she know you smoke it, Penny?"

"But I don't!"

Frank laughed and sat down on the bed next to her. After taking a couple of pulls from the joint, he passed it to Penny.

"No, I don't think I should. I've already had too much to drink."

"Come on, you're sixteen now, you're all grown up. I expect all of your friends smoke dope."

Penny reluctantly scrutinised the joint before putting it to her lips. The more pulls she took, the more she began to recline on her bed. After a short while she lapsed into semi-consciousness. Frank lifted her legs and swept them up, so that she was now laying on her back.

"Go and check on Deborah, Jamie, then wait outside the room and warn me if anyone comes. I wont be long."

Jamie did as he was told, but left Penny's door slightly ajar. He thought his father might notice, but Frank was too busy removing Penny's clothes.

Frank was only in Penny's room for about ten minutes, before he was disturbed by a girl shouting from the top of the landing.

"Penny! Penny! Where are you? There's two boys fighting. What shall we do?"

"Fuck it!" Swore Frank, pulling up his zip, as he heard the sound of breaking glass.

Jamie stood back as his father charged out of the room and headed off downstairs. He peeped through the crack in the door and saw that Penny was naked. He feasted his eyes hungrily on the teenager's slim body.

"Penny, are you okay, it's Jamie - can I come in?"

There was no reply, so Jamie crept into the room and closed the door quietly after him. As he sat on the edge of the bed, Penny opened her eyes and immediately began to pull the bed covers over herself.

"Go away, don't touch me." She pleaded.

"Please, let me stay with you for a while." Begged Jamie.

"Where's Frank?"

"He's downstairs sorting out some trouble. Are you Dad's girlfriend now?"

"I want my mother, can you ring her, she's at Lizzie's?"

"But you were letting him touch you?"

"I thought I was dreaming. It was all a bit of a blur. I think it was that stuff I smoked."

"I knew you shouldn't have smoked it." Smirked Jamie, laying down next to her.

"It must have been a dream. Your father wouldn't touch me like that would he?"

"I don't know, perhaps."

"But he said he was my friend. He told me all about the time when he was a little boy and his brother put chicken guts inside his teddy bear - isn't that gross?"

"My Dad told you that?"

"Yes, I felt really sorry for him."

Jamie started giggling.

"I think he was having you on, Penny. That's what he did to my sister, Tina."

"What? He put chicken guts in her teddy - his own daughter. I don't believe you!"

"Suit yourself. She told some lies about him years ago, so he did that to Treacle to punish her."

Penny froze and felt physically sick.

"But Jamie, you don't seem upset that she's dead?"

"Don't be stupid," he replied, angrily. "My sister's not dead, she's in hospital."

Penny felt herself go cold, as she realised nobody had told Jamie of Tina's suicide. It was then that she became aware of his arm moving across her body. Before she realised what was happening, the boy had reached under the covers and was cupping her breast.

"Stop it, Jamie, take your hand away!" She protested, reaching up to remove his hand.

"But you let my Dad do it?" Was his reply, as he moved his hand between her legs.

"Jamie, please stop. What if someone comes in?"

"If you don't let me, Penny, I'll tell your mum about you smoking dope and about what you and my dad were doing in here." He replied with a chilling menace in his shrill, unbroken voice.

Penny cringed as she endured Jamie's slobbering mouth at her breasts, and his fat, stubby fingers exploring her below. She thought of poor Tina, then of her poor mother.

Fortunately, no serious damage had been done. A few glasses had been smashed and there was a nasty crack in the back door window pane. Frank was just in the process of clearing up the mess, when Sally appeared.

"What on earth's been happening?"

"We had a bit of trouble with some young thugs, but it's sorted now." Replied Frank.

"Yes, I just passed one with a bloody nose. Did you do that Frank?"

"They were going to wreck the house Sally, I had to do something."

"Where's Penny?"

"She's upstairs, had a bit too much to drink. Leave her, she'll be fine."

"That's it, no more parties."

"Come on Sally, don't be too hard on her, she's a lovely girl, and you don't turn sixteen every day."

"I suppose I ought to be grateful you were here, Frank."

"It was nothing, Sally. Here, let's have a drink."

"I don't want one Frank. I just want you to go. It's not working, and I just can't go on like this."

"What? How can you say that, after all I've done - you ungrateful bitch!"

Suddenly, the music began to blare again. Frank stormed into the lounge, pushing teenagers out of the way as he made his way towards Penny's new stereo. He ripped the plug from the socket viciously, before lifting the apparatus high above his head, and smashed it down to the floor. The room went silent, and all eyes turned to watch him. Frank then marched back to where a terrified Sally was standing.

"Right, there shouldn't be anymore interruptions!" He glared.

"I'm calling the police. Get out of my house now!" She cried, taking a step back.

"I'll be back, you can count on that. After all, Sally, we're an item now, aren't we. You can't go kicking out little Frankie over a lover's tiff!" He said, inching closer towards her.

"Get away from me you bastard!" She screamed, reaching for a carving knife.

"I'll teach you to pull a knife on me!" He snarled, easily knocking the weapon from her hand.

Sally scrambled to retrieve it, but as she bent down a backhander sent her sprawling to the floor.

"Don't wait up!" He cursed, turning to go.

Frank screeched off into the night. He was angry about Sally, angry about the Penny interruption and angry about missing what would have been another opportunity with Deborah. He could have had three women that night, but now he would have to be content with one of the girls at the club if he could get lucky, or Pauline, of course, and that thought irked him greatly.

It was left to Kyle and a couple of Penny's friends to come to Sally's assistance. While one of the girls put a cold compress to the side of Sally's face, the young man watched, very perturbed by what he had just witnessed.

"I wish I could have done something to help, I just felt so useless."

"It's probably a good thing you didn't, Kyle. He's a very nasty and dangerous man."

"I think you're going to need a steak on that eye, Mrs. Peddlescoombe."

"Kyle, please don't ever mention steak to me again." Replied Sally, trying to laugh the matter off.

Penny came down in her dressing gown, looking pale and distraught. The sight of her mother receiving first-aid was distressing to her.

"Mum, what's happened?"

"Nothing to get upset about Penny. I just fell and had an accident that's all, and your nice friends are helping me."

"It was Frank wasn't it?"

"I really don't want to hear his name mentioned again Penny. Frank is history. So how did the evening go, and why are you in your robe?"

Penny couldn't bear to give her mother any more bad news, and decided to keep quiet about Frank and Jamie molesting her.

"Oh, I spilt a drink over myself, and just decided to get changed." She replied, rather unconvincingly.

"Penny."

"Yes, Mum?"

"Come over here and give me a cuddle, I need one."

For Sally, it had been one of the most restless night's in memory. She was over tired and didn't get to bed until late. The awful argument with Frank certainly hadn't been conducive to a relaxing evening, and to top it all, the side of her head throbbed like mad. She was the first one up the following morning and sat stroking Pepys for a while, before finding the energy to pull back the curtains and get started on the clear up. The whole house seemed to reek of stale smoke and alcohol, so she opened the kitchen door and as many windows as she could.

The party had finished earlier than expected, due to Frank's unforgivable behaviour, and as a result a lot of the food had remained uneaten. Sally made herself a coffee. It was 07.30, and she thought about waking Penny, but then decided to let her have a lie in, since she probably wouldn't be too much help anyway.

As she was filling a black bag with rubbish, Sally heard the most appalling noise. It sounded like a terrifying, high pitched scream, but it certainly didn't seem human. Dropping the bag, she hurried out into garden, where the noise seemed to have originated, then she heard it again. As she stepped onto the patio, she saw Pepys running for his life across the lawn. Both Frank's dogs, Conan and Thor were in hot pursuit, and soon caught up with the Border Collie. With frightening savagery, they tore into Pepys, pulling him around like a rag doll. Sally screamed at the dogs to stop, and not thinking of her own safety, grabbed the broom and went running towards them.

Conan growled at her, but Sally yelled back at the Pit Bull Terrier, and raised the broom to strike it. The blow was enough to send the animal scurrying off to a safe distance. Thor, however had Pepys's neck in his powerful jaws, and didn't look like letting go. Sally brought the head of the broom crashing down with a ferocity she never knew she possessed. She hit the dog hard across the back and it immediately let go of Pepys and yelped in pain, before running off to join its partner.

Sally scooped up the bleeding Pepys and ran back towards the house. Conan and Thor began to chase after her, quickening their pace as they sensed their prey escaping. She practically flew into the kitchen, feeling the dogs inches away. Conan leapt up at her, sinking his teeth into the back of Sally's dressing gown. Fortunately, he only got a mouthful of material and released his grip. Sally cursed him, and slammed the door hard into the animal's snarling face.

Penny appeared in the doorway looking horrified.

"Pepys! What's happened to him?"

"It's Frank's dogs. They've attacked him."

"Is he going to be alright, Mum?"

"I don't know Penny!" Shouted Sally, panicking. "Come and help me, there's blood everywhere!"

Sally laid the dog on the kitchen table, and gasped as she took in the extent of his wounds. Both his neck and hind leg had been badly bitten through, and he was bleeding profusely.

"I'll get the first-aid box."

"No, Penny - there isn't time. Get a couple of hand towels from the drawer and come over here."

Penny fetched the towels and rushed to her mother's side.

"What shall I do?"

"Don't panic Penny, remember when Tina was here and cut herself, it's just the same. Fold the towels and put them over his wounds. His neck looks the worst - just apply a little pressure and see if you can slow up the bleeding."

"But Mum, where are you going?"

"I'm going to get dressed, I'll have to take Pepys to the vet, and while I'm at it, I'll phone that bastard, Frank and tell him to get these monsters out of my garden before I shoot the damned things."

"Please hurry, Mum."

"He's very traumatised, Penny. Try and talk to Pepys and re-assure him."

It was midday by the time Sally got back from the vet's. She looked tired and pained as she sat at the kitchen table where Pepys had lain a few hours earlier.

"Is it bad Mum, will Pepys die?" Asked Penny, sitting down next to her.

"Yes, it's bad, but we don't know yet. The vet is operating on him as we speak."

"The dogs are still loose in the garden."

"I left a message for Frank, that's all I can do."

"Poor Pepys, he's such a friendly dog. He doesn't deserve this."

"None of us do, Penny." Replied Sally, her voice a mixture of despair and anger. "Where's that revolting son of his, still in bed I suppose?"
Penny nodded.

"Well, let's get the horrible little swine up. He can get those bloody dogs under control and clean up all the mess they've made."

"Leave him, Mum." Pleaded Penny. "I don't want to see him."

"Do you bloody well think I do, Penny, do you? He's got to accept some responsibility." Barked Sally, about to charge off up the stairs, only to be side tracked by the telephone ringing. "Yes, who is it?" She asked abruptly.

"Hello, Sally - it's Pauline."

"Pauline? I'm sorry if I sounded a bit off. I've been having a bad day, and now's not a good time to talk."

"You've been having a bad day? Why, what went wrong, some of your underwear turned pink in the wash!" Remarked Pauline caustically.

Sally wasn't in the mood to humour her caller. But she suddenly remembered the torment she must be going through having recently lost her daughter.

"No, Pauline, not quite. I was meaning to call you about the terrible news," said Sally, totally unprepared for the conversation. "I just don't know what to say, poor Tina. It's just so awful. Are you coping, I mean, is there anything I can do to help?"

"Could you come over, Sally? You said you would visit. I need someone to talk to."

"Let me check my diary, Pauline." Sighed Sally. It was the last thing she felt like doing.

"I feel so desperate. I've tried to bury my feelings about Tina. You are my friend aren't you?"

"Yes, of course Pauline." Replied Sally, feeling that under the circumstances, she had no choice but to go and see this strange, disturbed woman.

28. REVELATIONS

"What about this one, a bit formal I suppose?" Asked Mark, trying to be helpful.

"No, I wouldn't wear that, I want something youthful, something to match my new image." Replied Pauline, as she searched through another rack of designer clothes in the Knightsbridge boutique.

Mark was greatly relieved when Pauline eventually found what she was looking for and they could finally go to the till and settle up. They had spent the whole afternoon shopping for outfits to go along with Pauline's latest whim. Following her meeting with Claire, she had realised that things had to change, and a new, stronger, slimmer, fitter and calculating Pauline was about to emerge.

Mark hated shopping trips with the boss's wife. It wasn't even the tedium of hanging around, feeling uncomfortable, and having to try and say the right things. No, it was the embarrassment of it all. Pauline was a huge embarrassment. Sometimes he wished the ground would simply swallow him up, the way she spoke to some shop assistants. Frequently, she had them in tears, or calling for the manager after she had torn a strip off them for no apparent reason, other than she felt like it. Then, she would always hate the clothes once she got them home and tried them on again. This meant trips back to the shop, always on his own to exchange the items and get a refund. Today, however, Pauline had been satisfied with her purchases, and seemed at one with the world for a change. But, had a change come over Pauline, wondered Mark, or was there something rumbling underfoot he had no knowledge of.

He had been surprised at Pauline's indifference to Tina's death, and at times he began to have serious doubts about her sanity. He was also very much aware of the suffering she had endured at Frank's hands. But to show no outward emotion over something as serious as the death of a daughter was unnatural and impossible for him to comprehend. If anything, Mark himself had been more upset and shocked by the tragedy, rather than the girl's mother. He was the first to offer his condolences and send flowers and a card to both Frank and Pauline, despite their obvious shortcomings.

He liked to remember Pauline how she was when he had first met her, as a young and somewhat naive mother of a little girl. She was in love with the man of her dreams, and her head was way up in the clouds. Now he hated himself for even thinking for a moment that she might be insane. He accepted her behaviour by convincing himself she was in shock, and the real impact of the event hadn't had time to be assimilated into her troubled mind. He felt that it was only a matter of time before she cracked under the strain and gave full vent to her oppressed emotions. Mark, however remained loyally by Pauline's side and put up with her unpredictability with unbending resolution.

It felt strange, driving her around without Jamie. There had been countless times when he had wanted to speak in private with Pauline, without the spoilt child being present. On occasions, Pauline would sit up front with Mark, while Jamie was content to occupy the back seats, lost in his own vivid imaginative world. He and Pauline were able to talk quite freely, but now he had the chance, the words didn't come easy to him. But since Jamie had been sent off to stay with a 'friend' of

Frank's, Pauline had once again taken to sitting in the back and saying little.

Frank had made it very clear that he didn't want his son to know about Tina's death. It was this, and his opinion that Pauline's mental state would deteriorate further that finally convinced Frank that Jamie would thrive better away from his mother.

"I want to go and have tea near the Serpentine." Said Pauline, quite out of the blue.

Mark parked the car around the perimeter at Hyde Park, and before sitting down to their tea, they took a gentle stroll together around the lake. Pauline then surprised him again by linking her arm through his.

It was rather an overcast day with a light breeze, and as they walked, geese and ducks eagerly followed their progress in the hope of being tossed the odd morsel of bread or two.

They headed over to a cafe, situated by the water's edge. They walked purposely and silently, as if both were heavy in thought.

"I used to bring Tina here when she was a little girl. I would walk miles with her in the pushchair, or we would take a bus or get on the tube. Tina used to find it so exciting." Reflected Pauline.

"I'm sorry Pauline. It must be so difficult for you. I sometimes wonder where you get your inner strength?"

"Thank-you Mark, always as thoughtful as ever."

"If you want to talk Pauline, I'm always here to listen, you know that."

"In fact, I do want to talk to you, Mark, but not about Tina. I'll deal with my grief in my own way, just as I did with Albert."

"Yes, of course, if that's what you want. So what is it you want to talk about?"

"Your son!"

"My son?"

"Yes, Mark. Jamie is your son."

"I don't believe you!" Exclaimed Mark, looking totally bewildered.

"He's your son. Think about it."

Mark went silent and gazed at Pauline blankly.

"The occasion is far too serious for you to be joking, isn't it, Pauline?"

"I don't joke Mark." She replied, before taking a seat at one of the cafe's outside tables.

"I realise that Pauline."

"I'm telling you now Mark, while there's still time. Jamie is going to need you soon."

"I take it, Frank doesn't know of this?"

"No, of course not. Well, not yet anyway." Replied Pauline coldly.

"What do you mean, not yet? If you tell Frank, it'll be like signing my death warrant, and probably yours too. He dotes on Jamie."

"Don't worry about Frank, I'll deal with him." Remarked Pauline, as she studied the menu. "These cream scones sound nice."

"Does that mean you're finally going to leave him, Pauline?"

"I'll never leave him, Mark. In fact, Frank and I are going to be together for eternity." She said icily. "Now listen, I've informed my solicitors of the situation, and I've also changed my will accordingly. Frank has left everything to me. His father insisted on that when Tina was born."

"What does all this mean?"

"It means you've got to be there for Jamie. I know he can be a horrid, spoilt brat at times, but he's young. You can change him, Mark - you can make him a better person. Besides, he thinks the world of you."

"This is all too much, Pauline. I just can't believe it. After knowing him all these years, after watching him growing up, now I discover that Jamie is my son!"

"Now, don't go getting any ideas. You must keep it to yourself, just for the time being. Can you do that, Mark?"

"Yes, I think so, Pauline."

"Good. Now order our tea please."

Pauline's house certainly wasn't everyone's cup of tea. It was situated in Kew, a beautiful, leafy part of South West London, famous for the nearby, botanical gardens. But the house lacked character and seemed out of place compared to some of the other houses in the area. It was an ugly, square, ultra-modern building with a sloping roof and large rectangular windows. A double garage seemed to take up most of the ground floor, and as far as Sally could tell, the living areas looked as if they were located on the first and second floors.

It was a frightfully humid day and Sally was sweltering, even going bra-less in the light dress she had opted to wear. Not wanting to be noticed, she quickly put on her sunglasses. She didn't actually know anyone living in the area, but felt uncomfortable being associated with Pauline Gant. Although the side of her face still ached from the blow she received from Frank at Penny's party, the redness and swelling had thankfully disappeared over the last couple of days.

Ringing the doorbell, Sally took a deep breath and decided to stick it for no more than an hour, she would think up some sort of excuse to make her exit if things weren't going well. Although there was no real reason to think that, since it had been Lizzie who had managed to rub Pauline up the wrong way the last time the women had met. Sally had decided to bluff her way through her meeting with Pauline, and since Frank was now hopefully history, she could leave and have no further contact with either of them.

Pauline resembled a cheap hooker and looked ghastly. Her make-up had been smeared on, she was wearing bright red lipstick and her eyes were bloodshot and puffy, through drinking and crying. She welcomed Sally inside as if her visitor were royalty, and led her through to the lounge.

While Pauline went to sort the drinks out, Sally surveyed the room with its beige, leather furniture and cream-coloured carpet. Staring out through the green patterned blinds, Sally could see her car parked directly across the road, and longed to get back inside it, and flee off into the waiting sunshine. She was still very worried about Pepys, but as yet there had been no real news from the surgery. Fortunately Lizzie had taken a day off from the boutique and was able to go over and stay with Penny.

Sally peered into an enormous glass cabinet which contained Pauline's best crystal and a collection of her favourite photographs. There were a couple of old pictures, which Sally presumed to be of Pauline's parents. Another photo showed a proud old man standing outside a prestigious-looking bank. There was another which interested Sally, it was Pauline when she was much younger and slimmer. She was wearing a mini-skirt and standing outside what looked like a nightclub with an elderly-looking man, in rather a provocative pose.

"I can't be bothered doing tea, Sally. We'll have a drink instead. Is vodka alright?" Asked Pauline, causing Sally to jump.

"Yes, vodka's fine."

"That was me with Mr. Bloom, he was a very dear friend of mine."

"It was a few years ago, Pauline, judging by the length of your skirt," replied Sally, a little nervously.

"Mid-sixties I'd say. He was such a nice man, a jeweller, but he died in very suspicious circumstances."

"How sad," remarked Sally.

"People often tend to die in suspicious circumstances when Frank's around."

"I'm sorry?" Asked Sally, a little puzzled.

"Don't mind me, I'm always speaking out of turn." Pauline then started laughing, which Sally found most disturbing. It wasn't a normal happy sort of laugh, there was something sinister and very disturbing about it.

"It must all be very painful for you at the moment, Pauline?"

"I've tried to get on with my life, Sally. I thought I could do it. First I lost my grandfather, and now it's Tina who's gone."

"But isn't Frank helping you get through it all?"

"Frank? He's no help, in fact he's the problem. Besides, he's got himself another whore." Replied Pauline, glaring at Sally.

Feeling decidedly uncomfortable, Sally picked up her drink, and wondered what on earth she could say to this woman. In the back of her mind she kept thinking about Frank, and whether Pauline's odd behaviour meant she actually knew about the affair.

"Pauline, I'll try to help you all I can. I lost my husband not that long ago. It was the most awful feeling. I thought I had nothing left to live for."

"That's just it Sally - I don't have anything left to live for."

"But you have a son don't you?"

"Yes, I have a son of sorts. But Jamie has no time for me now. Anyway, Frank's taken him away from me, to live with that other bitch. I may as well be dead."

"Pauline, you mustn't think like that, there has to be something worth living for?"

"Like what?" With that, Pauline began to sob.

Sally was completely taken aback, and was again in torment about what she ought to do. She moved closer to Pauline, and placed an arm around her shoulder. It made Sally cringe, but it was the least she could do to offer comfort to a woman she both feared and detested.

"Thank-you, Sally. I think I'm okay now." Said Pauline, after a few moments, which seemed odd. She then turned to face Sally, and wiping her eyes asked; "You are my friend, aren't you?"

"Yes, of course I am, Pauline," Replied Sally, removing her arm.

"I think we both could do with another drink." Said Pauline, again fixing an icy stare on her guest.

"What a wonderful idea, but may I use your bathroom?"

Sally breathed a huge sigh of relief as she locked the bathroom door. She was glad to be away from Pauline, even if it was only for a few minutes. Sally needed time to think and regain her composure. Pauline's behaviour was making her feel extremely nervous. But she needed to bide her time, perhaps just finish her drink, then say she had to go, yes, that was the best idea. She would then put the whole Frank, Pauline and Tina episode behind her.

As Sally looked around, she noticed that Pauline appeared to have every single brand of shampoo on the market. There was also an abundance of conditioners, soaps and body lotions of every kind. For a moment it reminded her of her own bathroom at home, until she thought back to where she was and the cold, sterile interior. However, there was something else that caught Sally's attention. Just as she was washing her hands, she looked up to see where the towels were, and saw a robe. There was something familiar about it. Sally took the garment down from the hook and opened it out. She then noticed that it was exactly the same as the robe Frank had given her. This one however, had Pauline's name emblazoned on it. Sally was aghast and felt a sickness building up in her stomach.

There was a selection of men's toiletries on one of the shelves, and Sally glanced through the bottles, realising Frank had several of the same in her bathroom. She noticed a distinctive, horse-shaped bottle of aftershave, and knew immediately what it was, even before she had opened it. The smell made her gasp, and again she found herself having to sit on the edge of the bath. There could be no mistaking the vile, sickly smell of, 'Mane.' It had been a smell that had permeated Sally's life for the last few weeks. It haunted her, and made her want to retch.

Sally knew she had to start thinking clearly. She sensed great danger, and had to get out of Pauline's house as quickly as possible. She put the top back on the bottle and unlocked the bathroom door. As she came out and started to make her way towards the stairs, she noticed Pauline's bedroom door was ajar. Peeping inside, she saw more photographs on top of the dressing table. She was inquisitive and wanted to take a further look. Standing perfectly still for a few moments, she could hear Pauline crashing around down in the kitchen. Then, before she had time to consider the folly of her actions, she had slipped off her sandals, and found herself standing in the middle of Frank and Pauline's garish bedroom. She glanced at the ugly maroon wallpaper and matching king-size duvet. A large fur rug made up of several different animal skins was laid out in the centre of the floor. The furniture was pure white and modernistic. Two large television sets were attached to one of the walls, like you would expect in a hotel. A floorboard creaked as Sally reached across to pick up a photograph of Pauline and Frank. It was an old wedding photo, and she couldn't help noticing how insane and angry Frank looked, it was as if he was being forced to marry Pauline, and unbeknown to Sally, he was. Seeing him again as he was all those years ago made her blood go cold, it brought back such horrendous memories of when he got into William's house and attacked her. If it hadn't been for David, who knows what could have happened. She hurriedly put the photo back down, but couldn't help being drawn to another set of three pictures further along. One was Frank with Jamie, another was him with Tina as a baby, and the last was Frank alone. Sally gazed intently at all three. She felt nervous and her heart was pounding wildly.

She had been having an affair with Pauline's husband, a man she had detested since her days at university, a criminal, a violent sexual predator, and a man directly responsible for the death of his daughter, not to mention any other poor souls that Sally was unaware of.

She closed her eyes for a brief moment and began to realise the full horror of her predicament. However, as she opened them again, she saw Pauline standing in the doorway, clutching a carving knife.

"Pauline, what are you doing? Please put the knife down, you're scaring me!" Pleaded Sally, as Pauline, with hatred etched into her face, moved menacingly towards her.

"You tried to take him from me, you slut!"

"Pauline, he tricked me. He said your marriage was over. He pretended he wanted to buy my house."

"What the hell do you take me for? Coming here lying to me, telling me you're my friend!"

"I'm sorry, Pauline, I can explain," Begged Sally, falling back onto the bed.

"You put your arm around me, Sally. You tried to lure me in, like you did with my Frank!"

"We had a row, Pauline. He doesn't want me anymore, it's you he wants, not me, you're his wife!" Gasped Sally, scrambling up the bed.

"How dare you lie to me anymore, you bitch! I deserve better than that."

"I don't want him Pauline, I don't honestly. Please don't come any closer."

"What do you mean you don't want him? Is he not as precious as your dear William? Is my Frank not good enough for you?"

"No, I never meant it to sound like that, Please Pauline, put the knife down!"

Pauline halted her advance, and leered at Sally, whose dress had now ridden up to the top of her legs, in her desperation to flee her tormentor.

"Look at you, not so special now are you? You're like a cheap tart. I knew you were seeing him, I'm not stupid you know."

Sally could only nod, she would have screamed, but was certain Pauline would have stabbed her to death.

"I was curious to see how he would treat you," continued Pauline, her voice low and threatening. "Why, you've lost some of your airs and graces. You're no better than me are you?"

"No, Pauline, I've never been better than you."

"You lying bitch! You've always thought you were superior to me, you and that other bitch friend of yours!"

"Pauline, please let me go, this will only make things worse for you."

"You certainly look different now, in fact Sally, you look a bit rough! Bags under those lovely blue eyes, a few wrinkles here and there, and what's this, I do believe you've put on a few pounds - a bit too much of the old booze eh?"

"Pauline. Please trust me, my daughter's a nurse. I can get you help."

"Well, you're very fortunate, aren't you? I had a daughter once, she was a nurse too."

"Let's go back downstairs, Pauline - we can have another drink and talk things through?"

"Has he made you walk around with root vegetables and giant dildos stuck inside you?"

"I don't know what you mean?"

"That'll come soon, he likes that. It gives him some sort of a power thrill."

"I don't believe you!"

"It's true. You could ask Tina, but I don't think you'd get a reply. Frank saw to that, like he saw to your precious husband!" Pauline then started giggling again, in the same pathetic, but disturbing manner.

"What do you mean, Pauline?" Gasped Sally.

"Frank killed your husband, cut his brake pipes, and he'll kill you as well, now that you know."

"I don't believe you, Frank wouldn't do such a thing?"

"You stupid, naive cow, Frank will do whatever it takes if he wants something." Glared Pauline. "Has he forced you to have sex with other women yet? Has he tied you up and beaten you?"

"No, of course not!"

"That'll come too. He likes to see two women doing it. Do you know what it's like to have sex with another woman?"

"Get away from me!" Screamed Sally as she leapt up from the bed and attempted to get past her assailant. The thought of Frank killing William polluting her mind.

However, Pauline caught her by the neck, and yanking her head down, brought the knife up to Sally's stomach.

"I asked you a question, Sally. Do you know what it's like to have sex with another woman?"

Pauline then slit the front of Sally's dress open, and pulled it apart. She drooled at her victim's shapely breasts before pushing her backwards onto the bed.

She then leapt on top of Sally and began kissing her forcibly on the lips. Fighting for her life, Sally managed to wrench herself free from Pauline's probing tongue, and tried to wriggle out from beneath her. But Pauline wouldn't give up, and began biting viciously at Sally's breasts. Sally screamed in terror as Pauline then reached down and began to forcibly remove her underwear. Out of desperation, Sally grabbed a handful of her attackers hair, and tugged as hard as she could, but it just made Pauline bite deeper into her flesh.

"Please stop!" Begged Sally, as Pauline brought the knife up to her throat.

"Keep still, or I'll cut you!" Growled Pauline, her eyes full of hatred.

Sally could only lay back and sob, as Pauline pulled off her knickers, and lowered her head down between her thighs.

Pauline moaned with pleasure, as her tongue eagerly explored between her victim's legs.

"You taste good, Sally - we should have done this sooner."

The assault went on for several minutes, before Pauline came up for air and moved up the bed to kiss Sally again. The smaller woman was at last able to push herself away, and make a dash for freedom. However, the door was on the other side of the room, and once more, Pauline had the escape route blocked.

"Please let me go, Pauline. You've had what you wanted?"

"What's up Sally, don't you like being a lesbian? Frank wont like that - he likes his women to be versatile!" Pauline leered at Sally's naked body and began to move towards her. "I've only just started with you. You're my bitch now!"

Sally took a deep breath, and put her hands up to defend herself. Then, as Pauline went to make another grab for her, she pulled back her arm and sent her fist crashing into the side of Pauline's face. As her attacker crumpled up on the floor, Sally grabbed what was left of her dress and fled from Pauline's house.

"Lizzie! Lizzie! Open up, let me in, hurry!" Shouted Sally, hammering at the front door.

Lizzie, never one to be hurried, eventually opened the door and stared out tentatively. Sally pushed her out of the way and rushed inside, shutting the door quickly behind her, before slamming the bolts in place.

"What's going on?" Exclaimed Lizzie, totally puzzled. "What's happened to you? Your dress is all torn!"

"I'll tell you later. We must lock all the doors and windows, Lizzie. There's great danger, we have to call the police."

"Sally, I must speak with you, it's very urgent. Please calm down and listen."

"There's no time, Lizzie - it'll have to wait. Where's Penny, we've got to keep her safe?"

"Look, Sally, I can take Penny to Gloucester, my parents would love to have her for a while, but what's going on?"

"No, Lizzie, we have to stay together."

"But, Sally - I have to speak to you, it's about Penny. There's something you need to know."

"What's wrong, is Penny alright?"

"She's up in her room. She's safe, but something has happened to her."

"I think I can guess what you're about to tell me, Lizzie. Gasped Sally with a look of terror etched into her face.

"Sally, it's so awful, I just don't know how to put it into words."

"It's Frank isn't it?"

Lizzie nodded.

"My baby!" Shrieked Sally, losing all control of her emotions. "I'm going to kill him, Lizzie. I'm going to kill that evil bastard. He murdered William."

"Oh my god, Sally. It's like a horrid nightmare. I can't believe it." Replied Lizzie, in a state of shock. "You have to be rational Sally, and think about what you're going to do."

"I know what I'm going to do, Lizzie, and there's going to be nothing rational about it!" Screeched Sally, slamming shut the kitchen windows and locking them. "I must go up and see Penny."

"It's not a good idea, Sally, I mean, the way you are at the moment."

"It's okay, Lizzie, I'm calm enough."

Sally knocked lightly on Penny's door, before entering, what looked like an empty room.

"She's not here?"

"She is," replied Lizzie, looking concerned. "Try the wardrobe."

Sally stepped across to the wardrobe, and opened it slowly. It was packed full of Penny's clothes, which she had to push to one side as she desperately searched for her youngest child.

"Penny, for god's sake, answer me, if you're in there!" Called out Sally, pulling out numerous pairs of shoes and paraphernalia, which she tossed behind her.

When she eventually found Penny, the teenager was sitting on the floor of the wardrobe, curled up in a foetal position. After clearing a small space, Sally managed to ease herself inside, and cuddled up next to her daughter.

"Penny, darling, Mummy's here. He wont hurt you again. I wont let him."

Penny reached out and put her arms around her mother and sobbed.

"Mum, don't ever leave me will you?"

"Penny, listen to me - you have to go and stay with Lizzie's parents for a while, they'll take good care of you."

"But I want to stay here with you, Mum." Replied Penny, her voice child-like.

"It wont be for long. It's too dangerous for you to stay here. Frank is liable to come back at any time."

"What about you, Mum?"

"I'm staying, Penny." Replied Sally, defiantly.

Helping her daughter out of the wardrobe, Sally hesitated before asking Penny what Frank had done to her.

"It was nothing, Mum. I think I was more worried about Pepys."

"Penny, you don't have to put on a brave face just for me. I know you're hiding something. You're still my little girl, even if you are sixteen. Tell me what he did."

Penny sat on the edge of the bed like a frightened rabbit, clutching one of her old teddy bears tightly in her hands.

"He only touched me, Mum."

"Where, Penny?"

"Up, here, and down there." Replied the girl, feeling ashamed of herself. "I was a bit drunk, and he gave me dope to smoke. It made me feel ill."

"So he didn't...?"

"No, Mum," Replied Penny, starting to cry again. "There was some trouble downstairs, and he went to sort it out."

"You're not telling fibs are you, to protect my feelings?" Demanded, Sally, glancing towards Lizzie.

"No, Mum - I'm telling you the truth." Replied the girl, in a barely audible whisper, but choosing to say nothing of Jamie's attack on her.

"Why didn't you scream or try to fight him off?" Asked Lizzie in a matter-of-fact manner.

"I told him not to touch me, but he just kept doing it. I was too scared to do anything else."

"That's okay, darling, it wasn't your fault." Said Sally, as she glared icily at Lizzie, and reached across to comfort her daughter once more.

"Please make him go away Mum, and Jamie, and those horrid dogs that hurt Pepys."

"I will Penny. Nobody is ever going to hurt our family again, you can count on that. Now pack a bag, and come down when you're ready. I need to talk to Lizzie."

As the two women went back downstairs, Sally began to tell Lizzie about her horrendous ordeal at Pauline's house.

"Oh god, Sally - so Pauline knows you've been seeing Frank. Now you've got two psychopaths to contend with."

"I think he wanted to break me into submission, Lizzie, so that I became a pitiful wretch like Pauline." Said Sally glumly. "Poor Penny could have ended up like Tina. It's just too awful to comprehend."

"This is frightening, you've got to do something."

"I'm going to ring the police," replied Sally, going towards the telephone. However, as she did so, Lizzie stopped her.

"Let's just think about this for a moment."

"What do you mean?"

Lizzie looked deep in thought, and beckoned Sally to sit down.

"Firstly, we have you, Sally. Technically you're the other woman in an adulterous marriage. Then we have your lover molesting your drunk teenage daughter at a kids drinks party. Penny's not underage and he didn't apparently rape her. Finally, we have you frolicking around naked, having lesbian sex with your lover's wife. They wont buy it. In fact, you'll probably end up on the front page of a tabloid newspaper."

"But Lizzie, he murdered William, and Pauline will tell him that I know. He'll try to kill me to shut me up."

"Do you really believe that, Sally. It could have just been Pauline trying to get at you?

"Yes, maybe you're right. I just can't think straight, Lizzie, but whatever, I've got to think of the children's safety."

Just then, Penny came down clutching her overnight bag.

"Mum, Frank gave this to me for my birthday. It's a real diamond, but I don't think I want it now."

Sally took the necklace from her daughter and examined it closely, before opening the door cautiously and leading Penny out to the car. Lizzie put the bag in the boot, and walked back around to her friend.

"Sally, please come with us, I don't think it's a good idea you being here alone."

"Thanks Lizzie, but I've got to stay and get it sorted out. I want to call Jonathan and Laura and tell them to keep away. Besides, there's still Pepys to think of."

"Okay, if that's the way you want to do it."

Sally nodded.

"There's one other thing, Sally"

"What's that?"

"As soon as I drop Penny off, I'll be coming back. It may take a few hours, but we'll face him together, you and I."

"There's no need," said Penny out of the blue. "I'm not going, I'm staying here with you, Mum."

"Penny, I can't let you stay. Frank could return at any time."

"I mean it, Mum - we have to stick together, and I'm staying!"

Sally had to smile and went across to hug her daughter.

"Okay, but on one condition, you stay in sight of Lizzie while I have a shower. I feel so dirty."

Lizzie turned to face Sally.

"It looks like you're stuck with us, so you had better get used to it."

Sally had to accept that Penny and Lizzie weren't going to leave her. As they went back inside the house, she picked up the necklace that Frank had given Penny. She looked down at the imitation diamond. Poor Penny, she thought, it wasn't even a good imitation. Then with anger in her heart and torment in her soul, Sally opened the front door, and threw the necklace with all the strength she could muster, just as William had done, over twenty years earlier.

The rain and thunder was unexpected and abruptly brought to an end the short spell of warm weather London had been basking in.

The humidity made Pauline sweaty and uncomfortable, and the journey from her home to Frank's office later that evening hadn't made things any easier.

The Gant Carriage Company was busy when Pauline arrived, as taxi firms often are in severe weather conditions. A chatty, overweight blonde receptionist somehow managed to answer the phone calls, speak to the drivers, and deal with people coming in off the street, in a calm, efficient manner.

Pauline pushed past a group of people and went to the front of the queue.

"Where's my husband?" She demanded of the peroxide blonde.

The woman, however was too busy taking a call from a customer to pay any attention to the gaudily-dressed, raven-haired woman standing before her.

"I said, where's my husband?" Shouted Pauline aggressively, as she snatched the receiver from the receptionist and slammed it down with a loud crash.

"You've just cut me off!"

"I don't give a damn, you common tart! Where's my husband?"

"I don't know who your husband is, what do you think I am, a bloody mind-reader!" Retaliated the peroxide angrily.

"Frank Gant! Now find him!"

Instead, the receptionist put her face into an intercom system and pressed a button.

"Mark, are you there, we've got a problem with a drunk woman at the desk!"

A few moments later, a large bearded figure came through the door.

"What's the trouble, Sharon?"

"I think I'm the trouble, Mark." Called out Pauline. "I've come to see Frank, where is he?"

"He's at a restaurant in the city, Pauline, with a corporate client." Replied Mark, none too convincingly.

"Are you driving him tonight, Mark?"

"No, Barry is."

"Where's Barry?"

"Out the back," replied Mark, as Pauline pushed past him.

"Is that rude bitch really Frank's wife?" Asked Sharon, in amazement.

Mark nodded and followed Pauline out to where the offices and driver's area were situated.

"Who's Barry?" She barked at the three drivers watching television.

"I am!" Replied, a skinny, balding man in his fifties.

"Where are you picking up my husband?"

"At Rochelle's, why?"

"Where are you taking him?"

"The Royal Kensington Hotel." Said the driver, totally bewildered.

"I'm his wife, Pauline Gant. I'll go in place of you, so if you don't mind handing over the keys."

"With all respect Mrs. Gant, I don't think I should." Replied Barry nervously, looking towards Mark for support.

"Give her the keys, Barry, after all, she is the boss's wife." Said Mark, sensing it the best course of action.

"Thank-you gentlemen, that wasn't too hard, was it, and what am I driving tonight?"

"It's one of the jags. It's got a 5.3 litre engine, so be careful Pauline."

"Oh, I will, you needn't concern yourselves about that. Don't wait up for us, we'll be rather a long time."

The heavy rain had eased off a little by the time Pauline reached Rochelle's restaurant. She parked the car directly outside and called over to the doorman, who was standing like a sentry, clutching a large umbrella.

"Thank-you, driver, I believe Mr. Gant and his companion are going straight back to the hotel. I will let them know you are here." He said, haughtily.

It was twenty minutes before Frank finally came out. Pauline knew he was drunk from his loud voice and lecherous laugh. There was a girl with him. She was young, slim, in her twenties and very pretty. Frank and the girl giggled and cavorted in the rain, before the doorman opened one of the car's back doors. Frank slapped the girl on the bottom as she got inside, and lit up a cigar, before staggering around to the other side.

"The Royal Kensington, Barry, and put your foot down!" Roared Frank, as he groped the girl on the back seats. It wasn't until Pauline had driven nearly a mile that Frank realised that it was his wife driving the car.

"Pauline what the hell do you think you're doing? Where's Barry, he's supposed to be driving tonight?"

"I think it's time we had a talk, Frank, just as soon as we drop the tart off." With that, Pauline slammed the brakes on hard, and pulled over to the side of the road. She then got out of the car and opened the back passenger door. Grabbing the girl violently by the hair, she dragged her screaming out of the vehicle, and dumped her in the gutter.

Frank was about to get out and intervene, only to find Pauline glaring at him with a crazy look in her eyes.

"Get back in the car, I've not finished with you yet!" She screamed.

"That was a corporate client you stupid bitch!"

"I don't give a damn who it was." Continued Pauline, still venting her anger. "There's something you need to know about your so-called son."

Frank returned Pauline's glare and leapt into the front seat, as Pauline hit the accelerator and sped off into the darkness.

"This had better be good, Pauline, as your life depends on it, believe me - you'll be history, you worthless pile of shit!"

"I think you've got it wrong Frank, you're the one who's history." Replied Pauline bitterly.

"What the hell are you talking about?"

"I'm talking about us, Frank. I've loved you since the time you flirted with me in the student's bar, back in the sixties. I've never stopped loving you and have always supported you, even through the hard times."

"I don't want to hear this shit, tell me about my son!"

"I'll get to him later, I want you to hear me out first."

"You're mad, Pauline, fucking barking mad!"

"You hurt me Frank, and for that you have to be punished. Just like when you had to go into prison, remember?"

"Just get to the point, I'm a busy man!" He shouted, searching for his cigarettes.

"I said nothing when you murdered poor, Mr. Bloom, and stole his money. I liked him, Frank - but as with everything I like, you have to destroy it."

"That was bloody years ago. He was old, he was going to die anyway. I did society a service." Sneered Frank. "Anyway, he died to get us where we are today. You'd be wise to remember that."

"To get us where we are today? God, you're a heartless bastard. I turned a blind eye to all your criminal activities, and all your women. I knew I was better than them, and you would come back to me. I was never wrong, until now."

"Yes, you're wrong, Pauline. I've got someone else. I don't need a loser in my life like you anymore."

Pauline suddenly speeded up, and went through a red light, leaving the sound of screeching tyres and blaring horns, far behind them.

"You murdered my grandfather and stole his money, didn't you Frank?"

"I did it for us, Pauline. We now own Swann's."

"Don't try and con me, Frank. I'm not one of your cheap tarts. I know how you operate, remember!"

"He fell down the stairs, Pauline!"

"How do you know?"

"I don't know, but it's not important. You must have told me?"

"No, I didn't, Frank. You killed him, like you killed Mr. Bloom, like you killed Tina and William Peddlescoombe!"

"You can't pin Tina's death on me, you twisted cow. She was a parasite, she loved being one of life's pathetic victims."

"How dare you talk of your daughter like that. It was you that made her like she was. You're responsible for her death. You were her executioner Frank, just as if you'd strung her up yourself."

"Enough! Tell me about Jamie?"

"Jamie told me you killed William Peddlescoombe. Is that true?"

"So what if it is. He deserved it."

"You killed him so you could have his wife, didn't you?"

"Wow! Pauline, clever! I can see you went to university!"

"Well, I had a bit of fun with your little blonde whore too, and I just happened to tell her what you did."

"You conniving bitch, I'll have to shut her up, or deny it. So Jamie told you, did he?"

"It doesn't matter who told me. You're not taking him from me, I've lost everything because of you, my daughter, my grandfather, my marriage, my happiness and my life. And now you want to leave me and take my son too? Well, I wont let you."

"Look at you, you're no mother to Jamie, you're a disgrace - you disgust me! You wouldn't have a leg to stand on if I take it to the courts. You're mentally unstable."

"Wouldn't I, Frank?" Replied Pauline, glaring across at him. "At least I'm his natural parent, which is more than can be said for you."

There was a disturbing silence, and all that could be heard was the sound of the rain hitting the windscreen, over the soft purr of the Jaguar's powerful engine.

"What are you saying to me, Pauline?" Yelled Frank. "What are you saying to me?"

"Mark is Jamie's father, that's what I'm saying, Frank!"

"No, it's not true. Tell me it's not true, you lying whore!"

Pauline hit the accelerator, and the big cat leapt into action.

"You're mine Frank, the sooner you realise that the better. But if I can't have you, nobody else will."

"Slow the fuck down, Pauline! What are you trying to do, kill us both?" Screamed Frank as the car hit ninety along the dual carriageway.

"We're always going to be together, Frank. You, me and Tina, our baby girl."

Pauline yanked the steering wheel hard right, as she crossed the reservation and sped the car into the path of on-coming traffic. Frank was dazzled by the headlights of a large truck bearing down on them. He literally had split seconds to avert an impending disaster. Quickly, he swung his right foot over into the driver's foot well, knocking Pauline's feet away from the peddles. Out of sheer fright, Pauline had covered her face and was waiting for the impact that would ultimately re-unite Frank and herself with Tina.

Leaning across, Frank grabbed the steering wheel, and swung the car back towards the correct lane. He could recall hearing the blare of car horns, and the flashing of lights, as several vehicles skidded, before colliding with the heavy goods truck. Fortunately, the lane he had managed to manoeuvre the Jaguar into was clear, and he was able to steer a straight course until they were safely away from the carnage he and Pauline had left behind.

29. RETRIBUTION

Laura lay awake in her bed at the nurses' home deep in thought. She could hear all the activity going on around her as her colleagues got up for the early shift. There was always a rush for the bathrooms at this time of day, and if you listened carefully, you could also hear the hushed voices of boyfriends and lovers as they stealthily crept out before the eagle-eyed home warden came on duty.

Her thoughts returned to Dr. Lincoln Greene and the night of unalloyed pleasure she had spent with him. She couldn't understand her feelings or emotions. She felt guilt, she felt sated, she felt decadent, but above all, she felt free, and was glad she allowed things to happen as they did. Even if she had initially slept with him to get back at Nick, that thought no longer entered into the equation. It was as if Lincoln had made her a real woman, like he was the last piece of the jigsaw, the key to her sexual awakening. It wasn't like she was madly in love, or wanted to spend her life with him, it was literally down to lust in its purest form, and why should she feel ashamed of herself, after all, she wasn't the first student nurse to sleep with a doctor and she certainly wont be the last.

Forgiving herself, she settled back beneath the covers, running her hands up and down her naked body, allowing her fingers to explore herself, just as Lincoln had so expertly done.

She must have dropped off back to sleep, as the alarm woke her with a start. Laura was glad she didn't have to work on the ward at St. Mary Abbot's this week. This was because she was due to start her secondment in the Accident and Emergency Department at Westminster Hospital shortly and was obliged along with some of the other girls in her set, to attend a week of school.

Wolfson School of Nursing was just a stone's throw away from Empire House. School was easy and she didn't even have to be there until nine, so she could take her time and make full use of any bathroom she chose, without the fear of interruption. The student nurses were also able to wear their own clothes, which the girls liked. Many would simply wear jeans, which Laura had opted to wear today. Although the day was meant for learning, it was a welcome relief to get away from the practical side of nursing, and gave the girls the opportunity to see old friends and catch up on all the gossip.

Laura was dreading going to A&E. Some of the nurses actually looked forward to it, believing it to be real, front-line nursing. But for most, it represented stress, panic, fear, equipment, monitors and most importantly - blood! The potential for seeing lots of blood and gory sights in A&E was enormous, and Laura tried to divert her thoughts from it. She consoled herself that she wouldn't be alone, and even though she was very proficient caring for the elderly, she and the other girls would be mere novices in casualty and would have to be closely supervised.

"Welcome back ladies, it's lovely to see you all again!" Said Mrs. Drayton, the Nurse Tutor. "I do hope the spectre of the Accident and Emergency Department isn't giving you all nightmares?"

Some of the girls laughed nervously as they took their places in the large, airy classroom.

"As you will see from your handouts, the whole of this week will be dedicated to what happens in a busy city casualty unit, along with the policies and procedures that go with it. Now doesn't that sound interesting?" Mrs. Drayton laughed as she heard a series of moans and groans from the wary, unsuspecting nurses. "Listen girls, it really wont be that bad, and some of you will actually enjoy working in such an environment. The fear of the unknown is often more terrifying than the real thing."

Mrs. Drayton, was a tall, elegant-looking woman of around forty, with red hair, tied up in a bun. She was a confident teacher but always had time for a joke with her charges, which made her probably the most popular tutor at the school.

"Now, we'll just go through the admissions procedure for patients entering the A&E unit, and then, after coffee, I have a surprise for you."

"What, we can all go home early!" Called out one of the students from the back of the class.

"Nice try young lady, but perhaps on Friday, if we get through our schedule." Replied the tutor, peering over her spectacles.

Laura, along with the other girls studied the photocopied handouts that were in front of them, and listened intently while Mrs. Drayton took them through the whole admissions process. It was a tedious hour as it involved lots of paperwork and form-filling, and the girls were glad when coffee time finally arrived.

"I wonder what this surprise is, Mrs. Drayton has in store for us?" Asked Amanda, putting down her plastic coffee cup, to open a chocolate bar.

"She sometimes brings in donuts?" Replied Laura, trying to remain optimistic.

"No, donuts are always on a Friday. Maybe she's going to take us over to A&E?"

"God, I hope not!" Gasped Laura, feeling herself go red.

"Oh, you might see Lincoln?" Smirked Amanda. "So how did it go?"

"It was just as you said it would be, very intense and very, very erotic!" Replied Laura, trying to keep her voice down.

"So are you going to see him again?"

Laura glanced around to see who may be listening.

"No, probably not. He said something about working in the states as a locum. Besides, I could hardly walk when I finally got out of his flat - he was enormous!"

"Laura, what are you like!"

"But Amanda, that's the thing, I'm not really like that. I was upset because Nick stood me up, and I'd had far too much to drink. But I have to say, it was fun!"

"So studious, Laura Peddlescoombe has taken her first black cock, and probably, the first of many!"

"Shhh, Amanda, don't be so crude. Someone will hear you!"

"So what did he do to you, that's got you so excited?" Giggled Amanda.

"He did pretty much everything!" Replied Laura, blushing.

There was no time to go into anymore details as Mrs. Drayton suddenly appeared and beckoned the group back into the classroom.

"Now, girls, the surprise I told you about." Said Mrs. Drayton, in her pleasant

Lancastrian accent. "I'm pleased to introduce, Dr. Lincoln Greene, who's kindly agreed to give us an insight into a busy day in the Accident and Emergency Department."

Gasps went up all around the classroom, as Lincoln strode in with an air of arrogant confidence. He was wearing his white, doctor's coat, with blue scrubs underneath. Around his neck, he wore not only his customary stethoscope, but also a heavy, gold ingot on a thick chain. He looked as if he had just come straight from an emergency, as he surveyed his all-female audience.

Laura knew Amanda was smirking. She turned to face her friend, and noticed that Amanda, along with a fair few of the other girls, had turned a magnificent shade of scarlet too!

Lincoln cleared his throat, but instead of sitting behind the desk, that Mrs. Drayton had set up, he preferred to lean back casually against it to address the girls.

It wasn't long before the black doctor caught Laura's eye. She felt distinctly embarrassed under his intense gaze, but the attention she was getting excited her, and caused her to writhe on her seat. The electricity of their evening together returned like a thunderbolt, and Laura found it difficult to maintain her equanimity.

Lincoln had a slow, easy way of talking, and the girls were soon mesmerised by his seductive tones. Even, Mrs. Drayton had remained in the classroom, which was unusual with guest speakers, and was busy fanning herself, as she eyed him with keen interest.

"We cannot rely solely on what the patient is telling us." Continued Dr. Greene, as he sat himself on the desk in one swift, agile movement. "We also have to look for physical signs and symptoms, and ask probing questions." He said, again catching Laura's deep blue eyes.

"So how much more important is the nurse's role to the doctor in an emergency situation?" Asked Amanda, with a devilish grin.

Lincoln responded immediately, and stood up to walk over to where Amanda and Laura were sitting.

"As you well know, Amanda - the doctor can't function effectively without the back-up of the nurse, and the nurse can't function efficiently without the input from the doctor, so it's very much a team thing." Replied Lincoln, now closely addressing Laura. "This relationship becomes much more heightened and intense in the hot bed, that is the A&E department."

Laura immediately caught that same alluring, musky scent as he purposely brushed against her while moving cat-like between the desks. By this time, the nurses had stopped taking notes, and were eagerly watching the movements of the tall, muscular registrar.

"Well, that about concludes Dr. Greene's talk." Stuttered Mrs. Drayton, putting her fan down. "I've never known a group of young nurses to be so quiet and attentive." She said. "You must come more often."

"Oh, I intend to, Mrs. Drayton." He laughed, showing his perfect, white teeth.

"Now, ladies - it's lunchtime, and I shall see you all back here in an hour," Remarked the tutor, as the girls began to pack their things up. "I have a few little jobs that need attending to, so I'll leave the classroom open, should you want to come back early." She added, putting on her coat.

Now completely alone with Lincoln, Laura was all fingers and thumbs, and struggled to put her notes into her bag.

"It's an unbelievable pleasure to see you again Laura. I've been thinking about you a lot." He smiled, moving to within inches of her.

"I thought you may have gone to the states?" She replied awkwardly.

"What, and not see you before I go. I could never do that. I must say you look very different, and very pretty with your clothes on!"

"Oh, you mean not being in my uniform?" She giggled, getting his joke. "I thought you meant something else!"

He laughed his deep, sensual laugh and let his smouldering eyes latch onto hers once more.

"I could have meant that too!"

Laura felt her face burning, and turned to see if anyone was watching them, but the classroom was empty. Her heart was beating fast and she felt tingly. She longed to be taken by this handsome doctor again, and felt herself turning to jelly.

"I've been thinking about you too." She heard herself say.

"Pleasant things I hope." He replied, placing his hands on her hips, and drawing her closer towards him.

"Yes, very pleasant," she whispered, glancing at his lips.

He leant down and kissed her passionately, taking her by complete surprise.

"No, not here Lincoln, what if we're caught?"

"Let me worry about that. I'm just giving you a private lesson in anatomy." Was his reply as he ran his long fingers through her glossy, blonde hair. "I want you so much. I want you here, now!" He murmered.

Laura couldn't answer and her breathing was shallow. She felt his enormous erection pressing against her stomach, and longed to free it and take it in her mouth.

"I want you too, Lincoln."

He reached up and began to unbutton her blouse, and Laura did nothing to prevent him. Once he had removed it, he put his large hands around her back and expertly unclipped her bra. Removing it completely, he eased her pink nipples towards his mouth.

"You have the most beautiful breasts I've ever seen Laura. I have to lick them."

She sighed and leant her head back, noticing people walking past outside, but she didn't care, she was lost in the passion of the moment, and could think of nothing else.

Lincoln eased his massive penis out from beneath his white coat, and Laura gasped as she placed her hands around it. She felt a strong trickle of semen already seeping out, and instinctively knew what he wanted her to do.

He sat back on one of the classroom chairs and beckoned her down. Now dressed only in her tight jeans and shoes, Laura sank to her knees, before taking Lincoln firmly in her mouth. She gagged at first because of his size, but she soon got the measure of him, and began to run her tongue up and down the length of his rigid manhood.

He groaned and thrust his hips, in order to get deeper inside her mouth. Laura coughed, but she was determined to show this black doctor what a white student nurse could do.

She felt the tip of him against the back of her throat, and fighting her gag reflex, swallowed as many inches as she could.

Within minutes Lincoln began to gasp and reached down to grab her hair. Then, with one elongated moan, he lifted his hips from the chair and ejaculated hard into Laura's mouth.

"Didn't you have any lunch, Laura?" Asked Amanda, as she walked back into the classroom eating an apple.

"Yes, I managed a morsel!" She replied guiltily.

"Lincoln looked hot didn't he?" Continued Amanda, taking her place next to her friend.

"I didn't really notice to be honest."

"Don't give me that nonsense, Laura - you couldn't take your eyes off him!"

"Was it that obvious?"

"Yes, Laura, I'm afraid it was!" Grinned Amanda. "Don't go getting too involved with our Dr. Greene. You know his reputation and he's broken a lot of hearts. You do pick them don't you, Laura? First a married man, then a serial womaniser! Any more news about Nick?"

"Nothing." Said Laura flatly, "And I don't care, his wife is welcome to him."

"Sounds like you need some time at home to relax."

"I would love to, but my mother's got involved with some crazy, mixed up psychopath."

"Like mother, like daughter eh?"

Laura laughed, she could still taste Lincoln's sperm in her mouth and wondered if Amanda had noticed any on her face.

"I'm worried about my mother. I got some garbled message saying she's having man trouble and to stay away."

"Sounds like another reason to go home, Laura. She may need you."

"I'm stuck here in school with you until Friday, and I simply can't afford the fares back to Twickenham."

"Oh dear, the rigours of being a student nurse." Replied Amanda, taking out her lecture notes.

Pauline sat up and moved to the edge of the bed. A noise out in the corridor had distracted her. Her nerves were still in tatters following her unsuccessful attempt to kill both Frank and herself.

Fearing Frank's vengeance, Pauline had taken a room in a Knightsbridge hotel. She had escaped from him the moment he'd brought the car to a halt. Pauline had ran from the scene, taking refuge in a nearby service station complex. Frank had searched for a few minutes, but as other people were around and emergency services were heading to the accident Pauline had caused, he thought it best not to linger.

Pauline drained the remnants of her vodka and tonic, before padding over naked to the mini-bar to pour herself another. She had met Claire earlier that afternoon, and had told her about the events of the previous evening.

"Do you want another drink?"

Claire sat up in bed, running a critical eye over Pauline's nakedness.

"I want to see you looking how you did, when I first met you, Pauline."

"I can't even think about that now, Claire. Please don't put further pressure on me. Look, I'm a bag of nerves."

Claire observed Pauline's shaking hands as she brought the drink up to her lips.

"The booze is your biggest problem. Cut it out and you'll lose weight, and feel much better mentally."

"How can you be so damned cool, after all that's happened?" Asked Pauline with an agitated tone to her voice. "You haven't answered me, do you want a drink?"

"No, Pauline I don't. Come back to bed."

"It's not going to work, Claire, I can't concentrate." Replied Pauline, referring to their earlier attempt at having sex.

"I think you need the secret office, Pauline and the table of pain!"

"That would be the first place Frank would look. If he caught us together, who knows what he would do."

Claire got up from the bed, walked over to Pauline, and put her arms around her.

"My word, you are jumpy. Listen, I've got something that may help." Claire then went across to her handbag, and after rummaging around inside it, placed a small pouch on the table.

"What's that?" Asked Pauline, suspiciously.

"Come on Pauline, you've been in the nightclub business long enough to know what this is. It's something we both need." Replied Claire, making up two separate lines of cocaine.

"It'll make me feel worse."

"I think it'll make you feel better, Pauline. You certainly can't feel any worse. Come over here."

The two women both snorted their lines together and returned to bed. They kissed and touched each other, with Claire even going down on Pauline, but the younger woman still couldn't become aroused.

"You're wasting your time. I just don't feel like it. I should be running the club." Said Pauline after a few moments.

"Okay, you win." Sighed Claire, as she manoeuvred herself back up the bed.

They both lay in silence, before Pauline eventually spoke.

"Perhaps, you're right. Maybe the table of pain would make all the difference?"

"Now you're talking!" Giggled Claire, licking her lips. "I think we'd be safe going back to the club. The police would have it staked out. Frank would be stupid to go back there."

"Yes, you're right," Replied Pauline, leaping up from the bed laughing and prancing around the room like the sugar plum fairy. "I'm not scared of him. I run that damned club. He should be scared of me."

"That's my girl. I can see the coke's having an effect on you!"

Pauline's mood had changed drastically, and now Claire wanted to get her back to the club before the effects wore off and she went into a downer. Claire had realised that Frank's reign was coming to an end, one way or another, and sticking closely to Pauline could get her involved with the club once again.

Pauline insisted on ordering a bottle of champagne, against Claire's advice. When it arrived, the waiter got more than he bargained for as he pushed the trolley into the room, only to serve the hotel's best plonk to two half-crazed naked women.

"I want you to pour it all over me, then lick it off!" Giggled Pauline, once the waiter had left.

"That sounds yummy, let's take the rest of the bottle to the club, and you'll have your wish!" Replied Claire with a cunning grin.

Sally stood in the doorway, with Lizzie right behind her, and like two frightened animals, they listened intently for any signs of impending danger. The road was quiet, so Sally crept out, looking all around as she made her way to the front of the house. Here, she placed a bin liner full of Frank's clothes onto the gravel drive. Lizzie was following close behind and placed a second bag down next to Sally's.

"I can't see the police out there? Let's get back inside and lock up." Said Sally, anxiously.

After bolting the door, Lizzie made straight for the drinks cabinet.

"I'm sure the police are out there Sally, they said they would be." She added, trying to re-assure her friend. "Well, at least one thing could be said of him, he kept the booze supply well stocked up."

"He's far worse after he's been drinking."

"Thanks Sally!" Muttered Lizzie, looking worried. "We'll sort him out, don't you fret. Pour yourself a drink and we'll go over the plans again."

Sally didn't argue. Her nerves were in tatters, and she fixed herself a gin and tonic even larger than Lizzie's.

Pepys had earlier come out of surgery successfully, although the vet could only give him a 50/50 chance of pulling through. The much-loved pet would be put into an animal sanctuary until he was well enough to come home. However, this was in the hands of fate.

"I wish I had a gun, Sally. I would personally go and shoot those bloody dogs dead. Then, I'd do the same to that bastard who interfered with Penny, and murdered poor William. I wouldn't even give it a second thought." Lizzie immediately wished she hadn't mentioned William's name, it was a mistake, and she searched Sally's face for a reaction.

"Don't go getting yourself worked up again Lizzie, why you're worse than me." Replied Sally, swallowing hard, and trying to fight her emotions.

"You're far too good-natured Sally, that's your trouble. You really need to toughen up in this world."

"Lizzie, I'll be tough enough when he gets here, don't worry about that!" Replied Sally, getting rather angry with her friend.

"I'm sorry darling, you know what I'm like after I've had a few. Wouldn't like to do this sober though!"

"Me neither," replied Sally, trying to make herself comfortable on the hard kitchen chair.

"He might not come?"

"Maybe not tonight, but he will tomorrow, to get his dogs. You can never tell with Frank, just what he's going to do."

"Do you really think he might try to kill you, Sally?"

"I don't know, Lizzie, but I have to take every precaution. The police know he killed William so he hasn't really got a reason to kill me for that. I've told Laura and Jonathan to stay away for the time being."

"Have you told them about William's murder?"

"No, Lizzie. I didn't know how to. I'll cross that bridge later."

"Frank may come here to get money. Have you thought about that?"

"Yes, I have. He knows about the safe where I keep my jewellery, but there's not much cash in there."

Just then, a loud clattering noise came from the garden which set the dogs off barking incessantly. The two women almost leapt out of their skins, since they seemed to think Frank would try and gain access via the front door.

The idea was, they would stay together no matter what. Although, Penny had now fallen asleep in the lounge, the plan still remained. Sally would confront him with what he had done. As a precaution, the women had left weapons in specified places in all the rooms in the house which they were likely to use. The armoury included; kitchen knives, a couple of brooms, an electric iron, a power drill and hairspray. The hairspray was Lizzie's idea. Apparently, she had seen a film, where a woman was able to temporarily blind her attacker by aiming the spray into his eyes.

"Well, at least when the police come to arrest him, his eyebrows would have kept their shape." Said Sally dryly.

"The woman in the film hit him with a golf club after that!" Exclaimed Lizzie.

"Golf clubs? That's a good idea. We've got some old one's in the garage, they may come in handy."

It took a couple of minutes before the dogs finally calmed down, and everything went a deathly quiet. Both women now realised at the same time, that the dogs knew Frank, and he would easily be able to stop them barking. They looked at each other in a high state of alarm, before slowly inching their way towards the front of the house to see if he could be trying to gain access there. Lizzie didn't quite look the part of a commando as she crept along the hallway, her back hunched over unnaturally and clutching a golf club in one hand, and hairspray in the other. Suddenly, they heard the noise once more, this time it was definitely coming from the front of the house. It was enough to start the dogs off again, but now Sally and Lizzie were both quite relieved to hear that it was two cats fighting that had been causing the commotion.

"Phew, I'm too old for all of this!" Gasped Lizzie, downing her drink, before sprawling out on one of the armchairs.

"Thanks for staying, Lizzie," said Sally, placing a blanket over Penny. "I really don't know what I would have done if I'd been here on my own."

"Try thanking me in the morning, if we ever get there!"

Claire had been right about the police presence at the club. Although, with two uniformed officers standing near the door, and others posted at various exits, it was by no means discreet.

"Look at them, those silly policemen, they'll drive away all our customers." Exclaimed Pauline, lurching forward when the taxi pulled up, and still under the influence of the cocaine. "Just leave Frank to me, I'll sort him out. I nearly did it last night!"

"I know you did, Pauline. You told me all about it, remember, and you damned well nearly killed yourself too." Replied Claire, as she opened the door for Pauline. "But I don't think we'll be seeing Frank tonight, so we can just forget him and have some fun."

"Perhaps we can get one or two of the girls to join us?"

"That would be even better!" Said Claire, eyeing up a shapely, young blonde hostess as they made their entrance.

"Emily, get one of the other girls to take over from you, I want you to come up and see me later in the office." Called out Pauline to the unsuspecting blonde.

Frank was dressed in jeans, T-shirt and trainers. He pulled the baseball cap down over his eyes as he casually walked past Lake's, the club he owned with Pauline.

The police didn't notice him, they were too interested in the women who were starting to form a queue to gain access to what was now, one of the most popular venues in London.

Frank needed money desperately. His accounts had been cleaned out to raise cash for the deposit on Swann's, and the takings from the cab company had already been banked. Now his only option was the safe in the club's office. There was usually around £20,000 deposited in the safe at any one time, and that was more than enough to get him out of the country. Once he'd got even with Pauline, Frank had planned to visit Sally. She would probably be aware now about him murdering William, and he was sure her house would be closely watched by the police just like the clubs. The cash and jewellery in Sally's safe could amount to several thousands and there was also the possibility of him raiding Lizzie and plundering the takings from Scarlet's. If there had to be blood spilt, then so be it. But none of this was a foregone conclusion, and for now he needed to concentrate on getting inside the club.

Frank knew the entrance was a no-go area, and as he walked around the building he soon realised the exits were all being watched too. However, there was one other way in, which he was sure the police hadn't discovered yet. This was the waste disposal area. Just inside the alcove where the half dozen or so wheelie bins were stored was a slightly obscured door. It was always locked, but Frank had the key. The door was only ever used to gain access to the rubbish chute, if it got blocked, but it also led to another door, which in turn led to the service area of the club.

As Frank crept through the dirty, dank corridor, he heard the familiar sounds of club life, the music, the guest singers, the sounds of slot machines and the jollity. He wished he could be there, drinking whiskey, playing poker, feeling up the young hostesses, and of course, seducing them on occasion. His mouth watered as he inhaled the delicious aroma of a char-grilled steak being prepared in the kitchen. He cursed as he hit his head on a low pipe, and saw a rat scurrying off into the darkness.

Eventually he came to the service stairs, and began to make his way up towards the office. As he neared his destination, he heard a woman's laughter. It was Pauline. This surprised him as it was rare that Pauline even smiled, let alone laughed. He stood in the lobby, just outside the office and brushed cobwebs from his clothes, before gently pushing the door open, to see who was inside. It was reminiscent of something he had done many years earlier, when he had caught Claire, the previous owner seducing his wife. Now, for some reason he seemed to expect he would stumble upon a similar scene.

The office was empty, with just a banker's light for illumination. Frank immediately noticed the desk was laden with food, much of which was untouched. There were two racks of lamb, caviar, prawns, and a platter of smoked salmon. Frank was ravenous and greedily helped himself to what was on offer. Again, he heard Pauline's laughter, emanating from the secret office. This angered him greatly. Why should he skulk around like a common criminal, while she was living it up and enjoying herself so soon after Tina's death, and so soon after trying to kill him.

Gnawing at a rack of lamb, he approached the secret office. The door was closed, but instead of opening it by the handle, he simply kicked it open. Inside, he saw Emily, the blonde hostess, who usually worked the front lobby. She was naked and strapped to the table of pain. Both Pauline and Claire were dressed in dominatrix outfits. Pauline was pouring champagne over Emily's body, so that it trickled down between her legs, where Claire was eagerly lapping it up.

Emily looked terrified, but the sight of her being enjoyed by two mature, dominant women caused him instant arousal. He wanted to have Emily there and then, the other two could watch if they wanted, he would deal with them after he'd satisfied himself.

The scene was surreal. Both Pauline and Claire had frozen like startled rabbits, while Emily, lifted her head to glance across at him, her mouth tightly gagged.

"While the cat's away?" Leered Frank, moving menacingly towards the women, hurling the rack of lamb to one side. He reached the table and licking his fingers, gazed down at the helpless, Emily. He ran a hand across her breasts, and felt he was about to burst through his flies. The poor girl looked petrified and tried to scream, but she couldn't make a sound. It was then that Pauline rushed at him like a woman possessed.

"Leave her alone, you animal!" She yelled, her face full of hatred.

"Look who's talking eh? One rapist to another!" He shouted back.

Pauline however, wasn't quick enough with her attack. For as she leapt at Frank, he struck her hard on the side of the head. She fell to the floor heavily, while Frank hovered over her kicking at her from every angle.

"Stop!" Pleaded, Claire. Now it was her turn to come at him.

"Come on you scrawny bitch!" He growled, clenching his fists. But Claire, turned towards the door and fled. Frank continued kicking Pauline, who had now curled up into a ball.

"So you tried to kill me, did you? I'll show you how to fucking kill someone!" He then cracked a couple of Pauline's ribs with another vicious kick.

As Frank was about to stamp on his wife's head, he was brought to a halt by Claire's ear-piercing scream.

"I'll kill you Frank!"

He looked up to see Claire standing a few feet away, pointing a pistol in his direction.

"You haven't got the guts, you bitch!" He jeered.

"Just try me, you murdering swine!"

Claire had ran back into the office to retrieve a pistol from a concealed drawer in the desk she once used to own. Fortunately, she hadn't told Frank of its existence, when he had cheated her out of the club during their ill-fated poker game years earlier.

Frank again raised his foot to bring it down on the stricken Pauline. Claire now raised the pistol and aimed it at Frank's face.

He grinned as he noticed her hand shaking from the weight of the weapon, and sensed her resolve weakening.

Pauline let out a long groan, which was answered by another hard kick from Frank.

"Touch her again, and you'll die!"

Defiantly, Frank now trod on one of Pauline's hands and began to grind her fingers into the floor.

"Come on then, bitch, shoot me if you're man enough!" He began to laugh at his own joke and twisted his foot down again on Pauline's broken hand.

"Go to hell!" Hissed Claire, as she squeezed the trigger. There was an almighty bang and smoke filled the room. Claire was in shock and was staring straight at Frank. She wasn't sure if she'd hit him or not, as he was still standing there, his eyes crazy and dangerous.

Suddenly he began to move towards her, and as the smoke cleared, she saw a massive blood stain on his T-shirt, near his left shoulder. He reached up, and cupped his right hand over the wound and looked at Claire with a surprised expression on his face.

"I'll shoot again if you come any closer!" She cried out, struggling to keep the pistol aimed at its target.

Claire then noticed Pauline rise up on her knees and grip Frank's leg.

"Don't shoot him, please, Claire!"

As Pauline tried to pull herself up, using her husband's body, he raised his fist to strike her again.

Claire closed her eyes and fired another shot. This hit Frank in the chest, and after staggering backwards, dropped to his knees. He was babbling incoherently, and blood was oozing out of his mouth. Pauline clasped her arms around him as Claire fired a third shot, which hit Pauline. Frank was dead as he hit the ground, and Pauline fell across his body, just as she had done one Christmas, when she had found him dying in the snow, and the warmth of her body had kept him alive.

Claire then dropped the pistol, and ran from the secret office sobbing uncontrollably.

Sally, Lizzie and Penny did manage to get through the night in one piece, after they all eventually fell asleep in the lounge. However, it was the loud hammering at the door that suddenly brought the terror of reality back into their hearts.

"Oh my god, who's that, is it Frank?" Called out Lizzie, her head pounding and make-up smudged.

"I don't know, I can't hear myself think with those bloody dogs barking." Replied, Sally nervously.

Again they armed themselves, and crept towards the front of the house.

"It's Frank!" Gasped Sally, her voice quaking as the large frame of a man became apparent through the glass panel of the door.

"Sally, there's a huge white limo parked in the drive!"

"Oh my god, I'd better wake Penny, she's got to get out of the house. Lizzie, ring the police now!" Exclaimed Sally, trying to think straight, as the hammering continued. "I can't understand why the police didn't stop him?"

"Sally, I think I've wet myself." Said Lizzie, her eyes wide with terror.

Sally sank down to her knees and bit her knuckles.

"I think he's going to kill us."

"Come on, let's try and get out through the back," sobbed Lizzie, crouching down next to her friend. "I'd rather take my chances with the dogs."

The hammering was deafening as the women crawled back along the hallway on their hands and knees. Sally, then saw Penny appear in front of her, and beckoned the teenager to run for safety.

Suddenly Jamie was standing in front of them.

"What are you doing?" He asked, looking puzzled by the actions of the women. "Aren't you going to open the door?"

"Don't open it Jamie!" Screamed Sally, as the boy walked past her.

"You're all mad in this house!" He replied in amazement. "It's only Mark, and he wouldn't hurt a fly!"

Jamie was right. Standing in the doorway was the amiable giant with the neatly trimmed beard.

"Is Mrs. Peddlescoombe here, Jamie?" Asked Mark, his face long and drawn.

"That's her down there." Replied the boy, pointing a chubby finger towards Sally, who was still on her hands and knees next to Lizzie.

"Look, I'm sorry I've called at a bad time," he continued, trying to maintain his composure. "I'm afraid I have some very disturbing news, can I come in?" As he walked through the house he was dismayed to see bottles and rubbish strewn everywhere. A typical Frank Gant trait.

Sally rose to her feet, she felt ashamed and didn't know how much more she could take. She couldn't bear anyone to see her and her home in such a disgusting state.

"Please, help us Mark?" She uttered fighting back tears. "Frank murdered my husband and attacked my daughter. He's coming back to kill us, I know he is."

"You and your family are safe, Mrs. Peddlescoombe, I can assure you of that." Replied Mark, noticing how physically shaken she was.

Sally reached out and put her hand on his forearm.

"Thank-you, for your kind words, Mark, but I wish I could be as sure as you." She then began to sob, and Mark couldn't help but put a re-assuring arm around her.

"Please, Mrs. Peddlescoombe, you must listen." He said, releasing Sally. He then looked over at Jamie and asked the boy to come and sit next to him. "Late last night there was a serious incident at Lake's and Frank was killed."

"What on earth's happening?" Asked Lizzie, walking into the lounge, clutching a glass of Alka-Seltzer.

Mark ignored her, and turned to Jamie.

"Your mother was involved too, son." He held the boy tightly. "She's alive, but I'm afraid she was badly wounded."

Mark expected Jamie to be the most upset, but it was Sally, who seemed to take the news the worst.

"What happened?" She asked, holding a tissue up to her eyes.

"They were both shot by the former owner of the club." He continued. "She had a grudge against Frank."

"But why my Mum?" Asked Jamie, looking up to Mark for an answer.

"I don't know, son. Maybe she tried to help Frank and just got in the way?"

"Have they got the person who did it?"

"Yes, her name's Claire. She'll go to prison for a long time, I imagine." Mark then looked into the boy's cold, indifferent eyes. "Listen Jamie, I know on the face of it, you must think you've lost your Dad."

"Leave me alone!" Said the boy, pushing him away.

"Jamie, please listen to me. What I have to say is very important. You still have your Dad."

"Are you my father, Mark?"

"Yes, Jamie, I am. But, you seem to already know?"

"Mum told me a while ago."

"Jamie, I loved your mother, but she wouldn't leave Frank for me."

"That's because he would have killed all of us." Said Jamie, surprising Mark with his insight.

"Yes, I realise that now."

"Are you crying, Mark? Frank wouldn't let me cry." Replied Jamie, still showing no emotion.

"I'm going to look after you, the best I can, Jamie, and the dogs too. So you run along now and pack up all of your stuff, and I'll take you to see your mother."

As Jamie went back upstairs, Mark buried his face in his hands and wept for Pauline, the woman he could have made so happy, if only the circumstances had been different. This time it was left to Sally to go over and comfort the man who used to be Frank Gant's number two.

"I can see that you love Pauline very much. I'm glad she has someone who cares for her." Whispered Sally, sitting down next to him.

"Pauline means the world to me, but it was never meant to be, Mrs. Peddlescoombe." He replied, turning to face her.

"Please, call me, Sally." She smiled. "I know how it feels to love someone with every bone in your body, and not to be able to be with them."

Feeling awkward, Mark stood up to leave.

"I'm sorry I had to give you the news about Frank."

But it was Lizzie, who answered for Sally.

"Sally hasn't been crying about Frank's death. She's been crying tears of relief, that it's all finally over."

"Did he treat you very badly, Sally?" Asked Mark, saying her name for the first time.

"It was nothing I can't handle." She replied, feeling more in control of her emotions. "So you knew I was seeing Frank, and that he was practically living here?"

"Yes, it was quite common knowledge." He replied, rather uncomfortably. "Pauline told me, after she had been to visit you."

Just then they heard Jamie crashing down the stairs.

"I'm ready to go Mark. I want to see my Mum, come on, let's get the dogs."

Mark watched while Jamie shouted and kicked at the two hungry animals, as he led them out to the car. He wondered if he really was his son. If so, he would certainly have his work cut out trying to change him. However, there was still the matter of telling the boy the other piece of bad news, that his sister was also dead.

30. SUMMER INTERLUDE

The next few days were absolutely vital. Sally had managed to speak to the estate agent and get the proposed viewing put back by a week. It would take at least that time and probably longer to tidy things up and get the house back into shape again. The damage to the garden caused by Jamie and the dogs was far worse than Sally had anticipated. Inside, all the carpets needed shampooing, and the ones in the lounge and the hallway would either have to be patched up or replaced, due to drink stains and cigarette burns. Parts of the wallpaper would also have to be renewed because of the harm done by Jamie's graffiti, plus there was the upholstery that needed attention as well.

It was an absolute nightmare. No sooner had Sally and Penny cleaned up one area, when they were horrified to discover even more dirt and damage. Unfortunately there was no hope for the beloved mahogany coffee table. It was far too badly burnt and scratched to be of any further use.

Things only really started to get a move on when Laura and Jonathan came over to help. Eventually the family's combined efforts paid off, and the couple came to see the house, liked what they saw, apart from the garden and said they would put in an offer.

Sally now felt more inclined to sell the house. Her fond memories of the happier times she, William and the children had enjoyed were all contaminated by the recent events with Frank. However, to the children, the sale of the house would herald the family's ultimate destruction. It would destroy the most important things they had, their unity, their past and their future. They knew Sally's feelings, and there would never be a good time to challenge her about it, but now that time was ticking away fast.

"Laura, I think we have to speak to Mum again, before it's too late."

"Rather you than me, Jonathan. What have you got in mind?"

"I think we just have to state a few facts that's all." He replied, taking a seat at the kitchen table. "She's got to think about the disruption to Penny's schooling, plus there's you and I, where will we go if she sells the house?"

"You've forgotten Pepys!"

"Exactly! You're beginning to understand the urgency of it all. How is he anyway?"

"Well, the last I heard was that he's alive, but only just. They had to remove his hind leg. It doesn't look good Jonathan."

"That's awful, the poor little fellow. I hope he pulls through."

"That's why Mum has put all her energy into cleaning the house, to take her mind off him. She's really upset by it all."

"Laura, listen to me, we've got to tell her that the injuries to Pepys are another reason to keep our house."

"Okay, we'll give it another go, but you've got to keep your cool, Jonathan and not have another blazing row with her."

As they went to find their mother, Jonathan surprised Laura by asking if she'd heard anymore from Nick.

"No, nothing." She muttered, going bright red, as her thoughts returned to the two bouts of rampant sex she had enjoyed with Lincoln Greene. "He's back with his wife and good riddance to him. Besides, I've met someone else!"

"Really!" Replied Jonathan, in a mocking tone. "It didn't take you long! So who is he, another student?"

"No, he's a registrar actually!"

"A doctor eh, so my little sis is going up in the world!"

Laura however, decided to leave it at that. She thought it best not to mention that she'd been seeing the most prolific womaniser in the hospital's history.

The following morning brought with it blazing sunshine and a welcoming southwesterly breeze. However, to Sally, it just didn't seem right attending a funeral on such a lovely day, but it was a day she could have done without. She had awoken during the night and had vomited again. It was something that had been happening for about a week now. While the others were still stirring, Sally had gone out to the chemists, just as it was opening and had brought a pregnancy testing kit. Unlike those of today, this involved taking a urine specimen and a wait of two hours in order to get the results. Her worst fears were eventually confirmed mid morning, and the thought of knowing she was carrying Frank's child mortified her. She couldn't think straight and tried to avoid her family as much as she could, but it wasn't working and she knew she would have to bluff the day out.

The coroner had released Tina's body the week earlier, and the solicitors, anxious to put her to rest, in order to concentrate on Frank's estate had organised the funeral at short notice. The whole of Sally's family had decided to go and pay their last respects. Whether Frank Gant would receive similar was still open for debate. Sally had already received a written request to attend Tina's funeral, but in a sad twist of fate, the request had been sent by Pauline shortly before she was shot by Claire. Since Frank and Pauline's solicitors had now taken control of all the arrangements, there weren't many expected to be present at the service.

The Peddlescoombe women's choice of attire differed greatly. Sally had elected a more traditional, knee-length, plain black dress, complete with matching hat, while the girls preferred everyday dresses, but dark in colour. Jonathan, not even possessing a tie, let alone a suit had to be content wearing one of his father's old suits that Sally had got out of the attic for him.

The car was booked for 2.30pm, and the women were ready and waiting patiently. Jonathan caught his mother staring at him, dressed in his father's clothes, and felt awkward.

"Perhaps, I shouldn't have worn Dad's suit, Mum. I think I'll go and change."

"No, Jonathan, you look just fine. I'm just a bit touchy about funerals. You know what I was like at your father's." Replied Sally, giving her son a hug.

Jonathan smiled and kissed her on the cheek. His mother looked different now. She seemed so much quieter, and had a far more distant air about her. Even physically, she had changed, she had lost weight not only around her bust and hips, but it was noticeable in her face, where she now had the beginnings of crows feet, and even a few grey hairs were clearly visible. But none of this really looked out of place on Sally. She was still a stunningly beautiful woman, and her new attributes only served to give her a certain, graceful, accomplished look.

"What are you staring at, Jonathan?" Asked Sally, fearing he could read her mind and tell she was pregnant.

"I was just thinking how proud I am to have a mother like you."

"Don't get me crying again, Jonathan!" Part of her wished it was her own funeral that was taking place, instead of Tina's. She wanted to be with William, but now she was tarnished, and to make matters worse, she had fallen pregnant to the man who was his killer.

Just then, the doorbell rang.

"It's only two o'clock, the car must be early?" Called out Laura, checking her hair in the hallway mirror.

Sally opened the front door, expecting it to be the driver. She wasn't prepared to see David standing on the doorstep, and looking so much like William.

"You're not going to faint again, Sally, are you?"

"David, but you're here!" Sally gasped. "I can't believe it's actually you!"

David's delight at seeing Sally, quickly turned to despair, as he noticed her black attire, and the limousine pulling into the drive.

"Sally, what's happened? Is everyone alright?"

"Yes, we're all fine, David." She lied, still in a state of shock. "Laura and Jonathan lost a friend recently."

"Oh, that's terrible. Look, I should have rang first. It's a bad time, I shouldn't have come."

"Please, David, come inside." Replied Sally, reaching for his hand.

"Sorry, I'm a bit sensitive where funerals are concerned." He said, stepping into the house.

"I know, David, it's the same with me. In fact, I just said as much to Jonathan."

"I was so worried about you, Sally. You didn't reply to my letters?"

"I was a bit pre-occupied with things going on."

"Carol, my housekeeper said that was probably why you didn't answer."

"You look well, David."

"Thank-you, but are you sure everything is okay?"

Sally practically collapsed into his arms, her heart heavy from the pain and torment of the past few weeks. He held her tightly, wishing he could rid her of the demons that ravaged her soul.

"I'll not leave you again, Sally," he whispered into her ear, not wanting to let her go.

Sally was taken up to her room by her daughters. They laid her on the bed and remained at her side, while their mother retched into a bowl. Penny switched on the electric fan, and the effect of the cool air, and the reassuring sound of the girls' voices soon brought Sally around.

"I must go to the funeral." She said in a determined tone, making her way into the bathroom to freshen up.

"I don't think you should, Mum." Called out Laura anxiously, "You've just been sick!"

Sally didn't respond, and a little later went downstairs to David.

"Can you wait for me?"

"Of course I can, Sally."

"Lizzie will be here to keep you company. She's trying to sort the garden out."

"What, Lizzie from Falcondale?"

Sally nodded and tried to smile at him, as her two daughters led her out to the waiting car.

"Don't let her get you drunk, David!"

He recognised Lizzie immediately, even clad in an old pair of jeans, a man's shirt and green gardening gloves. Her make-up looked fantastically overdone as usual.

"No wonder Sally fainted when she saw you, David." She exclaimed.

"That's the effect I have on women!" He replied, jokingly, as he surveyed the garden.

"No, I mean you look just like William. That's what made her faint."

"I think that may have happened before." He said, shocked at the state of the garden.

"Dogs and a motorbike!" Replied Lizzie, picking up a tray of plants.

"Can I help you, Lizzie, it looks like you've got a massive job on your hands."

"Yes, thank-you, David. Sally's going to get a professional company in to do the turf and landscaping. But, if you can just help me re-plant these last few."

David hesitated as he bent down awkwardly to a kneeling position. The artificial leg he'd had fitted was rather restrictive where some movements were concerned.

"Sally looks very different to the last time I saw her, Lizzie. In fact, she looks like she's been to hell and back."

"She has, David."

"What on earth has happened to her?"

"Sally cares a lot about you, David. I don't think she would ever tell you what really happened. Sally is the type of person who prefers to live with her pain, rather than inflict it on others."

"Was I wrong to come here today, Lizzie. Does she have someone else?"

"No, there's no-one else, David. Her heart, or whatever's left of it, belongs to you."

"I came here to ask her to marry me."

"Be careful, you must give her time. Sally has been through quite an ordeal."

"Will you tell me about it, Lizzie?"

As Sally and her family alighted from the black limousine, they couldn't help noticing there were more undertakers present than Tina's relatives.

Jamie was there, along with his father, Mark and a few others who Sally assumed were related to the deceased. A haughty, and very aloof-looking woman stood a few feet away from the rest. Sally wondered who it could be, and was later informed that the woman was none other than, Irene Gant, Frank's mother.

Laura nodded in acknowledgment of Mrs. Drayton, the nurse tutor, who had been in charge of Tina's training while she was carrying out her nursing. Next to her, was a student nurse called, Sonia. It was Sonia who had always been first on the scene when Tina was tormented by the most horrific nightmares. She worked wonders with her troubled colleague, re-assuring her, and making certain she was safe, even in the middle of the night.

The service was short and concise. Inevitably there were tears, but these were from Jonathan, and later, Jamie, who had to be consoled by his father.

The floral tributes were sparse, but impressive, the most beautiful being the huge angel-shaped wreath ordered by Pauline before she was shot. There was nothing from Frank. Perhaps he merely expected his wife to arrange everything, or had he planned to send something spectacular, no-one would ever know.

It was while Sally was looking at the flowers and reading the messages that she began to feel unwell again. Jonathan was immediately at her side.

"Can you please take me back to the car, Jonathan. I think I'm going to pass out. It must be the heat."

Sally felt as if her life had literally come to a halt. She felt as if all of her systems had suddenly packed up and stopped working. She was totally drained, and shaking profusely when Jonathan and Laura helped her into the car. Laura offered her mother's apologies to all concerned, and asked the driver to take them home.

"Is he waiting for me, is William still there?" Uttered Sally incoherently.

"It's David, Mum! David is waiting for you at home. He just looks like Dad." Replied Laura looking deeply concerned, as she clutched her mother's hand.

"You're early!" Exclaimed Lizzie. "David and I were just having a glass of wine and a chat."

"Mum's ill, she nearly passed out at the funeral." Said Jonathan anxiously.

"I'm okay, Jonathan." Replied Sally, a little tetchily as she was helped into the house. "I'm just tired, that's all. It's too hot."

"You look very pale, darling." Said Lizzie, examining her friend in great detail. "I think it's all been a little too much for you."

"Where's David?"

"Don't worry, Sally, I haven't stolen him, he's sitting out in the garden. In fact, he's been helping me plant some flowers."

"I don't want him to see me like this."

"Don't be so silly. Look, I've got something to tell you, Sally."

"It's Pepys isn't it, he's dead?" Gasped Sally.

"Gosh, no - it's nothing like that." Replied Lizzie, puzzled by her friend acting so strangely.

Sally sighed and sat herself at the kitchen table.

"You look very guilty, Lizzie, what have you done?"

Lizzie sat down, and reached across for Sally's hand.

"I've told him, Sally. I've told David all about Frank, and everything else that's happened. I'm sorry, I know I shouldn't have, but I thought I was helping."

"Lizzie, you had no right to do that." Replied Sally, angrily. "I'm surprised he's still here. He must think I'm nothing more than a cheap tart!"

As Lizzie was about to explain further, in walked David from the garden, with his shirt sleeves rolled up and grass stains on the knees of his white chinos.

"David, you must be hungry? Sit down, and I'll fix you something to eat." Said Sally, trying to act as if nothing was wrong, while Lizzie quickly disappeared from the scene.

"No, thanks, Sally I'm fine. I'm glad you're feeling a bit better?"

"Yes, I'm okay now, thank-you. But you really should have something. I'll make you some tomato soup, we've got some lovely crusty bread in the cupboard."

"That sounds nice!" Replied David politely.

"I really can't get over seeing you again, David. I had been meaning to answer your letters."

"Don't worry about that, Sally. I understand."

"I expect you've guessed I wont be taking up the course in October." She said, opening what looked like a tin of rice pudding.

"There'll always be other times, Sally. You have to feel ready for it in your own mind."

"You see, the children don't want me to sell the house, and I was a fool for even putting them through such torment. I was only thinking of myself."

"Yes, Sally you're right putting your children first," he replied looking into her eyes, to see if there was any of the old spark still there. "But you also need someone to be there for you."

"Perhaps, we can keep in touch, if I ever go back to Falcondale we can meet up?" Replied Sally, choosing not to answer his last question.

"Would you ever have a reason to go back there, Sally?"

She swallowed hard, and looked down.

"No, David, probably not."

"Sally?"

"Yes, David?"

"Did you hear what I said about having someone to take care of you?"

"Yes, I heard what you said."

"I also meant what I said earlier. I'm not leaving you again."

"It wont work David, you don't understand."

"I love you, Sally - that's all I need to understand."

"Is it, David, is that all?" She put the plate of food down in front of him, but he barely noticed.

"Will you marry me, Sally? I could sell up in Wales and come and live here with you and the children."

"No, David, please."

"But Sally, we've both been battered and bruised by life. I can't bear to be without you anymore. We were meant for each other."

Tears welled up in her clear, blue eyes as she looked into David's handsome face.

"I can't marry you, David. I'm your brother's wife!" She then ran from the kitchen in tears and fled to her room, where she lay on her bed sobbing and clutching her stomach.

"I told you not to rush things, David!" Remarked Lizzie, who had obviously been listening to the conversation. "Why do you men always think you know best?"

David glanced down and noticed that Sally had served him up tinned rice pudding on toast.

"Yes, she's very troubled, David," added Lizzie, looking down at the plate.

He returned to Falcondale that same day, with Sally's current mental condition weighing heavily on his mind, and Lizzie's words of wisdom ringing in his ears.

It was a little later in the evening when Laura went upstairs to check on her mother. Lizzie had finally gone, Penny was listening to some music on her Walkman, and Jonathan was watching TV and making inroads into Frank's alcohol supply. Laura had been thinking about Lincoln, and was tempted to return to London in the hope of seeing him again, but the welfare of her mother now had to come first. She thought Sally had taken something, but could see no sign of any tablets or bottles. She called out her mother's name and shook her gently, but she couldn't be roused from the tortured malaise she had fallen into.

"Jonathan, come up here. It's Mum, she's got worse."

"I knew there was something wrong at the funeral." He replied despairingly. "It's like she's having some sort of breakdown or something. What shall we do?"

"I think we'd better call the doctor," said Laura with anguish in her voice, as she ran down to the telephone.

It was mid-morning and the large expanses of vacant beach were now disappearing at a rapid rate as holiday makers of all nationalities descended on the quiet, Catalonian fishing village. It was only the third day of Sandra and Nick's holiday, but already Sandra was jumpy and pre-occupied about something.

"I'm bored Nick, I think I'll go and have a look around the shops."

"That sounds good," he replied, sitting up from his inflatable sun bed. "I'll come with you, it's getting on for lunchtime, perhaps we could find a place to eat?"

"You don't have to come with me, Nick. I'm a big girl now, I wont get lost. Besides, I might take the car and drive into Calella."

"Okay, if that's what you want." He replied, a little disappointed. "I'll just stay here then until you get back."

He watched as Sandra put on her sarong, and gathered up her bits and pieces, before heading off to find the little Renault they had hired. Nick wasn't quite sure why she was acting like this, and simply put her mood down to PMT, which she regularly suffered from. Putting his sunglasses back on, Nick noticed a couple of nubile, young beauties set up close by him. He watched admiringly as they removed their bikini tops and took turns rubbing lotion into each other's skin, before settling down to soak up the sun. Perhaps, it wouldn't be quite so bad waiting for Sandra to return after all, he thought.

The nearby village of Calella was rather hilly, and what with the narrow streets, Sandra decided it would be best to park up somewhere, and wander around on foot. It was a beautiful, rustic village and more rugged and bohemian than its smarter, more exclusive neighbour, Llafranc, where Sandra was staying in a hotel with Nick.

She stopped and had a coffee in a sea-front cafe, before continuing her fact-finding mission.

"Gracias, Senorita!" Said the waiter, as he collected the bill.

"Excuse me, but do you speak English?"

"Yes, Madam. How can I help you?" He smiled back.

"I'm trying to find the Hotel Antonio?"

"It's not far, just up the hill a little, and you will see it in front of you."

Before going up to the hotel, Sandra walked along the sea front, taking in the wonderful view of the natural harbour. Although, becoming increasingly popular with tourists, Calella de Palafrugell was still a working base for a small fleet of fishing boats. It was the busiest and hottest time of the season, but the area, including Llafranc certainly wasn't overwhelmed by visitors. Sandra called in at a couple of shops, and in one, purchased a new slinky bikini. She certainly had the figure to wear something so revealing, and couldn't wait to see the effects it would have.

The hill was rather steep, so Sandra slipped off her sandals and continued in bare feet. As she turned a slight bend, the hotel suddenly came into view, just as the waiter said it would. It wasn't a huge, ugly tower block like those which blighted the landscape of some of the more popular resorts. It was more like a stately villa, complete with a spectacular garden, where one could have dinner, or enjoy a quiet drink and gaze down at the incredible sea view below.

Sandra walked into the hotel and went straight up to reception.

"I'm looking for Mr. Craig Winter, who I believe is staying here with the Stone House Corporation, for their summer convention?"

"They're not here at the moment, Madam." Replied the chubby, middle aged hall porter, allowing his eyes to wander up and down the attractive blonde standing before him.

"Will they be having dinner here tonight?"

He opened a large book on the desk and peered inside it.

"No, they have reservations at Giselle's Restaurant. Is that any help to you?"

"Yes, thank-you," replied Sandra, putting her sunglasses back on. "You've been very helpful indeed."

It was about three in the afternoon by the time Sandra finally returned to the beach where Nick was still sunbathing.

"Sandra, where the hell have you been? I'm like a bloody lobster!"

"I'm sorry Nick, I went to Calella, there were lots of little shops!"

"Have you eaten yet? I'm starving!"

"No, I haven't, but we can have a meal here tonight in Llafranc, just the two of us."

The restaurant Sandra chose was the Estrada, which just happened to be next to Giselle's. Both the restaurants were situated along the promenade and gave the diner a superb view of the beach, along with the marina, and its impressive collection of yachts.

After studying the menu for a few minutes, Nick ordered the mussels in white wine and garlic sauce as a starter, while Sandra opted for a delicious, local soup, called Gazpacho, which was served cold. Nick was pleasantly surprised that Sandra had so far managed to keep off the bottle, a feat he never thought she could achieve.

It was a wonderful, warm evening, and the sound of the waves lapping gently against the shore, soon removed any lingering doubts in Nick's mind about being there on holiday with his estranged wife. As he sipped his chilled wine he was convinced that returning to Sandra was the best thing to do under the circumstances.

Sandra barely touched her soup, and after a short while got up from the table to leave.

"Nick, I'm sorry, but I've got the most awful headache. I think I'll go back to the hotel."

"Sandra, wait, I'll come with you. Is everything okay?"

"Please, Nick, don't fuss. I'll be fine. You stay and finish your meal. Don't hurry back, have a nice walk along the front, there's some lovely cafe's and bars to have a drink in."

"Well, alright then, but as long as you're sure?"

She smiled and left him, as he ordered the restaurant's famous black paella, made its rich, tarry colour by the addition of squid ink.

Sandra checked behind her to make sure Nick wasn't watching, before walking into Giselle's. She scanned the tables for Craig. He wasn't hard to spot, with his loud voice and immature laugh. He was sitting with a group of four men and two women, and by the look of it, they had consumed a fair amount of the local plonk between them. The conversation was bawdy and the two women were contributing to it with as much gusto as the men.

Craig's mouth suddenly dropped as Sandra appeared at the table. She knew two of the others and smiled her acknowledgment. One of these, Derek, was a director of the Stone House Corporation, and had been boss to both Sandra and Nick in the past.

"Sandra, I can't believe it!" Exclaimed Craig, looking more than a little nervous. "But what are you doing here?"

"Hello, Craig. I'm on holiday with my husband."

"Sandra, it's wonderful to see you again." Said Derek, equally uncomfortable, as he pulled up a chair for her. "It's like old times, you really must stay and have a drink with us?"

"Thanks, I would like that." She replied with a hint of sarcasm in her voice.

"So where's Nick?" Asked Derek, looking around.

"Oh don't worry about him, he's gone off exploring somewhere I imagine."

Sandra sat next to Craig, and eagerly accepted the glass of sangria offered her.

"I'm sorry about what happened." Said Derek, quite genuinely. "It was all out of my hands, I was just the axe bearer. We certainly miss you, Sandra."

"Forget it. I'm doing something else now." She replied in an abrupt manner.

"Or someone else!" Smirked Craig.

Derek coughed and looked embarrassed.

"So what's the new job?" He asked, chancing a leer at her full cleavage.

"It's public relations, Derek."

It took quite a while before she could finally get away from Derek's attention. By this time, Craig was up on the small dance floor with one of the women.

Sandra waited for a slow one to come on, before edging the woman out of the way, and taking Craig over to a more secluded area of the restaurant.

"Avoiding me Craig?"

"I don't know what you're playing at Sandra, but I've told you, it's over between us."

It can't be finished Craig, not when you owe me."

"Come on Sandra, you know as well as I do, nothing formal was agreed."

"Craig, I bloody well won those contracts by sleeping with those vile characters you set me up with. Now you've frozen me out and done the dirty on me."

"It was Derek who fired you, remember."

"Yes, but it was you who put him up to it."

"What you did was starting to look bad on the company."

"Without me, you wouldn't have got those contracts, and you wouldn't be here now!"

"Come on Sandra, let's not argue, we're on holiday. Besides, I'll speak to Derek, I'm sure we can come to some arrangement."

"I'm going to make you sweat for what you did, you little bastard, in more ways than one. Perhaps, Derek would be interested to hear that you pimped me out to get the contracts." With that, Sandra led him back out onto the dance floor and held him intimately while they danced.

"You wouldn't dare, Sandra." He replied, searching her face. "It would make you look worse than me."

"You seem to forget, Craig, that I've got nothing to lose."

"Maybe you have. Why did you bring Nick?"

She put her hand against his chest and held him tighter.

"I brought Nick thinking it might make you jealous, and to possibly act as a witness, but he's just getting in the way now."

"So he doesn't know?"

"No, I haven't told him. There's some things best left unsaid."

"He's still as stupid and gullible as ever then?"

"Don't be like that Craig, after all, Nick's still my husband."

Craig laughed as he let his hands run up and down Sandra's shapely body.

"I must say, you look damned horny tonight!"

"See what you're missing!" She replied, pulling away from him, and thrusting up her bust. "How about a bit of married woman, Craig?"

Craig had a hired car parked within walking distance of the restaurant, and it took less than five minutes to drive the short distance back to Sandra's hotel room.

It was almost one in the morning by the time Nick got back. Even at such a late hour there were still many people out on the streets and sitting outside the various bars and restaurants. Nick however, felt particularly guilty about being out so long and leaving his wife alone and unwell in a strange hotel. When he let himself in, he was relieved to feel the coolness of the room. He hadn't been abroad a great deal in his twenty eight years, but the different climate and environment was already making him feel better and more alive than he'd felt in a long time.

Even with the air-conditioning on, there was an odd odour to the room, like stale smoke and perfume, or was it aftershave, he wasn't sure. He noticed Sandra's clothes strewn across a chair, and wondered if she would still be awake.

"Sandra, are you feeling better?" He called out gently.

"No, I've still got a headache," she replied in a slightly hoarse voice.

Sandra was tired and desperately wanted to go to sleep. However, she had literally only just got Craig out of the room, before Nick arrived.

"I'm sorry I'm so late back." He said, going in to use the bathroom. There was only a grunt from Sandra, so he continued. "I bumped into Derek, and some of the old crowd from the insurance days. What an amazing coincidence, can you believe it?"

"Really?"

"Yes, we walked along the esplanade and found there was a fiesta going on. It was wonderful, they really made us feel welcome."

"I want to sleep, Nick!"

"Derek said he saw you."

"Where?" Gasped Sandra.

"In the restaurant, where they had their meal."

Sandra squirmed, and was glad Nick wasn't right in front of her, to see her face blush up.

"Oh, that's right, I remember now. I walked past to go to the shop, I needed some water. That's when I saw Derek. I literally just called in to say hello."

"So that explains it." Laughed Nick, going over towards the bed. "I did wonder a little."

"Anyone else there of interest?"

"Just one or two. I didn't know the others, but I didn't see Craig, perhaps he doesn't earn enough commission to qualify!"

Sandra got up to brush her teeth. She knew it would only be a matter of time before he smelt the alcohol on her breath. She staggered a little as she reached the bathroom door, and had to hold on for support.

"Are you sure you're okay, Sandra, shall I call a doctor?"

"No, I'll be fine. It's probably just a bug I've caught."

"Yes, I suppose so," he replied, noticing a damp patch in the bed.

"If I feel up to it, I might go into Barcelona tomorrow and do a bit more shopping." She called out.

"Damn it, I've arranged to meet a couple of the others for lunch. Can't we go to Barcelona the following day?"

"No, I want to go tomorrow. Besides, you'd only get bored shopping. I'll go on my own."

"Okay, if that's what you want, Sandra."

It had been three days since Laura had called out the doctor for her mother. Dr. Mitchell was upstairs with Sally for the best part of an hour, but still there was no change in her condition. During the visit, as with the first, he had asked Laura to act as chaperone.

"Well, your mother's blood pressure is still very low. Is she drinking?"

"Only sips of water occasionally, but she wont eat anything, Dr. Mitchell."

"I'm not overly concerned about the eating just at the moment, Laura. Try her with meal replacement drinks, and keep her hydrated. I'll look in again tomorrow. Has she been taking the medication I prescribed?"

"Yes, I've been giving it to her myself."

"Good, just ring the surgery if there's any change."

"I will doctor, and if there's not?"

"We'll probably have to admit your mother to hospital, Laura."

"It's that serious then?" Asked Jonathan, as the doctor and Laura came back downstairs.

"Yes, it could be that serious, Jonathan. It's like she's in deep shock, and it doesn't help if she's not communicating."

"I don't want my mother going into a psychiatric hospital." Pleaded Jonathan, as his thoughts went back to Tina at Greenfields.

"Well, let's hope it doesn't come to that, but she may have to be drip-fed and monitored in a general hospital."

"But what's wrong with her?"

Dr. Mitchell saw the concern on Jonathan's face.

"Well, judging from what you've told me, your mother seems to have had a massive nervous breakdown. The human mind can only take so much, before it simply switches off."

"But surely she wont stay like this, doctor?" Added Laura. "She's always been such a strong, positive woman."

"Unfortunately, she's lost her will to live. We can only pray that it's a temporary condition, and it'll pass eventually. Just give her all the love and attention you can, and see to it she keeps drinking and taking the tablets."

Sally however, remained in a semi-coma-like state, totally oblivious to everybody and everything going on around her. Fortunately, Laura had taken some time off work and together with her brother, younger sister and Lizzie, they took it upon themselves to try and pull their mother back from the dark, depressing void into which she had descended.

"I didn't think I'd be doing nursing here in my own home, and with my mother as a patient." Said Laura, after they had just lifted Sally out of the bath.

"I want to be a nurse!" Replied Penny, excitedly.

"So, you want to be an interpreter, a vet, now it's nursing is it?" Remarked Laura, angrily. "This is not a game, Penny."

"Don't be nasty to me, I'm doing my best." Shouted the younger girl, as she ran from the room in tears.

"There's no need to speak to her like that, Laura." Said Jonathan, unaware that his sister was feeling guilty about pining for her doctor lover back in London.

"I know, I'm sorry. I'll go and apologise." Replied Laura regretfully. "It's just so frustrating. Mum's not getting any better, and the doctor's bound to put her in hospital soon."

"What the hell are we going to do?"

"I don't know Jonathan. We need a miracle to happen."

The following day, the telephone rang for the umpteenth time.

"I'll get it," said Penny. "I bet it'll be Lizzie or Uncle David phoning to see how Mum is?"

Moments later she came bounding into the kitchen, shouting excitedly.

"Guess who it was?"

"Not bad news, Penny." Replied Laura, anxiously. "This family can't take anymore bad news."

"It's good news, Laura! It was the animal sanctuary, they said Pepys was well enough to come home! Isn't it marvellous?"

It was indeed marvellous news, and it lifted all of their spirits at a very crucial time. Jonathan set off immediately to fetch the much-loved Border Collie back home.

Many vets would have simply put Pepys out of his misery, considering the wounds that had been inflicted by Frank's dogs, but the veterinary surgeon, Mrs. Wilde had known Pepys since he was a puppy, and knew just what he meant to the Peddlescoombe family. Although a great deal of soft tissue damage had been done to the animal's neck, there didn't appear to be any major arterial or nerve damage. Mrs. Wilde, demonstrating her remarkable suturing skills was then able to perform quite an impressive patch-up job on the injured dog. However, the vet with over twenty five years of experience, could do nothing to save Pepys' hind leg, and reluctantly had to amputate part of it. She hadn't been sure if the little animal could survive such a traumatic event, considering his age, but felt the risk was worth taking under the circumstances.

It was like coming back to a new home, what with the new carpeting, wallpaper and fresh paint. The garden though, was still in a bad state, and Pepys was very reluctant to venture out there, until he was satisfied the devil dogs had really gone. He was fine after that, and trotted around his old territories quite content on his three legs, even if he was a little clumsy.

Nick was surprised to see Craig at the Sugar Shack the following day. He was also angry, but this was an emotion long past its sell-by date. As far as Nick was concerned there was nothing he needed to say to his love rival.

Craig, at first kept his distance from Nick, and went to sit at the bar. Someone later suggested hiring a boat and exploring the bay, and as Nick seemed to be the most sober of the group, he elected to go along to the tourist office and make the arrangements.

Finishing his rum and coke, Nick put on his shirt and began to head off. It was then that Craig approached him.

"Nick, can I talk to you?"

Nick turned and glared at the other man with contempt.

"If you must Craig, but don't expect me to be civil to you. Just say what's on your mind and leave me alone."

"Sandra brought you here just to make me jealous. She's only using you." Said Craig, sweating in the hot sun, as he tried to keep up with Nick's pace.

"What do you mean? She doesn't even know you're here."

"Nick, you're such an arsehole at times. Of course she knows I'm here. She wants me to go back to her, she's missing the good times and the money. She's threatened to tell Derek certain things about me."

"I don't believe you Craig. Why on earth should she want a little toad like you back?"

"Because, unlike you Nick, I'm a winner."

Nick looked to see if anyone was watching, then quickly brought up his knee into Craig's groin.

"You're a wanker Craig, I wish I had done that the first time I laid eyes on you."

Craig sunk to his knees and gripped his genitals in agony. A couple of pretty Spanish girls walked past and looked down horrified at the stricken man.

"It's okay, he's English - too much beer!" Called out Nick. The girls giggled and carried on, but Nick felt tempted to give Craig more of a beating.

"Don't hit me anymore, please." Begged Craig as he lent on a low wall and tried to pull himself up.

"You're just scum, Craig." Called out Nick, as he began to walk off.

"So where was your precious Sandra last night?"

Nick stopped abruptly and turned to look back at Craig, who was now sitting on the wall.

"What do you mean by that?"

"It means that Sandra is a prostitute. Your wife is a whore, or haven't you worked that out either, you stupid bastard."

"You're going to die, Craig."

"It's true. Haven't you ever asked her about her lifestyle, the money, the clothes?"

"No, it's not true. Sandra would never do that!" Exclaimed Nick, unable to accept what he was hearing.

"She first started wining and dining the corporate customers, soon some of them became her own, personal clients. We couldn't understand how she was pulling off these huge deals, and got suspicious. She had to go, Nick. She was bad for the company image."

"I bet you had a part in all of this, Craig?"

"I only brought it to Derek's attention."

"That was very commendable of you." Replied Nick, sarcastically.

"I've always put the company first."

"You mean, you've always put yourself first. I smell a rat, and I think it's you, Craig."

"I turned a blind eye, that's all."

"If this is true, and I know it isn't, where does she work from?"

"Sandra's high class. She uses top hotels."

"I still don't believe you, Craig. Why should I?"

"Okay, I'll tell you the truth. I introduced her to most of the clients, she then took it upon herself to win the contracts. We had an unwritten agreement about fees, but Sandra became greedy. She thought I was ripping her off."

"So you were her pimp? I knew it."

"It was just a business arrangement, Nick that's all. But Sandra wanted more, and I couldn't give it. I wanted out."

"You wanted out Craig before the shit hit the fan, right?"

"Yes, I suppose so, but I had a lot at stake."

Nick sat on the wall next to Craig and hung his head in his hands.

"I don't want to believe you, but I know it's true. It all adds up now." He stood up, a heavy dark cloud had blighted his life. He would go back to the hotel, pack his things and go home, wherever that may be. "Just one more thing," he said, as Craig stood up next to him.

"What's that?"

"Didn't you say something about where she was last night?"

"Yeah, I'm sorry, Nick."

"Were you in our hotel room?"

Craig nodded and looked down.

Nick then punched Craig so hard, that he fell back against the wall, and toppled down the ten foot drop to the beach below.

"What about the boat trip, Nick?" Shouted one of the others from the Sugar Shack.

"Bugger the boat trip!" He replied angrily, before storming off.

As He walked back to the hotel, Nick wondered how he could have been so easily taken in again by Sandra. He felt bitter and angry that all along he had only been the second choice, the back up if Craig turned her down again, or if things turned nasty. He thought about Laura and what she would be doing. He longed to be with her again and enjoy those wonderful, uncomplicated times they had shared together. Was there still a chance to win her back? He wasn't sure, but it was certainly worth trying.

Nick thought it a little odd that the 'Do not disturb' sign was hanging from the door handle of the room. He had left Sandra earlier, just as she was putting on her make-up, ready to go shopping. At first, he thought she may have fallen ill again, and decided not to go after all. The thought of her being in Craig's arms last night suddenly flicked vividly across his mind's eye. He put the key in the lock, only to find it had been locked from the inside. He glanced along the corridor and saw a maid, busy at her work. He wondered perhaps if one of her colleague's was in the room cleaning it, but why would they lock the room?

Nick tapped lightly at the door, unsure what he would find inside. There was no reply, so he summoned the maid over, and asked her to unlock the room. The door opened immediately with the maid's master key, and Nick was about to enter, when he heard his wife's voice.

"Get out! We don't want to be disturbed!"

"Sandra, it's okay, it's me. What's going on?"

He noticed the room was in semi-darkness as he ventured inside, closing the door after him.

However, it wasn't Sandra he saw first, but Derek, sitting naked on the edge of the bed. Sandra was lying down next to him, having just lit a cigarette.

"Nick, I didn't expect you back so soon!" She exclaimed looking more than a little surprised."

"Obviously not! So it's true, this is your new job is it, Sandra?"

"Nick, look you don't understand!"

"I think I do, Sandra. Now, where's my suitcase?"

"Listen, I'm going to leave you folks. I'm sure you've got plenty to discuss!" Called out Derek, as he grabbed his clothes and made for the door.

Nick turned angrily towards him, "That's right Derek, just get out!"

"Listen Nick, this was the first time with Sandra, if that means anything to you?"

"Get out, Derek!"

In a fit of temper, Nick punched the wall hard. He then turned to Sandra, but she had already leapt out of bed and had locked herself in the bathroom.

"Nick, please listen to me, I was just using Derek so I could blackmail him and get my job back!"

"It sounds to me like you don't need your job back Sandra, you seem to be doing rather well as you are!"

Nick didn't have much with him, and packed his case quickly. After calling the airport, he found there was a flight back to Heathrow later that evening.

"Yes, book me a seat please. That's right, single ticket, one way only." Putting his suitcase by the door, Nick walked over to the bathroom. He was about to tell Sandra he was going, but judging by the sound of running water, guessed she was in the shower. He then glanced across at the table and saw a piece of paper sticking out from beneath an ashtray. He went and picked it up. It was a personal cheque for two hundred pounds, made payable to Sandra. Craig was right, she was big time. He tore the cheque into tiny pieces, and scattered it over the bed, before picking up his suitcase and letting himself out.

31. THE STORKS

It was the most strangest of things. Laura had only worked a morning, and now she was looking forward to a couple of days off. It would actually amount to three mornings curled up in bed if she included the afternoon shift on the day she was due to return to the ward. She would go back to her room, meet Jonathan and then they would both travel back home to Twickenham. There had been no change in Sally's condition, but Laura, as with her brother felt it was a duty to be with their mother during her hour of need.

It was while she was on her way to the tube station that she felt the unusual, compelling urge. In fact, she became quite desperate and found she was forced to act upon her newly acquired whim. Laura simply had to buy a cucumber.

Her mind constantly flashed back to the night of unbridled passion she had shared with Lincoln, and the day recently, when he had come to the school of nursing to give the girls a talk. The mere thought of what she had done not only filled her with guilt, but made her tingle below and long to be taken by him again. But this sudden urge for a cucumber wasn't in the least bit sexual. It may have been the sight of someone walking past her, eating a sandwich of some kind which had put the thought into her head, but whatever it was, the compulsion was there, and she had to have a cucumber sandwich.

Despite feeling a little sick earlier that morning, the feeling had gone away, and she racked her brains wondering if she had any edible bread left in her room, and more importantly, was it the right type?

Eating a cucumber sandwich was something she couldn't recall ever doing, neither could she remember a time when her mother had made them, but she had a vision of how her sandwich should be, and marched directly into a supermarket to buy what was required. The cucumber would have to be cut into wafer thin slices, and laid out on equally wafer thin, lightly buttered bread. There was already some salt and black pepper in her room, now all she would need to make the perfect sandwich was some vinegar - not too much, just a single drop on each slice of the cucumber.

Laura's hard work had been worth waiting for. The sandwich lived up to all its expectations, it was magnificent, in fact it was so delicious, she had to go for a second round, now that she was eating for two.

Laura needed to speak to Lincoln. She had worked out the dates and the child was definitely his. Part of her was saying she had to get it aborted. Potentially having a baby would finish her nursing career, and she daren't think what damage Lincoln would suffer professionally. However, the more she thought of the reasons not to keep the child, her natural extinct as a mother was beginning to cloud her judgement. She wanted Lincoln's child, she wanted the world to know that she was Lincoln's woman.

A little later, there was a gentle tap on the door, and Laura assumed it to be one of the other nurses, wanting to borrow some lecture notes, or just to catch up on gossip.

However, her heart leapt as she saw the tall, muscular shape of Lincoln standing in the doorway. He looked both ways along the corridor, to ensure he hadn't been seen.

"Laura, I got your message. So are you missing your Lincoln?" He smiled.

"Yes, I do believe I am!" She replied in a sexy whisper, before leading the handsome black registrar into her room. "I wasn't expecting you quite so soon though, I haven't even got changed yet."

He gazed around at the posters and prints adorning the walls in her spacious room, before surveying the trinkets and curios that young girls had a penchant to collect. But his eyes were soon drawn back to the pretty, blonde student nurse standing in front of him.

"I want you so much, Laura." He uttered in a low voice, as he moved forward to ravish her. "You look so unbelievably sexy in your nurse's uniform. I want to rip it off!"

"I think you need to improve your bedside manner, Dr. Greene!" She giggled, teasingly.

"I hope you have some spares?" He asked mockingly.

"About half a dozen. Why, do you want to borrow one?"

"Young nurses who are cheeky to doctors get their bottoms spanked!"

"You wouldn't dare!" Exclaimed Laura, with a wicked grin on her face.

Without another word, Lincoln reached up and gripped the front of Laura's dress. He then ripped it open to the waist, exposing her firm, ripe breasts. She gasped as he bent down, licking and biting at each nipple until they grew hard and sensitive under his touch.

Lincoln then reached into the pocket of his long white doctor's coat and pulled out a pair of silver handcuffs. He then instructed her to climb onto to the bed, and go on all-fours, before taking each of her wrists, and handcuffing them to the headboard.

Next, he slowly eased her shoes off, before yanking what remained of her uniform up around her hips.

"Mmm, stockings and suspenders, how deliciously erotic!" He moaned, admiring her shapely rear.

Lincoln then took hold of Laura's skimpy black knickers and tore them apart with his strong hands, before tossing them by the side of the bed. He then marvelled at her bare buttocks, giving them a hard slap, which made her wince. He followed this up with more equally hard slaps, causing her pale, flawless skin to redden in blotches.

After a few minutes of this, he started to massage her tingling bottom, it was in direct contrast to the rigorous spanking he had just given her. Laura gasped, as he then plunged his fingers deeply inside her, and was more than delighted to find she was wet and ready for him. Despite her hands being cuffed, she was still able to shift her knees slightly, in order to give him greater access to whatever he wanted.

Just down below, at the entrance to the nurses' home, Jonathan buzzed constantly at the intercom system. Either Laura wasn't back yet, or she couldn't hear the buzzer. He was early, and now began to think perhaps he should go and grab a coffee somewhere and come back later. It was then that he noticed Amanda, a colleague of Laura's, walking towards him.

"Hello Jonathan, what's up, wont she let you in?"

Jonathan smiled and greeted her warmly.

"She's either not back yet or she's got her walkman on and listening to Spandau Ballet knowing her!"

"Or maybe she's got a secret man in her room!" Joked Amanda, letting him in with her key.

"I doubt it, she's still a bit upset about Nick." Replied Jonathan, ignoring the lift and choosing to take the stairs instead.

"Poor Laura, she doesn't deserve a rat like that." Said Amanda, trying to keep pace with him. She lived on the same floor as Laura, and Jonathan knew they were quite close friends.

"I just need to go to the bathroom first," said Jonathan.

"Okay, I'll let Laura know you're here." Replied Amanda, helpfully.

When she arrived at her friend's room, she noticed the door was slightly ajar, and assumed Laura had just gone out for a moment. As she was about to knock, she heard what she thought was heavy groaning coming from within. This was accompanied by a banging noise and the sound of springs squeaking. It was as if someone was inside practicing the trampoline. The moaning was becoming louder and more intense as Amanda gently pushed open the door and poked her head around to see what was happening. To her surprise, she saw Laura kneeling on all-fours with her wrists handcuffed to the headboard being taken roughly from behind, by a well-built black man she recognised as, Lincoln Greene.

Amanda was not only shocked to see Laura in such a compromising position, but to her surprise, found herself becoming extremely aroused. Her mouth went dry and she couldn't swallow as she watched Lincoln ramming his huge manhood in and out of her pretty friend. The sound of Laura whimpering and gasping with each powerful thrust was driving Amanda crazy. She knew she shouldn't be looking and would surely be caught, but she couldn't stop herself, and this in itself was adding to her excitement.

As Lincoln withdrew and re-positioned himself, ready to thrust into Laura once again, Amanda felt herself getting all damp below, and knew that she would explode at any moment. This time, he started more gently and eased himself into her with short bursts. These grew in magnitude until he began to pound her with an intense determination.

Lincoln had placed his arm over Laura's hips, so that he could continue touching between her legs, as his weapon totally filled her. Within minutes, she let out a yelp of both pain and pleasure, before climaxing noisily while straining at the handcuffs that held her. Lincoln, feeling the intensity of her orgasm, groaned and arched his back. Unable to contain himself any longer, he thrust deeper inside her and coming heavily at the same time.

The sight must have had a similar effect on Amanda, for she was now squirming trying to contain herself, and desperately needed to get back to her own room. It was the tapping at her shoulder that brought her back to earth. She turned and was shocked to see Jonathan standing directly behind her.

"What's going on?" He asked innocently, as he peered into Laura's room.

"Laura's got Lincoln Greene in there!" Whispered Amanda.

Jonathan couldn't speak, he was far too overcome with embarrassment. He fled back down to the bathroom to regain his composure. Amanda was just about to quietly close the door, when Lincoln saw her.

"It's you Amanda, I thought I heard a noise." He laughed. "Care to join us?"

"Maybe next time Lincoln!" She giggled. "I think everyone in the building must have heard that!"

"Oh my god!" She heard Laura scream. "Was it that loud?"

It took Jonathan a good ten minutes to recover. He felt thoroughly embarrassed, but knew he would have to face his sister at some stage. In the end, he decided to sneak back downstairs, go out of the front door and press the buzzer again as if he had just arrived.

It was sods law that it was Lincoln who let him in just as he was departing, with his pager bleeping erratically. Jonathan watched as the tall, broad-shouldered doctor rushed back to the accident and emergency unit having just satisfied his lust with his sister.

Laura was in a state of panic when Jonathan appeared. It was difficult to work out who felt the most uncomfortable, but they both acted as if nothing had happened.

"Hi Jonathan. I wasn't expecting you quite so early." Said Laura, now wearing her robe. "I was just about to take a bath."

"Yes, sorry, I didn't mean to surprise you. Shall I go and have a coffee while you get ready?" He replied awkwardly.

"No, of course not, come in and wait, I wont be long."

Jonathan couldn't help staring straight at the bed as he walked in. The covers were all in disarray, a bottle of baby oil lay on its side, and a pair of handcuffs were dangling from the bedpost.

"So have you just finished work?" He asked stupidly, noticing her torn uniform on the floor.

"Yes, I finished late," she replied, following his gaze. "Silly me, I somehow managed to rip my dress."

He frowned and sat on the edge of her bed, deep in thought.

"Look, I think I'd better go."

"No, Jonathan, I want you to stay. Are you still upset about Tina?"

"I'm beginning to accept it now," he replied, reaching for a bottle of wine he had noticed. "I know she would have done something else if I hadn't given her the tape."

"I'm glad you realise that Jonathan. Tina was very ill and very desperate."

"I just don't understand why. She was such a wonderful person. I could have made her happy, Laura. I really could have."

"Some things are never meant to be. You loved her didn't you?"

"Yes, I suppose I did." He replied in a faltering voice. "But I'm not going to let it destroy me. In fact Tina's death has made me come to a decision."

It hurt Laura to see her brother in so much pain.

"You wont forget her, Jonathan. Time will help heal your wounds, and you'll meet someone else who you'll love. I promise."

"Meeting someone else who'll cause me pain is the last thing I feel like at the moment, Laura."

"Yes, I understand where you're coming from Jonathan. So what's this decision you've come to?"

"I'm quitting university!"

"You're what?"

"I'm going to take up nursing."

"Nursing? You must be mad."

"Not general nursing, like what you're doing."

"Don't tell me, psychiatric nursing?"

"Spot on! It was the whole Tina thing, and seeing her there in that secure unit, I just wanted to help her. But I realise now that I was going the wrong way about it."

"Nothing you did was wrong Jonathan."

"I felt wrong Laura. Just being a man was wrong. I felt ashamed, I was ashamed of my own gender, because of what Frank had done."

"But it wasn't you who hurt her."

"I know that, but I so desperately wanted to help. I'll make a good nurse Laura."

"I know you will. But what about your degree?"

"It's not what I want anymore. Besides, you can get a degree in nursing can't you?"

"Yes of course you can, but I just don't know what to say to you Jonathan, you obviously know your own mind."

"You chose nursing Laura, because something inside you wanted it, you felt it was your vocation, right?"

"I suppose so, but this is different. You're letting an emotional issue cloud your judgement. I would think about it for a while longer."

"I've already thought about it, and my mind is made up. They'll be two nurses in the family!"

"That's where you might be wrong."

Jonathan went silent and looked at his sister intently.

"What do you mean by that?"

"I've got to have a bath, I'll tell you when I come back." As Laura collected her towel and wash bag, Amanda suddenly appeared at the door again.

"Wow Laura, you're a bit of a dark horse!"

Laura squirmed and tried to indicate that her brother was in the room.

"I'm just off for a bath, Amanda. Jonathan's here." She said nervously.

"Yes I know, I saw him earlier, and what a show you and Lincoln gave him!" She smirked.

Laura's face was now bright red, and like Jonathan earlier, she rapidly fled to the bathroom.

"I'm sorry, Jonathan, I take it Laura didn't know you had seen them?" Asked Amanda.

"No, she certainly didn't," he laughed, realising the absurdity of the situation.

"I think I've put my foot in it!" With that, Amanda disappeared as quickly as she had arrived.

Laura was away a good hour and still seemed embarrassed when she finally came back.

"So you saw everything did you, Jonathan?" She asked a little sheepishly.

"No, of course not. I think you had just finished, but you should have locked the door." He replied with a grin on his face.

"Well, I'm glad you seem to find it funny."

"Well, it is really if you think about it. It's not every day you see your sister having sex!"

"Did anyone else see anything?"

"Only Amanda."

"That's bad enough, she'll tell everyone."

"Look, Laura it's no big deal is it?" He replied, trying to reassure her. "Come on sit down you're making me feel uncomfortable. That's if you can of course!"

"Oh my god, I just can't stand the indignity!" She gasped, putting her hands up to her face.

"Listen Laura, we're both people of the world. You're a nurse, nothing should shock you, and I like to think I'm very broad-minded."

"Well, I am shocked Jonathan. To think that my brother has seen me having sex is unthinkable."

"Let's just forget it and put it behind us!" He replied, pleased with his pun.

"There's something else, Jonathan." Said Laura uneasily.

Jonathan was all ears and looked at his sister intensely.

"What's wrong, what's happened?"

She hesitated and hung her head in her hands, before turning to face him.

"I'm pregnant, Jonathan. That's what's happened."

"What, just from doing that?"

"Oh don't be so stupid, you can't get pregnant doing that thing we just did," she replied irritated. "It happened a while ago, in his flat. It was the night Nick stood me up, if you must know."

"You mean it was that black doctor I saw you with?"

Laura nodded.

"His name's Lincoln Greene." She replied. "What am I going to do, Jonathan? I'll have to give up nursing."

"Laura, look, just hold on a second and let's think this through." He replied, putting his arm around her. "Have you told anyone else yet?"

"I've only just found out myself." She said, wiping her eyes. "Lincoln doesn't even know. I asked him to come over, so I could tell him, and well, the rest is history."

"Perhaps Mum could look after it, that would give her something to focus on?"

"Mum's got enough on her plate as it is. Besides, how can I tell her I'm pregnant with a black baby?"

"Mum will understand. She's never been racist."

"You just don't get it do you?" With that, she suddenly ran off back to the bathroom. Jonathan simply assumed she was just being emotional, but in reality, Lincoln's sperm was still trickling out of her.

Penny watched as her mother slept. She noticed how pale her skin looked and how shallow her breathing was. Every so often Sally would twitch and gasp, as if in pain, before drifting back into oblivion again.

Penny called out her name several times, but there was no response, so she went over and sat with her mother on the edge of the bed, softly stroking her face.

"Mum, I know you must be able to hear me. Please get better, we all miss you and want you to come back to us."

Sally sighed and slowly looked over in the direction of her daughter's voice. Although her blue eyes were still crystal clear, they were devoid of the warm sparkle that lifted so many hearts. Penny took her mother's hand, and gripped it tenderly.

"Uncle David called earlier. He calls every day. He asked how you were. I said you were still resting. He loves you Mum, and wants to marry you. He's very much like Dad, isn't he?"

Just then, Penny noticed a tear emerge from Sally's eye. She watched as it trickled slowly down her face, before disappearing onto the crisp, white pillow case. Penny then felt her mother beginning to grip her fingers, and reached across to hold her in her arms.

"I want us all to be happy again. Please marry him Mum, I know he's not Dad, but he's the next best thing."

Penny eventually got Sally to take some liquid nourishment through a straw. The fact that she continued to do this was just enough to keep her out of hospital.

It was a little later when Penny took Pepys in to see her mother. The little dog barked and wagged his tail excitedly, as he jumped up at the bed and began to lick Sally's hand.

Penny's heart raced as she saw the slightest hint of a smile on her mother's face. She looked on in amazement as Sally slowly opened her eyes, and turned to gaze at her.

"Penny, what time is it, what day is it for that matter?" She asked, in a barely audible whisper.

"Mum, you spoke!" Gasped Penny excitedly. "It's Wednesday, and it's 2.30 in the afternoon! Can I get you a cup of tea or something?"

"Yes, thank-you, that would be nice. Where's Pepys?"

"He's here, next to you, and he's better. He was licking your hand!"

"Yes, I know he was, the cheeky little thing!"

Penny went silent for a few moments, before cuddling her mother again. "Have you come back to us Mum?"

"I hope so Penny, I'm sorry I had to leave you for so long."

"I think the tablets worked after all?"

"Yes, perhaps they did, Penny, but it wasn't just the tablets that got me through."

Penny smiled.

"Can I call Jonathan and Laura and tell them the news?"

"In a moment, Penny. Just hold me for a while longer and tell me the nightmare is really over."

"It is Mum, now we're all safe and back together again."

"I feel hungry Penny, have we got any food in the house?"

"I don't know, I'll have a look. What do you fancy?"

"Just a sandwich will do. Yes, that's it, I'd love a peanut butter sandwich. Can you make one for me?"

"Yes, I think so, that's an odd request, you don't usually eat peanut butter sandwiches, Mum - that's children's food!"

"And don't forget the tea!"

"Yes, Madam!"

As Penny was about to close the door, Sally called her back.

"I can't marry David, Penny. So please try to get it out of your mind."

Penny looked sad, she couldn't understand her mother's decision.

"Why can't you, Mum? It would be the perfect solution to everything. We would all be so happy."

"David is your father's brother, Penny, it wouldn't be right. In fact I've already told him I can't marry him." Sally sat up in bed, her mind still in turmoil. Of course, it wasn't the real reason for her refusal to marry him.

As Penny went downstairs, Sally placed her hands on her stomach, and tried to think of the right solution, she had to think of a way of both telling her family she was carrying Frank Gant's child, but more importantly, she had to come to terms with giving birth to the offspring of the man who murdered her husband.

Jonathan, laden with a heavy rucksack decided to get off the bus a few stops further ahead, and begrudgingly paid the driver the extra fare. He had heard from Penny that his mother's illness had improved and he was now on his way to the family home in Twickenham to see her.

However, he had a few things preying on his mind, apart from his mother's health. His thoughts were constantly returning to the brief moments he had spent with Tina. If only she could have remained in the hospital longer, instead of being transferred to Greenfields, he felt he could have made a difference, perhaps even preventing her untimely death.

Now, with Tina in mind, he was unsure whether to put his plans of becoming a psychiatric nurse into action or return to university in a couple of week's time. He desperately needed time to think and plan what he had to do.

It was still warm and sunny, but with a fair amount of cloud cover. Rain was due later that day, and Jonathan decided to enjoy what remained of the fine weather and walk along the towpath, before slowly heading back into East Twickenham. Perhaps the soothing sound of the river lapping against the bank, and the chatter of birdsong would give him the opportunity to think his future through.

He began to eat a sandwich he had brought earlier and stopped outside a riverside pub called the White Swan. The pub was close to Eel Pie Island, a popular music venue from the sixties. There were several other people sitting outside on benches, either having lunch or just enjoying a quiet riverside drink. Jonathan was soon surrounded by a group of ducks, eager for a few crumbs of his long-awaited sandwich. As he tossed them morsels of bread he thought how pleasant it would be to have a nice cold beer to wash his belated lunch down. He went through his pockets gathering up loose change, and cursing the fact that, as a student, he was always so broke. He was just about to give up on the idea when he was momentarily distracted. He couldn't quite believe what he was seeing, and forgot all about the ducks gathering at his feet. For his attention was completely focussed on the young, flame-haired barmaid collecting glasses and plates at the front of the pub.

Jonathan hadn't yet seen her face, but he had been totally mesmerised by her long red locks and petite figure as she went about her job clad in the tightest of jeans. He shielded his eyes from the sun and watched eagerly as she went from table to table, expertly holding aloft a full tray of empty glasses. As she disappeared back inside, Jonathan knew there was nothing for it, but to go in and meet this beautiful apparition.

It felt remarkably cooler once inside. There were just a few regulars drinking at the bar as he made his entrance.

"Hello, can I help you?" Smiled the barmaid.

Jonathan thought he detected an accent as he smiled back.

"A pint of Guinness please." He replied, trying to sound a bit cool.

"It'll take a few moments to settle. Where are you sitting? I'll bring it over for you."

"I was outside, but you don't have to do that. I don't mind waiting."

"Your ducks might be missing you!" She smiled.

"Oh don't worry about them, they'll be fine!" He laughed as he watched her put a heart-shaped emblem on the head of his drink, before placing it in front of him.

"Will there be anything else?" She asked helpfully.

"I'll let you know!" With that Jonathan headed off back outside, feeling embarrassed that he'd said such a stupid thing. Perhaps, he should have stayed inside, then he would have been able to speak to the barmaid a bit longer.

He sat at a table, and putting the girl out of his mind, began to think about his future again. Continue at university or go into nursing? It was a big decision. Perhaps he ought to discuss it with Laura once more, but obviously his sister now had problems of her own. He would discuss it with his mother, when he got home. Yes, that would be the best thing, plus it would give her something else to think about, besides her illness.

He was still deep in thought and didn't notice the barmaid was back outside again.

"It's lovely out here isn't it?" She called over.

"Yes, It's my first visit. What happens when the tide comes up really high?"

"Well, you either get wet or you sit inside!"

"Yes, of course, how silly of me!"

"Are you from around here?" She asked, going over to his table.

"Yes, about two miles away. What about you?"

"I'm from a little further away, Canberra!"

"Wow, really?" Replied Jonathan, gaining confidence. "I thought I noticed an accent."

"So are you on your lunch break from work?"

"No, I'm a student. I'm still on my summer break." He replied, unable to take his eyes off her. She had a beautiful smile and the most adoring green eyes he had ever seen. "So do you work here full-time?"

"No, just part-time, I'm a student too," she added. "But I always work Thursdays, like today. So what's your name?"

"Jonathan. What's yours?"

"My name's Beth. Pleased to meet you, Jonathan."

They continued chatting for a couple of minutes, before Beth noticed more customers going into the pub. Jonathan finished his drink and handed her his glass. He wanted to stay for another and carry on talking to her, but his meagre student grant wouldn't stretch to it.

"Look, I have to go. Perhaps, I'll see you here another time?"

"That would be nice." She replied, dazzling him with her radiant smile. "I'm sure the ducks would like to see you again!"

Jonathan laughed and picked up his rucksack. He waved to Beth and carried on with his walk along the towpath. He seemed at peace with himself for the first time in a long while, and his thoughts turned back to his mother, as he quickened his pace, looking forward to seeing her again.

Laura felt distinctly nervous going into the doctors quarters. In fact, she felt more nervous than the time she had visited Lincoln a few weeks earlier. Probably because she was sober now and it was during the day. The security wasn't nearly so tight where the doctors were located, as it was in the nurses' home. However, if the cleaners went to lunch at the same time as they did at Empire, then Laura would have got her timing spot on.

The building wasn't as big as the one where Laura stayed, and was spread over two floors, with Lincoln's flat being on the second. The stairs creaked as she slowly ascended them, going over in her mind what she would say to him. Laura knew she had conceived in Lincoln's flat the same night that Nick had stood her up. They had both been so stupid, not using protection, but like so many other couples, they had simply just got caught up in the moment. But, there was more to it than that. For Laura, sex with Lincoln without protection was so risky, so taboo, and so incredibly erotic. It was like walking a tightrope without a net, and it was something she could never consider doing any other way.

Still not seeing or hearing anyone, she tiptoed along the corridor until at last, she came to Lincoln's apartment. She had to speak to him in person. If he wasn't there, she would just have to keep trying, or leave him more messages to call her at home in Twickenham, where she was proposing to go straight after.

She took a deep breath and tapped on Lincoln's door. The image of him standing there with his shirt off came flooding back, and made her spine tingle. She didn't even know how he would take the fact that he was going to be a father to their child. She didn't know how it would affect his career, or even their relationship.

Laura wanted to be with him, but up until now, their sultry meetings had been spontaneous and animalistic. She never quite knew when she would see him, or what would happen, and that both thrilled and excited her. No-one had ever done things to her like Lincoln had. He owned her body and her soul, but would he view her pregnancy as an insight into their future together, or would he see it as a trap to ensnare him, after all Lincoln Greene was something of a free spirit. He was almost mythical in her mind, a force of pure lust, of strength, of wanting, of how a man could satisfy a woman in every way possible.

There seemed no activity from within the flat, so Laura called out and tried the handle. The door opened and she tentatively stepped inside. The furniture was all still in place, but it seemed cold and lonely. The atmosphere was so different to the night of raw passion they had shared together.

"Lincoln, are you in? It's Laura. I really need to speak to you." She called out nervously. There was still no answer, so she headed towards the bedroom. The bed where Lincoln had made such passionate love to her was still there, but it was empty and totally devoid of any sheets or bedding. In fact, there was no personal effects in the room at all. She walked into the kitchen, but again, there was nothing to indicate that Lincoln had ever been there.

Laura then heard a noise and knew she wasn't alone in the flat. As she walked back in to the lounge, she came face to face to with another woman.

"He's not here. He went yesterday."

Laura recognised the woman as one of the cleaners.

"Where did he go?" She asked desperately.

"There's been one or two nurses asking the same thing." Came back the dead pan reply.

Laura chose to ignore the cleaner's last comment, and tried to make things look professional.

"I need to see Dr. Greene. Do you know where I can find him? It's very important."

"They all say that darling!" Laughed the middle-aged woman. "I think he's gone to America."

"For how long?"

"I don't know, I just clean here. I'm not married to him! You shouldn't even be in here. These quarters are for doctors only."

"Yes, I'm sorry, I'm going." Replied Laura, walking back out into the corridor. "You wont say anything will you?"

The woman was taking a vacuum cleaner out of a cupboard and looked around at the young nurse with sympathy in her eyes.

"No love, I wont say a word."

Laura's heart sank as she walked back down the stairs. She wasn't sure if the woman had been joking about the other girls, but right now she didn't care. She was carrying Lincoln's child, and he had gone off to the states without telling her, and unaware she was even pregnant.

32. MARK

It was a miserable wet October day, and Pauline was relieved to be finally rid of the police officers who had been constantly questioning her about the shooting incident that had led to Frank's death. From what Pauline could ascertain, the case could go either way, depending on whether Claire chose the right lawyer. There was a possibility she could be charged with manslaughter, but more surprising was the fact that she could actually get off totally free. A case could be made that Claire acted in self defence, shooting Frank when she genuinely believed he was about to attack her for being with his wife. However, that still didn't let Claire completely off the hook regarding using an unlicensed pistol, and for the dreadful assault on Emily. Fortunately, Pauline had arranged for a substantial sum of cash to be offered to the young hostess, and the possibility of promotion in order to keep her from testifying against Claire, and herself.

The shot on that fateful evening had hit Pauline in the shoulder and the bullet had successfully passed straight through without damaging any major organs. Pauline's shoulder was still heavily bandaged and she had to wear a sling, but the doctors had assured her that she would eventually regain most of the use in her arm. Although the pain had been excruciating and she had lost a great deal of blood, Pauline's biggest wound was to her soul. Part of her wished that Claire had finished the job, and killed her too. How she yearned to be re-united with Frank and the daughter she had lost so tragically.

Immediately after the police had gone, a nurse came into Pauline's private room at the hospital to tell her that Mark had arrived to take her home. This had come about because Pauline had discharged herself against doctors orders as soon as she felt well enough, and was able to move from her bed.

"I've got details of your first physiotherapy appointment, Mrs. Gant. It will be here at the out-patient's department next month. Now we just need to wait for your medication from the pharmacy, then you can go." Said the staff nurse, in a cheerful, but efficient manner.

"Thank-you," replied Pauline, putting her last few possessions into her case, before glancing at the nurse with sadness in her eyes. "My daughter was doing her nurse training."

"Was she? That's a coincidence." Replied the nurse. "You said 'was' so has she stopped her training now?"

Pauline had to look away.

"Yes, she had to stop. She's gone away. I had hoped to be with her, but it wasn't to be."

"I'm sorry to hear that," continued the nurse, sensing something wasn't quite right. "Mrs. Gant, please stay a little longer at the hospital. What you've been through was very traumatic and you need time to get over it. I can arrange for one of our therapists to see you."

"Thank-you, but that wont be necessary. I have two nightclubs and a cab company to run. I haven't got time to be talking to therapists." Uttered Pauline, not wanting to come across as weak.

"Very well, Mrs. Gant. I'll show your driver in," replied the staff nurse, as she turned to leave the room.

Pauline shut her case and sat on the edge of the bed, closing her eyes, and trying to come to terms with all that had happened. As she opened them again, she saw Mark standing in the doorway.

"Pauline, you're up and ready." He said, looking surprised.

"Yes, Mark. I can't be laying here in bed all day on my own, there's too many things to do."

"You're certainly a fighter Pauline, I give you that."

"Where's Jamie?" She asked, staring up at him.

"He's back at school. I thought it best. But, he's desperate to see you."

"I'm glad someone wants to see me." She uttered, her face devoid of all emotion. "Where's Frank?"

"Frank?" He replied, looking at Pauline, and trying to work out in his mind, her fragile mental state. "He's dead, Pauline. You have to accept that. You really ought to stay in hospital, you're on very strong pain-killers."

"I'm alright Mark. I'm just having trouble realising that he's gone. Talk to me, tell me about Jamie, about the clubs, the cab company. I need to focus on other things."

"I know you do, Pauline, and I'm here to help you all I can."

"You've been a great friend to me Mark. I don't know how I'll ever repay you."

He went and sat on the bed next to her and put his hand on hers.

"I'll always be here for you." He said, his voice low and meaningful. "But I want to be more than a friend to you Pauline."

Pauline stood up and went to the window. Mark knew she was deeply troubled, but knew better than to smother her too much.

"Why do you want me Mark? I'm just a hollow shell, everything's gone, everything that mattered. I've lost my daughter and the man I loved. I can't love again. It hurts too much when you lose them. Go and find someone who'll love you back. I'm not for you."

He sat motionless for a few seconds, before getting up and going to join her.

"Pauline, you haven't lost everything. You have a son who loves and needs you." He put his hand up to her face and made her look at him. "You may have lost one family, but you have another. You have Jamie, and you have me. I will never stop loving you Pauline. Let me be your husband. Let me love you. Let me take care of you?"

She looked up into his sensitive, brown eyes. It seemed strange for her to see a man emotional. She had only known a life of brutality and terror at the hands of Frank, and she couldn't quite understand this new, unfamiliar side of the male character, especially from someone as big and powerful as Mark.

Just then there was a knock at the door, and the staff nurse re-appeared.

"Mrs. Gant, I have your medication, you're free to leave now."

Sally had said she would probably be back home around 6pm. This was supposed to give Laura and Jonathan more than enough time to prepare the dinner and little surprise party for their mother. It wasn't planned to be anything too stressful, just Sally, and her three children. It was meant to be a show of love and appreciation for their mother rather than anything else. Sally had hit rock bottom, and it had been Laura's idea to let her just sit back and relax, while the rest of the family did all the work.

Lizzie had taken Sally out earlier that morning so she could get her hair done, and typically, Sally had insisted on going to the boutique afterwards to see how things had been coming along. She had been thinking about getting more involved with the business once more, now she getting well again. This had worked out fine for Laura and Jonathan, who along with Penny were busy cleaning the house, adding flowers and generally getting in each other's way.

"Look, it's only a family dinner party, Laura. I don't know why you're getting so stressed out?" Called out Jonathan, as Laura struggled with the new fangled oven Sally had recently brought.

"I'm not getting stressed out, Jonathan. It's just that I've got things on my mind at the moment." Replied Laura, sweeping her hair back behind her ears.

"You mean that doctor and his child you're carrying?"

"Jonathan, not so loud." Exclaimed Laura, glaring at her brother. "Penny will hear you."

"Listen Laura, you have to set the temperature first before you put the timer on!"

"Now you tell me! How come you know so much about Mum's new cooker?"

"Because I took the time to read the instructions, that's why!"

Eventually Laura got the oven to work and placed the basted chicken inside.

"Jonathan, have you peeled and cut the potatoes?"

"Yes, they're over there! Anything else madam?" He replied, standing to attention.

"Just the rest of the vegetables, and oh yes, the table needs setting up." Came back Laura's stern reply. "Where's Penny?"

"Why are you cooking a roast? It's Saturday!" Asked Penny, after Jonathan had prised her from her Walkman.

"It really doesn't matter, Penny. You can have a roast any time."

Penny shrugged her shoulders and pulled a face.

"I suppose so. What do you want me for?"

"Can you set the table for four, while Jonathan and I sort the vegetables out?"

"You're very bossy Laura!"

"Come on Penny, this is for Mum. I'm not doing it for myself." Was Laura's irritated reply.

Jonathan watched intently as his sister began chopping carrots. He waited until she picked out an extra large one and was about to make a witty comment when she turned on him.

"Don't even think about saying anything Jonathan!"

"I'm sorry sis, but I can't stop thinking about seeing you with that Lime Green bloke!"

"His name's Lincoln Greene, and please stop going on about it. Being pregnant is no laughing matter."

"Have you decided what you're going to do yet?" He asked.

"I'm going to tell Mum later tonight."

"Wow, heavy stuff, do you think that's wise?"

"Yes, I do. She'll find out soon enough anyway, and I need all the support I can get."

"Rather you than me."

Laura went on to tell her brother how she had gone to Lincoln's flat, only to find it empty, with him supposedly having gone to the states.

"Hey, I've got an idea. Mum could look after your baby while you finish your course. Then you wouldn't have to give up nursing."

Laura broke into a smile for the first time that day.

"Yes, it might give her something to focus on. You see Jonathan, you can come up with some good ideas. You being at university hasn't been a total waste of time!"

Scarlet's was going through an extremely busy spell. Lizzie had recently introduced the new autumn line and it seemed very popular.

"I'm glad leg-warmers are finally going out of fashion!" She exclaimed, clearing some space on a shelf. "We've got that damned, Fame show to thank for those! What's the point of wearing a nice pair of boots just to cover them up with a load of knitting?"

Sally laughed as she picked out a garment from a rail, and inspected it.

"I see you've been managing rather well without me!"

"On the contrary, Sally. Yes, I've taken on another girl to work the sewing machines and someone to help me with the designs, but it's out here I need you, on the shop floor." Replied Lizzie glancing over to a bored-looking assistant flicking through a magazine. "These girls today don't know how to interact properly. You have to engage with the customers and find out exactly what they want."

"Yes, I couldn't agree more Lizzie. Perhaps I could start back part-time and see how things go?"

"My words exactly, Sally. Get to know the new ranges again, then we can start taking out samples to the bigger organisations, just like before!"

"It sounds perfect Lizzie. I really need something to get stuck into."

"You're looking wonderful Sally," Remarked Lizzie changing the subject. "Perhaps you need to put some weight on, but the new hairstyle suits you. We can be a great team again."

"Thank-you, that's nice to hear, but don't worry about me putting weight on." Added Sally dryly. "Maybe we could design a few things for the older woman too?" She continued, glancing around at the young girls surrounding her.

"You see, you still have your wonderful insight!"

"What about pregnant women, now there's a good market?"

"Sally, I love it! Come on, let's go to the wine bar, we've got so much to discuss!"

"Oh Lizzie, you never change do you?"

Sally was more than pleased to leave the busy shop, as she desperately wanted to confide in her old friend, and the best time to talk to Lizzie was always over a glass of wine.

"Why have you never had children?" Asked Sally, out of the blue, as they found themselves an empty table. "You would make a fantastic mother."

Lizzie laughed and lit up a cigarette.

"It's not from the want of trying darling."

"What do you mean?" Asked Sally, puzzled.

"Well, Jeremy has always wanted children, and we have said if it happens, it happens. But it never does. I don't know if it's him or me, but anyway it's far too late now." She replied, summoning the barman and eyeing Sally suspiciously. "But why do you ask?"

"Oh, it's nothing really. I was just curious that's all."

"Pull the other one Sally. I've known you too long. You can't hide anything from me."

Sally looked around to see if anyone was within earshot.

"I'm pregnant Lizzie."

Lizzie gasped and stared at Sally with a look of absolute astonishment on her face.

"My god, you're a bit of a devil. Congratulations must be in order, or are they not?"

Sally looked serious and closed her eyes for a few moments.

"No Lizzie, congratulations are not in order, not this time."

Lizzie inhaled sharply as the realisation hit her that Sally was carrying Frank's child.

"Oh my god, is the father who I think it is?"

Sally nodded and took a mouthful of her wine.

"What on earth am I going to do? I can't possibly keep it, knowing it belongs to Frank, not after all he's done."

"Yes, I quite agree, oh dear, you poor thing. But how many weeks are you?" Asked Lizzie concerned.

"I'm not a hundred per cent, but I'm sure I conceived when he took me to Paris."

"I think we need to act fast Sally. Does anyone else know?"

"No, Lizzie. I just can't think straight, that's why I had to talk to you. Part of me wants to keep it, but I can't. Frank murdered William and did all those other appalling things, and there's poor Tina and Pauline to consider. I simply can't keep the child, it's not an option."

Lizzie poured herself another drink and scrutinised her friend.

"You can't go through this on your own Sally."

"I know, that's why I'm going to tell the children. Penny is old enough to understand."

"Are you sure that's wise, Sally. You're such a brave open person, but I wouldn't like to be in your shoes right now. Some things are best left unsaid."

"Maybe you're right, but I was planning to tell them tonight, after dinner."

"Be it on your head Sally. I think you're making a big mistake. Whatever will they think?"

"Thank-you. I know we don't disagree on many things, but I will give it a bit more consideration." With that, Sally finished her drink and stood up to leave. Lizzie watched, still in shock as her elegant, blonde friend walked proudly to the door, with many an admiring eye watching her.

Jonathan, Laura and Penny were overwhelmed when their mother returned at six, just as she said she would.

The hairdresser had only taken a few inches off Sally's hair and had put in some ash blonde highlights, which really suited her. Her make-up had a professional look to it, and despite appearing somewhat thinner, Sally still looked much younger than her thirty nine years suggested. Laura was the first to notice that her mother was dressed in a different outfit to what she had originally gone out in.

"Mum, you look fantastic in jeans. I wish I had your figure and long legs." She remarked, amazed at Sally's appearance.

"Come off it Laura, you've got a figure super models would die for!" Laughed Sally, delighted with the compliment.

"Well, I must have got it from you, Mum!"

Sally was in fact wearing an outfit Lizzie had picked out for her back at Scarlet's. It was quite a youthful look and much in vogue with the times. It comprised of designer jeans, set off by a very dark purple silk blouse, gathered at the waist by a thick, patterned leather belt.

"You two look like sisters!" Added Jonathan, not wanting to be out-done in the compliment department.

"Thank-you Jonathan, what a considerate son I've been blessed with." Joked Sally. "So how much money are you after?"

"Well, now you come to mention it, twenty pounds wouldn't go amiss, until my grant comes through. I'd like to go the White Swan for a drink later."

"I'll think about it Jonathan. perhaps there's some jobs you can do around the house." Then, turning to Penny, Sally asked; "So where's my compliment from you, or don't I get one?"

"Sorry Mum, but Laura and Jonathan got in first."

"Why are you looking so grumpy Penny?"

"It's Laura, she's been bossing me around again."

"I wish you two would learn to get along." Sally then sniffed the air and glanced towards the kitchen. "Something's burning!"

"Oh my god, the chicken!" Exclaimed Laura, jumping up and rushing out of the room.

The dinner actually turned out wonderful, even though the chicken was a little well-done, it did have a lovely crispy skin.

"Laura, you've done parsnips. That's unusual with roast chicken?"

Laura blushed and took a sip of her water.

"Yes Mum, I've really been fancying parsnips lately. I just had to have some."

"How very odd." Remarked Sally, looking at her daughter with a puzzled expression.

"This is wonderful, all of us sitting here together again, without a certain person who shall remain nameless." Said Jonathan, raising his glass for a toast.

"Yes, we've all come through everything remarkably well. That just goes to prove that you can't beat family love and unity."

"Well said Mum," giggled Penny. "You sound just like a politician!"

"Thank-you Penny." Replied Sally, struggling to finish her meal.

"Let's toast our wonderful mother, Mrs. Sally Peddlescoombe, fashion icon, matriarch and politician!" Called out Laura, as they raised their glasses. The mood was jovial and relaxed, which helped Sally with the timing of her announcement.

"Now, listen carefully all of you. I have something very important to say." As she searched for the right words, Jonathan suddenly interrupted.

"That's a coincidence Mum, I have something very important to say too." He then glanced across at Laura, who was squirming in her chair.

"I have an announcement as well." She added sheepishly.

"So, that only leaves you Penny. I'm sure you must have something you want to say?" Asked Sally, a little peeved at being side tracked.

"Only that I took Pepys for his check up at the vets, and they said he was fine and didn't need to go back anymore."

"How wonderful!" Remarked Sally, as she called the Border Collie over to pet him. "Pepys is a great example in how to take all that life throws at you, and still have the courage to stand up and be counted."

"Mum's doing her politician bit again!" Said Jonathan, laughing. "Here's to Pepys, the greatest dog in the world!" He cheered, pouring himself some water.

"So Jonathan, you being the oldest son, what do you want to say that's so important?"

He felt a little embarrassed as they all looked towards him. Then, clearing his throat, he turned his attention towards his mother.

"I'm giving up university. I'm going to become a mental health nurse instead."

Sitting back in her chair, Sally took a few moments to consider what Jonathan had just said.

"I don't want to sound patronising Jonathan, but I take it you've given this a great deal of thought?"

Jonathan nodded.

"Yes, mother, I have. I've even spoken to Laura about it, and she thinks I'd make a good nurse."

Sally looked across at Laura, but for some reason her daughter was avoiding eye contact with her.

"I think you would make a good nurse too, Jonathan. Has this come about because of Tina?"

"I suppose it has. But seeing how she suffered, I just feel that I have something to offer. I really want to help people like Tina, people who don't deserve to be hurt. Can you understand that Mum?"

"Of course I can, Jonathan. I have no problem with you becoming a nurse, if that's really what you want to do."

"It is Mum."

"Well, that came as a surprise." Said Sally, turning her attention back to her oldest daughter.

"You've been quiet, Laura, so what is it you want to say?"

"It's nothing Mum, really." Replied Laura, thinking that Jonathan's surprise would pale into insignificance, when her mother heard her announcement.

"Come on then, out with it, you're among family." Said Sally, watching Laura, and wondering why she was being so vague.

"We're waiting, Laura," Smirked Jonathan, enjoying his sister's discomfort.

Laura glanced back at her mother, and before she had time to think it through any further, she blurted out;

"I'm pregnant Mum."

Sally's face dropped.

"You can't be," she gasped.

"I am, Mum, I'm sorry. I had to tell you, as I didn't know what to do."

Laura's disclosure had hit Sally for six. It was a cry for help from her daughter that she couldn't ignore. Obviously Laura still held her in high regard, despite her affair with Frank.

"I'm glad you told me. Have you checked your dates, and have your periods stopped?"

"Yes, Mum. I haven't really had much morning sickness yet, but I've had cravings for odd things."

"Well that'll certainly explain the parsnips with the chicken," added Sally dryly.

"So does the father know?"

"No, Mum he doesn't yet. I tried to tell him but he's gone away."

"That's convenient. Have you decided what you want to do?"

"Yes, I'm going to keep the baby."

"But you'll have to give up your training?"

Laura glanced across at Jonathan, before turning back to her mother.

"I was hoping you might be able to help and look after it, Mum?"

"That's quite a responsibility to lay at my door, Laura. Looking after a small child isn't easy, believe me, I know."

"Yes, Mum, I know you do. That's why I wanted to ask for your help."

Sally was aghast and tried to hide her emotions. How could she look after Laura's child when she might possibly have her own to look after.

"Laura, you have to tell this Nick chap. He must take responsibility. Perhaps you can get help from his family? I can't do it, I really can't look after a child."

Laura suddenly realised that her mother, and quite rightly so, had assumed that Nick was the father. Now for the hard part, how could she tell her shocked mother that Nick wasn't the father, it was a black doctor, who had since gone away and left no forwarding address, It all became too much for Laura to bear, and bursting into tears, she ran from the table, up to her bedroom.

"I think I may have been a bit hard on her?" Said Sally, as Jonathan and Penny looked on speechless.

"Hormones Mum. We learnt about them at school." Added Penny trying to be helpful.

"Thank-you, Penny, but I think I had better go up and speak her."

Sally found her daughter lying on the bed sobbing into a pillow. She sat down next to her and placed a hand on Laura's shoulder.

"Laura, please listen to me. I'm sorry I came across as unhelpful. It was just the shock of it, that's all. You are my flesh and blood, and I'll stick by you and support you through thick and thin."

Laura stopped sobbing and sat up, to face her mother.

"Mum, I know you've been so ill recently. I had no right presuming you could just drop everything and look after the baby."

Sally thought hard about what she was about to say, and stood up.

"Laura, there's another reason why I can't look after your child. Do you remember earlier when I said I had an announcement to make?"

"Yes, but what's happened?"

"I'm in the same predicament as you Laura. I'm pregnant too."

Now it was Laura's turn to gasp in surprise.

"Oh my god, you mean Frank?"

Sally nodded and sat down next to her.

Yes, I'm afraid so, and like you Laura, I need someone to talk to."

"Mum, I'll help you all I can. We can get through this together."

"Thank-you, sweetheart, but I think in view of who the father is, I had better have a termination."

"That's a really big decision to make. I was thinking the same, but I just can't do it."

"Our circumstances are very different. I couldn't love Frank's child after knowing what he's done. It's best this way."

"Oh Mum, we've been so stupid." Said Laura, reaching out to cuddle her mother.

"Perhaps in a few weeks I might be in a different situation and could possibly help you. We all make mistakes in life, it's just a pity some of them are so costly."

Laura gazed lovingly at her mother.

"Is this a secret between us?"

"Yes it is, Laura, woman to woman."

"I love you Mum." Sniffed Laura, wiping her eyes with a tissue.

"And I love you too Laura, more than you could ever know. Now, we'd better go back downstairs."

"Is everything okay?" Asked Jonathan, rolling a cigarette on the dining room table.

"For the moment. So, where's this trifle we're supposed to be having?" Asked Sally, taking her seat back at the table.

Laura and Jonathan came through into the dining room carrying bowls, spoons and the huge strawberry trifle that Laura had made earlier. It looked delicious, topped with custard and double cream. It was just unfortunate, that both Sally and Laura couldn't face any of it.

"So what was it that you wanted to tell us, Mum?" Asked Penny, clearing her bowl.

"It was nothing really," replied Sally feeling distinctly uncomfortable.

"It must have been something, Mum. You said it was important?"

Sally felt she was being nudged into a corner, and glanced over at Laura.

"I'm thinking of going back to help Lizzie at the boutique, that's all it was."

It was mid morning, the following day and Lizzie had come over for a coffee. Both Sally and Laura had been up for some time, while Jonathan and Penny were content to catch up on their sleep.

"So how did it go?" Asked Lizzie, taking a seat at the kitchen table.

"Not that great, and certainly not as expected." Replied Sally, filling the percolator with boiling water.

"I only told Laura I was pregnant, and that was only after she had told me she was pregnant too."

"Gosh, you Peddlescoombe women certainly know how to put it around!" Remarked Lizzie. "So how is Laura coping?"

"Fine, she's having a bath right now, but unlike me, she wants to keep the child." Replied Sally, joining Lizzie at the table.

"So I take it the father's this young student chap she was seeing?"

"Yes, I would imagine so, his name's Nick, but apparently he's gone back to his wife!"

"Men!"

"Laura has suggested that I look after the child when it's born, so that she can continue with her nursing."

"That's a big ask, Sally. It would put an end to you coming back into the business."

"Yes, that's what I tried to explain to her."

Just then Pepys began barking and alerted them to a van pulling up in the drive.

"Are you expecting a delivery, Sally?"

"No, I'm not. I'll go and see who it is."

Sally opened the front door, with Lizzie standing right behind her, and was surprised to see Mark and Jamie heading towards them.

"Hello, Mrs. Peddlescoombe," called out Mark with a cheery smile. "I hope I haven't called at a bad moment?"

"No, not at all. What can I do for you?" Asked Sally, a little puzzled by the visit.

"I've come to repair your garden. There's a truckload of turf due to arrive at any minute."

"But Mark, you don't have to do that. The damage to the garden wasn't any of your doing."

"Most of the damage was done by Jamie on his motor bike, and since he's my son, it's the least I can do."

"That's very British of you!" Called out Lizzie, admiring the huge man in his jeans and polo shirt. Mark looked embarrassed and turned away.

"Look, do you want to come in for a coffee, we're just about to have one?" Asked Sally, catching Mark's eye.

Both Mark and Jamie followed the women through to the kitchen, with the latter feeling more than a little ashamed of himself.

"I know you've been putting in some plants yourself, but I've got more coming. Jamie and I will plant them." Said Mark, taking a seat.

"That's very nice of you, but it's going to cost a fortune to re-turf the entire lawn, Mark."

"Please Mrs. Peddlescoombe, I want to do it. Besides, I've taken over the general running of Frank's business affairs while his wife is recovering. That's where the funding will come from."

"But what about Pauline?" Asked Sally, feeling chilled to the bone at the mere mention of the other woman's name.

"It was Pauline who suggested that the money comes from Frank's estate. I told her about the damage to the garden I hope you don't mind?"

Sally didn't quite know how to react. Part of her was delighted that the garden was going to be restored to its former glory but she shivered at the thought of Pauline being involved and having to feel indebted to her. However, repairing the garden was an enormous job, and one which Sally couldn't even think about at the moment, so she reluctantly agreed.

"Thank-you Mark, I really appreciate you helping me."

"You're more than welcome, Sally," he replied, feeling awkward using her first name. Mark finished his coffee and motioned to Jamie to follow him back out to the van. "Oh, by the way, Jamie has something to say to you."

The young boy, looking just as uneasy as his father, turned to Sally, before running over to her and giving her a big hug.

"Thank-you, for being like a second Mum to me." He said in his unbroken, shrill voice. "I'm sorry for ruining your garden, and for being nasty to you and Penny."

Sally felt a little overcome and bent down to kiss him on the cheek.

"Thank-you, Jamie - that means a lot to me."

"Can I go and say sorry to Penny?" He asked excitedly. "Where is she?"

"She's still in bed, Jamie like a typical teenager." Replied Sally, a little concerned. "No, it's probably not a good idea you going up to her room. I'll tell her for you."

Sally and Lizzie watched with great interest as Mark and Jamie unloaded their tools from the back of the van.

"I see you've taken quite a fancy to Mark." Said Lizzie, out of the blue.

"Lizzie, whatever gave you that idea?"

"I saw the way you were looking at him, and the way he was looking back at you."

Sally couldn't help but turn crimson.

"Yes, he's a very handsome man, but that's absurd Lizzie. Besides, he has a thing going with Pauline, and I certainly wouldn't make that mistake again."

"Sometimes you have to take your opportunities when they come along Sally, before someone else beats you to it."

"Lizzie, I don't need a man in my life right now, and certainly not another of Pauline's, so just forget it." Remarked Sally getting a little irate. "I just want to live a boring existence without any mega emotional upheavals."

"Well, I think you're wrong Sally, you do need a man in your life."

"Well, it's not going to be, Mark."

"If I didn't have Jeremy, I would probably give Mark a try myself!"

"Lizzie, you're incorrigible!"

Lizzie laughed, and beckoned her friend back into the kitchen.

"I have something for you, Sally." She then began to rummage through her sizable handbag before producing what looked like a pamphlet.

"What's that?" Asked Sally, glancing across.

"It's details about a clinic in the west end. You're only in for one night. Then your problem will be solved."

Sally took the pamphlet from her friend. Although she knew it was inevitable, she simply couldn't bear the thought of taking such drastic action. It was such a huge decision to have to make, and one that was so desperate, and so final in its outcome.

"I just don't know, Lizzie. Laura wants to keep hers."

"Listen Sally, if you keep this child it will be a constant reminder of the man who killed your husband. Plus, what if the child turns out to be just like Frank, a monster? You have your own children to consider, remember."

"I know you're right, Lizzie. But I just wish it didn't have to come to this."

"I'll go to the clinic with you, and bring you back. If the circumstances had been different then you would have kept the child. You have to go ahead with it Sally, there's no other way."

Sally was rather glad to finally see her friend go. Although she meant well, Lizzie could often come across as over-bearing, or even bullying. But deep down Sally knew the woman she had met at university all those years ago, only wanted what was best for her, and the rest of the family. As Sally read through the pamphlet, she decided to call the clinic after the weekend, that would at least give her a bit more precious time to think about what she had to do.

After making up some orange juice, Sally added ice cubes, before placing the jug on a tray, along with a couple of glasses. She then carried it out to where Mark and Jamie were working in the garden. Jamie was content to pot plants around the border, while Mark, with his shirt off was carrying the heavy turfs and putting them into place on the lawn.

His eyes once again met Sally's, and for a brief moment there was a surge of electricity in their lingering glances. She couldn't help but admire his rippling muscles, as he thanked her for the drink, and downed it in one.

"You're doing a fantastic job out here, and it's so hot." She smiled.

"Thank-you, but I think I'll have to come back again tomorrow and finish it. Jamie's not much help, but at least I can keep an eye on him, since his mother can't do an awful lot at the moment."

"You've come along a way with Jamie, he's a totally different person."

"I've just added a bit of structure and discipline to his life that's all."

"Well, I think you've done wonders, Mark. So how is Pauline? The news was so dreadful about the shooting."

He looked up to the sky and shrugged his shoulders.

"Pauline discharged herself against medical advice. She's back at home now, but she's in a lot of pain."

"I'm sorry to hear that," added Sally, none too convincingly.

Mark put his glass down and mopped his brow.

"Look Sally, I wont beat about the bush, Pauline has agreed to marry me. I know there's a lot of bad feeling between you both, but I would really like you to come to the wedding."

"Gosh, things have moved fast for you both." Replied Sally realising the bond between him and Pauline was stronger than she had first imagined. "That would be nice. So yourself and Pauline would carry on running the businesses as normal?"

"Yes, that's correct. It's far too much for Pauline to do, and we have a number of employees who we want to remain loyal to."

"I see," said Sally, a little disheartened. "I'm glad you've found your soul mate in Pauline. Some of us search our whole lives to find the right person, and when we finally do, we lose them."

Mark moved to console her, but as he did so, he found that she had already gone, and was heading back into the house.

33. WALES

Sally was a little nervous. Although she had modelled the boutique's ranges in the past, she always felt jittery when the time actually came to tread the catwalk. It wasn't like an international fashion show in front of thousands of people, but more like walking out onto a length of carpet in front of about a dozen buyers, but still she was on show and it made her anxious. This particular show was for a leading airline and Sally would be modelling different styles of uniforms. Lizzie was very excited, as a good response could get them into the profitable world airline business, and lead to many more exciting contracts. The outfits had to be glamorous, practical, and crease-resistant, and Lizzie had seen to it that they ticked all the boxes.

She had also arranged for her partner, Jeremy to do the driving and bring the rails and samples up to the modelling area, where she would conduct the sales presentation.

Once they arrived at the plush offices near Regent Street, the two women headed off towards the changing rooms, but Lizzie had an inkling something was wrong.

"How are you feeling Sally? I know you do get a bit edgy before these shows."

"I'm fine Lizzie, I've just got stomach cramp that's all, but I'm sure it's just nerves." Sally didn't mention that she had been bleeding down below for most of the day, as she knew how much the presentation meant to Lizzie and to cancel it would probably mean not getting the opportunity again.

"Any luck with the clinic?"

"Yes, I've spoken with them," replied Sally carefully removing her jeans and camisole top. "I've got an initial appointment on Wednesday, and if that's okay, they'll book me in straight after."

Lizzie reached across and took Sally's arm.

"It's for the best you know, darling."

"Yes, I know it is." Sally was just about to slip on the skirt when Lizzie cast her a disapproving look.

"Underwear off too Sally, we don't want any tell-tale panty lines."

"The bra can come off Lizzie, but the knickers are staying on!" Replied Sally defiantly. She then put on the skirt, blouse and jacket, and checked herself in the mirror.

"Excellent darling, my word you would make a wonderful stewardess! Now, there's three outfits in total, and they all come with a tabard."

"Don't worry Lizzie, I wont forget. I have modelled clothes before!"

"Yes, of course you have. I'm sorry, but you know what I'm like!" Muttered Lizzie. "Now, just come through this door when I give you the signal. There will only be about a dozen people out there. So just walk straight out onto the carpet, do a couple of turns, remove the jacket and come back wearing the tabard, and simply repeat with each outfit. Got it?"

"Yes, Lizzie, just go and get on with it and leave the modelling to me!"

The show went like clockwork and the buyers insisted that Sally come back and do a repeat performance. All three of the outfits were ordered and Lizzie was beaming ear-to-ear. Sally also did her fair share at the presentation, explaining how personal the service was and how many distinguished customers Scarlet's could boast of.

"That went very well," Exclaimed Lizzie, waltzing into the changing room clutching an order form. "This will keep us busy up until Christmas."

As Sally was getting changed back into her own clothes, she suddenly came over faint and had to sit down for a moment. The stomach cramp she been suffering with earlier had returned, but it felt far more severe. As soon as Lizzie had disappeared into the lift with a rail of clothes, Sally checked herself. She was still bleeding, but heavier than before. She couldn't understand it as her periods had ceased some time ago. She heard the lift coming again and knew Lizzie and Jeremy would step out at any time. She quickly gathered her things and made a dash for the toilets. The pain was excruciating now, and she only just managed to reach the cubicle in time.

"Sally darling, we're all ready to go. We'll be downstairs in the van."

"Yes, all right," gasped Sally as she tried to stop herself from collapsing. "I'll be with you shortly."

Lizzie sensed something was amiss and sent Jeremy back down, while she checked on her friend.

"Sally, is everything alright in there, is something wrong?" She called out desperately.

She heard Sally sobbing and tried to push the door open, but it was locked.

"Lizzie, I'm okay, I'll be out in a moment. Please wait for me."

Obeying her friend's instructions, Lizzie went back and waited in the changing rooms. It was another five minutes before Sally eventually came out, looking distraught.

"Sally, what on earth has happened? You look so pale!" Gasped Lizzie, as her friend stood trembling in the doorway.

"I wont be needing that appointment after all, Lizzie. I've lost the baby."

"Oh my god, a miscarriage?"

Sally nodded and Lizzie ran to support her.

"I should have realised what with all the cramps."

"Oh you poor girl, what an ordeal to have to go through. Look, come and sit down for a while, Jeremy can wait."

"No, Lizzie let's just get home. Fortunately I had a spare towel with me."

"My word we've been through some things together, you and I." Said Lizzie, hugging Sally tightly. "Perhaps we should take you to the hospital?"

"No, that wont be necessary, but I'm glad I wont have to go to the clinic now."

"Yes, I know it's a horrible thing to say, but really, it's a blessing in disguise." Added Lizzie. "It has all worked out naturally, just how it was meant to be."

"Yes, you're right. I wont have to explain why I was going away for the night either."

Lizzie smiled.

"I think you probably will have to explain why you're going away Sally."

"What do you mean?"

"Well, your conscience is clear now, you can go back to Falcondale, and finally claim your husband."

"What, you mean David?"

"Yes, Sally, I mean David."

Sally was back home an hour later. Although her ordeal seemed to be over, she felt empty inside, as if something had been ripped out of her. It was hard to quantify, but the loss of any life, no matter whose it was, touched her very deeply.

Penny came downstairs with her Walkman attached to her ears, humming along to some nameless tune.

"I'm going up to lay down, I've had an exhausting day, and just want an early night."

"Okay, mum, but it's not even seven yet!"

"I know Penny, dearest, but when you get older you find you get tired more easily."

"Well, I'm glad I'm not old, that's all I can say," replied Penny, scrutinising her mother. "Shall I bring you up a cup of hot chocolate, Mum?"

"Yes, that would be nice," said Sally as she wearily climbed the stairs.

Ten minutes later there was a knock at her bedroom door.

"You look like you've been crying Mum?"

Sally tried to laugh it off.

"No, Penny, not at all. I've been helping Lizzie model some clothes. I'm just tired, that's all."

"Wow, modelling clothes, how absolutely glam!" Beamed Penny excitedly. "Do you think Lizzie would let me try it?"

"Yes, I don't see why not. Perhaps in a couple of years time." Replied Sally, putting on her dressing gown. "So where's Laura and Jonathan?"

"Laura had to go back to London, she's on duty tonight and Jonathan has gone to the White Swan again."

"How odd, I wonder why he keeps going there?"

"I think there's a girl who works behind the bar he fancies!" Giggled Penny.

"Oh, so that explains why he wanted twenty pounds!"

Penny reached across to give her mother a hug goodnight, and suddenly remembered the phone call.

"David rang while you were out. That's the third time this week he's rang. Why don't you want to speak to him, Mum?"

"Did he leave a message?" Asked Sally, side stepping Penny's question.

"He just asked how we all were and said he would try again another time." Replied Penny, looking at herself in Sally's long mirror and trying to pose like a model. "Oh yes, he said he was thinking of you."

"How very sweet."

"I miss Uncle David, I wish we could go and see him in Wales again."

"Yes, I know you do, Penny."

"Well, goodnight Mum. If there's anything you need, just call me."

"Goodnight sweetheart, I will," smiled Sally. But just as Penny was about to go back downstairs, her mother called out to her.

"Penny."

"Yes, Mum?"

"Do you remember when you asked me to marry David?"

"Yes, but why bring all that up again?"

"No reason really. Do you still want me to marry him?"

Penny broke into a huge grin and ran back to embrace her mother.

"Oh Mum, I want that more than anything in the whole wide world."

It was October, and the mild weather continued as Sally at last finished packing the clothes she would take with her to Falcondale. She stepped out of the kitchen and glanced up at the sky. It was still cloudless, although it was meant to turn fresher and more overcast over the next few days. She and Penny were due to set off on the long drive early the following morning. Although Sally was looking forward to seeing David again and re-visiting the town where she once went to university, she felt a little nervous, a bit like a schoolgirl about to go out on her first date. However, she put the nerves down to the mere thought of having to drive on the motorway, which she utterly detested, and made a start on Penny's packing.

Both Jonathan and Laura were back staying at home. Jonathan had at last applied to become a student mental health nurse with the local health authority, but as he had heard nothing back yet, he had decided to carry on as usual at university. This weekend though, he had come home earlier than usual for some unknown reason.

Laura had finished her stint of night shifts, and had seven days off. These, she preferred to spend at home, rather than be stuck in her room at the nurses' home, thinking about Lincoln Greene.

Jonathan had talked Laura into going for lunch with him at the White Swan, but Sally and Penny had politely declined the invitation. Sally still wasn't feeling her best, and found she needed to take frequent rests during the day. It would take a while for her to get fully back into the swing of things again. Penny, on the other hand used the excuse that her brother and sister were no longer cool enough to be seen with.

Even Pepys had changed. He was much quieter, and would become very upset if other dogs came too close to him. He had also begun to spend more time in the smaller front garden, rather than roam around out the back, like he used to. It wasn't a problem, as he never ventured out onto the road, and it turned out to be rather convenient in view of Sally's brand new garden. All the same, she still felt saddened by it, and knew the affectionate little animal must still be suffering in his own way.

It was when Sally heard Pepys barking, and went out to see what it was, that she noticed the man walking up the drive.

"Hello, can I help you?" She asked, as Pepys stood cowering behind her.

"Yes, I hope so," smiled the tanned, handsome young man. "I'm looking for Laura. This is where she lives isn't it?"

"Possibly," replied Sally, placing him under scrutiny. "She's not here at the moment. Who shall I say called?"

"Well, she might not want to see me. My name is, Nick."

"Nick!" Gasped Sally, surprised. "I'm Laura's mother."

"Yes, I can certainly see the resemblance," he replied a little awkwardly. "I'm very pleased to meet you, Mrs. Peddlescoombe. I don't know if Laura has ever mentioned me?"

"Yes, she's mentioned you, although not in the most glowing of terms recently."

"That's understandable."

"Please come inside, Nick. You look thirsty?"

Sally could easily see in Nick what had attracted Laura to him in the first place. He was a likeable chap, tall, with a good, solid build, a shock of dark hair and a smile that would knock any woman dead.

"Will Laura be long?"

"It's hard to say. She's gone to the pub with her brother."

Nick petted Pepys, and glanced around while Sally fixed them both a cold drink.

"Thank-you Mrs. Peddlscoombe. This is delicious." He remarked politely as he took a sip of the fruit cordial.

Sally led him into the lounge, where they sat opposite each other.

"Nick, please call me, Sally. You're a student aren't you?"

"I was a student, but I've recently taken my finals."

"A first I presume!"

"I hope so," he replied laughing, "But I'm not counting my chickens."

"Do you have a job, Nick?"

"Yes, I have. I'm due to start work in the insurance industry next week."

"Good for you." Replied Sally, still watching him with a critical eye. "Could I be rude and ask you a personal question?"

"Yes, of course, Mrs. Peddlescoombe."

"My daughter is very upset that you stood her up and apparently went back to your wife in her hour of need. Is that true?"

Nick coughed and had to put his glass down.

"Yes, it's true, but my marriage is well and truly over." Although, looking rather uncomfortable, he seemed willing to continue. "You see I had to find out if my marriage was worth saving, after all, I didn't take my vows lightly."

"So you've left your wife again have you?"

"Yes, I have, there's nothing to be salvaged from our relationship."

"Do you have any children, Nick?"

"No, Mrs. Peddlescoombe, we didn't have any children."

"So what was your intention coming here to see my daughter today?"

Nick wasn't prepared for Sally's direct line of questioning, but knew he had to make an impression.

"I wanted to get Laura back. I didn't realise just how much she meant to me. I was foolish to return to Sandra. Do you think she would have me back?"

"I really don't know. She's still very angry at the moment and unsure about her future. You can't just walk out on a pregnant woman, Nick."

"Pregnant! What, Laura?"

"Yes, that's right."

"But I didn't know. I would never have even thought about going back to Sandra if I had known that."

Sally watched him closely, trying to detect the slightest hint of deception in Nick's voice and mannerisms.

"Laura has been trying to contact you."

"Oh my god, what have I done?" He sighed, feeling utterly ashamed of himself. "Laura must really hate me. I just can't believe it, I'm so sorry."

Sally was quite touched by Nick's reaction. Although she was still very concerned about Laura's pregnancy, she couldn't find it in her heart to scold a young man, she had quickly grown to like.

"Do you still want her back after hearing that, Nick?" She asked looking directly into his brown eyes.

He didn't hesitate in the least with his answer.

"Yes, Mrs. Peddlescoombe, I want Laura back desperately. I love your daughter with a passion I can't describe."

"In that case I suggest you go along and convince her, like you've just convinced me."

She watched from the window as Nick walked back down the drive. She knew she shouldn't have mentioned anything about Laura's pregnancy, that was really up to her daughter to discuss with him. But more importantly, was the fact that she had unknowingly, led Nick to believe that he was the father of Laura's child.

Hoping it would improve his sister's mood, Jonathan led her along the scenic towpath to the White Swan. The ploy didn't work though, she remained ratty and wanted the whole world to know. Laura's sleep pattern was still disrupted from her night shifts, and she had now been suffering bouts of morning sickness. Yes, she was still hurt over Nick's actions, but more importantly, it was Lincoln Greene, or the lack of him that preyed on her mind. She tried to convince herself that he would never have abandoned her if he'd known she was pregnant, after all they had a very special bond together. She thought it would only be a matter of time before he got in touch. But as time went by, Laura became increasingly disheartened by the situation. Her secondment at St. Mary Abbot's had also come to an end, and her next placement would be the dreaded Accident and Emergency Department at Westminster Hospital, and this depressed her greatly. Laura felt absolutely desperate, and now the offer of lunch at the pub that her brother kept raving about seemed like the perfect distraction from her problems, even if it was only temporary.

Jonathan, on the other hand was now having deep misgivings about inviting Laura in the first place. His main mission was to ask Beth out. He had wanted his sister to go with him both as company and also as someone who could spur him into action if he found he was losing his nerve. But now, because of her dark mood, it was like she was draining all the positive energy from him, and making him wonder if he'd been better off simply going on his own.

"So what's this girl's name?" Asked Laura, attempting to be sociable.

"Her name's Beth. She's Australian." He replied chirpily.

"Okay. So what does she look like?"

"She looks absolutely beautiful!" He reminisced excitedly. "She's got glorious, long red hair and the most enchanting green eyes!"

"You're very poetic today." Came Laura's begrudging reply. "So she doesn't look anything like Tina then?"

He went quiet and picked up a large twig, which he then tossed into the river.

"No, nothing like Tina."

"I'm sorry Jonathan. I shouldn't have said that."

"It's okay. I don't get choked up about her now."

"That's good. It's best to move on, no matter how much it still hurts." Replied Laura, taking her brother's hand.

"Yes, that's good advice. I do need to toughen up sometimes."

"You'll have to detach yourself from lots things if you do take up nursing, Jonathan."

"Is that what you do, Laura?" He asked innocently.

"I try to, but it doesn't always work."

They reached the riverside pub just after 1.30pm. The nice weather was still holding out, but it felt distinctly cooler down by the water. Just like the previous Thursday, when he had visited, the pub was busy with lunchtime customers.

"Wow, it's lovely, Jonathan!" Gasped Laura, as she glanced up at the over-hanging baskets of cascading flowers, which adorned the white-washed walls.

"We can sit down next to the river's edge if you like." He replied proudly. "What do you want to drink, Laura?"

"I'll have a coke please." She said, going to find a free table.

Jonathan disappeared inside the bar, looking around anxiously for Beth. However, he didn't see her, and had to be content being served by someone else.

Laura put her cardigan on as she waited for her brother to return with the drinks. But, she doubted if he would remember to bring back a menu.

It was then that she first noticed Beth emerge from a side door carrying a tray of food. She was walking about fifteen yards behind Jonathan, but he was concentrating so hard on not spilling the drinks, that he didn't notice her. He put the drinks down on the table and began to search his pockets for his rolling tobacco. Laura saw Beth again, gathering up some empty glasses. She knew it had to be her, the red hair, the pert figure, and now, the sullen expression. Beth caught Laura's eye, before glancing back at Jonathan. He still hadn't noticed her, but Laura could tell immediately by the other girl's body language exactly what was happening. Beth obviously thought Jonathan and Laura were an item, and it appeared to be having a negative effect on the normally, high-spirited barmaid.

"Hey, Laura, we could have a party tomorrow when Mum goes to Falcondale?"

"I can't really say I'm in the mood for a party Jonathan."

"No, of course not." He uttered, trying not to antagonise her any further. "So when are you going to tell Mum, that the child belongs to Lincoln?"

Laura sighed and put her glass down.

"I really don't know. I suppose I should have said something when I told her I was pregnant, but something happened and the moment wasn't right. I'll tell her when she gets back from Wales."

Jonathan didn't reply. He had now seen Beth and was distracted, his eyes eagerly following her, as she went about her duties.

"Look, there she is!"

Laura glanced over, but the flame-haired Aussie wasn't playing the game this time.

"I don't think she's seen me. Perhaps I should go over and say hello?"

"Just wait a moment," said Laura reaching to stop him. "Where are the toilets?"

Jonathan pointed her in the right direction and continued rolling his cigarette.

Laura then followed Beth back into the bar area.

"Excuse me, but are you still serving lunch?"

"Yes we are," replied Beth helpfully, as she passed Laura a menu. "We also have today's specials written up on the board."

"Thank-you," said Laura. She could easily see why her brother had taken such a fancy to the petite redhead. "I'm here with my brother, it's such a beautiful place. I'm amazed I've never been before."

The transformation was immediate, and Beth's face broke into a broad smile.

"That's so nice of you to say. My parents own it. We've only been here a year ourselves."

Job done! Laura took the menu and went back out to join her brother, knowing that Beth would soon be following.

"Silly me, I forgot the menu didn't I?"

"Yes, you did Jonathan, but you are a man, so I can't expect too much!"

He laughed and began to read the contents out loudly.

"The ploughman's are enormous here, I think I'll have one of those."

Laura took her seat again. She had done her part, but she just didn't feel hungry, and eyed the menu with little enthusiasm. Her earlier, despondent mood had returned.

"It's getting colder Jonathan, perhaps we should go inside?"

Jonathan was distracted again, but this time it wasn't by Beth.

"I can't believe it!"

"Jonathan, what are you going on about?"

"That bloke you went out with who stood you up."

"You mean Nick?"

"Yes, that's the one. He's here!"

"He can't be!" Gasped Laura, looking shocked.

"I've just seen him walk into the bar."

Just then Beth appeared right on cue.

"Hi Jonathan, nice to see you again!" She beamed.

"Wow! Beth! What a lovely surprise. I forgot you said you worked on Thursdays!" He babbled excitedly. "This is my sister, Laura."

"Yes, we've already met. So are you ready to order?"

"I'll have a ham ploughman's. What about you Laura?"

"Nothing thanks," she muttered, as she watched Nick emerge from the bar, and begin to walk towards her.

It had been Nick who had noticed Laura first. He had observed her for a couple of moments while she and Jonathan chatted to the barmaid. He saw how her mind was wandering, and how she kept staring out across the river. He surveyed her blonde locks, her beautiful neck, that he loved to kiss so much. How could he have been such a fool.

As he neared the table she saw him. But, he couldn't make out if it was a look of pleasure or disappointment on her face.

"Hello Laura." He said hesitantly, before acknowledging Jonathan. There was a long pause, as Laura's blue eyes met with the brown of his.

"This is an unexpected surprise. So what brings you here?" She asked, her tone mocking.

"Laura, I've been to your house. I wanted to find you. Your mother said you would be here."

"Well now you've found me, what do you want?"

Jonathan squirmed uncomfortably in his chair.

"Look, I think I'll leave you lovebirds to get on with it." He remarked, standing up to make good his escape.

Nick took over the vacant seat, and sat looking directly at Laura, however, she chose to turn away from him.

"Please Laura, I know you're angry with me. I've made a terrible, stupid mistake, which I'm paying for."

"Nick, why didn't you tell me you didn't want to see me anymore? A phone call, or even a letter would have done. But no, you let me wait all alone in that cafe. I even went to the Devonshire Arms to look for you. It was there I learnt from Roberto that you had gone back to your wife."

Jonathan could hear his sister's voice getting louder as he stepped into the pub, glad to be away.

"So, I've finally got you all to myself have I?" Smiled Beth, watching him approach the bar.

"I'm escaping!" He replied, looking relieved. "My sister's long-lost boyfriend is here. Things are getting a bit heavy!"

"I thought you two were together when you first arrived. Your sister is very beautiful, she's like a model. I couldn't compete with her."

Jonathan gazed deeply into Beth's green eyes. He wanted her so badly.

"You can compete, Beth. I think you're absolutely stunning!"

"Thank-you!" She replied, delighted with his compliment.

"I want to ask you something Beth."

She quickly stopped what she was doing and listened intently.

"What do you want to ask me, Jonathan?" She asked, fluttering her eyelashes.

"How long is my ploughman's going to be? I'm famished!"

She laughed and mockingly went to hit him.

"You're a funny one! I'll go and see."

He pulled up a bar stool and looked out of the window. Laura and Nick still appeared to be in deep discussion. He was glad he never got into problems with women like that, he surmised as he finished off his pint of Guinness. Beth returned a few seconds later and placed the most gigantic ploughman's lunch he had ever seen in front of him.

"You need fattening up!" She grinned.

"I'll be the size of a house if I keep coming here!" He replied, biting into the crusty bread hungrily.

"Your sister looks upset." Remarked Beth, glancing outside.

Laura had stood up, and now had her back to Nick. He then got up and moved behind her.

"I know about the baby." He said.

It only took Laura a few seconds to realise where he must have got this information from.

"My mother had no right telling you that." She snapped.

"I'm pleased she did, Laura. I want to be here for you, after all I am the child's father." He put his arms around her, but she pushed him away.

"Please Nick, you don't understand. Just go away and leave me alone."

"But Laura, you don't realise what you're saying. I've left Sandra. I only want you. I want us to be happy."

She sat back down, with her head in her hands.

"Nick, you're not the father of my child."

There followed a silence that seemed to last an eternity.

"What do you mean, Laura, of course I'm the father, who else could it be?"

She turned to face him, tears streaming down her cheeks.

"That night you stood me up. I went out. I was angry. I got drunk." She sobbed, turning away from him again.

"You're saying, you slept with someone else?"

"Yes, I slept with someone else. There, you have it now. I did it because I was so upset with you."

Nick looked down, his face a mask of pain.

"Is it really true, Laura?"

"Yes, Nick. It's true."

"So who was it, anyone I know?" He asked sarcastically.

"Lincoln Greene." She replied, with a hint of rebelliousness in her voice. "He's a registrar in A&E."

"Yes, I know who he is, and I know of his reputation too."

"I can't put the clock back, Nick."

Now it was his turn to get up, and stare out at the river.

"So, is he going to stand by you?"

"I don't know." She answered back abruptly. "He doesn't even know I'm pregnant. He's gone off to America."

Nick wanted the ground to open up, and swallow him whole. He couldn't come to terms with what she had just told him. He glanced across at her one last time, before turning, and walking away.

Beth suddenly reached across the bar and gently shook Jonathan's arm.

"I think your sister needs you."

Jonathan got up and walked out of the bar, returning to where Laura was still sitting.

"He's gone Jonathan. I turned him away. Why do we always hurt those we love the most?" Said Laura, remorsefully.

He placed his arm around his sister and held her tight. She sobbed into his chest, huge tears of grief. She sobbed for herself, for Lincoln, for Nick, and for her mother. But most of all, she sobbed for the baby and the terrible realisation of what she would have to do. She remembered seeing the pamphlet about the clinic at home, and had taken a note of the number just in case, but never thinking for a moment that it would ever come to this.

"Did you ask Beth out Jonathan?" She asked, trying to put a brave face on things.

"No sis, I didn't." He replied softly, still holding her tight.

"What a pair of losers we are."

"Perhaps not." Said Jonathan, noticing Nick walking back along the towpath. He nudged Laura, and she glanced up, her heart beating wildly.

"I thought you had gone?" She whispered, as Nick pulled up another chair.

"I can't go Laura. I can't leave you again. I'll be the child's father. I'll bring the child up as if it were mine."

"That could be rather difficult Nick, the baby will be black!" Replied Laura, trying to laugh through her tears.

"I don't mind, I'll love the child like I love you. If you'll let me."

She looked up at him, and wiped her eyes. She then left Jonathan's arms and went to Nick's.

"I'll let you," She heard herself whisper, as she fell into his embrace.

"You look like you need another drink?" Asked Beth, as Jonathan wandered back into the bar.

"Do you believe in true love Beth?"

"I don't really know. I've seen it in movies, but why do you ask?"

"Because, I think I've just witnessed it!"

"You're a right old softy, aren't you?" She joked looking into his watery eyes.

"Yes, I really think I might be." He replied with a mischievous grin. "Beth, there's something I want to ask you."

She placed her hands on her hips and looked at him squarely.

"You want another pint?"

"No, in fact I wanted to know if you would do me the honour of coming on a date with me?"

"Very nicely put for a student. I thought you would never ask!" She smiled.

"Well, I'm asking."

"And I finish at three!"

"I'll wait for you then." He replied, trying his hardest not to do a cartwheel in front of her.

It had taken Mark a little longer than expected to lay the turf in Sally's garden. But after placing the final piece, he had a good look around to ensure everything was perfect before leaving. He didn't say goodbye to Sally, he knew she still had her crosses to bear, and as far as things went, he had fulfilled his obligation to repair the damage done by Jamie.

Mark had made a phone call a couple of days earlier and now wanted to act on the result of that conversation. He would drive back, have a shower, make sure the businesses were running okay, and then go over to see Pauline with the good news.

Although Mark was overseeing the two nightclubs, he didn't really have a great deal to do on the face of it. Both locations had experienced managers. Anne was doing a wonderful job looking after Lake's, and with great hindsight, Frank had decided to retain the original manager at Swann's. So it was only the day-to-day operations of the Gant Carriage Company that concerned him the most, and this he could do blindfolded.

Pauline had given Mark his own key to the house she once shared with Frank, and had told him to come and go as he pleased. Mark though, felt very uncomfortable viewing this as his new home, what with the constant reminders of his old boss being ever present. Pauline however, was content to remain there and had said nothing about moving, so it was just a case of Mark having to live with his feelings and get used to his new surroundings.

It was mid afternoon and Pauline had asked him to take her to Lake's so she could re-establish her authority over the highly ambitious Anne, whom she suspected of having an affair with her late husband. Pauline also wanted to totally transform the office and secret area. She couldn't bear the thought of having to sit in the same area where Frank had been slain. The possibility of selling Lake's was also an option she was seriously considering. First, though, Mark wanted to present her with the surprise he had gone to such great lengths to bring about.

Pauline was already downstairs when he arrived and was busy trying to fix her raven hair with one arm still in a sling. He always had to be wary approaching Pauline, as he could never quite tell what sort of mood she would be in. Oddly, the demise of Frank, seemed to have had a positive effect on Pauline, although she would be the last to ever admit it. Her life was now her own, it was easier and a lot less traumatic than living in fear of suddenly being beaten by a drink-crazed brute, intent on causing mayhem. Having Jamie living there, also had a settling effect on Pauline. She would busy herself helping him with his homework and getting his school uniform ready. She rarely spoke of Frank, or her lover, Claire and appeared totally unfazed by the thought of the up-coming court case. But to Mark, he sensed she was missing something. Perhaps, it was Frank. Perhaps in some sort of perverse way she had grown to accept the beatings and harsh treatment as a sign that he loved her in his own deluded way. Mark could only ever offer her his unconditional love, loyalty and a steady platform in which to plan for the future. But could a woman like Pauline Gant ever be content with this, to live and function in an ordinary lifestyle. He didn't know, but if he persevered, perhaps one day, Pauline would love him, like she had Frank.

"What are you looking so happy about?" She asked suspiciously.

"Next year, is going to be our year, Pauline. The businesses are going to thrive, we'll expand and take on new staff. The world is going to be our oyster." He replied cheerfully. "But first, I think you, Jamie and I need a break."

"You're full of it today," she remarked sarcastically. "What are you going on about?"

"I've booked us a week's holiday in New York. We're going on Concorde!" He exclaimed proudly, while casually tossing the envelope containing the tickets onto the table.

"What about the court case?" Asked Pauline, picking up the envelope.

"That's not for a while yet, besides, they've got Claire, she's the one who did it. It'll be her who goes down."

Pauline wasn't entirely convinced.

"What about Jamie, and taking him out of school?"

"I've already spoken to the school, and they agree, he needs some time away."

"I hate flying, Mark."

"It's Concorde Pauline, you'll love it. We can even go shopping to get you some new outfits to take, or you can just buy them in New York!"

It was working. Pauline started to warm to the idea of the big apple, and began to visualize herself as an international, high-flying business woman. Jamie was equally excited about the trip and went to the library and asked endless questions about the super sonic jet.

The big day finally arrived, it was Pauline and Mark's wedding, although it had all been somewhat of a rush. Mark was desperate to make Pauline his wife at long last, and had booked their ceremony at the local registry office to coincide with the trip to New York. It would be perfect, a small wedding with no fuss, just close family and a few friends and acquaintances, then off, across the Atlantic the following day. It would be the perfect honeymoon.

Pauline's weight had plummeted recently, what with all the stress and strain surrounding Tina's suicide and Frank's murder. But the weight loss couldn't have come at a better time, for she fitted perfectly into her cream-coloured, size twelve wedding dress. It was meant to resemble a 1940s film star look; long, and tight-fitting, with a plunging neckline complete with huge shoulders pads.

Pauline for once felt proud and dignified as she climbed out of the white Rolls Royce, gripping her elderly father's arm, and making her way into the registry office.

Compared to a formal church wedding it was dismal. The council offices were grey, drab and barren. However, once inside things did start to improve. The actual room where the ceremony was to take place was very light and airy, and was pleasantly bedecked with beautiful flowers of all colours, shapes and sizes.

Mark smiled warmly at Pauline, and it lifted his heart to see her smile back at him. It was rare to see any emotion on her face these days, other than pain. The wedding was also a far cry from her earlier farce of a marriage to Frank. He had gone through with it against his will and had made sure everyone was aware that he was marrying Pauline under protest. Now she was marrying someone who actually loved and cared for her. Perhaps, in hindsight she should have left Frank much earlier, and Tina could well be alive today.

It wasn't a long ceremony and was attended by no more than thirty guests, mostly from Mark's family, although there were some senior employees from both the clubs and the car company present.

Once Pauline and Mark had signed the register and photographs had been taken, the guests were ushered back out into the foyer. It was during this time that Pauline noticed the registrar in deep conversation with the police inspector who had questioned her about Frank's shooting when she was in hospital. She didn't say anything to Mark as it may have been purely innocent. But why would a police inspector investigating a murder case be talking to the registrar at Pauline's wedding? A chill ran down her spine as the abrupt, grey-haired registrar approached her.

"Is there a problem?" Asked Pauline innocently.

"No, not as far as the wedding was concerned." Replied the woman, sternly. "But the police want to speak with you in private. There's a room just over here, if you care to follow me."

Pauline glanced at Mark in a re-assuring manner. He then turned and went to speak to the guests while she followed the registrar and police inspector into the side room.

"What do you want. I've told you everything I know." Said Pauline, as she was asked to sit.

"Perhaps you left something out, Mrs. Gant?" Replied the middle-aged, stout detective in a sarcastic tone. "Perhaps you chose not to tell us about something that would have considerable bearing on the case."

Pauline thought there was something familiar about the inspector. Could he have been the young, cocky, over-confident policeman who had questioned her nearly two decades earlier over the murder of Mr. Bloom?

"I can't possibly think what you mean?" She replied, shaking.

"Mrs. Gant, I have to inform you that Claire Lake has made a new statement in which she claims you attempted to murder your husband by trying to bring about a fatal road traffic accident, in which two members of the public were critically injured. Is this correct?"

There was a long pause.

"Yes, that's correct." Replied Pauline, in a barely audible whisper.

"Can you please speak up Mrs. Gant!" Barked the inspector, as two uniformed female officers stood by.

"Yes, it's correct. I've just told you." She cried out, putting her hands up to her face.

"Pauline Gant, I'm arresting you for the attempted murder of your husband, for conspiring to commit murder with Claire Lake as an accessory, and for the abduction, imprisonment and sexual assault of Miss Emily Crickleford." Said the inspector in a precise manner. "Further more, anything you say, may be taken down, and used in evidence against you. Do you understand the charges, Mrs. Gant?"

Pauline nodded and was led back out into the foyer, where Mark was waiting anxiously. She was ashen-faced as she reached out to him, flanked by the two female officers. The guests then surged forward cheering and throwing confetti over the happy couple. Pauline stopped in her tracks and stood staring at the well-wishers. There was an eerie silence that seemed to last an eternity, until it was eventually broken by Pauline herself. It wasn't a scream or even a cry. It was more like a deathly wail that seemed to come from Pauline's very soul. She clung to Mark desperately, knowing that she would soon have to leave her new husband. The two female officers moved either side of her, but before they could handcuff the distraught bride, Pauline collapsed to the ground, a sobbing heap of anguish, the confetti still falling from her hair. She never did get to fly on Concorde or visit New York.

They had waited several minutes for a space, and Sally was starting to get agitated. She wanted to get out of the car, stretch her legs and freshen up. She was just about to drive off and find somewhere else, when Penny thought she saw someone leaving.

"Look Mum, there's a car going. Can you park in such a small space?"

"Of course I can, Penny. I've been driving for more years than you've been on this planet."

It was tougher than she had anticipated, and Sally had to concede defeat, and ask Penny to get out and guide her into the narrow bay.

"How many years did you say, Mum?"

Sally had to laugh as she squeezed herself out through the half-open driver's door.

It was an unusually busy period for the Black Lion, and Sally and Penny were fortunate to get a room, even though they would have to share.

Penny lifted Pepys out from the back of the car, as he was still unable to jump, and was terrified at even the slightest of heights.

"Well, he certainly looks happy enough now!" Remarked Sally, as Pepys barked and ran around excitedly.

"I'm glad we brought him with us, Mum."

"So am I Penny, even dogs need a holiday sometimes."

After dumping off their bags in the room, Sally and Penny just had time to go down and have a bite of lunch in the Black Lion's genteel dining room.

"It'll be so romantic Mum. Are you going to tell him we're here, or will you just turn up at David's house?"

"Penny, just calm down!" Replied Sally, slightly embarrassed, as other guests glanced across with interest. "I'll do nothing of the sort," she continued. "I just want to have a nice, cool shower, then I'll have a walk around town, and perhaps have a browse in the library."

"Can I come?"

"Yes, of course you can. Did you think I was just going to leave you here?"

Penny laughed and finished her soup, as Pepys waited patiently out in the yard, gnawing on a bone the chef had found him.

It was tea-time when they finally arrived at the library. The university was open and in full swing for its autumn semester, and many of the new first year students were still trying to find their way around the various departments.

As Sally was about to enter the building, she noticed an employee of the university walk past her. She immediately recognised the woman as Carol, whom David had engaged recently to be his cook and housekeeper. The woman seemed to recognise Sally, for she smiled and gave a wave, before continuing on her journey.

Sally glanced around at Pepys and wondered whether to tie his lead to some railings while they went inside.

"Don't worry Mum, I don't really want to go inside, it's much too stuffy and it reminds me of school." Remarked, Penny. "It's such a lovely evening, I'll just take Pepys for a walk around the grounds and we'll come back and meet you in about half an hour."

"Okay Penny, I'll see you then." Sally gave her daughter a kiss on the cheek and ruffled Pepys's fur before making her way into the library.

Ten minutes later Carol arrived at David's house. She wasn't sure if he would even be there. Sometimes he would work late, or go up into the hills and walk. There were occasions when he would even drop into one of the local pubs on his way back from his office at the university. Carol had been thinking about what he had said to her about being bored and having nothing in Falcondale. The town could indeed be a lonely place for someone without a family around them and a loved one to confide in. She wanted to apologise to David, perhaps she had over-stepped the boundary a little by concerning herself too much with her employer's personal life.

Carol called out his name, as she let herself in. There was no reply but on this occasion she seemed to sense that he would be there. The back door was open and a draught of wind caught some papers he'd left on the table, and sent them flying across the room. After picking the papers up and putting them back, Carol, headed out into the garden.

"What's this, nothing better to do than sit here tanning yourself, Mr. Peddlescoombe?" She smiled, as she ran an approving eye over David's shirtless torso.

"Hello Carol. I wasn't expecting to see you."

"Likewise, Mr. Peddlescoombe. Are you expecting any visitors?"

"No, none that I can think of, but why do you ask?" He replied with a puzzled look on his face, as he got up to go back into the house.

Carol hesitated for a few moments, before following him inside wondering if she should say anything. She was certain it was Sally she had seen near the library, and looked up at the portrait of her hanging on the wall.

"Well, it's just that I saw someone a little while ago."

"Who did you see, Carol? I don't understand."

"It was her, it was Sally." She said, pointing towards the picture. "She had a young girl with her and a dog."

David looked at the picture, his eyes widening.

"You mean Sally is actually here, in Falcondale?" He exclaimed.

"Yes, it was her all right. She even smiled and waved back to me. That's why I came over. I thought you would have said something if you were expecting her."

"Yes, you're right, I would have. But Carol, where did you see her?"

"She was going into the library."

David grabbed his shirt and headed towards the front door.

"Don't wait for me, I don't know how long I'll be."

"Just do what has to be done, Mr. Peddlescoombe!" She called out after him.

The library was almost empty by the time David arrived. The duty librarian looked bored, and glanced up at the clock stifling a yawn.

"Good afternoon Mr. Peddlescoombe, you'll be a bit lonely in here today, I can't believe it's so quiet." She remarked. "I was thinking of closing up for the day."

"Just give me a few minutes, Miss Tibbs, then you can lock up." Replied David, trying to get his breath back. He had just called out to Penny and Pepys after he had seen them strolling in the campus. Now his heart was beating wildly as he trod the well-worn carpet and began to look around for Sally. He knew it was here that she had met William over two decades earlier. He knew what he was doing was right. William wanted it that way, he thought, feeling inside his jacket pocket to ensure he still had his brother's letter.

Going down a couple of steps, David didn't pass a soul, when he entered the inner sanctum of the older part of the library. Only sounds of the odd, distant cough broke the silence, as he walked through an aisle stacked almost to the ceiling with musty, antiquated books. This was quite a secluded area and was only really used by the more serious students of Classics and English literature. For a brief moment he thought he detected a hint of feminine fragrance. He followed the scent as it grew stronger. He now knew where to find her, and began to quicken his pace. Reaching the end of the aisle, he came to a study area, dominated by a large, sturdy writing table. There was someone sitting at the table. She was not reading, or revising, but simply gazing out of the window, looking across at the sun, setting behind the lush green hills. He saw how the rays of the fading sunlight lit up the highlights in her blonde hair. He noticed the odd strand of grey, which he had never seen before.

She didn't hear him at first, but soon became aware that she wasn't alone.

"Sally," he called out gently, as she turned to face him.

"David, it's you. I hoped you would come." She whispered.

He moved slowly towards her, taking in her beauty, her fragrance, her love.

"Promise not to faint," he smiled, as she rose to her feet.

"Would you take me in your arms again, if I did?" She replied, gazing deeply into his eyes.

"That's why I'm here Sally, to take you in my arms."

Her mind began to race, and she felt unable to put into words how she felt.

"David, you know when you asked me to marry you?" She heard herself utter.

"I know, I rushed you, I'm sorry. Look, there's something I need to show you." He replied, reaching into his pocket for the letter. "I found this when I was clearing through some of William's personal effects. It concerns you, Sally."

He passed her the letter and they sat back down. He watched anxiously, as she stared motionless at her husband's writing. She examined the envelope in great detail, holding it as if it were a priceless museum artefact. Eventually, she took the letter out, again handling it as if it could simply just disintegrate at any moment. He could hear her soft breathing, and for a moment, thought he could hear her heart beating.

She let out a whimper as she began to read the first paragraph, her hands now visibly shaking. She stopped reading half-way through and glanced up at him, like she needed an assurance that it was alright to continue. Her eyes were dewy, yet still so beautifully blue. He loved to watch her, and so wanted to take her in his arms, and tell her everything was meant to be.

He followed the trail of her tears as they trickled down her face. Each poignant word touching not only her heart, but her very soul. She came to the end and looked up at him.

"I've changed my mind David, can I do that?"

"Of course you can Sally, it's a woman's prerogative!"

He reached out to grasp her hands, pulling her closer towards him. As he held her, he kissed her hair, and buried his face in its glossy silkiness. She delved into her bag, searching frantically for something to wipe away her teardrops.

"You don't need anything, Sally." He said, as he lent forward and began to kiss her tears away. As each new one appeared and rolled down her cheek, he kissed it away, until there was no more.

"I'm not the woman you once knew." She sobbed, pulling away, and leaving the table.

"I've always loved you, Sally. It's our future that's important. We can't change the past."

"It hurts me David, when you say you love me. I'm not worthy of you."

"I know what happened Sally. I know all about Frank, Lizzie told me everything."

"Everything?"

"Everything she could."

Sally's mind raced back to when Lizzie and David last spoke. It must have been the day of Tina's funeral, but he didn't seem aware of her pregnancy and subsequent miscarriage.

"Do you still want me, David?" She asked him hesitantly.

"More than life itself, for without you Sally, I have no life." He replied.

"Do you mean it, David?"

"Yes Sally, I mean it."

She clung tightly to his hands and looked into his eyes.

"Then will you marry me, David?"

He embraced her, never wanting the moment to pass.

"Yes, of course I'll marry you, Sally." He smiled. "Just try and stop me."

They held each other for what seemed like an eternity, until the moment was eventually broken by the shrill tone of Miss Tibbs' voice.

"I'm sorry to interrupt you when you're so busy, Mr. Peddlescoombe, but you're the last one's here, and I want to lock up the library now."

"Yes of course, Miss Tibbs. You go ahead, we'll be right behind you." Replied David, a little awkwardly.

"I do believe you're blushing, David?" Smiled Sally, feeling like a scolded first-year student again.

"Whatever will she think? I am the Dean of Students!"

"And I'm going to be your wife, so she can think what she likes!"

Outside, Penny and Pepys were waiting anxiously. Pepys took to David immediately, and ran up to him wagging his tail excitedly.

"He likes you, David!" Said Penny, linking her arm through his.

"It's probably because we've got something in common, Penny. We've both got a leg missing." He laughed, giving Pepys a pat on the back.

Penny glanced across to her mother, who was now linking David's other arm.

"Is everything okay, Mum?"

"Everything is just fine, Penny." She replied with a knowing glance.

They walked across the narrow bridge that spanned the tiny river Teifi, and Sally recalled how she and William used to pass across it when they were young students back in the sixties. It all seemed so long ago, but now it was all flooding back, the past, the present, and the future, merging, and joining together as one.

THE END